Praise for *The Conqueror*

"Bryan Litfin brings a historian's background to the story he tells about Constantine the conqueror, giving you a feel for the time and actions of a historic figure. This is still fiction, but it tells a good story well. Enjoy."

Darrell Bock, Executive Director for Cultural Engagement, Howard G. Hendricks Center for Christian Leadership and Cultural Engagement; senior research professor of New Testament studies

"With an eye for detail and an engaging fictional story, Dr. Bryan Litfin makes history come alive. If you've ever wondered what life was like for early believers, you will love *The Conqueror*."

Chris Fabry, author and radio host

"*The Conqueror* is a wonderful mix of excellence in storytelling and keen insight into the setting's historical context. This is what you get when a historian crosses over the authorial divide into the world of fiction. Read this book! Read all of Bryan's books! They are enjoyable from beginning to end. This is certainly on my list of Christmas presents for the readers in my family."

Benjamin K. Forrest, author and professor

"A deftly crafted and fully absorbing novel by an author who is an especially skilled storyteller."

Midwest Book Review

"I thoroughly enjoy a well-researched novel concerning ancient Rome and Litfin did not disappoint. *The Conqueror* is filled with rich Roman history and lush tidbits of the early church in Rome. If you're a fan of this time period and history, it will definitely need to find a way to your bookshelf."

Write-Read-Life

"Entertaining and overall well-done. Litfin gives readers an enjoyable and thought-provoking story with relevant theological themes."

Evangelical Church Library

EVERY KNEE
SHALL BOW

Books by Bryan Litfin

CONSTANTINE'S EMPIRE

Book 1: The Conqueror
Book 2: Every Knee Shall Bow

EVERY KNEE SHALL BOW

BRYAN LITFIN

Revell

a division of Baker Publishing Group
Grand Rapids, Michigan

© 2021 by Bryan M. Litfin

Published by Revell
a division of Baker Publishing Group
PO Box 6287, Grand Rapids, MI 49516-6287
www.revellbooks.com

Printed in the United States of America

Library of Congress Cataloging-in-Publication Data
Names: Litfin, Bryan M., 1970– author.
Title: Every knee shall bow / Bryan M. Litfin.
Description: Grand Rapids, Michigan : Revell, a division of Baker Publishing Group, [2021] | Series: Constantine's empire 2 |
Identifiers: LCCN 2021006641 | ISBN 9780800738181 (cloth) | ISBN 9781493431892 (ebook)
Subjects: LCSH: Church history—Primitive and early church, ca. 30–600—Fiction. | Rome—History—Constantine I, the Great, 306–337—Fiction. | GSAFD: Historical fiction. | Christian fiction.
Classification: LCC PS3612.I865 E94 2021 | DDC 813/.6—dc23
LC record available at https://lccn.loc.gov/2021006641

This is a work of historical reconstruction; the appearances of certain historical figures are therefore inevitable. All other characters, however, are products of the author's imagination, and any resemblance to actual persons, living or dead, is coincidental.

21 22 23 24 25 26 27   7 6 5 4 3 2 1

To my mother,
Sherri Litfin,
who first showed me
what a godly woman looks like

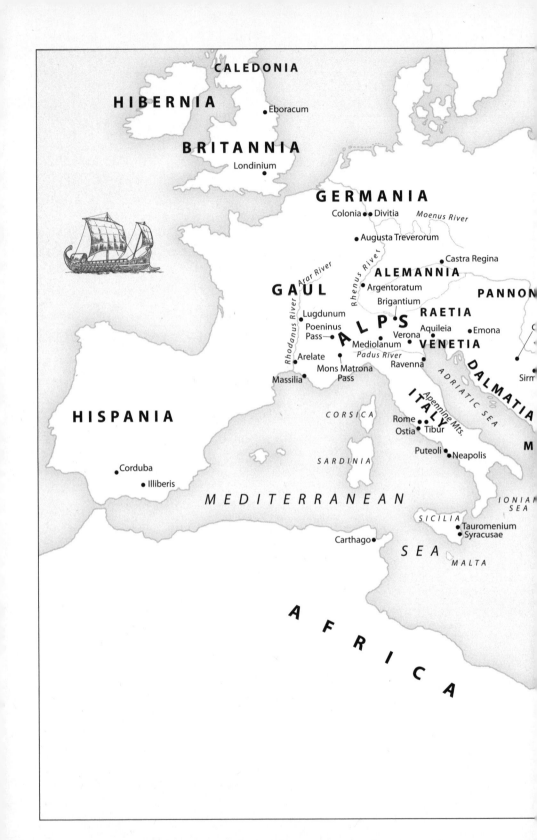

NIA

Cibalae

GOTHIC TRIBES

Danubius River

rmium

DACIA

Serdica

MARDIAN PLAIN

A

Hebrus River

Stobi

MACEDONIA

Thessalonica

Aenus

GRAECIA

Demetrias

AEGEAN SEA

AN

Corinthus

Athenae

Pylos

Ephesus

PELOPONNESE

Kythira Strait

CRETA

Hadrianopolis

THRACIA

Byzantium

BITHYNIA

Propontis

Nicomedia

Nicaea

ASIA

EUXINE SEA

SARMATIA

CYPRUS

Antiochia

SYRIA

THE EAST

Tigris River

MESOPOTAMIA

Euphrates River

Caesarea

PALAESTINA

Hierusalem

Alexandria

LIBYA

AEGYPTUS

Wolf City

Nilus River

RED SEA

ARABIA

to Aethiopia

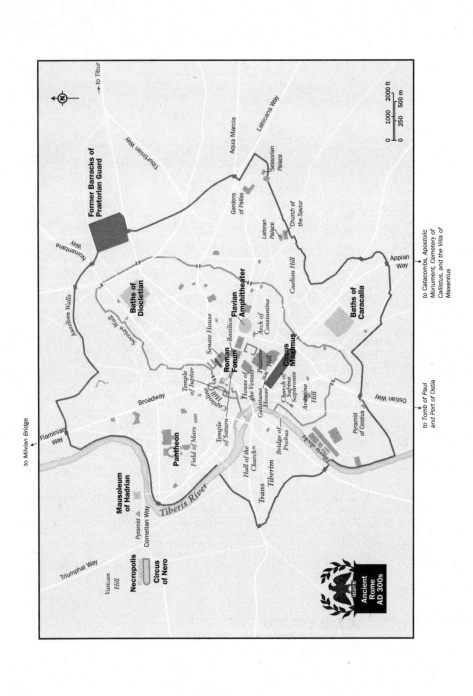

Ancient Rome AD 300s

to Milvian Bridge

to Tibur

Former Barracks of Praetorian Guard

Tiburtinian Way

Nomentana Way

Aqua Marcia

Labicana Way

Sessorian Palace

Gardens of Pallas

Lateran Palace

Church of the Savior

Aurelian Walls

Servian Wall

Baths of Diocletian

Caelian Hill

Appian Way

to Catacombs, Apostolic Monument, Cemetery of Callistus, and the Villa of Maxentius

Senate House

Basilica

Roman Forum

Flavian Amphitheater

Arch of Constantine

Baths of Caracalla

Temple of Jupiter

Capitoline Hill

Palatine Hill

Circus Maximus

House of the Vestals

Gelotiana House

Church of Sabina Sophronia

Broadway

Temple of Saturn

Aventine Hill

Ostian Way

to Tomb of Paul and Port of Ostia

Pyramid of Cestius

Flaminian Way

Pantheon

Field of Mars

Hall of the Church

Bridge of Probus

Tiberis docks

Trans Tiberim

Mausoleum of Hadrian

Tiberis River

Pyramid

Cornelian Way

Triumphal Way

Vatican Hill

Necropolis

Circus of Nero

0   1000   2000 ft
0   250   500 m

Contents

Historical Note

THE CONSTANTINE'S EMPIRE TRILOGY TAKES PLACE in the fourth century after Christ, when the Roman Empire was starting to be Christianized. By this I do not mean that earlier Christians had done no evangelism. The church had been growing for about three hundred years before the time setting of these novels. What was happening now, in the early 300s, was that the Roman Empire itself was in the process of accepting the Christian faith as its official state religion.

Emperor Constantine initiated this radical change. Unlike previous emperors who ignored, favored, or persecuted the church but remained pagans, Constantine actually converted to the new faith. A major turning point came as an important battle drew near. Constantine experienced a heavenly vision of the cross, followed by a dream in which Jesus (so he believed) told him to mark his soldiers' shields with a Christian symbol. He went on to defeat his opponent at the Battle of the Milvian Bridge in AD 312. Since the emperor attributed the victory to Jesus, he immediately issued a letter that instructed his governors to restore Christians' property and not persecute them anymore. These dramatic historical events provided the basic plotline for book 1 of this series, *The Conqueror*.

Constantine also gave money for the Christians to build beautiful new churches and make expensive copies of the Bible. Some people believe this means Constantine founded the Roman Catholic Church. But this isn't true. The characters in my novels cannot be considered Roman Catholics in the strict sense of the term. Instead, they were part of the one holy, catholic, and apostolic church. The word *catholic* means "universal." Ancient believers used the term to describe Christianity's worldwide unity. It is anachronistic to read later terminology or controversies back into previous times. I have tried to present the spirituality of the early church just as it was in the fourth century, without imposing modern categories on ancient people. That is why I use the word *catholic* with a little *c*—to describe the ancient and universal body of Christ, not a specific institution.

Another aspect of ancient terminology that might be confusing to today's reader is the word *pope*. The Latin word *papa*, from which we get *pope* and *papacy* in English, simply meant "father." In the early fourth century, *papa* was a term of respect for one's paternal bishop, whether in Rome, Alexandria, or some other place. Only later did the term come to define the bishop of Rome alone. So when you read about Pope Sylvester in this story, you should think of him as a fatherly, pastoral, and respectable figure. That is what *papa* meant at the time.

A third term that might be confusing is *nun*. We tend to think of nuns as women wearing distinctive garb who have made lifelong vows never to marry but to live hidden away in a convent. However, ancient Christian monasticism—for both men and women—was a much more fluid situation in the early fourth century. Many different ascetic lifestyles were being tried by various individuals and groups. In the case of Flavia, Cassi, and Sophronia, we should picture them not as modern nuns following a formal rule but as women who had, for a time, made vows of devotion and celibacy as they came to live in a shared house. They were not expected to maintain this for their entire lives. They could leave the convent for important purposes and were free to exit the sisterhood altogether if life demanded it.

Modern readers might also find the characters' delay of baptism strange. Christians today are baptized either as babies or relatively soon after their conversion. Children or teenagers often take this important step before reaching adulthood. But in the first few centuries of church history, baptism was so important that people did not enter into it quickly. They remained unbaptized until they were absolutely certain they could accept the challenges and hardships—including the risk of torture and death—that being a Christian entailed. Infant baptism did not become the standard practice in Christendom until after the time period of this trilogy. That is why my characters have to confront the issue of when they should be baptized.

In any historical novel, some of the core events are real, while others are part of the fictional story the author is telling. Perhaps you may wonder about my book: What parts of it actually happened?

In the book's fourth-century setting, the Roman Empire was indeed ruled by an Imperial College consisting of two emperors called augusti and two junior emperors called caesars. The creation of this so-called Tetrarchy led to a lot of murderous competition and civil war. The report of Bassianus's assassination attempt on Constantine's life at Senecio's instigation is found in the historical sources. Licinius did cast down his brother-in-law Constantine's statues at Emona. Then Constantine and Licinius fought each other at two major (yet inconclusive) battles at Cibalae and the Mardian Plain. They reached a tentative peace at Serdica in 317.

After this stabilizing moment, Constantine embarked on a major church-building campaign around the empire, including at Rome. It was through his imperial patronage, or that of his immediate successors, that some of Rome's greatest churches were built: the Lateran Basilica of the Savior and its baptistery (today called the Papal Archbasilica of St. John Lateran); St. Peter's Basilica; the Basilica of St. Paul Outside the Walls; and San Sebastiano, which is the church that now stands over the original catacombs, or burial grounds of the early Christians. In addition to these, a large hall in Helena's Sessorian Palace was transformed into Santa Croce in Gerusalemme (which supposedly preserves fragments of the Holy Cross, along with ancient soil from Jerusalem). Today there is also a beautiful church, the Basilica of Santa Sabina, on the site of Flavia's imaginary house on the Aventine Hill. That building, however, dates from a century later than the age of Constantine, so I only describe a hypothetical house church in this trilogy. All these churches can be visited in Rome today, though they have been modified or completely reconstructed over time.

Also, the Patriarchal Basilica of Aquileia in northern Italy preserves the incredible paleo-Christian mosaics described in the story, as commissioned by Bishop Theodore in the early fourth century.

What about the bones of Saint Peter? Beneath the altar of today's St. Peter's Basilica, encased within the rubble of many intervening centuries, lies a little structure called the Trophy of Gaius. This was a marker that the ancient Christians erected to remember where Peter's grave was originally located. In 1968, Pope Paul VI declared the human remains found there to be the actual bones of the Prince of the Apostles. But do they really belong to the Lord's most famous disciple? It is quite possible that they do—perhaps even likely. Yet no one can say for sure. For a discussion of the various traditions about Peter and all the apostles, see my book *After Acts: Exploring the Lives and Legends of the Apostles.*

The following characters who appear in *Every Knee Shall Bow* are actual historical figures:

- Emperor Constantine
- Emperor Licinius
- Constantia, Constantine's half sister and Licinius's wife
- Helena, Constantine's mother
- Fausta, Constantine's wife
- Julius Constantius, Constantine's half brother
- Crispus, Constantine's son (by Minervina, not Fausta)
- General Valerius Valens
- Bassianus
- Senecio
- Pope Sylvester of Rome
- Sophronia (however, the name Sabina that I have attached to her is imaginary)
- Alexamenos (nothing is known about this person except his Christian faith)
- Bishop Ossius of Corduba
- Bishop Chrestus of Syracusae
- Bishop Theodore of Aquileia
- Bishop Marinus of Arelate
- Bishop Melitius of Lycopolis ("Wolf City")
- King Chrocus of the Alemanni

- Vincentius, a Roman priest
- Abantus, a naval officer
- Arius, a heretic
- Athanasius, a presbyter of Alexandria
- Alexander, bishop of Alexandria

One event that is not known to actual history but has realistic contemporary parallels is the plot point in which the characters seek permission from Constantine to hold a council about the canon of scripture, then make a beautiful copy of the book. We have no evidence of such an event in Rome. However, this was the sort of thing that was happening at the time. Meetings of bishops were being held, lists of canonical books were being determined, and complete "Bibles" were being formed. Although a single volume containing the Old and New Testaments is not known to have been created in Rome within the novel's time frame, only a few years later, in AD 331, Emperor Constantine ordered the creation of fifty such books. The ancient church historian Eusebius of Caesarea records this noteworthy imperial commission in his well-researched book *Life of Constantine* (Book Four, chapter 36). Therefore, it is not impossible that there was a precursor volume a few years earlier in Rome. Today there are several surviving Greek manuscripts of Bibles just like these, such as Codex Sinaiticus or Vaticanus, and some with both Greek and Latin like Codex Bezae, all of which come from a slightly later period than the age of Constantine.

As you can see, the story in *Every Knee Shall Bow* takes place against the backdrop of real historical events. It is my sincere hope that you will enjoy this blend of history and entertainment. When you finish, please know that the story is not over. The Council of Nicaea, at which the doctrine of the Trinity was defined for the ages, and Queen Helena's discovery of the relics of the True Cross form the important historical background for Rex and Flavia's final adventures in book 3. I trust you will find it a fitting conclusion to the story of these two energetic protagonists.

Dr. Bryan Litfin

The Dynasty of Constantine

KEY:
+ marriage
↓ children
= siblings
(*not all siblings and relatives are depicted*)

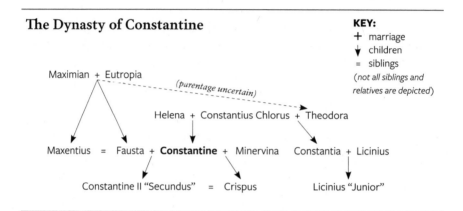

Maximian + Eutropia

(parentage uncertain)

Helena + Constantius Chlorus + Theodora

Maxentius = Fausta + **Constantine** + Minervina   Constantia + Licinius

Constantine II "Secundus" = Crispus   Licinius "Junior"

Gazetteer of Ancient and Modern Place Names

Note: the modern names of *Rome* and *Italy* are used in this book because of frequent appearance.

Aegyptus. Egypt

Aelia Capitolina. Pagan name for Jerusalem, Israel

Aenus. Enez, Turkey

Aethiopia. Ethiopia

Africa. Corresponds to Libya, Tunisia, Algeria, and Morocco

Alemannia. Corresponds to southwestern Germany

Alexandria. Alexandria, Egypt

Alps. Mountain range across northern Italy and central Europe

Antiochia. Antioch, Turkey

Apostolic Monument. Outdoor dining facility at the original catacombs, believed to contain the relics of Peter and Paul

Aquileia. Aquileia, Italy

Arelate. Arles, France

Athenae. Athens, Greece

Augusta Treverorum. Trier, Germany

Beroe. Stara Zagora, Bulgaria

Brigantium. Bregenz, Austria

Britannia. Roman Britain corresponds to England, Wales, and parts of Scotland

Byzantium. Istanbul, Turkey

Caledonia. Scotland

Carthago. Ancient Carthage, near Tunis, Tunisia

Castra Regina. Regensburg, Germany

Catacombs, the. Catacombs of San Sebastiano, Rome

Cenchreae. Kechries, Greece (eastern port of Corinth)

Cibalae. Vinkovci, Croatia

Colonia. Cologne, Germany

Corduba. Córdoba, Spain

Dacia. Corresponds to parts of Bulgaria and Serbia

Danubius River. Danube River

Demetrias. Volos, Greece

East, the. Diocese of Oriens, at the eastern end of the Mediterranean Sea, corresponding to parts of Israel, Jordan, Lebanon, Syria, and Turkey

Eboracum. York, England

Emona. Ljubljana, Slovenia

Euxine Sea. Black Sea

Floating Mat Island. Psathoura, Sporades chain, Greece

Gaul. Corresponds to France, Belgium, Netherlands, and portions of a few other countries

Germania. Corresponds to areas northeast of the Rhine and upper Danube, including Germany, Poland, Czechia, Austria, and other central European countries

Graecia. Greece

Hadrianopolis. Edirne, Turkey

Hall of the Church. Basilica of San Crisogono, Trastevere neighborhood, Rome

Hebrus River. Maritsa River, Bulgaria, Greece, and Turkey

Hibernia. Ireland

Hierusalem. Biblical Latin name for Jerusalem, Israel

Hispania. Spain

Illiberis. Granada, Spain

Kythira Strait. Waterway off the southern coast of Greece, known for hazardous passage

Lake Brigantium. Lake Constance, with shoreline bordering Germany, Switzerland, and Austria

Libya. Libya, North Africa

Lucky Tree. Arbon, Switzerland

Lugdunum. Lyons, France

Malta. Republic of Malta, an island nation in the Mediterranean Sea

Mardian Plain. A region of the Upper Thracian Plain near Harmanli, Bulgaria

Massilia. Marseille, France

Mediolanum. Milan, Italy

Moenus River. Main River, a tributary of the Rhine

Mons Aetna. Mount Etna, Sicily, Italy

Mons Matrona Pass. Col de Montgenèvre, France

Neapolis. Naples, Italy

Neviodunum. Drnovo, Slovenia

Nicomedia. İzmit, Turkey

Nilus River. Nile River, Egypt

Ostia. Ostia Antica, an archaeological site today, but formerly the original port of Rome

Padus River. Po River, Italy

Palaestina. Corresponds to parts of Israel, Jordan, Lebanon, and Syria

Pannonia. Corresponds to parts of Austria and several Balkan countries in southeastern Europe

Peloponnese. Large peninsula comprising all of southern Greece

Piraeus. Port city in Greece that is today part of the Athens urban area

Portus. Secondary port of Rome, which eclipsed Ostia; today it is at the tip of the runway at Rome's Leonardo da Vinci International Airport

Propontis. Sea of Marmara, Turkey

Pylos. Pilos, Greece

Raetia. Corresponds primarily to eastern Switzerland

Ravenna. Ravenna, Italy

Rhenus River. Rhine River

Sardinia. Sardinia, Italy

Savus River. Sava River, a tributary of the Danube

Serdica. Sofia, Bulgaria

Sicilia. Sicily, Italy

Sirmium. Sremska Mitrovica, Serbia

Stobi. Today the town is an archaeological site near Gradsko, North Macedonia

Syracusae. Syracuse, Sicily, Italy

Tauromenium. Taormina, Sicily, Italy

Thessalonica. Thessaloniki, Greece

Thracia. Corresponds to parts of Bulgaria, Greece, and Turkey, bordering the Black Sea

Tiberis River. Tiber River, Italy

Tibur. Tivoli, Italy

Trans Tiberim. Trastevere neighborhood, Rome

Vemania. Vemania Castle, a ruin at Isny im Allgäu, Germany

Venetia. A region in northeast Italy, which later included the city of Venice

Verona. Verona, Italy

Vindonissa. Windisch, Switzerland

Wolf City. Lycopolis, modern Asyut, Egypt

Glossary

agora. The central marketplace of a Greek town, equivalent to the Latin *forum.*

argenteus. A silver coin of significant value, though not as much as a solidus.

augustus. A traditional title for the emperors, used within the Imperial College to designate one of the two highest leaders.

ballista. Mechanical weapon for projecting darts and missiles with great force.

bema. A raised platform in a Greek city from which speakers carried out civic and legal functions.

bireme. A rowed warship (usually also having a sail) with two banks of oars on each side.

caesar. A traditional title for the emperors, used within the Imperial College to designate one of the two junior rulers.

calda. A warm drink made of wine, water, and spices.

caldarium. A hot room in a Roman bath.

capsa. A tube-shaped container for carrying books or scrolls.

catechumen. A person who has believed in Christ and entered into preparation for baptism.

chiton. A simple, loose-fitting dress worn especially by Greek women, held in place by pins.

codex. A book of papyrus or parchment pages bound inside covers, readily adopted by Christians to replace the scroll.

cognomen. The third part of the threefold Roman naming system, usually an identifying nickname.

colleague. One of the members of the Imperial College.

decanus. The leader of a typical army squad of approximately eight soldiers who shared a tent.

denarius (pl., *denarii*). In late imperial times, it was no longer an actual coin but a monetary unit of low value; e.g., an unskilled laborer would make twenty-five *denarii* per day.

domus. A Roman city house, as opposed to a country villa.

Donatists. A strict schismatic group that broke away from catholic Christianity under Donatus; they viewed clergy who apostatized during persecution as forbidden from serving communion.

donative. The periodic distribution of large monetary gifts to soldiers to increase their annual pay and keep them loyal.

fossor. Gravediggers employed by the church to oversee Christian cemeteries.

genius. The inner spirit (in fact, a kind of deity to be worshiped) that empowered and protected a man or inhabited an everyday place or object.

Gnosticism. Ancient heresy that took many forms; centered on the idea that knowledge (*gnosis*) of heavenly truth, not the historical work of Jesus on the cross, leads to salvation.

mile. A Roman mile, equal to a thousand paces, or about 4,860 modern feet (nine-tenths of a modern mile).

monoreme. A rowed warship (usually also having a sail) with a single bank of oars on each side.

nummus. (pl., *nummi*) The general name for a coin, including bronze coins of little value, like a penny.

optio. A Roman army officer with various duties, serving under a centurion.

ornatrix. A domestic slave specializing in hair and makeup for the lady of the house.

ostracon. (pl., *ostraca*) A piece of broken pottery reused as a writing surface by ink or incision.

peristyle. The rear garden in a Roman house, surrounded by pillars supporting a shady arcade.

posca. A cheap drink of soldiers and lower classes, made from diluted vinegar and herbal flavorings.

solidus. A late imperial gold coin of significant value.

spatha. A long sword that had come into common use by soldiers of the late imperial era, replacing the shorter gladius.

speculator. A Roman special-forces agent, like a spy (from *speculari*, to observe, explore, examine, watch).

trireme. A rowed warship (usually also having a sail) with three banks of oars on each side.

votive. A religious gift given after a sacred vow is fulfilled.

Prologue

Though I wanted to speak about the terrible thing I had seen, I held my tongue.

At first, I told myself it wasn't a woman's place to address such a respectable group of men. This was, after all, a council of eminent bishops and theologians in the catholic church. Who was I to speak before such an august gathering? Just a nun from a faraway island—a mere girl, only twenty years old. Why would they care what I had to say?

Yet in truth, I cannot blame my silence on my female sex, for the catholic church has always welcomed prophetic women into its midst. No, it was more than my feminine soul that silenced me that day. I kept quiet because I felt afraid to do what the Lord was asking. I wasn't sure my words would be well received. What I had witnessed was shocking, and the accusation I needed to make would have caused a rowdy disturbance. The images were clear enough in my head. But if I had described them to the bishops, I would have had to express my testimony with eloquence and clarity. Further, I would have been submitting my memories to judgment and critique. It scared me, for it seemed too hard to bear.

And so I held my tongue.

Do I wish now that I hadn't? Looking back, I do. But in that moment, my courage faltered.

26

Bishop Chrestus of Syracusae was the man who had brought me to Arelate for the important council. "Why me?" I had asked him.

"All the bishops will bring along a few priests or deacons, and some nuns," he replied. "I have been allowed five assistants by Constantine. We will be staying for several weeks in Gaul, and there are always tasks that need doing. Some will require a woman's expertise."

"I understand, Your Holiness, but why *me* in particular?"

Chrestus looked at me closely, a slight smile on his wise and godly face. He leaned close and raised his wrinkled finger at me. "Because, Flavia, you are a handmaiden of the Lord."

He didn't elaborate further, and I didn't press the point. Yet during the long sea journey, I thought often about what he said. He was alluding to the Annunciation at the beginning of Luke's gospel. By the time we arrived in Gaul, I still wasn't sure what I had in common with the Virgin Mother of the Lord. Yet Chrestus must have seen something in me that reminded him of Blessed Mary.

The Council of Arelate had been convened by Emperor Constantine himself. Pope Miltiades—may his soul rest in peace—had been forced to confront a church heresy soon after the emperor won his great victory at Rome. Now that Miltiades had passed into the underworld to await the resurrection, Sylvester was the new bishop of Rome. His representatives were at Arelate with Chrestus and all the other righteous bishops who opposed the heresy of Donatus. The Donatists believed in harsh treatment of clergy who had succumbed to the pressures of persecution. These priests had denied Christ or handed over the scriptures for burning. Such sinners were forbidden forever, said the Donatists, from serving the holy bread and wine. But my own bishop, like Pope Sylvester, believed in forgiveness from the church for these fallen brethren.

I was visiting the market after the council's deliberations were over for the day when I happened to see the Aegyptian bishop of Wolf City sneaking down an alley with a voluptuous prostitute. Melitius! He was an ally of the Donatists—an especially outspoken advocate of legalistic punishments for the disobedient. Yet there he was, cavorting with a streetwalker!

I decided to follow him.

Melitius was short and quick, like a little rat darting here and there in the busy lane. At times he disappeared in the crowd. Unfortunately for him, the prostitute was a tall, yellow-haired Goth who was hard to miss. I saw the pair dart into a scribe's shop next to the brothel. I entered after them but turned immediately to examine a stack of papyrus sheets, as if I were oblivious to anyone else in the store.

"Come on, church man," the girl whispered in a sultry voice. "Let's not delay."

"It will only take a moment, and then this job will be done," said Melitius. "I want to finish it first so I can take my time with you."

The bishop of Wolf City went to the back room, where the scribe copied documents for his customers. Melitius began to dictate a letter to an unknown recipient while the scribe took it all down. I crept closer to the back room, listening through the doorway. What I heard shocked me.

"The fool Sylvester and his lackeys are going to prevail over us," Melitius said to the scribe. "There are too many supporters of cheap forgiveness here in Arelate. But we will win in the end. The emperor's mind will soon be turned away from Rome to the capitals of the East." The letter went on to describe secret tactics and upcoming travel arrangements that I could only half hear. Finally, Melitius ended the letter with a startling farewell. "You are the Aegyptian Asp," he declared. "With God's help, I pray you will slip in silently and bite the church hard—with deadly poison."

Praying for God's help to bite the church with poison? What kind of bishop would say such a thing?

The prostitute wandered over and called to Melitius from the doorway of the back room. "Hurry up, handsome," she whined, wiggling her hips as she spoke.

"I'm coming in a moment! Just wait, woman."

Melitius finished his transaction with the scribe, who promised to post the letter the same day. After the pair left the shop, they went inside the brothel next door. I watched them go, then purchased some parchment for my bishop and exited into the hot August sunshine.

What a hypocrite! Melitius feigns godliness before the council, yet he visits prostitutes unseen! And he is plotting against Pope Sylvester! And who is the Aegyptian Asp?

When the council convened the next day, I found a seat among the delegates from Sicilia, my island home for the past few years. During the course of deliberations, Melitius took his usual haughty stance against the fallen priests. "Hander-overers," he called them, for they had handed over the holy scriptures to the persecuting authorities. Some had even cursed the name of Christ! This was surely a grievous sin, but that is exactly why the Savior shed his blood—as medicine for even the worst crimes. Melitius, however, believed in a rod of iron—for everyone but himself.

That day at the council, I did not speak up. Nor the next three. It wasn't until the final day that I gathered my determination to state what I had seen. The righteous bishops assembled before me could decide what ought to be done about it.

The Lord himself gave me the opportunity to speak. The host of the council, Bishop Marinus of Arelate, announced that thirty-four of the gathered bishops had decided to censure Melitius for heresy and schism. His Donatist views were to be utterly rejected.

The defeated man rose, gathered his Aegyptian associates, and left the proceedings with a huffy air. Everyone could sense the tension in the room. Some men—mostly fellow Africans—began to remark on Melitius's holy character.

"Perhaps we were too hard on him?" one delegate suggested.

A murmur of assent rippled through the crowd.

Bishop Marinus clapped his hands for attention. "Quiet, please!" he cried. "Let us have order, as we are in the presence of God."

The council settled down, though the aura of unease remained.

A wax tablet was passed to the hosting bishop. After reading it, he announced that some of the Africans were suggesting the removal of any formal condemnation of Melitius by name. He would remain a bishop in good standing at Wolf City, though his views about withholding grace and forgiveness would be rejected in the council's decrees.

And that is when the Lord gave me a golden opportunity.

"Does anyone here have reason to object to this deletion?" asked Bishop Marinus.

The council chamber fell silent.

I knew then that I should speak up. I was the only person in the room who had information that ran counter to the narrative of Melitius's sanctimonious piety. The bishops needed to know what I had seen. God was prompting me to speak. Obediently, I rose from my place and started to collect my thoughts.

Yet as I stood there, I felt overwhelmed by a powerful sense of isolation. As the only erect person in the room, I felt alone. As a woman, I felt out of place. Reaching out my hand, I sought stability but felt only empty air.

And so I fled.

Yes, I fled. I ran out of the room like a frightened doe. Outside the council chamber, at the end of a long colonnade, I paused, leaning against the wall to catch my breath.

Bishop Chrestus had surely misnamed me. *A handmaiden of the Lord? Hardly!* The Virgin Mary had offered a resounding yes to God when he promised to incarnate his Son in her womb. If she could assent to something so momentous, could I not face a simple challenge like speaking the truth? Where Mary had said yes, I had looked God in the face and said no.

I raised my eyes heavenward. "Grant me courage next time, Lord," I whispered to the sky, "the courage to do your will even when I am afraid." Then I followed my prayer with an even more sacred request. "Look upon me, Lord, and make me your handmaiden in spite of my failing."

And in that moment of great failure, I knew that, even so, God had accepted me. My heart was bound to his.

Yet I also knew that the time would come when God would put me to the test again.

ACT 1

NAVIGATION

1

MAY 316

The first lash of the leather whip was like hot fire on Rex's back.

Don't cry out, he told himself, gritting his teeth. *Just take as many stripes as you must until the time is right.*

"Death by the lash" was the sentence decreed upon him.

But I am not going to die today!

The second stroke fell, slicing another molten line across Rex's bare shoulders. He sagged a little, kept upright only by the rope that held his wrists above his head. The rope dangled from the ship's yard above. A brisk wind buffeted the imperial navy warship *Deadly Encounter* as it rolled in the open sea like a speck of driftwood.

"Had enough already?" the centurion sneered. His real name was unknown to the rowers and soldiers gathered on deck to watch the execution. Everyone just called him Brutus. The nickname was fitting, for he was a brute, more animal than man.

"Give me the best you've got!" Rex shot back, unwilling to show fear to his tormentor. The rejoinder brought him a third lash, which he took again in silence.

A few moments later, a fourth.

Then the perfect wave hit, and everything changed.

Rex had been waiting for it: the kind of doubled-up breaker that outsizes the other waves, hits the ship broadside, and throws the men off-balance. Great swells of seawater had been slamming into the craft all day, so when

33

this one crashed into the hull and everyone was reaching for a handhold, Rex knew it was time to move.

Grasping the rope that bound his wrists, he lifted his body and planted his feet on a water cask tied to the rails. Turning quickly, he launched himself at Brutus as the unsteady centurion sought to recover his stance. Rex wrapped his legs around his enemy's neck, locked his ankles tight, and began to squeeze his thighs.

The suffocating leg choke was one of the many weapons in a speculator's arsenal. Rex's body remembered his combat training even if his mind had forgotten it over the years. At the age of sixteen, after a period of intense preparation, he had been commissioned into the Roman army as a speculator. They were the most elite soldiers in the legions: highly skilled operatives who spied on enemy lands, entered locked buildings, and took out opponents by stealth. Swords and spears weren't their only weapons; they also knew the Greek martial art of *pancratium*, an ancient method of hand-to-hand combat. Even the toughest street fighters were no match for a trained speculator. Certainly this overweight centurion with an appetite for cruelty wouldn't be.

But while Brutus was out of shape and flabby, he was nonetheless a heavy man. He dragged Rex back and forth as he stumbled across the deck while the crew cheered the sudden brawl. The furious centurion sputtered curses from his red face and struggled to separate the legs that clenched his throat. His fingernails raked Rex's thighs, gouging bloody grooves, but Rex only pressed harder. He dangled like a carpenter's plumb line from the yard above, following Brutus's zigzag path. In a moment, the man's blood flow would be cut from his brain and he would go limp. A hard stomp to his throat would crush his windpipe. After that, Rex hoped the mutiny aboard the *Deadly Encounter* would begin.

Mutiny had been brewing for a long time. Even more than the legions, the navy was notorious for the harsh discipline it imposed on its crewmen. But the *Deadly Encounter*, under Brutus's sadistic regime, had gone far beyond the normal standards of the fleet. "Death by the lash" was decreed for infractions as minor as stealing an extra bread crust or laughing in the presence of an officer. The sacrifice of toes to the surgeon's scissors was one of Brutus's favorite penalties. Half the rowers on the ship were missing a digit on their bare feet, and even some of the marines had suffered this punishment despite it weakening their combat readiness. As for salaries, none of the men had received payment in almost a year. A request for what was owed would have been answered with a beating, or worse, the scissors' snip. Rex had been telling himself for weeks that the warship was ripe for a mutiny—but only if domineering Brutus could be taken out first.

"Argh!" the centurion grunted as he struggled against Rex's strangling grip. "Let . . . me . . . go!"

The rope around Rex's wrists bit hard into his skin, and his shoulders burned from the lashes he had taken. Yet he had no intention of letting his prey escape.

Although the marines on deck—many of whom had been brutalized by their centurion—were in no mood to intervene, Brutus's optio finally sprang into action. Since all weapons were stowed during routine patrols, the junior officer didn't have a blade. Instead, he began looking for a chance to whack Rex's shins with a stout rod.

Rex renewed his grip on the blood-slick rope above his head. Twisting his body midair, he spun Brutus around just as the optio's stick was about to make contact. Instead of striking Rex, the blow landed squarely on the centurion's spine. He let out a squeal and backpedaled until he crashed against the ship's rail. Though his feet remained on deck, his upper body arched backward over the gunwale with Rex still attached to his neck. The two men dangled precariously over the choppy sea.

High above, the old salty rope that had been thrown over the spar for the whipping, pulled taut by the deadly struggle, now lurched out toward the yardarm. The sudden slack in the line was all it took for the two combatants to topple over the rail.

But Rex refused to let go of his enemy. He swung at the end of the rope with Brutus still clutched between his legs, trying to choke the life from the centurion rather than let him escape into the sea. Someone had to die today, and if Brutus survived, Rex wouldn't. A groan escaped his lips, for the terrible strain on his wrists was unbearable. Lightning bolts of pain ran down his forearms and into his shoulders.

And then the rope snapped.

Rex and Brutus separated now, each becoming a slingstone launched by the release of tension on the ship's broken line. Their trajectory took them toward the bireme's double bank of oars protruding from the hull. Brutus struck first, his skull smashing into a pinewood shaft with a solid *thunk!* that could be heard above the churning ocean and shouting men. Rex glimpsed a burst of red mist as he also hurtled toward the sea. His ankle painfully clipped an oar. Another wooden shaft slammed his hip. Then he hit the swells.

The water felt cold, even in the relatively warm Aegean. Rex surfaced beneath the oar banks, sputtering and shaking salty droplets from his eyes. Fortunately, his wrists hadn't been bound in a knot, merely wrapped in coils as he was strung up for the whipping. Now the rope was loose enough for him to extricate his hands. Bloody streaks encircled his forearms like bracelets.

Although most other men would have paused to recover in such a moment, Rex was a trained operative who knew the circumstances called for immediate action. Grasping one of the oars in both hands, he lifted himself from the sea and swung his leg over it. Astride the shaft like a horse, he inched his way up its length until he could slip through a portal in the hull. Angry men met him below deck—but they were the right ones, the ones Rex had marked as possible mutineers. Their pent-up fury was directed at the officers and the faction of the crew that supported them. All they needed was a leader brave enough to harness their rage.

"I can't believe it!" cried a long-armed rower whom everyone called the Thracian because of his birthplace. "You killed Brutus!"

"You sure he's dead?" someone else asked.

"His body was floating facedown in a cloud of red water," the Thracian replied.

"You're gonna be executed!" exclaimed another man, one of the marines who made up the fighting crew. It was a ridiculous thing to say to someone already condemned to death.

Rex raised himself to his full height. As a Germanic warrior from the tribe of the Alemanni, he was taller than most of the men aboard the ship. He glanced at the expectant faces staring back at him. When he finally spoke, it was in firm tones with emphatic jabs of his finger. "You're all going to be executed," he declared, "because you stood around and cheered while a crewman killed your centurion."

Stepping back, Rex let that reality sink in.

"It's time," the Thracian said at last. "It's either them or us." Everyone else nodded, steeling themselves for what they were about to do.

The battle was intense and violent, though mercifully brief. Since the unexpected rebellion had caught everyone without a sword, the fighting was hand-to-hand; not the skillful work of a speculator, but the brutal struggle of animals trying to survive by clawing, choking, punching, and gouging.

Only about half the rowers and a few of the soldiers joined the mutineers, so Rex thought at first that his inferior numbers might lead to defeat. However, the mutineers proved to be on the more ferocious side. They fought with a deep hatred accumulated from countless acts of abuse. One by one, the defenders fell before the mutineers' rage. Fists pummeled them into submission on the planks. Many others were thrown overboard. Eventually the deck quieted as the defenders capitulated. The victors panted as they gazed at the bloody bodies strewn around the ship. Some of the defeated were still groaning. Others would never make a sound again.

"Help us!" came a cry from the water.

"Toss lines to our brave men!" Rex shouted. "Bring them up!"

The Thracian assumed a kind of second-in-command status. He organized the mutineers into groups of three, who helped their comrades aboard. But those who had fought against them were left in the turbulent sea. Dejected, they clung to the oars, awaiting their fate.

"Heave the dead over the rails!" Rex ordered, and his men complied. Many of the bodies sank right away, though some floated on the surface like gruesome lily pads in a swamp of death.

The Thracian brought a short, stocky rower to Rex by the collar of his tunic. "This one didn't pick a side but refused to fight. What should we do with him, Captain?"

Captain? Now, that's an interesting term . . .

Rex decided he would run with it.

"Stephen, why didn't you rebel against your evil lords?" he asked the heavyset young man, though he already knew the answer.

"I am a priest of God," Stephen replied. "The Lord told us to love our enemies and obey our authorities, as you know."

Rex did know. He had learned much about the Christian religion in a former life that seemed distant to him now. At one point, he had almost converted to the catholic faith—until his path in life took a drastic turn.

For the last three years, Rex had been forced to row in the imperial navy. It was hard work at first, but eventually he had settled into the naval routine. His galley had sailed from one end of the Aegean to the other on various missions. Gone was the era when great seafaring powers like Carthago or Graecia challenged the warships of Rome. These days, the navy's only foes were pirates, smugglers, and the occasional rebel in a civil war. Yet many galleys like the *Deadly Encounter* still patrolled imperial waters, enforcing the will of the two Roman emperors, Constantine and Licinius. Rex remained loyal to Constantine, despite being banished by him to the navy. The charge of treason was unfair—Rex had not, technically, fled the emperor's side in battle—but he had been sentenced nonetheless. And he had endured the drudgery of rowing ever since.

He smiled at Stephen, a man who had been kind to him from the beginning. "Join us," Rex offered. "You're a good oarsman."

"I will join, but only to restrain you from violence. I won't fight for you."

Rex gave his captive a long stare—and Stephen, to his credit, returned the steady gaze. Finally, Rex nodded to him. "Very well. Restrain me if you can, Brother Priest." He turned and faced his waiting men. "To the oars! We're mutineers now, but we aren't pirates! For almost a year, the navy has abused us and denied our salary. Merchant ships should have been taxed to pay us. But since that duty was refused, we must do it ourselves! It's up to us to take what we're owed for our labors and suffering."

"And look at us!" crowed the Thracian, puffing out his scrawny chest. "We're the best-looking band of tax collectors the empire has ever seen!"

All the men erupted in a cheer.

"Sir, our enemies are still clinging to the oars," said the red-haired pilot who manned the steerboards. "Others are lying around the decks. What are your orders?"

Rex thought for a long moment. Everyone waited expectantly. "Leave them all in the sea," he said at last. "The living and the dead."

The mutineers carried out the grim order without delay. The injured men on deck were tossed overboard. Those who could swim managed to grab an oar. Many of the sorely wounded, however, sank beneath the surface after a brief attempt to stay afloat.

"To the oars!" Rex cried again. "Shake loose those barnacles, and let's get going."

Heading to their benches, the mutineers raised their oars high and began to wobble them hard. One by one, the desperate men outside the hull lost their grip on the wet shafts and fell into the sea.

Stephen approached Rex and put a hand on his new captain's shoulder. "Rex," he said quietly, "our boarding gangplank will float. Leave it for those men. They can cling to it and kick their feet. And give them a cask of water. There's an island on the horizon. They can make it."

"We'll need that plank if we want to capture any ships, Brother Priest."

"We can get another one somewhere."

"In what port?" Rex shot back. "We're outlaws now."

"God will provide a way."

Rex stared at the boarding plank for a moment, then looked back to his friend. "Your captain will provide a way," he declared. "Now go find your seat. It's time to row."

—◦/◦/◦—

When Pope Sylvester entered the reception hall of the Lateran Palace, he didn't just see the space with his eyes; he also inhaled its scent through his nose and savored its sweet, pungent aroma. The smell of frankincense, myrrh, balsam, and aloe permeated the air. Although Titus Junius Ignatius's washed and anointed corpse was wrapped in a shroud, the scent of the grave spices couldn't be contained by mere linen. The mourners—a large crowd of them, for the deceased man was a wealthy senator—had gathered around the body as it rested on a table. The men wore dull colors, and the women were veiled. Everyone awaited words of godly comfort from the bishop of Rome.

Sylvester stepped to an ornate wooden pulpit and laid a book on its flat surface. The elegantly carved ambo was one of the many additions that his predecessor, Pope Miltiades, had installed in the spacious reception hall. Before that, the Lateran Palace had been in the hands of the city prefect, a wicked man who decorated the room with all the lewd and idolatrous finery one would expect of a pagan. But Emperor Constantine gave the palace to the catholic church after he won a great victory at Rome. Cleansed of its secular trappings, the palace now housed the city's bishop, and its reception hall had been converted into the so-called Lateran Church. Although the room wasn't originally designed for church gatherings, it would serve that purpose well enough for now.

But not forever, Sylvester reminded himself as he turned the pages of his codex to find his chosen reading.

The text he had selected for Ignatius's funeral came from the *Acts of the Apostles.* Everyone agreed this book was within the church's rule of faith. Like the gospel that went before it, the *Acts of the Apostles* was written by Saint Luke, an apostolic man and companion of Paul. One of Sylvester's deacons had urged him to read instead from the *Acts of Peter,* a much more exciting story than Luke's plain account of the earliest church. The deacon had recommended the *Acts of Peter* because in its pages, the heroic apostle did mortal combat with the evil magician Simon Magus and defeated that sorcerer through a series of divine miracles.

But Sylvester had refused the deacon's suggestion. He knew, along with all the church scholars, that those other "acts" were imitations of the first one by Luke—more fanciful and flightier in their narration than the original, and not always historically valid. Although the common believers loved such entertaining tales, the bishop knew that only the *Acts of the Apostles* conformed to the church's rule of faith, which the Greeks called the "canon."

"Beloved, I greet you in the name of the Lord," Sylvester said from the pulpit, his arms raised over his little flock. "Peace be with you!"

"And with thy spirit!" came the unified reply of the mourners.

Rather than move to his chair, Sylvester proceeded through a short funeral liturgy while standing at the ambo. His homiletic text from *Acts* was the account of Saint Paul raising Eutychus from the dead after the youth fell from a window. Clearly, this miracle was due not to Paul's power but to God's. In the same way, Sylvester told the mourners that God's power would raise all Christians to new life, including the senator whose body lay on the table. Like the meaning of Eutychus's name, every believer would one day have the "good fortune" of being ushered into Paradise.

The bishop gestured toward the senator's linen-wrapped corpse as he

40

closed his homily. "My people, fear not! Consider how the blessed Paul said to those first Christians, 'Do not be afraid, for indeed, his life is in him.' And that same power of life is within our brother Ignatius—the life of the Savior who declared, 'I am the Way, the Truth, and the Life.' Ignatius will rise up when the final trumpet sounds and the underworld gives up its dead. This is the promise of Almighty God. Let it never be forgotten!"

The comforting reminder from Rome's pastor prompted the mourners to offer grateful murmurs and nods of assent.

When the liturgy was finished, the gravediggers stepped forward and put the body in a wooden casket for transport. The funeral procession made its way to the city gate and out onto the Appian Way. The destination was an ancient quarry pit that unbelievers first turned into a burial ground but that now belonged to the catholic church for exclusively Christian use. The Apostolic Monument was there too: a shrine that housed the relics of Peter and Paul, with an attached dining room for funeral banquets. Long ago, in a time of persecution, Paul's bones had been moved here from his tomb on the Ostian Way. As for Peter, no one remembered anymore precisely where he had been buried. The veneration of Peter was focused here now, not at his original grave on the Vatican Hill. Wherever that spot may have been, the memory of it was lost today—and probably forgotten forever.

Though a large crowd had come to the countryside, only a few of the mourners, along with the gravediggers and the bishop's assistants, made their way underground. The senator had chosen a good burial site in this cemetery that everyone called the *Catacombs*, a Greek term which meant "down in the pits." Senator Ignatius was to be interred near the grave of Sebastian, a Christian soldier from Mediolanum who was martyred in Rome.

The lamps in the deacons' hands cast flickering lights on the bare rock walls as the gravediggers slipped the body into its niche and sealed the opening with a marble slab. The milky-white plaque was engraved with the senator's name, age, date of burial, and the words *rest in peace* enclosed in palm branches. Sylvester sprinkled holy oil on the grave, said a final prayer, and returned to the surface. The rest of the mourning party proceeded back into the city, though without the usual racket of weeping and wailing that secular funerals generated. The *First Epistle to the Thessalonians* said it was not right for Christians to grieve like those who have no hope.

Once the mourners dispersed, Sylvester called for his most senior assistant, the scholarly Archdeacon Quintus. He had served Pope Miltiades effectively and had continued his faithful service in the Lateran Palace after the bishop died. The new pope had made only one request of Quintus: Sylvester had asked him to shave his beard as a sign of loyalty to the bare-chinned Emperor Constantine. A beardless face was the new fashion among the Roman Christians. Sylvester actually enjoyed the feel of it, though not the endless shaving and plucking required to maintain his smooth cheeks.

"Did you not find the document, Quintus?" Sylvester asked when his assistant arrived empty-handed. "I see you have brought nothing with you."

"It has been unrolled already for your examination, Your Holiness. Please follow me."

The two men entered the bishop's study and hunched over an expensive scroll that had been laid flat upon the desk, its corners held down with weights. The ink on the parchment was still bright and clearly legible. It was the last will and testament of Senator Titus Junius Ignatius.

"The lawyers have determined its legitimacy?"

Quintus nodded. "All is regular and in order. Fortunately, its provisions are quite simple. Look here."

Sylvester examined the paragraph to which Quintus pointed. "Aha!" he said. "A generous gift to the catholic church! We can begin a building program with that."

Quintus stepped back in surprise, his eyes widening. "A building? Wonderful news! So you have gained the emperor's permission?"

"No, not yet. We must secure his agreement before the construction can begin. I consider it the foremost mission before us now. An embassy must be sent to Constantine."

"He is in Gaul. Travel for a party that size will be costly. But I'm sure we could borrow some funds from our distributions to the poor. Should I arrange it?"

Sylvester snorted at this suggestion and waved his hand. "Never! The hungry must always be filled and the unclothed be warmed, not just in word but in deed, as the *Epistle of James* reminds us." That apostolic letter was believed by many bishops—though not all—to be included in the canon too.

"I knew you would say that," Quintus replied with a chuckle, "but I had to make sure. So by what other means might we pay for the mission?"

Sylvester paused for a moment, gazing at Quintus's expectant face. He allowed a mischievous grin to turn up his lips. "We will rely on the charity of someone who is newly rich," Sylvester declared, "someone with great piety and a holy desire to pay for such an important mission as this."

"Are you thinking of someone specific?" Quintus asked, though both men knew the matter had already been decided in the bishop's mind.

"Indeed, I am," Sylvester answered, playing along. He pointed to a passage farther down in the scroll. "I will petition Senator Ignatius's sole heir, who is now fabulously wealthy."

Quintus stretched his neck and inspected the bequest in the senator's will. After reading the name of the heir, he looked up and met the bishop's eyes. "A wise plan, Your Holiness," he said with a nod. "I will make arrangements for a ship. And may the Lord grant us success."

—◦◦◦—

The fire inside Mons Aetna was so hot that the earth itself would melt and burst forth. Flavia had seen it a few times during her three years on the island of Sicilia: how the bubbling lava would explode from a fissure, red-hot and steaming, then cool into a torpid sludge that smoldered with unbearable heat. The lava was no doubt the hottest thing on the island. However, as Flavia had come to learn the hard way, the heat of the Sicilian sun was a close second.

"It is only May!" Flavia complained to her friend Cassiopeia, a fellow nun rescued from harsh slavery by the catholic church. "How can it be so hot already?"

Cassi had no explanation for the unusually hot weather, but she did offer a smile as she handed her friend a kerchief. "Mop your face, my sister," she said in halting Latin. It was her third language, and she was still learning it. "Your brow is misty."

"We would say 'drenched' or 'wet,'" Flavia corrected. "But thank you," she added as she wiped the sweat from her forehead. "Is it this hot in Africa? I have heard your land is like an oven at times."

"Ah, yes, my sister. So hot in Africa. How else am I like this?" Cassi pointed to her face, which was the dark color of polished ebony. Her eyes were bright with a playful expression. "I am Aethiops, you see? 'Burnt face' in Greek. My people bake under God's sun. We are his favorite raisin cakes!"

Flavia took her friend's hand as the two women walked side by side on the road. "Such beautiful skin," she murmured, caressing Cassi's wrist. Suddenly she looked up and gestured to the south. "Let's visit Africa together some day!"

"Ha! You dream so big!" Cassi exclaimed with a giggle. "We are poor sisters of Sicilia. Not senators' wives, to go all about the earth!"

Not a wife, but once I was a senator's daughter, Flavia thought. *Yet Cassi is right. I am something much humbler now. I am a nun—a daughter of Jesus Christ. Thanks be to God.*

"If we cannot visit Africa," Flavia continued, "we can at least gaze across the sea and imagine such a journey. The harbor is just ahead now. Stay close to me. We are two women traveling alone, and ports often collect some unsavory characters."

Cassi made the sign of the cross on herself. "God be with us," she prayed.

The harbor at Tauromenium was old. Though the Roman Empire controlled Sicilia now, and the Roman Republic had annexed it before that, the island itself was first settled by Greek and Phoenician sailors who established trading posts, then settled down and founded towns. Some of the most authoritative historians whom Flavia had read considered Tauromenium to be even older than Syracusae. The beautiful theater here was made of Roman brick, yet the town followed an ancient Greek street plan rarely seen in Italy, which testified to its great age.

"Sister Flavia, I have the—" Cassi broke off, seemingly searching for the right word. "*Deltum?*" she tried, then grinned and shrugged. She had only Latinized the Greek term *deltos.*

"Tablet," Flavia said. "It's called a tablet." She took it from Cassi and showed her the words scratched into the wax, sounding out each one. "Fish ... vinegar ... dates ... cloth ... needles ..."

"We have much to buy," Cassi observed after repeating all the words on the list.

"Fortunately, a port is the best place to buy whatever you need. Come now, let's get started. I'm in the mood to bargain."

The two women proceeded up and down the market stalls, with Flavia doing the haggling and Cassi carrying the growing load in a sack over her shoulder. Although both women were social equals as sisters in the Tauromenium convent, Flavia was the recognized leader among the nuns, so Cassi had naturally adopted a supporting role. The arrangement worked well for both women, in light of their respective backgrounds.

When the shopping was finished, the pair made their way to the end of the pier and sat down on its edge, dangling their legs over the water. They broke apart a loaf of coarse bread to share and poured some vinegar in a clay bowl for dipping. Though the sun was still hot, the sail of a nearby ship cast its shadow over the women. An ocean breeze rustled Flavia's plain woolen tunic. Contented, the two friends lapsed into a companionable silence.

Flavia found herself staring at the other ships in the port, examining them one by one. Finally, Cassi broke the silence. "All for trading," she observed with a compassionate tone to her voice. "I see it too." She put her dark hand on Flavia's pale one and caressed it soothingly.

Does she know? Are my feelings that obvious? Intrigued, Flavia glanced at her friend. Cassi's glossy hair was woven into tight braids.

She smiled back at Flavia with her perfect, white teeth. "Perhaps that is the ship you seek?" she said with a dip of her chin to indicate the direction.

Flavia's head spun around. "The imperial navy!" she exclaimed as her eyes fell on a trireme making its way into the harbor by the steady rotation of its oars.

"Let us meet it and look at the sailors," Cassi suggested.

She does know!

Flavia scrambled to her feet and dropped her unfinished loaf into the shopping bag. The two women watched the ship pull alongside the pier and tie up. When the job was done, the crew hurried down the gangplank with the enthusiasm that navy men always have for the taverns and brothels of a port town.

Flavia scanned their faces but saw none she recognized. She sighed. "Aegyptians and Carthaginians, from the look of them," she said glumly.

"No white Germani," Cassi agreed.

Flavia turned and looked more closely at her friend. Cassi's face was sympathetic but not pitying. She remained silent, offering gentle understanding and quiet acceptance. Over the past three years, Flavia had tried to keep hidden her most private feelings. Yet at times it was impossible to conceal the one thing she longed for more than anything else in the world. Tears gathered in her eyes as she let the pain of searing loss come into her conscious mind.

"He will come, Sister Flavia. Someday, he will come for you."

"I hope so. But it's hard to wait."

So hard! How long, O Lord? How long will you ask this of me? Another year? A decade? Till death?

Cassi pointed over Flavia's shoulder. "Look! There is the captain. His face is kind. He will speak to us, I think."

"Let's find out."

The women approached the captain, who was squatting on the dock as he scraped a barnacle from the hull. Flavia waited until he stood to address him. His insignia showed he held the rank of centurion.

"Sir, we thank you for keeping the emperor's waters safe for us," she said politely. "What news of pirates and slavers? I'm sure you must have them all on the run."

The leather-faced centurion examined the nuns with an appraising eye, though not with the lecherous stare other men might have given them. "Aye," he said agreeably, "the sea lanes are mostly clear. A few rogues will always hide here and there. But our boys can take care of whatever comes along." The man chuckled and scratched his head. "Since when do young girls care about naval operations?"

"This region isn't very productive, sir. We rely on the goods that come in from the sea. It's nice to know the commerce will keep flowing." Flavia waited a moment, then asked, "Are you part of a fleet?"

Again, the centurion's expression was quizzical, yet he remained friendly. "If you must know, aye, we got a couple of biremes up in the straits. And a whole flotilla is out in the Ionian right now. So don't worry about any pirates, little lady. Other than a recent mutiny, the waters are calm."

"Are any of those navy ships headed this way, perhaps?"

"Hey, what's the matter? My boys ain't handsome enough for ya?" The centurion's tone was teasing, though he also seemed slightly irritated now. Flavia sensed he was ready to move on to other business.

"Oh, they're plenty handsome," Flavia insisted, smiling broadly to keep the banter going. "It's just that I'm partial to the northern men. Girls love that blond hair, you know."

She paused, her heart beating rapidly. *Just ask. Don't hesitate. Do it.* "Have you seen any Germani on those other ships?"

Now the captain took a step back, and the look in his eyes turned suspicious. "Germani? There ain't many of those in the navy. They ain't good seamen. Strange that you'd mention it. Why do you ask?"

"Um . . . I like their blond hair?"

The centurion ignored that reply. "Have you heard something about a specific German?" he demanded.

"Should I have?"

"Of course not! You shouldn't even be asking about sailors! Look at you. Plain clothes, simple hair, cross around your neck. Ain't you one of those Christian girls that prays in the wilderness?"

Flavia gestured to Cassi, whose eyes were cast to the ground. As a former slave, she always remained quiet in the presence of powerful men. "Yes," Flavia acknowledged, "my friend and I are sisters at the Tauromenium convent. But we are interested in any news of the sea to report to our spiritual mother."

"Well, little lady, you're in luck. The news of the sea is that there's a churchman from Rome aboard my ship, and he's looking for the sisters of Tauromenium."

A churchman from Rome? Who? And what does he want?

"Will you . . . introduce us?" Flavia asked uncertainly.

"Of course. Wait here."

The captain left the pair of nuns on the dock and went up the gangplank to his galley, then disappeared below deck. Flavia gazed over the water to the horizon, fighting the ever-present urge to curse the vast and arrogant sea. The dark-blue expanse always felt like an enemy to her, for it had stolen her heart's most earnest desire. Somewhere, far to the east, was the object of that desire. And it was exactly what she had said to the captain: a German.

A specific German named Brandulf Rex.

Footsteps sounded on the gangplank. Flavia turned and immediately recognized the man coming toward her. He was Archdeacon Quintus, a respected scholar and the highest-ranking assistant to the bishop of Rome. Only a matter of great significance would bring such a man here.

Keep your mind sharp, Flavia told herself. *Things are about to get interesting.*

—◦◦◦—

The imperial warship *Deadly Encounter* was turning out to be more than capable of living up to its name. Now that Rex was its captain instead of a mere oarsman, he was delighted to discover all the craft could do. Twice he captured fishing vessels, and soon after, he caught a grain ship with a decent treasure chest aboard. The Roman navy had a real wolf here—quick, fierce, and dangerous. But the navy had kept the wolf in a pen. Rex's philosophy was to open the gate and let the beast do its thing.

The seas were calm one morning, and the sky was clear, when the lookout called, "New sail on the starboard horizon, sir!"

Instantly, the men were on high alert. Rex felt the ship surge as the rowers instinctively quickened their pace. He ordered the beat-keeper to slow them down. "Draw near at one-quarter speed," he shouted from his position in the stern next to the red-haired pilot. "Keep the imperial standard visible! Do nothing to make them nervous. And let me know right away if you see any other craft."

The two ships converged at a gradual pace for most of the day. The merchant vessel was large, with a red-striped mainsail and a smaller foresail on a raked mast to aid in steering. A delicately arched gooseneck decorated the stern, the symbol of the bird goddess Isis who protected sailors. The boat was tubby, and it had a deep draft—which meant lots of cargo and little maneuverability in the event of a boarding. It was a pirate's dream.

Or a tax collector's dream, Rex corrected himself. He smiled at the thought.

Around the ninth hour, when the sun was past its zenith and the winds had died down, a second ship appeared in the distance—a monoreme warship making for the merchant vessel at a fast clip. The new style of warship, with its single bank of oars, was noted for its speed and maneuverability in battle. The monoreme's sailors must have known the *Deadly Encounter* held an unauthorized position and was engaging in stalking behavior, because they had moved to intervene. Evidently, today's taxes weren't going to be collected without a fight.

Fine, Rex decided. *Let's see what they're made of.* He instructed the beat-keeper to speed up in anticipation of the battle.

"You've been waiting for this moment!" Rex shouted to his band of mutineers, encouraging them to row harder as they increased their pace on a collision course with the oncoming warship. What the crew lacked in numbers on the oars they made up for with enthusiasm. "That fat boat is bound to have riches in its hold! You'll finally earn the pay you've been denied—but you'll have to fight those navy boys first!"

A cheer rose up at this exhortation, which Rex took as a good indication of his men's high morale. The red-striped merchant vessel was trying to get away, but Rex paid it no mind, for he knew it couldn't get far on this windless afternoon. The imperial monoreme was his main concern now. As the warships drew near, the enemy vessel launched a volley of arrows across the intervening water. Most of the shafts fell harmlessly into the sea or thunked into the hull, but a scream of pain indicated that at least one of Rex's men had been hit. Battle was imminent now. Rex ordered a full-speed ramming, loosened his spatha in his scabbard, and braced for impact.

The stupendous crash of the two ships rattled every oarsman to his bones and staggered the officers in the stern. Normally, the *Deadly Encounter*'s bronze ram was effective at smashing the timbers of an opponent's hull. But in this case, the skilled enemy rowers had maneuvered their ship so the two rams banged into one another. The great metallic *clang!* reverberated like Vulcan pounding his hammer on his underworld anvil. Both ships shivered with the impact, yet neither hull was breached, so a sinking wasn't imminent.

"To arms!" Rex shouted as the boarding bridge was heaved across the rails of the other ship. It was a wide plank that allowed Rex's fighters—some of them former marines, others just brawny rowers with an aggressive streak—to swarm to the enemy's deck under cover from archers. The air was thick with deadly arrows crisscrossing in both directions, but the mutineers held their shields high in defense. More importantly, they possessed an urgent will to attack. Any loss in battle would be followed by merciless execution. It was fight now or die, and the mutineers knew it. They pushed across the plank and leapt onto the prow of the enemy warship. Immediately, the clamor of swordplay and the screams of dying men rang out from this island of death in the middle of the Aegean Sea.

While the fighting continued near the prow, two clever mutineers managed to snag the opposing ship's stern with a grappling hook. They began hauling the line to bring the enemy vessel alongside.

Rex ran to the stern, away from the fray up front. Leaping onto his ship's rail, he beckoned to his Thracian lieutenant and a group of brave fighters. "We jump across!" he cried. "We can make it! Let's go!"

Most of the men made the leap, though one jumper miscalculated, fell short, and plunged into the sea with a scream. But the battle was raging, and there was no time to help the fallen man. Armored and helmeted like a legionary, with a spatha in one hand and shield in the other, Rex felt battle lust surge through him—a feeling he hadn't experienced in a long time.

He led his band in a pincer move that surprised the enemy from the rear of the ship. They were so preoccupied with the attackers on the boarding bridge that they were unprepared for an assault from the stern. Five or six men went down before the defenders realized they had to fight on two fronts. Though they gave it a try, it was hopeless. Whirling to fight in one direction meant the soldiers' backs were exposed to the other. The defenders fell like wheat stalks at harvest. Soon the deck grew quiet as the last few soldiers dropped their weapons, sank to their knees, and awaited the hope of mercy.

"Victory!" cried the Thracian, raising his blood-smeared blade to the sky as the mutineers cheered. Crimson droplets were spattered across his cheek. His ear was cut, and reddened sweat soaked his throat.

"Victory and great spoils!" Rex shouted, drawing yet another acclamation.

The mutineers collected the dropped weapons and herded the survivors to the stern under the Thracian's watchful eye. "Should we push them overboard, sir?" he asked.

Rex felt a hand on his shoulder. He turned to see his friend Stephen, the Christian priest. Rex was gratified to find him dripping with sweat, for Stephen had been one of the few men on the oars who had kept the ship in position after the initial collision. Though he refused to take up arms against an enemy due to his religious convictions, Stephen was willing to guide the ship. *And now he's trying to steer my conscience,* Rex realized. Perhaps that should have angered Rex, but it didn't. He was grateful for Stephen's presence aboard.

"Do not fear, Brother Priest," Rex said before his friend could speak. "I do not plan to drown these men."

"They fought valiantly and did their duty," Stephen agreed.

"Duty is a strange thing, with many motivations. Let's find out whether their duty was born of freedom or compulsion." Rex leapt onto a barrel and addressed his captives. "Soldiers of Rome, I salute your courage! Today I offer you two options. If you are happy with your lot in life, take your chances out here in the sea. You have some water, though I intend to take your food with me. And of course, your oars will be taken as well, lest you get the idea that a second engagement might turn out better for you. So you can remain here if you wish, floating under Sol's hot face until someone rescues you or you drift to an island or—may the gods forbid it!—you run out of water in this moist desert which we call the sea."

"What's the second option?" demanded a broad-shouldered captive with a scruffy likability about him.

"Join my band of tax collectors! We haven't been paid in a year. Have you been given what you deserve? Or does your centurion skim off what is allotted to you from the tax income? Why not seize what is rightfully yours? If you come over to my crew, yes, it's true that you'll always be hated as a mutineer as long as you are at sea. The navy will hunt you constantly. But capture a few ships with us, bring in some good treasure, and soon you can start a new life on land with the kind of riches a navy career could never provide you!"

Rex could see that many of the men were aghast at the idea of mutiny or rebellion, while others recognized the attractiveness of what he had offered.

"Make something of your lives!" the Thracian urged. "Be free!"

In the end, about a third of the monoreme's crew came over. Rex made them swear a blood oath to serve him, just as he had done with the original mutineers. Now the *Deadly Encounter* had a full crew again. Rex confiscated the warship's money chest, all its rations, and every weapon he could find. The oars were also collected for disposal far from the enemy's reach.

Waving and laughing, the mutineers left the glum soldiers on the deck of their crippled ship, their honor intact even if their hope for the future wasn't. The sailors who had joined the mutineers were the most boisterous in waving goodbye. Evidently, the harsh conditions on their ship hadn't been much better than what Rex had experienced.

Now it was time for treasure. Though the red-striped merchant vessel tried to make a run for it, the *Deadly Encounter* caught up to the tubby freighter just before sunset. The next morning, the mutineers awoke to find the merchant vessel had tried to make a run to escape, but the winds were unfavorable and it wasn't far off. Rex captured the vessel and boarded without incident. The crew comprised only ten men, led by a portly captain with a bushy white mustache.

"What are you carrying?" Rex demanded of the frightened seaman. "I'll leave you alive and well supplied if you cooperate, or sailless and thirsty if you don't. I want mobile wealth only."

"We're a grain ship, sir," the captain answered in a respectful tone. "That's bulky freight, unfortunately. Not something you can take along in a warship."

Rex grabbed the man's tunic and pulled him close. "Listen, skipper, I'm gonna find whatever you have aboard. If you have something mobile, tell me now. Because if I find it later and you didn't tell me, it's overboard for you. With that belly of yours, I imagine you'd sink pretty quick. But until you do, you'll have plenty of time to think about how much the sharks are gonna like your taste."

"Bit . . . bit . . . bitumen," the captain managed to say, his eyes wide. "Take the bitumen! It's valuable!"

Rex knew the tarry substance well. In certain places in the empire, it could be extracted from the ground or collected in gobs from pools. Heated up, the gooey, black stuff became runny and could be spread on wooden surfaces. When it cooled again, it made a waterproof seal. Wherever ships were being constructed or repaired, bitumen was in high demand. In some ports, it was literally worth its weight in silver coins.

Turning to his men, Rex ordered, "Find all the jars of bitumen! But leave the grain alone. And don't touch their food and drink. These men didn't fight us. We're collecting a tax here, not plundering. The bitumen will be our only levy."

The men went below and began to remove the clay jars of expensive bitumen, though not without some grumbling at the limit imposed on their looting. Stephen, however, gave Rex an affirming nod.

Rex approached the captain again. "So, sailor, what port are you out of?"

"Caesarea of Palaestina. The bitumen is from the salty sea beyond Aelia. Nothing can live in those waters. We loaded the bitumen in Caesarea, then took on a full load of grain at Alexandria."

"And where were you headed next?"

"Rome. The capital always needs bread, so I suppose we'll continue there, if it please you. We're grateful for your mercy, my lord."

"Yeah, you can make it to Rome. But that's the last place we want to get near. Where would that bitumen fetch the best price? Preferably somewhere close."

The captain tapped his chin and thought for a moment. "Syracusae is your best bet," he said at last. "The shipyards are busy there. They always need sealant. The competition will drive up the price. And the Syracusans won't be troubled by where it might have come from. In Sicilia, there's a long history of backdoor deals and looking the other way."

Rex clapped the man on the shoulder and smiled gallantly at him. "Kind sir, the empire thanks you for your cooperation in this modest tax transaction. May the gods speed you on your way."

Approaching the ship's rail, Rex shouted across to his men, most of whom now had returned to the *Deadly Encounter* with the confiscated loot. "Set a western course, you scoundrels!" he cried. "We're making for the island of Sicilia!"

Sicilia!

Saying the word aloud hit Rex hard. Stepping to a hidden place behind the mainmast and a stack of crates, Rex reached to his neck and softly caressed an amulet around his neck. The golden medallion had been incised with the Christian symbol of the cross.

"Jesus," he muttered, "you have no reason to answer me, and I have no right to ask. But if somehow you could hear me—"

Rex broke off his petition, aware of its futility. Yet something urged him to press on. "Jesus, could you somehow lead me to—"

Again, he quit, feeling unworthy to finish the prayer.

A hand touched Rex's forearm. He turned to see who it was.

Stephen.

"Lead this man back to Flavia, O merciful God," the priest whispered to the sky.

Rex nodded at these gentle words, for they expressed the deepest desire of his heart. Somehow, some way, he hoped the prayer might be answered.

———◊◊◊———

Flavia couldn't help but feel that every eye in the streets of Rome was looking at her, even though she knew it wasn't actually true. "Keep your veil down, Mother!" she hissed. "You're supposed to be dead!"

"But I can't see through it," Sophronia complained. "I just want to look at my old house. I lived there twenty years. You were born in that house! Rome is all I ever knew, until recently."

Flavia pulled her mother into a shadowy alley on the Aventine Hill. "I understand, but you have to be careful. If anyone recognizes you, they'll know you're alive. It will change everything."

"If anyone sees me, they'll die of fright because they'll think they've seen a spirit. Just give me another moment. Then we can go. I'll probably never come back here, so I just want to look at the place one last time."

The Roman mansion's exterior was mostly unchanged since Flavia left it three years ago. The only difference was the installation of a plaque above the door to indicate the building was no longer a private residence but a full-time church where Christians met weekly. THE HOUSE CHURCH OF HOLY SABINA SOPHRONIA, the plaque declared.

Everyone in Rome believed pious Sophronia had taken her own life rather than be arrested, ravished, and executed by the wicked Emperor Maxentius. But the suicide had been a ruse: a superficial dagger wound combined with a potion to induce a deep sleep. When the emperor's henchmen found what they thought was a corpse, they left in disappointment, and Sophronia went into hiding after she woke up. Then her lecherous husband, Neratius, ran off to a distant estate with a teenaged bride, which enabled the catholic church in Rome to purchase the house.

Although those times had been hard, everything turned out for the better. Now Sophronia's position as the spiritual mother of the Tauromenium convent offered her a quiet and obscure life that brought her more peace than she had ever experienced as a senator's wife. Flavia, too, thought the convent was an improvement in most respects.

A handsome, dark-haired man came out of the mansion and proceeded down the street, accompanied by a doorkeeper whom Flavia didn't recognize. *I wonder what happened to sweet old Onesimus?* The new doorkeeper was a younger, beefier fellow, and the handsome man was Felix, the priest appointed to lead the Aventine church after its former pastor, Miltiades, became the pope. Evidently, Felix was now living in Flavia's old home, probably along with some monastic brothers, to take care of the place. The congregation used to gather in the large hall that Neratius had allowed—after much badgering from his wife and daughter—to be constructed from two unused rooms. Flavia hoped the Christian community here was still thriving under Felix's leadership.

"He's certainly a good-looking man, isn't he?" Sophronia remarked. "How old do you think he is?"

"Too young for you, Mother, if that's what you're thinking."

"Bah!" Sophronia scoffed. "I'm only thirty-nine. He can't be much less than that."

"Midthirties, I'd say. But why do you care? You're a nun!"

Sophronia turned and gave her daughter a playful stare, arching her eyebrows and smiling a little. "Do not fear, my love. It was merely an observation. I am not looking for a man in my life—and certainly not a Roman priest!" The distinguished matron lowered her veil, signaling that the secret visit was over. "It was nice to see the house again, but it's time to get going. We mustn't keep the bishop waiting."

Flavia and Sophronia returned to the foot of the Aventine Hill and met Archdeacon Quintus where they had left him, in front of the enormous bath complex of Caracalla. The archdeacon had commissioned a litter to travel the hectic streets of Rome, so the women rode alongside their friend, leaving the draperies open to catch what breeze they could.

"I imagine that visit must have been hard for you both," Quintus said. "Your memories of that house run deep, and some are painful. But I pray that, in the end, your excursion left you with good hope." Quintus was one of the few men in Rome who knew Sophronia's true identity.

"It was a delight to see the old place," Sophronia acknowledged, "and to know it is in Felix's capable hands."

Quintus shifted uncomfortably but made no reply. Instead, he changed the subject. "Have you recovered from the rigors of travel? A week aboard a ship isn't the easiest thing for delicate bodies to endure."

Sophronia smiled. "Ah, you forget, Archdeacon, we are no longer delicate! Though we were once ladies of luxury, we are ascetics now—accustomed to the hardships of a simpler life. The trip up from Sicilia was fine, and we are none the worse for it."

"I actually enjoyed it," Flavia said. "Sea travel is a delight to me. I love the feel of a ship rolling beneath my feet and an ocean breeze in my hair."

"That is good to hear. Pope Sylvester is anxious to see you. I believe a meeting will be possible this afternoon, since you seem rested from the long journey."

The travelers lapsed into silence while the porters made their way through the streets. Eventually they halted in front of the Lateran Palace, a large urban domus that used to be called the House of Fausta. She was the wife of Constantine, so when he took over the western half of the empire after defeating Maxentius at the Battle of the Milvian Bridge, the magnificent house came into his possession. Constantine's first act was to bequeath it to the catholic church. A few years back, he had seen a heavenly cross that told him to fight under Christ's banner. The Lord had given Constantine victory, so he was favorably disposed toward the Christians and wanted to grant them his largesse. The bishop's new palace was a major example of that generosity. Other plans were probably in the works too, though Flavia didn't know what Sylvester had in mind for the city.

Stepping out from the litter under the hot sun, Flavia shaded her eyes as she examined the palace's gleaming façade. The place hummed with activity. Priests, nuns, and monks were constantly entering or leaving this building that had become the hub of the Roman church. Strangely, however, a large property adjacent to the palace was vacant. Grass and weeds grew up between chunks of rubble from what must have been a substantial building.

Flavia drew Quintus's attention to the vacant lot. "I cannot recall what used to stand there. Can you remind me?"

"It was the camp of the imperial horse guard—the Emperor's Personal

Cavalry. Constantine disbanded them and destroyed their base because they supported Maxentius."

Of course! The horse guard! Rex's old unit . . .

The memories seemed to be from a different world. Flavia recalled how Rex had come to Rome as an undercover spy who joined the cavalry to gather intelligence about Maxentius. In those tension-filled days, Flavia never visited Rex here at his military headquarters, lest she give away his secret identity. Now the camp was gone—razed to the ground to show everyone what happened to army units that fought for false emperors.

"Who owns the land now?" she asked Quintus.

He smiled slyly. "Your friend Miltiades, God rest his soul, had the audacity to ask Constantine for the title to that property too, as if the palace weren't enough."

"Did he agree?"

"Yes, eventually. We have the deed in our archives."

"What will you build there?"

"So many questions, Sister Flavia! Perhaps you should come inside. His Holiness might be able to provide better answers about the church's plans for the city of Rome."

"Yes, Daughter, you must stop pestering the archdeacon with these inquiries," Sophronia added. "Let's get out of the hot sun and await our audience with the bishop."

Quintus escorted the women to a cool sitting room that caught a breeze from an adjoining atrium. He left them there with two silver cups of water flavored with blackberries and sage. While they waited, Flavia couldn't help but get up and take a peek at the former reception hall that now functioned as the Lateran Church. Large Roman houses like this one typically had a grand room for meeting clients and guests. Such rooms could accommodate a large group of visitors, so with the right decorations—lampstands, a pulpit, and an altar instead of idols and scenes from mythology—the space could work well as a church. Apparently, a Christian congregation was thriving here at the Lateran Palace. The idols had been replaced with elegant furnishings suitable for the worship of God.

Flavia returned to the sitting room and finished her drink. A servant, a man with a wine-colored birthmark splashed across his cheek, noticed her empty cup. Most people believed such disfigurements showed disapproval from the gods, which would make the man a social outcast. But not here at the Lateran Palace. The true God looked not at a man's outside but at his heart.

"I will bring you more to drink right away, m'lady," the slave said as he scooped up the empty cup.

"Thank you, sir," Flavia replied—a thing only a Christian would ever say to a slave.

The man returned with more flavored water, and shortly after that, Quintus arrived to take the women to meet the bishop. Sylvester had invited his guests not into the grand reception hall but into the more intimate setting of his personal study. The stocky, middle-aged man sat behind his desk. Three wicker chairs with cushions were arranged before him. Though his hair was thick and white, he wore no beard. His height was average, and so were his looks. He had an intangible aura of pent-up energy that Flavia sensed immediately.

The slave with the birthmark arrived again, this time pushing a wine cart. He poured a beautiful golden vintage from a carafe into four goblets.

"I'm trying to use up all the Falernian that Pompeianus had stocked in this house," Sylvester explained. "He was a horrible man, but he had excellent taste in wine."

Flavia shivered at the mention of her old enemy Pompeianus. "I think that's the only good thing we can say about him."

"He is under God's judgment now," Sophronia observed, and the pope nodded sagely at this.

Once the wine was distributed, Bishop Sylvester pointed to a parchment spread on the desk. "I have two matters to discuss with you ladies today. Both are momentous, and they will change your lives forever."

"Tell us," Sophronia said as Flavia nervously sipped her wine.

"Lady Sabina, your brother-in-law, Senator Ignatius, has gone to rest beneath the earth. His soul is in the care of Christ, who will surely raise him up on the last day. In the meantime, his body rests in the Catacombs, not far from the prayers of holy Sebastian."

Oh, no! My beloved Uncle Ignatius!

Flavia remained quiet at the sad news, maintaining her dignity and decorum as she had been raised to do. Sophronia likewise kept her peace, staring at the ground with her hands folded in her lap. Nevertheless, the news was shocking, for Ignatius had seemed healthy the last time Flavia was with him. And she had loved him dearly. He was a godlier paternal figure than her own father ever had been.

"As usual," Sylvester went on, "a senator's wealth passes to his heirs. But in this case, Ignatius had no living descendants of his own, nor any adopted children. A nephew or niece would be next in line. What this means, Lady Junia"—the bishop used Flavia's formal name to emphasize his point—"is that you are the sole heir of your uncle's huge fortune. It is established without doubt in this legal document laid before us. You are now among the richest citizens of Rome."

The bishop's announcement was staggering, and the shock of it caused Flavia to fumble with her glass and spill some wine on her tunic. When Quintus motioned with his hand, the slave immediately stepped forward with a towel and blotted the stain as best he could, then retreated to his position at the wine cart.

Sophronia found her voice first, speaking like the stately Roman matron she was. "Your Holiness, this is a lot for my daughter and me to comprehend. Surely God will help us consider all the ramifications of this news. In the meantime, I can hardly bear to ask about your second topic, when the first was so fateful! Yet I feel compelled to ask what it is, if only so the suspense of waiting will be relieved."

"Let me relieve you of that distress, my friends—though unfortunately, my plans will lay upon you an even greater burden than what I have just told you."

Flavia shifted in her seat. *My goodness! This pope isn't anything like gentle old Miltiades. Sylvester is always on the move toward his goals!*

"Speak," Sophronia said, "and we will embrace the will of God, whatever it may be."

"Dear sisters, today I send you forth to Gaul on a special mission. Ossius of Corduba shall be the leader of your embassy—but you, Flavia, shall pay for the entirety of this journey from your new wealth. You will meet Emperor Constantine in Gaul, presenting him with a twofold petition that is absolutely vital to the future of the Roman church."

"But this will take us out of our life of holy seclusion," Sophronia remarked.

"For the sake of the catholic church, it must be so. The petition is that important."

"And what is the substance of that petition, Your Holiness?"

"First, you must secure the emperor's permission and financial support for a great construction campaign. I plan to raise up a new Christian architecture in this city like the world has never seen. Only the funds of the imperial treasury are sufficient for such a task. And through these grand buildings, everyone shall see that Jesus is the empire's future, not the temples of the gods."

So far, Flavia had remained silent out of respect for her mother's seniority, but a powerful sense of anticipation finally overcame her deferential spirit. Sensing that something marvelous was happening, she leaned toward the bishop. "And what, Holy Father, is the second part of your request?"

"It is time for the church of Jesus Christ to have an official copy of the holy scriptures," Sylvester declared. "No more guessing about which texts do or do not belong within the canon of faith. We must have a beautiful version of the book of God—two testaments united to form one sacred writing. It will be the basis for all the copies that are used in the Roman churches. This, too, will be expensive! But Constantine has shown himself to be a willing patron of our faith."

The bishop's bold plan immediately captured Flavia's mind. Buildings and books—a dual strategy to change the people's devotion from paganism to the one true God. "Oh!" she exclaimed as she contemplated the possibilities. "I feel eager and frightened at once!"

"As you should. This mission is both exciting and dreadful." Sylvester instructed Flavia to rise from her chair. "Do you sing, dear one?" he asked when she had arisen.

"Well, I . . . yes, I used to have music tutors, like most girls of my upbringing."

"And do you know the Song of Mary?"

"Of course. I only ever sang psalms and hymns, for mine was a Christian home."

"Then sing it, Lady Junia Flavia. Sing the beautiful song that gives your answer to my request. We will listen as you perform for God alone."

Flavia's heart was beating rapidly now. "Holy Father, I declare to you in plain words—I am already willing to do this thing that you ask."

"I know you are. Nevertheless, sing it to us, dear one. Sing your obedience to your Lord and Master."

"But I—"

"Do as I say."

Recognizing the futility of further delay, Flavia took a moment to gather her thoughts and calm the butterflies inside. After clearing her throat and finding her pitch, she intoned the opening line from Mary's Song. "*Magnificat anima mea Dominum*," she sang, "*et exultavit spiritus meus in Deo salutari meo*." Flavia followed the first line with the rest of the stanza—but then the intense faces of her mother and the bishop made her words trickle away.

"Is that enough?" Flavia meekly asked the pope.

Thankfully, Sylvester relented. "Yes, it is enough for today, dear child," he replied. "But I am certain you shall need to find the rest of your voice in the days that are to come."

Most men went to the barber for a shave, but not the man in the brown hooded robe. He interacted with the world as little as possible—a figure more at home in the shadows, moving at dawn or dusk, not the bright light of day. Doing his own shaving meant one less reason to have to be seen in public.

The polished bronze mirror revealed his face well enough when he brought it near the window of his Roman apartment. After rubbing his cheeks with olive oil, he scraped away the stubble with an obsidian razor, a tool infinitely keener than iron. Working with such a sharp instrument took a practiced hand. But the man in the brown robe had such a hand. Sharp blades were well known to him.

For a variety of uses.

After wiping away the oil with a rag, the man inspected his face in the mirror. His snake tattoo was clearly revealed now that he was shaven again. The emerald color of the serpent that glided up his left jawline and beside his ear stood out against his dark Aegyptian skin. Two yellow eyes stared at the world from the man's forehead, and a forked reptilian tongue seemed to taste his left eyebrow. The serpent was a beautiful animal, a delightful creature of God. The so-called catholics, those unenlightened Christians, had it all wrong. The dragon in holy scripture was not evil but instead was a glorious bearer of mental healing and mystic insight.

Did not the *Book of Genesis* call the serpent crafty?

Did not the prophet Moses tell the people in their sickness to gaze upon a snake lifted on a pole?

Did not the Jesus, the archangel of God, tell his disciples to be as wise as serpents?

Real believers, the spiritual Christians known as Gnostics, understood that the snake was a symbol of good. In fact, it was an emission of the Heavenly Fullness.

The man in the brown hooded robe touched his forehead with two fingers and whispered a prayer for good fortune. No one knew the man's real name. He himself had forgotten it. Everyone referred to him by his serpentine tattoo, and that was as it should be. The "Aegyptian Asp" was a better alias for him than whatever name he had borne in a former life, when he had served in the Roman legions. Now he was a secret assassin in the army of Christ.

A knock signaled the arrival of the Aegyptian Asp's visitor. The fellow's name was Primus, and he came often these days, for there was much news to report out of the Lateran Palace. The Asp set his razor and mirror on the windowsill and went to open the door.

"I salute you," said Primus, though he didn't dip his chin as a good slave should do.

"Come in and give your report. Be quick about it. We haven't much time."

Primus stepped inside, and the Asp closed the door behind him. The apartment was sparsely furnished, with only a mattress, a wooden chest, a table, and one chair. Some water pots and food jars sat in the corner. The Asp seated himself while Primus remained standing to reveal what he had learned.

The report was brief yet significant. Sylvester, the arrogant bishop of the catholic Christians, was planning a major initiative. He intended to raise the profile of the Roman church through an extensive new building program. He also wanted to obtain an official copy of the scriptures to define which books belonged in the canon. Of course, the catholic Christians always misinterpreted those books by taking them literally, and they also refused to read other ones—the mystical ones that revealed the Heavenly Fullness. All these plans would require Emperor Constantine's permission and funding, so an embassy was being sent to Gaul, paid for by a Sicilian nun who had just come into a large inheritance. If Sylvester's plans were successful, it would certainly increase the standing of the Roman church at the expense of the Aegyptians. Bishop Melitius was going to want to know about this, for he had aspirations to be the next pope of Alexandria. Wolf City on the Nilus River was just a stepping-stone for him.

The Asp retrieved a pouch from under his mattress and fished out an argenteus. The silver coin was worth a significant amount, and he resented having to pay it to such a menial slave. Whenever possible, the Asp preferred threats and violence over bribery. Yet in the present circumstances, a quick payment was the best way to secure up-to-date intelligence from inside the catholics' stronghold. Money would keep the information flowing. This wretched fellow couldn't expect to get that kind of money anywhere else— not with that hideous purple blotch across his face.

After paying Primus for his report, the Asp dismissed him, then set an inkwell and sheet of papyrus on the table. He dipped the reed pen into the ink and began to write in Greek:

The Servant with No Name, The Serpentine One, The Secret Poison of Aegyptus;

To Bishop Melitius of Wolf City, Prelate of the True Church, the Perfect and Pure:

Greetings to you in God, the All-Wise Monad.

According to information recently supplied to me, I now advise you that Bishop Sylvester and his earthly minded devotees are seeking to expand the stature of the Roman church. Unless intervention is made right away, the glory of Peter and Paul will eclipse the sanctity of Mark, our own apostle to Aegyptus, and the sacred patron of Alexandria. Surely this news is alarming and requires utmost attention. Nothing shall prevent me, glorious lord, from putting an end to this mischief. I will report to you when I have accomplished this goal by devious and secretive means.

Send money to me by the courier who carries this letter. I am recruiting him to our society; you can trust him. Do not withhold funds, but open wide your purse. Now is the time to strike a death blow from which our enemies cannot recover.

With prayers for your empowerment by many high-ranking angels, I write this letter and seal it with my own hand. I remain ever your faithful servant.

After rolling the papyrus and sealing it with wax inside a leather tube, the Aegyptian Asp set it on the table. Quickly, he packed his belongings, then slung his bag over his shoulder on his staff and went downstairs. The landlord of the apartment block had his dwelling on the ground floor behind his hot-food restaurant. It was late afternoon now, so most people were at the baths or taking a nap. It was a good time to conduct business without being noticed.

"Here is all my rent, plus three months in advance," the Asp said, laying several coins on the counter.

The landlord's greedy hand swept up the money. "Why in advance?" he asked, though he didn't object to the arrangement.

"I shall be traveling for a while. Other than the courier who comes for my letter, keep my room locked until my return. If anything seems to have been disturbed, you shall lose me as a resident."

"Listen, snake man, you keep paying in advance like this, and you can have whatever you want! Your room will be waiting when you return—untouched."

"Except for the letter."

"Agreed."

The Aegyptian Asp said no more but turned abruptly to the street and proceeded to the Emporium on the Tiberis River. As always, the riverport was bustling. The Asp kept his face deep in the shadows of his hood as he arranged for passage on a grain barge to the harbor town of Ostia. From there, or from nearby Portus, he could catch a ship that would take him out to sea.

Though the barge was packed with crates, there was a small open space in the stern. The Asp reclined on a pile of empty sacks. They would be filled again at Ostia with newly arrived wheat from across the empire; but for now, they made a decent mat upon which to rest. He lay there with his arms folded across his belly, each hand inside the opposite sleeve of his baggy robe.

"Push off!" shouted the helmsman to his assistant in the bow, who held a long pole. Slowly, the barge began to drift downstream in the sluggish current of the Tiberis.

To Ostia within a few hours. And from there to the open sea.

Using an often-practiced move, the Aegyptian Asp slid the obsidian razor from a secret sheath bound to his forearm. With his other hand, he removed an apricot from his bag. Though he drew the blade across the fruit's surface with the lightest possible touch, the edge still bit deep, carving out a slice with virtually no effort. After spearing it, the Asp plucked the juicy morsel from the tip of the blade with his lips. He savored the taste for a moment, then gulped it down.

What a delightful little tool, he thought as his razor sliced the apricot again. *How easily it cuts the flesh of this fruit.*

Or whatever else I might wish.

2

The Greek city of Pylos was a natural harbor, having served to protect watercraft since the long-lost days when Odysseus plied the ancient seas. But Rex didn't care about the mythology of Homer; he cared that the Roman navy didn't have much of a presence here. The fleet's capital at Ravenna was far away, and its commanders were more concerned about patrolling the Adriatic Sea for pirates than looking for mutineers off the Peloponnese. Yet while this was good news for Rex, he still had no intention of sailing into Pylos's harbor and getting trapped by an unexpected blockade.

"That little cove will do nicely," he told the pilot of the *Deadly Encounter*, who had the ship under sail and was guiding her by the light of a full moon. "Tuck us in there, and let's get a few hours of sleep before dawn."

"Looks sandy over that way," the pilot said, pointing to a flash of white amid the scrub along the shoreline. "Shall I beach her?"

"No. We'll drop anchor near the mouth, nose out, and be ready to make a break if trouble comes our way."

"Very good, sir. I'll send one of the rowers up the mast to keep a lookout." The pilot motioned to his navigator, an expert in the lore of stars. "Go wake Stephen," he said.

"Not the priest," Rex countered. "Send another. Let Stephen finish his rest. He's coming with me today, once the sun is up."

The navigator went to fetch another crewman while the red-haired pilot brought the ship around until she was in the mouth of the cove with the prow facing out yet hidden by a spit of land. After the anchor was set, Rex retired to the captain's leather tent and caught a quick nap until the sunrise grew bright enough to wake him.

Everything was quiet aboard the *Deadly Encounter* when Rex emerged from the goatskin structure at the stern, a snug little space under an arched roof that could be vented for fresh air or to catch a view of the sky. The tiny cabin was furnished with a cot, a sea chest, a hanging lamp, and one of the true luxuries of shipboard life—a chamber pot that allowed for privacy instead of the undignified practice of relieving oneself straight into the sea. Only the captain had the privilege of sleeping and conducting his other necessary business apart from the crew.

"Morning, sir," the Thracian said as Rex yawned and stretched. He spoke quietly, for almost everyone else was asleep, sprawled wherever they could find sufficient space on the deck. Normally a galley would be beached over-night and the men would disembark, but navy sailors knew how to sleep aboard the ship when necessary. The only crewmen awake were Stephen and the Thracian, who had stripped to their loincloths. The rest of their clothing and gear was in an oiled leather bag.

"You need to eat better, you skinny stork," Rex replied to the tall, lanky oarsman who had become his first mate. The fellow was good with a sword and even better with his fists. Few enemies could match his long reach. His many years at the oar had made him lean and hard. Rex was glad to have him around.

"The money is packed inside this waterproof bag, Captain," Stephen said. "All we need is your clothing and we can get going."

Rex stripped like the others, handed his dirty tunic to Stephen, and dove into the water. The three men swam ashore and quickly re-dressed in their dry clothes. Both Rex and the Thracian carried daggers. The Christian priest was unarmed, and he kept the coin purse hidden beneath his garment.

The town of Pylos had roused for the day by the time Rex and his companions reached it after hiking over a low ridge. The travelers needed to obtain only three products, and the waterfront would be the place to buy them. "Try not to be noticed," Rex ordered his men. "Let's move quickly and get what we need. Don't take extra time to bargain. Money isn't our problem. Recognition is. Meet back at the tavern in an hour."

Stephen doled out some coins to each man as they separated. The priest's job was to purchase salted sardines and vinegar wine—standard fare for men at sea. The Thracian had been told to secure two pack mules to transport the supplies. But only Rex knew the third product he was about to buy; for once his men learned of it, they'd likely protest and might even resist. He was waiting until the last moment to let them find out.

A baker's shop at the waterfront had just opened for business when Rex entered. The smell of fresh bread usually greeted bakery customers, but not here. Soft white loaves weren't this establishment's specialty.

"How much for a day's ration?" Rex asked him.

"Depends on how much you buy. Bigger order will get you a better deal."

"Fifty men. Six days."

The baker quoted a decent price—not cheap, but worth a little extra because, he boasted, his flour was especially tasty. Rex asked to try it, so the man tossed him a sea biscuit. The round wafer felt as dense and hard as a stone in Rex's hand.

"Sour wine?" he asked.

The baker poured some weak vinegar in a bowl. Rex dropped the biscuit into the liquid and poked it with a spoon to make a mushy porridge. When the concoction was well mixed, he tried it.

"Not bad," he said. "The salt helps a lot. And it's got decent flavor." He nodded to the baker. "I'll take seven days' worth—just in case."

The baker filled several sacks and tied them together with a hank of rope. Rex paid him, then hoisted the load to his shoulders and returned to the tavern. Stephen was already there with his supplies, and the Thracian arrived a short time later with the two mules.

"We should get going, sir," the first mate said. "These beasts are due back by noon."

"I have one more errand before I return. One of you will remain with me. The other can return to the ship and load the supplies, then bring the mules back."

The two crewmen glanced at each other. Neither wanted to volunteer for the more arduous task. To stay in town with the captain would probably mean a stop at the tavern instead of leading two stubborn animals over a

ridge and back again under the hot sun. Though Rex could have ordered one of the sailors to do the job, he decided to provide some incentive.

"The pack train driver gets the use of the brothel when he gets back," he announced. "Paid for by me."

As Rex had anticipated, Stephen only rolled his eyes while the Thracian's hand shot into the air. "I'll do it, sir," he said eagerly.

Rex grinned and gave him a wink. "Somehow I thought that would be the outcome."

The men began to load the mules. Stephen had just picked up the sacks of sea biscuits when he stopped and raised an eyebrow at Rex. "This doesn't feel like loaves," he observed.

Rex shook his head. "Loaves spoil quickly."

Now the Thracian was interested too. "That doesn't matter near land," he said quietly. "You eat it before it molds, then get more."

After regarding his two men for a moment, Rex finally replied, "True—if you are near land."

Stephen and the Thracian examined the sacks again, then exchanged glances. They understood what it meant to victual a ship with that much hardtack. Rex decided to confirm their suspicions. "We're headed into open waters," he announced. "Straight across the Ionian Sea to Sicilia."

"In a warship, sir?"

"Yes, but mostly by sail. Six days, if the winds are right. We can do it! Remigius is an excellent navigator."

The Thracian shrugged and grabbed the halter of the lead mule. "The crew won't like it. They're navy boys. They ain't used to leaving sight of land."

"Then it's your job to get them comfortable with the idea until I return."

"Aye, Captain," the Thracian replied. He saluted and began trudging toward the ridge that lay between Pylos and the ship.

When he was out of sight, Stephen glanced at Rex with a curious expression. "Straight across the sea, eh? What's the hurry?"

"None of your business. Follow me."

"Yes, sir," Stephen said meekly. "Where are we headed?"

Rex gestured to his filthy tunic. "Look at this thing! It's not worthy of a sea captain. I look like what I am—a mutineer from the oars. I'm going to need to appear more respectable if I want to bargain for a good price on the bitumen in Syracusae."

"You never know who you might run into there," Stephen agreed.

The two men found a tailor's shop and were met inside by a wizened little fellow with a bald pate. He sold Rex an exquisite dark-blue tunic with gold trim. "It looks perfect against your yellow hair!" the tailor exclaimed.

"You should have seen my hair when it was long, my friend. Down past my shoulders when I was a youth in Germania."

"A youth? You're a youth now!" The tailor smoothed Rex's tunic as it draped his tall frame. "Look at you—wide shoulders, narrow waist, thick chest. Your arms barely fit in those sleeves! How old are you?"

"Twenty-two."

"Ach! What I wouldn't give to be twenty-two again," the tailor muttered with a shake of his head. Rex held up the hand mirror and examined his new outfit while Stephen chuckled at the exchange.

When the transaction was finished, Rex found a tanner from whom he bought a pair of calfskin boots, a belt, and a fine leather scabbard. Since a barber was next door, he also got a trim of his long, ragged hair and thick blond beard. The two men then stopped at the tavern before they headed back to the ship. Though it was only midmorning, Rex's philosophy was to drink the good stuff whenever he could get it.

The end of the bar was unoccupied, so Rex found a place there. He ordered two cups of strong wine and a bowl of olives.

The bartender served him but seemed nervous as he brought the tray. "Don't stay long," he whispered, bending close. "The locals don't like strangers in here."

"We'll keep to ourselves," Rex said as he took a swallow of his wine.

But the bartender's warning proved accurate. Four ruffians rose from a corner table and bellied up to the bar, two on each side of Rex and Stephen. "This place ain't for foreigners," one of them growled.

Rex wanted no trouble. He casually drained his cup, then set it on the counter. After laying down two copper coins, he turned to go.

A hand grabbed Rex's collar. "Fancy tunic you got there, stranger," the leader of the ruffians said with an edge to his voice. He was a mean-faced fellow with breath like a donkey's rear end.

Rex eyed the man calmly. "You have some good tailors in your town."

"Sometimes their thread don't hold up," said Donkey Breath. He yanked hard on Rex's collar, tearing open a seam with a loud ripping sound.

Rex's hand went to his dagger, but Stephen grabbed his wrist. "Don't involve the law!" he hissed.

Releasing his dagger, Rex instead locked eyes with Donkey Breath and refused to avert his gaze. The two men drew close until they were nose to nose. Suddenly Rex's knee shot up into his opponent's groin. As the man doubled over with a cry of pain, Rex seized his hair and slammed his head into a steaming bowl of fish stew sitting on the counter. The bowl's contents splashed the other three ruffians, who drew back in surprise as the hot liquid burned their exposed skin. While the scalded man squealed and wiped his eyes, Rex used the opportunity to withdraw to the tavern's door. His long dagger was in his hand now.

"Get him!" one of the other bullies shouted. Yet no one moved. They were unarmed men facing a tall German with a fierce-looking blade.

The bartender raised an amphora. "Free cup of wine for all the men of Pylos!" he announced to the room, drawing a few cheers. "Strangers, you can move along now."

"We thank you for your hospitality," Stephen said, tugging Rex out the door.

They hurried away and found a secluded alley where they could regroup.

"He tore my collar!" Rex complained to his friend. "I should've stuck him with my knife!"

"You did the right thing. You said before we set out that we don't want to attract attention."

Rex nodded and sighed. "You're right, as usual, Brother Priest." He looked down at his shoulder. "Maybe we can find someone on the *Encounter* to sew it."

Stephen examined the torn seam, then brushed a few bits of fish from Rex's chest. "With some care and attention, that rip can be fixed. But look here. There's a stain from the soup. Now it needs to be washed too."

Rex stared at the greasy blotch on the front of his tunic. "Ugh! It'll never come out. It's ruined forever."

"No," Stephen countered. "It can be cleansed. All it needs is a good washing."

71

"That would have to be some washing. The stain is deep."

Stephen looked his friend in the eye. "You might be surprised, Rex, what a good washing can do."

———❦❦❦———

The morning sun slanted through the skylight of Bishop Chrestus's lovely Syracusan villa, providing the illumination Flavia needed as she repaired his clerical robe. A decorative patch depicting the chi-rho symbol had come loose from the fabric, but a few quick stitches would make it fast again. It was the least she could do for the man who had provided her such gracious hospitality for the past week.

And not for the first time, Flavia remembered. Her mind went back to her visit here six years ago with an awkward Christian boy named Magnus. She had to laugh as she recalled how Magnus was afraid to visit an underground cemetery, while she—a mere sixteen-year-old!—had boldly followed Chrestus into the tunnels. All that seemed like a different world now.

After putting the final stitch in the bishop's robe, Flavia tied off the thread and set aside her needle. Sewing was a household art she employed often as a nun in the Tauromenium convent. It was a practical skill for a woman, and Flavia liked to use it as an act of service for those she loved.

Oh, how I wish, someday . . .

Flavia let her mournful thought slip away. Indulging in fantasies always ended up hurting because reality eventually barged in and shattered the dream. It was a lesson she had learned the hard way.

Her mother entered the little parlor that adjoined the atrium and took a seat next to Flavia on the divan. "Your things are packed, my dear?" Sophronia asked. "We head for the harbor within the hour."

"I've been packed since yesterday. I'm so excited! It will be an honor to meet the emperor. Do you think I shall get to talk with him?"

"Probably not. Bishop Ossius is the spokesman for our embassy. We have to do this in just the right way. No social mistakes. A lot is riding on this mission for the church of Rome."

"Oh! I hope Constantine is favorable to us. I heard that Sylvester is planning a council when we get back to decide which books belong on the list of truth. I imagine we'll follow the *Seventy* for the Old Testament. It's the

New that I'm worried about. Some of the common people favor strange books that clearly aren't from the apostles."

"The theologians will sort that out," Sophronia said.

"And the buildings!" Flavia went on. "Can you imagine all the splendid new churches rising within the city walls and out by the cemeteries? It will tell everyone that the old gods have lost. Their temples will crumble as the true houses of God rise up to replace them!"

Sophronia smiled at Flavia. "I can see our pope has chosen the right donor for this mission. The only thing more abundant than your gold is your enthusiasm!"

The women spent the next hour putting the finishing touches on their packing until a mule-drawn coach arrived to take them to the harbor of Syracusae. Cassi met them in front of the villa. Flavia had chosen her for the mission because she was strong and capable, always finding ways to be helpful. She sat beside Flavia in the coach, humming an African folk song as the three women rode along without speaking.

Bishop Ossius of Corduba met them at the docks. He was a trim, distinguished Spaniard with silver hair that swept back from his forehead in a dashing curl. Though he was about sixty, he looked much younger and had the energy of someone half his age. His voice was deep and resonant, yet Bishop Ossius was known to speak sparingly.

"Greetings in the name of Christ, ladies," he said with a gallant bow. He helped each of the women from the carriage while porters removed their baggage from the wagon and carried it up the gangplank.

The ship for the journey to Gaul was called the *Concordia*. It was primarily transporting Sicilian wine to Massilia, but from its luxurious appointments, Flavia could tell the captain did a nice side business with well-to-do passengers who could pay for a more comfortable voyage. Several men in elegant tunics were visible on deck, and the women accompanying them appeared to be fashionable too. Flavia smiled at the realization that although she was probably richer than any of them, her gray woolen dress and plain shoes would never reveal it. Christian women were taught in the *Epistle of Peter*—the first one, not the second one more recently discovered—to avoid external displays of wealth and beauty like braided hair or expensive jewelry and clothes.

The pier was crowded today with all sorts of people: brawny dock hands, navy rowers and marines, salty old sea captains, barmaids and fishwives, scrawny boys making mischief, and imperial tax collectors with their styluses and wax tablets. The whole range of human coloration could be found there too, because the island of Sicilia formed a convenient intersection between Europa, Africa, and the East. In one quick glance, Flavia saw a tall, thin Aethiops with obsidian skin; a swarthy Aegyptian sailor hobbling on a peg leg; a bushy-bearded Greek playing knucklebones; and a blond Gothic soldier in chainmail armor.

"Syracusae is surely exotic," Flavia remarked.

"Look at that tattoo," Sophronia whispered. She giggled and rolled her eyes toward a shirtless man with a leaping porpoise emblazoned on his chest.

"I saw a fellow yesterday with a snake crawling up his neck and beside his ear," Ossius added.

"A real snake?" Cassi asked with a horrified expression.

"No, just a tattoo. But it looked real at first," said the bishop.

Cassi shivered and let the subject drop.

The traveling party finally boarded the *Concordia*. As Flavia had guessed, she found the accommodations to be as nice as could be expected aboard a ship. A section of the hold had been divided into sleeping berths, each with a curtain for privacy. The area reserved for female passengers was partitioned with planks, accessible only by a door that could be latched from the inside. Flavia and Cassi exchanged a nod, grateful that if they had to sleep aboard the ship, they wouldn't be bothered by any amorous sailors during the night.

The winds were favorable, so the crew hoisted the foresail and left Syracusae on the Nones of June under a blue sky speckled with puffy clouds. The passage to Gaul would require stops in Carthago and Sardinia along the way, taking a total of two weeks, or perhaps more depending on the weather. Flavia was glad she had tucked a few books of the scriptures in her luggage. She hoped to use the long voyage to refresh her schoolgirl Greek with help from Cassi, who was fluent in that tongue, along with her native Aethiops dialect.

On the second day of travel, just as the *Concordia* had rounded the southernmost tip of Sicilia and was preparing to make the run to Carthago, a ship was spotted abaft, bearing down hard. At first Flavia hoped it might be the imperial navy, but her hopes were quickly dashed. Instead, it was a cargo vessel whose sail was the dusky color of fog. Though Flavia squinted and stared, she could barely discern the hull, which was painted a blue-gray shade to blend in with the sea.

As it drew near, the *Concordia's* crew spotted a bank of oars in addition to the sail. The craft was too long and sleek for a merchant ship—clearly built for speed rather than cargo. Its aggressive behavior and stealthy appearance had all the marks of piracy. The captain ordered evasive maneuvers and instructed every able-bodied man to take up arms in case of an attack.

Despite the *Concordia's* best efforts, the enemy ship proved too fast to evade. It closed quickly under its large sail, yet it still had the swift agility that its oars could provide. Since it wasn't a warship and didn't have a ram, it drew alongside its prey to ensnare it with grapnels. A few crossbow bolts were exchanged, but in the end, the *Concordia* was taken without putting up much of a fight.

The attackers turned out to be pirates out of Malta, a tiny island notorious as a hideout for criminals and fugitives of all kinds. Their skipper was a disgustingly fat man with a burn scar on his left cheek that pulled his eye socket out of shape.

He waddled over to the *Concordia's* captain, whose wrists were shackled behind his back. "Where's the bishop?" the pirate skipper demanded, jutting his deformed chin into his captive's face.

"Get away from me, you knave," the proud captain replied—then took a backhanded slap to his jaw for the remark. A splotch of blood smeared his lip after the wicked blow.

"You got a bunch of rich nobles on this boat!" the skipper screeched. "I know it! And one of them is a bishop who's friends with the emperor!"

"I don't know what you're talking about."

The pirate skipper whirled, grabbed an aristocratic lady, and shoved her to the rail, where he dangled her over the water as she squealed. The evil man pushed her so far out that if he released the wad of her dress in his fist, she would surely topple into the sea.

"I can drop them one by one till you bring me the bishop!" he shouted.

Ossius stepped forward. "There is no need for that, sir. I am the bishop you seek. There will be a large ransom paid by a grateful emperor when all these folks are delivered safely to the nearest port."

"We ain't goin' to the nearest port, church man," the skipper said. He yanked the terrified matron from her dangerous perch and hurled her back into her husband's arms. "I got too many ladies in my hold who will fetch a better price farther away."

Ossius wrinkled his nose. "You're a slave trader."

"We move human cargo," the skipper replied with a smirk, "and we add to our shipment whenever we get a chance."

"The emperor will pay more to ensure these women remain untouched," Ossius said, gesturing to his companions. "*Much* more."

The remark made the skipper and his band of raiders burst into laughter. "What a waste of good women—keeping little virgins sacred to your god."

"They are far more valuable to you in that state," Ossius repeated.

"You're right. They're valuable, old man, but it ain't 'cause of what you think! First-timers like them are worth a whole lot to the pimps—and even more to the priests of Aphrodite!"

Aphrodite!

Flavia felt a bolt of fear run through her body. She glanced at Cassi, then at Sophronia. All three women knew what the name meant. They were about to be sold into sacred prostitution.

"Ransack this ship for anything valuable!" the fat skipper shouted to his men. "Take whatever can travel. Tie up the crew and throw them in our hold with the whores. We'll sell 'em in the next slave market. But keep the bishop's ladies apart with him. The goddess of love don't want her sweethearts violated." The skipper turned and sneered at Flavia with his twisted grin. "Not yet, anyway."

"Where are you taking us?" the captain of the *Concordia* demanded.

The obese skipper pointed to the east. "That way. Where the Great Harlot lives!"

"Bishop, where will it be?" Sophronia whispered to Ossius.

"Stay strong," he replied. "We're going to Corinthus."

———◈◈◈———

The cove near Pylos turned out to be a better place to take a break than Rex had first realized. It was a secret little spot with virtually no maritime traffic passing its mouth. And Rex hadn't realized how badly his men needed some time off. The pressure of rebelling against the navy, then staying on the run for several weeks, had taken its toll. The mutineers needed a few days to loaf around or do easy chores. In the end, Rex had allowed the *Deadly Encounter* to be run aground on the beach for hull maintenance. He had even stored the sea biscuit below deck and made the trip into Pylos a few times so the crew could have real bread.

It was on one of his bread runs that Rex first heard the news that launched him into action again. He was waiting in line at the bakery with Stephen—Rex wanted to limit how many crew members were seen publicly—when he overheard another customer repeat some waterfront gossip.

"They say the Maltese pirates have been at it again," said a weather-beaten old man with dark-brown skin.

"Slavers, ain't they?" asked his companion, a somewhat younger fellow, though equally tanned.

"Aye. They make a run from Africa to Graecia. Usually they just raid villages and take captives to the flesh houses of Corinthus. But now they've started hitting passenger ships. They paint their boat gray so they can sneak up from behind. Gettin' bold, they are, while the navy's busy with the mutinies."

Rex pretended to examine his fingernails while he waited to be served. Mentally, though, his attention was focused on news about the "mutinies." It was interesting that the old man had used the plural. Rex didn't know there had been more than one mutiny—though it didn't surprise him, given the rampant abuse in the fleet.

"I heard they scooped up a famous bishop," the leathery old man continued. "Adviser to the augustus."

"Which one?"

"Constantine."

The younger man laughed. "No, I figured it was Constantine! I meant 'Which bishop?' My brother's a priest in Libya, so I've heard a few names."

"I don't know who it was, but apparently, he's one of Constantine's favorites. Sits at the right hand of the throne. A Spaniard, they say."

"A Spaniard! The Maltese pirates are hitting Hispania now?"

"Naw," said the old sea dog with a wave of his hand, "the Spaniard was visiting Sicilia. They got him there. And some of his nuns. Ha! Won't those girls be in for a rough time at the Temple of Aphrodite? The Corinthians love to defile those little angels."

At those filthy words, a feeling of unease settled upon Rex. He had every reason to think Flavia might have been captured in this raid. When he was forced into the navy three years ago, she told him that she planned to take up the life of a nun in Sicilia. Now an important bishop had been captured after departing from that same island. It could only be Ossius. Long ago, while Rex was an imperial bodyguard, he had seen with his own eyes how the emperor relied on the prominent Spanish churchman. If the slavers had seized some Sicilian nuns who were in Ossius's company, Flavia was likely among them. She was one of the rare Christian sisters with the social ability to function in those high aristocratic circles.

And if there's even the slightest chance that she's been kidnapped, I'm going to find out! The gods can curse me to Hades before I let the brothels of Corinthus swallow the woman I—

What?

Love, Rex admitted. *Yes, I love her.*

By now, of course, Flavia didn't love him back.

But I'm still going to save her from that terrible fate!

The two sailors' conversation moved on to other topics. Yet their words had caused an instant pivot in Rex's plans. He would no longer be headed to Syracusae to sell bitumen to the highest bidder. He was now on the hunt for slave ships trying to round the Peloponnese—if he could convince his men to agree.

After the sailors left the bakery, Rex purchased the loaves he had come to buy. He would have split the load for the return hike to the ship, but Stephen insisted on carrying all the bread himself. He was sturdy enough to do it, and Rex appreciated the gesture of loyalty and obedience.

An hour later, the men arrived at the cove. The *Deadly Encounter* was still aground on the beach, yet the tide—meager as it was in the Mediterranean—was high now, so the greater part of the hull's length was in the water. Rex gathered his men and informed them about the change of plans, using an argument he had devised on the way back from Pylos. He would try to convince his crew to intercept the pirates and collect the emperor's reward themselves.

"You think those jars of bitumen are valuable," he said, "and they'll certainly make us some silver when we get around to selling them. But that bishop is worth a whole lot more! I'm talking about the kind of wealth that only emperors deal with. Constantine won't want to lose his main adviser for church affairs. Christianity is becoming the centerpiece of his domestic policy. He needs Ossius alive. That man is easy money!"

A scruffy marine named Marius, who had come over from the captured warship, raised an immediate protest. He was a likable, broad-shouldered fellow, very popular among the crew. "Wait a moment!" he complained. "Your plan will make us not just mutineers but slave traders and kidnappers! I didn't sign up for that when I left my ship. I thought we'd pretend to tax a few merchantmen and take some booty, then run off somewhere and be done with it. Now you're talking about demanding a ransom for the emperor's favorite adviser. That's high treason!"

Rex smiled at Marius and held up a cautioning hand, hoping to mollify not only him but also the men around him who seemed to agree. "I'm not suggesting we hold Ossius for ransom. Just the opposite—we'd be *rescuing* him from the hands of kidnappers! See the difference? We'd return him to the augustus safe and sound. So Constantine would be rewarding us out of gratitude, not paying a bitter ransom."

Marius looked skeptical, but he held his peace for the moment.

"Where do we find these slavers?" the red-haired pilot asked. "That sea-colored ship of theirs sounds hard to find."

"We can do it. If they're headed to Corinthus, we'd just have to patrol the southern Peloponnese until they show up."

The announcement drew immediate murmurs from the men. "That's the Kythira Strait," the pilot griped. "It's one of the deadliest spots in the sea. There are crazy currents and bad storms all the time. Sometimes even earthquakes. The sea floor is covered in wrecks. I don't want to join them!"

"What makes you think they won't take the western route to Corinthus?" Marius asked. "It would be a much safer voyage. Then they could use the road across the isthmus."

"I thought about that," Rex admitted, "but there's too much naval presence over there. They'd never slip by with their captives. And to ransom the bishop properly, the slavers will need to go to an imperial capital with a prominent church. The western route would put them on the wrong side of the isthmus. Only one city would work for them: Nicomedia. And getting there requires using Corinthus's eastern port."

"It's true," the Thracian agreed. "I'm from near Nicomedia. I've been across the Propontis and seen that city. The church there is closely tied to imperial politics. It's the kind of place that has access to big money for Christian purposes."

"Men, there are no great rewards without great risks," Rex declared. "Let's get the *Encounter* afloat again. With good winds, we can be in the Kythira Strait by tomorrow, and that's about the time the slavers would get there too. We'll patrol the sea lane with eagle eyes until we find them."

Though some of the men grumbled, they got to work nonetheless. Heaving with their combined strength, they lifted the keel of the *Deadly Encounter* and shoved her back into the water. It took no more than ten sweeps of the oars to leave the mouth of the snug cove and emerge into the open sea again.

The fair weather held, and Rex's prediction came true: by late afternoon the next day, the lookout atop the mast spotted Kythira Island. Rex overtook a local fishing boat, and for a few copper coins he obtained a report on recent traffic. The men had seen a sea-colored ship with an oar bank before, but it hadn't been observed passing through the sea lanes any time lately. Although the slavers might have slipped past unseen since stealth was always their intent, Rex thought it more likely that they hadn't arrived yet. Not much evaded the observant eyes of the fishermen who spent every single day on the patch of ocean they knew so well.

Another day passed, and still there was no sign of the slave ship. Rex ordered the *Deadly Encounter* to weave a back-and-forth pattern between Kythira Island and the next island over. Numerous ships went by, yet none fit the description of the enemy vessel. Civilian ships that combined sails with oars were uncommon in these waters, and none would be painted for camouflage. Rex knew the ship would be recognizable if his crew were to lay eyes on it.

Which they did, at dawn the next day.

She was indeed a fast-looking craft, with a big mainsail for speed, plus a raked bowsprit with a foresail for steering. A single bank of twelve oars on each side allowed for lightning-quick thrusts when needed. Although this was clearly a merchant vessel—with a deep hold, a high stern, and a rounder shape than a warship would have—she nonetheless had a long, sleek profile that could slice through the surf like a knife. Rex knew it was going to take everything his men had in their wiry bodies to catch the slavers before they reached Corinthus.

"They're fast, but we're strong, boys!" he shouted to his crew. "I want a light hand on the steerboards and a steady pace on the sweeps. We sail in straight lines and dark waters where there's plenty of wind. That boat might be faster than ours, but we'll overtake them by seamanship!"

The men seemed enthusiastic, so Rex left them to their work. The slavers immediately realized they were being pursued and picked up their pace. Yet the *Deadly Encounter* stayed with them all day—never able to close the gap, while never losing contact.

When darkness fell, Rex ordered a stop. The night was overcast and still, so neither ship was going anywhere. The cook broke out a little brazier and let the men warm their porridge of sea biscuit and posca. The mush was surprisingly filling, and the men were sleeping well when Rex finally retired to his goatskin cabin.

At first light, the *Deadly Encounter* resumed the chase. Despite the slavers' faster ship, they were sloppy sailors, so Rex's direct lines—and the skill of his crew at avoiding lulls in the wind—always kept him close.

On the third day, they rounded a mainland cape and hit the Saronic Gulf. Now it was a straight shot into Corinthus. A stiff breeze was blowing from aft, and both ships were running before the wind. Yet the air was unsettled, and the sky had the look of an afternoon thunderstorm. Rex realized the new conditions would favor the enemy craft, so he ordered all his rowers to the oars for a full-speed surge. Navy patrol boats would prevent an attack in Corinthus's harbor, so Rex knew that if he wanted to capture the slave ship, it was now or never.

But the enemy also realized that the end of the chase was at hand. They used the wind to their advantage and began to pull away. Rex stared at the blue-gray vessel that had tormented him for three days. It was hard to believe Flavia was possibly aboard that ship! The prospect of her suffering at their evil hands angered him—all the more now that the ship seemed to be escaping.

He descended to the rowing deck. The timekeeper's pace sounded frantic as he pounded the beats with his mallet. Their staccato concussions reverberated in Rex's ears and seemed to rattle his brain. He challenged his men to pull harder.

"Take me off, sir!" came a voice from the benches.

Stephen . . . But why?

"Take me off," the stocky youth repeated. "Send me up the mast!"

"What are you talking about?" Rex shouted above the crash of the waves outside and the creak of forty oars. "We need every hand pulling!"

"You need God's hand pulling, Captain!"

God's hand? Since when is God a rower?

"Prayer is your answer," the priest continued. "Show God you believe in him! Pull me off the oar and send me up the mast to beseech the throne of heaven."

"Shut up, zealot!" the Thracian yelled from his seat. "Leave the captain alone and keep sweeping!"

"No! Stephen is right," Rex declared.

All the men stopped talking, though they continued to pull with maximum effort. Every eye was on Rex. He approached Stephen's bench and ordered him to stand. "We do need God's help," he admitted. "Brother Priest, get up there and lift your hands in prayer. I rowed for three years, and I can do it again now. Either we'll catch that ship by divine help or we won't catch it at all. Not in a wind like this."

Rex took Stephen's place on the bench as the youth hurried topside. Grasping the oar for a moment, he felt its smoothness in his palms. Rex let the rolling shaft of wood take his arms in one complete revolution. Then, as he raised the oar and felt the blade catch the sea, he flexed his shoulder muscles, leaned back, and pulled hard.

The crew exploded into cheers. "Captain Rex!" they cried in unison, heartened by a leader who was willing to join them in the lowly labor of an oarsman. Now they pulled with renewed vigor, striving to close the final distance to the enemy ship.

"We're gaining on them!" the pilot called down.

Lightning flashed and a thunderclap boomed. The seas were rolling now, and the ship pitched and heaved as it pierced the waves. Rex could see heavy rainfall through the portals that gave the oarsmen an outside view. They were in a real storm, and the sail had come down. Even so, the men kept rowing with all their strength.

"Approaching their stern!" the pilot cried.

"Full speed ahead!" Rex answered. "Take out their steerboard, then turn aside."

"Very good, sir. Impact in ten! Nine! Eight!"

Rex left his bench and ran up to the main deck. The wind whipped his tunic, and the driving rain soaked him right away.

"Six! Five! Four!"

The high stern of the slave ship towered ahead. The *Deadly Encounter*'s bronze ram was about to smash the enemy's portside steering oar from behind. The blow would probably also breach the ship's hull. She wouldn't sink, but she'd be immobilized right away.

"Three! Two!"

Rex tugged his pilot's cloak and pointed. "Look! She's turning hard! Follow them!"

"One!"

"Turn now!" Rex shouted.

But it was too late.

The enemy craft had executed a sharp right turn to perfection. The ship listed far to one side as it curved away with both steerboards strained to near breaking. Meanwhile, the *Deadly Encounter* surged ahead, its bronze ram striving toward its mark like an arrowhead.

But the arrow whiffed into open sea as the slave ship dodged out of harm's way.

Rex looked up to see two harbor patrol boats dead ahead. A third was about to ram his starboard side.

WHAM!

The crashing sound of the impact made the thunderbolts seem tame by comparison. Rex staggered for a handhold. The *Deadly Encounter* shook like a sapling in an earthquake.

"Hull breached!" someone shouted.

"Cease rowing!" Rex ordered.

"God help us!" came a cry from on high.

83

Rex looked up. Stephen was there at the top of the rigging, clinging to the mast with one arm curled around it. His other arm was still raised in prayer.

"You might as well come down," Rex said bitterly. "Apparently, God's hand doesn't pull for me."

———❦———

The village of Cenchreae was Corinthus's eastern port on the Saronic Gulf, and an equally busy port lay on the western gulf as well. The city of Corinthus was situated between the two harbors on a narrow isthmus that separated the Greek mainland from the Peloponnesian peninsula. It was this strategic location—an intersection by land and by sea—that made Corinthus such a useful destination for traders and sailors from all over the empire.

And where traveling businessmen go, Flavia thought glumly, *prostitutes would always follow.*

She lifted her eyes from the deck of the slave ship and gazed across the plains at the mountainous height of Upper Corinth, a walled citadel on a crag above the city that was crowned by the Temple of Aphrodite. It was there that the goddess's elite prostitutes met their customers in a supposedly spiritual union. The sex act was a means for humans to copulate with the goddess and thus be joined to the divine world. Flavia winced at the notion, for it was a primitive, pagan concept—a practice utterly foreign to the ways of the true God.

"Bishop Ossius, what should we do?" Sophronia whispered as the captured girls emerged from below deck and were hustled down the gangplank onto the pier. "Did you not say the emperor would wish to ransom us?"

Ossius closed his eyes and shook his head in a mournful expression. "I've been trying for several days to tell that to our pig of a captain, but he insists otherwise. He says he brought you here for a more lucrative outcome. I believe prayer is our best hope now. Stay strong, dear ones." The bishop beckoned for Sophronia, Flavia, and Cassi to come near. "Know this too, my beloved friends. Holiness is a matter of *intent*. There is no sin in things that can't be avoided. You are only defiled by the free choices you make, not what is forced upon you. Do you understand what I mean?"

Flavia's eyes filled with tears, and she gripped her mother's arm. Cassi drew close as well.

"Has it come to that, then?" Sophronia asked with steely resolve.

Ossius's face was tender and compassionate, yet he offered no false hope. "I am afraid it may have," he said at last.

Flavia recoiled at the thought of what was being suggested. It was revolting . . . repugnant . . . unthinkable.

The Lord will surely save me!

Yet in her heart, Flavia knew the truth. *God does not always deliver a woman from her greatest fears.*

Most of the kidnapped girls were standing on the pier now, their wrists in chains. A few of them had been separated and remained on the slave ship's deck. One obvious reason for their separation stood out: these women were exceptionally beautiful. Though the slave lords treated the captives on the dock with crude disdain, their rough manhandling didn't extend to the separated women. "The dedicated," they were called. Women whose bodies would be given over to the goddess in sacred worship.

The obese skipper waddled up to Ossius on the ship's deck, followed by a beefy Goth whose hands were behind his back. "This is where you say goodbye to your lady friends," the skipper snarled. His smug look suggested his words were not a final mercy but cruel delight in the suffering of others.

"Stay strong, sisters," Ossius murmured.

The Goth drew his hands from behind his back and held up a single pair of handcuffs. "I think you mean 'sister.' Only the pale girl is pretty enough for Aphrodite. The mother and the Aethiops don't meet the divine standard."

A new height of terror seized Flavia's heart. *Oh, God, no! Not alone!*

"You can't take her!" Sophronia screamed, grabbing Flavia's arm and trying to drag her daughter away. But it was no use. The Gothic guard shoved Sophronia and pried loose her grip, then slapped the manacles onto Flavia's wrists.

"The Lord will be with me!" Flavia called desperately over her shoulder as she was dragged down the gangplank with the other dedicated girls. It was a proclamation of hope that she didn't truly feel.

Sophronia and Cassi could only huddle and cry, but Ossius did not break off his gaze. "It is not your fault!" he shouted, then Flavia lost sight of him as she was hustled along with the other sex slaves.

From Cenchreae, a good road led to Corinth. The captive women were made to march the full seven miles under the watchful eyes of their Gothic overlords, who were slaves themselves. The sun was low now, and an afternoon thunderstorm had cooled the air. Even so, by the time the girls arrived in the city, they were sweaty and exhausted. Flavia trudged with her forlorn companions but did not try to make contact with any of them. They were too dejected for conversation, much less any attempt at escape.

The captives passed the night in a grain warehouse near the central marketplace, known in Greek as the *agora*. A meager ration of bread and water was given to everyone, though the dedicated were allowed a handful of oily sardines as well. Periodically during the night, some of the girls destined for street work—mostly Africans from coastal villages around Carthago—were removed, kicking and screaming, from the warehouse, only to come back in stunned silence. Flavia said prayers for their emotional wreckage until she finally lapsed into a fitful sleep.

The next day was the auction, and it was as raw as anything Flavia had ever experienced. Her only consolation was that as one of the dedicated, she was not put on display while disrobed. But most of the other girls were subjected to that indignity, paraded in front of the pimps and passersby from a high platform called the *bema*. The women were nothing more than property for sale, so they were inspected and evaluated like animals in a cattle market. The street pimps bought them up one by one. Then it was time for the priests of Aphrodite to bid on the sacred prostitutes.

Flavia was led with about twenty other beautiful women onto the bema. She gazed out at the arrogant men in priestly garments, their eyes eager and bright. Competition was fierce for the prettiest girls who would fetch the best return on the priests' investment. Apparently, the wealthiest citizens paid exorbitant sums to climb to Upper Corinthus and have intercourse with elegant prostitutes. It was believed that Aphrodite would certainly hear the prayers of men who "worshiped" her in this way. Virgins were especially valuable, for they had the most to sacrifice to the goddess.

The horde of pedestrians in the agora strolled past the sordid affair without giving it much attention. Flavia could hardly keep from shouting at them as they wandered by. *Wake up!* she wanted to scream. *Don't you see what is happening here? We are kidnapped women about to undergo a terrible fate! Do you simply accept this?*

Yet even worse than the oblivious bystanders were the Aphroditean priests waving their fingers as they threw in their bids. A biblical curse came to Flavia's mind, but she refrained from praying it. Instead, divine pity flooded her heart. "Love your enemies, and pray for those who persecute you," the Lord had commanded his disciples in Matthew's gospel. Flavia managed to ask God to open the eyes of these wicked men and reveal their deeds to be as hideous as they truly were.

When it was Flavia's turn to be auctioned, the bidding turned intense. She had always known that men found her attractive, with her curvy figure and wide hazel eyes. Yet as a senator's daughter of high station, her suitors had been few, and none had meant anything to her. Only Rex had ever captured her heart, and he was far away now. *Oh, Lord! If only Rex were here!* She recalled the day, much like this one, when cruel enemies had cast her in chains before a ravenous crowd. Brave Rex had intervened then. He had saved her life while risking his own.

But today, no such help would come.

"Five solidi!" cried one of the so-called priests, who was really nothing more than a high-end pimp. The solidus coin was very valuable, made of nearly solid gold, as its name implied. Only the richest clients could afford to be with a girl who had cost so much to purchase.

In the end, Flavia went for eight solidi. The twenty dedicated women were herded from the bema into a nearby shop with an empty back room. Most of the street girls had already been dragged off to the brothels. Now the sacred prostitutes were loaded into enclosed wagons, then the doors were firmly locked behind them. They were driven up a steep road to a gate in Upper Corinthus's ancient wall.

"Get out and begin walking!" one of the Gothic slaves commanded as he swung open the wagon door.

Upon entering the citadel, a decadent scene met Flavia's eyes. Men caroused in the streets with women whose gauzy outfits left nothing to the imagination. The wine flowed freely as the men pawed at their companions and the women pretended to enjoy it. It seemed like every other building was a house of prostitution, all of them leading up to the Temple of Aphrodite on the mountain's summit. The aura of sensuality was palpable, and there was nothing beautiful or praiseworthy about it. Flavia recoiled at its horrors. Sexuality wasn't supposed to be like this. There was no love here, no gentleness, no marital fidelity. Such promiscuous behavior was befitting only of wild animals.

The women trudged uphill until they arrived at the temple itself. It was surprisingly small: a shrine just big enough for the cult idol inside, with a porch supported by Corinthian columns. There was no altar out front, for the bloodshed here was of a different type.

One of the Goths delivered Flavia to a mansion a few steps from the temple. The Aphroditean priest who met her was a ratty little man with tufts of nose hair bursting from each nostril. "Welcome to your new home, my lovely," he crooned.

"My true home is in a city far away."

"And where would that be, young lady?"

"The glorious city of God."

"Aha! A Christian! The men who come here love to encounter resistant girls like you. I shall start the bidding higher than usual. It will be a very rich man who first takes you."

The Goth grabbed Flavia's elbow in a firm grip and followed the rat-man into the house. An upstairs room was designated for the new guest. Its window was barred, and its bed linens were expensive. Flavia stared at the painted wall instead.

"Look away if you must," said the ratty priest, "yet even so, it is here that you shall be given to the Great Harlot. Your body shall become Aphrodite's dwelling place as her presence inhabits your flesh. Only in this way can a mere man join with the divine."

"Wrong!" Flavia cried. "I'm not the temple of a goddess! I belong to Jesus!"

"Not anymore, my lovely. The pitiful bread and wine of your Christ creates a union that is far less"—the man paused to offer a wink and a sneer—"*intimate* than the one you are about to encounter."

Flavia sagged at these ominous words. She steadied herself against the wall, refusing to collapse onto the sumptuous bed that was actually a pagan altar.

"Take off her chains!" the priest instructed the Gothic guard.

The blond man removed the manacles, which had chafed Flavia's wrists. The Goth laughed at this, but the ratty priest came and inspected the damage. He took Flavia's hands in his own and began to caress them with his fingers.

"So much holy work for these hands to do," he whispered softly. "For many years to come."

At these words, Flavia's resistance finally broke. Faced with the awful reality of what was about to happen, all she could do was cry.

"There, there," soothed the priest. "Do not be afraid. Aphrodite will take good care of you."

To this evil word, at last, Flavia had no bold reply.

———

Rex dangled a rope ladder over the gunwale and clambered down the side of the *Deadly Encounter*. Reaching the waterline, he dropped into the sea. After taking a deep breath, he went under and began to inspect the gaping hole from yesterday's ramming.

Holding his face close to the hull, Rex peered at the opening through the cloudy water. The Corinthian patrol boat that had carried out the attack wasn't a huge warship, so the hole was only about the size of a large melon. Although a major hull compartment had flooded with sea water, making the ship unstable and dangerous, the compartment could easily be pumped out if the ship could be dry-docked. Unfortunately, no one was looking to make the *Deadly Encounter* seaworthy again. Instead, the ship was chained to a buoy about a mile from Cenchreae's harbor until the imperial navy could arrive to tow away the vessel and punish the mutineers.

Probably with death.

And a slow one, at that.

Rex, however, had no interest in a long, painful death at the hands of Roman justice, so he finished inspecting the hole and climbed back up the ladder. The Thracian met him at the top.

"How bad is it?" he asked.

"Not as bad as you might think. Clean edges. About this big." Rex held up his hands to indicate the size.

"Fixable with the timber and tar we have aboard," the Thracian observed, "if she were up and out of the drink."

"Right. Dry-docked or beached or—"

The Thracian arched his eyebrows, waiting to hear what his captain would say.

"Listing far to port side," Rex finished.

Now the Thracian broke into a grin. "Roll the ballast over?"

Rex nodded vigorously. "It wouldn't take much because the breach is near the waterline. Just tip her enough to lift the hole so we can pump out the compartment and patch it. Then set her back down, and no one's the wiser."

"A single day's job?"

"Or a night's. Then at dawn, we go."

"Sir? Aren't you forgetting the chain?"

Rex grinned at his first mate. "Do I ever forget things like that?"

"No, sir. That's why you're the captain of this ragged bunch of mutineers."

"As I should be. Now follow me."

The two men went to the stern and peered over. After the port authorities had disabled the ship, they had dragged her to the buoy at which Rex and the Thracian were now staring. It was just a wooden barrel attached to an anchor on the sea floor, but the *Deadly Encounter*'s steering oars were fastened to the buoy by a heavy chain. Nothing aboard was sharp enough to cut through iron like that, and tearing the chain away would destroy the twin steerboards. Even if the ship could be sprung loose, it was incapacitated by its flooded hull. And the shore was too far away to reach by swimming. Rex's men had seen all this immediately and resigned themselves to lounging around the deck while they awaited some future means of escape. But they didn't have the inner motivation their captain did.

"That chain sure is thick," the Thracian said, gesturing to the tether that secured the ship to the buoy. "It would take us a week to file through it, working in shifts night and day. And that's if we had a thousand files to use up."

"Have you ever anchored a ship?" Rex asked him.

"Not until we rebelled. Until then, I was just an oarsman."

"I have, many times. When I was new to the navy, I spent a year on an anchor crew when I wasn't rowing. It'll give you a lot of wrist strength, hauling up all that line." Rex bunched his fists and flexed his corded forearms to prove his point. "So I know a lot about anchoring," he went on, "and one thing I know is, you don't make the whole rode out of chain."

The Thracian's head swung around. "Yeah? Why not?"

"In a storm, there's maximum pull on the ship, and a chain will go taut like a bar of iron. That'll tear a ship apart if there's no flex in the line. You have to make some of it from rope so it'll stretch."

"You're telling me some of the line under that buoy is rope?"

"Most likely."

"How deep?"

"That's what I came back here to find out," Rex said with a cocky grin. And then, without saying another word, he bent his knees and launched himself over the rail. He surfaced quickly after an arcing dive and looked up in time to see the shocked expression on the Thracian's face.

"Back in a moment," he called to his friend.

After taking a deep breath, Rex plunged beneath the buoy and found the chain. Pulling himself hand over hand, he went down into the murky depths. After ten hard pulls, he still felt nothing but iron, so he released the rode and kicked his way back to the surface.

"Find anything, sir?"

"Not yet. I'll try again."

This time Rex went down twelve pulls but still didn't find the rope. It wasn't until his fourth try—at seventeen pulls—that he located the place where the chain ended and the flexible rope began. He mimicked twenty slices with the edge of his hand against the line, then began to run out of breath. Leaving the rope, he propelled himself upward, gasping as he finally burst from the water.

"Seventeen pulls down," he shouted to his first mate up on deck. "And five hundred cuts with a sharp blade would probably sever the line. So that's only twenty-five dives."

The Thracian let out a whoop. "And then with the hull patched up, we could get out of here!"

"That's right. Since I don't know when the navy's going to show up, we're doing it tonight. I want you to lead the repair team. As soon as the sun sets, get a crew moving those ballast stones portside to tip us over. When the hole is high enough, pump out the hold, then get our shipwright on the job. Demosthenes is a hundred times better at carpentry than rowing. Finally, he'll be worth something to us."

91

"Aye, sir. You can count on me."

"I want Marius leading the diving crew. He's a fish, that one. Not afraid of the deep. Ten men with knives taking turns at the rope, seventeen hands down. It'll be dark and scary, but not nearly as scary as being in a dungeon awaiting crucifixion."

"Marius is the man for it! He'll get it done." The Thracian paused. "But what about you, sir? What do you plan to do?"

"Me?"

"Aye."

"I'll be in Corinthus. Now throw me the ladder and let me up."

—————

Ships had been passing the *Deadly Encounter* all day, heading in and out of Cenchreae's harbor while ignoring the disabled and impounded warship with its doomed crew. No doubt those passing sailors assumed the mutineers deserved a terrible punishment. Soon the navy would arrive to serve up a dose of imperial justice. Until then, the rebels would have to float in boredom on a remote sea anchor designed to keep them isolated.

Rex could only chuckle as he watched a grain ship go by in the reddish light of dusk. *Won't they be surprised tomorrow when they find this buoy bobbing alone in the sea?*

By then, his men would be long gone. And if all went well, he would be in Corinthus. *With Flavia!* But he would have to hurry if he was to spare her the terrible fate that awaited her.

When the sun had finally set over the isthmus of Corinth and his men had started shifting the *Encounter*'s ballast, Rex slipped overboard once again. The sea anchor was in a good location for holding impounded ships. The spot was much too far to swim to Cenchreae, so without a dinghy, there was no way to get to land. Rex knew he would have to get there with the aid of a passing ship. Unfortunately, everyone was forbidden from helping the mutineers, on pain of death. Yet those weren't the sort of details Rex had ever let stop him before. He wasn't about to start now.

Down in the water, Rex lay on an old hatch cover and paddled toward the sea lane that the passing ships had been using all day. Few would be coming along anymore now that it was so late, yet there were always a couple of stragglers hurrying into port as full darkness set in. Rex hunkered down and waited on his little wooden raft, churning his arms and legs to stay in the same position. Fortunately, enough junk was bobbing in the sea that he was confident he wouldn't be noticed.

In the distance, a harbor patrol boat materialized in the gloom. Though it was returning to the port at a good pace, Rex let it go by. It wasn't the right sort of ship for what he had in mind.

A crescent moon hung over the water now. The sky, though not yet black, was a deep blue that signaled night was at hand. Rex waited for a few tense moments, fearing that no more ships would pass—until he spotted a fishing boat making its way toward the harbor with whatever catch the day's nets had brought in. It was a smaller vessel than Rex had hoped for, but he didn't want to risk waiting for another. He began to paddle toward it on an intercept course.

When he was near to the ship and slightly ahead of it, Rex reached over his shoulder for his crossbow. It was a useful weapon for naval combat, with a greater draw weight, and thus shooting power, than a bow could provide. Lying on his back upon the raft, Rex set the weapon against his belly, drew the string with a hard pull, and latched it. After placing a bolt in the groove, Rex rolled over, aimed at the passing ship, and depressed the trigger.

It was too dark to see the bolt make impact, but a faint thump indicated a hit. Since the bolt's head was barbed, Rex surmised that once it pierced the ship's hull, it would stay put. At least, that was the hope.

Before shooting the bolt, Rex had attached a length of ship's cord to it. Now he grabbed the line floating in the water and wrapped it around a plank on his makeshift raft. For a long moment, the rope remained slack. Only when it went taut did Rex know for certain he was secured to his target. The moving ship began to tow its secret rider through the waves, making a little wake of bubbly white water. He was like a tuna being hauled in by an angler—except this tuna *wanted* to be hooked.

Rex rode behind the ship for about half an hour under the dim light of the crescent moon. Occasionally the fishermen's voices wafted across the water, but their tone was normal and they raised no alarm. Their cheerful laughs and the clink of their copper cups suggested they had things on their minds other than checking for a freeloading mutineer being dragged abaft.

The fishing ship finally approached a torch tower at the end of Cenchreae's longest pier. Slipping off the raft, Rex wondered what the fishermen would think in the morning when they discovered their overnight stint as unwitting tugboat captains. But by then it wouldn't matter, for he would be far away.

After swimming to the pier, Rex hauled himself up. The Corinthus Gate on the other side of sleepy Cenchreae was easy to find. From there it was seven miles to Corinthus. Rex exited through the gate and began trotting toward the city at a double-time pace that would have impressed even Aratus, his demanding centurion back in cadet school.

Less than an hour later, he arrived at the gates of Corinthus. For a place with an infamous reputation for carousing, the city seemed unexpectedly quiet as it lay on the grassy plains beneath the looming bulk of the acropolis. Rex gazed at its height. Something white could be seen at the apex—no doubt it was the Temple of Aphrodite gleaming in the moonlight. Was Flavia there? If she had indeed been captured in Ossius's company, she would be within the vicinity of the temple. The prettiest and classiest women were always taken there, and Flavia was strikingly beautiful. Many men would want to . . .

Ach! Jesus, may you guard her! Though Rex wasn't normally a man of prayer, he thought it would help to ask Flavia's own god for help in a time like this. Jesus would probably come to her assistance more quickly than any other god.

Despite the prayer, a sense of urgency settled on Rex as he began to hike to the mountain's summit. He soon reached the walls of Upper Corinthus and was stopped by a sentinel, who peered through a little window in the wooden gate. The light of an oil lamp flickered on his unshaven face.

"The citadel is for high-class customers only," the man said gruffly.

"And such am I," Rex replied. "I'm looking for new girls who have never been with a man."

The gatekeeper's face grew sly. "There's a fresh batch of 'em right up near the temple. But they're reserved for better folk than you."

"I can pay. In pure silver."

"You don't have no silver," the man sneered. "Look at you in your cheap tunic, dripping with sweat like a farm boy. You're just a peasant. Be off now, you yellow-haired German! Go find a cheap whore on a street corner. You ain't got enough money to open these doors."

"You're wrong." Rex untied the thongs of his pouch and dug out a handful of shiny silver pieces. "I have whatever it takes."

The guard could see that the coins were valuable. "Fine, then," he grumped as he unlatched the gate. "But why does a commoner like you want to spend so much?"

"Because some things are priceless," Rex replied.

It was a dark night. And it was about to get much darker.

At the mansion next to Aphrodite's temple, Flavia sat on the edge of the bed in the little room to which she had been assigned. The bed was the only furniture in the room, pushed into the corner against the stone walls and anchored to the floor. There was a ring in the wall for wrist chains. Flavia was glad she hadn't been made to suffer that indignity.

Dejected, she stared out the window for lack of anything better to do. Ragged clouds now obscured the crescent moon. For probably the twentieth time, she tried to shake the bars on the window, but they didn't budge.

Help me to escape, Lord. I'm so scared!

She had heard male voices in the house all night, and even some female laughter, but no one had come to Flavia's room except a maid who brought her a tray of food and a little vial of perfume. Flavia had wolfed down the meal and pitched the perfume out the window.

Footsteps creaked on the stairs, a sound Flavia had come to dread. So far, the visitors had all passed by her room. But this time, a hand began to turn the door latch.

I'll fight . . .

She bunched her fists. *Punch! Dodge! Flee!*

The ratty priest stepped into the room, followed by a tall man in a dark hooded cloak.

Now!

Flavia burst from the bed and threw a fist at her rat-faced tormentor. But instead of being knocked aside, the man simply seized her arm and hurled her back onto the mattress. The bed's coverlet fell onto the floor, making Flavia feel helpless and exposed.

"Seen it all before, my lovely," said the priest. "Customers love it. Keep it up."

Now the truth sank into Flavia's mind that there would be no escape. Only endurance. *Go far away in your mind, and endure.* It was all she could do now.

"You should feel proud," the priest announced. He gestured to the hooded figure behind him. "This worshiper paid a huge sum for you. Truly you are an incarnation of Aphrodite on earth."

The priest turned to his customer and gave him a polite bow. "Enjoy yourself," he said with a slimy grin, "and may the Great Harlot favor you." Then he slipped past the man, locking the door behind him as he exited.

Flavia stared at the frightful figure looming before her—a monster who had emerged from the woods, a demon risen from hell to bring anguish and destruction to her soul. She wanted to scream curses at him, but words evaded her. Instead, she recoiled from his malevolent presence and withdrew into the corner at the head of the bed. The wall at her back was the only solid thing in her unsteady world. Everything seemed to be happening slowly, as if in a terrible dream.

The hooded man was silent. Flavia could not see his face, yet she knew his expression must be bestial and corrupt.

He stepped close.

Rage finally burst from Flavia. "I hate you!" she screamed, drawing her knees up to her body. "Get away! You're disgusting!"

The man knelt beside the bed. His hand reached out, slithering toward her like a snake, creeping like a predator on the prowl. Flavia's heart was hammering now.

Perhaps I can overpower him! Run past him! Surely the door can be yanked from its hinges!

She kicked hard at the man's face, but his hand was lightning quick. He caught her bare foot in his firm grip.

"Let me go!" Flavia squealed, but his grip only tightened as she squirmed. *Perhaps he truly is a demon?* Terrified now, she fell still.

The man drew Flavia's foot toward his face.

Will he bite me? Is he some kind of weird torturer?

"Don't . . . don't hurt me," she pleaded.

Softly, the man pressed Flavia's foot to his bearded face. And then he did something strange. He kissed her toes with a gentleness she could scarcely comprehend.

"I am not here to hurt you," came a deep and resonant voice from within the depths of the hood.

Outside the window, the clouds shifted, causing a beam of pale moonlight to flood the room. The man's kneeling form was washed in a luminous glow. Hardly daring to believe, Flavia leaned forward and touched the man's hood. Suddenly she grasped it and threw it upon his shoulders.

Rex stared back at her in the moonlight. His gaze was more tender and adoring than any husband had ever given to his bride on the night of their first embrace.

"You found me," Flavia whispered, at a loss for other words.

"I will always find you," Rex replied.

Like no other, she realized.

And softly, for the second time that night, Flavia began to cry.

3

The city of Sirmium had been named by the great Diocletian as one of the four capitals of the Roman Empire. Yet out of those four cities—none of which came anywhere close to the splendor of Rome—little Sirmium was the most pathetic. At least the other three had something significant going for them: Mediolanum could boast of splendid architecture, Nicomedia was a great crossroads and trading city, and Augusta Treverorum bustled with a sizable population. But to Emperor Gaius Valerius Licinius, who had reigned as Augustus of the East for more than three years now, his capital of Sirmium was a piece of caca. And that was one of the many reasons why Licinius wanted the whole empire for himself.

"How much longer before the envoy arrives?" the emperor asked his trusted adviser, a powerful duke named Senecio. Although the man was as ugly as an ape, he had a grasp of political strategy like no other. Licinius was glad to have him around.

"About an hour, Your Majesty," Senecio replied with a servile dip of his head. Somehow the fellow managed to be scrawny in his shoulders while having a potbelly at the same time. "The throne room is almost ready. I ordered some extra lampstands of gold to give the appearance of great wealth."

"Excellent! When Julius Constantius returns to his brother, I want him to go back suitably impressed and give a fine report to dear old Constantine."

Licinius fanned himself with the folds of his toga as he reclined under a shady portico that caught what little breeze was available. Unfortunately, the stink of horses also wafted on the wind, though Licinius understood that the charioteers needed to practice in the adjacent racetrack. Returning his attention to his homely adviser, he asked, "What is the latest gossip about Constantine's pick as his caesar?"

Senecio did not reply right away but seemed to choose his words carefully—always a wise move in front of an emperor. The politics here were delicate, and extremely consequential.

About three decades ago, Emperor Diocletian of blessed memory instituted a new means of ruling the Roman Empire. It had come to be called the Imperial College, and it divided power among four rulers: two senior emperors called *augusti*, assisted by two junior emperors called *caesars*. Splitting power into a fourfold tetrarchy like this was a good move, for the empire was too vast for one man to control. However, a tetrarchy had the inherent flaw of being prone to civil wars, because power-hungry men with loyal armies always viewed themselves as legitimate contenders for one of the four spots.

Civil war did indeed occur for many years, until Licinius and Constantine finally joined in a Christian alliance against two pagan warlords. With the help of the newfangled sun god named Jesus, they defeated their enemies at war, thereby reducing the Imperial College to two augusti—themselves— while leaving vacancies for the caesars. Each augustus would now get to pick someone for the junior role.

To seal their great alliance, Constantine offered Licinius his sister Constantia in marriage. The wedding took place at Mediolanum. After too many tries, Licinius finally managed to spawn a son with fat Constantia. They named him Licinius Junior. Somewhere nearby, the cute little cherub was crawling around the palace right now. *Little did that baby know he was about to be made a caesar!*

Senecio finally found his voice. "It goes without saying, Your Highness, that we already know who the better of the two caesars will be. That boy of yours will make a fine emperor someday—just like his father."

Flattering as always, Licinius thought, *yet correct as always too.*

"The latest gossip about the fourth spot," Senecio went on, "is that my brother Bassianus will get the nod. As you know, he's married to Constantine's sister. That's why Constantine will choose him. The clever rascal likes to keep things in the family."

"As do I. It is the Roman way." Licinius rubbed his chin stubble as he thought it over. "The elevation of Bassianus is a good idea. One relative of Constantine's to be his caesar, and one pick for me: little Junior, when he comes of age. We each get a family member in the college. It will cause both our dynasties to prosper for the glory of Rome."

"So, if Bassianus is the emperor's choice, you will agree?" Senecio eyed his lord carefully, as if to test his response.

"It's Constantine's right to pick whom he wants. I have no reason to object."

"Indeed, you do not. My brother is a good man. I just wanted to make sure."

A servant appeared in the shady portico and tinkled a bell for attention. "The envoy is ready to meet thee, O great Augustus," he said with the new formality that emperors now demanded.

"Send him in, once I am seated in full splendor," Licinius ordered.

After Licinius had taken his place on the throne, the envoy from Constantine was ushered into the palace basilica with a trumpet fanfare. Julius Constantius was younger than Constantine but had many features in common with his older brother. He was a tall fellow with big brown eyes and a dimpled chin. After exchanging the greetings and formalities necessary at such a high diplomatic occasion, Julius finally revealed who the proposed Caesar of Italy would be. Indeed, the choice was Bassianus, just as the recent gossip had suggested. Licinius glanced over at Senecio, who seemed delighted that his brother had just been named a member of the Imperial College.

"And now it is time to offer my master's second appointment," Julius continued in his bombastic way, "to complete the sacred number and once again have four harmonious colleagues ruling over the four corners of our fertile and peaceful realm. Let there be no doubt, gentlemen—my master Constantine has identified a wise pick."

Licinius turned to a servant stationed beside the throne. "Go tell Constantia to be ready to bring in the baby," he instructed the slave in a whisper. "That is, if she can pry herself away from her pastries and cakes."

"Esteemed gentlemen!" cried the envoy. "As the senior emperor of the

College, my master Constantine exercises his right to declare"—Julius swept his hand toward his diplomatic retinue—"Flavius Julius Crispus, his own firstborn son, as the new Caesar of the East!"

Crispus!

Enraged, Licinius gripped the armrests of his throne until his knuckles turned white. Yet he betrayed no emotion on his face. Certainly, he would never let this treasonous appointment go forward, even if it meant starting a war with Constantine. But for now, he would display no response that could help his rival gain an advantage. He calmed himself with a deep breath.

"How convenient for Constantine," Licinius said when he had gathered enough composure to speak, "to have his brother-in-law and his firstborn son as the two caesars."

"Truly the young man is worthy," Julius agreed. He gestured at Crispus, who had stepped from the crowd. He appeared to be about eighteen, with the good looks and rust-brown hair that proved his mother was the red-headed Minervina, not the current queen, homely Fausta.

"I salute you, dear uncle, with all the respect due to such a great augustus as yourself," Crispus said with perfect diplomatic decorum, plus an added touch of boyish charm.

"I salute you in return, dear nephew," Licinius replied with equal politeness, even as he briefly fantasized about strangling the youth with his bare hands.

Now that the big announcement had been made, a few more strained pleasantries were exchanged, then the meeting came to an end. The envoy Julius and his retinue retired from the throne room to their personal chambers. Licinius and Senecio immediately went to a private garden with a bubbling fountain in the corner that would drown out sound. It was one of his favorite places to strategize.

"Senecio, we cannot let this stand," Licinius said as the potbellied duke sat beside him on a stone bench. "Constantine cannot be allowed to install two family members in the Imperial College! Before long, he will oust me, and then what will happen to my legacy?"

"Surely your family would suffer the ultimate penalty of proscription. Your descendants would be blotted from the earth. Your clan's name would come to an end. This whole affair must be stopped, Your Majesty."

"Yes—but how?"

Senecio was silent for a long moment. Licinius could almost see the ideas flitting around inside his head like butterflies. The wily duke licked his lips, then finally spoke up. "My brother Bassianus is driven by very lofty ambitions," he remarked. "There is nothing he wouldn't do to achieve his aims."

"Nothing, you say?" Licinius narrowed his eyes and stared at his savvy adviser. "Where is he now, by chance?"

"In Gaul."

"Where in Gaul?"

"Arelate."

"Near Constantine, then."

"Oh, yes. One might even say at the emperor's side."

"Day and night, he is at the emperor's side, you say?"

"At all times, Your Highness, for he is highly trusted. No one ever questions him."

Licinius nodded sagely at these words. "And yet he is driven by lofty ambitions. So I wonder, Senecio, to what lengths might your brother go in his quest for imperial power? Would he kill a man? Ah, indeed, I wonder that."

"It so happens that I am curious about that as well. Perhaps I should travel to Arelate to find out?"

Licinius couldn't suppress a devious smile; and when Senecio saw it, a wide grin also came to his face.

"An excellent idea!" the emperor burst out. "I shall send you to Gaul with my full blessing. No doubt you can persuade your ambitious brother to use all possible means to deal with the problem of Constantine."

"We shall do whatever it takes, my lord."

"Yes, that's right," Licinius agreed. "Whatever it takes."

—◦◦◦—

The wooden floor was hard and uncomfortable—not a good place for sleeping. Of course, the architect of the mansion in Upper Corinthus had never meant for its occupants to sleep anywhere but the beds. Rex rolled over onto his side and tried to put more of his cloak between him and the planks. Though the garment was expensively tailored, he wished he had stolen a thicker one when choosing a disguise to blend in with the rich guests of the citadel.

"Are you awake?" Flavia whispered from the bed.

"Mm-hmm."

"The sky is a little lighter, I think."

Rex glanced at the window and saw that Flavia was right. Still uncomfortable, he shifted his position at the foot of her bed. Customers could, of course, exit the room by knocking for the night watchman. But new girls were always locked in their bedrooms because they spent the first few weeks trying to escape. "Dawn is less than an hour away," Rex said in response to her observation. "How did you sleep?"

Flavia didn't answer right away, and Rex wasn't sure why. Finally, she sighed deeply. Then, after a little rustling, she appeared at the foot of the bed, looming over him on the floor. "So much better than I thought I would," she said earnestly. "Thank you."

"For coming to get you?"

"Yes. And for saving me from something terrible. For pursuing me without stopping. For lying there all night at the foot of my bed, guarding me."

"Like a faithful dog," he joked.

"Like Brandulf Rex," she replied, and the two of them fell silent again.

When the sky had lightened to a pale gray, Rex stood and signaled it was time to make their escape. The Aphroditean priest had told him he had "rights" to Flavia until dawn, after which she would begin seeing other customers for the remainder of the day. He threw the stolen cloak around his shoulders and fastened it, then handed Flavia her mantle to put on over her chiton. She had been dressed in archaic Greek fashion like some kind of sex nymph from the ancient past. But even today, in sensual Corinthus, such attire would easily blend in.

Outside the door, footsteps sounded on the stairs. "Listen! The rat-faced man is coming," Flavia said urgently.

"I hear him. Be ready to move."

The priest jiggled the lock, then entered a little too eagerly. He seemed surprised to find the pair standing up.

"How was the—" he began, but was brought up short when Rex smashed him in the larynx with his knuckles.

Before the priest could escape, Rex put him in a chokehold from behind. Though the man struggled in Rex's viselike grip, he could make no sound other than a faint gurgle. After a few moments of this, Rex felt him go limp from the blood flow being cut from his brain—one of the many paralyzing attacks taught to speculators in the Roman army. Quietly, he let the priest drop to the bed.

"Walk beside me like nothing is wrong," he said to Flavia. But as he was about to leave, he turned and was surprised to discover her attention focused on the priest, not the door. Flavia stood over the ratty man, grimacing and raising a balled fist above his unconscious form.

"I want to punch him!" she snarled through gritted teeth.

Rex gently touched Flavia's arm, lowering it to her side. "You once called me to a better way," he said. "Now I do the same for you."

Flavia blew out a long breath as she stared at the evildoer on the bed. She uncurled her fingers. Rex could feel the tension leave her body and the rage depart her soul. But then, just as Flavia was about to exit, she turned and spat on the floor. "That is my curse against all the pain you cause," she declared.

"It needed to be said," Rex agreed as he led Flavia from the terrible room.

The front atrium of the mansion was guarded by one of the Gothic slaves who worked the brothels of Upper Corinthus. He rose from his stool when the pair entered, his hand casually gripping the club on his belt. "The lady can't leave with you," he said gruffly to Rex.

"Her stomach is upset," Rex replied without missing a beat. "Must have been some bad sardines. She needs to visit the latrine. The ones here are being used."

"She can't leave," the guard insisted. "It's forbidden, especially for the new girls."

Some manacles hung on a wall nearby. Grabbing a pair from the peg, Rex clasped one cuff onto Flavia's wrist, then attached the other cuff to his own. "I have to go too," he said. "See? She can't escape. I'll bring her right back." He hustled Flavia out the door before the Goth could intervene.

Flavia lifted her arm to display the shackles as the pair headed toward the public toilets. "This might make things a little awkward in there," she remarked.

The jest made Rex smile. "Well, I have to admit, it's certainly not the first jewelry I wanted to buy you. I guess it will have to do for now."

"I'll treasure it forever," Flavia replied with a little laugh. "But seriously, what are we going to do? The key is back at the house, and we don't want to go back there."

"Yeah, I know. I did that on impulse. I'll think of something. Let's duck into the latrines before the guard gets suspicious. He's probably watching us."

The dark, smelly building was a simple square, with toilet seats around three walls and the entrance door on the fourth. Fortunately, the latrine was unoccupied at this early hour. The citadel of Upper Corinthus had a natural spring, so there was fresh water running through a trough on the floor, as well as beneath the seats to carry away the filth. Several buckets held sponges on sticks for bodily cleansing. A clay lamp burned on a stand in the corner, next to a mop that hadn't been used in far too long.

Tugging Flavia behind him, Rex climbed onto the marble bench of seats and peeked through an air vent. "Uh-oh. Three guards are coming this way. I guess they don't trust us."

"Ugh! Why do they have to be so cautious?"

"You're an expensive investment. They aren't going to just let you walk away."

"Can you fight them?"

"Not really. I'm sort of regretting this decision." Rex dipped his head toward the handcuffs. "One-armed attacks against three men usually don't work."

"What should we do, then?"

"Buy time. Quick, hike up your chiton and sit down."

"What? Right here next to you? No!"

"Just fluff your dress around you. I'll do the same with my cloak."

"Rex, I can't!"

"Do it!"

Rex plopped down on one of the toilet holes and dragged Flavia beside him. They had just arranged their garments around their hips to make it seem as if they were using the facility for its intended purpose when the three guards burst in.

"Good morning, gentlemen," Rex said. He broke wind loudly in the little room. "Can you give us a moment longer?"

The guards' suspicions seemed to be relieved upon finding the pair where they had said they would be. They exited the facility with a little grumbling.

"Now we need a diversion," Rex said.

"Like what?"

Rex rose from the seat with Flavia following. He grabbed the oil lamp with his free hand and held it above one of the toilet holes. "Flammable gas," he said, then dipped the lamp into the sewer.

A flame burst to life in the space beneath the marble benches. Fiery orange tongues licked out of every hole. "Guards, help us!" Rex shouted. "Fire!"

The three Goths burst into the latrine and instantly snatched up the buckets, for a building on fire was a grave danger to any city. They started scooping water from the trough and pouring it into the toilet seats. Rex snatched the mop and exited behind the men while they weren't looking. After slamming the door, he wedged the mop handle between it and an upturned cobblestone.

"Hey!" cried a voice from inside. "Get him!"

"That won't hold them long," Rex said. "Let's run."

United at the wrist, the two fugitives hurried through the streets, looking for a building in which to hide. But Upper Corinthus was still asleep, so its doors weren't open yet. Footsteps and shouts in the distance told Rex that the guards had escaped the latrine. Glancing over his shoulder, he saw the pursuers—and they spotted him too.

"This way!" he urged Flavia. "We can still lose them!"

After switching directions three or four times in the tight alleys, they rounded a corner and found themselves staring at the Temple of Aphrodite on the citadel's summit. Unlike the other buildings, its entrance was wide open. Religious awe, not wooden doors, kept intruders out of this particular edifice.

"We can't hide in there," Flavia protested.

"It's our only option. Come on!"

The idol of the goddess, naked from the waist up, loomed inside the temple as Rex and Flavia entered. She was svelte and full-figured, painted in lifelike detail as she held out her arms to offer seductive pleasures to her worshipers. Rex could understand why so many people venerated Aphrodite. Sexual desire was universal to the human race, and its intense hunger could easily be turned into an object of worship.

"She disgusts me," Flavia said.

"That's part of what makes her attractive."

"Maybe so. But there's a better way."

Rex had no answer for that. Instead, as he gazed up at the marble statue of the goddess—dominant and alluring as she reigned over ancient Corinthus— a plan formed in his mind. The guards outside were running everywhere, shouting and searching for their prey. Although Rex and Flavia were safe for the moment, it would only be a short time before they were discovered. He turned to Flavia to propose an idea.

"When I was a cadet in speculator school, my trainer, Aratus, used to talk about three options. He taught us that in situations like this, you have to pick the strategy of an animal—a mouse, a badger, or a hornet. Sometimes you sneak around quietly like a mouse, sometimes you fight like an enraged badger, and sometimes you smash the hornet's nest and lose yourself in the confusion. Right now, I think it's time for the third option."

"That sounds better than fighting. And sneaking hasn't gotten us anywhere. But what would create a hornet's nest like that? Should we start a giant fire?"

"How about if we topple a giant goddess?" Rex replied.

Flavia arched her eyebrows and her mouth fell open. She pointed up at the idol. "You mean—"

"I'm not pious. I would do it."

"I *am* pious, which means I would too! But how?"

Rex led Flavia onto Aphrodite's pedestal. Using the folds of the goddess's lower garments as footholds, they climbed to the bends of her outstretched arms, one on either side. Together, they threw their conjoined wrists over the statue's head so that the manacle chain was at the nape of Aphrodite's neck.

"The guards are outside now," Rex whispered. "Get ready. When I say go, we jump!"

One of the Goths ascended the steps to the porch. "I'll check inside the temple, boss!" he yelled.

Rex cupped his free hand to his mouth. "We're in here, you loser!"

"Comrades! Over this way!" the guard called to his friends.

A moment later, the three Gothic thugs were silhouetted in the doorway. They began to approach the idol. Two of them held clubs, while the third had a knife.

"Oh, Rex," Flavia murmured, "I don't want to get caught again!"

"Just hold steady. Wait for it . . . a little more . . ."

Flavia shifted and groaned as the men drew close.

"Jump!"

The pair leapt from the goddess's arms to the floor, dragging her with them by the chain at the back of her neck. Shrieking, the guards tried to dive out of the way as the idol bore down on them like a bare-breasted demon from hell. Rex and Flavia used their momentum to land in front of Aphrodite's massive form as she crashed onto the paving. A chunk of flying marble struck Rex in the back of the head, stunning him, but he kept his wits enough to keep running for the door in a cloud of debris and powdered stone.

Coughing from the dust and dizzy from the blow, Rex emerged into the sunlight with Flavia at his side. He squinted and shook his head, trying to regain his bearings. People were yelling and dashing toward the temple.

"Three Goths have rebelled!" Flavia shrieked. "They attacked us in the temple while we worshiped. They knocked over Aphrodite!"

"How dare they insult our goddess!" roared a beak-nosed Greek with an unruly mop of curls on his head.

"Where are they?" demanded another Corinthian patriot.

"Inside!" Flavia replied, extending her finger. "Don't let them get away!"

The crowd pressed toward the temple entrance and seized one of the guards as he stumbled out. A smack with a broomstick sent him to his knees. Everyone started kicking him and hurling insults while Rex and Flavia melted away in the confusion.

They didn't talk for a while, but instead hurried to one of the citadel's minor gates. Exiting onto a path that wound through some trees, they descended toward the suburban estates around Lower Corinthus.

After establishing some distance from their enemies, Rex called for a halt at a little clearing that gave a view back up the mountain. His foggy mind had cleared now. Though the blood on the back of his head was sticky, it was no longer flowing. He examined the main road coming down from the citadel but saw no signs of pursuit.

"Those were some fierce hornets we stirred up," Flavia said to Rex as they took a final look at Upper Corinthus.

"Yes, because those hornets were guarding their queen. The Queen of Love."

"*Pfft!*" Flavia scoffed with a wave of her hand. "The Queen of Love is flat on her face, while the King of Kings still reigns on high."

Rex didn't answer right away, because Flavia's observation struck him as profound. She just stood there smiling at him with her beautiful white teeth. Gently, he pulled her close by the wrist chain. She didn't resist. Yet neither did she come all the way to him. "I can say amen to that," he told her, "even if I'm not a Christian."

Flavia sighed and glanced away, then muttered something Rex couldn't quite hear. He was halfway to the city of Corinthus when he finally realized what she had said.

"*Not yet.*"

———

Perhaps the only positive aspect of Flavia's experience with cult prostitution was that her lavender-colored chiton had come with a set of expensive pins that held the garment together. One of them allowed Rex to dredge up his lock-picking spycraft and pop open the handcuffs. Flavia rubbed her chafed wrists, then glanced at Rex's deeply calloused hands. Only many months at the oar could cause such a thing. She didn't comment about it. Yet she felt sad that the strong, masculine hands she knew to be so capable had been so sorely abused.

The pair now left the countryside and passed through the gate of Lower Corinthus. Before Rex came ashore, he had instructed his friend Stephen to leave the ship and look for him at the city's famous Pirene Fountain at the sixth hour each day. Supposedly, this gushing spring once watered the winged stallion Pegasus. Since Flavia didn't believe those silly pagan myths, she was disappointed to notice Rex touch his forehead and salute the idol of Hercules when they arrived at the fountain. Rex had always favored that deity, though he seemed to respect Jesus too. Flavia offered a silent prayer that her friend might find his way to the one true God.

"Thirsty?" Rex asked, handing Flavia the dipper before he sipped from it. *That's the Rex I remember! Always attentive to my needs. Never taking something for himself that he could give to me instead.* She sighed as she received the dipper from her friend. The water was so cold and refreshing, she almost believed it could make horses fly—which sounded like a lovely idea right now.

"There's Stephen!" Rex said after the pair had slaked their thirst.

He was a short, stocky man with bangs combed forward. Flavia liked him right away, not only because he was a Christian priest but because of his sturdy, reliable demeanor. He had a no-nonsense way about him.

"Did the *Encounter* get away?" Rex asked excitedly. "Did you get the hole fixed?"

Stephen chuckled. "Yeah, old Demosthenes patched it up so tight, you can't even tell it was there. When we rolled her back into the water, not a drop came in. And you should have seen Marius's crew! 'The dolphins,' we called them. They dived down and hacked that rope till it broke. The chain slipped right off the steerboards, and we left the buoy by the light of the moon. Everyone was eager to row. They dropped me on the coast, then got out of there at full speed. I've never seen such relief on men's faces!"

"Are they waiting for us in some hidden cove?"

"Yes. But they won't sit still for long. The boys still want that bishop's ransom, if they can get it."

Ransom? Flavia hadn't heard anything about that. "Rex, you can't—"

Rex stopped her with a soothing gesture. "It's not a ransom," he assured her. "We would just let the government know we rescued Ossius from pirates, and we're hoping for a hefty reward."

"Where?"

"Nicomedia."

"Constantine is far from there. He's in Gaul."

"It's still one of the imperial capitals. They're all in communication with each other. And the church is powerful there. They'll know what Ossius means to Constantine and arrange to have us rewarded."

Flavia figured Rex knew what he was talking about, so she decided to leave such matters to him. The main thing was to rescue the bishop—along with Sophronia and Cassi. "My mother was with him," she said. "Will she be safe as long as she stays with Ossius?" Flavia believed it would be true, yet wanted to hear it from Rex.

"Your mother was on this trip with you?"

"She's the head of our convent, so yes, she came along. As a noble lady in the bishop's company, she should be treated well, right?"

Stephen intervened in the conversation. "I'm sorry, Flavia. I know I just met you, and I hate to bring bad news . . ." He frowned, then continued. "I did some inquiring around the agora while I was waiting for you to show up. Those slavers offloaded all their cargo here—street girls, captured sailors, and some aristocrats as well. A few noble ladies were bought by some Athenian businessmen. There's a market for 'civilized' women who can serve as respectable companions for older men. I don't think anyone was kept aboard that ship except Bishop Ossius. The pirates took on a new cargo of slaves and headed north. I'd be surprised if your mother was still with them."

"Oh, Lord Jesus," Flavia whispered. "Please don't let that be true."

"We can find out. The bill of sale at a slave auction is a public record."

Flavia turned to Rex, putting her hand on his forearm. "Can we check it? We can't leave Graecia without my mother! And my friend Cassi too. She would be viewed as my mother's handmaiden. They're probably still together. Can we look at the records?"

Rex nodded. As he did, Flavia was startled to see something unexpected in his eyes: compassion. Although Rex seemed much harder after his three years in a galley, even so, his old tenderness and empathy—traits that had surprised her in a Germanic barbarian—made a fleeting appearance again. His words also reflected this deeply buried softness. "Yes," he said simply. "Trust me. I'll always help you. We'll find your mother and your friend."

With this encouragement, Flavia felt herself relax. Rex was on the mission. Flavia could be borne along on his wings. Things were going to be alright.

He pointed to Stephen's coin purse. "How much money do I have left?"

"Uh, Captain—I think you're below zero. The boys were furious when they learned you had raided the treasure chest before leaving the ship."

"We still have the bitumen to sell," Rex protested.

"Even so, you're going to have some explaining to do."

Rex wrinkled his nose, yet he acknowledged Stephen's point. "I'll sweet-talk them," he said.

"You'd better sweeten your words with gold."

"Yeah, you're right. I'll find some loot somewhere and make it worth their while." Rex put that item on his mental to-do list, then switched focus and assumed the commanding role of captain that came so naturally to him.

"So here's our plan," he said to Stephen. "I want you to rendezvous with the *Deadly Encounter* wherever they arranged to meet you. Have them sail around and inquire in all the nearby ports about where to track down the Maltese pirates. Tell our boys that if they get the chance, they should attack those slavers and spring the bishop free. But don't keep following them all the way to Nicomedia! I need our ship back in the port of Athenae by the tenth day before the Kalends. Flavia and I will meet you there with her mother and friend."

"*If* the records show they were sold to an Athenian," Flavia added, though she hoped that wouldn't be the case. Maybe they were still with Ossius.

"Yes, sir," said Stephen. "I'll do it. Let's go to the tabularium now and check the bill of sale."

"It's just across the agora. But before I forget, Brother Priest, let me have some coins from that pouch. Flavia and I are going to need enough silver to live in Athenae for a few days."

"Sir!" Stephen protested. "You've already angered the boys by empty-ing the treasure chest! You can't turn around and borrow against the ship's purse. Remember, this crew has already mutinied once over their pay. Take away their loot, and they'll do it again!"

"Bunch of money-grubbers," Rex said irritably. "Alright, go ahead and sell my leather goods to cover it. Those calfskin boots I bought and the belt."

"It won't be enough. You're talking about several days of food and ac-commodations for two people."

"Then sell the scabbard as well," Rex said. He punctuated his command with a grunt of resignation.

"Sir, what about your travel to Athenae? You'll have to go overland from Corinthus. The navy's looking for you in the harbor."

"Fine! Sell that blue-and-gold tunic too!" Rex exclaimed with a swat of his hand. "I really liked it, though," he muttered.

"That should cover it," Stephen said meekly.

Flavia watched the exchange with a sense of awe. Though she had the wealth to pay for such matters, none of her money was available here. And Rex had no way of knowing about her riches. He didn't think he'd get any of his money back. Yet here he was, emptying the ship's treasure chest and selling off his prized possessions without another thought. *What drives this man?*

Gratitude overwhelmed her. She grabbed Rex's hand, squeezing it tight, then dared to dip her head until it touched his shoulder. Lifting her eyes, she looked up at him through her lashes.

"Thank you, Brandulf Rex," she whispered.

He chuckled at this affectionate gesture and nonchalantly waved his other hand. "Don't worry about it. I'm happy to do it. Some things are just priceless."

Flavia's heart melted. *Why me?* she wondered.

There was no obvious answer.

Gracious Father, she prayed with a hopeful heart, *please let me have this man forever.*

———◦◦◦———

Athenae was supposed to be one of the greatest cities in the world. Its amazing historic legacy was known by all. Long ago, Athenae had ruled the ancient Greek league that defeated the mighty Persians. It produced eminent philosophers like Socrates, Plato, and Aristotle. It was famous for its art, politics, and temples. Yet upon seeing this teeming, energetic city, Rex found it surprisingly run-down for such a celebrated place. Somehow it seemed prosperous and chaotic at the same time. He decided to reserve judgment until he had spent a little more time here.

The ride over from Corinthus had been uneventful. A coachman was hired easily, and since there was plenty of daylight this time of year, they had pushed on until late, then finished the trip by sunset the next day. Now it was early on the third day. Rex and Flavia found themselves at the foot of the most famous acropolis in all of Graecia. Instead of sensual Aphrodite, it was wise and warlike Athena whose temple—the Parthenon—crowned this rocky outcrop.

Poor Flavia was still feeling a little tired from the long journey; yet all things considered, Rex thought she was holding up well. As they had suspected, the records in the Corinthian tabularium did reflect the sale of an "Italian matron of noble bearing" and her slave, a "small female Aethiops," to an Athenian merchant named Orion. This man had made his fortune in speculating on the price of silver. That was all the information the record had provided.

Rex beckoned the waitress at a corner food bar. She bounced over and set down a breakfast of honeyed yogurt, bread, and melon slices. Gesturing up toward the Parthenon, Rex asked her in the best Greek he could muster, "Where is Mars Hill?"

The girl giggled at his terrible pronunciation but indicated a jagged height protruding from the flank of the acropolis. It was much lower than the Parthenon and formed a distinct knoll. With noticeable civic pride, she said something about the "ancient Areopagus Council," then left to serve other customers.

Flavia—who had studied Greek during her childhood and had been brushing up on it lately—explained what the waitress said. The Council consisted of the wealthiest and most influential city fathers. They met on the hill, not to try murder cases or debate civic legislation like the old days but to interact with the complaints of everyday citizens and so preserve the revered principle of democracy. "It sounds promising for us," Flavia concluded.

Rex agreed. "We'll either find Orion there or meet someone who knows where to locate him. Let's finish eating and go up."

Mars Hill turned out to be steeper and more rugged than it looked from a distance. The pair clambered up its flank and proceeded to the only structure on its summit, a pergola that covered a flat area where people could gather. A few umbrella pines shaded the space in addition to the wooden lattice that was interwoven with vines. With the breezes that blew across the hill, the place was surprisingly comfortable, even under a direct summer sun.

The seats for the Areopagus Council members were arranged in a semi-circle of three tiers. Directly in front of them was a speaker's podium facing toward the councilors. Any spectator who wanted to listen to the proceedings could find a place to sit on one of the many smooth boulders. Meanwhile, the day's lineup of concerned citizens waited for their turn to address the council. *This is democracy in action*, Rex thought. *Too bad the rest of the empire doesn't have a tradition like this.*

A man in a Roman toga—not well folded, Rex noticed—was just now finishing his speech at the podium. "Your Honors," the speaker concluded,

"I respectfully ask you to restore the statue of Winged Nike that once decorated our stately agora, despite the criticism it has received from the Jews and other Eastern cults. Thank you."

Flavia leaned close to Rex. "He means Christians," she whispered.

"The local disputes don't concern us now. We have to stay focused." Rex edged away from Flavia and sidled up to another bystander, a congenial-looking fellow who was chatting with a friend. "Greetings, sir," Rex said to him.

"Still learning Greek, eh, German?"

"Am I so bad?"

"Pretty bad," the bystander replied with a grin.

Rex decided to get to the point instead of wasting time with small talk that he couldn't conduct anyway. "Recently, I get inheritance of silver coins," he said bluntly. "You know silver man Orion? He is in Council?"

"Orion! Yes, he's filthy rich. I bet you can pick him out just by looking at those men."

Rex inspected the councilors. One of them had an oversized brooch holding his toga together. "Big silver fibula?"

The bystander winked and nodded. "You barbarians are less stupid than I thought!"

Since Rex had the information he needed, he simply smiled and let the insult go by. Arrogance like this was so natural to the Greeks that it wasn't even offensive. It was just who they were now, due to their many centuries of superior civilization. After giving the man a hearty *eucharisto*, Rex returned to Flavia.

"Orion is the pudgy little fellow with the silver pin."

"I see him. Should we follow him home when he's done here? Maybe you could sneak into his house and free my mother and Cassi."

"His mansion will have a staff of tough doorkeepers. Extractions like that are dangerous, so it needs to be our last resort. I'm thinking of a more direct approach. We know money is the language he speaks. Let's offer to pay him double for his two new slaves. What businessman wouldn't want to make a one hundred percent profit?"

"But we don't have any money."

"I will, once I sell that bitumen. The income would cover what we need here, if we paid him all of it."

Flavia shook her head vehemently. "Rex, your crew will string you up by your neck if you try that!" She paused for a moment, then said, "Do you remember my rich uncle Ignatius?"

"Of course. He had an estate at Tibur."

"He died, and I was his sole heir. It's all in a bank at Rome. I'm affluent now."

"Really? That's fantastic. Do you have any letters of credit?"

"Yes, if we can get Ossius back with us. He has a plain-looking walking stick with a hollowed-out core. I put the rolled-up letters in there, just in case."

"Then all we have to do is get the bishop back!" Rex said excitedly. "In the meantime, we'll offer Orion some silver as earnest money."

Flavia nodded, so the plan was confirmed. However, it didn't go at all like Rex had hoped. He waited until the Areopagus broke for a midday meal. When he followed Orion off the hill and hailed his litter as it proceeded through the street, a bodyguard shooed him away. Though Rex was insistent and Orion finally granted him a brief audience, the wealthy silver speculator laughed in Rex's face.

"More wealth is the last thing I need!" he scoffed. "But well-bred slaves like Sophronia rarely come along. She's to be my escort at an important festival in a few days. Keep your pennies, German! I've got the woman I want, and no amount of money will change my mind. Be off, now! I have a busy day."

The flat rejection made Flavia wince when Rex reported it to her. "Don't worry," he soothed. "We'll just have to do an extraction. I can pull it off."

Yet even as he spoke, Rex knew his promise held far more bravado than real capability. A team of elite speculators with a month of advance planning would have a hard time infiltrating a guarded mansion to extract two specific people and get them out of the city. *How am I going to do that by myself at a moment's notice?*

Rex didn't know the answer.

But he was determined to try.

The first task was to learn where Orion lived, which would be easy enough to do by following him home at the end of his day. Rex and Flavia found a quiet spot on Mars Hill near the back of the shady pergola and sat down to wait. Two speakers—an artist seeking permission to create a public mosaic and a philosopher wanting to debate his pet theory of Platonism—addressed the Areopagus while Rex recalled basic infiltration tactics. The philosopher was waxing eloquent about the Platonic Forms when a sudden idea struck Rex like an inspiration from the gods.

This could work. And it would be so much more promising than a one-man extraction!

He escorted Flavia to a rocky outcrop with no one nearby. "I think I've found a solution," he told her. "Look at those councilors over there. They have everything they need in this city—power, wealth, prestige, family name. They have it all. They're at the top. There's only one thing they seek anymore, and they're all fighting for it constantly—prestige. The esteem of their peers. And the opposite is true too. The one thing that horrifies them is the prospect of being shamed in front of their rich friends. So that's what we have to do! We have to shame Orion for dealing with low-life pirates and enslaving an innocent noblewoman like your mother. He'll do anything to avoid losing respect. We have to make it so his two new slaves are the last thing he wants in his house. Then we'll just take them off his hands."

"So instead of taking them out by force, we'll make Orion do our work for us and expel them!"

Rex grinned at Flavia's sharp tactical mind. "Exactly. It's just like they taught us in cadet school—use your opponent's inclinations against him. It's easier to dig a trench to lead water downhill than to pump it uphill."

"So how do we shame him? Maybe we could circulate flyers outside his home? Or we could paint graffiti on his house at night. Wait, I know! This is almost like an election campaign. We could hire sign-makers like when there's a tight political race."

Instead of answering, Rex eyed Flavia with genuine respect. Her ideas were good, but there was an even better solution staring them in the face. "All his peers are gathered right here on Mars Hill," Rex said at last. "We don't need to hire a painter or a scribe. We need to hire a rhetorician—a man who knows the art of eloquence."

"I see! Someone to give a great speech to the council. A lawyer on our behalf."

"Actually, no, it doesn't work like that here. Look at that podium, Flavia.

They don't have advocates and lawyers. It's not a courtroom but a place for public discourse. Anyone can speak here."

"Hmm, good point." Flavia tilted her head as she considered Rex's words. "So why do we need the orator?"

"To shape the speech that a gifted and courageous woman is going to deliver on Mars Hill. A woman I admire very much."

"No!" Flavia cried, recoiling. "I could never do that! Not in front of all those powerful men!"

But Rex was having none of it. He offered Flavia his open palm. When she did not respond, he took her hand in his and held it firmly. Looking her in the eye, he said, "This is your moment, Lady Junia Flavia. I can help you with this task, but this is for you to do. Will you take it on your shoulders?"

"Oh, Rex . . . I . . ."

"Will you do this noble thing?" he persisted.

Flavia closed her eyes and lowered her chin. "I will," she said with a little nod.

"Then put your trust in God and turn your voice loose," Rex told her with a gentle squeeze of her hand. "Your words will go out with great power. And I will be with you the whole way. There's no one on earth who believes in you more than I do."

———◦◦◦———

When Flavia met Rex the next morning, he stank of horse manure, and it was the sweetest thing she had ever smelled.

He had slept in the stable of an inn so the money for a room could be spent on a few hours of an orator's time instead. They had found a good man near the civic basilica—Thales was his name—but in order to pay him, something had to be given up. Rex had insisted on foregoing a bed and a meal but was unwilling for Flavia to do the same. "You need to keep your strength up," he kept saying.

"Are you hungry?" she asked when she met him not long after dawn. "Look—I brought you a pear. It was all they'd let me take out."

"I'll save it for later. I'm full right now."

"You're full? Of what, Rex? Hay?"

"I found some groats in the bottom of a bag."

"Groats! You ate horse feed?"

"They're not too bad if you grind them up and soak 'em in water. It makes a little porridge."

"Brandulf Rex," Flavia said with a shake of her head, "you are an amazing man."

He chuckled and waved his hand. "It's nothing. Let's go meet our orator."

Thales was a tall gentleman with well-oiled hair and a distinguished bearing. He had spent three decades trying cases before the judges in the basilica. Now he had taken up a more relaxed life as a teacher of rhetoric to young boys. "Come in and have a seat," he said, welcoming the pair into his rented rooms. He set out a bowl of olives, and since time was money, began to explain the basics of oratory. Flavia noticed Rex eyeing the olives without taking any. She finally sampled one, then immediately wrinkled her nose. "Ew," she whispered, handing the bowl to Rex. "Much too salty for me. I don't want another one of those."

"I don't mind it," Rex said. His stomach growled loudly as he began to eat.

Thales explained that rhetoric had five main parts. The first, invention, was the process of determining exactly what the orator would argue. After much discussion, the threesome decided that Flavia would attack the disreputable character of the pirates with whom Orion had done business, then celebrate the noble dignity of Sophronia, who deserved to be honored instead of degraded into slavery.

The second canon of rhetoric was arrangement. Again, working together, the teacher and his two students outlined a speech with a tight introduction, two central points, and a powerful conclusion in which Orion's actions would be revealed as dishonorable. His character would stand in stark relief to the brave young daughter pleading on her mother's behalf.

With the basic structure in place, Thales moved to the third aspect of rhetoric: elocution, or the style to be used. Although Thales wanted Flavia to employ the bombastic "Asiatic" technique, she insisted on using the more plain and rational "Attic" style, which relied not on flowery exaggeration but on logic and reason. Several figures of speech were devised, all centered on Rex's suggestion that "tarnished silver" be used as a running theme. Flavia would function as a diligent "polisher," using a rag and quicklime to restore the luster of Orion, whose nickname was Argyros, or silvery, after his chosen profession.

The aspect of the speech that Flavia feared most was the fourth canon, memorization. She knew she wouldn't be able to recall the whole oration word for word. Thales had arranged for an appointment before the Council at the fifth hour tomorrow, which did not leave enough time to attain complete mastery of the speech. Rex suggested using the myth of Orion the Hunter as a memory aid. Just as the legends told how Orion hunted his prey, violated innocent Merope, and was blinded and stung by a scorpion, so the silver speculator of Athens committed the same crimes and became blinded by his foolishness. Flavia's chastising speech would be the scorpion sting that awakened him. Only by making a wise decision could he be elevated into the stars like Orion's heavenly constellation. Thales applauded the idea as an excellent rhetorical device.

"Pronunciation is the most often overlooked aspect of oratory," Thales said next, moving on to the final canon. "It deals with how you deliver your speech—your pitch and intonation, your posture, your gestures, your facial expressions." He told Flavia to smile often, since her teeth were pretty and should be shown. She must keep her back straight and make eye contact with the councilors at all times. Her voice should sound sweet at first, then turn fiery in the second point, create pathos in the third, and conclude with a powerful invitation to greatness.

"Rex, I'm terrified about all this," Flavia admitted to him when they took a break. "I wish I hadn't agreed to it! At every moment, I question my abilities."

"I don't," he replied. "Where you feel questions inside, I only hear exclamations. Have courage, my friend. Stand up and speak, and trust your God, like your scriptures say."

"My scriptures? How do you know what my scriptures say?"

Rex pointed to Thales's library. "I glanced at that Christian book while you were outside. Right there, see it? *The Letters of Paul.* We just came from Corinthus, so I read the beginning of that one. Take a look at what your apostle wrote. I think it applies to you."

"Show me."

Rex removed the codex from the cabinet and laid it on a table. He turned to the *First Epistle to the Corinthians* and moved his finger to the selected passage. "Read that," he said.

Flavia bent over the page and began to recite. "'I will destroy the wisdom of the wise, and the intelligence of the intelligent I will frustrate. Where is the wise one? Where is the grammarian? Where is the orator of this age? Has God not made foolish the wisdom of the world?'" She stopped there and looked up, trying to comprehend a crazy reality: that this handsome Germanic warrior who worshiped Hercules and smelled like horses was pointing her to the exact scripture she needed right now.

"It says not many of the Corinthians were wise or eloquent, but that doesn't matter with God," Rex observed.

"You're right. I needed to hear that."

Rex gestured to the book. "Read a little more."

"'God has chosen the foolish things of the world to shame the wise,'" Flavia went on, "'the things that are weak to shame the strong, so that no one should boast.'"

"'Let him who boasts, boast in the Lord,'" Rex finished.

After setting the book back on the shelf, Flavia was quiet for a long time. Finally, she could only say, "You confound me, Brandulf Rex."

"That doesn't surprise me. Sometimes I even confound myself." He uttered a goofy laugh and shrugged.

Suddenly Rex's face lit up. "I almost forgot!" he exclaimed, then reached into his belt pouch and brought out something in his fist. "I saved that pear. You need to eat it now to keep up your strength." When Rex tossed her the fat yellow pear, Flavia caught it midair, took a bite, and pitched it back.

"Want to share it with me?" she asked.

"Sure," he replied and bit into the fruit with a satisfied grin.

———

Mars Hill.

The very name of it brought biblical associations to Flavia's mind. It was here that, two and a half centuries ago, Saint Paul gave a speech before the same body that Flavia would be addressing today. *Did he have this intimidating place in mind when he told the Corinthians not to trust in human eloquence?* Flavia didn't know, but she imagined it might be true.

A stiff breeze blew across the hill as she climbed up. It mussed her hair, swirling tendrils of it this way and that. Though she tried to smooth them down, she knew some locks would go astray despite her best efforts. Earlier this morning, Rex had sold his cloak to pay for her visit to a public ornatrix. Now her hair was all windblown, and beads of sweat ran into her makeup. But there was nothing she could do about that. If she looked like a mess during her speech, so be it. It was up to God to soften the councilors' hearts.

"This way, please. Follow me," Thales said as he led Rex and Flavia to the speakers' area under the latticework pergola. Probably thirty councilmen faced her, including Orion. The chubby fellow had no idea he was the subject of today's speech—but he was about to find out.

After a cursory introduction from the orator, Flavia approached the podium. Her heart was hammering, and her wobbly legs seemed unable to support her.

"Be strong," Rex whispered in her ear, then gently guided her toward the pulpit.

With aristocratic dignity, Flavia straightened her shoulders, stretched her neck, and lifted her chin. For a long, silent moment, she stared at the men. A sense of tranquility descended on her. The nagging questions in her mind evaporated. And then she began to declaim.

"Esteemed gentlemen of Athens, I greet you from Italy in the mellifluous language of Greek. The story I shall narrate today has a central character in it—either a hero or a villain. The man is seated in your midst right now, and only after my oration is finished shall we discover which one he is." The councilors exchanged glances, each wondering if he was the man to be named. Now Flavia could see she had hooked them.

After the speech unfolded, she revealed that Orion Argyros was the man in question. The revelation elicited many grunts of surprise. Some men heckled and jeered. In fact, the whole scene was far more interactive than Flavia had imagined it would be. Raucous shouts often interrupted her words, which she either ignored or acknowledged with a clever riposte, then continued.

"Look at her sweaty forehead!" one of the councilors mocked. "It's dripping off her nose!"

"May I use your kerchief, kind sir?" Flavia asked sweetly.

"Give it to her, Alexander," his friend chided. "Be gallant."

Flavia received the cloth and mopped her brow, then held it up. "Just as I wipe the moisture from my face, so I seek to polish away the tarnish on Orion's reputation!" she exclaimed, then resumed her speech from the point of her interruption.

Rex's analogy of Orion the Hunter proved to be a helpful memory device. Flavia painted a terrible picture of the Maltese pirates: their rapacious cruelty to their prey, their wanton destruction, their crude and vulgar talk. In contrast, she described Sophronia as a true exemplar of the Greek word *sophrosune*, which meant respectable modesty and chastity.

"O! What a tragedy that so great a woman should fall into slavery," Flavia declared. "And O! How great is the sorrow at the doe's last breath, when she succumbs to the huntsman's blood-stained shaft. Who will stay his cruel hand?"

By the time Flavia reached the speech's conclusion—known as the peroration—she was deep in the flow and surging toward the end. The crowd and the councilors were enthralled now, while stunned Orion could only stare at his feet with his arms folded across his chest. Flavia raised her cadence and lowered her pitch. Her gaze was intense, and her body was an extension of her voice. Every word was more than a sound; it was a living, breathing thing, an inexorable call to action. The speech had taken on a life of its own.

A thunderous ovation erupted after Flavia's final appeal for mercy toward her mother and her friend. Shouts of acclamation rose into the sky above Mars Hill. "What say you, Orion?" demanded Alexander, who had mocked Flavia's sweaty brow. "Get rid of those slaves that tarnish your name!"

"Never!" Orion spat. "I will not be manipulated by a girl!"

"Orion the Silver is no more! He is Orion the Tarnished now!" shouted another councilor.

"Here is some bright silver if you love it so much!" a third man exclaimed, tossing shiny coins onto the ground in front of the podium. Others followed suit, until there was double, then triple the price of two slaves at Flavia's feet.

A white-haired statesman stood among the councilors. Brandishing his wax tablet, he began to read aloud what he had just written: "I release . . .

Sophronia . . . and the Aethiops!" Then he set the tablet and stylus on the speaker's podium as Flavia stepped aside.

"Sign it, Orion!" shouted someone from the crowd.

Chastened by the unanimous urging from his friends, the pudgy business-man rose from his seat and approached the podium. For a long moment, he stared at the tablet. Then, slowly, he put the stylus to the wax. Everyone waited in hushed silence.

And Orion hurled the tablet off the edge of Mars Hill.

Boos and jeers exploded from the crowd, but the wealthy silver investor held up his hands for calm. When the council had quieted a little, he cried, "Since when has the word of Orion Argyros not been enough to seal a deal? I need no tablets!" He bent to the ground and picked up one of the coins. "Today I accept your generous compensation for my ill-gotten slaves. I will emancipate them immediately!"

Now the crowd of onlookers and the Areopagus Council burst into cheers. Flavia retreated from the podium, the last of her energy spent. But as she took a step back, her foot slipped on the uneven ground. She started to fall backward—and to her surprise, she found strong arms supporting her. Tipping back her head, she looked up into the clearest blue eyes she had ever seen.

"I knew you could do it!" Rex exclaimed.

"And that's why I could," Flavia replied.

4

JUNE 316

Pope Sylvester took a seat in his chair at the Lateran Church and received the book of the scriptures onto his lap. His congregation stood before him in the spacious hall of the palace, their eyes eager and expectant. Clear sunlight cascaded through the windows, seeming all the brighter on this summer morning of the Lord's day. As always, the liturgy had four parts: the processional entrance, the readings and homily, the Eucharistic celebration, and the concluding benedictions and dismissal. The clergy had already entered in solemn procession, then the lector had stood at the ambo to read selections from the Old and New Testaments. Now it was time for Sylvester to preach.

The text for the day was from Saint Matthew's gospel, the anointing of Jesus's feet. Sylvester described how the woman—Mary, the sister of Lazarus, according to John's gospel—came to Jesus with expensive perfume and poured it on the Savior's feet. The disciples protested that something so valuable should have been used to help the poor. But while Jesus certainly cared about the needy, in this case, he also blessed Mary's extraordinary deed because it was an act of pure worship.

"That jar was made of alabaster," Sylvester went on, "and the perfume is described as *barytimos*, 'very costly.' For a woman like this, it would represent her life's savings. Only the Lord is worthy of such extravagance." The bishop paused and stared intently at his congregation before making his final application. "And we, too, dear children, must be willing to lavish great beauty on the God who is beauty himself. That is why, today, I propose to you a new plan! We, the ancient and venerable church at Rome, shall embark upon a building program. With the Lord's help, we will raise beautiful structures around our city to glorify God, replacing the temples of demons that for so long have stained—"

"Heresy!" came a cry from the congregation. A nervous silence immediately descended on the Lateran Church.

"I say it again—heresy!" shouted the same voice. The man stepped forward. It was handsome Felix from the church on the Aventine Hill that was named for Lady Sabina Sophronia.

"Felix, you are out of line, brother," Sylvester said gently. "A priest should never interrupt a worship service like this, nor dishonor a pastor in front of his people."

"If the bishop is a heretic, I must!" The rebellious comment sent a horrified murmur through the congregation.

"I am no heretic," Sylvester replied. "What error have I committed?"

"To construct churches is sin! Since the earliest days, true believers have met in houses. That is the only meeting place of which Almighty God approves. Nothing else is found in the holy scriptures."

"House worship is certainly *described*, Brother Felix, but it is not *prescribed* in holy writ. The earliest Christians were simple folk with no other place to meet. But that was long ago, and times have changed. God has given us new opportunities. It is not a sin to take advantage of them."

"It is a sin to change ancient practice! Whatever is not revealed by the word of the Lord is not to be done by his holy people."

"Christian funerals are never mentioned in scripture, yet you are not against those. Many new things arise after time passes. The church must learn to adapt to later times, while never changing essential doctrines."

"I am not talking about funerals, Sylvester!" The use of the bishop's name in such a casual way drew gasps from the congregation, but Felix plowed ahead undeterred. "I am talking about your wicked intent to waste church money by putting up buildings and decorating them with art. To suggest that God cares about material things is idolatry!"

"No, Brother Felix. It is the Incarnation."

The wise statement put Felix on his heels and silenced him as he tried to think of a good rebuttal. Bishop Sylvester used the sudden hush in the hall to press his point. "When the Son of God became incarnate, he took a body to himself. Understand this, my people! In the womb of a virgin, the eternal God joined himself forever to material existence. The physical world is elevated and dignified in Jesus Christ. God in flesh—what a great mystery! Material things are used by God to bring us salvation. The wood and iron of Calvary, the bread and wine of the table, the water and oil of the font—by these things, God mediates his blessings to us. It is no part of Christianity to scorn physical things like the Gnostics do. Yes, our bodies can sin, but the bodies themselves are good gifts of the Creator. We worship him in our bodies—and it honors him when we become beauty makers too. To build great halls and decorate them with art reflects what God did when he spanned the heavens with the vault and filled the earth with loveliness."

Felix's face was red now, and he shook his fist at Sylvester. "You spout fancy words, you so-called bishop, but your theology is corrupt! Our true home is in heaven. We care nothing for"—Felix pinched the flesh of his forearm—"this wicked and dirty stuff."

"Be careful! Remember in *Acts* how the divine voice warned Peter, 'What God has cleansed, do not call unholy.'"

"Bah!" Felix shouted with a swat of his hand.

"Leave us, disrespectful priest!" cried a voice from the crowd. And with that, Felix stormed from the church.

"Take a deep breath, my beloved flock," Sylvester said soothingly from his chair after Felix slammed the door behind him. "And once you have quieted your souls in prayer for a moment, we shall break bread together and drink wine, as the Lord himself taught us to do."

The rest of the service proceeded without a problem, and the people were sent on their way with the benediction of God. Afterward, Sylvester retired to the rear garden of the Lateran Palace. Its former lascivious statues had been removed, replaced with potted plants and elegantly carved marble columns. Archdeacon Quintus joined the bishop there to debrief the day's interruption.

"That outburst was deserving of discipline," Quintus concluded after the matter had been discussed in detail. "I think we should act."

"Let us first send a wise man to hear Felix out and see if we can reach common ground."

"You are a more patient man than me, Your Holiness."

"And God is the most patient of all. Let us always remember it."

Quintus sighed as he nodded. "Very well. I myself will go talk with him, to see what he is trying to say. Perhaps there is something we can learn from Felix. As for patience, I think it is going to be needed in the days ahead if we hope to get the rescript from Constantine. I just received some bad news on that front."

"Tell me."

"Bishop Ossius's ship was attacked by Maltese pirates off the coast of Sicilia. He and the three women were taken east. We think they went to Corinthus, but we don't know for sure. I suggest we send someone after them."

The news was sobering, and the bishop took a long moment to consider it. Finally, he said, "There is no one to send, and even if there were, where would he go? It would be like searching for a pea in a pigsty. A pointless waste of resources."

Quintus frowned at this. "You will do nothing?"

"I did not say that. I only said chasing after the bishop would be fruitless. We must trust God and await word from our friends. If Ossius is alive, he will find his way to some Christian community. We will hear of it, for news of the churches always flows to Rome."

"Your words are wise," the archdeacon acknowledged, "yet this is so frustrating! Day after day, the temples of the gods loom over our people in proud arrogance. Meanwhile, the true faith contents itself with converted houses and a few plain halls. Why should such great beauty be lavished on foul demons, while the truly deserving God gets nothing? The Lord should have a house worthy of his name, like David realized and Solomon implemented."

"It will require Constantine's permission and financial support. We cannot do it ourselves without compromising our mission to the poor, the widow, and the orphan."

"And that is why we should send someone after Ossius! He needs to be freed so he can get to Gaul and meet the emperor."

"God can bring the emperor to Ossius if he so wishes."

"Ha! I'm ashamed to admit it, but I find that hard to believe."

"Then you must pray. Even faith as small as a mustard seed can move mountains."

"You are right," Quintus said quietly. "Thank you for the reminder. Let us pray for this."

"Come with me, my friend, and we shall pray in the church."

The two men rose and exited the garden. Yet Sylvester did not lead Quintus to the palace basilica that had become the Lateran Church. Instead, he took his loyal archdeacon outside.

Quintus glanced upward. "Praying under an open sky is good too," he remarked.

Rather than answer, Sylvester walked to the ruined barracks of Maxentius's cavalry troops. The former military camp had been leveled by Constantine when he defeated his old enemy. Now it was a weedy expanse of grass and mud, with bits of debris everywhere.

Sylvester bent to the ground and pulled a rusty javelin from the dirt. "Stay here until I come back," he said to Quintus.

Thrusting the javelin's point into the ground, Sylvester began to drag it behind him, making a shallow groove in the mud as he went along. He walked in a long, straight line, then turned and walked at a right angle for a shorter distance. Again, he turned, and again, until he had completed a large rectangle and returned to Quintus.

"What are you doing, Your Holiness?" the archdeacon asked, but Sylvester only smiled and left his friend again. This time, however, he did not drag the javelin. He walked to the far end of the rectangle, lifted the spear, and jammed it point-first into the ground. Now he called for Quintus to join him.

When Quintus arrived, Sylvester gestured to the spear. "We shall pray here," the bishop declared.

"In a muddy field next to the Lateran Palace?"

"No," said Sylvester as he swept his hands toward the rectangle around him. "At the altar of the Church of the Savior, which shall one day rise at this place. Now kneel with me, my brother, and let us pray that God would do this mighty thing."

—◦◦◦—

When Flavia saw her mother arrive at the docks, she couldn't help but run and embrace her. She hugged Cassi too—a threefold reunion too joyous for words.

"Were you hurt? Mistreated in any way?" Flavia asked them both. Her eyes were tearful from the flood of emotions at the release of her constant worry.

"We are fine," Sophronia said. "Orion is a strict man, yet no abuser of slaves. A few days more, and yes, things would have grown difficult for me. But praise God—we were released just in time."

"The men in that house had hungry eyes," Cassi agreed. "However"—she made the sign of the cross on her forehead—"the Lord was our defender."

Thank you, holy Father!

Flavia felt an arm slip around her shoulder. "Hey, don't give all the credit to God," Rex said with well-meaning sincerity. "Flavia deserves a big share too! She gave a speech before the city council like I've never seen. I was—" Rex broke off his words and remained silent for so long that Flavia glanced over at him. His jaw muscle flexed as he struggled for words. "I was very impressed," he said at last. Rex's admiration was so sweet that Flavia easily overlooked his misunderstanding of Christian humility before God.

Although Rex already knew Sophronia from years past and needed no introduction, he had never met Cassiopeia, so Flavia introduced them. Reticent as she was in the presence of powerful men, Cassi kept her eyes down, but Rex's congenial nature soon won her over. He told her about the time his bad grasp of Greek caused him to ask for a drink of water from a *krepis* instead of a *krene*—a boot instead of a fountain—and Cassi started smiling. When Rex cried, "The man gave it to me, so I had to drink it!" Cassi burst into laughter. Flavia could see that from now on, her shy friend would accept Rex as one of her own.

The foursome loitered around the Athenian port of Piraeus all afternoon, for it was the tenth before the Kalends of June, the day that Stephen was due to meet them. In exchange for a few copper coins, a stevedore on the dock let the group wait in a small warehouse stacked with jugs of Greek wine. It was a private, out of the way place, so Rex left the women there at dusk and went out to wander along the pier.

Flavia was peeking out from the door of the warehouse when she saw

Rex returning with another man. Even in the faint moonlight, she could tell from his stocky physique it was Stephen.

"Did you fly here like a bird, Stephen?" she joked when the men reached the warehouse. "I can't see your ship anywhere."

"We didn't want to draw too close, but trust me, she's out there in the bay. I came in by rowboat. It was the first thing the men bought once we got free."

"Let's hope we'll never be trapped aboard our ship again," Rex said. "Come on, I'll row us back. Your captain isn't too proud to take his turn on the oars. It will be good for me."

An hour later, Rex had the three women and Stephen aboard the *Deadly Encounter*. Although the crew seemed glad for their captain's return, there was no time to celebrate the recovery of the captives. Rex immediately ordered the ship to anchor farther from Piraeus, lest a harbor patrol boat wander by and ask to see their credentials.

After the ship had come to rest again, Rex showed the women the little goatskin cabin in the stern. "You can sleep in there," he told them.

Flavia peeked inside. Although only one person could fit in the tiny bed, there was enough room for the two other women to recline on the deck beside it. Rex had made some pallets for Flavia and Cassi from folded sailcloth, with woolen blankets on top. The door flap on the cabin could be tied down, assuring that the female guests would have some much-needed privacy. They entered the cabin gratefully. Soon the entire vessel fell silent as everyone succumbed to the fatigue of a long day.

It was just before dawn when Flavia awakened. The cabin was stuffy and closed, so she loosened the flap and exited onto the deck. Her bare feet made no sound on the cool cedar planks. A soft breeze stirred the sheer fabric of her chiton as she stood at the deck railing. The eastern horizon was lined with a pale pink glow, though the sun had not yet risen. Suddenly an unexpected voice spoke over her shoulder.

"Sleep well?" Rex asked quietly.

Flavia's heartbeat quickened—although she didn't know why. She didn't feel any danger from Rex. Nor did she sense that some kind of romantic encounter was imminent. Perhaps it was nothing more than being so close to an attractive man in this quiet, intimate setting. *Not just any man*, she realized. *It is this man's presence that quickens me.*

"I slept deeply," Flavia said without turning around, "because for the first time in a long while, I was at peace."

Rex came to her side. They stood silently at the rail, enjoying the stillness as they stared across the sea at the rosy line of dawn. High above, in the deep blue darkness, the morning star glinted like a diamond—last remnant of the night, harbinger of things to come.

"I missed you these past three years," Rex said at last.

Flavia nodded sadly. "We both have stories to tell, I suppose."

"When I rowed away from you, I thought our story was over."

"Somehow I knew it had just begun."

"Where is that story headed, do you think?"

"I don't know," Flavia said carefully. "All I know is, I want to—"

Be with you forever, she wanted to say. Yet she wasn't prepared to admit it yet.

Rex allowed Flavia's deepest desire to remain unspoken for now. "How about if we just follow the story and see where it goes?"

"That works for me," she agreed.

Slowly, Rex reached out and caressed Flavia's hand, which was resting on the ship's rail. The two of them made eye contact, then smiled at each other. After they both uttered an awkward laugh, Flavia averted her eyes, and the moment was gone.

Rex took a deep breath as he stared at the horizon. "Look there," he said. "The sun has finally risen."

The warmth of the dawn rushed across the ocean like an incoming wave. It felt good on Flavia's cheeks as she welcomed its gentle heat. Glancing at Rex, she noticed how the orange glow seemed to light his blond beard on fire. His chin was strong, and his eyes were clear as he gazed at the morning sky. Tendrils of his long blond hair swept back on his head and draped onto his shoulders. One stray lock dangled over his forehead, and it was all Flavia could do not to reach out and tuck it behind his ear. He was tall and strong, with well-defined arms, a thick chest, a slim waist, and a virile masculinity that radiated from him like a tangible force. She could sense the energy that always drove him forward.

"We're headed to Demetrias," he announced.

"Why there?" she asked, content to let Rex's confidence carry her into whatever the future might hold.

"That's where the Maltese slavers are headed next," Rex explained. "All the waterfront gossip agrees about that. People heard them say it. Demetrias is at the head of a gulf up north, and it has a big slave market. They're taking a bunch of captured Gothic warriors to sell, then I suppose they'll continue to Nicomedia with Bishop Ossius. We have to find out for sure."

"So we're leaving for Demetrias today?"

"We'll weigh anchor in less than an hour. The Thracian is about to stir everyone now that the sun is up."

"Sailors awake!" cried a loud voice a few moments later, as if to prove Rex right. "Get out of your blankets, you lazy tomcats!"

"I'm ready to get moving again," Flavia agreed.

The sun was still low but growing hot when the *Deadly Encounter* set out with favorable winds under the steady hand of the red-haired pilot in the stern. The ship made good progress northward, its bowed sail saving the rowers' strength throughout the day. After beaching in a remote cove, they continued the next morning and took on food and supplies at a fishing village. Though the weather had cooled a bit, the winds stayed brisk. The only frustration was that no one had seen a sea-colored ship, not even the fishermen, who usually noticed everything.

A few hours after leaving the village, Flavia and Cassi relieved the cook of his normal duties and made a lunch of cucumbers in oil with chunks of crumbly cheese and bits of tuna. The crew reacted as if the girls had accomplished a miracle. Their effusive praise—along with a few more frisky comments—seemed to have no end.

Flavia was below deck putting food back in the storage pantry when she sensed someone behind her. "Need help?" the voice asked. It wasn't Rex.

She turned to see the broad-shouldered mutineer named Marius. He was smiling, yet it was a strange grin, almost forced. And his eyes certainly held no mirth. Instead, they roved across her body with bestial hunger. Though Marius didn't make any aggressive moves, Flavia was painfully aware of being alone with him in the ship's cramped larder—and the lustful sailor stood between her and the exit.

"I'm finished here now, but thank you for the offer, Marius." Flavia thought that using the man's name would make him feel accountable for his actions.

"It's mighty nice having a woman on board," he remarked. "I ain't used to that. You sure I can't help ya somehow?" Marius took a step forward, the strange smirk still on his face.

"Actually, there is something a strong fellow like you could do for me," Flavia said sweetly. She pointed to a hidden nook behind a stack of crates. "Maybe you could clear a little space back there for me. If you could move that heavy sack, there would be room for . . . whatever I need."

Marius's eyes brightened, and he took an eager step forward. "I can serve your needs," he said lecherously.

After Flavia stepped aside, Marius bent down and grabbed the sack of grain by its corners and tried to manhandle it out of the way. He bumped against the crates as he yanked it—and at that moment, from behind him, Flavia swatted a heavy clay jar and toppled it from the crates. The jar broke open upon impact, sending oily sardines slithering across the floor of the storeroom.

"Oh, what a mess!" Flavia exclaimed. "It wasn't your fault, Marius. I'll go get a mop." She dashed from the pantry before her would-be suitor could protest. Only after the ship was underway again and the sailors were oc-cupied did she return to clean up the spill, bringing Cassi along to assist as well as deter any more advances.

On the third day of the trip, the *Deadly Encounter* arrived in the Gulf of Demetrias and made its way to the namesake city at the gulf's northern end. Demetrias had a nice, wide harbor and a bustling waterfront. Houses and shops filled the flat area behind the port and climbed partway up the encircling hills. As usual, the ship anchored a good distance from the pier, using the new rowboat to transport any crewmen who needed to go ashore. Nobody wanted to get trapped by the navy without room to escape quickly into the open sea.

There was no sign of the sea-colored pirate ship at the harbor, so Rex decided to go ashore and investigate. When Flavia asked to accompany him, he protested a little bit. "Waterfront towns can be dangerous," he said.

"So can ships full of rough men," she replied. And that was enough to convince him.

Stephen dutifully rowed them to the pier, along with Cassi, who also did not wish to remain behind. Sophronia, however, was feeling the effects of exhaustion, so she stayed back to rest on her cot in the goatskin cabin.

Since a tavern did not seem like the right kind of place to take the women, Rex led everyone to a shipwright's business. Such men knew all the comings and goings in a port, because whenever sailors came in for repairs or supplies, they gossiped about the latest news.

"You can wait out here while I make a few inquiries," Rex said to his friends before he entered the shop. "I won't be gone long."

Strangely, though, Flavia found herself not wanting to be separated from Rex. She took pleasure in watching him do what he did best. Rex excelled in situations like this—a bold and confident man who took charge and got results. Flavia delighted in his skills and liked to be alongside him in his endeavors.

"Can I come too?" she asked.

"It's easier for me to do it alone."

"Let me go with you, Rex. I like to see you do your thing."

The remark seemed to take him by surprise, but from the little smile that crept to his lips, she could see it pleased him. He relented, and they entered the building.

The shipwright's shop was a mess, with every conceivable item a sailor could need sitting somewhere on one of the shelves. Rope, tar, nails, sailcloth, saws, planks, oars, planes, chisels, paint—all of it was visible in one sweeping glance at the room. But the shipwright himself was nowhere to be seen, until Rex hailed him and he emerged from his work yard in the back. As it turned out, he was an immigrant from Barium in southern Italy. The two men chatted for a long time in Latin about the winds and waves. Finally, when the weather had been thoroughly discussed, they got down to business.

"So what can I do for ya today?" the grizzled old fellow asked. "I got everything ya could need." As he gestured around his shop, Flavia noticed he was missing two fingers on his left hand, probably from a woodworking accident.

Rex gave the man a congenial grin. "I can see that! Quite a place you've got here. I've been needin' some paint for my rostrum. Just five pots would do it."

"What color, my friend?"

"I'd say it's sort of a blue-gray," Rex lied, "like a mornin' sky or the sea on a cloudy day." His voice had a seafarer's ring to it, though he didn't normally talk that way.

"Ach! I be all out of that color, mate. Sold out."

"Really? That's surprisin'. It ain't a common choice."

"Aye, 'tis true. But a ship was in here two days ago and took all I had. Eighty pots! I couldn't believe it. Glad for the sale, though."

"Poseidon curse 'em!" Rex cried, slapping his palm on the wooden counter. "I really needed that paint." He rubbed his beard for a moment, then glanced at the shipwright. "Eighty pots would paint a whole ship, eh?"

"More than enough. Mebbe they'd have a few pots left over."

"I'd surely buy it! They say where they was goin'?"

"Well, now, them fellas weren't a talkative sort. But their bos'n did mention he's headed out the Sporades chain. All the way to the end, then up to the Propontis."

"Me too!" Rex exclaimed with a big grin. "Now don't that take all? I'll hafta keep a double eye out for 'em as we go along. That's what I needed! *Eucharisto*, old-timer."

Rex and Flavia exited the shop. "You're good at that," she told him.

"I'm a man of many talents," Rex agreed with a cocky grin.

"You are indeed. Do you have any flaws?"

"Ha! None that you need to know about."

"Rex, I see all your flaws. Including the ones you don't even know you have."

He glanced at her, looking not offended in the least, just intrigued. "So far, you haven't run away from me, despite my flaws."

"Of course not! How else are you going to learn what they are?"

"So you can take me down a notch, eh?" he teased.

Flavia grabbed his sleeve and stared intently at him. "No, Rex," she said in a more serious voice. "To help you rise above them."

He looked back at her, considering the words she had just uttered. Finally, he admitted, "You're perceptive about such things. I need that."

Now it was Flavia's turn to play the cocky one. "I'm a woman of many talents," she said with a grin.

Rex chuckled at her saucy words, then unexpectedly, he leaned toward her. The smile on his lips and the invitation in his eyes made him seem incredibly charming. He came very close.

"Want to go sailing with me, Flavia?" he asked softly.

"Anywhere you want to go, my captain," she replied.

Geta was about to commit murder.

And not just any murder. This was treason. Assassination. Regicide. The brutal stabbing of Emperor Constantine. But perhaps the strangest thing about it was that Geta had been in this exact hiding place before—except on that occasion, six years ago, it was to prevent the murder of Constantine. The assassin back then had failed in his secret task. Geta then strung him up from the rafters and hung him to death. Now the roles were completely reversed. *And unlike that day, I'm going to get away with it!*

The tall Germanic speculator shifted his position behind the curtain in Constantine's bedroom and dried his sweaty palm on his tunic so the knife wouldn't slip when the time came. The window behind him was open, allowing the night breeze to waft in. The cool air felt good on the back of his neck, so he reached to his long braid and draped it down his front instead. Periodically, Geta could hear the escape horse nicker as it waited in the courtyard below. Since this part of the palace was sparsely occupied, he didn't think anyone would notice it.

Footsteps sounded outside the door. Geta froze, waiting to see if it was Constantine. But the person—whoever it was—went away.

It had not been difficult to gain access to the emperor's bedroom in the imperial palace at Arelate. Geta was, after all, a member of his personal bodyguard. Yet prior to that—long before he entered Constantine's service—Geta pledged himself to Licinius. Ever since then, he had been a double agent, waiting for the time when he could help his true lord the most.

Now, that time had arrived. Senecio had come from Sirmium and deviously planned the assassination of Emperor Constantine so Bassianus might take his place as Augustus of the West, forming a glorious alliance with Licinius.

Soon, Geta told himself, *I will stand at a grateful emperor's side. No longer a mere bodyguard but a mighty general and a respected commander of men!*

Yet this would come to pass only if the assassination were carried out perfectly. Each step had to be executed with precision. Geta wiped his hand again, making sure he had a good grip on the dagger's hilt.

Twice more as the night wore on, Geta heard footsteps approach the door, then recede. The moon had gone behind the buildings of Arelate when the bedroom door finally creaked open. It was after midnight now—the third watch. A man came in, alone. He lit no lamp, so the room remained dark. First, he went to the tall wardrobe in the corner. After fumbling inside it for a moment, he went straight to the bed and lay down. He was just ten paces from Geta's hiding place.

The bedroom fell silent. Only the faintest light from the window illuminated the chamber. Geta listened to Constantine's breathing become steady and deep. It was time to move.

He slipped from behind the curtain and began the swift yet stealthy approach that all speculators had mastered. His trainer, Aratus, had taught him the essentials in cadet school: wear black garments, move efficiently but without running, and above all, do not try to tiptoe or avoid noise. Instead, glide smoothly like a snake. "Speed has its own kind of silence," Aratus used to say.

The victim did not stir as Geta strode across the room. He moved well despite his limp from an old injury—a broken leg suffered in a one-on-one battle that he had lost. *Be sure to strike the heart*, he reminded himself. Instant death was vital here.

He neared the bed and raised the knife. One more step and he would bring the blade plunging down. But at that moment, the sleeping man raised a crossbow from his side and triggered it.

"Argh!" Geta cried as a hard blow smashed his right forearm. He staggered backward, then a hot streak of pain shot up his arm and into his shoulder. The crossbow bolt protruded from his wrist, its tip lodged in his bone. Only by chance had Geta's arm been in front of his body as he approached the bed. Otherwise, the deadly bolt would now be in his chest.

"Traitor!" shouted a man who burst from the wardrobe. "Guardsmen! Come in! Come in!"

The man in the bed leaped to his feet, swinging a knife of his own. Geta parried with his blade as he retreated to the window. Across the room, the door banged open and more soldiers rushed in.

"Arrest that man!" Constantine screamed from beside the wardrobe.

The imperial bodyguard who had been impersonating the emperor swung his knife again, and Geta only barely managed to block it. The two blades locked against each other. "You're dead, Geta!" the man snarled.

Heaving with all his strength, Geta managed to thrust his opponent backward. "No, you are," he spat, then hurled the knife into the stunned bodyguard's throat. Before the first trickle of blood had time to dribble out, Geta turned and jumped from the window.

The hard impact against the haystack below sent agony coursing up Geta's arm, even though he landed on his feet and kept his injured wrist high. He groaned and stumbled to the horse, clutching his arm against his chest. Hot blood soaked his sleeve, but he paid it no mind. Grasping the saddle with his good hand, he mounted the postal pony and turned it toward the courtyard's gate.

"Hit him!" Constantine screamed from the window.

A crossbow bolt ricocheted off the gatepost as Geta passed beneath the arch. He turned around to see a guardsman land in the haystack and begin running with his sword in hand. But the pony was at a gallop now, and Geta lost his pursuer after he turned the corner.

He exited Arelate onto the southern road toward the sea. His entire arm throbbed, and the thoughts flitting through his mind were jumbled as he rode. Like a heavy millstone, the gloom of failure began to descend on Geta's shoulders, but he pushed the emotion away. If he didn't focus on the present, he wouldn't live to see the future. Fortunately, he had already been planning a quick escape. All he had to do was ride and endure . . . ride and endure . . . ride and endure.

But it was supposed to be a ride with the exhilaration of success!

Geta galloped for longer than he should have if he wanted the pony to make it all the way to the postal exchange station. About a mile from the city gate, he finally let the poor beast slow down. It was thirty miles to the stable, where he could obtain a fresh horse. From there, it was another thirty miles to the port of Massilia, where the escape ship would be waiting.

After a while, Geta sped up again. He cantered his mount through most of the trip, not wanting to kill the pony yet not unwilling to push it to the limits of its strength. Eventually the pain in his arm dulled to a steady, pounding ache. Nausea swamped him and cold sweat drenched his forehead, but he gritted his teeth and ignored it. He was a highly trained warrior. He knew how to suffer pain and remain in the saddle.

Arriving at the station, he dismounted and hurried inside to meet Bassianus. Surprisingly, the man wasn't there. Instead, the monkey-faced Senecio greeted him.

"Where is your brother, sir?" Geta asked. He leaned against a table to remain upright, for his injury had clouded his vision and made him dizzy.

"They got him. Someone tipped off Constantine."

"I didn't think anyone else knew of the plan. Who was it?"

"How should I know? Maybe it was an angel in a dream! What difference does it make? You failed, and now Bassianus will be put to death."

"They were waiting for me. Somehow they found out. The plot was foiled." Geta hung his head, deeply ashamed. "I let down Emperor Licinius. I deserve execution too."

"This is no time for your execution!" Senecio snapped as he headed for the door to the stable. "I need you to get me to Massilia. If we can't get there ahead of our pursuers, we'll both be dead by sunrise. Now get your arse onto your new horse, soldier, and let's get out of here."

Rex's ship had been following the slave traders for three days now, usually about a day behind them, though sometimes only a few hours. Flavia admired his perseverance. She had come to realize that Rex wasn't truly convinced a reward for rescuing Ossius would be forthcoming in Nicomedia. As it turned out, the promise of compensation had been a ruse to keep his men going. Rex was pursuing the bishop for her sake, and Flavia recognized his dogged determination as one of the many ways he took care of her. She couldn't really explain why he was like that. For such a rugged man, he was surprisingly gallant.

Sailing along the Sporades chain had been a delightful experience as the *Deadly Encounter* hopped from village to village and isle to isle. The sun was hot each day, but not extremely so, and the winds were fair. Flavia had never seen such a deep-blue color in seawater before. She stared at it often, marveling at its cerulean beauty. Surely this was what the ancient poet

Homer meant when he spoke of the "wine-dark" Aegean. This was truly an exquisite place, and Flavia resolved to remember this journey forever.

Rex wandered up one day and joined her at the prow of the ship. Below them in the sea, the mighty rostrum created white foam as it punched the ship through the waves.

"I think we'll catch the slavers tonight," Rex said. "They'll want to go ashore at the last island before heading north into the open sea. We'll hit them tonight before they leave."

"What's the place called?"

"Floating Mat Island."

"What an attractive name," Flavia joked.

"Apparently, the place is extremely flat, like a floating mat. It's just a low patch of rock without much elevation. The highest point is no higher than a ship's mast, so it's hard to see it from a distance. There are dangerous reefs that restrict your approach. And it's uninhabited."

"Sounds like the perfect place for pirates and slavers to hide."

"Yes, but that also makes it perfect for sneaking up on an unsuspecting enemy. It's going to be dark tonight. No moon. We should have the bishop back with us by dawn."

"If anyone can do it, you can, Rex."

He smiled at this but was summoned away by the navigator before he could respond.

Although the *Deadly Encounter* reached Floating Mat Island in the late evening, it was high midsummer now, so the days were long and the sun was still above the horizon. A little fishing vessel had been testing the waters nearby, but when it saw the naval warship approach, it tried to scoot away. Rex ordered his men to overtake it.

"Hail to you, good men of the sea," Rex called to the fishers in his atrocious Greek accent. Flavia and Cassi had been working with him in the evenings, so his vocabulary and syntax had improved. Yet somehow his native Germanic tongue just didn't mesh with Greek. He sounded like a wild barbarian whenever he spoke. At least now, though, he was a grammatically correct barbarian.

"We ain't done nothing wrong," the skipper replied to Rex's greeting. "Just humble fishermen, that's all."

"I know it! I mean you no harm. How would you like to earn an easy jug of wine?"

The sailors brightened at this suggestion and quickly agreed to Rex's proposal. In exchange for the amphora, they allowed Rex to board their ship and took him on a quiet circumnavigation of Floating Mat Island. Rex brought with him the youngest of the five crewmen who manned the *Deadly Encounter*'s sails, a sharp-eyed youth who often ascended the mast and served as the mutineers' lookout.

Rex did not return until after the sun had gone down. He immediately assembled a small group of men in the stern. Stephen was among those chosen, along with the lanky Thracian, the sharp-eyed lookout, and a few others. Flavia noticed the brawny oarsman Marius was not invited, despite being an informal leader among the crew.

"Our lookout was certain that he saw Ossius on the beach," Rex told his rescue team. "He was the only older man among them, and he had silver, wavy hair like the bishop. They were letting him walk around freely."

"And he carried a tall walking stick," the youth added.

"Then let's go hit 'em!" the Thracian said eagerly. "We've been waiting for this chance for weeks!"

Rex shook his head. "They're too well positioned—guarded by reefs all around. The water is shallow and tricky. If we try to go in there at night, we'll run aground for sure. They'll be mocking us all the way to Nicomedia."

"At first light, then," the Thracian suggested.

"Still too dangerous. Remember how quick and nimble they are? They'd run circles around us in that tight space. Ram us, breach us, push us onto a reef. Again, they'd be laughing in the taverns while we're stuck in the middle of nowhere, watching our food run out."

The Thracian swatted his hand. "Bah! So we have to give up, after all this? Some captain you are!"

"I'm not suggesting we give up," Rex replied with a confident swagger. "Just wait. I have a plan."

You always do, Flavia thought, smiling to herself.

Rex's plan was to approach the island and hide the rowboat in one of the secret caves that dotted the western shoreline. With a hideout secured, he would ascend to the island's flat surface and cross to the beach on the southern side where the enemy ship was moored. The pirates would be asleep in the hushed hour before dawn, and a watchman was unlikely to be posted in such a remote place. The moon was new, so it would be very dark. After awakening Ossius, Rex would slip him out of camp. Guided by a signal fire maintained by Stephen, the fugitives would work their way back through the thorny underbrush to the bluffs above the waiting boat. From there, the threesome would descend to the cave and make good their escape before the pirates even knew that Ossius was gone. Rex's crewmen agreed that the plan would work, so everyone dispersed to make the necessary preparations.

As Rex was about to depart for the rescue mission, Flavia approached him. "I don't want to be left here without you and Stephen," she told him. "These men are untrustworthy. Especially Marius and his faction."

"I know they're rough men, but they're harmless. They won't bother you."

"Don't be so sure. Marius made a pass at me the other day, and I only barely escaped."

Rex's mouth fell open. "What? Why didn't you tell me?"

"It wasn't worth bothering you about. But I don't feel safe without you or Stephen aboard. You two are the only good men. Could you leave him behind?"

"I need Stephen to maintain the signal fire. He's one of the few I can trust to get the job done."

"There's another who could do it."

"Who?"

"I could go with you, Rex."

"You? No, it's much too dangerous. I don't want you sneaking around the island with enemies nearby."

Flavia frowned at this and folded her arms across her chest. "Brandulf Rex, how short your memory is! You once sent me into a deranged emperor's palace to spy it out. And don't you remember the coins in the bread? We plotted treason against Maxentius! You should know I can do this job. You can trust me to keep that fire going. Then Stephen could stay behind to watch over Mother and Cassi."

Rex seemed unexpectedly chastened by the firmness of Flavia's rebuke. "I do trust you," he said in an earnest voice. "Please don't think I don't. I

143

remember all those brave things you did. I just want you to be safe." After hesitating for a moment, he sighed, then nodded. "Alright. You can come with me. Grab your mantle and let's go. I'll tell Stephen about the change."

After retrieving her woolen wrap, Flavia descended the rope ladder by the light of an oil lamp and dropped into Rex's waiting boat. He rowed them to the crags along Floating Mat Island's western shore, searching for a good place to hide the watercraft where it couldn't be found even if the escape were delayed until after sunrise.

"That looks promising," he said as he approached an overhang that came within arm's length of the water's surface.

"I don't think we can fit under there."

"Lie down in the bottom of the boat, and I'll drag us under."

Flavia complied, reclining on her back and staring up at the night sky. She felt a cloth land on her stomach and heard a small splash immediately after. *Rex's tunic!* Her heart began to beat a little faster as she realized what that meant. She forced herself not to dwell on the matter.

From down in the water, Rex maneuvered the boat under the overhang. The oil lamp rested on the planks beside Flavia, its glow illuminating the jagged rocks not far above her face. Suddenly the rocks disappeared and the space opened up as the boat glided into a secret cavern. Sitting up, Flavia held the lamp high. Dancing orange light flickered on the walls and gave the water a glossy sheen. The grotto's atmosphere was eerie and enthralling at the same time. It was like being in another world, a secret den hidden from outsiders.

"Beautiful, isn't it?" Rex asked. She glanced over to find him waist deep in the pool, his physique sharply defined by the lamp's soft glow. Though he was examining the ceiling, Flavia suddenly found the cavern far less interesting than the powerful shape of Rex's shoulders, the rippling of his arms, and the tight, square cut of his chest.

"It . . . it certainly is," Flavia agreed.

"Toss me my tunic, then I'll pull you over to dry ground."

Flavia threw him the garment, then forced herself to look away as he clambered out of the water onto some rocks. She waited until she was certain he was dressed before turning back. "How do we get out of here?" she asked.

"I think we can ascend through that crevice and reach open sky. I feel cool air coming down. Let's tie off the boat and go up."

After Rex had secured the rowboat and donned his cloak and sword belt, he approached the opening of the crevice. It did in fact lead through the craggy bluffs to the island's flat top. Instead of open fields, Flavia found the terrain to be like the labyrinth of the Minotaur, with tiny paths meandering everywhere through low, spiny bushes and scraggly heather. Some paths made connections to others, but more often, they resulted in dead ends.

Yet with the help of the oil lamp, the pair was able to pick their way through the maze. Once Rex had ascertained the correct path to the enemy camp on the beach, he backtracked to a flat area that was sheltered among some mastic shrubs. The spot was adjacent to the nearly invisible crevice that led down to the waiting boat.

"We'll make the fire here," Rex said. "After I have Ossius, I'll follow a direct line to the fire. It doesn't have to be a big one, but make sure you keep it burning or I'll be wandering all night trying to find my way back to that cave."

"I'll make sure the blaze is visible," Flavia promised. "Are you heading out to rescue him now?"

"Not until the hour before dawn. Speculators call it the 'magic hour' because we do our best work then. The human body is most sleepy at that time. It's perfect for stealthy operations."

"What do we do now?"

"We just wait. Let's get the fire going."

The wood on Floating Mat Island was abundant and dry, so it wasn't hard to start a small campfire. Rex and Flavia piled enough sticks nearby to feed the flames until dawn. A wide, smooth boulder served as a convenient backstop to lean against. Rex gathered his rough woolen cloak around his body and sat down, reclining against the boulder with crisscrossed ankles and his feet nearly in the fire. He offered Flavia the place next to him with a tip of his head.

"Don't you think it's a little . . . okay, fine," she said as she dropped down beside him.

For a long time, they sat comfortably side by side, staring into the campfire as they chatted. Rex seemed relaxed despite the dangerous mission to come. His listening ear combined with the cozy setting made Flavia feel talkative. She told him story after story about her life in the Sicilian convent, and he asked questions that showed he was truly paying attention. Wrapped in her mantle, Flavia felt she had appropriate separation from Rex. Yet she was acutely aware that her shoulder was resting against his while they reclined together.

"I've always loved staring at the night sky," she murmured with her head tipped back. "You can really see the Milky Way out here. So much more visible than in Rome. I wonder what it is?"

"Zeus let the infant Hercules suckle from Hera to make him divine. When Hera didn't recognize the baby, she pushed him away. That streak in the sky is her milk that spurted out."

Flavia was silent for a long time. Finally, she said, "You know that's just nonsense, right? Those mythological stories about the gods are all made up."

Rex fiddled with a mastic branch in his fingers. "Yeah, I know," he acknowledged. "And I know what you're going to say next."

"What?"

"That the stories in your scriptures aren't like that. You don't have gods doing crazy things to explain the world. The Christian stories are more historical."

"I was going to say that," Flavia admitted with a little laugh.

"Because you want me to convert."

Subtly, as if merely shifting position, Rex rolled toward Flavia. He looked into her face in a way that showed he was intrigued by her, yet he wasn't threatening in any way. "Why is that so important to you?" he asked.

"It's the true faith, Rex. It really is. Eternal salvation is found only in Jesus Christ."

"What would happen if I converted and got baptized?"

"You would live a wise life. And you would be with God forever when you die."

"Any other good things?"

"I . . . I don't know. Only God knows that."

"What would happen if I never converted?" he asked with an impish tone in his voice.

"I don't want to think about that," Flavia said as she stared into the campfire.

A big yawn overcame Rex. He stretched his powerful frame, and when he settled against the rock again, his hands were folded behind his head, leaving the side of his body in contact with hers. "I'm so sleepy," he said.

"Me too," she admitted, inching slightly closer to him. "It's warm here. Warm and nice."

"Want some gum?"

The question was so unexpected, it almost made Flavia burst into laughter. "Some what?"

"Some mastic gum." He rolled a piece of golden resin in his fingers. "People chew it. It's kind of piney, and it makes your breath fresh. Because, you know . . . if we're going to sit this close, we might as well enjoy it." His laugh was playful yet very charming too.

Flavia tried the gum, chewing it thoughtfully to assess its flavor. It was bitter at first, but then it released a pleasant, resinous taste.

"I really like this," she announced.

"The gum?"

"Sure. The gum."

"Flavia, can I kiss your cheek?"

She turned toward him, aware she was blushing tremendously. "How come, Rex?"

"I don't know. Because I want to. It just seems right."

"A different kiss once seemed right to us," Flavia dared to say.

"That was another world. We're in this one now, and I think this is right for the present."

"I agree, Rex."

She offered her cheek to him. His first response was to cup her chin and draw her close in a gentle, protective way. Then he leaned close and kissed her cheek. Rex lingered long enough for Flavia to be aware how soft and tender his lips felt against her skin. At last, he drew back and settled against the rock again.

Flavia's heart was fluttering. *That was sooo nice . . .*

"Shall we doze a bit, right here under the Milky Way?" he asked.

"Mm-hmm," she murmured as she closed her eyes and snuggled against his side.

Bishop Melitius was just that: a mere bishop of a small town in Upper Aegyptus that no one in the wider world cared about. "Wolf City," they called it. Named for the wolf-god Osiris. Even the temple of that false deity was bigger than the crummy little hall that passed for the bishop's church in Wolf City.

But all that was about to change!

Melitius had spent the last two days traveling down the Nilus River and navigating through its adjoining canals to reach Alexandria, a truly great city by anyone's estimation. He stood on the street corner and gazed up at the leading episcopal church of Aegyptus, the beautiful Church of Theonas. Located in a prominent position next to the Moon Gate on the city's main thoroughfare of Canopus Avenue, the church served as the headquarters of Melitius's enemy and rival, Pope Alexander.

That man was a weakling—full of "grace" and "forgiveness" for anyone who sought it. Did he not know that grace and forgiveness always came at a price? Only through hard penance and years of self-abasement could one earn it, especially when the sin was the worst one of all: capitulation during a persecution. The true church was the church of the martyrs—rigorous, holy, and full of manly endurance. *One day*, Melitius vowed as he stared at the church, *I will become the powerful and influential Pope of Aegyptus*. Then Alexander's lenient theology would be replaced with doctrines more worthy of a strict and fearsome God. And nobody would get "grace" simply by asking for it!

Turning his back on the basilica, Melitius began walking down Canopus Avenue toward the other side of Alexandria. Unfortunately, political maneuvering within the Aegyptian church wasn't the only thing he had to worry about. A man like him had to think worldwide, and that was why the report from Rome today was of such great importance. Though Melitius knew he was a physically small man, he prided himself on having giant-sized ambitions. What good would it do for his Melitian faction to defeat the catholic bishop of Alexandria and take over his church only to find that Rome or Antiochia had risen to even greater prominence in the meantime? Those bishops had to be stopped for Aegyptus to rise.

After arriving at the east-facing Sun Gate, Melitius went out to the overgrown area of animal pasturage called the Boukolia district. It was a wild neighborhood whose gritty herdsmen were known to be ruffians. Soon he came to a chapel used by his supporters: the Martyrium of Saint Mark. Entering its dim and musty interior, he proceeded toward the altar, which lay above the apostolic relics.

"Shall I leave the doors open or closed?" asked the priest who was making the chapel ready for the meeting.

"Close them," said Melitius. "I want no listening ears, nor prying eyes."

"As you wish, Your Holiness," the priest answered with a bow. His use of such a formal title indicated his hope that Melitius would one day be the local pope. Melitius resolved to remember this and to reward the man once he came into power.

The visitor arrived at the sixth hour, just as he had promised in his letter. He had come from far away, from the den of iniquity, from the city of arrogant bishops who claimed supremacy through Peter and Paul. Yes, the stealthy operative known as the Aegyptian Asp had come all the way from Rome.

"I greet thee with due esteem," said the tall, olive-skinned man with the snake tattoo on his face. The hood of his brown robe was around his shoulders, so Melitius could see the tattoo in full detail. It was a wicked-looking thing, yet strangely beautiful too.

"Welcome to the Martyrium of Saint Mark," Bishop Melitius said.

"Is it true, then? Did the apostle of the Heavenly Teacher actually visit this city?"

Melitius gestured to the chapel around him. "This church was built many decades ago, though not in the time of the apostle. It stands on the site of what all believe to be Mark's grave, outside the city walls. No one knows when people started saying that Mark founded the Alexandrian church. Perhaps he came here, perhaps not. We have few records from the apostolic age."

"I choose to believe it," the Aegyptian Asp said. "His gospel tells how he fled naked from the garden, unlike Adam, who was naked in a garden but fled away clothed. Man must be spiritually naked, unclothed from earthly wisdom, in order to reenter the Garden of the Divine Presence." The Asp's cryptic words were accompanied by a little smile that was neither happy nor sad but simply content with his inner enlightenment.

"I forgot how much you Gnostics like your allegories," Melitius remarked. "But come, let us change the subject. We have no time for exegesis of the ancient gospel. It is the more practical matters of today's world that we must discuss."

"Yes, my lord," said the Asp with a bow.

Melitius led his guest to a pair of couches set up by the priest. Wine had been poured into two jeweled glasses before he left. Little did the priest know that the visitor drank no wine, nor indulged in sex or baths. He was an ascetic—a "monk" they were calling such men these days—part of a secret brotherhood that Melitius knew little about. No matter, though. As long as the Aegyptian Asp remembered his former skills from his days as an army scout and assassin, Melitius didn't care what ascetic brotherhood he was part of now.

"Two cups will suit me well," the bishop told his visitor. "I will drink them while you give me your report. Go ahead and begin."

"As you wish, my lord," came the humble reply once again.

The Aegyptian Asp proceeded to tell all that he knew about the activities of the catholic church in Rome. The news was indeed dire. Proud Sylvester, always a busy bee, was on the move in the capital. He had a twofold plan: build great churches around the city and secure a reliable text of the scriptures, defining the list of books that came from God himself. Buildings and a bible—this double approach was truly clever, for it united the eye and the ear to win the people's hearts. Some leaders in Rome opposed the plan, but most of the clergy were in support. If Sylvester succeeded, the Roman bishop would gain prominence over all other clergymen across the empire.

But there was one flaw in Sylvester's evil scheme: it was pricey. To erect such great buildings, or gather bishops from far and wide for a council, or make multiple copies of expensive books—these things required money. And not only money but permission as well. Emperor Constantine would have to be petitioned by a formal embassy to allow such meetings and churches. Since he was in distant Arelate, that, too, would require an expensive outlay. The costs were daunting. Even so, Sylvester had started the plan in motion.

Yet the Aegyptian Asp had not been without countermeasures. Spying around, he had learned that the embassy to the emperor was led by Bishop

Ossius of Corduba, the pompous Spaniard with luxurious hair more suited to a famous actor than a humble cleric. A couple of Sicilian nuns, one of whom had come into a rich inheritance, were funding the mission and accompanying Ossius—probably for sexual favors at night, the Asp suggested. They had departed Sicilia on the Nones of June, intent on their prideful plan to gain imperial favor for Rome at Alexandria's expense.

It was at this point that the problem had been especially well-handled by the Aegyptian Asp. Using his stealthy ways and many shady connections, the former speculator made contact with some Maltese slave traders who plied the waters between Africa and the Aegean Sea. Tipped off to the nearby presence of the emperor's favorite bishop, the slavers were easily induced to capture that man in hope of winning a big ransom. By now, those virginal nuns had been despoiled two hundred times in Corinthus, while Ossius was on his way to be ransomed in Nicomedia at the opposite end of the empire from Constantine.

"Every single thing," the Aegyptian Asp concluded, "went according to the plan of Divine Wisdom."

"But where is Ossius now?" Melitius inquired. "Perhaps he shall be freed, and then he might return to his quest. I must admit, that concerns me."

"With what money? The girl who was paying for it is lost in the brothels."

"Be that as it may, you must locate the bishop and make certain his mission has truly come to an end."

At this command, a crafty gleam came to the Asp's eye. For a moment, Melitius did not know why. Then he realized what had entered his visitor's mind.

"No!" Melitius exclaimed, waving his hands in a dismissive way. "Do not even think of such a thing. Clergy cannot be harmed. It is an inviolable law of God! Vengeance is one of his primary attributes. I would surely come under the strict hand of divine justice if I commanded such a thing. So hear me tell you now, in plain words—you may not kill the bishop."

"There are many ways to thwart a man's plans," said the Asp mildly. "Violence is only one of them."

"Violence is sometimes necessary," Melitius agreed, "but never against those in holy orders."

"Then I will crush the structures that surround and support that man.

His mission will end when he has no resources upon which to draw. It is a well-known tactic to those with my training."

"Excellent! See to it that Bishop Ossius is left with nothing but dead ends at every turn. When he can do no more, he will give up in defeat. Once this is accomplished, return to Rome and keep watch on Sylvester. I think you can foresee the terrible things that would happen if he got the rescript from Constantine. That kind of monumental architecture . . . the definition of an official canon . . . the establishment of Peter and Paul as the foremost apostles . . ." Melitius's words trailed off as he let his point sink in.

"I understand, my lord," said the Aegyptian Asp.

"Do you?"

"Yes, of course! If this plan succeeds, Rome will stand as the foremost Christian church forever. Alexandria will be eclipsed, and your own glory will be much diminished."

Melitius took a slow sip of his wine, then set down the cup in dramatic fashion. He dipped his chin toward the Asp, acknowledging his correct assessment of the situation. "Those things must not happen," the bishop declared.

"They shall not. I vow it. The brotherhood exists to serve purposes like yours."

"What is this brotherhood, anyway? I know little of it."

"We are those who were taught the military arts for the sake of human conquest—then came to discover a higher use for our training. That is enough to be said, I think."

Melitius shrugged, for he cared only about final outcomes. "Once upon a time, you were a soldier. Now you are a surgeon, whether you know it or not."

"A surgeon, you say?"

Melitius rose from his couch and went to the chapel's book cupboard. He returned with the *Four Gospels* that had come to be standard among the non-Gnostic Christians. Flipping the pages of the codex, Melitius found his text in Saint Mark's gospel and began to read: "'If your hand causes you to stumble, cut it off. It is better to enter life crippled than have two hands, but go into hell, into the unquenchable fire.'" He closed the book. "Attend to the wisdom here, my servant. The word of the Lord tells us to cut off the hand that is guiding the body to hell. That is what you must do—sacrifice some of the infected appendages for the sake of the whole. Sometimes you have to amputate a hand in the body of Christ so the rest of it can thrive. I give you permission to cut away any of the laity who need to go. This is a holy sort of violence. Although the cutting hurts, the main body is healed."

The Aegyptian Asp held up his empty palm. Then, in a motion too quick for Melitius to see, he flicked his wrist and a razor appeared in his grip. The blade must have been up his sleeve—but it felt more like the work of magic.

"Aha! It seems I was correct," said Bishop Melitius. "You are indeed a surgeon."

"I am a master of knives, Your Holiness. And that means there are certain kinds of surgery I know how to perform."

"See that you cut cleanly," Melitius advised. "Be quick and deep. The future of the Alexandrian church depends on it."

⸺◦/◦/◦⸺

It wasn't the crackling sound that awakened Rex, nor the heat, nor the flickering light. All those things entered his awareness as soon as he woke up. But it was the acrid smell of burning heather in his nostrils that first made him bolt from the rock at his little campsite.

"Flavia, get up!" he cried, rousing her from sleep as well.

"Wh-what?" she mumbled, thoroughly disoriented as she got to her feet.

"We've got to get out of here!"

She coughed as a cloud of smoke billowed over them. "What about Ossius?"

"Impossible now. The whole island is on fire! The slavers will know we're here. Let's go!"

He grabbed her hand and they stumbled toward the crevice in the cliffs, dodging errant sparks and smoldering bushes along the way. Though it was still an hour before dawn, the sky was alive with a ruddy, flickering glow. After scrambling down the crack into the secret grotto, they untied the boat, and Flavia lay down in it like before. Rex didn't even have time to remove his tunic as he pushed the boat under the overhang and out into the open sea.

"What just happened?" Flavia asked while Rex rowed. The turn of events was stunning to her, and she was struggling to comprehend it.

"I'm a fool. I let the fire escape our ring while we slept, and it just ran out of control on this parched little patch of dirt."

"We can't abandon the bishop. Can we keep chasing the slavers?"

"I'm not sure. I'll know more when we get back to the ship."

Unfortunately, Rex's reception when he boarded the *Deadly Encounter* was worse than anything he had experienced since the mutineers first rebelled. The crew was restless and surly, even the ones who had been supportive. It was a delicate situation for a captain who had not yet provided any loot to his crew.

"The slavers have left, Rex," announced the Thracian. Apparently, he was done with the term *captain*.

"How do you know?"

"We just checked. They aren't at the beach."

"You're lucky we came back for you!" Marius shouted from across the deck. He had a gang of angry-faced oarsmen around him. "We should have left you on the burning island!"

"Everybody get ahold of yourselves," Rex barked. "Don't start panicking just because we had a sudden change of plans."

"We want a change of captains!" cried an anonymous voice. A few others quickly added their agreement.

Rex glared at his rebellious crew. "I'm still in charge here. Now I want everyone—"

"Enemy to starboard!" shouted the lookout. "Arrows incoming! Get down!"

The slave ship, its camouflage paint making it almost invisible in the predawn twilight, came barreling out of the mist with unbelievable speed. Although five or six of the mutineers had the courage to grab bows and return a few shots, most of the crew ducked behind the rails as the enemy vessel swept by. Several of Rex's men screamed and went down under the hail of arrows. A few of them even tumbled into the sea, including two of the brave archers who had shot back.

After its first pass, the enemy ship immediately started coming around for a second attack. It executed the turn and began to gather speed again. This time, a horde of crossbowmen stood at the rails, eager for a closer approach. After their intense barrage, the enemy would surely grapple and attempt to board.

"To the oars!" Rex cried. "We've got to get moving!"

His crew scrambled to the benches and immediately commenced an evasive maneuver, trying to pull away from the imminent assault. But the sleek pirate ship had already built up too much speed. The crossbowmen would be in range at any moment.

"They're gonna smash us right up our stern!" the Thracian whined, panicked now that he realized his predicament. "We got no protection back there! We'll be dead in the water! Do something!"

So Rex did.

Dashing below deck, he grabbed two huge bitumen jars by their handles and hauled them topside. After shoving one into the arms of the Thracian, he broke the other jar's neck against the rail and started pouring the gooey black substance into the ship's wake. "Do the same," he ordered, and the Thracian immediately complied.

A black smudge appeared on the ocean's surface, like the ink of an octopus when it jets away from danger. The slave ship continued to barrel on, oblivious to the gunk in the water. Rex snatched an archer's bow from the deck, then plunged an arrow into the broken amphora. The head came out globbed with bitumen. Ducking into his stern cabin, Rex lit the arrow from his lamp, nocked it on his bow, and sent the missile arcing into the deadly stain upon the sea.

Bitumen was known to burn even when it floated on water, and Rex was glad to see its reputation proved true. The enemy ship was passing through the center of the splotch when a seaborne bonfire burst to life around it. The crossbowmen dropped their weapons and backed away from the rail as tongues of flame engulfed their ship. Sticky bitumen lapped onto the hull and started new blazes wherever it touched. Suddenly an aggressive attack was the last thing on the slavers' minds. Every sailor dreaded fire, knowing how vulnerable their ships were to its ravages. The formerly bold attackers now seemed to want nothing but to escape their burning vessel.

The exodus started slowly but spread without delay. One man jumped into the water, then another, then a whole host of sailors started leaping into the sea as fire swept along both flanks of the ship. Soon, the entire crew was in the choppy surf, while the captured Gothic slaves were making a tremendous racket in the ship's belly.

Bishop Ossius was the hero who let them out. Rex saw the distinctive man—tall, well-dressed, with his silvery hair blowing in the wind—

struggling with the main hatch to the ship's hold. He finally pried loose the locking bar and popped open the hatch. Yellow-haired Goths swarmed from the opening like angry bees.

The enemy ship was fully ablaze now. There was nothing to do but abandon it, so everyone jumped overboard, including the elderly bishop. Rex saw Ossius hit the water with his staff in his hand. He surfaced a short distance away. Fortunately, the ship had floated out of the patch of burning sea, so Ossius did not emerge into a conflagration.

"Come about!" Rex ordered. "Hard to port!"

The *Deadly Encounter* made the tight turn, and Rex guided it toward the bedraggled bishop. The rest of the enemy sailors—along with their now-released captives—were swimming toward the blackened island. That scenario would be interesting. It was going to result in either a colossal battle with only one side left standing or an enormous multiethnic effort to signal the first fishing boat that happened to drift by. Rex hoped the men would find a way to cooperate, but knowing the Germanic Goths as he did, a fight with their captors would more likely ensue. Either way, it wouldn't be his problem. He was headed for the open sea.

"Would you like a ride, sir?" Rex called to Ossius as he dropped the rope ladder.

"Who are you?" asked the lone man bobbing in the surf.

Different responses flitted through Rex's mind, for there were many answers to that question. Before he could make a reply, Flavia appeared next to him, leaning over the rail.

"He is Captain Brandulf Rex, my supporter and friend," she announced with a smile. "Climb on up and meet him. I think you're going to like him a lot."

ACT 2

EXPEDITION

5

Licinius Junior was about to do something amazing: he was about to take his first step.

"You can do it," his father urged, palms extended toward the toddler. "Come to Papa!"

The baby released the table leg and balanced precariously on his tiny feet. Licinius could see the child wanted to come but was struggling to figure out how to make his body do it.

"Don't let him fall," Constantia warned, hovering over her son like a broody hen.

Licinius scoffed at his wife and swatted away her protective hands. "Back off, woman! Let him fall on his face if he must. It is good for a boy to overcome pain."

Fortunately, no pain was in store for little Junior at the moment. In a series of steps that was more like a barely controlled tumble, he shuffled toward Licinius and fell into his father's arms. Licinius scooped him up and held him high. "Good boy!" he exclaimed with a smile.

"He has all the makings of an emperor," Constantia boasted.

"And I will make that happen—even if it means war."

Snapping his fingers, Licinius summoned a nursemaid to take Junior from him. "See if he can walk the distance between those two pillars," he told the slave. "Give him a sweet if he makes it." The maid nodded and carried the boy to a nearby colonnade to practice his walking.

Licinius crossed the atrium and stared at a sun-washed garden centered on a mosaic with a floral pattern. Fine mosaic art was one of the few good things they had going here in Sirmium. He inhaled deeply as he gazed at the manicured shrubs and potted flowers without really seeing them. Finally, he turned back to Constantia.

"Your brother vexes me," he said.

She was lounging on a divan, snacking on a fruit tart, as if she needed to get even fatter. "We must find a way to elevate Junior into the college, my love."

"It is only Constantine who prevents it. That conniving brother of yours."

"I agree, he's a conniver," Constantia said diplomatically. "Yet I think he means you no harm. He is merely competitive when it comes to politics. Just like you, really. With God's help, you can handle him."

Licinius uttered a disgusted grunt. "I don't need God's help."

At this remark, Constantia set down her tart but did not rise from the couch. "We can all use some help from heaven, my love. Perhaps you could come to church with me tomorrow. Should I inform the bishop you will be attending?"

"I'm not interested in that, Constantia." Licinius went to the wall, where a pair of crisscrossed swords had been hung on pegs. They were for ornamental purposes only, so they were unsharpened, yet Licinius drew one of the blades from its sheath anyway. "Rome was founded more than a thousand years ago on the Palatine Hill, and its empire has always rested on this." He brandished the sword toward his wife. "I have come to wonder whether the peace-loving God of the Christians is our helper after all. I think accepting that faith may have been a mistake."

"Licinius, what are you saying? You're in a Christian alliance with Constantine. You even purged your territory of the church's persecutors! When you executed the families of the persecuting emperors, you made your decision. You sealed your destiny with their blood. Now you have to stay with Christ. It's the religion of the future."

"But what kind of future will it be when it makes men so weak? Jesus told his followers to turn the other cheek. What use is that? If I stick with

Christianity, all I will have is a shrunken kingdom overrun by Goths and Sarmatians."

Constantia finally rose from her divan. Cautiously, yet with sincere affection, she came to Licinius's side and put her hand on his arm. "Consider your wars against Daia. Only three years ago, you defeated him by God's power. He fought by Jupiter's might, while you fought by Christ—and you won! An angel gave your troops a prayer to say before the battle."

"Constantine's bishop wrote that prayer. I lied and told the men it had come down from heaven. There was no angel."

"Be that as it may, my love, your decision is made. You have aligned with the Christian God."

"Sometimes a man comes to regret his decisions." Licinius couldn't veil the bitterness in his voice. "Then he must decide what to do about it."

At this, Constantia fell silent, and Licinius was glad for the change. But the peace didn't last long. "Your best and most loyal courtiers today are Christians," she observed.

"They would put their loyalty to Jesus above me."

"If you would be a better Christian, they wouldn't have to choose."

The remark finally moved Licinius from simmering frustration to outright anger. He drew back from his wife, staring at her round face with disdain. "I don't ever want to hear you mention Constantine or his religion again!"

"*His* religion? Is it not yours too?"

"Not anymore!" Licinius stamped his foot and threw the ornamental sword across the room with a loud clatter. "I'm done with that foolish faith! It's back to the old gods for me. They served us well for a long time. Some of them will be glad to have me back. They're not defeated yet!"

In the nearby colonnade, Junior began to cry. "The loud noise has upset the baby," Constantia said.

She started to go comfort the child, but as she turned away, Licinius grabbed her arm. "You'd better decide your allegiances here, woman."

The stern warning caused Constantia's eyes to widen. Since she did not reply, Licinius continued with his ultimatum. "Your brother won't be around much longer to look out for you. I sent Senecio to his court in Arelate with an order of assassination. Bassianus can arrange things like that. It's probably taken care of already."

Now Licinius could see he had his wife's full attention. She sagged a little, and perhaps would have fled the room if he didn't have such a tight grip on her arm. Nearby, Junior was wailing despite the nursemaid's soothing, making Licinius feel even more tense. He wanted to release Constantia so she could take the boy away, yet he had one more demand to make.

"Me or Jesus?" he barked.

Constantia began to shake in his grip. For a moment, Licinius actually considered whether he would have to make his queen into a Christian martyr. But finally, her face fell. He released her arm and she collapsed at his feet. Kneeling and grasping his hand, she kissed his imperial ring. Licinius felt warm tears against his fingers.

"Caesar is Lord," Constantia whispered. And with those words, she rose to her feet, scooped up the crying baby, and hurried out of the room.

—◦◦◦—

July 316

The *Deadly Encounter* had finally met its match: not pirates, nor slavers, nor even the imperial navy, but a band of Thessalonian scavengers who ran the ship aground and picked her apart like termites on an old log. Taken together, all the timbers, planks, rigging, sails, and shipboard equipment ended up being worth even more than the cargo of bitumen, which was also sold at a good price. Once the scavengers had hauled away everything of value and settled up, Rex's crewmen each received a decent sack of coins that would hold them until they found something to do next. A few days earlier, the mutineers had decided that life on the run wasn't all it was cracked up to be. They had voted unanimously to take whatever money they could get and disappear into the underbelly of the nearest big city, which happened to be Thessalonica.

"At least you freed us from Brutus," the Thracian acknowledged gruffly to Rex as they stood on the city's main dock. "Not many men would have had the guts to start a mutiny."

"Nor the thighs to pull it off," Rex answered, recalling his desperate strangulation of the cruel navy centurion.

"That too! You're a great warrior, my friend, but you were a terrible pirate."

"We were *tax collectors*," Rex corrected, and the two men burst into laughter.

"Farewell, Captain," the Thracian said when the laughter finally subsided. Watching him go, Rex felt gratified that, in the end, the man considered him worthy of such a title.

He turned to face the small band that was left: Flavia, Cassi, Sophronia, Bishop Ossius, and Stephen the priest. "It's just us now," Rex said to his friends. "Where to?"

"To Gaul," Ossius replied. "On the first ship we can charter. We must make our way to Emperor Constantine."

"Ha! From Sicilia to Gaul—through Graecia." Rex chuckled at the thought. "Not exactly the direct route."

"Be that as it may," the bishop insisted, "Gaul is our destination."

Rex hefted the sack in his hand. "This isn't bad money, but it's not enough to get six people all the way across the empire."

"Pope Sylvester would not send us on a mission with inadequate funds. Fortunately, Lady Junia Flavia has the resources to cover the costs of such a journey."

"Maybe in the Roman banks," Rex said, "but not here in her purse." Though he didn't want to argue with the bishop, he felt it was essential to make realistic plans in light of the present situation. "What about those letters of credit? Flavia said you have some hidden inside your staff."

The bishop held up his walking stick. "Yes. It's hollow. The letters are rolled up inside, safe and dry, and redeemable at any government bank."

A burden lifted from Rex's shoulders at those words—the burden of a guard dog whose flock was shelterless and exposed. "Excellent!" he exclaimed. "There will be a bank at the imperial palace. Emperor Galerius made Thessalonica a capital before he died. They say he got a bowel cancer that burst open, and worms ate him from the inside. Anyway, he's gone now, but his palace is still here. We can get some money tomorrow morning. Now all we need is an inn that's safe enough for the women. Let's find someplace away from the harbor before it gets dark."

Rex started to move, but Flavia intervened. "I have a better idea. There's an ancient church in Thessalonica. The Christians will give us hospitality. We should seek out the bishop."

"I agree," Stephen said, and Ossius seemed inclined toward that option as well.

Rex shrugged and decided to go along with the plan. The Christians were known for being harmless and generous. Staying with them probably would be safer than a public inn.

After asking directions, the party of six headed toward the House of Demetrios, a church named for a recent martyr. The building was situated near the Rotunda of Galerius, which had been intended as a temple to Jupiter but was left unfinished when the cancer took the wicked emperor's life.

"I wish the Christians could buy that rotunda and make a church from it," Flavia mused as they passed by.

"Perhaps someday it will happen," Ossius agreed.

Rex let the bishop take the lead as everyone approached the House of Demetrios. Despite its name, it wasn't a personal residence like the churches of earlier ages. Though it had originally been a domestic building, a marble plaque above the door indicated the structure had been converted for full-time liturgical use. A few deacons probably lived there to care for it, but it was no longer a private home. Many congregations across the empire were doing the same these days. The era of house churches was coming to an end.

Ossius rapped on the exterior door. A man in plain wool emerged, squinting in the late afternoon sun. "We are Christian travelers in need of hospitality," Ossius declared. "A bishop, a priest, three nuns, and our bodyguard."

"If you are Christians, you will surely know the acronym spelled by the word *fish*."

"Of course. It is Jesus Christ, the Son of God, the Savior."

Rex silently considered the letters of the Greek word *ichthus*. Indeed, they did make the acronym Ossius had supplied. *A clever Christian password!*

"Come with me," said the deacon, opening the door wide and closing it behind his guests.

It turned out that the bishop was in the House of Demetrios, reading some books in what had once been the master's study. He came out and greeted the visitors in the atrium, introducing himself as Basil.

"Aha! Ossius of Corduba!" he exclaimed when he met the silver-haired Spanish bishop. "Your reputation is known across the empire! It is an honor to make your acquaintance."

"I am only a humble pastor like you, Brother Basil. In fact, I am beneath you. It is my honor to visit one of the founding churches of our faith."

Basil nodded at this. "Truly, our roots go back to the time of Saint Paul's visit." He paused, then beckoned his guests toward the study. "I don't do this often, but for you, I will. Come see our greatest treasure."

Rex followed his five friends into Basil's study. The bishop went to a cabinet and removed a tightly sealed wooden case. After setting it on his desk, he opened it. Peering over Flavia's shoulder, Rex could see several loose sheets of faded and decayed papyrus resting on a cushion. The writing was in Greek. Basil removed a page with a pair of tweezers and laid it on the desk.

"Is that what I think it is?" Ossius cried.

"These pages are many decades old," Basil said, beaming with delight.

"The original epistles? Truly?"

"Yes, brother, the actual letters written to the Thessalonian church. Touched by the hand of Paul himself. What you see here is the original manuscript of *First Thessalonians*—the first piece of the New Testament ever written. It was composed only twenty years after Jesus Christ returned to heaven."

"Amazing," Flavia whispered with awe in her voice.

"Now look here, Brother Ossius," said Basil. "Let me correct something about which many churches are mistaken. Be sure and let the church of Rome know." He pointed to a sentence and asked for it to be read aloud.

Ossius stooped over the parchment and read, "'But we were infants in your midst, as a nursing mother would care for her own children.'" He glanced up at his host. "It says 'infants' here, but I have heard 'gentle in your midst' instead."

"The difference is only one letter. *Nepioi* or *epioi*. Infants or gentle."

"It would make more sense if Paul had said *epioi*," Stephen chimed in. "He'd be saying he was gentle, like a loving mother. It seems strange to call himself an infant, then immediately switch and refer to himself as the mother too."

Basil nodded. "That is why some scribes have changed it to *epioi*. It is an easy mistake for a copyist to make, especially if he only hears it read to him while copying. The previous word ends in *n*, so the sound runs together."

"But it clearly says 'infants.' I can see it with my own eyes right there: *nepioi*," Ossius observed.

Carefully, Basil picked up the page with his tweezers and laid it back in its case. "Tell your friends back home to get it right. It says 'infants.' The precise words of God matter a great deal."

These Christians sure are devoted to their sacred books, Rex thought as the visitors were invited into a dining room to receive refreshments.

After some light conversation while the food was being served, the topic turned to the reason for Ossius's arrival in Thessalonica. He explained the recent travails of his friends, then thanked Basil earnestly for giving them such a warm reception. They were all in need of safety and rest. Ossius went on to explain the mission of Pope Sylvester: to secure the emperor's permission for a building program and for holding a council about the correct list of biblical books, from which a beautiful version would be made for the bishop's use. Based on the official text, other copies of God's word could be multiplied among the Christians.

"Surely the two Thessalonian epistles must be on the list," Basil said. "Now you know without doubt they are apostolic and authentic."

"Oh, yes, the Pauline letters will be included for sure. It is some of the other books about which we must debate."

"This is truly an important mission, Brother Ossius. Rest assured that we will supply you with everything you need for the journey—above all, with prayer. You may stay here as long as you wish until you are ready to resume your travel."

"Your hospitality is worthy of Christ's love," said Flavia. "We thank you so much. It is a long way to Gaul, and we must recover all our strength."

Basil arched his eyebrows at this. "To Gaul?"

"Yes, Bishop, to Gaul. To meet with Constantine, like we said."

Now a wide grin spread across Basil's face. He set down his wine cup with a hearty chuckle and a shake of his head.

"What is it?" Ossius asked.

"God's ways are surprising, my friends. Sometimes we struggle with his will, but other times, he grants us great blessings. I believe this time he has done the latter."

"How so?"

"By stirring up Licinius against us. Many are saying he has abandoned the Christian faith, and in so doing, he has broken his alliance with Constantine.

Just two days ago, a ship arrived in our port from Gaul. We learned that an assassination attempt was made on the emperor's life—and the belief is that Licinius was behind it."

"That's terrible!" Flavia exclaimed. "His own brother-in-law?"

Such treachery was shocking, especially within the royal family. But Rex was concerned about more than the moral implications of the attack. "His Highness survived the attempt?" he asked urgently.

"He did. The plot was foiled."

And with that, the pieces fell into place as Rex discerned the steps that surely must ensue. He turned toward Ossius. "Do you know what this means?" he asked with a smile that now equaled the one on Basil's face.

"Tell me, Rex! I know little of such things."

"It means we don't have to sail across the sea to Gaul. Constantine isn't going to let an assassination attempt go unchallenged. He will immediately marshal his forces and march against Licinius."

"So he's coming to us?"

"Not all the way to Thessalonica, but to Sirmium, at least," Basil said.

"And when he arrives," Rex added, "we will be there to meet him."

After a long week on the road, Flavia had grown tired of riding in a wagon. A day of rest in Stobi was going to do the six travelers a lot of good.

Though the trip had been boring, at least it was as comfortable as Flavia could have hoped for. Bishop Basil knew a high-placed Christian in the Thessalonian bureaucracy who had granted the emissaries special access to the imperial travel system. Then Flavia's letters of credit secured enough money to hire a well-appointed coach for the journey. Every night, they stayed at the government inns, stationed about a day's journey apart. Fresh mules could be obtained at each inn, but more importantly, the travelers slept in two private rooms—male and female apart. Public inns were notoriously rowdy places, so Flavia was glad for the safer accommodations and personal privacy that the imperial establishments provided.

The coach itself, a covered vehicle handled by a professional driver, was capable of doing about twenty-five miles a day. Though the windows were usually left open for fresh air, they could be closed with shutters in the event of rain or to ward off the early morning chill. Cushions and planks served as seats but could be reconfigured so the travelers could stretch out and take naps as the wagon rolled along the highway between the Aegean Sea and the Danubius River. Ten-hour days were the norm, with brief stops for meals or necessary business. When the weather was nice, the travelers often strolled alongside the coach for a mile or two. In this way, they covered the 175 miles to Stobi in good time and decided to reward themselves with a day of rest.

"This place doesn't look like much of a town, but at least it will be nice to hold still for a day," Rex said to Flavia as the wagon approached the city's southern gate in the fading light of dusk.

"To me, it'll be a paradise compared to rolling down a highway," Flavia replied with a tired smile.

The imperial way station was located on the central town square. Since it was clean and secure, Flavia slept late the next morning with her mother on one side of the bed and Cassi on the other. It was midmorning before she finally arose, splashed water on her face, and got dressed. Then she combed out her hair and secured it in a bun with the simple wooden pin she had been using since the silver one she had brought with her went missing.

Rex greeted her in the common room. "Come have some Macedonian wine with me," he offered, pushing out the opposite bench with his foot and pouring her a cup. "It's famous."

Flavia sat down across from him and found the sweet wine to be as good as advertised. Between sips, she ate bread with honey and downed a bowl of figs as well. Something about sitting on a stationary piece of furniture made the meal especially appealing, even though it was just a rough-hewn bench.

"So, Flavia, what are you doing at the twelfth hour this evening?" Rex asked when the meal was finished. A mischievous look was on his face.

"Oh, probably reading one of Basil's books in my room," she replied nonchalantly. The bishop had given her a volume of Eusebius's *Church History*, and it truly was interesting. But Flavia had no intention of staying in her room tonight. She only said it to make Rex work for whatever he was about to propose.

He didn't hesitate. "I'd like to offer something better," he said with resolve.

Flavia pursed her lips and arched her eyebrows. "Go on. I might consider it."

"Have dinner with me. And then let's go to the theater. There's a play on tonight."

Flavia looked straight at Rex and flashed him a big smile. "I would love that, kind sir," she said with playful formality. "But can you still get tickets?"

"I already have them," Rex said proudly. The tall German reached into his belt pouch and produced two discs made of bone. On one side was a picture of Stobi's theater, and on the other was the date and the name of the play: an adaptation of Lucian's *The Death of Peregrinus*. "I found a man who would part with his for the right price."

"You bought two! What if I had declined?"

"Well, there are plenty of pretty girls in Stobi," Rex remarked with a shrug. At this rejoinder, Flavia's mouth fell open and she feigned indignation, prompting him to add, "And I would have sold my tickets to them, because I only want to go to the play with you."

Ah, Rex, you know just what to say. Suave as well as handsome—a deadly combination!

With her heart racing more than she liked to admit, Flavia said, "Then I will meet you here at the twelfth hour, prepared for a delightful evening."

Rex eyed Flavia with a devilish look. A cocky smile curled up one corner of his lip inside his blond beard. He leaned forward, putting his elbows on the table as he brought his face close to hers. She looked back at him from her seat, drawn to him, yet slightly aflutter as well.

"You can't prepare for me," he said with brash confidence. He winked at her, stood, and swaggered out of the common room without looking back.

After he left, Flavia realized she had been holding her breath. She finally exhaled and shook her head at the exhilarating exchange. "I'd sure like to try," she murmured, and the truth of it made her giggle.

Flavia spent the day around the inn, chatting with Cassi and her mother and shopping at a nearby cloth merchant's shop. Ever since her stay in Corinthus, she had been wearing the same lavender chiton, which she typically covered with a wool mantle since the chiton was gauzy and left her shoulders bare. Now she purchased a different sort of wrap, a more elegant one made of silk. She thought it was the sort of thing a lady would wear to the theater. A new pair of shoes with decorative trim completed the outfit. They seemed more fitting for such an occasion than her plain leather slippers.

Rex met her that evening as the sun was going down and the hot July day had turned pleasantly cool. Though he was always handsome, he looked especially dashing with his long barbarian hair pulled back with a thong at the nape of his neck. He, too, had purchased new clothes: a tunic of light gray fabric that came to his knees, and under it, the common trousers of the Germanic north. Their color was dark red, matching the trim on the tunic. As always, his long sword hung on his belt, giving him the commanding presence of a warrior.

"You look ready for the Danubian provinces now," Flavia said casually as they walked along. "No longer an Aegean pirate."

"And you, Flavia, look gorgeous no matter where you are," Rex replied.

Oh my . . .

"Take my arm," he offered. "The ground is uneven here."

Delighted by the compliment as well as the chance to be close, Flavia strolled beside Rex with her arm in his until he stopped at a flower shop. They entered, but instead of purchasing anything, Rex led her to a rear courtyard. When she saw it, she gasped at the scene that met her eyes.

"You like it?" Rex asked.

"It's stunning!"

The little courtyard served as a kind of storage area for the shopkeeper's wares—but this was no mere closet. Thousands of flowers overflowed from vases on racks around the walls. Clay urns on the floor erupted with eager blossoms. Many other bouquets had been inserted into a vine-covered trellis that overhung the space. At every turn, red roses mingled with yellow sunflowers and purple irises and white orchids. Innumerable bunches of wildflowers cascaded from a backdrop of leafy greenery. A sweet floral aroma permeated the air. Everywhere Flavia looked, her eyes met a multi-hued abundance. The place was magical, like entering a rainbow itself.

And in the center of the space, on the cobblestone pavement beneath the deep blue sky, stood a single table, lit by a silver lamp. Two couches were on either side of it.

"Come lie down," Rex said, beckoning to Flavia's divan. After she took her place, he plucked a white rose from a bouquet, dropped it into a small glass vase on the table, and reclined across from her.

"This place is unbelievable!" Flavia gushed. "I've never seen anything more beautiful!"

"I have seen only one," Rex replied, and Flavia felt her heart skip.

At that moment, the shopkeeper approached. "Welcome, guests," the old fellow said warmly. "Miss Flavia, I must inform you, this is a special arrangement by Rex, so you'll have to excuse me if I don't know the proper method of serving food. Yet my wife is a good cook, so I'm sure you'll be pleased tonight. I will bring it out shortly."

"You planned all this yourself?" Flavia asked when the owner had stepped away.

Rex nodded. "I was just going to buy some flowers, but then he took me back here and I got the idea for a meal. I thought, *Why not?* So I asked to rent the space. He was happy to oblige."

"You're sweet to me," Flavia whispered. She stared at the white rose, trying to comprehend Rex's unceasing affection and care for her.

"Here's something else that's sweet. A little present I picked up."

"Oh! What is it?" Flavia received the leather-wrapped package that Rex handed across the table. After untying the strings, she folded back the flaps and found two things inside. One was a small box of candy: delicate pink rose petals, dried and honeyed to increase their sweetness. Next to the candy was an ivory hairpin. It was carved to depict a lioness with proud, dignified eyes. Flavia removed the pin from its box and gazed at it in her palm.

"I think of you like that," Rex said.

Oh, God, let this man become a follower of you! Then let him become mine as well!

Flavia thanked Rex profusely for the gifts and immediately rearranged her hair with the new pin. By the time she had finished, the food was ready and the shop owner brought it out. The fare was simple yet delicious: a traditional Macedonian dish of salted butter beans and onions, served hot in an earthenware bowl. Slices of roast lamb accompanied the dish, and to drink, there was a sweet beverage made from apricots and raisins. At the end of the meal, the host served a local yogurt made from goat's milk, topped with a dollop of honey and berries. Flavia felt that she had eaten like a queen.

"Shall we head to the theater now, m'lady?" Rex asked gallantly.

"Indeed, we shall." The couple stood, and before they left, Flavia made sure to snatch the white rose from the table as a keepsake. She slipped it into her bun next to the ivory pin.

Stobi's theater was impressive for such a provincial town. It served a dual purpose. The orchestra pit was enclosed with a low wall so animal games and gladiator combat could be held there on occasion. However, plays were the main attraction on pleasant summer evenings, and tonight was such a night.

"I don't know much about the works of Lucian of Samosata," Flavia said as they found their seats on one of the risers. "He was a writer of satire, I believe, not a dramatist."

"They say this is an adaptation by a local playwright. It's about the philosopher Peregrinus. He committed noble suicide by throwing himself on a fire at the Olympic Games. It happened long ago, during the reign of Marcus Aurelius."

"I guess we'll see what he's all about. The actors are coming out now."

Seated beside Rex, Flavia followed the story of Peregrinus, who immediately embarked on a series of terrible crimes. Not only did he commit adultery with a woman, he then procured a young boy for sexual favors by bribing the parents, and he even murdered his own father. The jokes were bawdy and crude. Though Flavia tried to laugh along with Rex, she found herself growing increasingly troubled. Even Rex began to squirm, sensing Flavia's discomfort. And then the play turned blasphemous.

"I know what I shall do!" declared Peregrinus from the stage, supposedly sojourning in Palestine. "I shall join the sect of the foolish Christians who worship a crucified liar!"

What came next was a terrible mockery of the Christian faith. The martyrs were portrayed as deluded idiots who met a meaningless death like Jesus himself, who was a charlatan and a fool. Then the common believers were made out to be gullible buffoons, duped by Peregrinus's slick words into giving him high office in the church. Even after they learned about his crimes, they did not demote him but honored him as a god.

"What easy money!" Peregrinus exulted. "Any trickster can get rich among these Christians by spouting nonsense and taking up a collection!"

"I can't stand this," Flavia whispered to Rex. "It's insulting to my faith."

"Yes, but that's what satire does. It mocks things to make a point. Could you try to see it as humor?"

Flavia stood. "Blasphemy isn't humorous to me," she declared, then slipped down the row past the other raucous onlookers.

Holding back tears, Flavia found a quiet place beneath the theater's risers and tried to collect her thoughts. She pulled her silk mantle over her head like a hood, seeking privacy and solace in the quiet place. *Why did I even buy this wrap?* she wondered. *It's just part of an empty fantasy! Dreams and hopes and girlish whims, all with no basis in truth.*

"Want a sweet roll, lady?" cried a street urchin with a few buns for sale from his cart. Unfortunately, the rolls were smashed by careless fingers and looked like blobby lumps of dough.

"No, thank you."

"Come on, lady! Honey and raisins. Two for a nummus!"

"I'm not hungry."

"They're still warm!" the boy insisted. "Don't miss out!"

"No! I don't have any money," Flavia snapped, then turned toward the wall so the boy would leave her alone. A tear rolled down her cheek as she realized how far she really was from Rex. Strong emotions swirled inside her as she fought to reconcile her dreamy thoughts with actual reality. Drawing the hood even further around her cheeks, she rested her forehead against the wall, wishing earnestly she could disappear.

A hand squeezed her shoulder. Flavia whirled, inhaling sharply at the unexpected touch. At first, she feared she would be accosted—then immediately saw it was Rex.

"Have a roll, Flavia," he said, offering her one of the misshapen buns. His face had a gentle expression. "Go on. Take it. I want you to."

"How come?"

"Because even though it's imperfect, at least it's sweet."

Flavia sighed and accepted the treat from Rex's hand. *I can live with that for now*, she thought, then smiled at her beloved and took a bite of the roll.

The entire journey to Sirmium ended up taking three weeks, including a few final days on a riverboat. *Not bad timing*, Rex thought. *We're here ahead of Constantine, and that's what matters.*

He sat on a stone bench in the hot room of a public bath, dripping with sweat as he enjoyed the intense heat against his skin. Stephen sat beside him, equally sweaty, and apparently just as content with it as Rex. The two men were alone in the caldarium.

"Have you found everyone here to be as obsessed with war as I have?" Rex asked his friend.

"Absolutely! The whole city is thick with fear. War is coming, and the people know it. It's only a matter of when."

"Many of them know about Senecio's failure with the assassination too."

"Yes, it seems to be common knowledge. He returned here a few days ago, but the rumors had arrived ahead of him. He's disgraced before Licinius. And Constantine is insane with rage. He executed Senecio's brother. Now he wants Senecio too."

Rex wiped a salty droplet out of his eyes. "Nobody likes him. They say he's ugly. Looks like a monkey."

"I heard that too."

"Licinius should just hand him over. It might avert the war."

"He won't," Stephen said with a wave of his hand. "Licinius is too stubborn. War is on the way for sure. Everybody is terrified of hearing hoofbeats on the western horizon. It's not going to happen tomorrow—but it's definitely going to happen. A month or two, it looks like."

"Constantine will crush Licinius."

"Don't be so sure! I heard Licinius is recruiting a horde of Goths from Dacia. They could definitely swing the battle in his favor."

Rex let out a frustrated growl and slapped the stone bench of the spa. "So the emperor is coming here, and he needs troops, and I'd be happy to serve him. But I can't! I'm an escaped mutineer whom he sentenced to row in the navy forever. You might find this hard to believe, Brother Priest, but I used to be his favorite bodyguard! Now I have to hide so he doesn't get rid of me for good."

"How did you fall so far, Rex?"

"It's a long story."

"I'm still enjoying the heat. Tell me."

Rex fiddled with the Christian amulet at his neck, the only thing he was wearing on his body. Finally, he decided to tell Stephen the story—or part of it, anyway. He described how, ten years ago, he was just a rowdy boy of twelve in Britannia when Constantine was acclaimed as Augustus of the West by the Victorious Sixth Legion and the Alemannic mercenaries who served with them. Unfortunately, Rex got into a schoolyard brawl the same day, and he ended up killing a centurion's son. Hauled before the new emperor for justice, Rex feared for his life. As a last resort, he challenged Constantine to a duel. Impressed by his youthful audacity, Constantine sent him to military school to become a speculator. Rex excelled, and before long, he found himself a guardsman in the imperial retinue.

"So what caused the big downfall?"

Rex shrugged. "I put Flavia before all else," he said. "She was constantly threatened by the Praetorian prefect in Rome. One time, he even threw her to the wild beasts, but I saved her. An evil man, he was. Then a war started. I wounded him in battle, but he got away. At the same moment, Constantine fell into mortal danger on the field. Faced with a choice, I decided to . . ." Rex's voice trailed off as he discovered he didn't want to speak about his actions that day.

"You decided to pursue Flavia's enemy instead of defending your lord."

Rex nodded. "I caught him and thrust my sword into his throat. Only then did I know she'd be safe."

"But Constantine considered leaving his side in the heat of battle to be treason."

"Yes, and maybe it was," Rex acknowledged. "But I'd do it again."

The two men fell silent for a long time. At last, Stephen spoke up. "I know how you could get back into Constantine's good graces."

Rex sat up straight at this. "How?"

"Licinius is hiring some Goths, right? They're good fighters. What if you brought a barbarian army as well? You're Alemannic. Why couldn't you go to Germania and recruit a bunch of them? Those mercenaries who served Constantine in Britannia are only ten years older now. Many would still have a lot of fight left in them. Maybe they'd enjoy a chance to come to the aid of their old master again. You could convince them, I imagine."

Especially since I'm the son of their king, Rex mused, though he had no intention of revealing that fact right now. Yet Stephen's idea was exciting, and Rex thought it actually might work. A waiting platoon of loyal, battle-tested Alemanni would certainly be a welcome surprise when Constantine arrived at Sirmium. Then the emperor might not only forgive Rex for his flight in battle but also be favorably disposed to Ossius's mission from the Roman bishop. It would be a double victory—if only Rex could convince the Alemanni to rise up for war.

Ha! Since when has it been a problem to get the Germani to fight?

Rex gave Stephen a slap on the shoulder. "That's a good idea, Brother Priest. I'm going to make some inquiries."

That evening, Rex made sure he was seated in a tavern where good Germanic beer was served. He listened intently to the various accents he overheard, since not all German was spoken the same way. Sometimes the dialects differed so much, they weren't even mutually intelligible. Rex had downed three foamy mugs before he finally caught the distinctive sound of an Alemannic accent in a man's voice. The fellow was a seasoned warrior of about forty, with leathery skin and a huge mustache that draped on either side of his mouth to below his chin. He was laughing heartily with the stranger he had just met at the bar. Rex liked his demeanor immediately. As soon as the stranger left, Rex approached him.

"This stuff's not bad," he said in Alemannic German, lifting his mug to the man, "but there's nothing like beer made from a cold stream of the Moenus valley."

"The Moenus! Bruder, it's been too long since I've seen that mighty river. You from the homeland?"

"Aye, grew up along the Rhenus. Spent most of my life on the Roman side of the lines."

"Soldier father, eh?"

Rex nodded but didn't linger on that subject. He extended his hand. "My Latin name is Rex, but I was born Brandulf. What about you?"

"Gundomar," the mustached man replied as he clasped Rex's hand in greeting.

"What brings you to Sirmium?"

"Ach! A desperate quest! My lord the king was overthrown by a rebel and his band of warriors. Now my lord is in exile, and this pretender—Aoric, his name is—has taken over. We heard Constantine was coming this way. So I was sent to petition him to restore the rightful king."

The rightful king . . . overthrown?

Rex's heart was beating fast now. His own father had been the king of a prominent Alemannic tribe, which made Rex a prince, even though his mother was only an innkeeper beloved by the king, not his formal queen. The Latin name "Rex" had been given to him in military school when he bragged about his royal lineage. A decade had passed since little Brandulf Rex had seen his father. Now the adult Rex wasn't even sure he was still alive.

Tentatively, he set down his mug and wiped foam from his beard. Fiddling with a piney knot on the table, he asked in a casual voice, "So, what's your king's name?"

"He is the great Chrocus, famous throughout the land. Have you heard of him?"

My father lives!

As a trained speculator, Rex knew how to keep a straight face and adopt a fake persona while on a spying mission. Yet it took all his skill to conceal the turbulent emotions that welled up inside him. "Of course I've heard of him," he said evenly. "Chrocus the Great of the Alemanni. A mighty warrior."

"Not anymore. He's dejected by his defeat and hiding in exile."

And then in a flash, Rex knew exactly what he was going to do. He often found his life was like that: the pieces would suddenly fall into place, opening a clear and obvious path ahead. Rex would go to Germania and rally his father's men to serve Constantine again. Gundomar would help him. Upon returning to Sirmium, Rex and the band of Alemannic warriors would fight bravely against Licinius. A victory in battle—if it could be attained—would favorably dispose Constantine toward them. King Chrocus would be restored, Rex would be forgiven for his treason, and Pope Sylvester's petition would be granted to the emissaries. A lot would have to come together for all that to happen. But Rex's unshakable self-confidence made him believe he could get it done.

"Gundomar," he said, "I believe the gods have brought us together today."

"How so, Bruder?"

"It just so happens that I am a representative of the imperial government."

It was a big lie, but Rex was wearing his new gray tunic, so at least he looked the part of a well-to-do government functionary. And he had found that boldness was the most essential part of convincing someone of a false identity. When you tried to scale back and make something more believable, people grew skeptical. But when you spoke plainly and didn't hesitate to go big, people naturally wanted to believe you.

"I've been sent here by Emperor Constantine with the power of troop recruitment," Rex went on. "I had hoped to get the Goths first, but Licinius has already sewn them up. Doesn't matter, though. I'd rather have Alemannic warriors any day—they're twice as good as the Goths."

"Three times!" Gundomar boasted.

"Indeed! So that's why I need your help. With a good riverboat, we can be in Germania in—what? Two weeks?"

"Ten days, if you use the imperial system. They change row teams at each station. I used it to get here. Swift rowers, those oarsmen."

"I have both the permission and the funds to use the system," Rex said. "How soon could you leave?"

"Nothing's keeping me here except waiting for Constantine. But now the word is, he's a month or two away. I'd rather meet him with a band of faithful warriors than empty-handed! Let's go get some fighters and come back."

"So then . . . shall we meet at the riverfront at dawn tomorrow?"

"Aye! I'll be there!" Gundomar grabbed his mug and raised it. "And now a toast, Bruder!"

"To what?" Rex asked, lifting his own mug.

"To Chrocus, true King of the Alemanni!"

The words caught Rex by surprise. And once again, they caused an upwelling of powerful emotions. Yet he covered it like a professional, smiling broadly at his new friend.

"To mighty King Chrocus," Rex said, clinking mugs with Gundomar. "After a long absence, may we see him soon."

———❧———

The Aegyptian Asp slithered into Sirmium under cover of darkness. The moon was merely a crescent, but it was enough to see by. He found lodging in a cheap inn near the riverfront, knowing he would have business there the next day. Very important business. Hopefully, blood would not have to be shed. But he was prepared for that if necessary.

In the morning, the Asp took up his staff and exited the city gate to the docks along the Savus River, a tributary of the Danubius. He knew exactly the prey he was looking for: not the top men who ran the imperial travel system, nor the slaves who were scared of a beating if they did something wrong, but a bureaucratic underling who was weak-minded and disgruntled yet knew all that was going on at Sirmium's busy docks.

The right man was easy to spot by his messy uniform and slovenly appearance. He was one of the thousands of underpaid worker bees in the great imperial hive. Such men actually did more work than the bosses. They knew it and resented it. They could usually be bought for a price. Or be intimidated by threats. Or both.

From the shadows of an awning, the Aegyptian Asp observed the man he had selected. The fellow was portly and had the veiny, red nose of someone who drank too much. The Asp watched him bustle around the main pier, shouting at people to get out of his way. Finally, someone cursed him by his name: Dignus. That was just what the Asp needed.

"I have a business deal for you," the Asp said to Dignus after approaching him outside the riverport office. The building was too run-down to be the headquarters. It was obviously just a minor outpost near the waterfront. From the ink on the man's fingers, the Aegyptian Asp took the man for a clerk. No doubt he was skimming the money box and adjusting the books. Such men always did.

"I got no business with you, stranger," Dignus replied. "If you want to hire a government boat, show me the tablets. Otherwise, it's the merchant system for you. They can get you where you want to go, just a lot slower. Show me the permissions or run along!"

Such bluster. But the man is weak. Time to strike.

"I've been watching you for a long time, Dignus," the Asp intoned.

At this, the man's eyes narrowed. "What are you talking about?"

"I know all about your ledger books. And I mean everything." The Asp leaned forward menacingly. He knew the snake tattoo on his face was offputting, to say the least. Dignus stepped back, and in that moment, the Asp realized he had snared his prey.

"Ledgers? Wh-what ledgers?"

"Just step inside, Dignus, and perhaps we can talk about a deal."

"How do you . . . how do you know me?"

"I know everything about you," the Asp repeated. "Let's go into the office, where people can't see you. Enough is suspected about you already."

Dignus's eyes were wide as he hurried into the shabby office. The Asp didn't waste time with pleasantries. "You have two choices here. One, you tell me what I want to know, and I'll even pay you for it. Then I'll disappear forever. Or two, if you refuse, I go straight to your boss."

"About what? I ain't done nothing wrong!"

A ledger book was on a nearby desk, so the Asp wandered over to it before Dignus could stop him. Removing a folded sheet of papyrus from his sleeve—blank on the inside, but that did not matter—he held it up. "Shall we compare your records to the accurate ones I've got here, my friend?"

Now Dignus's face turned pale. "Let's do a deal," he whispered.

"A wise choice indeed. Here is my request. I seek information about a traveler who recently arrived in Sirmium. Tell me everything, and I shall pay you well. Then you'll never have to see me again."

"Who was it? I will reveal all that I know."

"A famous bishop, a Spaniard with a mane of silver hair. No doubt he was traveling with some kind of retinue."

"Yes! I remember him! I registered him only two days ago! The man had the right documents from the palace in Thessalonica. Everything had already been paid for. I wrote it down myself."

"Who was traveling with him?" the Asp demanded with more urgency than he intended. He was very curious about this, for it would determine his tactical approach. So far, his spying had only discovered the bishop's journey to Sirmium. But since the bishop himself could not be harmed, it was his retinue that had to be destroyed to bring Rome's mission to failure. The Asp needed the facts to know how to proceed.

"It was a strange crew! I remember there was an Aethiops girl. You rarely see skin so dark as that around here. And a young Christian priest. And a Roman matron, with a girl that seemed to be her daughter."

Aha! So they escaped the brothels! Apparently, my enemies are more adept than I first believed. Or perhaps they were aided? It is no easy thing to thwart the pimps of Corinthus.

Hiding his surprise, the Asp asked, "Were there any others in the group?"

"I have named five, but I remember there was one more."

"One more?"

"Yes, but I can't remember that one."

"You have a weak memory, Dignus. Perhaps the imperial torturers will help you recall the details of your fraud and embezzlement?"

"No!" he bawled. "Just wait! Let me look it up!" Dignus hurried to another ledger and flipped through it. "Yes, here it is! A Germanic warrior by the name of Rex."

"So a party of six arrived in Sirmium?"

"No more and no less, sir. I'm sure of it. But some of them just departed on another riverboat. Not all of them, though."

"Which ones left?"

"Four of them set out with someone new, another barbarian with a droopy mustache. It was Rex, and the two girls, and the young priest."

"Not the bishop, nor the distinguished matron?"

"No, sir. They didn't depart with the others. Only the four young folks went away, plus the older barbarian."

"And where do your records say that these people were headed?"

"All the way to the end of the navigable Danubius, sir. To Germania. The homeland of the fellow with the mustache."

"He was Germanic too?"

"I believe so, yes."

"You *believe* so, or you *know*?"

"I know it, because I remember when he came down from Alemannia about a week ago."

"Do not say *believe* when you actually know something to be true."

"My mistake, sir. I'm sorry, sir. It won't happen again."

"And what was the purpose of their trip to Alemannia?"

"Well, they didn't say, but from what I overheard, I guessed it was to recruit troops. Every barbarian with a sword knows there's money to be made here when Constantine shows up. One army or the other will hire them as mercenaries."

181

Mercenaries! Nothing is more precious to an emperor at war. He who provides them is certain to gain imperial favor and rewards. This development has to be prevented at all costs. Pope Sylvester's lackeys cannot be allowed to win Constantine's generous gratitude.

The dire news made the Aegyptian Asp fall silent, which seemed to make Dignus even more nervous than when he was being interrogated. "Are we finished?" he finally asked in a shaky voice. His brow was very sweaty now.

"We are. Let us settle up." The Asp reached into his coin purse and brought out some silver. "I wish to purchase passage to Germania, to the same destination as my friends."

"Do you . . . do you have the permission documents?"

"I do not. Does that matter?"

"Not in the least," Dignus mumbled. "I'll give you some."

The Aegyptian Asp paid him for the transit, then added a few coins for the clerk's "helpful assistance."

"Thank you, sir. Thank you very much," Dignus said as he took the coins in his greedy fist. The relief in his voice was obvious.

"It has truly been a pleasure doing business with you," replied the man with the snake tattoo.

6

Lake Brigantium was, Flavia decided, more like an inland sea than a mere lake. She gazed across its vast blue surface, so unlike the lakes she had known in arid Italy. Its water volume was huge by comparison. Beyond this, the hillsides seemed more lush, the mountains more snow-capped, the fields more fertile than the region around Rome. As it turned out, Germania was quite a beautiful place. Flavia was more than a little impressed with Rex's homeland.

"Does it look familiar to you?" she asked him as they rode side by side on horseback. A short overland journey from the river port on the Danubius was required to reach the Alemannic capital of Brigantium.

"I've been to this lake a few times, though I grew up north of here. We lived in several villages and forts along the Rhenus frontier, until my father took me on campaign to Britannia."

"How did a soldier get to take along a twelve-year-old boy?"

"Oh, it was common for officers to bring their wives and children. My mother was a second wife whom my father truly loved. She set up an inn at Eboracum. As far as I know, she's still there."

"And your father?"

"I don't know," Rex said and fell silent.

As the five riders rounded the southern edge of the lake and drew near to the citadel of Brigantium, Gundomar began to offer a lay of the land. He swept his hand in a wide arc. "This whole region is the Roman province of Raetia," he explained in fluent Latin. "Until about fifty years ago, the boundary with the barbarians was north quite a ways. It was a reinforced military line with many forts and watchtowers. But then the Alemanni broke through, and the Romans had to pull back their frontier. The Rhenus River runs into this lake and out the other side. That is essentially the new line. Romans on one side. Germani on the other."

"So Raetia belongs to the Alemanni now?" Stephen asked.

"The northern part of it does. The mountainous southern region is still Romanized. There's a mix of both people in Brigantium. It's a true border-land. The peace is fragile."

"Are the Alemanni considered invaders or provincials?"

Gundomar smiled at the complexity of Rex's question. "Both. It just depends on the day. And the mood of the chiefs. And the opportunity for plunder. And whether the Romans are paying good money for mercenaries. As you can see, the loyalties of our people can shift on a whim. Sometimes, we fight on behalf of Rome. Other times, we're barbarian invaders, looting our way into the Roman Empire."

"The emperors allow that?" Stephen asked with a look of surprise.

"Bruder, up here on the Rhenus frontier, the emperors don't always have a choice about what they allow. Welcome to life in the age of Constantine! It's not like the days of Julius Caesar, back before your Savior was born. The Romans were the aggressors then. Now the Germani are on the offensive."

"Tell me about Aoric," Rex said.

"He's a scoundrel. The problem is, he's a likable scoundrel. A lot of men follow him because he's so manly and brave. Yet he has a cruel streak. Ambition drives him. He cast out a respected king without a second thought. Then he slaughtered several of Chrocus's chiefs in cold blood. It was a bitter day. Many men had to flee. Those of us who love Chrocus want to see him restored to the throne."

Rex nodded. "He will be."

"Don't go saying that out loud, Brandulf Rex, or you'll find yourself in chains—or worse."

"I think I'll just go by my Latin name around here."

"Fine with me. My point is, we're in Aoric's land now, and Brigantium is his headquarters. It was a fine Roman town until it got plundered and ruined in the invasion. Now the Alemanni have rebuilt it and made it their capital. The Romans let us keep it as long as we don't push south. Constantine's army turned us back a couple of years ago when we gave it a try, and we've stayed put ever since. However, Aoric wants to start raiding into the empire again."

"But not Chrocus."

"Definitely not. He's still loyal to Constantine. He thinks the Alemanni should be a respected wing of the army, not a bunch of uncivilized marauders who loot farms and burn villages."

Flavia felt the weight of Gundomar's words. *That used to be Rex's view, too*, she realized, *until he was forced to give up the job he loved*. The magnitude of his loss made her sad. *Lord, help Rex find his way back to Constantine!*

"As we arrive in the city," Gundomar went on, "we need to think about appearances. Rex, I believe Aoric will receive you with hospitality since you come to us on the emperor's business. We can make up a full Latin name for you. Whether he will release any troops to go fight, I don't know. Stephen and Cassiopeia will seem to him like servants, so I suggest they play that role while you're here. But Flavia needs an explanation because she's clearly an aristocrat. Can she be your wife?"

Rex glanced at Flavia. When she saw him raise his eyebrows in inquiry, she quickly shook her head. "Probably not a good idea," she said. "Too complicated." *I definitely don't need to be playing that role. It's hard enough to hold back already!*

Fortunately, Rex came up with a better story. "Let's say she's a senator's daughter who wanted to see Germania. Her powerful father made me take her along."

"Very well," said Gundomar. "Aoric will accept that reasoning. That kind of thing has happened before. And look—there's his city on the horizon."

Brigantium was, like Gundomar had said, a fifty-year-old wreck that had been given a little recent attention by Alemannic builders, who weren't nearly as skilled as the Romans. The most ancient part of town, ringed by a defensive wall, sat on a bluff above the lake. After the initial city was founded, during the ensuing peaceful centuries, nice Roman villas were constructed outside the walls on terraces that stepped down to the water's edge. While some of them were still in good repair, others looked like they hadn't been inhabited since the Germanic takeover. The original walls of the old city were intact, but their breaches had been filled by stonemasons who didn't have the technology the Romans did. Their shoddy work created an ugly patchwork along the wall's length. Like an old warrior in his final years, Brigantium combined vestiges of former greatness with the prospect of imminent decay.

The traveling party passed through a necropolis and approached the main gate. Immediately, a band of warriors rode out to meet them. Since Gundomar was known to the guards, he did the talking. After explaining that he had brought high-ranking Roman visitors with him, he requested an audience with Aoric.

As the warriors conversed among themselves, Flavia had to marvel at the height and muscularity of the Alemanni. *No wonder these barbarians are such a threat to the empire. Every one of them is big, powerful, and aggressive!*

The men agreed to admit the visitors and ushered them into the city. Aoric had taken up residence in a large mansion that sat across from Brigantium's old forum. A doorman welcomed the travelers inside the house. Flavia noted that its architecture differed from Italian homes in one main way: less of it was open to the sky, no doubt due to the northerly climate. Yet it did have a feature common to all Roman houses: an atrium in which to greet guests. The spacious hall with a small skylight had been turned into Aoric's throne room. His retinue of guards lined both sides of a central pool, while he waited in royal dignity at the far end.

"I welcome you in the name of Wodan," Aoric boomed, rising from his chair with a toothy smile. He was a tall man, broad-shouldered and lean, with impeccable taste in clothing. A fur-lined cape of expensive fabric was around his shoulders. His thick hair was the auburn color of new bronze, and instead of bushy whiskers like his men, his beard was cropped close to his chiseled jawline. He spread his arms in a gesture of greeting, then bowed his head to show his heartfelt welcome. "Any friend of Rome is a friend of mine," he declared.

That's not what we heard about him before, Flavia thought. *But maybe his opinions have changed.*

"Hail, King Aoric," said Gundomar, speaking a little more icily than he probably should have. "I hereby introduce to you Publius Claudius Rex, a legate of Emperor Constantine." The made-up names were so common that they said nothing about Rex's actual family lineage. Many Germanic families had adopted names like that over the years in a desire to Latinize. The aura of imperial prestige was always attractive to the barbarians.

Aoric looked directly at Rex. "May I call you by your cognomen, sir?" he inquired. When Rex agreed, he continued, "Then I greet you with genuine warmth, Legate Rex, and I ask what brings you to my realm."

Rex stepped forward with his back straight and his head held high. Flavia could see that he was establishing his equality with the king, though without showing any disrespect.

"The details of my petition need to be worked out," Rex said, "but I will tell you in plain language the reason for my visit. I come to you on behalf of the world's greatest ruler—the Augustus of the West, His Glorious Majesty, Emperor Flavius Valerius Aurelius Constantine. As you may have heard, Constantine has been betrayed by his own kin. The treacherous Licinius, no longer worthy to be called Augustus of the East, has made an attempt on his life. War looms between them. As Constantine was once served by faithful Alemannic auxiliaries, so he wishes to be again. My mission is to hire four thousand of your soldiers for the true emperor's field army."

Aoric folded his arms across his broad chest, seeming neither angry nor pleased, but only thoughtful. "It is a matter for prudent consideration." Suddenly a bright smile widened in his russet beard, and he jabbed his finger into the air in a jubilant way. "We must feast tonight and talk it over!" He glanced around the hall at his retinue. "My men, what say you? Shall we feast?"

"Hear, hear!" they cried, pounding the butts of their spears against the mosaic floor.

"A feast indeed!" the king went on. "Of venison steak and pork sausage and rye bread and hot cheese—and of course, more thick beer than any man ever ought to drink!" The announcement brought further cheers from the guards.

But then Aoric's face went from exuberant to debonair. "And yet, alas, my manners have escaped me," he purred as his eyes shifted to Flavia. "I have spoken of a feast without being properly introduced to the lovely lady in our midst."

Rex quickly intervened. "This is Lady Junia Flavia, a senator's daughter from Rome. Her family is of very high rank, going back to ancient times. She was intrigued by the land of Germania, so she requested a visit. Her father allowed it, but only in the safety of my company."

"Your betrothed?"

"No."

"Your consort?"

"Not that either."

"Then what, Legate Rex?"

Flavia shifted her feet. *What will he say?*

"A dear friend, a worthy woman, very close to my heart."

"In that case," Aoric said, taking another step forward, "I shall enjoy getting to know such a worthy woman. Perhaps my heart will become close to hers as well."

"It is always proper to honor a king in his realm," Flavia said with a dignified bow. "So I thank you for your greeting."

Gundomar spoke up again. "We have traveled far, Lord Aoric. Might your guests now take some rest until it is time for the banquet?"

The king agreed, ordering one of his men to show the travelers to their rooms. Stephen was assigned to wait upon Rex, while Cassi was lodged with Flavia as her maidservant. Apparently, the ruse about their identities had worked in every way. Now the only question was, Would Aoric part with any troops?

While Flavia was resting on her couch in her quarters, Cassi poured water from a pitcher into a bowl and set it on the floor of the quiet bedroom. "How you keep up so many lies?" she asked in her broken Latin. "It is like mimes in the circus." She smiled as she made a frantic juggling motion with her hands. "So many balls!"

"I thought the same when Rex told me his plans to come here. But he's a speculator, so he knows how to deceive the enemy. I was skeptical at first, yet I understood his strategy. And my fate is bound to his. So I had to come."

Cassi knelt beside the bowl of water. "My eye sees he is bound to you too." Gesturing to a nearby stool, she said, "Come, now. Come sit and be washed."

"No, Cassi! You aren't really my servant! You don't have to wash my feet."

Again, the tenderhearted Aethiops girl pointed to the stool. "Sit here, my sister, and receive. Rex is not the only one who loves you."

Flavia obliged, and when the foot washing was finished, the two girls relaxed in the room for the afternoon. The sun was low in the sky when they finally heard a knock at the door—a servant summoning them to the banquet.

The mansion's dining room wasn't set up like an Italian one would have been. Instead of the traditional Roman couches on which to recline, the northern barbarians liked to sit upright to eat. A long wooden table was in the center of the room, with benches lining either side, while a great chair for Aoric was at the head. He stationed Rex on his right and Flavia on his left. Gundomar was nearby too. And despite being viewed as servants, Stephen and Cassi were also invited to the table since they were guests from a faraway land. Other important figures from Aoric's retinue were seated there as well.

As the banquet progressed, the mood in the room grew more relaxed and convivial. The food was rich, the beer flowed freely, and because the Rhenus valley had recently started growing grapes, there was even a crisp, aromatic white wine available to the diners. As stomachs were filled and tongues were loosened with drink, the conversation grew more intense. Soon Aoric began to opine on feminine beauty.

"The allure of Germanic women is of a certain sort," he announced. "They tend to have stout frames. Long-limbed and buxom. And who doesn't like a long leg? But Italian women are different. More truly feminine. Many of our women look like they could go out to war. In fact, some do! But I prefer the curvy beauty of Italian women—women like you, Flavia. You are more my type. Petite and slender and shapely, just like a woman should be."

Before she could reply, Rex spoke up. "That is because Lady Junia comes from a warmer climate. Consider this. We Germani have always had to fight against the elements. Only the big and strong survive to pass their traits on to their children. Our harsh winters weed out the weak before they can bear young. But in Italy, life is much easier. Therefore, the Romans are a smaller and less robust people, generally speaking." Deftly changing the subject, Rex asked, "Have you ever been to the south, Master Aoric? The warm sun there is truly a pleasure."

"Only as far as the Alps, never over them. Perhaps I should go sometime soon?"

"If you have good reason."

"I could think of some profitable ones, Legate Rex."

"I am sure you would be welcomed, if your purposes were friendly."

The men bantered a little more, and the lively conversation continued around the table until the banquet came to an end. Most of the diners stumbled off to their homes, though some fell asleep on furs scattered upon the dining room floor. After Aoric retired with a gracious farewell, Rex escorted Flavia to her room. Feeling a little heady from the wine, she leaned on his arm.

"Be cautious about Aoric," he warned as they arrived at her door.

"I will, Rex. I can see his interest in me. Yet I believe I could use it to turn him our way. There's a big festival coming up for his god, Wodan. If he trusts me by then, and he's in a good mood, he might grant our request for soldiers."

"I'd prefer if you didn't do that."

"Oh, so you're the only one who can go undercover as a spy?" she teased. "Guess what Aoric told me when you stepped out."

"Tell me."

"He suspects many of his warriors still favor Chrocus, and he's worried about it."

Rex remained silent for a long time. Finally, he said, "I need to find that exiled king. It was he who served Constantine. He is likely to have many loyal soldiers to send to the war."

"Does Gundomar know where he is?"

"Yes, I believe so. But he refuses to tell me. Doesn't fully trust me yet. I'll have to figure it out on my own. I can do it, though. I'm trained for such things."

"Go find him, Rex. I'll stay here and see if I can soften up King Aoric."

Rex bent close so he could whisper in her ear. "Don't call him king," he said softly, then lightly kissed Flavia's cheek and bid her good night.

———✻———

The next morning, after a breakfast of bread and beer, Rex told his friends he was going to do some spying around Brigantium. It was a decent little town, though its recent lack of upkeep had taken a toll. The pavement was cracked and uneven, the sewers were backed up, and half the shops were now abandoned. Rex's biggest problem, however, was that everywhere he turned, he seemed to run into Aoric's warriors. Rex could tell they were watching him closely.

He decided on a change of strategy. Returning to the mansion on the main square, he changed into his plain woolen tunic that no one had yet seen him in. Then, after slipping out through the slaves' door, Rex used some alleys and narrow lanes to dodge the observant eyes of his watchers. When he was certain he hadn't been followed, he proceeded to the lakefront and rented a sailboat. He would have to get out from under his enemy's gaze if he wanted to learn anything about his father.

The next village up the coast was called Lucky Tree. Rex reached it in the late afternoon and spent an hour dozing under the shade of a chestnut tree—though whether it was the original lucky one, he didn't know.

Around sunset, the local fishermen and vegetable farmers began to come into town for a beer. A single tavern called the Grey Heron served the thirsty villagers. Rex sat in a corner with his chair tipped back against the wall. Finally, he approached some congenial old-timers playing knucklebones for small bronze coins. The men were absorbed in their game, so Rex stood over them and watched. When one man finally had to leave, Rex offered to take his place, and the others agreed.

After playing the game of chance for a while—winning some nummi and losing some too—Rex struck up a conversation about local weather. From there he progressed to business prospects, then taxation, then politics. "I've been away for many years," he said. "Aoric is a fairly new king, right?"

"Aye," said a straggly haired geezer with a hunched back.

Rex shook the cup as he prepared to throw the bones. "How long?"

"Less than a year."

"What happened to the old king?" Rex asked nonchalantly. "Chrocus was his name, if I recall. Did they kill him off?"

Now the men fell strangely silent. One of them said, "Just make your throw, stranger."

After tossing the sheep bones on the table, Rex counted up the score and added it to his tally. It was a decent roll, so he scooped a few more nummi into his pile. "It's hard to kill old warrior kings like that," he said, as if making a general observation while he stacked his coins.

"I used to fight for him," said the hunchbacked geezer. "You can't kill Chrocus without shedding some blood yourself. But he's not a god. He can be wounded."

"Where is he now?"

Again, a stony silence descended on the group. "That's the sort of thing you don't ask out here in the front room," said another wheezy fellow with tufts of hair in his ears.

Rex smiled good-naturedly. "Sorry, friends! I didn't know there was a back room where people can freely talk politics."

"If there were such a room, would you want to enter it?" asked the hunchbacked veteran.

"I might."

"How come?"

Rex weighed his answer carefully. He knew he was onto something here, yet he didn't want to appear overeager. "I'm in Germania hiring soldiers for a distant army," he said at last. "No threat to Aoric. Just giving work to good men with swords for hire, so all the Alemanni can prosper. Everybody wins."

The veteran cocked an eyebrow at Rex. "So you'd meet with Chrocus if you could?"

"If that were legal, yes." *Or even if it's not. But let's see where that answer takes me.*

"Wait here." The man rose and limped away to the back room.

A short time later he returned to the table and the game resumed. The conversation was just small talk until the man who had gone to the back muttered, "Meet me at the dock when the moon rises above the hill."

"I'll be there," Rex said.

Eventually, the old-timers grew tired and decided to call it a night. They thanked Rex for playing and went their separate ways. After paying for his beers, Rex wandered outside for some fresh air. When the moon began to show its face above a distant rise, he started toward the dock. The hunchbacked veteran was standing there alone, gazing across the water.

SMASH! Something hard clobbered Rex across the back of his head, and he tumbled forward. Yet even as he fell, instinct and training both told him to tuck his shoulder and roll as he hit the ground, increasing his distance from whoever had struck him. Dizziness and pain fogged his mind, but one thing was clear: it was fight now or fall into the hands of enemies.

He had just scrambled to his feet when five or six men surrounded him and began to grapple. Rex's hand-to-hand combat skills were deeply ingrained, so without thinking, he was able to throw one man into the lake and sweep the legs out from another before he was overwhelmed. There were too many assailants to resist, and all were big, strong men. They wrestled Rex to his knees with his face above the water, holding him there in a fierce grip. A strong hand grabbed a fistful of his hair at the back of his neck, then yanked his head back.

"Loyal to Chrocus, are ya?" snarled an attacker who seemed to be the leader. He kicked Rex in the jaw, sending bright stars swirling around his brain. Rex spat a wad of bloody saliva into the lake but did not respond.

"You tryin' to raise a rebellion against the king?" the same man demanded.

Rex knew he shouldn't speak, but he couldn't help himself. "Aoric isn't my king," he declared.

"How dare you!" shouted the leader. "Dunk him, boys!"

Rex managed to grab half a breath before his head was forced underwater. He struggled and thrashed, but the men's hold on him was too strong. He turned his head right and left but couldn't lift his face from the turbulent water. Terror swept over him as the urge to breathe intensified. These men were going to drown him in the knee-deep water of a muddy lake. It would all end here—his dreams, his goals, his ambitions. He would never see Flavia again . . .

I wanted to make you mine! I should have! Jesus, give me another chance!

The pain in Rex's lungs was like a searing fire now. The sound of cruel laughter began to fade. Somewhere, far off in the distance, a flute began to play. Gentle voices spoke to him. *If I just inhale, the pain will end . . .*

The hand gripping Rex's hair yanked his head from the water. He immediately gasped out the old breath and sucked in new air. The desperate, high-pitched sound of it was like a woman's shriek, but Rex didn't care. His lungs heaved as he gulped air, sputtered, then gulped once more.

The leader shoved Rex onto the shore with his boot, tumbling him onto his back in the mud. "You'll tell us what you're up to when you start losing your fingers one by one!"

"Let's do it now!" another voice suggested. "My knife's sharp!"

"No! Tie him up and put him in the boat. And you, Lothair! Get on your horse and ride to Aoric. Find out what he wants us to do with this guy. The rest of you, get in the boat now and let's shove off."

Rex lay unresponsive in the mud as the men bound his hands in front of him. Exhaustion had taken hold of him now that the terror of imminent death had passed. He began to shake all over.

Thank you, Jesus, he prayed as the ropes were pulled taut around his wrists. *Thank you for second chances.*

The distant sound of a cock's crow wakened Lady Sabina Sophronia at first light. The rooster probably lived on some farm outside the walls, yet it was close enough to be heard because the house church where she was staying was near the edge of town. It abutted the racetrack in the southeast corner of Sirmium—not because the bishop liked chariot racing but because he often had business with the government, and the imperial palace adjoined the track. The former mansion was now a thriving church in a convenient location. If that meant putting up with some early awakenings, so be it. Good Christians didn't need to lie abed anyway.

Sophronia sat up and put her feet on the floor of her tiny bedroom. This wing of the house was otherwise unoccupied, for the full-time residents who lived here were all men, and the bishop of Sirmium did not want the sexes to mingle at night. The men were ascetic brothers who called themselves monks, from a Greek word meaning "alone" or "solitary." It was a new and respected vocation in the church.

The only other guest in the house was Bishop Ossius, and he, too, was forbidden to lodge near Sophronia. But Ossius didn't mind. He was among the theologians who were strict about such matters, though others allowed for cohabitation as long as celibacy was maintained. While those Christians considered their arrangement a "spiritual marriage," Ossius frowned on the practice because of its ongoing sexual temptation.

Before doing anything else, Sophronia began her day in prayer. Standing at her little window, she lifted her face to the brightening sky. With earnest words to the Lord, she interceded for Flavia, who was so far away in Germania on her mission with Rex. Although such a journey had seemed too arduous for Sophronia and Ossius after all they had already endured, the two of them had covenanted to pray for Flavia and Rex and their friends like spiritual parents.

"Bring them back soon, mighty God," Sophronia whispered to the sky with her palms upraised. "And please, O gracious Lord, keep my girl safe from all harm."

After her prayers, Sophronia washed her face and fixed her hair while staring into a little hand mirror. As a Christian woman, she tried not to put too much emphasis on appearance. Yet styling her hair in a dignified way seemed appropriate, and so did the application of a little makeup to her cheeks, eyes, and lips. Not a lot, but enough to be respectable. After all, she would be turning forty in a few weeks. She didn't want Bishop Ossius to think she had become slovenly in her middle age.

Ossius was in the rear garden of the church when Sophronia finally emerged. Often, the bishop of Sirmium joined him there for theological discussions, but today he was absent. Ossius was reading a book alone. From the sound of his reading, Sophronia discerned it was *Against Heresies* by Irenaeus of Lugdunum.

"A fine refutation of the Gnostics," Sophronia said brightly as she entered the garden. A songbird chirped at her from the branch of a potted tree, fluffing its feathers at such an intrusion yet content to remain on its perch.

"You know it?"

"Certainly Irenaeus is highly respected in Rome. I was tutored in basic theology by the priest of the church that used to meet in my house. I asked that he use *Against Heresies* as a text."

Ossius brushed a stray lock of hair from his brow, sweeping it into the silver mane that crowned his head. "Why that text, Sophronia?"

"Because when you study the things you don't believe, it clarifies the things that you do."

"Well said! A keen insight indeed." Setting down his book, the bishop smiled. "A female theologian is a rare thing, in my experience."

"Then consider yourself to have entered a wider world, Bishop Ossius."

The saucy rejoinder made the Spaniard chuckle. Sophronia understood that few women would dare speak to him like that. Yet few women had ever traveled with him for two months straight. There was something about traveling together that helped one get to know a person—their strengths as well as their flaws. Sophronia had settled into a warm, enjoyable friendship with the dashing and intelligent bishop.

Ossius rose to his feet, a mischievous look on his face. "Do you know what happens when monks run a house instead of a lady?"

"I could think of many things. For one, it would not smell as nice."

"In truth!" cried Ossius with a laugh. "And for another, they let the place run out of bread. However, there is a farm across the bridge whose ovens are near the road. They sell warm loaves every morning until the third hour. How would you like to take a stroll with me across the Savus and do a service for the brothers?"

"I can think of nothing I'd like more, my friend. Let me get my wrap and a basket, and I shall meet you in the atrium."

The pair left Sirmium's enclosing walls and followed a paved road to one of the three bridges that spanned the Savus. The farm villa's baker was at his ovens when they arrived, and his good white bread still steamed when Ossius sliced open a loaf.

"Do you have any oil?" he asked.

"Yes, but try it with this." The man offered a pale yellow substance in a bowl.

"What is it?"

"It's called butter. Lots of the Germani use it. Tastes great on bread."

"I want to try it," Sophronia said. She spread some of the creamy stuff onto her slice with a wooden spoon and bit into it. "Delicious!" she exclaimed.

Ossius good-naturedly slathered the butter on his breakfast as well, then bought a bowl of it from the baker. After feasting on the warm, buttery bread, the pair made their way back toward the bridge. Sophronia thought it was sweet that Ossius carried the basket of loaves for her. Glancing over at him, she noticed a little smear of butter on his clean-shaven chin.

"You, uh . . . you have a little something . . ." She touched her own chin in the same place.

Ossius wiped his jaw with his thumb. "Right here?"

"A little above."

He tried again. "Here?"

Taking a kerchief in hand, Sophronia dabbed the spot herself. "Got it," she said.

"Thank you, madam," Ossius replied playfully. He halted in the middle of the bridge, setting down the basket. "The current is swift today. It must have rained in the mountains."

"The Savus is hurrying to the Danubius. And the Danubius hurries to the Euxine Sea."

"If I had to guess, I'd imagine you more often consider from whence the river comes, not where it goes."

Sophronia sighed. "Yes, I do. My sweet Flavia is at the Danubian head-waters, up in Germania. She's probably getting into the kind of trouble that only God knows. It's always on my mind."

"Such is the way with children, I suppose."

"Yes, Bishop, it is. Thank you again for entering into prayer with me for those four children who have gone so far away. Like sons and daughters, they are! So young and inexperienced."

"And yet so capable too. All of them are wise for their age. And I have rarely met a man as resourceful as Rex. He does what needs to be done without a second thought."

Sophronia put her hand to her bosom. "I know. I have a scar from a dagger wound to prove it."

"That was quick thinking on his part. You would not be here right now if not for that deed."

"Truly! Ah, what can I say about Rex? He is a good man in so many ways. A complex man. Few people see how tenderhearted he really is behind his warrior nature."

"Flavia sees it, obviously. She is the recipient of his kindness quite often."

Sophronia glanced over at her friend. "You have noticed it too?"

"Of course. The bond between them crackles like lightning at times."

These words caused Sophronia to let out a heavy sigh. "Rex would make a very fine husband for her, except . . ."

"Except he is not in the catholic faith," Ossius finished.

"He might convert, though."

"Perhaps. However, I have seen few signs of it."

Sophronia had to nod her agreement. "Marriage is a strange thing. God invented it for Adam and Eve. Yet even theirs was harmed by sin. Becoming well-married is quite a difficult task."

"As you well know."

Yes. I am so much happier now than when I was married to that philandering Neratius! The realization was disconcerting to Sophronia. Although the fact was true, it wasn't something she wanted to admit to the respected bishop.

She changed the subject, raising a theological debate that she had never discussed with him. "Why do you take the position that clergy must be celibate?" she asked.

"Well, first, let me say, I acknowledge that this point is debated among Christians. Yet the apostle makes his views clear in his first letter to the Corinthians: an unmarried man is concerned solely about the Lord, but a married man must also be concerned for his wife. Such a man cannot give full attention to ministry. Paul says 'his interests are divided.' He writes that he offers this teaching for our own good, so that our attention may be single-minded. The pastors of the church should give their full devotion to the things of God. It is a blessing, not a burden."

"But we know Peter was married, since the gospel declares he had a mother-in-law. And does not Paul instruct Timothy that bishops and deacons should have one wife?"

Ossius glanced at Sophronia with an appraising eye. "Again, I commend your knowledge of scripture and theology! Yes, my friend, you are correct. To clarify these difficult matters, I called together a council of Spanish clergy about ten years ago. We held it at Illiberis. There we decided that if a pastor was already married when he entered the priesthood, he must abstain from further intercourse with his wife and certainly must not procreate. If unmarried, he should remain in that state, as *First Corinthians* says. The main thing is that a priest's ministry must not be divided. Saint Paul himself taught us this, by divine inspiration. Therefore, I must assume that both Peter and Paul adopted a celibate life when they began to serve the Lord."

"That is a very hard calling, yet many today have adopted it." Sophronia traced her finger along the bridge's railing, wanting to broach a related subject, yet unsure if she should. Finally, she took the plunge. "Why do you reject the concept of spiritual marriage? Could it not be a very holy thing?"

"How do you define spiritual marriage?"

"A man and a woman living under one roof in chaste love, treating each other as 'beloveds,' yet without sexual expression. A brother and sister in Christ serving the Lord in partnership and harmony, though not as husband and wife."

"Is that even possible?"

"In theory, it should be, if the word *beloved* means anything. The Greek is *agape*. A different kind of love than *erotic*. Scripture offers us *agape* as an attainable ideal. I know you believe that."

"I do. But even so, at Illiberis, we decided against such arrangements. I understand the holy intent. I also understand the convenience, for a woman is needed in any home, even a priest's home. Yet the temptation of this lifestyle is too great to bear after night has fallen. It is unwise, my friend."

"In all cases? No exceptions?" Sophronia was surprised to find her tone sadder than she intended it to be.

Ossius gripped the railing in both hands and stared down at the Savus's current for a long time. Finally, he said, "Yes, in all cases where there is cohabitation."

"But . . . do you believe . . . do you believe that a deeply spiritual love could exist apart from sharing a roof? A devoted love, true *agape* love, an abiding friendship grounded in the holiness of Christ? Do you think, Ossius, that such a thing could exist?"

Now Ossius fell silent for an even longer time than before. He continued to stare at the river. Sophronia could see his jaw clenching and unclenching as he gathered his thoughts.

Finally, he raised his eyes to her. Taking her hand in his, he pressed something into it. "I know for certain that it exists," he declared. "And it always will."

Yes, it always will.

"Come now, my friend," said the bishop as he picked up the basket. "Let us return to the city with the bread for the monks."

Sophronia swallowed the lump in her throat and began to follow Ossius back into the city. Only when she was sure he wasn't looking did she decide to examine what he had given her.

She glanced down. There, in her open palm, lay the gold finger ring he normally wore. On its face was an *alpha* and an *omega*.

The beginning and the end.

Eternity.

"I accept," she whispered to the bishop as they walked along. And though Ossius smiled slightly at this, he made no audible reply.

———

King Aoric didn't know the name of the priest of Wodan who was planning the big party. He was a puny little fellow who wouldn't have made much of a warrior. Probably he'd be dead already if he had tried to be a fighter. Men like that always went into the priesthood instead, and thus they gained power in a different way. The gods were nothing to trifle with—certainly not Wodan the Allfather. The planning for his festival tomorrow had to be just right. Fortunately, the priest seemed to know what he was doing.

"There will be even more lights by the time the celebrations start, sire," the priest said as he gestured to a huge tree called the Grand Old Oak. It stood on a forested hilltop not far from Brigantium, gazing out at the surrounding landscape with dignified indifference. A troop of agile boys had already festooned the branches with candle lanterns. Now that it was nighttime, the little flames were visible far up into the canopy as they flickered and danced among the leaves. Aoric thought the tree already looked great, so he could only imagine how splendid it would be tomorrow, on Wodan's Day.

"Nice work, my good man," said the king. "Now show me the firepit too."

The priest led him to a low stone enclosure with a sandy bottom. A huge stack of logs stood next to it, comprised mostly of applewood. Several large iron spits spanned the roasting pit, each ready to receive a wild boar.

"Where are the hogs now?" Aoric asked.

"Soaking in brine to keep them juicy."

Aoric's stomach rumbled at the mere thought of it: the crispy skin, the moist pork falling off the bone, the drippy sauce made from berries and honey and vinegar. All washed down with a hearty ale. *My first Wodan's Day as king! It's going to be a feast worthy of someone like me!*

He was still imagining the feasting and dancing when he caught the sound of hoofbeats approaching. Turning, he saw it was Lothair, a skillful warrior, especially with a throwing ax. The man dismounted and hurried to the king, bowing before him.

"Rise, noble son."

Lothair stood up and saluted the king with his fist on his chest. "We followed the legate from Constantine, just like you said."

After dismissing the skinny priest with a wave of his hand, Aoric returned his attention to Lothair. "What did you discover?"

"He was inquiring about Chrocus! In a tavern at Lucky Tree, he struck up a conversation with some old warriors. One of them fought with Chrocus but bears a grudge against him now. He reported to us that Legate Rex was trying to recruit warriors from your enemy."

"So what did you do?"

"We apprehended him, of course. Roughed him up a little. I don't think he respects you."

Aoric grunted at this. "Where is he now?"

"Not far offshore, tied up in a boat."

Aoric paused to consider all the implications. To reject the overtures of an imperial legate and send him disgruntled back to Constantine could easily invite war. More often than not, the Roman army would beat the Alemanni through superior armaments and organization. Aoric didn't want to give Constantine any pretext to invade the area and establish a new frontier.

At the same time, Aoric realized he couldn't let the arrogant young legate find the exiled Chrocus and rally his men. Even if they ended up fighting on some distant battlefield, they'd return to Germania enriched with spoils and energized for more battle. That was the last thing Aoric wanted while his hold over the Alemanni was still so tenuous.

"Lothair, you lived at Colonia for a time, did you not?"

"Yes, sire."

"Was Constantine ever there?"

"I saw him a few times, yes."

"Tell me about the Romans. Do they make alliances by marriage?"

"Very often, sire. I believe all people do that."

"What about second marriages? Do those count as well?"

201

"The Romans do not take multiple wives like our royalty. However, they recognize all our marriages as legitimate unions."

"Here is my dilemma. I do not wish to anger Emperor Constantine by sending his man back empty-handed. It would do me great harm to stir up those Roman hornets against me right now. Just the opposite, I need a respectable Roman connection to put me in good standing with the generals at Vindonissa. And what do you know? It seems I suddenly have a satisfying opportunity right in front of me."

"The senator's daughter?"

"So I was thinking. She's pretty, isn't she?"

"If you say so."

Aoric chuckled and slapped Lothair on the shoulder. "You may speak freely, noble son. I am not a jealous man."

"Then, yes, sire. She is a true beauty."

Aoric's eyes flared. "How dare you speak about Lady Junia like that!" he roared. When Lothair shrank back in terror, Aoric burst into laughter. "I am joking with you!"

"Oh . . . ha! Yes, that's funny, sire," said Lothair in a shaky voice.

"So now I find myself with these Roman visitors in my midst," Aoric went on, speaking more to himself as he sorted his thoughts. "One of them would make an excellent wife and open up some political advantages. But the other is a real burr in my breeches. Possibly treasonous, and at the very least, an obstacle to moving things along with Flavia."

"So why not just eliminate him?"

Aoric stroked his close-cropped beard. "Kill an imperial legate in cold blood? I stabbed Chrocus in the back, but this would go far beyond that. I'd bring down the full wrath of Rome on the Alemanni!"

"Not if no one found out."

"Hmm. A quiet disappearance? No one the wiser?"

"Why not? There's no reason you have to trump up charges against him or execute him in the town square. He's out there in a boat right now. Just say the word, and we'll drown him in Lake Brigantium before the sun comes up. Then all you have to do is play dumb—tell Flavia and her friends you have no idea where he went. Maybe it was bandits. Maybe it was a bear. Somehow the fellow just disappeared. Life has to go on."

Aoric considered the suggestion for a long time. The plan was risky. If the generals at Vindonissa heard about the crime, there would be total war. It would be the ultimate breach of diplomatic relations. Revenge would be demanded, and the Alemanni couldn't withstand Rome's concentrated might. And yet, how would they ever find out about the murder? Lothair said his comrades had abducted Rex on a dark night from a no-account village. Now he was tied up and floating in the middle of a deep sea. With no corpse to be discovered and no witnesses to report anything . . .

It could work.

King Aoric gripped Lothair's sleeve and brought him nearer. He bent his head and whispered into his man's ear. "Noble son, I have an important job for you."

"Yes, my lord?"

"Send that legate to the bottom of the lake with an anchor attached to his leg. Wrap him up tight so the corpse will never surface. Then I order you to never speak about this man again."

Lothair smiled and saluted once more. "What man?" he said.

It was the quiet hour before dawn when all was still. Rex lay unmoving in the bottom of the boat, blindfolded and bound. The cords dug into his wrists, but that was the least of his problems. Losing his fingers was a much bigger threat. And there were even worse possibilities beyond that.

"Quit your whispering," barked the leader of the band to a pair of his men. By listening to the distinct sounds of their voices, Rex had discerned there were five of them in all. The sixth man, named Lothair, had ridden away on horseback. At their master's sharp command, the two whisperers fell silent.

Across the water, Rex could hear an occasional barking dog or drunken carouser, so he knew he had been rowed close to Brigantium. A tangible dampness in the air suggested a fog had rolled in. Faint moonlight filtered through the cloth that covered Rex's eyes.

Before long, he caught the gentle slap of oars against water. Someone was rowing a boat toward them.

"It's Lothair," said the cruel leader. "Light the lantern or he'll never find us in this soup. But stay quiet until he's here."

A few moments later, a voice hailed the men. Lothair was given permission to approach. Rex felt the new watercraft bump against the one he was in.

A vigorous exchange of whispers ensued as Lothair and the leader discussed Rex's fate. Their evil snickering made Rex fear the worst. In his mind, he went over his escape options, but no solution presented itself. He couldn't swim with his wrists bound. Nor could he fight. His best plan would be to remain quiet and be taken to land. At least then, he might find a chance to run. The thought of torture came to his mind, but he pushed it away. *Wait until the right moment to act*, he told himself. Of course, there was no guarantee that such a moment would come.

Strong hands seized Rex's legs, holding them immobile. Then someone began to encircle both of his ankles with a rope.

"Let's cut him up first," said a wicked voice.

"You're obsessed with that!" the leader snapped. "Put your knife away! The king said no blood, no mess, no evidence. You want to disobey him? If he finds out about it, we'll all be drowned too!"

"Drowned too?"

Now Rex realized he was destined to be thrown into the deep. He started to thrash, but the leader called for help. Once again, many hands pinned him down. The rope kept encircling his lower legs.

An alternative escape plan—unlikely to succeed, but better than nothing—instantly formed in Rex's mind. *Struggle when they try to throw you out. Don't go without grabbing someone's dagger! Deep breath. Hit the bottom. Cut that rope fast, even if you have to leave a chunk of flesh behind. Surface and . . .*

An agonized scream pierced the night, followed by a tremendous splash. Shouts broke out in the boat as the men began to scramble. In the chaos, Rex's mind identified the sound that had preceded the scream: the familiar *swish-WHAP!* of a whistling arrow smacking into flesh.

They're under attack. Now what?

Hold steady, he told himself. *An enemy of theirs is a friend of mine.*

"Archers to the portside!" screamed the leader. "Douse the lantern! Man the oars!"

The remaining rowers immediately got the boat moving so they wouldn't be such an easy target. None of the men had bows, so they couldn't exchange shots with whoever was attacking. All they could do was run.

Lying in the bottom of the boat, Rex used the chaotic moment to reach up with his bound hands and work the blindfold off his eyes. The night had indeed become foggy, and the lantern was put out now, so it was hard to see anything at all. Rex heard the whizzing sound of a few more arrows, though none made impact. Then a gust of wind parted the wisps of fog, washing the boat in white moonlight.

"There they are!" came a voice across the water.

"They're going to ram us!" cried one of the rowers.

And they did.

The crash of the impact was so loud, it probably woke up half of Brigantium. Wood splintered, men shouted, and the clang of swords rang out all at once. Rex squirmed to a kneeling position, struggling against the tangles of the long rope that his enemies had been wrapping around him. He was about to make the leap to the attacking boat—whoever they were, they would surely be better than his abductors—when Aoric's lieutenant grabbed his collar from behind.

"The king wants you gone, Roman," he snarled in Rex's ear, then gave him a fierce shove. The force of it toppled Rex into the water, and for the second time that night, the possibility of drowning struck terror into his soul.

The rapidly sinking anchor pulled hard on Rex's ankles, as if a sea monster had grabbed him and was dragging him into its gloomy lair. Though he undulated his body upward, his bound wrists couldn't generate enough force to counteract the weight attached to his leg. Desperate urgency seized Rex as he plunged into the murky depths of Lake Brigantium.

An abrupt yank on the trailing rope suddenly arrested his descent. Its counteracting pull spun Rex upside down. Now one great weight tried to drag his ankles toward the abyss, while an even stronger force began to draw him back to life. Rex could only hold his breath and wait as the rope that was intended to be his doom instead became his lifeline.

At last, his feet broke the surface. A hand grabbed his belt. His back scraped against a wooden edge. And then Rex was dropped, sputtering and gasping, into the bottom of a boat.

"Bruder, you're quite a handful!" Gundomar boomed.

"Wh-what?" Rex shook water out of his eyes and panted hard, trying to regain his bearings. Other men were in the boat too, none of them threatening. Someone's helpful knife cut the ropes that bound Rex's wrists, immediately ending the sharp bite into his skin. The tight loops of the anchor line around his ankles disappeared too.

"You're gonna be alright," Gundomar went on. "Just take a moment to catch your wind, then grab an oar. We've got some rowing to do before the sun comes up."

"You . . . you want me to row?"

"Sure, why not? You can't let a little swim in the lake throw you off. It's just water."

Rex uttered a laugh at this and shook his head. *That's just like the Germani. Tough men, these northerners!*

The lake had fallen silent now. "Where are the others?" Rex finally asked as his head cleared.

"We scared 'em off. Sent two to the underworld before the rest got away. But I grabbed ahold of that anchor line before they escaped. Hauled you up from the deep like a fat carp." Gundomar bent down and pulled something from a sack. "Here you go, Bruder. Drink this."

The leather-faced warrior with the droopy mustache handed Rex a gourd flask. He put it to his lips and found it contained strong ale. After three long guzzles, he handed it back.

"Thank you, Gundomar," Rex said earnestly. "I thought that was going to be my end."

"Nein! Couldn't let that happen. Our boys are hoping to get into a good scrap with a Roman army, and we need you to lead us to the fight. Just point us toward Licinius, and unleash the dogs."

"I'll get you there as soon as I can."

"Good man! You're made of strong stuff."

Rex sat up straight and gave his new friend a grin. "These hands know how to row," he said, holding them up in the moonlight. "And I'm definitely ready to get out of here."

"We are too. Sit over there on that board and start pulling on my command. I'll navigate."

When the other five men were in place and Rex had taken the sixth spot, Gundomar called out the strokes and the boat began to slice through the water. The craft was well-built, for the Germani were excellent woodworkers. It felt good to Rex to be pulling an oar again.

"I have one question for you," he said to Gundomar after they had rowed in silence for a while. "Where are we going?"

"You just dodged death by drowning. Does it matter?"

"Not really. But since I'm not destined for Hades just yet, I might as well know where I'm headed in the meantime."

"Ah, Rex! You surely live up to your name. Always trying to be the king of wherever you are."

The remark made Rex smile. "Better to be a king than a servant," he quipped.

"Don't fool yourself," Gundomar warned. "A man can't always be the one in charge. You'd better learn to bow your knee real soon."

"Why is that?"

"Because it's time for you to meet the real king of the Alemanni. In a few hours, you're going to be face-to-face with King Chrocus the Great."

7

AUGUST 316

Though Flavia had rarely seen anyone as proficient as Rex on horseback, she had to admit, Lord Aoric was his equal. The cocky king of the Alemanni—the so-called king, Flavia reminded herself—was so naturally comfortable as a rider that he seemed to be one with his horse. As he rode around the ring, man and beast appeared to merge into a single organism, like the centaur of pagan mythology. Flavia could understand why warriors would charge into battle behind such a confident and skillful leader.

One of the most anticipated features of the Wodan's Day festival was the riding contest at high noon. The men would gallop in a large oval, throwing javelins through iron rings if their aim was good enough and cleaving melons on posts with sweeping strokes of their swords. The game was meant to imitate battle, of course. Just about everything in Alemannic culture glorified war in some way. It was a thoroughly violent society, and in it, Aoric had hacked his way to the top. He was likely to win the competition today not because he was the chieftain of the men but because he was the most talented among them—which was exactly why he was their chieftain.

It was still early, however, and Aoric was only practicing on his private riding grounds. Although the sun hadn't yet cleared the treetops, the day was already warm and humid. Aoric wore only trousers and boots, for a tunic surely would have been soaked by the sweat glistening on his alabaster body. He made a successful throw of his javelin, then wheeled his horse in

208

a tight turn and drew his sword from its scabbard. A large melon exploded into a burst of pulp as Aoric leaned from his saddle and hewed it with a mighty blow.

"A fine performance, lord!" Flavia exclaimed, alerting him to her presence so he would ride over.

Rex could have done it better, she told herself. Although exactly how he would have, she didn't know.

"Lady Junia, how good of you to come see me," Aoric said with genuine warmth as he trotted to the railing.

"Look, I've brought you some refreshment. It is a hot morning, and you must have worked up a thirst." Flavia held up a pewter pitcher of mead and one of the drinking horns the Germani favored so much. This was the king's special one, taken from an aurochs bull, so it was exceptionally long and curved. Its opening was trimmed with silver.

"Fill it for me, m'lady," said Aoric, showing his sweaty forearms to her. "I'm afraid I would drop it."

Flavia filled the horn from the pitcher and handed it up to Aoric in the saddle. His muscles glistened as he reached for it, prompting her to wonder how he maintained such a powerful physique despite his frequent drinking and feasting. *Probably by an equal amount of riding and fighting*, she surmised.

Aoric took a long draught from the horn, sighed deeply, then took another. A ray of sun shone on his copper-colored hair, making it seem to blaze as if on fire. With his smooth skin and chiseled body, he looked like one of the marble sculptures that adorned the Roman Forum. Many brave fighters would surely give their loyalty to such a man—but Flavia was here to learn about those who did not. There must be some secret rebels who favored the old king. *Time for a little spying.*

"Your games are practice for war," she observed. "Accurate throws and vigorous blows are even more important on the battlefield than in the ring."

"Indeed! Among the Alemanni, life is practice for war, war is real life, and the afterlife is simply more war." The king took a smaller sip of his mead this time. "I intend to be ready for whatever battles confront me."

"I am sure you will be. Do you have many enemies, or have you defeated them all by now?"

"I defeated most of them when I claimed my throne. The warlords of Chrocus met their fate after he went into exile. But here and there, traitors still exist. I'm always on the lookout, in case they rise up against me."

"Rise up against you? They would be like fleas on the back of a wolf! A mere nuisance, it would seem." Flavia knew she was laying on the flattery pretty thick, yet it seemed to be working.

"Perhaps they are a nuisance," Aoric acknowledged with a charming grin. "Yet what wolf wouldn't wish to be free of fleas? I intend to rid my fur of all such pests."

Flavia couldn't tell if his response accurately represented his enemies' strength or was just masculine bravado. "What glory is there in fighting fleas?" she asked. "Aren't your enemies worthy opponents in battle?"

"They have some good warriors among them, to be sure. Many went into exile with Chrocus. And like I told you before, I suspect some in my realm are secretly loyal to him. At times, I even wonder about Gundomar, though I have no evidence of treachery."

"The number of rebels cannot be high, my lord, for who would fight for a decrepit old king instead of a brave warrior like you?" Again, Flavia chided herself for the blatant flattery. Yet such words always worked on men like Aoric when they were spoken by a woman who seemed to have interest.

"Ha! You're exactly right, Flavia!" Aoric's use of her familiar name signaled she had been accepted into his inner circle. "I keep wondering the same thing. What do they see in old Grandpa Chrocus? Why does anyone want to follow him? It seems stupid. Yet, apparently, some do."

"But not many."

"More than you might think, actually."

"A force you could easily defeat, sire! A few hundred men compared to your thousands."

"I think he's got about two thousand men loyal to him. Not a trivial number."

Flavia suppressed a smile. *Thank you, Aoric. Duly noted. Rex will be so proud of my clever spying!*

Tipping back his head, Aoric drained the rest of his drinking horn and dismounted. With the easy dexterity of an elite warrior, he swung his leg over the railing of the riding arena, then swung his second leg over too, crossing the barrier almost as if it weren't there. He approached Flavia and loomed over her with his cup. Suddenly she found his masculine presence unnerving, for it had an aggressive edge.

"My horn needs a little something more," he said, "for I am an unusually thirsty man."

"Fortunately for you, I brought a lot of mead." Flavia took the horn in her hand, emptied the pitcher into it, and gave it back.

Aoric took another swig from the cup, then wiped his ruddy beard with the back of his hand. A groom came to lead his horse to the stable, and before he left, Aoric unbuckled his belt and handed over his sword too.

"From now on, that blade will only have blood on it, not melon guts," he vowed. "By Wodan's Day next year, I will have defeated all the rebels in my kingdom."

"No doubt, sire! Can you march out against them immediately?"

"I would if I could find them. They disappeared into the great forest. Much of Raetia went back to wilderness after the Romans pulled out. There are scores of abandoned forts in the deep woods. He's probably hiding in one, but it would take a long time for scouts to ride around and check them all. And whichever scout found the right one, well . . . that man probably wouldn't return."

"So you have no idea where King Chrocus is now?"

A fierce scowl came to Aoric's face. "He's not the king, I am!" he barked. "And why do you care so much about warfare, anyway? Why all the questions?"

Uh-oh! I pressed too hard. I'm clearly not a professional at this!

"I d-didn't mean to offend," Flavia stammered, taking a step backward. "You've been such a gracious host. I was only trying to converse about things that matter to you. My questions were intended to honor a great warrior who is conquering his enemies one by one."

The soothing words seemed to mollify Aoric, turning his angry frown into a satisfied smile. He made a fist and pounded his sweaty chest. "It's true. There is no one in Alemannia who can defeat me."

"Not with a physique like that!" Flavia exclaimed. Though she sensed she might be close to crossing a dangerous line with that one, she was rattled by Aoric's harshness and wanted to deflect the conversation in a new direction.

"Aha! The little Italian girl can charm with her words as well as her looks," Aoric said with the return of his previous warmth. "So how do you like it here in Germania, my dear Flavia? Is our realm all you imagined it would be?"

"Yes, sire, the land is rugged and fertile, and open to a big sky. I like it."

"Could you . . . could you see yourself staying here for a long time?"

"I think that would be difficult, to be honest. I was only intending a brief visit."

"Why not longer?"

"Well, for one thing, I'm a Christian. There are no bishops here, nor even a priest. How would I partake of our sacred ceremonies?"

"This is a border area. Many Romans are still around. We could surely find one of your priests and bring him here. Perhaps some of our people would even be drawn to your Jesus. He was a victor who conquered death, wasn't he? Brave and mighty, like Wodan. Both of them even hung on a tree! Perhaps they are the same god?"

"No, Aoric, my Jesus is not like Wodan. They cannot be equated."

Aoric grunted and flicked his hand dismissively. "Fine! If you say so, I will not debate you. It is a matter of your own expertise. However"—his green eyes grew bright—"I would be willing to accept your Roman Christianity, if that would please you."

Aoric would convert to the Christian faith? Truly? Lord, are you at work in this man? Are you bringing the Alemanni to belief in the Savior? And are you using me to do it?

"That would please me very much!" Flavia gushed. "I think you should strongly consider it!"

"And what would the generals at Vindonissa think? Would they be happy as well?"

"Yes, they would be delighted! Now that Constantine has converted, many of his generals have joined him in the catholic faith. The imperial army is full of Christians now. They would look on you with great favor if you became a believer in Christ."

Aoric folded his rippling forearms across his broad chest as he contemplated the idea. His raw masculinity seemed a little more benign now, touched ever so slightly by the softness of the Lord.

"I will make it a matter of serious consideration," he announced at last.

Flavia bowed to the king of the Alemanni. "And I, Lord Aoric, will make it a matter of prayer."

———⦿⦿⦿———

Rex rowed until dawn across the quiet, misty surface of Lake Brigantium. Around sunup, the travelers came to a river whose entrance into the lake was swampy and braided with multiple channels. Yet Gundomar knew how to thread the boat through water deep enough for the keel. Rex trusted his friend's judgment and gave himself over to the rhythm of rowing.

The rolling of an oar was a hypnotic sort of motion, helping Rex forget the dull ache in his skull and his chafed wrists. He lapsed into his own mental world, allowing random thoughts to flow through his mind as they happened to come. Memories from his days as a navy oarsman soon gave way to more distant recollections. Images of his boyhood began to resurface: his favorite swimming hole, his first pony, his father chopping firewood.

Will I really see my father today?

The idea was hard to believe. Though many years haad passed, Rex could still recall his noble bearing, fierce eyes, and hearty laugh. Yet one image stood out more clearly than any other: a blue-sky day in Britannia when the two of them were sparring with wooden swords. Boisterous young Rex had swung his weapon with gusto while Chrocus parried and feinted. His father then stepped back, beamed with pride, and tossed Rex a honeyed fig as a reward for his fine swordplay. Delighted, Rex was about to bite into the treat when his father knocked it from his hand, toppled him into the mud, and gave him a hard whack on the rear end.

"My son, never lower your guard to an armed man," he said sternly, "or you may find the next sword piercing your ribs, not smacking your arse."

That hard lesson was one Rex had never forgotten.

The sun grew hot as the rowers labored at their oars. After proceeding upriver all morning, with a brief stop for some bread and sour wine, the six-oared boat finally reached an area of thick forest with steep bluffs on either side.

Gundomar pointed to a rocky outcrop that was overgrown with briars. "Can you make out anything in that foliage?" he asked Rex.

"To be honest, no, and I have pretty good eyesight."

"Good. There's actually an abandoned fort up there, which we chose because it's hard to see. We'll be there within an hour."

After tucking the boat into a swampy side channel that petered out in a patch of cattails, the men disembarked onto dry ground. They scrambled through the underbrush and emerged onto a game trail.

"Stay close behind me," Gundomar said, "and keep quiet. No talking at all."

The party of seven warriors hiked up the flank of a wooded promontory and finally topped onto a flat, open summit. The game trail continued ahead into a dense stand of trees. Gundomar was about to enter the tangled copse when a man's voice rang out. "Halt!"

Gundomar held up his fist, and his followers froze.

"Every one of you has an arrow aimed at his heart," warned the voice. "Identify yourselves!"

"I am Gundomar the Left-Handed, and these are my trusted men."

"Bees know how to make honey . . ." declared the unseen speaker.

"But only men can make mead," Gundomar finished.

For a long moment, there was nothing but silence. Then the voice said, "Password accepted. You may proceed."

Rex followed his six companions into the thicket. A few moments later, he found himself staring at the gate of a decent-sized fortress built by the Roman army. Currently, however, it was surrounded by creeping vines and dense shrubbery that no legionary would have left there to provide an enemy with cover. Nevertheless, the construction was clearly the work of imperial masons, and its location followed standard army protocol: on the brow of a ridge with good views of the surrounding terrain and with defensible drop-offs on two sides. Deep ditches protected the walls on the remaining two sides. It was a well-built castle, though now in poor repair. Rex thought he could even discern scorch marks on the walls from a blaze in the not-too-distant past. A stone inscription above the entrance indicated its name was once Vemania, but with the Romans gone, it had no name anymore.

The gatekeeper asked for another password, and Gundomar knew this one too. The visitors passed through a stout gate and emerged into an open courtyard whose wooden barracks had indeed burned down several years ago. Though they were now reduced to blackened debris, about a hundred men had set up leather tents beside them to garrison the castle. Fortunately, the original headquarters building was constructed of stone, so it alone was still intact. It was a two-story structure with a tiled roof, built with traditional Roman sturdiness. When Rex looked up at it, his heart began to beat faster as he contemplated what he might find inside.

"Wait here," Gundomar said. After disappearing into the headquarters for a short time, he returned and beckoned to Rex. "You alone may enter with me."

The two men were escorted inside by a guard who was surprisingly young, contradicting Rex's assumption that only the older generation of warriors still followed Chrocus. The youthful warrior took the visitors upstairs and brought them to a doorway blocked with a heavy drape. In every military fort Rex had ever seen, this would have been the commander's personal quarters. He felt strangely shaky as he imagined his father inside, seated on a chair, staring at his visitors with his steely gaze. *Should I bow before my own father? Should I even tell him who I am? Or perhaps he already knows?*

Another thought occurred to Rex: *Will I weep?* He hoped he would not.

Sweeping aside the drapery, the youth gestured for the two visitors to enter. The room was darker than Rex had expected, for the shutters had closed off the window and only a single lamp was burning on a stand. There was no throne in the chamber, just two simple chairs, a cabinet, and a bed. Unexpectedly, a hand gripped Rex's shoulder as someone emerged from the gloom to his left. He jumped at the touch, but the voice immediately identified the speaker as an old woman.

"Do not say anything startling," she warned in an ominous tone.

Gundomar turned to Rex and looked him in the eye. "The king is near death," he explained. "We have kept it a secret—for without him, the resistance would crumble, and we would be stuck with Aoric forever. No one must ever learn what you see in here."

"Be sure not to startle him," repeated the old hag. Rex noticed an herb pouch draped over her shoulder, identifying the woman as a healer. "Any great shock could be the end of him. He's very fragile."

Now Gundomar led Rex to the bed. The two chairs were close beside it; yet because the shadows were deep, Rex could not see the lumpy form under the heap of blankets. Then the healer brought the lampstand a little closer, and for the first time in a decade, Rex beheld his father.

Chrocus's face was gaunt, and his beard had grown long and tangled. The thick locks that once flowed to his shoulders were thinner and grayer than before. His eyes were closed, and his breathing was slow and regular. Although at first he appeared to be sleeping, he eventually adjusted his position in such a way that signaled he was awake, even if his mind was elsewhere. Clearly, he was listless and drowsy. Yet his brow wasn't sweaty, nor did he seem to be in pain. That much, at least, was positive.

"Sit here," said the healer woman, gesturing to one of the bedside chairs. "Do not touch him, especially not here"—she hovered her hand over his rib cage—"where the wound is festering."

"How was he wounded?" Rex whispered to Gundomar.

"Aoric invited him to a great banquet. While he was offering a toast, he walked around the table. Suddenly he pulled out a dagger and stabbed the king in the back. The blade went all the way through. Then Aoric's men leapt from the forest like wolves and attacked the king's retinue. Several warlords gave their lives to help Chrocus escape that day. The memory of their bravery will never be forgotten in Alemannia. Surely they are feasting right now in the Heavenly Hall."

"And Chrocus has not recovered?"

"The wound festers," repeated the healer woman. "A terrible spell has been put on him, and the dark magic prevents him from getting well."

"Does he speak?"

"Of course I speak," croaked the old king, making everyone gasp in surprise. He opened his eyes and stared at the new arrival for a long time, though no recognition appeared on his face. "Who are you?" he said at last.

Rex put his fist to his chest and dipped his chin. "A messenger from your former master," he announced.

"I have no master but Thor."

"You once had human masters too: Emperor Constantius, and after him, his son Constantine. Your mighty men fought for them at Eboracum."

Chrocus lapsed into silence at this. Finally, he said, "It is true. But it happened long ago. The world was different then."

"The world was surely different, yet some things remain the same. War is one of them. Emperor Constantine is in need of troops once more."

"You are troubling the great king," warned the hag. She gently caressed Chrocus's arm, which lay outside of the covers that swaddled him. "Rest easy, my lord," she whispered.

"I am sleepy," he admitted.

"I know, sire. I shall make you a restful potion when the guests leave."

Rex interrupted the conversation. "King Chrocus, you will not always lie abed. The day will come when you are healed. Then what will you do? You cannot hide in this overgrown fortress forever."

"Thor will show me the way, young man." Chrocus paused, his eyes narrowing. "What is your name?"

"I have no name right now," Rex replied. Strangely, the king accepted his answer. "There are many men who follow you," Rex went on. "Gundomar says two thousand are known, but I believe more would come to your side if Aoric were gone."

Now Chrocus's eyes flared, and he raised himself a bit from his mattress. "Do not utter the name of that wench-spawn in my presence! He is—" Though Chrocus wanted to say more, a coughing fit overcame him and he collapsed back onto the bed.

"Look what you have done!" the hag scolded. "You must leave now."

But Rex was undeterred. "King Chrocus, listen to me! The older warriors side with you—and so will many of the young ones. They see that your enemy is strong but not honorable. You could rally them to your side!"

"No. I am ill."

"Open the window and let in light and fresh air. Drink good wine, as much as you want, and wash the wound in it too. Begin to walk on your feet like a man, a little more each day. You will quickly improve—I have seen it many times in the army! Lying abed drinking potions is no way to heal. You need food, exercise, clean bandages, wine upon the wound, and above all, hope! This is how the Roman army repairs its men."

"Thor will decide my fate," Chrocus repeated.

"Let Chrocus decide his own fate." The statement was bold, and Rex knew it. Even Gundomar flinched a bit at the strong words. Yet Rex knew it was what the king needed to hear.

217

The healer woman stood up. "It is time for you men to go," she said firmly. "Gundomar the Left-Handed, please escort your friend away from this room. I do not even know why you brought him here."

"We must do as she says," Gundomar whispered as he rose to his feet.

Rex stood up as well. "Since when do warriors get shuffled here and there like servants?" he asked his friend, then turned back to the king. "Your Majesty, a slow decline does not have to be your fate. Rise up as the chief of your men once more. Emperor Constantine calls you back into his service. The spoils of that war would crown your men with great wealth. You would return to Germania as a conquering hero, restored to your position by a grateful emperor. Rise up, I say, and issue a call to arms! Rally your men to battle!"

Shaking his head slowly, Chrocus stared at Rex and gestured toward his side. "My wound festers. I am too weak to do what you suggest."

"Leave this room," the hag insisted.

"Come," Gundomar added, tugging Rex's sleeve. "We must go, Bruder."

For a long, tense moment, no one said a word. Rex knelt beside the king and took hold of his wrinkled hand. "Perhaps you are too weak to do this thing alone. But your prince could stand at your side, giving you strength."

"I have no prince," said the old king sadly.

"You do now," Rex declared. "I am Brandulf, and I am your son."

———✦✦✦———

The witch lived about a mile outside of Brigantium, deep in the woods of the former Roman province of Raetia. The Aegyptian Asp had found that women like this always lurked on the outskirts of every city. Often they were knowledgeable about local herbs that would affect the human body in ways no one else understood. With their ancient lore, they could brew concoctions and mix tinctures that would heal the sick of virtually any disease. Or, if they wished, they could kill a man in a foaming delirium of pain and confusion.

Yes, they were useful women, these witches.

The Asp had completed an uneventful riverboat trip to the end of the navigable Danubius. From there he had traversed the land of Germania in the direction of Brigantium. His quarry had arrived two days before him: the

Alemannic warrior Rex and his consort, Lady Junia Flavia. Their dynamic cooperation had become the driving force behind the bishop of Rome's wicked endeavors. It was this intrepid warrior and his rich girlfriend who kept the pope's mission alive—and their strategy of winning Constantine's favor with hired mercenaries had raised the stakes considerably. But out here on the edge of the empire, where imperial power barely held any influence, the Asp hoped to extinguish this vexing problem once and for all. The assassination of a man like Rex wouldn't be easy, but it was certainly possible with the right tools. And that was why the Asp had come to the witch's house.

"I need a poison," he told the white-haired woman at the door of her cottage beneath a giant yew tree. The underbrush was thick here, the forest lush in every direction. *A good place for gathering herbs*, he observed.

The old woman brushed a strand of stringy hair out of her eyes. "I can probably help you for the right price. But I'm going to need more than money before I give you what you seek."

Flipping the hood of his brown cloak onto his shoulders, the Asp asked, "May I come in?" When the witch eyed him suspiciously, he followed with an appeal he knew she would understand. "Madam," he said in a respectful tone, "is it not evident that we are both travelers along dark paths? I am a friend to the likes of you. We are creatures of the occult world. In this, we share a common bond."

The witch pursed her lips and nodded. "Yes, I sense it too. The serpent upon your face speaks to me. Come inside and have a cup of tea." She turned, then glanced over her shoulder and added, "If you dare to drink it." The Asp could only smile at the cheeky remark.

While the tea steeped in the pot, the pair discussed their business deal. "I need something that can be absorbed through the skin," said the Asp. "Something in powdered form. Death must be caused by even a small amount."

"Ah! You need bitter almond powder."

"Almonds are not poisonous."

The old woman cackled at this. "No, indeed, but a poison can be extracted from them with the right techniques. From the pits of fruits too—apricots, cherries, even apple seeds. Bitter almond powder sickens you within an hour and kills most men whose skin it touches. And you are in luck. I have some on my shelf."

"There is no luck. Only what the spirits ordain."

"I know," the witch agreed with a nod. "It is just a saying among those who don't know better."

She rose and went to her cabinet, returning with a vial of brownish powder. "Before I sell this to you, I need to know something about your purposes. If word gets out that you bought this from me, people might ask questions. I want to know what I'm dealing with."

"Madam, it is not too much to say that the politics of the world's greatest empire are at stake."

"Tell me a bit about it, or no sale can be made. Whose side are you on?"

"My brotherhood serves the true religion of the Sacred Divine, standing against the catholic church. We find salvation through inner knowledge, not the horror of a cross. The truly mystical are those who realize Jesus was a revealing angel, not God made flesh in our midst. Such an idea is hideous and unworthy of a deity."

As the witch contemplated these doctrines, she fiddled with a lone whisker on her chin. Finally, she said, "How do imperial politics come into play?"

"It is complex, but the essence is this. Emperor Constantine favors the catholic church, especially the bishop of Rome. I represent a movement that wishes to overthrow the current leadership of the church in Aegyptus. The false bishop Alexander must be replaced with a wiser man. Then, from that new power base, we can begin to challenge the church at Rome, until our gnostic truth has supplanted the primitive faith of the Romans—those simpletons who lack the Divine Light."

"And what could possibly be found in Raetia to occupy the attention of a man with such grand imperial concerns?"

"The Roman pope has sent a Spanish bishop and a rich girl on a mission. Along the way, they hired an Alemannic warrior for protection. Now he has come here to recruit mercenaries, which he thinks will impress Constantine. Then the emperor will be favorable to the pope's mission, launching the Roman church on a trajectory that would be hard to stop. So it must be prevented, which means this warrior must be kept from recruiting troops. Or even better, if both the warrior and the rich girl were to disappear in Raetia, the pope's mission would surely fail. That, in brief, is my holy purpose."

"So you must arrange a secret death instead of just attacking the man."

"Exactly. And I need your poison to do this job right, with no one the wiser."

The witch rose and removed the teapot from the flame, then poured two steaming mugs of herbal tea. One she kept and the other she offered to the Asp. After blowing on it, he took a sip. It was sweetened with honey and tasted faintly of mint.

"You could take this poison from me by force," the witch observed, gesturing to the vial on the table.

"Of course I could. But I wouldn't do that, would I? And that is precisely why you will sell it to me."

"I will indeed," she replied, and began to describe how to use it.

The next morning, the Aegyptian Asp arrived in Brigantium while the sky was still dark, as was his usual custom. He proceeded to the poorest quarter of town and fell in with the riffraff of the city. Such people did not ask questions of strangers, nor did the upstanding citizens take notice of their doings. The poor were always irrelevant to the rich, and that cloak of invisibility was often useful.

By asking around the seedy taverns, the Asp learned that Rex and Flavia were staying in King Aoric's mansion on the main town square. Gossip always spread quickly in a tightly packed city, especially when money was involved. Many warriors were eagerly awaiting details about the mercenary work that Rex was authorized to offer on behalf of Rome. Though the imperial legate hadn't been seen around town lately, rumor had it that he would announce the opportunity at the Wodan's Day banquet this evening. Many men had already started sharpening their swords in anticipation of a foreign adventure.

Aoric's mansion was likely to be busy right now, yet lightly guarded, for no one in Brigantium would dare rob the king. The Aegyptian Asp proceeded to the town square and observed the comings and goings at the house for about an hour. As every speculator knew, entering a residence in daytime was best achieved by bluffing, not stealth. Absolute confidence in one's excuse for being there was the primary requirement. The household slaves were unlikely to question a self-assured visitor, for slaves lived by the rule that attracting attention to themselves for any reason was never a good idea. All the intruder needed was a plausible reason to be inside the house.

Rising from his bench outside a bakery, the Asp went around to the back of the shop and peeked through the rear window. The bakers were scurrying around like madmen. Because of the great banquet, Wodan's Day was one of their busiest days of the year, rivaled only by Tiw's Day, Thor's Day, and Friya's Day. A basket of fresh loaves lay not far from the windowsill, but to lean in and snatch it was impossible with everyone running around.

The Asp returned to the front of the store. While other customers were being served, he examined the interior until he spotted what he wanted: the opportunity for a distraction. Going outside again, he found one of the places where the bakery's brick wall had crumbled from lack of maintenance. Poking a stick through the hole, he touched it to a heavy crock of butter on a shelf, then gave it a shove. The crock fell to the floor with a loud crash. While all the bakers were gawking at what was surely a slippery mess at the front of the shop, the Aégyptian Asp grabbed the basket of loaves through the rear window and quietly walked away.

After knocking on the door to the slaves' entrance of Aoric's mansion, he barged his way past the clueless doorkeeper who answered. Though the little fellow tried to protest, the Asp held up the basket and snapped, "Bread delivery for the king. He ordered it himself. Don't make me report you!" Before any more could be said, the Asp disappeared around a corner and left the slave to return to his work.

In virtually all Roman mansions, a few formal bedrooms were attached to the atrium, but smaller and more private ones opened onto the peristyle that surrounded the rear garden. Guests, of course, would not be accorded the privilege of sleeping in the master's lavishly decorated chambers up front. This meant Rex and Flavia would have their rooms in the rear. The Asp made his way to the peristyle with his basket of bread, striding boldly through the house as if he had every right to be there.

Each of the bedrooms that faced the garden was closed off with the kind of cheap fabric that barbarians could tolerate but no self-respecting Roman would have allowed. Only two of the niches outside the rooms held lamps whose wicks had recently been burned. One of those rooms had its curtain drawn, but the other was partially open. The Asp glanced in: a single bed, a pallet on the floor, a bronze table, and a wooden chest in the corner. A pair of men's boots stood next to the chest—muddy and recently worn. And next to them was indubitable proof that this was Rex's room: a soldier's sword.

After drawing the curtain behind him, the Asp hurried to the chest and opened it, wincing at the loud creak its hinges made. To be caught rifling through a guest's things would have cost a slave his right hand. Though the Aegyptian Asp was confident there wasn't a person in this house capable of inflicting such a punishment on a former speculator like him, even so, he wanted to finish the job and get out before he was seen.

Glancing into the chest, he found that its contents confirmed his belief that he was in Rex's room. The expensive tunic and trousers were large enough to be Rex's, and their colors fit the verbal descriptions of those who had recently seen him. An amulet incised with a cross also suggested that its owner had some affinity for Christianity. The evidence here was conclusive.

After unfolding the tunic, the Aegyptian Asp worked a high dose of the poisonous almond powder into the fabric with a brush, all the while holding a kerchief over his nose with his other hand. Then, using a second kerchief so that he never touched the fabric, he refolded the tunic and laid it back in the chest. He had just closed the lid and stood up when he heard a female voice outside.

"Rex, is that you?"

The Asp snatched his bread basket and set a loaf on a table at the same moment that the chamber's curtain was pulled aside. The woman shrieked in surprise, and the Asp whirled to face her. It was Lady Junia Flavia. She was holding a vase of flowers.

"What are you doing in here?" she demanded, stepping back from him.

"I'm from the bakery," said the Asp, holding up his basket. "Making a delivery to the house today. The cook said to bring loaves to the guests in case they were hungry. Are you the lady he mentioned? Would you like one too?"

Flavia ignored the offer. "I thought I heard the chest open," she said suspiciously.

"What chest?"

"The one right there with Rex's things." Flavia gestured toward it. "The hinges squeal."

"No, it wasn't the hinges. I moved this little table when I set down the bread. The legs are metal, see? They squeal when dragged on the floor. Now are you sure you don't want a loaf for yourself? It's fresh. We just made it today in our bakery."

"No, thank you."

"Miss Flavia?" inquired a male voice from the garden. Then a husky servant appeared behind her with a pewter pitcher. He, too, stopped short at the sight of the intruder in the bedroom.

End it now. Time to get going before this escalates. The Asp arranged the cloth that covered his bread basket and began to edge toward the door. "No problem about the bread, m'lady," he said with a polite tip of his head. "Just wanted to ask. I'll give the rest to the cook and be off."

He shuffled past Flavia and left the rear garden. After setting the basket on the kitchen counter, he took a loaf for himself and exited through the slaves' door. Wasting no time, he hurried away from the house, yet without ever breaking into a run.

In an alley several streets away, the Asp finally stopped for a rest. A flick of his forearm brought his wrist-razor into his hand. He carved off a piece of bread and popped it into his mouth, savoring its yeasty taste. The sight of the golden-brown loaf made him recall the one he had just left in Rex's room.

By God, I hope he eats it when he changes his clothes, the Asp thought as a satisfied smile came to his lips. *It will taste so good to him . . . until he vomits it up in the agonized throes of death.*

———

Of all the arrogant things Licinius had ever seen, the behavior of Constantine's half brother, Julius Constantius, had to be the worst. At least when he came before, he had carried himself with the proper deference of an envoy on a diplomatic mission. This time, Julius had shown up in Sirmium like a god from heaven and immediately started acting like he owned the place. Refusing to stay in Licinius's palace, he had lodged instead in a tent outside the walls, as if he had put the city under siege. His lone demand had been simple: hand over Senecio for extradition to Gaul or consider yourself at war with Constantine.

If Constantine wants war with me, he can have it!

Licinius cleared his throat, feeling dry and parched on this hot summer day. Across the atrium, Senecio was pacing like a caged animal—perhaps like one of the African monkeys he resembled so much, with his big ears and long, skinny arms. Periodically, the homely fellow would wipe sweat from his forehead, then resume his pacing.

"Quit your wandering and sit still," Licinius snapped.

"Are you *sure* you won't remand me to the ambassador?" Senecio whined. "Are you absolutely, positively sure?"

"I am, but if you don't settle down, I might change my mind!" At this warning, the disgraced politician's eyes widened and he froze in place. Glancing toward a nearby stool, he hurried toward it and took a seat.

Licinius turned away from the anxious man and signaled for a slave to fetch some wine. In truth, he had no intention of heeding Julius's demand to hand over Senecio to Constantine. Not that he cared so much for Senecio. Licinius wasn't particularly concerned about losing his counselor. The real problem was that before they killed the pitiful fellow, they'd squeeze information from him by torture. Then Licinius would be directly implicated in the failed assassination plot, losing the moral high ground. The rampant rumors of Licinius's involvement would be documented as fact. People would consider him a betrayer of his alliance rather than a noble defender of territories unjustly invaded. Licinius knew he had a tenuous hold on his troops. Any pretext for them to flip to Constantine had to be avoided at all costs.

The slave returned with a jug of wine and a full goblet. A twinge of pity for Senecio's distress made the emperor feel generous. "Go get another cup for him," he instructed the slave as he put his own goblet to his lips.

"Thank you, lord," Senecio whimpered.

"If my brother-in-law marches against me, I will be more than happy to meet him," Licinius declared after he had sipped the sweet red. The wine had been mixed with a little seawater, so the salty and sweet tastes made a nice pairing. "I'm planning a little something to greet him when he arrives."

"Wh-what is it?"

"Come here and see."

Licinius beckoned Senecio to follow him out to a sunny courtyard. An array of statues and busts were assembled in the open space, some made of marble, others of bronze. There were tall ones to be mounted on a great pedestal, smaller ones to stand on a column, and even a magnificent bronze casting of a rider astride a horse. Only one thing was common to all the sculptures: they depicted Emperor Licinius, and him alone.

Senecio bowed before the assemblage. "They are stunning, Your Majesty. Each is invested with the power of your imperial genius."

Licinius laughed at the flattering words, yet he enjoyed the compliment nonetheless. "Where do you imagine I will have them installed?"

"All over the province, I hope! From one end of Pannonia to the other. Perhaps even some here at Sirmium, so when wicked Constantine shows up, your imperial greatness will strike fear in his heart. In fact"—Senecio marched over to one of the smallest sculptures, a bust of Licinius—"why not hand this one over to Ambassador Julius?" The idea made him cackle. "Yes, indeed! So you want Senecio, do you? Take Licinius instead—for Licinius and Senecio are one!"

"You forget yourself. Watch what you say! I am not one with you."

At this stern rebuke, Senecio's jaw dropped, and he wagged his head in apology. "No, of course not! I only meant . . ."

"I know what you meant. But your words were poorly chosen. We are not men of the same kind."

"Not at all, Your Majesty! Yet I am one with you in total obedience." Senecio hoisted the bust in his arms and kissed its cheek to show his love for his emperor.

"Set it down, Senecio, and have some wine. I am not going to hand you over."

The disgraced politician returned the bust to its stand and took the wine goblet from the slave who had followed the men into the courtyard. He sipped it uneasily, still wiping sweat from his forehead with his fingertips.

"The statues are not destined to be spread across Pannonia," Licinius said. "Originally, that was the plan. Now I have a better one."

"Tell me, O Great One."

Although that title wasn't traditional for an emperor, Licinius ignored it as just more flattery. "Do you know the city of Neviodunum?"

"Yes, lord. It is on the road toward Italy, west of here."

"I propose to install my statues there—every single one of them. It is the first city Constantine will encounter upon entering Pannonia. When he leaves his territory and crosses into mine, I shall be there to confront him in all my regal splendor."

Senecio's face grew sly. It was a familiar expression that reminded Licinius why he had made this man his counselor for so many years. Senecio had a natural inclination for plots and intrigues. Licinius could tell he was mulling over an idea but was unsure if he should voice it.

"Go ahead," the emperor offered. "Speak your mind."

"Well, I was thinking about the symbolism."

"As always."

"As I must, Your Majesty. Neviodunum is the first town Constantine will meet when he crosses the line between West and East, from Italy to Pannonia. That puts you in the position of the responder. He acts. You react. Do you see the symbolism of this? The boldness is all on his side."

"Hmm. That is a good point."

"But why not turn the tables on him? Why not become the bold defender of your rights by marching out to war against him?"

"Because I don't want to fight in Italy. Strategically, that favors his resupply and reinforcement lines. He controls the naval station at Ravenna. He would have Aquileia at his back. It would give him multiple advantages."

"I am talking about symbolism, not military tactics. Fight him here in Pannonia if you wish. But the initial confrontation should be in Italy."

"What do you have in mind?"

"Take the statues beyond Neviodunum. Take them out of Pannonia altogether. March into Italy a few miles and tear down Constantine's images at Emona. They depict the two of you in harmony. Shatter them on the pavement! Then spread these mighty sculptures around Emona. Put them on the empty pedestals. It will infuriate Constantine! But it will also show that you are the aggressor, that you are not afraid to confront him in his own lands. He will enter Pannonia tentative and irritable because of the affront to his pride."

A smile now came to Licinius's face. He crossed over to Senecio and clinked goblets with him. "Now I remember why I kept you around!" he exclaimed. "What a clever little ape you are!"

"So . . . you will not hand me over?"

"I will not," the emperor promised, "but I'm putting you in charge of the Emona expedition. And you'd better do it quickly, because Constantine is coming soon. I'd sure hate for you to be there when he arrives. That, my friend, would not go well for you."

Senecio nearly dropped the cup from his sweaty hand. "I will leave tomorrow," he declared.

"See that you do," Licinius replied, then drained his wine and left Senecio trembling among the statues.

—◌◦◌—

For the first time in what must have been a long while, the window shutters were opened in the headquarters building at the Vemania fortress. Dust and debris crumbled from them when Rex threw them wide. A gush of fresh air wafted into King Chrocus's bedroom, immediately dispelling the mustiness that had gathered there. The rays of sunlight also helped to banish the gloom.

"It is good to see the golden light of the sun again," Chrocus admitted from his bed.

"That type of gold is nice, but I think this gold will please a Germanic heart even more." Rex went to a tray on a cart and filled two mugs, then brought them to his father. He took a seat beside the bed.

"Beer!" Chrocus exclaimed. "The healer says it saps my strength. But I don't care. Hand it over!"

"Not until you sit up."

It was a struggle, but Chrocus managed to do it. Rex thought he looked stronger in that position than when lying down. When Rex offered one of the mugs, the king snatched it and quaffed a big gulp. "It's been too long," he said with a sigh.

"Yes it has, Father."

Chrocus glanced over at Rex. "Tell me your story, Brandulf," he said.

"I warn you, it is rather complicated."

"We have plenty of time. I want to hear it all."

And so the two men, father and son, drank beer in an old Roman fortress, conversed in throaty Alemannic German, and laughed their way through a

228

decade's worth of adventures. Rex described his training to be a speculator, his meteoric rise to the imperial bodyguard, and his special mission to spy out Rome in advance of Constantine's arrival for war. There were some great battles to recount, and some even greater defeats. Rex used the term *misunderstanding* to explain how he got on Constantine's bad side and was sentenced to row in the navy. That punishment eventually led to mutiny, then piracy—it wasn't really tax collection, he admitted to his father with a grin—then to his current situation: an escort to Bishop Ossius on a mission for the Roman pope. Chrocus declared that this story, all told, made quite a saga.

"Tell me more about Flavia," he said. "She's a crucial part of your life, and you're obviously fond of her. Are you in love?"

"What does that word even mean?" Rex countered.

"Attracted?"

"How could I not be? She's gorgeous."

"The bed?"

"Those of her faith reserve it for marriage."

"Since you bring up that subject—why not marry her?"

"She wouldn't have me."

"How come? You're not of her station?"

"No, she isn't proud like that. She left that world behind of her own free choice."

"Then she must be extremely stubborn if she's holding out for someone better than you."

"Actually, she holds me in high regard. But we do not share the same religion."

"What's the big problem? Thor or Hercules are just different names for Jesus."

"Not in her mind. If there's one thing Flavia won't do, it's assimilate any other gods to Jesus. For her, he stands alone and unchallenged. She has no pantheon. She has only Jesus Christ."

"And the Father. And the Holy Spirit too. I lived among Christians in Britannia. I know what they teach."

"It's an interesting dilemma for a monotheist," Rex acknowledged. He wasn't exactly sure how Flavia put those three deities together and still claimed to worship one God. Perhaps she didn't even know herself. "In any case," he went on, "my religion doesn't fit with hers. I'm a heathen and a killer. She's a Christian and a nun. Those two things are about as opposite as you can get."

Chrocus didn't offer any fatherly advice but just downed the last of his beer and let out a loud belch. "I feel like a man again," he said.

"And that is why," Rex said, changing the subject to the one he had intended all along, "you must rise from this bed and reclaim your rightful throne."

At these words, Chrocus sighed and set his mug atop the cabinet beside him. "A ray of sunshine and a nice, foamy head can't heal this wound instantly, Brandulf. The knife pierced my ribs and came out here." He pointed to a spot beneath his left pectoral muscle. "The wound festers still."

"May I see it?"

"No! Even I cannot! The healer says deep magic is in the bandages. They must stay in place at all times and never be lifted or the magic will escape."

"The surgeons in the Roman army did exactly the opposite. They used clean linen strips and changed them frequently. Wine was used to wash the wounds, and honey and garlic too, which they said drives out infection."

"We do everything better here in Germania."

Have you seen the Roman amphitheater? Rex wanted to say, but he refrained, lest it sound insulting to his father. Instead, he asked, "Does it hurt?"

"Surprisingly little in recent days. The magic protects me from the pain. And I sleep a lot, thanks to the healer's potions. She takes good care of me. She thinks there is a chance I might not die."

"*Die?* Father, you do not look like a man close to death."

"But wounds can turn putrid and take a man down. It happens often."

Rex grimaced and decided to get back to the main subject. "Assuming you will not die, I think the day will come when you should challenge Aoric."

"I hate him," Chrocus admitted, then gestured to his side. "But what can I do?"

"Many men would abandon him if they had a reason. Not just your old warriors. The young ones too."

"It will be weeks, perhaps months, before I am in a position to move."

"But he grows stronger every day! Now is the time to confront him, before he solidifies his hold on the realm. It could be as simple as challenging him to a duel. Man against man to settle an offense, as has always been our tradition. Let Gundomar fight in your stead. He is a strong warrior. He could defeat Aoric in combat."

Chrocus shook his head. "I have seen Aoric fight, Brandulf. Few men are his equal. Even Gundomar is not. Perhaps I might have been his match in my youth. Or even now, in my forty-fifth year—if he hadn't stuck a dagger in my back."

The old king fell silent as he recalled the bitter day. Rex remained quiet as well, letting the hard memories and turbulent feelings flow freely through his father's mind. At last, Chrocus pointed to the cabinet beside the bed. "Look inside," he said.

Rex unfastened the latch and opened the door to find garments stored within, the rich clothing of a king. There was also a fur-lined cape. And one more thing: a sword.

"Is that what I think it is?" Rex asked. Although the scabbard was different now, the hilt looked familiar. Images from his boyhood rushed back, memories of that same sword on his father's hip.

"Yes, it is Blood-Maker," replied the king. "Hand it to me."

Rex reverently gave his father the sword. The sound of it being drawn from its sheath awakened even more memories from Rex's childhood. Chrocus gazed down its length, inspecting its line and balance, then slowly moved the blade in the classic thrusts, cuts, feints, and parries of a swordsman. Satisfied with its feel in his hand, he tipped the point into the scabbard and shoved it home.

"It is still a fine weapon," he declared.

"The great ones never decay. The passing of years only adds to their legend."

Chrocus smiled at this, then held out the sword to his son. "I want you to do it."

"What?" asked Rex, taken aback.

"I want you to challenge Aoric. You are my prince. You could challenge him to trial by combat. If he wins, you would leave Germania in shame and never return. I, too, would be exiled from my homeland until death. But if you defeat him, I would get my kingdom back, and you would get your mercenaries. The stakes are very high. But I believe you are worthy to fight a duel against that false king."

Rex rose from his chair, taking Blood-Maker in his grip. He stared down at his father reclining in his bed. The king's eyes were lively now, bright and very fierce. Rex's heart began to pound as he contemplated how truly momentous such a battle would be. The idea of it seemed outrageous. But Chrocus was undeterred. "Fight for me, Brandulf, my son," he said.

Rex drew the blade from its sheath again and raised it into a ray of light from the window. The barbarian steel glinted as brightly as the day it was forged. "On the memory and glory of this blade," Rex declared, "I will confront Aoric for his crimes."

"And when will you do it?"

"Tonight, at the Wodan's Day festival, beneath the Grand Old Oak."

"And why shall you do this thing?"

"For honor, and duty, and the timeless pursuit of justice."

"Now those are words of a king," said Chrocus the Great.

⟞⟊⟊⟊⟝

When Rex arrived around dusk, the Grand Old Oak was draped with lanterns. The warmth of the summer day had given way to a cool, breezy evening. Rex had exchanged his plain tunic for the more elegant one made of gray wool with burgundy roundels and piping. The long-sleeved garment fitted him well. It was perfect for dancing and feasting—and also for fighting, when the time came for that.

A large crowd had gathered at the oak tree. It seemed that all of Brigantium had turned out for the festival in the countryside. Everyone was jabbering about Aoric's performance in the horse-riding contest earlier that day. He had pierced eighteen of the twenty rings with his javelins, and he hadn't missed a single melon on the posts. Though the citizens thought this proved his great prowess in battle, Rex was more encouraged by the fatigue it would induce in his foe. *That will be good*, Rex thought, because he was feeling unusually tired this evening. *Probably from all that rowing*, he reasoned. It was quite a distance from Vemania back to Brigantium.

For all the guests who had gathered on the lawn beneath the tree's immense canopy, Aoric was the hub around which the wheel of the party turned. Revelers in colorful garments swirled around him, laughing as they talked or hoisting mugs of frothy ale to toast their king. Aoric seemed to know them all. With his copper hair, wide shoulders, fashionable clothes, and easy humor, people of all kinds were drawn to him. He was a charismatic man, no question.

As Rex sized up his foe, he was surprised to notice Flavia standing at his side. She wore a Germanic gown that someone must have loaned her, and a string of delicate white flowers had been woven into her chestnut hair. In the soft glow of the lanterns above, she looked exceptionally beautiful. Suddenly she giggled at something Aoric said, and the way she glanced at him made Rex grit his teeth. In fact, it bothered him more than he would have guessed, for he felt a hot flush rise to his neck and cheeks. Though the air was cool tonight, beads of sweat broke out on his brow. It literally made him feel nauseated to see Flavia cavorting with Aoric. *She's just gathering information*, he told himself. *So why does that make me feel sick?*

It was almost time for the priests of Wodan to carve the wild boars that had been spit-roasted all afternoon. The first cut would be tossed onto the coals to be consumed by the god. Then, once Wodan had received his share, the people would dig into their portions. Although Rex usually loved good pork, the thought of that juicy meat dripping with sauce didn't sit well with him. He sat down on a bench, feeling drained by the intensity of the looming confrontation. Usually, he felt nervous before combat, but then a powerful battle lust would kick in and empower him for the fight. Tonight, however, he only felt anxious, even a little dizzy. It felt good to sit for a moment. Once everyone had gathered around the firepit for the ceremonial carving, he would issue his challenge to Aoric. Until then, he would wait here and gather his strength for the combat.

A great cheer woke Rex from a semi-delirious doze. He opened his eyes to see that the priests had sacrificed a ham hock to Wodan. Now the people crowded around the firepit with empty wooden dishes in their hands. Rex rose from his bench and swayed for a moment as he regained his balance. Striding across the lawn, he forced his way through the crowd until he stood across the roasting pit from Aoric.

"King Aoric is . . . is a pig himself!" he shouted. *Was that how I was going to start this?* Rex couldn't recall the exact speech he had planned for this moment. *Maybe this will do?*

The circle of revelers instantly fell silent. No one dared to speak. Rex put his hand on his sword's hilt. He took a step forward. And vomited down the front of his clothes.

Vaguely, he was aware that everyone was laughing. Yet he could hardly hear it, for the world was spinning and the people were very far away. A fist seemed to reach inside him and grab his lungs, squeezing them so hard that they could no longer function. Though he panted and heaved, he couldn't get enough air, no matter how deeply he inhaled. The feeling was terrifying, yet at the same time, Rex was too deranged to care. He sank to his knees. Vomitus bubbled up from his mouth and oozed into his beard.

A tall red-haired man towered over Rex like a god. His skin was fair, and his eyes were green. "Throw this man into my wagon and take him back to Brigantium until I decide what to do with him," he said with a ring of authority in his voice. Apparently, he was some kind of king.

Someone's hand grabbed the back of Rex's collar.

"Wait!" shouted the god-like king. "He's disgusting. First strip him naked and dunk him in the horse trough. Then put him in my wagon and get him out of my sight."

A severe headache was pounding inside Rex's skull now, and his breath was coming in ragged gasps. Spasms of nausea shook him again and again. Dizzy blackness rolled through his mind like billows of smoke. Each time the darkness came, it brought relief. He only wished it could somehow become permanent.

Yet through the delirium, a driving purpose remained alive in Rex's soul, burning like a flame that could not be extinguished. He knew in some primordial, animalistic way that he was here to confront the enemy king who loomed over him. Strong hands were tugging the back of his garment, trying to stand him up. In a moment, all would be lost. Now was the time for action.

Rex's fingers tightened on the hilt of his spatha. He began to rise to his feet. Suddenly, in a movement born from untold hours of training and practice, he drew his blade and slashed it around in a speeding arc of death. A surprise attack like this had been known to behead a man so quickly that the severed head kept speaking until it hit the ground.

But not this time.

Somehow the red-haired king saw the blade coming and leapt back from it. Rex felt the sword's tip graze his enemy's chest. The king grunted in surprise.

Perhaps I was slow?

Dizziness overwhelmed Rex once again, and the exertion of combat had robbed him of even more air. He dropped his weapon, slumped to his knees, and tumbled forward. It felt good to lie prone in the grass. He was utterly spent.

"Lock him up," snarled the king.

"Rex! I'll come to you!" shouted a woman's desperate voice.

And then, mercifully, darkness took hold of him and the world was no more.

———————

The horror of what had just happened left Flavia staggered. It was beyond anything she could comprehend. Something was terribly wrong with Rex. Some sickness had taken hold of him from out of nowhere. *How?* He didn't look like he had been physically abused. Perhaps he had eaten some strange local food? Surely he couldn't have been drunk! Whatever the cause, she knew she had to go to him right away.

But can I?

With rising panic, Flavia realized that the problem went much deeper than Rex's illness. He had just attacked the king before many eyewitnesses. His delirious state wouldn't be an excuse for such a dreadful deed. He had made an assassination attempt against the lawful regent of the Alemannic people. Though Aoric probably wouldn't execute an emissary from Constantine, still, Rex had ceased to be the honored man he once was. He had become an instant criminal. And that meant . . .

I'm in danger too.

Flavia's urgent concern for Rex now mingled with fear for her own safety. When she was a respected member of an imperial entourage, her right of security was guaranteed. But with Rex as some kind of outlaw, who was left to protect her? Stephen the priest certainly wasn't strong enough to provide adequate protection. Stunned, Flavia realized she needed to get clear of this place immediately.

King Aoric had moved to the edge of the clearing beneath the oak to confer in private with his high-ranking comrades. The crowd of partygoers had likewise splintered into small groups, all of which were abuzz with heated conversation. A mood of outrage hung in the air. Several priests of Wodan were trying to calm the more vociferous voices, and one priest even started serving cuts of pork to restore a sense of normalcy.

"Flavia, we should leave," someone said in Greek. Turning, she saw it was Cassi. Fear was in the Aethiops's large brown eyes.

"I agree. Let's slip into the woods and figure out what to do. But don't run. Meet me at that hazel thicket over there."

"Then we will run," Cassi said, and the two girls parted.

Though she walked as nonchalantly as possible and didn't glance around, Flavia couldn't help but sense that many eyes were on her. Perhaps it was just her imagination. Or perhaps all the Alemanni wanted to lynch her on the spot. Anxiety had a strong hold on her now.

With great relief, she reached the hazel thicket without interference. The many branches spreading from each trunk created dense cover yet left adequate space to walk underneath. Flavia ducked under the foliage and made her way to where Cassi was waiting. Fortunately, the dusky sky had given way to full darkness now. And it was even darker here, outside the circle of light from the party tree.

"We must hurry," Cassi urged.

"I know, but to where? Perhaps we can find lodging in Brigantium. We could send word to Stephen to bring us money for a room."

"I think a small village is best. Let things settle down in the city."

"Or maybe we should just sleep under the stars? The night is warm enough. The trees of the forest might be better friends to us than the villagers."

"Let's start running," said Cassi, "and decide later what to do."

The two fugitives set out at a pace that soon left the sounds of the party behind. They traveled by moonlight along a deer path that ran parallel to the lakeshore. At one point, they crossed a stream, so they stopped to slake their thirst before continuing. A fishing hamlet was visible to the right, down by the water. Even if they didn't lodge there, Flavia decided it would be better to sleep near civilization than in the deep woods. Cassi felt the same way.

As they drew near the village, the two girls came across another hazel thicket on the outskirts of town. Though its boughs were dense, there were enough gaps in the foliage to slip inside. Once past the outer branches, Flavia found that the arching canopy made a kind of secret enclosure. The ground was soft beneath the leafy roof. It was a snug and dry little place, so the girls decided to spend the night there. They spread one of their mantles on the ground and covered themselves with the other, huddling together for comfort more than warmth.

"We should pray to Jesus before we sleep," Cassi said.

"Yes. Perhaps you could pray first, then I will."

"It is my delight to pray with you, my friend."

Wrapped in barbarian cloaks beneath the dangling hazelnut pods, the two Christian nuns joined hands and poured out their hearts to the Savior of the world. They admitted their fears and asked for courage. They sought God's heavenly protection and care. Both of them interceded for Rex, wherever he might be right now. And then, when the final amen had been said, Flavia fell asleep, still a terrified fugitive yet confident she was also the handmaiden of God.

8

AUGUST 316

Since ancient days, people had been calling on Artemis for help in childbirth because the virgin goddess had served as a midwife when her brother Apollo was born. Though the superstitious masses still prayed to Artemis when the labor pains hit, Emperor Constantine had found a better patron. When the Highest God decided to send his Son to earth, he did so through a different virgin: not Artemis but Mary, a Hebrew girl with exceptional faith. Who better to help a woman in labor than a saint who had experienced those pangs herself?

The emperor paced outside the bedroom in the imperial palace at Arelate. It was a hot day, and southern Gaul was famous for its intense sun. Feeling the heat himself, Constantine didn't dare imagine the sweaty travail that poor Fausta was enduring on the birthing chair right now.

"Holy mother Mary," he prayed with palms upraised, "the gospel says your womb and breasts are blessed because of the Son you bore. And you even said that all generations shall call you blessed! Though I am an emperor, I humbly bless you now. Please look down on the labor pains of my wife, which you yourself have endured, and ask your Son to grace her with a safe delivery. And please let it be a little boy."

Constantine had just finished the prayer when, from behind the bedroom's curtain, Fausta uttered a shriek more intense than any so far. "You can do it!" the midwife urged. "Push harder!" There was some more grunting and shrieking, and then came the sound that Constantine had longed to hear: the wail of a newborn baby.

"Well? What do we have?" he called anxiously through the curtain.

It was his mother, Helena, who stepped out to meet him. A triumphant smile was on her face. "You have a second son," she announced.

"Thank you, Mary and Jesus!" Constantine exclaimed. "A male heir!"

"You have a male heir already," Helena reminded him.

"From Minervina. She was a concubine, not a wife."

"I considered her a wife," Helena said with a sniff. "And Crispus is your firstborn son and heir, no matter what status his mother may have had."

"Bah! Don't worry about him, Mother. I will always love him, because I loved Minervina. But now is the time to rejoice at the birth of a new prince! Do you know what this means?"

"That he shall occupy a spot in the Imperial College, of course."

Constantine chuckled to himself, for his clever mother was exactly right. And like her, he rejoiced at the opportunity to advance the family name. The Imperial College normally consisted of two augusti and two caesars, but the caesars were vacant now. Licinius's wicked assassination plot had failed, and Constantine had ordered Bassianus beheaded. With him gone, and now with the birth of this new son, Constantine had two direct descendants to install in the college as caesars: Crispus and the baby. His family was going to rule the entire empire—a glorious thought indeed! The only downside was, a war would have to be fought with Licinius to make it stick.

"Come meet your second son," Helena invited. "He looks like you, not that woman you married."

"You mean my queen, Lady Fausta?"

"Yes, of course. That is the woman you married, after Minervina."

"She deserves your respect, Mother."

"I have always given her all the respect she is due. Now come see the baby."

Constantine entered the bedroom and found the exhausted Fausta reclining on a couch while the midwife rocked the infant. Bloody rags and other womanly things were on the floor, but the emperor averted his eyes and focused on the swaddled newborn. Although there was sticky stuff in the baby's hair, Constantine ignored that too. Instead, he folded back the swaddling cloth and was gratified to see that he did, indeed, have a little boy.

"His name shall be Flavius Valerius Constantine," said Constantine.

Fausta lifted her tired head. "Exactly the same as you?"

"We can call him Secundus, since he is the second with that great name."

"May he reach the same lofty pinnacle as the first," Fausta said.

"Alongside his brother, Crispus," Helena added, drawing a little sneer from Fausta.

But Constantine had no time for the petty wrangling of women as they tried to advance their favorite offspring. Bigger matters were at stake within the empire. War was inevitable now, not only because of the assassination attempt but because Licinius would never stand idly by while his little "Junior" was excluded from the college. And so, with a major battle once again looming on the horizon, Constantine faced the two most important women in his life and declared, "I have lingered in Gaul long enough. Within a week I shall depart Arelate at the head of a mighty army."

"By what route?" asked Helena.

"We shall take the Mons Matrona pass into Italy and keep marching eastward until we encounter resistance."

"Aha! The same pass by which you invaded Italy to destroy my accursed brother," Fausta said.

Fausta, you faithful devil! She was an unattractive woman, and she had a devious personality. Yet Constantine greatly appreciated how she had rejected her brother, Maxentius, to side with him in that prior crisis. Constantine also remembered that dark night several years ago when Fausta's father tried to assassinate him right here in this palace. Fausta not only reported the plot when she learned of it but also shed remarkably few tears when the speculators hanged her father from the ceiling beams. Clearly, Fausta was a loyal wife, and she would no doubt be a fierce mother as well. Helena was going to have her hands full keeping Crispus's career on track now that Secundus would be vying for imperial honors.

"Where do you imagine you shall confront Licinius?" Helena inquired.

"Hard to say. If he marches out to meet me, it might be somewhere on the Padus plain. If he waits, I'll have to go all the way into Pannonia and dig him out of Sirmium."

"Which legion shall Crispus command?"

The question was unexpected, and Constantine frowned. "Crispus is not a general, Mother. He cannot lead a legion."

"Why not? He is certainly capable! He's eighteen now, and he attended the best cadet school in Gaul. And he is a fine Christian. His tutor, Lactantius, speaks highly of his moral fiber."

"I am not averse to giving the young man high command," Constantine said diplomatically. "But he is untested."

"How better to test him than on a campaign?"

"Hmm. There is truth in what you say." After a moment of thought, the emperor said, "I'll tell you what. I shall bring him with me in this war against Licinius. If he comports himself well and the men respect him, I will put him in charge of all Gaul."

"A worthy appointment!" Helena exclaimed.

At this, Fausta rose from her couch and took the newborn from the midwife. "But look here," she said, bringing the baby to Constantine. "You can see from the shape of his hands that he is made to wield a sword. I foresee a great future for him as well."

The baby's tiny little hand didn't look capable of holding a twig, much less a sword. Yet Constantine knew Fausta was only trying to remind him of his obligations to their son. "Secundus shall find a place in the Imperial College as well," he promised. It seemed to satisfy Fausta, so she retired again to her couch.

"I believe I shall join you on this grand adventure, to witness Crispus's exploits," Helena announced.

Fausta had an immediate reply. "And I shall follow in my coach, that I might accustom Secundus to war from the very beginning."

Constantine merely shrugged, for who could resist the combined force of two determined women?

In the end, it took only five days to assemble the troops and leave Arelate. Following the ancient Domitian Way, the expedition marched northeast until it reached the foot of the Alps. Fortunately, the Mons Matrona pass was warm and sunny this time of year, covered with daisies and buttercups instead of snowdrifts. If Hannibal could get huge, lumbering elefanti over this pass in October, Constantine knew he'd have no problem getting a simple army of men and horses across the grassy pastures of late summer.

After descending the other side into Italy, the army left the mountain vales and joined the Postumian Way. The Padus River plain lay wide before them now, and none of the scouts were reporting enemy activity ahead. Constantine pushed eastward quickly with few stops because the marching was so easy.

By mid-September, he had reached Verona, where he called for a halt to rest the troops. Verona held a special place in Constantine's heart because it was the site of a dramatic victory a few years back. Though he won the battle that day, he had almost died when he found himself surrounded by deadly foes. Only the bravery of his valiant troops saved his life as they rallied to defend their lord—all except one, who had turned and run like a coward. That was too bad, because Constantine had liked that handsome young German, who possessed all the makings of a great soldier. *What was his name? Rex, I believe it was. I sentenced him to row in the navy for the rest of his life. I wonder what happened to him?*

Constantine returned his attention to the present. With so many urgent duties, reflecting on previous battles wasn't a priority. The field scouts were reporting that Licinius's forces had recently been in Italy, advancing as far as the border city of Emona, but they evacuated two days ago. Constantine decided to press on to that city before making a final drive toward Sirmium.

The gates of Emona were open to the emperor when he arrived, and the people gave him a hero's welcome. They clearly didn't want him to think they had been siding with Licinius, even though the impostor's troops had taken control of the city for a time. In reality, said the local town councilors, Emona was completely devoted to Constantine.

Yet one thing about the city did glorify the Augustus of the East: the imperial images. Not long ago, the civic statues in this boundary town had depicted the peaceful harmony of the Imperial College. But now, instead of Constantine and Licinius sharing pedestals like they once did, the current sculptures depicted only Licinius in triumphant poses. This change had been made during the recent occupation by the enemy troops. Constantine's images, the embodiment of his imperial majesty, had been thrown down in his own territory of Italy. It was a final outrage. War was the only possible outcome now.

"Should we pull these atrocities off their pedestals, Your Highness?"

asked one of the bodyguards who accompanied the emperor at all times. "We have ropes and horses. We could do it."

"No, leave them up," Constantine replied as he stepped close to the base of one of the statues. It was a bronze depiction of Licinius gazing across a battlefield with a military banner in his hand. "My dear brother-in-law actually looks rather handsome up there. The sculptor did a fine job."

"But he is your enemy," the bodyguard said.

Constantine shrugged. "Yes, he is. But he's family too. When you are an emperor, it all gets rather complicated." And with that, the Augustus of the West hiked up his tunic and began to relieve himself against the base of the Licinian statue that dared to call Italy its home.

———◇◇◇———

King Chrocus picked up the vial of medicine left by the healer woman and stared at the little green bottle. The potion had been remarkable in its ability to numb his mind and make all his sorrows go away. A blessed fog would descend, then everything that had happened—the excruciating shame of defeat and exile—would immediately fade. It was a sweet release.

Yet the mental fog had brought its own kind of pain too. *Running away isn't what a courageous king would do,* Chrocus had told himself over and over, probably a thousand times. *You don't need this stuff!* With that conviction now firm in his mind, he leaned over the bedside, poured the potion into the chamber pot, and hurled the vial against the bedroom's opposite wall. The sound of shattering glass was satisfying in its finality.

Reclining against his pillow, Chrocus dozed a little, trying to catch a nap because he hadn't slept well overnight without the medicine. A commotion in the courtyard awoke him midmorning. Hoofbeats and the jingle of horse tack signaled that riders had arrived at the fort. Chrocus's heartbeat quickened, for this was surely a report on the confrontation with Aoric at the Wodan's Day festival. Much would depend on what was about to be disclosed.

After a few moments of scurrying downstairs, Gundomar strode into the king's chamber and came straight to the bedside. Several other high-ranking warriors were behind him.

"Greetings, my lord," said Gundomar with a bow of his head. "I come with urgent news." Although his droopy blond mustache was streaked with gray, his stature was impressive and his physique was still muscular. He was a fine example of a middle-aged warrior who had kept himself in fighting shape.

"Tell me quickly. Leave nothing out, even if you would wish to spare me."

"Things at the festival did not go well."

Chrocus felt his stomach lurch. "Does my son still live?"

"Aye, but Aoric has imprisoned him."

"Wounded?"

"Not in battle, my lord. It was a very strange thing. Just as Brandulf stepped forward to confront the wicked usurper, he fell to his knees and puked. Clearly, his mind was clouded too. At first, we suspected strong drink. But we have since learned that the men who touched Brandulf's clothes got sick as well, and two horses died after drinking from the trough in which he was washed."

"He was poisoned."

"Yes, sire. It is the only explanation."

"By whom?"

"We do not know. But it wasn't a traitor among our own men. The tunic that was poisoned was not the one he wore here, but one that remained in Aoric's house in Brigantium. Aoric clearly wants him dead, though he's afraid to do it openly for fear of imperial retaliation. Only something secret could work."

"Gundomar, my son is in grave danger! He must be rescued."

"Actually, sire, we believe Brandulf is safe for now, since it is widely known that Aoric is holding him. An Alemannic king has no legal authority to execute a Roman legate, no matter what crime he's accused of. If the young man died while in Aoric's care, the legions would march against us for sure."

"Did Brandulf mention me? Have we been discovered?"

"No, we're safe. However, I am beginning to think Aoric suspects me of siding with you. It won't be long before he starts a purge of suspected rebels. I do not think we can keep hiding here much longer."

Chrocus frowned at this, though he knew it was probably true. "Perhaps we should send scouts to find another castle farther away. I could be moved there to continue my recuperation. The Romans left many forts in the deep forest when they withdrew from Raetia."

Now it was Gundomar's turn to frown. "Or perhaps," he said tentatively, "you could begin to command your men again. Summon all those faithful to you. Direct the resistance from here."

"It is much to ask of a wounded old man."

"Even wounded, you inspire great loyalty. And you have many supporters—more than you think. We could withstand a siege if they found us here. In fact, we could even besiege Brigantium. The walls are weak in many places. Two thousand men could surround the city and eventually break in."

"Perhaps we could try in a few weeks—if I am able to heal and the wound stops festering."

At this, Gundomar turned and received a wrapped object from one of the warriors standing behind him. Unfolding the cloths, he revealed it to be an unsheathed sword. "It is your mighty weapon, the Blood-Maker. We retrieved it from the ground at the festival. Take it in hand, my lord."

Chrocus received the sword and lifted it to the light from the window. As the king examined the blade, he noticed something staining its tip.

"It has been bloodied," he observed.

"Yes, my lord. Even as Brandulf was on his knees, delirious from the poison, he attacked the wicked usurper and drew blood from him. It was his last act before the poison took him."

For a long time, Chrocus was silent as he contemplated this news. Finally, he said to the warriors behind Gundomar, "Leave us, all of you."

When the men had gone and the king was alone with his most faithful retainer, he beckoned him to come close. "No one has seen what I am about to show you," he whispered.

Gundomar only nodded, so the king continued with his revelation. After laying aside the bedcovers, he showed Gundomar the hole that had been cut in his tunic to access the wound in his flank. A great mass of linen was there, darkened with old blood and crusty pus. The warrior did not flinch as Chrocus grasped the edge of the bandage. But when he pulled it back, Gundomar's jaw dropped.

"It has completely healed, Your Majesty!"

Chrocus looked down at the scar where the tip of Aoric's blade had exited. Indeed, it had closed up well. The skin around the scar was a healthy pink, not the raw red of a festering sore. Although it would no doubt leave a permanent mark, the king's body had done its healing work. The wound was in excellent shape.

"I have known it for some time," said Chrocus. "The entry wound in my back is the same. Neither of them pains me anymore."

"But . . . why then are you abed?"

Chrocus could not respond right away, for the emotions that took hold of him were powerful and complex, preventing him from uttering any words. Foremost among his feelings was shame—the awful realization that the indignity of his dethronement had been made worse by his own lack of kingly resolve. By putting the blame on his "festering" wound, he was able to avoid a response, even when he knew the injury was on the mend. Instead of rising to fight again, he had retreated into the solace of the healer's potions. Yet the comfort they provided lasted only until he could obtain the next dose. The cycle of craving, indulgence, shame, and despair was one he hadn't been able to break. Only the coming of his long-lost son had caused him to feel hope again. Surely it was a sign from the gods. And so he had decided to be done with potions and passivity.

But do I have what it takes to reclaim my throne?

Gundomar shifted uneasily at the long silence. "Sire? Do you wish me to leave?"

"No," Chrocus replied, then hurled the bedcovers off him. "I wish you to help me stand."

"Gladly, my lord!"

With help from his friend, Chrocus raised his stiff body and swung his feet to the floor. After pulling on a pair of leather boots, he stood up, leaning on Gundomar for support. "Bring me my royal cape," he said.

The warrior bent to the bedside cabinet and brought out a fur-lined cloak. When he wrapped it around Chrocus's shoulders, the invigorating effect was instantaneous. Gone was the feeling of being dressed like a sickly invalid. The dyed wool cloak, with its trim of marten fur, made all the difference in Chrocus's outlook. As he brandished his sword, a regal fire came alive within him.

"That is not the last blood of my enemies that shall ever stain this blade," he vowed.

"Sire! You must let your men see you like this. Can you make it down the stairs?"

"If I cannot make it down the stairs, I am no longer worthy to be called king."

"You shall always be our king! All the men will rejoice when they see you. They will think you have been miraculously healed."

"Perhaps I have. We will give praise to Thor for his mighty intervention. He sent my son to inspire me."

"And we must honor your own courage too, for you threw off the shackles of despair."

Slowly, with Gundomar's assistance, Chrocus left the upstairs bedchamber and descended to the main floor. Though Gundomar wanted to lead him directly into the bright courtyard, the king stopped him at the camp shrine. This room, which had once housed the legion's standards, had a pit in the floor that could be accessed through a trapdoor. During the time of Roman occupation, it had served as the treasury of the castle, a cellar that was guarded day and night. Today, however, the trapdoor was held fast only by a sturdy metal latch.

"Go down and fetch the chest that is there," said Chrocus. "I shall not appear before my men as anything but their king."

Gundomar obeyed and returned shortly with an iron-bound treasure chest. After setting it on the floor, he opened it. His eyes widened when he saw what was inside. "Your crown!" he exclaimed.

Taking the circlet of gold from his retainer, Chrocus placed it upon his head. He then arranged his cape so that it completely covered him, descending to the tops of his boots and hiding his undignified nightshirt. His unsheathed sword was in his hand. Now, at last, he felt ready to appear before his men.

When the door to the headquarters building was thrown open, Chrocus stepped into the sunlight for the first time in many weeks. The courtyard was full of warriors conversing with one another or lounging on the grass outside their barracks. Other men were on the ramparts keeping watch. For a long moment, nothing happened. Then, as if on cue, all the warriors fell silent at the same time.

"Hail, King Chrocus the Great!" Gundomar cried.

"Hail to the king!" the men chorused in reply.

Chrocus took another step forward. "Your lord calls you to action!"

"To what purpose, sire?" Gundomar asked, speaking for the men.

"Send out messengers to call the faithful to arms! Tell them to be ready within a fortnight. Then we shall march against the tyrant Aoric, a murderer who does not deserve the title of king!"

"To war!" shouted Gundomar, and all the men echoed the cry. "To war! To war!"

Lifting high his sword, Chrocus gazed at the expectant faces of his brave troops. "Yes, my men, to war we shall go. Ready yourselves to lay a siege. Gather many arrows in your quivers. Build ladders and bridges and battering rams. For this oath I make to you in Thor's mighty name: Before the new moon arrives, the true king of the Alemanni will be sitting on the throne in Brigantium!"

—⁊⁊⁊—

When Flavia woke up next to Cassi in their hut of hazel branches, for the briefest moment, all seemed right in the world—until, like a heavy weight descending, she remembered she was running from a ruthless king in a foreign land, with no one to give her shelter or protect her from bodily harm.

Except the Lord God, she reminded herself. *And that is all I need.*

Cassi stirred soon afterward. "I'm hungry," she said as the girls lay side by side in the dim twilight of the approaching dawn. Her stomach rumbled as if to prove her point.

"Perhaps we can find a nice fisherman's wife in the village—" Flavia began, but Cassi cut her off by gripping her arm and pointing.

"Look!" she exclaimed.

Flavia's eyes followed the line of Cassi's finger. There, interwoven into the hazel thicket in which they had taken shelter, was a bush of thorny brambles. And it was overflowing with huge red raspberries.

Hurling aside the mantle that had served as their blanket, the girls scrambled to the bush and began picking the berries. They were sweet and juicy, and there seemed to be no limit to them. Flavia worked on her knees with two hands, performing a steady rhythm of plucking and eating while Cassi harvested a different part of the bush. Finally, when the girls had eaten their fill, they flopped back on the grass with satisfied smiles on their faces.

"That was the best breakfast I've ever eaten," Flavia said.

"Like the manna of Israel," Cassi replied. "A provision from God's hand."

And that is all I need, Flavia repeated in her heart.

At that moment, far in the distance, they heard hounds.

The look in Cassi's eyes confirmed everything Flavia immediately suspected. No one in Germania hunted with hounds at dawn in August. There was only one type of prey being sought this morning: human.

"We must go," Flavia said, rising to her feet.

"Yes, but where?"

"Not into the village. I think it's called Lucky Tree. The old Roman road runs through it and goes along the lakeshore. It eventually leads to Vindonissa."

"Are you sure?"

"No, but all Roman roads run somewhere important. And Rex said that is the road that goes back into the empire. Vindonissa is the nearest manned fort. The army would protect us. We are imperial citizens."

"But won't the hounds catch us first?"

"I think we can lose them. Come on!"

Wrapped again in their mantles, Flavia and Cassi exited the hazel thicket and found the air outside noticeably cooler. Although the expensive clothes they had been loaned for the party didn't make for easy traveling, there was nothing they could do about that. Flavia led Cassi downhill toward the village, but on a line of travel that she believed would intercept the creek they had encountered in the night. The stream would eventually flow into the lake, probably near the village, for settlements were built near flowing water whenever possible.

The baying of the hounds continued to draw nearer while the girls trekked through the forest. Fortunately, just as Flavia had hoped, they did meet the creek not far above the village. It had grown wide here, and the water was about knee-deep. Flavia removed her sandals, hiked up her gown, and waded right in. "To make our scent disappear," she said.

Cassi followed her. "The hounds will smell where we get out," she observed.

"That is why we will not get out. I plan to go right into the lake, steal a rowboat from the village, and move us up the shore to where the road is close. We'll leave the lake far from the hounds. They'll be sniffing along both sides of this stream all day while we're speeding up a good Roman road to Vindonissa!"

"You are so smart, Flavia! I will go with you anywhere."

Together the two fugitives followed the tumbling creek downstream. As it flattened out near the lake, the current gradually slowed. A few docks jutted into the water, but no people were up and about at this early hour. Where the stream entered Lake Brigantium, several fishing boats sat on the sandy banks. Flavia spied a little dugout canoe with two paddles inside. *I'll only go a short way and abandon it,* she decided. *The owner will surely find it again.*

The girls had just begun to push the boat into the water when a man emerged from the underbrush with an accusatory shout. Before they could turn and run, he had seized each of them by the wrist. Flavia struggled, but the man's grip was fierce.

"Quit struggling or I'll headbutt ya!" he snarled. "And my skull is like granite!"

As he approached the village, dragging his captives behind him, he hailed a man in warrior's clothing. "Look! They showed up here, just like you said."

"Well done," said the warrior gruffly. "Take them to the dock. You can collect the reward there."

"No!" Flavia pleaded. "Let us go! I'll pay you ten times as much!"

"Sure you will, lady. How about if I let you run off into the woods to fetch your purse?" The man guffawed and handed over his captives to the warriors at the dock, receiving a few coins in return.

"I'm scared," Cassi said to Flavia as their wrists were bound in front of them with ropes.

"Stay strong. God is our mighty protector."

The captives were shoved into a rowboat that was immediately pushed away from the pier. The man in charge was a surly fellow with black, beady eyes like a crow. "Double-time," he instructed his rowers. "King Aoric wants his prize."

Flavia shuddered at these words. Prayer was her only defense now.

The trip from Lucky Tree to Brigantium's harbor was completed in about two hours. A dreadful silence hung over the boat during the journey. Apparently, the men had been instructed not to speak. Upon reaching the docks, the beady-eyed boss fastened a lead line to each of the captives' bonds, then twined the lines together. Holding the braid in his hand, he led them uphill toward the walled city, accompanied by the four rowers. After passing through the gate, they proceeded down the main street toward the forum.

"We're going to Aoric's house," Flavia whispered to Cassi.

"Shut up," muttered the boss, giving his braided line a hard yank that wrenched the girls' arms.

The leader stopped in front of the familiar mansion where Flavia had been greeted with dignity only a few days earlier. Now, of course, everything was different. Even the building itself seemed sinister and unwelcoming.

Like every noble Roman house, this one had a crew of burly doorkeepers and bodyguards. However, since the Germani weren't as much of a slave-holding society as the Romans, the guards here were not slaves but free warriors in Aoric's retinue, though low-ranking ones. They tended to be cruel dullards whose sullen demeanor and dim intellect had prevented them from rising higher in Alemannic society. Yet they knew their business. Rare was the stranger who could enter such a house undetected—or the resident who could leave unseen by their watching eyes.

The boat crew transferred the captive women to the doorkeepers, who immediately separated Cassi and Flavia. The young Aethiops was led to some other part of the house, while Flavia was taken to a private wing where only the household elite could go. A paunchy, unshaven guardsman hustled her into a lavish bedroom with erotic frescoes on the wall. He gave her a malevolent sneer, then left the room and locked the door behind him. Few Roman bedrooms had solid doors like that. Flavia did not like being imprisoned behind one.

She waited in tense silence for what seemed like an hour or two. Finally, she heard a key turn the lock on the door. When it opened, King Aoric stood in the doorway. His face was neither kind nor menacing. It was simply the placid face of a man in complete control.

"You are disheveled from your night in the woods," he said, "but even

251

so, you are beautiful." When Flavia made no reply to this, he entered the bedroom and closed the door. "Why did you flee?" he asked.

"I knew you would blame me. Was I wrong? Your men hunted me with hounds and arrested me like a criminal instead of a guest."

"Are you a criminal?"

"Of course not! I didn't know what Rex was going to do. I had no part in that."

"So you are not attached to that man in a meaningful way? If you are not, I see no reason to detain you. But if you are his companion, I would have to suspect that you played a role in his attack. To be honest, I would not take that very well."

Oh, God . . . there it is. How do I answer? If I lie, I betray Rex. If I tell the truth, I am in grave danger. What do I do?

Tell the truth. And never, ever betray the man you love.

Flavia's heart was beating rapidly as she met Aoric's gaze. The words she uttered next would have a profound effect on her future. Great pain might be in store. Perhaps even death. But there were certain words she simply could not say. And certain truths that could not be denied.

"I am attached to Rex," she declared at last. "He is the man I love. We are bound by an eternal devotion that will never be broken, no matter what else happens to us." Flavia gathered her courage and took a step forward. "Yet I also say to you, Lord Aoric, that I had no part in his attack on you. Something is terribly wrong with Rex, and I hope you can forgive him. He was not himself last night."

Aoric did not move, and his face was chillingly blank. It was impossible to discern if he was simmering with rage or utterly indifferent to what Flavia had just said. Then, very slowly and with deliberate motions, he began to untie the thongs that bound his shirt at his neck. Terrified, Flavia stepped back, but there was no way out of the bedroom. Its lone window was too high, and Aoric blocked the door.

"Look at me!" he barked.

When Flavia meekly obeyed, she saw him reach to the hem of his shirt and pull it over his head. Dressed now only in his Germanic trousers and tall boots, the warrior king seemed even more powerful than before. His body was luminous and pale, except for the fresh gash that crossed his broad chest. Though the wound had been cleaned and was not deep, it stood out like a red viper on white sand. Aoric pointed to it. "To attack a king with a sword deserves death," he said.

"I . . . I did not attack you."

"But you came here with Legate Rex. He sought to kill me. What else can I believe but that you are plotting my death?"

"I swear to you, I am not."

"That oath is not enough," said Aoric. "But there is one you could make that is."

The tall king approached Flavia swiftly, backing her against the bed, though not forcing her down upon it. Her mouth felt dry, and she swallowed hard as she tried to moisten it. "Wh-what do you want from me?" she asked in a shaky voice. "Leave me alone, I beg you."

"Swear an oath to be my second wife, and all will be well. Think of it, Flavia! You can reign in Alemannia as a queen. Everyone will respect you. We'll make trips into the empire together—not just to forts but to great cities with elegant life. I can make an alliance with the Romans, and you will be my noble lady who seals the deal. Can't you see it? This is an opportunity for greatness, if you will only take it."

The fear in Flavia's heart was strong now. She was sorely tempted to agree, just to buy herself some time. Yet once again, she found that there were certain words she simply could not utter.

Aoric pressed close, his body nearly touching hers. "Don't you want greatness, Flavia? Don't you want what I have to offer?"

"I want Rex," she replied.

At this, Aoric stepped back. Now his face was obviously enraged. He curled his hand into a fist but did not strike. Finally, he said in a cold and formal tone, "If you will not be my wife, then I hereby take you as my prisoner of war and concubine, by the law of the Alemanni."

"No . . . not that . . . please, Aoric—"

"The outcome of this is certain," he went on, "and I shall surely exercise my rights. The only question is, will a struggle be necessary?"

Flavia felt her knees sag at these words. Aoric grabbed her wrist in a grip far too tight to break. Agony gripped her soul as the evil man pulled her closer.

O God, hide me now in a secret place.

"Will a struggle be necessary?" Aoric repeated.

"No," Flavia whispered.

As she spoke, tears welled up in her eyes. A little rivulet trickled down her cheek and fell to the floor, disappearing into the dust like the precious gift that should have been given to someone else.

SEPTEMBER 316

The prison beside the judicial basilica on Brigantium's main square had served as Rex's pitiful home for two weeks. The first two days had been the worst, for that was when the poison still held him in its grip. He had retched and vomited, sweated and ached, moaned and gasped through the hot days and dark nights. Only Stephen brought him clothes and food, a truly faithful friend, despite the risk to himself.

A local butcher's wife had told Stephen that organ meats and pork cured with saltpeter were good for some kinds of poisoning, so he delivered meals of liver and ham to the jail. Apparently, the lady was right about that, for the symptoms eventually subsided—though not before a few times when Rex thought he would die. And he probably would have, Stephen said, if Aoric's men hadn't stripped him and dunked him the night of the party. Although they only wanted to keep his filth out of the king's carriage, the action had unintentionally saved Rex's life.

When the intense pain and delirium finally passed, Rex found himself exhausted and terribly hungry. Unfortunately, the rations Stephen was allowed to bring were meager, and Rex could tell that his frame had grown thin. In order not to become even weaker, he exercised frequently, pulling himself up on the high, barred window; shadowboxing around the cell; and doing other exercises that he'd learned in cadet school. His body felt leaner yet also harder after his two-week ordeal.

And the ordeal had no end in sight. No one had come to charge him with a crime or haul him before the royal throne in the basilica. Under Roman law, he would have at least been arraigned by now. But the Germani did whatever they wanted, so Rex had been totally cut off from the outside world. The isolation left him in a state of constant uncertainty about his own fate, accompanied by intense concern for Flavia's well-being. He sat on the floor, bored and discouraged, chewing a piece of straw from his cheap mattress. *I never should have come here,* he thought as he flicked the straw away.

The afternoon wore on, and night started to fall. Around dusk, the guard began to stir outside the cell. Rex watched him retrieve a key from a little jar on a shelf, which he thought Rex couldn't see. He opened a hatch near the floor and pushed through a bowl of fish broth that had been thickened with hardtack and lentils. The guard was a sullen fellow whose right eye was clouded. He glared at Rex through a small window in the door.

"Guess what I just learned?" he said with a sneer in his voice.

"That your breath stinks? I already knew that."

"No . . . yours does!" replied the guard, struggling for a witty comeback. Rex ignored him and picked a twig out of his stew. Though he was ravenous, he forced himself not to wolf down the food but to make it last.

"I heard some gossip from the king's mansion next door," the guard went on. "It turns out that your woman is Aoric's concubine."

Rex froze at these words. He stared blankly at a wall as he tried to comprehend the news. Slowly, he set the bowl on the floor and swallowed his bite. "That is a lie," he said at last.

"It ain't a lie!" The guard was grinning now, clearly enjoying himself. "Heard it straight from the doorkeeper who brought her in. She's locked in his special room, day and night. The king takes her often. How do you like that?"

The sadistic guard wanted to torment Rex further, so he kept giving more details. Though he presented many filthy scenarios, Rex refused to give him the pleasure of a response. Covering his ears, he went to the darkest corner of the cell and turned his back. Eventually, the guard gave up, leaving Rex to contend with his own dreadful imagination.

For the next several hours, he rolled through a cycle of excruciating emotions: helplessness, sorrow, loss, pity, rage, and even jealousy. He lay on his mattress and pounded his fist against the dungeon floor. The fact that such a terrible thing was happening to Flavia nearly drove him insane. "Argh!" he cried to the ceiling, trying to vent the fury that boiled in his soul. Rex's deep empathy for Flavia made her suffering his own. His inability to stop this moral travesty was like an icy knife stabbing his heart again and again. He reached over and snatched his half-eaten bowl of stew, hurling it against the wall with a crash. Yet the act of rage didn't help him any more than his groaning had. The knife of helpless empathy for the woman he loved stabbed him once more. *Oh, God, get her out of that house! Make it stop!*

It was deep in the night when Rex's emotions were finally spent. He had groaned and wept all he could. Exhausted, he fell into a dark and dreamless sleep.

He was awakened at an unusually early hour by a stirring in the prison. Groggy, he rose and peeked through the little window in his door. The entire prison consisted of three rooms: the cell he was in, a pit under the floor where murderers were lowered and left to die, and a front room where the guards congregated. Usually, four or five jailers were out front—husky men who locked up the rowdy drunks of Brigantium for an overnight stay or shoved food under the door to more serious offenders. But when Rex glanced out, all the guards were gone. They had even left the prison door ajar. He had never seen that before.

Rex crossed his cell to the window that looked outside. After jumping and grabbing hold of the bars, he pulled himself up so he could see the street below. Though the sun had not yet come up, people were already scurrying around. Their bustle seemed more urgent than normal for such an early hour. He dropped back to the floor, wondering what was happening in Brigantium today.

"Rex! Over here!" someone hissed. He turned to see Stephen's face at the little opening in the cell door.

"Hello, Brother Priest! You are a welcome sight. What's going on outside?"

"The city is surrounded by men! They came up during the night."

"Armed men, like invaders? A siege?"

"Yes! They have Brigantium encircled. Everyone is frantic. All able-bodied citizens have been summoned to the walls."

Rex was astounded. "You mean the prison has been left unguarded?"

"I guess so! I came with your rations this morning and found the place abandoned."

"Quick, then! Get me out."

Stephen jiggled the lock. "It's too strong to break. Maybe I can find an ax somewhere."

"Just use the key. Those jailers are so stupid. They hide it in my line of vision. See that jar of beans? Reach into it until you feel something metal. The bigger key opens the door."

After going to the jar, Stephen returned and put the key in the lock. It turned, and the cell door opened. Rex exited the cell, crossed the guardroom, and stepped into the sunlight for the first time in almost three weeks.

"It feels good to be a free man," he said.

"Where to now?"

Glancing across the forum toward the mansion of Aoric, Rex wanted to say, "To see Flavia." But now wasn't the time for that. Flavia was in no danger at the moment since Aoric certainly wouldn't be there. In fact, she was safer inside the house than in the chaotic streets. Flavia's future depended, first and foremost, on the outcome of this battle. So instead of rushing to the mansion, Rex pointed to the city walls. A continuous walkway ran behind the battlements.

"I'm headed up there," he told Stephen.

"To aid in the city's defense?"

"Of course not!" Rex answered with a snort. "To help the invaders get in."

Stephen's jaw dropped. "Help them get in? Why would you do that?"

At that moment, a ringing blast from a war horn sounded from outside the walls, followed by a ferocious roar as the troops began their assault.

"Because that is the army of Chrocus the Great, the true king of Alemannia," Rex said to his loyal friend.

"Is he your king?"

"He is my father," Rex replied, then snatched a spear from the guardroom and left the astonished priest alone in the street.

———⟆⟎⟆———

The defenders of Brigantium were lining the walls and hurling insults at the enemy below when Rex reached the walkway. He recognized two of the men as prison guards, but they didn't see him, for their backs were turned as they focused on the attackers. Occasionally an arrow whistled past, but that was a hard shot for an archer aiming from the ground, so the defenders were safe enough. An iron brazier had been brought up to the walkway behind the battlements. A cauldron of bubbling oil sat over it.

"Over here!" shouted a stocky ax-man from further along the wall. "They've got a ladder! Bring the pot!"

The two prison guards put a stick under the cauldron's handle and lifted it from the coals. Running to where their comrade had summoned them, they prepared to dump the boiling oil on the attackers' heads. Rex glanced over the battlements and saw that a party of about thirty of Chrocus's men had thrown a ladder against the wall and were bravely attempting to ascend. Little did they know that a terrible scalding awaited them.

"For the true king!" Rex cried, dashing toward the guards just as they began to tip the cauldron over the edge. Barreling into the nearer man with a forearm shove, Rex sent the pair of defenders sprawling across the walkway. The sizzling oil splashed both men before the pot clanged onto the city pavement below. While the guards screamed and squirmed from their burns, Rex leaned over the wall and beckoned to the first man coming up the ladder. "Friend of Chrocus!" he shouted. "It's all clear! Climb up!"

"Die, traitor!" someone screeched.

Rex whirled to see the stocky axman swinging his weapon in a wide arc. It was the inefficient attack of a woodsman, not a warrior, so Rex parried it easily. He locked his spear into the crook where the ax head met the haft, then spun the spear in a full revolution that wrenched the ax from the man's grasp and sent it spiraling over the wall. The man's mouth was agape as Rex high-kicked him in the chest, knocking him from the ramparts like a doll tossed aside by a distracted child. He hit the pavement below and did not move again.

Other defenders now rushed to the point of attack, but Rex met them with his spear and kept them from advancing along the narrow walkway. Only when he heard the war cry of the first man up the ladder did he step aside and give way to the newcomer, who was inflamed with battle lust. The man's whirling sword flashed like lightning as it caught the morning sun. While the defenders tried to deal with the furious onslaught, Rex helped more besiegers clamber over the wall. He spoke to them in good Alemannic German as they came up, insisting he was for King Chrocus.

As soon as they arrived upon the ramparts, the swarm of attackers charged after their leader toward the city's defenders. Terrified by the sudden change in the balance of power, the defenders turned and fled down the walkway. The attackers let them go, preferring instead to regroup and devise a strategy.

The leader who had come up first, a middle-aged fellow in leather armor, approached Rex. He was speckled with blood and breathing hard. "How did you get in?" he demanded.

"I was already inside when the attack started. Follow me with your men and we can open the gate."

"Is it heavily defended?"

"Of course."

"By how many?"

"Five times our number," Rex said with a dismissive wave of his hand, "but we're five times braver, so I'd call it even."

At this, the leader in leather armor broke into a wide grin. "You *are* a man of Chrocus!" he cried. "I'm one of his lieutenants. Show us the way, friend!"

After picking up a dropped sword and discarding the spear, Rex led the thirty warriors down to the street level and toward the main gate. One of the invaders had brought a flag of King Chrocus up the ladder, so he surged to the front of the attacking party with the proud banner waving in the wind.

They arrived to find the gate bristling with enemy warriors just like Rex had said. Immediately, the men of Chrocus pressed the attack. Since everyone's attention was focused outside, the defenders were caught off guard by the sudden assault from behind. Though some of them fell right away, others stood their ground and fought hard, while many more began to rush down from the battlements to aid their comrades.

"To the windlass!" shouted the lieutenant to his men. "We've got to open that gate!"

Now the entrance to Brigantium became the scene of a fierce melee. Because the city's defenders had been surprised by the overnight siege, they had no arrows to deploy. The fighting was sword to sword and eye to eye in the crowded gateway. It was fight now or die, and all the men knew it. Yet the tight confines actually helped the outnumbered attackers, for it limited how many opponents could engage them at once. Blood and sweat spattered Rex's face as he fought alongside the lieutenant in a desperate battle that seemed it would not end. But eventually, the lieutenant broke through the enemy's ranks and reached the windlass.

"Cover me!" he shouted as he dropped his sword and began to turn the mechanism with both hands. The great oaken portcullis rose up a little, groaning in its grooves. But the success was short-lived. An anguished cry burst from the lieutenant as a well-thrown hatchet split his skull. He fell to the ground with the blank expression of a dead man.

"We can take them!" screamed an enemy chieftain, a fat fellow with bushy, black whiskers. "Now's the time! Hold that gate!"

The defenders of Brigantium, encouraged by the lieutenant's death, pressed their attack with increased vigor. The invaders lost their position at the windlass and started fighting for survival. Several more brave warriors went down, including the flag-bearer. Rex ran to the banner and snatched it from the ground. Leaping onto a cart full of beer barrels, he began to wave it back and forth. "For Chrocus!" he cried. "Men of Alemannia! Come back to King Chrocus the Great!"

"Traitor!" accused the fat chief with the black beard.

"You are the traitor! You left your king for a knave! Aoric stabbed the true king in the back!"

Someone hurled a javelin at Rex, but he used the flagpole to deflect it. "Chrocus is coming to reclaim his city! Men of Alemannia, I call upon you! Will you defend the rebel or come back to your lord?"

The battle's intensity slowed as many of the defenders quit fighting and stared up at Rex. He could see the ambivalence on their faces. One voice rose above the others. "That is my war banner," said a grizzled old veteran with a huge scar on his cheek. "I fought under it before. And now I will again."

An unseen speaker from the crowd countered him. "You can't, Meredich! It's treason!"

"Fighting for Aoric is treason," Meredich replied. He turned and pointed to a handsome blond youth with a cleft in his chin. "You there! Turn that windlass and raise the portcullis. Then open the gate."

After giving Meredich a quick nod, the youth obeyed, and a cheer went up from the attackers as well as many of the defenders. Though some men now slunk away into the streets, understanding that things had just turned against them, the majority joined the cheering for King Chrocus.

The portcullis was no sooner lifted and the gate opened than the besiegers rushed into the city, surprised to find a boisterous welcome instead of fierce hornets with iron stingers. Though they were confused at first, Rex waved his flag and assured the invaders that the men standing before them were on the same side.

"Where's that filthy Aoric?" asked a broad-shouldered warrior with a huge sword. His sturdy helmet and coat of chainmail identified him as a high-status captain of the besiegers.

"A real leader should be on the walls with his men," Rex said, "but Aoric is probably hiding."

"Do you know where?"

"Now that the city's defenses have broken, they will have to rally to the center."

The captain in chainmail nodded. "Agreed. But Brigantium has no inner fortress."

"It will be the Jupiter temple. It's the last defensible place. Aoric will surely be there."

"Let's go," the captain said, pointing the way with his long blade. His men rushed behind him with war cries ringing from their bearded lips. Rex noticed that old Meredich with the scarred face was at the front of the pack.

Though many Roman towns had a temple devoted to the Capitoline Triad of Jupiter, Juno, and Minerva, the one at Brigantium was unusual in that it didn't directly face the forum. Nevertheless, like all capitols—including the original one on Rome's Capitoline Hill—it was situated on the highest point in the city. Jupiter's name was "Highest and Best," so no other location would do.

The capitol at Brigantium was located on a craggy bluff that overlooked the lake. Behind it ran the city wall, directly above the steep drop-off. It was a commanding position, and the building's stone blocks were solid. Rex could see immediately that the attackers had their work cut out for them. The temple formed an excellent makeshift fortress.

"Look at that!" someone yelled.

Following the man's gaze as he pointed toward the capitol's roof, Rex was astonished by what he saw. Aoric had climbed up there and was striding toward the temple's eave. He wore no shirt, so his body glowed white in the morning sun like the resplendent skin of a god. A longbow was over his shoulder, and he carried his shield like a basket, piled high with arrows.

"Take cover!" shouted another voice, but the warning didn't come fast enough. Aoric had reached the roof's edge and nocked an arrow in his bow. Before anyone could find shelter, he sent a feathered shaft speeding down like one of Jupiter's thunderbolts into the crowd. A man fell with a scream, and Aoric reached for another arrow from his pile.

Now the invaders began to scramble for somewhere to hide. They were all foot soldiers whose swords, axes, and spears could do nothing against a lone shooter from such a high perch. The captain in chainmail grabbed the sleeve of one of his warriors. "Go back to the lines and get the archers!" he shouted. "Bring them here, quick!" But even as he gave the order, another one of his men went down to Aoric's next arrow.

Rex, however, did not hide. *If Aoric can get up there*, he reasoned, *so can I*. He sprinted to the rear of the temple where it adjoined the city wall. As he had expected, he saw that Aoric had ascended to the wall's defensive walkway, then climbed a ladder from there to the temple's roof.

A nearby staircase gave Rex access onto the ramparts. After picking up a shield from a fallen soldier, he hurried to the base of the ladder. Stepping firmly on its wooden rungs as it leaned against the back of the temple, he began to ascend. By the time he reached the roofline, he was very high above the urban pavement, and even farther from the ground outside the city. He felt dizzy as he gazed at the rocky cliff that dropped off beyond the wall. Tearing his eyes away from the surrounding terrain, he looked back to the roof and clambered up.

Fortunately, the roof's pitch wasn't too steep, so Rex found he could stride across the terracotta tiles. Aoric was busy at the far end, loosing arrows onto the men below. At the sound of Rex's approach, however, he whirled to confront him.

"You!" he cried, drawing his sword from his belt with one hand and picking up his shield with the other. "How did you get out of the prison?"

"It wasn't hard. A fool of a leader has fools for servants."

"Bah! I should have killed you when I had the chance," Aoric sneered.

"You have your chance now," Rex replied, and charged his enemy.

Though Rex was well trained in the use of a blade, he quickly discerned that Aoric's skills, though different in style, were excellent too. The swordsmen battled forward and backward along the temple roof, hacking, blocking with their shields, and hacking again. Steel banged against wood as each man sought an advantage while protecting himself at the same time. Yet the adversaries were well matched, so no blood was drawn. At times, Rex pressed his attack and thought he had found an opening, but Aoric always had countermoves that would put Rex back on the defensive. It was an equal—and therefore exhausting—balance of power.

Finally, after a furious exchange of ringing blows, the men stepped back and stared at one another, breathing hard. Aoric's copper-colored hair was lank with sweat, and his face was ruddy from exertion.

"You're worn out," Rex taunted.

"Just like when I'm done with your woman," Aoric shot back with a throaty chuckle.

The barb infuriated Rex, and he renewed his attack with a barrage of slashes and lunges. Aoric deflected them all but was clearly having a hard time of it. At one point, he stumbled and had to take a crouching position with his shield in a defensive posture. Raising his own weapon above his head, Rex brought it down in a tremendous blow that he hoped would splinter his opponent's shield. The power of his strike did exactly that—but Rex's own cheap blade shattered under the massive force of the impact.

Now, although Aoric had been forced to his knees, his intact weapon was still in his hand while Rex had nothing but a useless hilt. He turned to run for the ladder. "You coward!" Aoric snarled as he scrambled to his feet and followed.

Rex dashed across the capitol's roof as fast as he could move on the uneven surface. Halfway across, he turned and hurled the broken shard of his sword, forcing Aoric to wait and dodge it. The delay gave Rex the time he needed. He was several steps ahead of his pursuer when he neared the eave where the ladder ran down to the city wall. Though the sound of his enemy's footfalls on the tiles was close behind, Rex could see he would make it to the ladder first. Now he sprinted even faster toward his escape.

"I'll run you through!" Aoric screeched, insane with bloodlust.

The false king's cry was still on his lips when Rex launched himself into the air. However, instead of leaping over the edge, he whirled in a spin move that brought his foot whipping around with incredible speed. The high kick was aimed at Aoric's head while his defenses were down—a move so fast the man never saw it coming.

Rex's boot smashed Aoric's jaw with the combined force of his own rotation and his enemy's forward drive. Aoric's head twisted sideways, sending blood, sweat, and teeth flying from his shattered face. The mighty blow knocked Aoric unconscious while he was still on his feet.

Yet he did not collapse, for his body had built up too much momentum to stop. Instead, he rushed over the temple's eave as if the roof went on forever. Limp as a rag, Aoric plummeted past the city wall. After a short freefall, he crashed headfirst into the craggy ground at the base of the bluff. His inert body bounced twice, then lay still.

Rex stared at the bloodied corpse while he panted to regain his breath. It was a long time before he could speak again. "You were right," he said at last to the dead man sprawled on the rocks. "You should have killed me when you had the chance."

—◈◈◈—

It was Cassi who came to Flavia and comforted her. The mansion was nearly abandoned, for everyone had fled from the uncertainty surrounding Aoric. The city outside was in chaos. But instead of running away, Cassi came straight to the king's bedroom.

"My friend?" she called through the locked door.

Flavia rolled over in bed, its blankets serving as a cocoon of protection in a terrible world. A curtain was drawn over the high window, yet even in the dimness, she couldn't help but see the erotic frescoes that adorned the bedroom walls. The sight of those lurid acts made her sick. Yet Cassi's voice was like a healing balm to her soul.

"The key is on the lintel above the door," Flavia shouted back. "Do not let Aoric see you touch it."

"No fear! The servants are returning from the streets. They say the master has been killed, and his last defenders have fled the city." After jiggling the lock for a moment, Cassi opened the door and rushed to Flavia's side. "You are free," she said with great tenderness.

But Flavia could not immediately rise from the bed. Instead, she fell into her friend's arms and wept with a grief that pierced her to the deepest place. It hurt so much, Flavia wanted to die. Though Cassi sat beside her and held her close, nothing could make the pain recede. The sudden release of her shame about all that had happened in this room—now that it was finally over—brought a gut-wrenching sadness to Flavia like she had never felt before.

"I didn't want this," she whispered when her sobs had abated a bit. "But there was nothing I could do to stop it." Though she shuddered often, she found she could talk in between gasps. Her eyes burned, and her nose was runny from so much crying. In fact, her entire body felt disgusting.

"I know, dear sister. I know."

"It didn't happen as often as I'd feared it would," Flavia went on. "I hardly remember it. My mind has blocked it. Perhaps that is a mercy."

"I am glad for that," said Cassi, stroking Flavia's hair. "I love you, dear sister."

"There is nothing left to love. I am defiled . . . no longer a maiden."

"In God's eyes, you are as lovely as ever."

"But not in Rex's," Flavia said forlornly.

"He is a man who overcomes," was Cassi's wise reply.

Yet Flavia could not believe it. Wails of anguish burst anew from her ruptured soul. She cried on Cassi's shoulder for a while, then pulled away and buried her face in her own hands. Bent over at the waist, she sobbed uncontrollably as grief and anger raged within. Cassi sat beside her in silence, for what else could be said?

After a long time of weeping, Flavia's tears were spent. She lowered her hands to her lap and whimpered on the edge of the bed with her eyes scrunched shut. Her lashes, her cheeks, her chin, even her gauzy gown were soaked with tears. A deep, dark sadness had ahold of her now. The world was a scary place. Flavia felt she could never open her eyes and face it again.

"I am lost," she finally whispered.

"You are found," replied a deep voice from the doorway.

Flavia's eyes popped open. Through her misty tears, she saw Rex smiling at her from across the room. Flooded with sudden joy, she leapt from the bed and flung her arms around him. Rex scooped her into his protective embrace. "You came to me!" she cried, overwhelmed by relief. She clutched Rex's tunic, holding him close.

"I will always come to you, Flavia. No matter what."

Cassi left the room at that moment but returned quickly with a mantle. She handed the garment to Rex, then quietly slipped away. The mantle was a modest wrap of winter wool. Rex draped it around Flavia's shoulders, covering her flimsy gown with its thick folds. Protected from her sense of shame and exposure, Flavia felt her voice return. "Am I less to you now?" she asked.

"You are more to me than ever, my beloved."

At those words, an abiding peace came rushing back into Flavia's heart. Rex held her close, one hand upon her waist, the other stroking the back of her head, as if to cradle her violated mind as well as her body. She laid her head against Rex's chest and squeezed him tight, trying in some measure to express how comforting his statement sounded.

"Flavia," he said tenderly, "do you want to leave this place forever, and all that it represents?"

"Yes, Rex. Yes, I surely do."

"Do you want to return to Sirmium with me, to see your mother and Bishop Ossius again?"

"That, too, is what I want."

"And do you want to stand beside me as we go outside and commission four thousand Alemanni for an expedition—the kind of army that will make Constantine proud?"

"No," said Flavia. "That I cannot do."

"Why not?" Rex asked with surprise in his voice.

"Because, my beloved, I am not finished listening to your heartbeat."

Rex laughed gently at this reply. "Alright," he agreed. "We can stay here a little longer. But only if you let every beat of my heart remind you that it belongs to you alone."

9

It looked to Rex like every riverboat in Castra Regina had been comman-deered for the crazy flotilla of Germanic warriors that was heading for Pannonia. Four thousand brave Alemanni, each with weapons, a horse, and three weeks' worth of rations, had mustered at the ancient Roman fort on the Danubius River.

At first, the regular soldiers of the Third Italian Legion had been suspi-cious of the barbarian horde that descended on their fort. Yet the Alemanni behaved themselves well, and they claimed to be staunch allies of Constan-tine, just like the legionaries. Not wanting to be known as having thwarted the emperor's mercenaries, the men stationed at Castra Regina rounded up every available military boat or merchant vessel. A few rafts had even been lashed together out of logs to send along supplies behind the troops.

At dawn tomorrow, the river journey would commence under the lead-ership of the restored King Chrocus. Rex felt honored to be following his father into battle, though he did wonder whether the hastily assembled flotilla would hold together for the eight-day journey to Pannonia. It would be an ugly fleet, full of decrepit and mismatched boats. But if the boats made it all the way, the warriors who disembarked were going to bring some serious hellfire to Licinius's legions.

The restoration of King Chrocus had been a sight to behold, an event Rex would always remember. After Aoric's death, his few remaining supporters melted into the countryside, leaving most of the Alemanni to switch sides and claim to have been loyal to Chrocus all along. The coronation in Brigantium's basilica had brought tears to Rex's eyes. He stood next to his father's throne in a place of honor, with Flavia at his side in an elegant Roman gown like the aristocrat she was. A wise city elder, a man who had openly resisted Aoric's rule, placed the crown on the king's head with a look of satisfaction. Everyone in the hall cheered and rattled their swords against their shields.

After the momentous ceremony, the lavish banquet at the Grand Old Oak eclipsed any party Aoric had ever thrown there. Flavia had come up to Rex under the lantern-decked branches and intertwined her fingers in his. "Now *this* is how I pictured the festival," she had whispered in his ear, to which he'd replied as the pipers began to play, "And this is how I had hoped we would dance." The feasting and dancing had lasted long into the night.

It was a crisp September morning when the awkward flotilla set out from Castra Regina's docks on the Danubius. The journey was proceeding with the help of the river's current, so Rex expected to make good progress. He rode behind the king's flagship in a barge that usually transported wheat. Flavia, Stephen, and Cassi were with him, along with Gundomar and a few other Alemannic warriors.

The travelers spent the eight days napping or caring for the horses as the boats made their way downstream. Fortunately, the weather was sunny most of the time, though the barge's leather awning came in handy during a few rainy spells as September yielded to October. Everyone slept at night in bedrolls along the banks wherever they happened to be when the sun went down. The townspeople and farmers along the river donated food as they were able, in hopes of being remembered as having aided the emperor's allies in his battle against Licinius.

Around noon on the eighth day, the flagship of King Chrocus was hailed by a military riverboat heading upstream. The legionaries aboard it were clearly worried about the swarm of fierce warriors they saw coming toward them.

"Cease rowing!" the decanus commanded.

He stood next to another soldier who was aiming a light ballista at the king's ship. Although a dart from that weapon would pierce even the best armor, the ten legionaries knew the barbarian horde floating their way could easily overwhelm them. They were putting on a show of command authority, but they knew they were in trouble if the Alemanni wanted to make a fight of it.

The king, however, was intent on being friendly—so long as the troops belonged to Constantine. "Show me your standard," Chrocus called back to the decanus, "and we might let you live."

The legionaries on the boat exchanged uneasy glances, for they had no idea who owned the loyalty of this huge Germanic flotilla. Yet there was nothing they could do but raise the flag and hope for the best. Rex was curious to see who they were. They might be scouts from Constantine's invasion army, or they might be a Licinian patrol boat from downriver. Their flag would clarify the matter.

"We serve Constantine," the decanus declared as he raised his war banner.

King Chrocus called over his shoulder to Rex, whose barge was just behind the royal flagship. "Is that the Christian symbol, my son?"

"Yes, it is the chi-rho. The first two letters in the name of Christ."

"Speak to him in Latin and tell him we are allies. My grasp of that tongue has faded over the years."

Rex cupped his hands around his mouth. "We come to you in time of need to fight for the true emperor, Constantine Augustus!" he shouted to the decanus. Immediately, the tension eased, though it did not entirely disappear.

The decanus put out his hand and turned away the ballista, signaling his own intent to be friendly. "The emperor could use some fresh cavalry," he acknowledged, "but I cannot authorize it myself."

"Lead us to him, then, and let him decide."

The decanus shook his head. "I cannot lead an unknown army to my master's camp."

After conferring with Chrocus briefly, Rex turned back to the patrol boat. "Our king, a former confederate of Constantine, will send a delegation to discuss the matter. It will be led by Gundomar, a warrior who fought in Britannia under Constantine and his father, Constantius. As the son of the king, I shall come too. And to show our goodwill toward the Romans, we will also bring a Christian priest and a senator's daughter who have been living among us as guests. They can attest to our loyalty to Rome."

The decanus seemed impressed by this. "Very well," he agreed. "Meet us ashore."

When both boats had reached the riverbank, the legionaries disembarked and surrounded the four emissaries to Constantine. Gundomar led four horses onto dry ground and began to saddle them. As Rex was helping out, he noticed that Flavia stayed close by him. Lately she had seemed less independent than she used to be—and Rex couldn't blame her, after all she had been through. He resolved to do everything he could to make her feel safe.

Though the emissaries now had horses to ride, the legionaries did not. However, the decanus—Burrus was his name—said Constantine's army was only fourteen miles away, and the soldiers could march that distance at quickstep and keep up with mounted riders. There was no time to waste, so after packing a few supplies, the party set out by early afternoon. The trail led through deep woods, moist and ferny and bursting with life. Three hours later, when the October sun was low in the sky, they arrived at a flat plain. Not far away, an army was encamped along the western edge of it. Everyone reined up where the forest ended and the plain began.

"The town over there is Cibalae," said Burrus, gesturing to a settlement upon a hill in the distance. "We are hearing that Licinius's troops are on the march. They are coming this way. The battle will happen soon, right there on the plain."

"How many men does he have?" Gundomar asked.

"The scouts are saying thirty-five thousand to our twenty."

Rex winced at the mismatch. "Then our four thousand will definitely help. All of them are mounted. And a good Germanic fighter is worth two regulars."

"We shall see if the emperor agrees."

At that moment, the runner whom Burrus had sent ahead to confer with the camp headquarters returned, breathing hard. "First thing tomorrow, sir," he reported. "An audience with General Arcadius—and also the Augustus himself!"

Rex's heart sank at this news, for he had been expecting to meet only with the military leaders. *Will he recognize me as the traitor he sentenced to row in the navy?* It had been three years since he had last seen Constantine. A man's appearance changed a lot between the age of twenty and twenty-three. Yet was it enough to make a difference? Rex's beard was thicker now, and he had the shoulder-length hair of his people instead of his former military cut. His frame was also more heavily muscled from his years at the oar. Still, Constantine was known for his sharp memory and eye for detail.

Flavia leaned over from her saddle and squeezed Rex's hand. "Jesus will protect you from the emperor's wrath," she said, obviously having read his thoughts—or at least the troubled expression on his face.

"We'll find out tomorrow, I guess." He shrugged and turned his horse away from the battlefield. "Nothing we can do until then. Let's find a place to sleep, away from the troops."

After scouting around a bit, Rex discovered a barn just inside the tree line that would provide adequate shelter from the chilly autumn night. He unfurled his bedroll in the soft hay, then went outside. It was dusk now, and in the distant military encampment, little cookfires glowed in front of the troops' goatskin tents. Occasionally, a loud guffaw or angry shout broke the stillness, but for the most part the men were quiet, as soldiers usually were when a battle loomed.

"Do you miss it?" Flavia asked, coming to Rex's side as he leaned against a tree and stared at the camp.

"I do, actually. That was my life for several years. It was a good life."

"For that time."

Rex turned and looked at Flavia. "Yes, for back then. I have other good things now," he said with a gentle smile.

"Stephen has a fire going back at the barn. Do you want to get some stew?"

"Sure. I'm starving."

"Okay. I dug up some wild onions for it. And I also put—"

When Flavia broke off, Rex glanced at her. "What?" he asked.

"I put my bedroll next to yours," she said shyly. "I hope you don't mind."

Intuitively, Rex understood what the gesture meant. It wasn't a sexual invitation, for even if Flavia's morals would have allowed that, her recent experience had made her tentative in that regard. Instead, it was a bid for acceptance. Rex knew Flavia still felt disgraced in his eyes, despite his affirmation that she was pure. Though he had been trying to communicate his love in various ways, he sensed that she still felt ashamed. It was courageous of Flavia to initiate closeness when she felt embarrassed and defiled. "I'm glad you did that," Rex told her reassuringly. "Your place is next to me, always."

She nodded at this. Together they walked back to the campfire in front of the old barn where Stephen and Gundomar were already eating the stew of dried beef, beans, and onions. A stack of barley cakes had also been cooked on a griddle, and the men crumbled them into their stew. Flavia ladled out a big bowl for Rex and sat down beside him with her own. They enjoyed a hearty meal and some quiet conversation before turning in for the night.

The hay in the barn was soft under the bedroll. Rex lay down next to Flavia, and soon she was breathing steadily at his side. He glanced over. The expression on her face looked so contented and tranquil in the moonlight. *At least when she is sleeping, she is at peace*, Rex thought with satisfaction. Rolling over, he closed his eyes, and it wasn't long before sleep took him as well.

At dawn the next day, a legionary came to escort the visitors to the meeting with the emperor. Fortunately, it was a chilly morning, so Rex felt justified in keeping his cloak wrapped around him and his hood up to mask his appearance. It had been decided that Gundomar, as the senior warrior in King Chrocus's warband, would do all the talking. The others would remain quiet, their presence simply proving the good intentions of the Alemanni to make an alliance with the Roman Empire.

The escort led the guests to the imperial tent and held aside the flap so they could proceed inside. The space was large enough to include some furniture, and it was brightly illuminated by two bronze lampstands. Emperor Constantine looked much like Rex remembered him: tall and commanding, with short-cropped hair, a Mediterranean complexion, and large piercing eyes.

Next to him stood General Arcadius, a stocky fellow whose forearms were corded with muscle. He spoke to Gundomar with gruff military directness. "Who are you?"

Gundomar identified himself as a warrior of Chrocus who had fought for

Constantine and his father against the wild Picts of Caledonia. After reminiscing about that for a bit, he gestured behind him to indicate that he was accompanied by a Christian priest, a Roman senator's daughter, and the son of Chrocus, who was formerly a soldier in the imperial army. Rex stared at his feet as Gundomar said this, praying that Arcadius would not press for details.

"What is your offer today?" Arcadius asked bluntly, and Rex exhaled the breath he had been holding.

Gundomar straightened his back, his height impressive. "The Alemanni of Germania recently learned that the great Emperor Constantine was in need of support against his enemy. As soon as King Chrocus heard it, he vowed to help his old lord—indeed, his old friend. We mustered the troops by invitation and not compulsion. Each man has come here by his free will, supplying his own arms and a horse trained for war. We have four thousand men nearby, all willing to serve as auxiliaries against wicked Licinius."

Arcadius sized Gundomar up and down. "If they are all like you, German, that must be quite a force," he said with an appreciative nod.

Constantine finally spoke up. "What do you seek in return for your service in combat? The finances of the empire are tight. Rome cannot hire mercenaries at will."

"We understand this, Your Highness," Gundomar replied. "We ask only to be paid from the plunder of war. Licinius's treasure hoard is famous. From its capture, an ample reward could flow to our men. But if we do not succeed in this task, we ask for no pay. Thus, there is no risk to you."

"Why would you take such a risk?"

"Without risks, there are no rewards in life. We hope to return to Germania with wealth we could not get otherwise, but we will accept the outcome regardless. And also, we fight for the love of King Chrocus. Our lord seeks a final campaign to seal his legacy forever."

In the far distance, a trumpet sounded. Arcadius and Constantine exchanged glances. "That was not one of ours," the general said.

"No, indeed. It seems we are finally at war. My brother-in-law has arrived at last." Constantine smiled with the supreme confidence of a man who ruled his world and expected to continue to do so. "Gundomar of the Alemanni," he said as he extended his hand, "kiss my ring, and you have yourself a deal."

The blond warrior bowed his head and seemed to absorb the jeweled ring into his bushy mustache. After he swore an oath of fidelity, the four emissaries turned to go. But as Rex was about to exit the tent, he heard a voice hail him from behind.

"Young man!" the emperor barked.

Slowly, Rex turned. "Yes, Your Majesty?" Though he maintained a humble expression, his dignity would not allow him to keep his eyes downcast. Even if it meant being recognized, Rex would hold up his head and carry himself like a warrior.

"It has been a long time since I have seen your father. How does he fare?"

"He is as brave and valiant as ever, sir."

"And is he still loyal to me?"

"Without a doubt, Augustus. The man is ever faithful to you."

Constantine nodded thoughtfully, staring at Rex with a strange look in his eyes. "What about you?" he asked at last. "Are you faithful to me as well?"

Rex saluted with his fist to his chest. "To the death, Your Majesty."

"To the death?" Constantine arched his eyebrows at this. "We shall see about that, son of Chrocus. Yes, we shall see very soon." He flicked his fingers toward the tent door. "You may go now. And be quick about your business. You have a battle to fight today, and I sincerely hope you will not fail me."

Rex bowed and exited the tent, grateful that Constantine did not add the final dreaded word.

Again.

———

OCTOBER 316

The Alemanni were milling around the southern bank of the Danubius for about a mile of its length when King Chrocus heard Gundomar returning with the Roman decanus. Chrocus was seated under a leather canopy, finishing up his breakfast, when the sound of hoofbeats alerted him that the emissaries had returned from Constantine's camp. He shoved his plate aside and stood up. "Tell me the news, Gundomar. What is the answer?"

"Get the men mounted up immediately," the old warrior said. "The Augustus summons you to his side once more, like days gone by. He shall soon be under attack."

"Constantine considers you a faithful ally forever," Rex added.

Chrocus felt a surge of pride in all that his son had achieved through his mission to Germania. "I knew you could do it!" he cried. "This was your idea from start to finish!"

"It was my idea, but the four thousand men followed you into battle, not me."

"Then we make a good team, I suppose. Father and son, making war together." Chrocus turned to Gundomar, assuming a more commanding tone. "We must depart within an hour. Tell the men to take only their arms, a bedroll, and one day's worth of rations. Pick twenty of the weakest fighters to stay back and bring the rest of the supplies tomorrow in a pack train. We travel light and fast today. Speed is essential. Battle is at hand!"

Gundomar's eager laugh burst from him. He pumped his fist while his other hand rested on his sword's hilt at his waist. "That's right, sire! We don't want to arrive too late and find all the good fighting is over!"

After the order to break camp was given, Chrocus couldn't suppress a laugh of his own as he watched the troops mount up with undeniable enthusiasm. Few of them wore armor, except for some of the older warriors who had chainmail coats or iron helmets from previous service with the Romans. Most Germani carried an iron sword these days, though a few still fought with battle axes, and the poorest had only clubs. Yet every man had a spear and a shield, since these were essential for fighting on horseback. It was the cavalry's job to break the infantry's ranks with a devastating charge—though, of course, the opposing horsemen would try to prevent such an attack. Chrocus hoped the element of surprise would win the day. Licinius had no idea that four thousand additional riders were bearing down on him.

Gundomar did a good job getting the men saddled up. They rode in pairs on the narrow track through the forest. Although the troops kept trying to trot their mounts over the fourteen miles to the battlefield, Chrocus insisted on holding them to a steady walk. He wanted the horses fresh enough when they reached the lines to break into an immediate charge if needed.

"The trees are thinning ahead," Rex said as he rode beside Chrocus. "When it opens up to a wide plain, you'll see the fighting."

But Chrocus didn't need a visual cue. The distant roar of battle was already in his ears, getting louder with each clip-clop of his horse's hooves. He loosened his spatha in its scabbard and adjusted the chin strap on his helmet. A bead of sweat stung his eyes, but he blinked it away. The sun was high now, and the day had grown warm. It was a good day to ride into battle like a man.

The trees thinned out like Rex had said, and then, there it was. The battlefield was arrayed with Licinius to the east and Constantine to the west. From a glance at the bodies on the ground, it seemed that Constantine's side had taken the greater losses so far; and his army was noticeably smaller to begin with. At the moment, several battalions of infantry were locked in a stalemate in the center of the battlefield while other units had pulled back and were exchanging arrow fire across the grassy plain. Though neither side yet had the upper hand, each was gradually taking a toll on the other. It was a classic battle of attrition—and in that scenario, time wasn't on Constantine's side.

"Ride back along the line and tell the men to divide into three groups," the king said to Gundomar. "Keep everyone in the woods and out of sight. Right now, we have the element of surprise. If we choose to use it at the right time, it could be devastating."

Gundomar immediately turned to carry out his master's order. In the meantime, Chrocus used Rex's better command of Latin to communicate with Burrus. The decanus agreed to take a proposal to General Arcadius. If the general agreed to the strategy, he would ride into battle under a white banner emblazoned with the chi-rho; but if not, the banner would be the tube-shaped standard called the *draco*, which was crimson and had the golden head of a dragon.

While Burrus rode off to communicate with his superiors, Chrocus took the opportunity to sit astride his horse and assess the battlefield from inside the tree line. "Brandulf, you were trained in Roman tactics," the king said to his son. "What do your eyes see out there?"

"The center is a killing zone that will eventually favor Licinius," Rex replied. "Both sides are rolling fresh troops to the front, but Constantine doesn't have the numbers to sustain that approach. If he keeps it up, his infantry will give way before sunset."

"Constantine has cavalry. Why not send them to disrupt Licinius's flanks? Make a hard charge from the side so that the rank and file break apart."

"Yes, that would destroy Licinius's infantry, but his general knows it too. His name is Valerius Valens. He's famous as a defensive specialist. Look over there." Rex pointed to the rear of Licinius's infantry formation. "Do you see how his horsemen are poised to defend an attack? Valens would immediately confront a cavalry charge and keep the riders away from his footmen."

Chrocus was impressed with his son's eye for tactics. "I remember the day you left for cadet school. You were just a scared little boy! Now you're a man—a soldier who knows the arts of war."

"The Romans trained me well. I owe it all to Constantine."

"No wonder you're so loyal to him."

"Even if he doesn't acknowledge it," Rex muttered, though Chrocus wasn't sure what was meant by that.

A trumpet blast from the battlefield signaled a new foray from the Constantinian side. Imperial cavalrymen were assembling for an attack on Licinius's infantry. "A white banner!" Chrocus exclaimed. "The Romans have accepted our strategy. Go find Gundomar and tell him to be ready to put the plan into action!"

While Rex rode off to convey the instructions, Chrocus focused his attention on the battlefield. He could see the Constantinian standard-bearer rallying a battalion of horsemen for a side attack against the densely packed foot soldiers. If those riders could gain the enemy's flank and penetrate their formation, chaos would ensue, just as Rex had noted. Then the forward press of Constantine's infantry would wipe out the broken ranks.

However, gaining the flank was going to be difficult for those horsemen. If General Valerius Valens was even half as smart as Rex said, he would stop it immediately—and he had a larger cavalry with which to do it. Chrocus could already see the Licinian side preparing to defend against the imminent charge.

Yet the Constantinian cavalrymen were bold. After another trumpet blast, they tried the charge despite the mismatch. As Chrocus stared at the battlefield, he spotted something that snatched his breath away. The man carrying the white standard wasn't wearing a lion skin draped over his helmet like a normal standard-bearer. Instead, to Chrocus's great surprise, the man's helmet was gold, and the tunic under his armor was imperial purple. Emperor Constantine himself was riding into battle!

Gundomar and Rex rode up to the king with the horde of Alemannic warriors stretched along the tree line on either side. The men had been given strict orders of silence—no battle cries, no sword rattling.

"Look there!" Chrocus exclaimed. "Constantine is fighting!"

"He's brave, you have to give him that," Gundomar said.

"That emperor is a true leader of men," Rex agreed.

As the threesome watched the scene unfold, Constantine's cavalry swept around the side of the Licinian infantry in a flanking maneuver. Valerius Valens, however, was ready for the attack. His own cavalry came thundering across the plain to confront the charge and turn it aside. Now the two sides found themselves locked in a fierce exchange. Spears broke against shields, swords rang against helmets, and horses tumbled to the churned-up ground as their riders went sprawling in the mud. Chrocus could feel the tension running high among his Alemanni. Their urge to gallop into the fray was incredibly strong. But Gundomar held them behind the tree line with a fierce expression and his upraised fist.

Eventually, the fighting around Constantine grew one-sided as his bodyguards fell before the greater number of opponents. The trumpets sounded a retreat to the Constantinian fortifications, so the emperor was forced to withdraw. The white banner turned to leave the field.

But now, drawn by the lure of imminent victory, General Valens's cavalry pressed hard as Constantine pulled back to his encampment. The move stretched the Licinian horsemen into a long, thin line as they followed the hasty retreat of their foes. It was a dangerous position to be in, yet they couldn't resist pursuit. Like a dog when it sees a rabbit turn and run, the Licinian cavalry surged toward the fleeing emperor, sensing the vulnerability of their prey.

That was the moment King Chrocus had been waiting for. He raised his spear above his head and let loose a war cry. "Strike with the hammer of Thor!" he cried in the ancient tongue of the Alemanni.

The shout was immediately joined by a mighty chorus of battle-hungry warriors. They exploded out of the trees in unison and began to gallop across the grassy plain.

The four thousand Germanic warriors now separated into three distinct attacks, like three arrows flying simultaneously toward the side of an unsuspecting stag. Gundomar led one arrowhead toward the stag's "rump," the reserve troops stationed at the rear of Licinius's army. Rex led an opposite arrowhead toward the stag's "head," the overeager pursuit of Constantine by General Valens. And between them both, Chrocus led a speeding attack on the stag's "flank," the infantry formation in the middle of the battlefield, which was now protected by only a thread of cavalrymen whose attention was focused elsewhere.

The thundering horde led by King Chrocus hit the drawn-out string of enemy riders before they could even stop their pursuit of Constantine and turn to face the unexpected threat. The Alemanni sliced through the enemy horsemen like a finger breaking a cobweb. But Chrocus's men did not stop to fight the riders. Their real quarry was the infantry that the cavalry was supposed to protect. Thanks to Constantine's feigned retreat, the flank of the opposing army now lay totally exposed.

Like a thunderbolt from on high, Chrocus's charge crashed into the infantry formation at full speed. The tight-packed footmen had no room to turn, no means of sideways defense, and no way to escape. The king's war horse plunged halfway through the rank and file before the beast finally slowed. Chrocus swung his spatha right and left, cleaving heads, severing arms, and sending the terrified soldiers into whatever underworld might await them. Everywhere, the men of Licinius were being ground into the mud by the churning hooves of the Alemanni riders who seemed to have fallen from the sky. The horsemen kept surging ahead, hacking at the enemy, mowing them down, disrupting the army that moments before had been on the brink of victory.

By the time Chrocus and his valiant warriors had ridden all the way through the enemy formation, everyone on the battlefield knew Licinius was defeated. Now the foot soldiers who were still alive were a disorganized mess, no longer presenting a united front to their attackers. The disciplined legions of Constantine immediately pressed their advantage, keeping their own lines unbroken as they advanced upon the doomed enemy. Instead of chaos, the Constantinian side presented a solid shield wall that bristled with stabbing swords. Any Licinian troops who tried to flee were killed from behind as they stumbled over the corpses of their fallen comrades. The few who did manage to break into the clear were run through by the spears of Chrocus's swift riders. Only the rear guard managed to escape into the forest, though Gundomar's division chased them right up to the edge of the trees.

"Victory!" Chrocus cried as Licinius's army fled in disarray. He raised his bloody sword to the sky. "Victory to the Augustus of the West!"

A white banner rippling in the wind signaled the presence of the emperor on the field. Chrocus scanned the swirling mass of troops around the flag until his eyes fell on the golden helmet and purple garb of Constantine. The officer next to him in expensive armor could only be General Arcadius. Rex was riding alongside them, though Chrocus had a hard time recognizing him at first because his son was wearing a helmet with a nose guard and cheek flaps that obscured his face. Perhaps Rex's original helmet had taken a hard blow and he had scavenged this one.

Chrocus held his head high as he swung his horse around and rode to meet the emperor and his general. Although Chrocus was a confederate auxiliary, sworn to serve Constantine, he was also a victorious champion today, so he had no intention of being overly deferential.

"Hail to the Augustus of the West!" he exclaimed when the two commanders had drawn near.

As Constantine approached, he answered with the words that Chrocus had come all this way to hear. "And hail to the rightful king of the Alemanni," the emperor replied. "Today you have proven yourself a man of valor."

Chrocus felt tears flood his eyes at this salutation. For so long, while he lay abed day after day, he had dreamed that this day might come. Now it had arrived. He glanced at Rex, who was staring back at him. There, upon the glorious field of war, father and son exchanged nods that signaled their mutual respect. And in that moment, Chrocus understood he had received a crown even greater than anything Constantine could offer.

———✳✳✳———

The feast to celebrate the victory at the Battle of Cibalae rivaled any great banquet Flavia had experienced in Rome. Four days after the battle, the troops reached Sirmium and found its gates thrown open in submission. Licinius and all his supporters had fled to Thracia, taking with them a vast treasure of coins and jewels. Now Constantine took up residence in the imperial palace, where his brother-in-law had been living only a few days earlier. Apparently, the new master of the house had decided he might as well make use of the well-stocked larders and the lavish dining room he found at Sirmium. The banquet tables were laden with innumerable dishes and bowls. The culinary delights seemed to have no end. Flavia could hardly wait to try the many foods spread before her.

Constantine, however, had not yet entered the dining room. All the guests—high-ranking soldiers, for the most part—were chatting quietly as they awaited the emperor's arrival. The head couch was reserved for him alone, while next to it were couches for General Arcadius and Bishop Ossius on one side, and King Chrocus and Gundomar on the other. Women were not allowed to recline with the men at a military feast, so Flavia and Sophronia sat next to each other on a pair of stools behind Ossius's couch. Other aristocratic women, including Helena and Fausta, were seated near the emperor as well. The only obvious absence here was Rex. He had taken a hard blow to the head at Cibalae and was still having dizzy spells—though the even more urgent reason for his absence was to avoid being recognized by Constantine in this brightly lit room.

At long last, a trumpet blast signaled the emperor's arrival. Dressed in a gorgeous purple tunic with gold roundels along the hem, he greeted everyone before the meal commenced. After a brief speech about the glorious comportment of the Roman legions in battle, he turned his attention to Chrocus. "And what can I say about the skillful cavalry charge executed by the king of the Alemanni?" he asked with a sweep of his hand toward his guest of honor. "The man knows how to ride, does he not?"

"Hear, hear!" cried all the troops in the hall.

"I truly believe the battle would have been lost without the aid of our auxiliaries," Constantine went on. "To reward these dear friends who came to us of their own free will, I proclaim a donative of one gold solidus per man, to be disbursed as soon as we capture the treasury of Licinius. Any noteworthy acts of valor will earn even more. And to make a pledge of this promise today, I award ten solidi to King Chrocus, with the hope of more to come."

A cheer went up in the hall as Constantine pitched a coin purse to Chrocus, who caught it midair and jingled it above his head with a grateful smile.

Finally, the preliminaries were done and the emperor lay on his couch so the serving could begin. Despite the bounty already upon the tables, the slaves brought in huge silver trays piled with haunches of venison, juicy sausages, whole roasted pigs, and legs of mutton. The meat and numerous side dishes kept coming in wave after wave, all washed down with a robust red wine, full-bodied and aromatic. It didn't take long for everyone to settle into a festive, even raucous, mood.

Sophronia leaned over to Flavia and spoke quietly. "Don't make it obvious," she said, "but keep one ear on Constantine. Everyone is talkative now. If the emperor mentions any church topics, Ossius is going to raise the matter of the pope's petition. I actually have it here to present to him if we get a chance."

"The augustus seems to be in good spirits," Flavia agreed. "Today is as good a day as any to present our request."

As the eating began to slow down and there was more time for conversation, Constantine started to reminisce with King Chrocus about their days at war in Britannia. Together, they laughed about a Pictish chieftain who went into battle naked except for his war paint but learned he could have used some armor in a few choice places once the arrows started flying. Then the talk turned to the momentous day, ten years ago, when Constantine was acclaimed as emperor by the Victorious Sixth Legion and the Alemannic mercenaries who served with them.

"That was a great day for me, one I will always remember," Constantine said. "To become an augustus of Rome is an awesome responsibility."

"You be worthy of it, my lord," Chrocus replied. Flavia had noticed his Latin was rusty, but he was trying to converse as best he could.

"I recall a remarkable thing about that day," Constantine went on. "You had a little boy who challenged me to a sword fight."

He remembers Rex!

Now Flavia's heart began to beat faster, and she shifted subtly in her seat to make sure she could overhear the exchange. Neither Chrocus nor Constantine was paying attention to her, but for her part, she was focused on their every word.

Chrocus gave a little chuckle. "That be my Brandulf. A fighter from start. Always ready to scrap."

"Ah, yes, Brandulf was his name," the emperor mused. "I sent him to cadet school to become a speculator. The soldiers gave him the name of Rex because of you."

"Aye. They saw him as a king."

"It was probably just a joke. But king or not, they trained him well. Eventually he became a great speculator. I took him into my bodyguard, then sent him on a spying mission to Rome. But he committed treason, you know. Fled in battle. So I sent him to the navy on the edge of the empire."

Chrocus's body stiffened at these hard words, yet Flavia thought he maintained his composure well and did not betray any emotions on his face. Although Constantine's expression was also unreadable, Flavia sensed he was testing his old friend.

"I love my son," Chrocus said firmly.

Constantine raised an eyebrow. "More than anything?"

"As much as a father should. No more. No less."

Though the comment brought a sage nod from Constantine, he said nothing further. After popping an olive into his mouth, he took a swig of wine, and the conversation moved on to other things.

Sophronia was seated a little closer to Ossius than Flavia, so she had been monitoring the bishop's conversation without seeming to eavesdrop. Flavia switched her attention there as well. Ossius had started a friendly discussion with General Arcadius about the propriety of Christians serving in the army. Ossius felt it was acceptable for a believer to be a soldier as long as no sacrifices were made to the gods. Yet other Christians held that armed service was completely forbidden to the followers of the Prince of Peace. At Constantine's direction, General Arcadius had granted exemptions from the cult of Jupiter and Mars to all soldiers who had been baptized into the catholic church.

"The emperor favors your faith," said Arcadius. "He tells me that he adheres to it himself, though he is not yet ready for baptism."

"I have advised him not to wait, for baptism is the mark of full commitment and entrance into the church."

"I don't really understand his reasons for conversion," Arcadius admitted. "The Christian religion seems new and irrational. Why does he like it all of a sudden? What was wrong with the old gods?"

"Perhaps you should ask him. Look. He isn't talking to anyone right now. Ask him what makes Christianity superior."

"I will," said Arcadius, beckoning for the emperor's attention.

From the corner of her eye, Flavia saw Sophronia's lips begin to move, and she knew her mother was uttering a prayer for God's favor. A conversation about the merits of Christianity would be an excellent context for submitting the petition from the pope to Constantine.

When Arcadius had posed his question—which was exactly the kind of thought-provoking question that rich banqueters loved to discuss at fancy dinners—the emperor wiped his mouth with a napkin and collected his thoughts for a moment. Finally, he said, "The Christian God is the Highest God. He is the Creator, and he reigns alone at the top of the universe, like the sun. The Jews found him first, but their laws for his worship are outdated. Now Jesus the Christ is his revealer, and the catholic church offers the right path of divine observance. So, if I want to receive aid from the Highest God, I must favor the church and keep its rules as best I can."

Though this seemed like a perfect segue to bring up the petition, Ossius couldn't help but hold off until he had corrected the emperor's theology. "Remember, Your Highness," he said gently, "God seeks the true allegiance of your heart, not just outward conformity to rules. He wants you to love him for himself, not merely for his rewards."

"Of course," Constantine agreed. "But when I learn to love God as God, then surely his blessings will flow to me as well."

Ossius smiled in a dashing and winsome way. "When your heart is attuned to God, you will hear his voice and know how to respond with prudence to all things. Therefore, Your Majesty, I know you will give good consideration to the petition that I have brought all the way across the empire. It is from Sylvester, the bishop of Rome and leader of the Latin-speaking church. I hereby submit it to you for wise consideration."

At these words, Sophronia reached into a satchel at her feet and handed the reclining bishop the petition they had carried through so many dangers and trials. He held it up for all to see.

"Hmm. Pass it over to me." Constantine's voice was a little sterner than Flavia would have liked. After scanning the document, he asked, "Bishop

Sylvester seeks my approval for a building program and an official copy of the scriptures?"

"Yes. And he needs government funds to make it happen. We consider this a much better use of the imperial treasury than what has flowed for so long to the houses of demons."

"So you seek my largesse. Is that right, Bishop Ossius?"

"We do, on behalf of the purposes of God."

A dark cloud seemed to pass over the emperor's face. "You desire my favor. But do you give me loyalty in return? Let us test you, bishop! Repudiate the traitor you have brought into your company: the soldier Brandulf Rex, who abandoned me at Verona! Hand him over to me and join me in condemning him. Then I will know I can trust you completely!"

At these startling words, Flavia couldn't help but recoil; and she wasn't the only one. Chrocus and Gundomar flinched on their couches, and Ossius had a shocked expression on his face.

It was King Chrocus who spoke first. "That is my son of whom you speak!" he thundered.

"I know who he is!" Constantine shot back. "You raised him well enough. Then I gave him the chance of a lifetime. And he squandered it!"

Now Chrocus and Gundomar rose from their couches, as did all the other Alemanni warriors in the dining hall. Though they were unarmed and presented no threat, it was clear to everyone that they were deeply offended by Constantine's words.

Even so, the emperor did not relent. "Anyone who fights for me must be loyal," he declared with ice in his voice. "I am the Augustus of the West, soon to be ruler of this whole Roman realm. I demand all or nothing from anyone who would serve in my army. I deserve nothing less than total devotion."

"Such pride is unworthy of the Christian faith you profess," Bishop Ossius accused. It was a bold thing to say, drawing a gasp from Flavia.

Constantine narrowed his eyes. "Perhaps it is. But there are limits on what God can demand from an emperor."

King Chrocus was standing in front of the emperor's couch. He took a step forward, prompting three imperial bodyguards to draw their swords. No one moved. The tension in the room was so high that Flavia felt physically oppressed by it.

The king's voice was careful and measured when he finally spoke. "You speak of your limits," he said. "There also be limits on what emperor should demand of father." Then, with Gundomar at his side and a train of Germanic warriors behind him, Chrocus exited the room as every eye watched them go.

Now it was Ossius's turn to stand up from his couch. "This is no way to win God's favor," he said with a frown.

"So you will not repudiate Rex?"

"I will not. He is a good man who has served us well." There was a long pause, then the bishop added, "And he served you faithfully too."

"Then be gone from my sight," Constantine said fiercely.

Righteous anger flared in Ossius's eyes. "Take care that God does not cast you from his sight in the same way! Though you are an emperor, you are but a man before the Lord of the cosmos. Take heed! He exalts the humble, and he humbles the proud."

"Now I have reason to question your loyalty, Ossius!"

"No, Your Highness. Only the most loyal servant would warn you of the danger you face from the God who tolerates no rivals." With those words ringing in the ears of everyone in the room, the bishop straightened his back, turned for the door, and left the diners gaping at him in stunned silence.

Once again, Rex was back in chains. He was starting to feel like the entire world wanted to lock him up and throw him away in some godforsaken corner of the world.

Don't wallow in self-pity, he reminded himself. *Instead, do something about it. Break free!*

It was a bold idea. Unfortunately, the iron shackles binding him to the dungeon wall had plans of their own. There was no way to snap them. Rex would have to wait for the right time to escape.

The soldiers had come unexpectedly to his guest room at the mansion in Sirmium where King Chrocus was staying. Though most of the Alemannic troops were encamped outside the city, a few warriors in the king's retinue had been given lodging inside the walls when Constantine triumphantly arrived. No one could have imagined that the king's son would be arrested while everyone was at the victory banquet. But Constantine was that kind of man: generous to his allies, unforgiving to his betrayers, with no middle ground in between. It was said that he'd execute his own family members if he thought they had turned against him.

The cold chill of the predawn hour made Rex pull his cloak tighter around him as he awaited the arrival of the four-man squad that would escort him to Thessalonica. The emperor had ordered Rex to be sent back into the imperial navy, and Thessalonica was the nearest seaport with a naval base attached. It all felt like Rome four years earlier: waiting in prison to be shipped out to sea, despairing of the future, hoping to see Flavia one last time before being consigned to the monotonous life of a rower.

Footsteps and rough laughter sounded outside the jail. A moment later, the squad of soldiers entered. "Get up, kid! It's time to get out of here," one man barked. He was far too chubby for a legionary, with saggy jowls and a paunch no soldier should have.

Rex stood up. "It's hard for me to go anywhere while chained to a wall."

The paunchy fellow only smirked and unlocked one of Rex's cuffs, attaching it to his own wrist before unfastening the second and doing the same with a second guard. Rex was now chained between two fat soldiers and guarded by two others with swords on their belts. Escape wouldn't be happening anytime soon.

A carriage drawn by two mules waited outside Sirmium's gate. Rex was about to be shoved inside it when he heard his name being called. He turned to see Flavia and Sophronia hurrying toward him from the city. Immediately, he moved toward them instead of entering the carriage.

"No time to delay!" screeched the first paunchy guard, holding Rex back by the chain.

But Rex was having none of it. He was going to see Flavia no matter what these sad excuses for soldiers had to say about it.

"I'll escape somehow," Rex promised when Flavia had drawn near. It was hard for Rex to see her frightened expression yet be unable to do anything about it.

"Oh!" she cried. "You must break free! I can't go through this again!"

The strain on Rex's wrist was intense as the soldiers tugged on his chains and hurled threats at him. He wouldn't have much longer to speak with

Flavia. "Don't come to Thessalonica," he urged. "Stay on the mission. The Roman church needs you. There's still time to change Constantine's mind."

"No, my place is with you!"

"Your place is with God," Rex replied, then the soldiers forced him to separate from the woman he loved.

After shoving him inside the carriage, they slammed the door. It had no windows. From outside, Rex thought he heard Flavia cry "I love you!" but he couldn't be sure. And with that, she was gone from him.

For how long?

Only God knew.

The overland journey didn't last more than a day. The party transferred to a riverboat, then after sailing a few days on the Danubius, they once again resumed the journey by carriage. Fresh mules were available at the military relay stations, so the squad and their prisoner made decent progress as they worked their way through the Macedonian mountains. Most of the time, the guards ignored Rex, which was his preference as well. But they always kept him chained, either to themselves or to an immovable object.

After two boring weeks, they reached Thessalonica. Rex was dropped off at a prison house at the city's naval base. The commandant's name was Lucius. Though his demeanor was brusque and aloof, he didn't seem cruel.

The news that Lucius delivered, however, was a cruel blow indeed. "You aren't being enrolled back into the navy," he announced to Rex when he brought the evening meal. "You're being reduced to the status of an imperial slave. Your job is to row troop transports between Greek harbors. In the wintertime, you'll do ship maintenance."

Anger welled up in Rex, and he would have punched the scrawny commandant if his hands weren't chained to a ring on the stone wall. Controlling his anger, since it would be no use to vent it, Rex said, "I'm skillful in war maneuvers and battle. This will be a complete waste of my abilities."

"Orders are orders. Get used to it." Lucius pushed Rex's bowl of gruel toward him with his toe, then left the cell and locked the door behind him.

A slave!

Being sentenced to row in the navy was bad enough, but at least it was a respectable position with certain rights and privileges. On a normal navy ship, Rex would have been paid for his work, though any advancement through the ranks was prohibited.

However, with this announcement from Lucius, he had just been reduced to the lowest possible status in his society. Not long ago, he was a respected prince of the Alemanni. Before that, he had been a highly trained speculator in the Roman army. Now he was nothing but the property of the vast imperial government. Even household slaves sometimes had the respect of their masters. But as an imperial slave, Rex wasn't owned by a person with vested interests in him. He was owned by an abstraction. The "empire" would direct his fate, and its brutal machinery didn't care what happened to its individual pieces. A replacement part was always available. Imperial slaves existed only to be used up, then discarded when fresh ones came along.

Dejected, Rex sat on his moldy straw pallet and ate his thin barley gruel with a seashell for a spoon. It was slave food, not a military ration. Such fare could hardly sustain a man. Rex told himself that somehow he would break free of this life. Yet his three years of rowing in the navy told him otherwise. The Roman system, honed over many centuries, knew how to lock in its victims. Escape from one's lot in life was hard enough for a free man. Escape from slavery was next to impossible.

I'll find a way, Rex resolved. Yet as he slipped into a fitful doze on the cold dungeon floor, he knew it wouldn't likely be soon.

Shortly after sunset, the commandant Lucius opened the door again. "You have a wealthy visitor," he said with a smirk. The jingle of coins in his palm explained the satisfied look on his face.

Squinting into the gloom, Rex tried to make out the shadowy form behind Lucius. *I know no one in this city*, he thought. *Who could it be?*

A moment later, when the visitor stepped past Lucius, Rex was reminded that he was wrong. He actually did know someone here. Bishop Basil of Thessalonica had come to see him!

"Greetings, friend," the bishop said, kneeling down beside Rex.

"Friend." It felt good to hear that word, and to hear it spoken in a gentle tone. Rex had grown used to being berated by everyone around him since his arrest two weeks ago.

"Why have you come?" he asked, surprised by the visit, though glad for it too.

"We Christians take care of our own," Basil replied. Even in the fading light from the window, Rex could see the kindness in the visitor's eyes.

"But I am not a Christian."

"Perhaps you are and don't know it yet," Basil said with the hint of a smile. "Regardless, you are a friend of our dear brother, Bishop Ossius. When I learned of your return here, I came immediately. It is something Ossius would want."

The explanation was enough for Rex. He glanced at a small sack the bishop had brought, which appeared to hold jars. "Is that what I think it is?"

"A man cannot survive on what a prison provides. There is food here: salted sardines, kale, oil, and garlic. Eat this with whatever they give you. Not only will it taste better, it will give you strength and health. I will bring more later." Basil withdrew a large raisin cake from the sack and handed it to Rex. "And this is for now," he added with a smile that spread inside his bushy Greek beard. "To lift your spirits and give you hope."

Ravenous, Rex ate the cake without talking. When he had gulped it down, he glanced at the bishop. "Your kindness to me is undeserved," he said after he swallowed his final bite.

"So is the grace of God, young Rex. We do not deserve God's grace, but he gives it anyway."

Rex had to admit, right now the Christian God had a lot going for him. He might not be powerful in war, but his constant outpouring of love through these Christians had a power of its own. The catholic church produced amazing people—people like Bishop Basil, who showed up unexpectedly when you needed him most, with friendship in his eyes and raisin cakes in his hands.

After some quiet conversation and words of encouragement, the bishop stood up to leave. The cell had grown dark. Basil handed Rex four more things before he left: an oil lamp, a fire striker, a piece of flint, and a wad of charcloth.

"A man shouldn't have to sit alone in the darkness," the bishop said. "Let the light of God be a comfort to you. I will bring more lamp oil when I come again with food."

"You are too kind to me," Rex said humbly, but the bishop waved him off and bid him good night. After he left, Lucius returned and made sure to lock the door tight.

By now, it was deep into the first watch of the night. The only illumination was the starlight that came through the window. Rex gathered his fire-starting materials and threw a spark onto the charcloth, then used a piece of straw from his pallet to ignite the wick of the lamp. The lively little flame brought a warm glow to the corner of the cell where Rex was chained. Basil was right—the light was indeed a comfort in the darkness of the prison.

"*We do not deserve God's grace,*" the bishop had said, "*but he gives it anyway.*"

True enough, Rex decided. The Christian God was loving and forgiving. He accepted all people, even when the rest of society cast them aside. The Christians were proof of that, for they were always reaching out to the poor, the afflicted, the downtrodden. Like Bishop Basil had done tonight, the Christians gave mercy to those who had no right to expect it.

But are there limits to God's mercy?

Surely the bishop knew that Rex was a killer. A soldier didn't go long in this dangerous world without shedding human blood. Rex had slain men in war, and sometimes he had killed for other reasons. Were those reasons good enough? Or was he a murderer in God's eyes?

For the next hour or two, Rex wrestled with his thoughts. On the one hand, he wanted to accept the idea that God could be merciful to him. However, another voice kept accusing him, saying he wasn't like Basil or Stephen. Those men were fundamentally gentle, whereas Rex had a violent streak inside him. He killed quickly and easily. Not so long ago, he had left an entire ship's crew to drown in the Aegean Sea! Such a coldhearted disposition was probably beyond the redemption of any god—even the Christian God, who defined himself by grace.

A cold autumn draft seeped from the window above. Rex tightened his cloak around him and lay on his side upon the straw mattress. The oil lamp was before his eyes, its flame bright and steady. For a long time, Rex stared at the burning wick, until at last he grew sleepy. Puffing his cheeks, he was about to blow out the lamp to conserve the oil when he realized he didn't want to do it. The little yellow flame brought him peace. However, if he let it burn all night, the oil would be used up more quickly. Soon, it would be gone.

But that doesn't matter, Rex reminded himself. *Bishop Basil promised to bring more.*

The promise was enough. The Christians would not fail him. Rex closed his eyes and settled in for sleep, confident that whatever the next day might bring, the mercy of God would be there too.

—◦◦◦—

Emperor Constantine had found that when chariot races weren't scheduled in circuses, they made nice riding grounds for his private use. The sandy surface of the racetrack was just right for horses' hooves, and there was plenty of space to open up to a gallop. Conveniently, the circus at Sirmium was close to the palace where he was now staying; and Licinius had, in his haste to escape, left behind a stable full of spirited Arabians. That was fortunate, because equestrian mastery was one of the many requirements of a good emperor.

Today, however, Constantine was only watching. Crispus was in the saddle instead, riding a gray stallion with an arched neck and the high tail carriage typical of the breed. At eighteen years old, Crispus was a grown man now—a good rider, well-built, and fully trained in the arts of war. Constantine was proud of him.

"What a magnificent beast!" the youth exclaimed as the horse slowed to a walk after galloping down the straightaway. "He could do ten more laps without a breather!"

"Five is plenty, my boy."

"He hardly breaks stride as he turns the posts," Crispus went on, still excited by the vigorous ride. Though it was a cool October day, the sun was shining from a cloudless sky, so sweat matted his reddish locks. He reached forward from the saddle and stroked his mount's neck. "This horse would be great in a battle!"

"Then he is yours. You may take him along as we chase our enemy into Thracia."

"Thank you, Father," said Crispus with a respectful nod.

There was something about the way Crispus nodded—the dip of his chin, the flash in his eyes—that instantly reminded Constantine of the boy's mother. *Ah, Minervina, so fair and sweet!* She was the complete opposite of bossy Fausta. But Fausta had possessed one advantage that outweighed everything else: her powerful father. Beautiful Minervina was just a peasant commoner, while Fausta's father had been a founding member of the Imperial College. That was the main reason Constantine had married her.

When Constantine entered into a political marriage with Fausta almost ten years ago, his new bride insisted that Minervina be sent far away. *Where are you now, my sweet companion? I miss you at my side!* Constantine's wistful longing for his former concubine led immediately to a pang of guilt. *How could I have banished Minervina like a five-penny whore?* It was the kind of coldhearted treachery that the Furies would normally avenge. Fortunately, Constantine didn't believe in those pagan myths anymore. He hoped Christianity didn't have something similar that he didn't know about.

Crispus dismounted from the gray stallion with the casual ease of a man accustomed to the saddle. He whispered as he stroked the animal's muzzle, thanking it for an excellent ride. After a groom came to lead it away, he turned and looked at his father. "How soon before we ride out after Uncle Licinius?"

"We will give the troops a decent rest. And we are awaiting the addition of some new legions. So not right away."

"Let's not wait too long, Father. It is said Licinius has abandoned his Christian faith. He's hostile to God now. In the Imperial College, that usually means one thing—persecution."

"It has meant that in the past. But at the wedding in Mediolanum, we sent a letter across the provinces requiring tolerance of the Christians. I do not think Licinius will start attacking the catholic church."

"If he does, we will crush him as an enemy of Christ!"

"Of Christ, you say?" Constantine eyed his son carefully. Crispus had turned out to be an upright young man with respectable Christian morals, unlike so many youths today. Constantine credited his tutor, Lactantius, for that. The wise African scholar was a skillful defender of the new faith, always refuting the pagans and instilling a Christian perspective in his hearers. Evidently, Crispus had absorbed much wisdom from his tutor, for he had become an ardent observer of the church's teachings.

"What do you believe to be the essence of Christianity?" Constantine asked his son.

To his credit, Crispus did not answer right away, for he recognized the profundity of his father's question. Finally, he said simply, "Love."

"Explain what you mean."

"Real love isn't part of the old religion. The gods run a system of bribery and rewards. If you only 'love' someone who can do something for you, it's actually selfishness. And if someone pays attention to you because of what you provide, then they're selfish too. The same is true of the gods. Give them blood and incense, or coins and votives, and they might do what you want. If your gifts stop, they ignore you, or maybe send a curse. It's all a transaction. Power and manipulation are the motivators between gods or men. So it's not true love."

"And Christianity?"

"Christianity starts with God loving us," Crispus explained, gesturing with his hands like a trained rhetorician. He was clearly well taught in theology too. "God the Father gave us his Son, the Savior Jesus. This demonstrates divine love. And the Christians form a community that is centered on self-giving. They share gifts with one another. Care for the poor. Consider others as equal to themselves, no matter their station in life. It's unique, really. No other philosophy teaches anything like it."

"But I'm an emperor," Constantine countered. "Sometimes that will require me to exercise power. I cannot show love to everyone. At times, I must dominate in order to survive."

Crispus pursed his lips and nodded. "There is a proper place for power. Any soldier must recognize that. The use of force is inevitable when men are evil. But when you have absolute power, it becomes too easy to consider your own selfish desires as noble and necessary. A wise emperor needs to know the difference. Otherwise, he can justify any action he can think up, and he becomes a tyrant."

"Am I a tyrant?"

"No, Father. You are a wise Christian emperor. Not perfect, but trying."

"And how am I imperfect?"

"You are unforgiving at times, if I may speak directly. And this leads to cruelty that is unwarranted."

"Your words to me are very bold, Crispus."

"I know. But Lactantius says candor is true courage. And it was you who assigned him to be my tutor."

Constantine couldn't argue with his son's logic. "Give me an example of my cruelty."

"Well, for one, you were unduly harsh toward Brandulf Rex at the banquet. That man served you faithfully. He brought you an Alemannic army that turned the battle at Cibalae. And to thank him, you sent him back to the oars for a second time. There was no need for that."

"But he abandoned me at Verona!"

"So that he could chase down your enemy. He single-handedly pursued Ruricius Pompeianus and slew him like a dog. Some would consider that extraordinary courage, not treason."

Constantine looked away from his dignified son and stared for a long time at the empty risers of the circus around him. He inhaled through his nose as he considered Crispus's words, then let out a heavy sigh. Finally, he said, "King Chrocus was deeply offended by my decision."

"Of course he was. You insulted his brave son in front of all his men. What if someone did that to you? You would be furious."

"Chrocus certainly was furious. He and all his men."

"Do you think the Alemanni will leave you?"

"They might. It remains to be seen."

"We will need them for the final confrontation with Licinius."

"I know. But what can I do?"

"Perhaps your sentence on Rex was unduly harsh."

"In other words, you think it was unworthy of a Christian."

"I am only saying it wasn't an act of mercy. Haven't you ever felt the need for God's mercy?"

Yes, Constantine thought, *when I sent your mother away*. It was a hard truth that he dared not utter out loud.

Crispus's expression softened. "I do not mean to disrespect you, Father, but only to exchange words of wisdom between Christian men. I hope you know that."

"I do. I'm proud of you, Crispus. You have indeed become wise."

"True wisdom is from above. Thanks be to God if I have received a tiny measure of it."

"Well, my son, be sure to share whatever wisdom you have gained with your father. His old religious habits die hard."

"Let them die. Turn to the way of love instead."

"The way of love," Constantine said. "Maybe I should try that."

"I think you should," Crispus replied.

10

It had taken several days, but Licinius was finally beginning to feel safe again.

The rout at Cibalae had shaken him; it was a defeat so terrible it seemed impossible to overcome. Licinius rushed straight to Sirmium from the battlefield. After gathering his family, the top imperial bureaucracy, and the treasury, he hit the road to the east. A cohort of crack troops served as a bodyguard in case of pursuit. But after a week of travel, he had finally reached the safety of Thracia.

On the distant horizon, he could see the faint, white line that marked the walls of Hadrianopolis, a city comfortingly close to the impregnable citadel of Byzantium. This was secure Licinian territory. The people of this region still supported him. Here, he would set up a new base, reassemble his army, and at the right time, take another shot at his accursed brother-in-law.

"I'm ready to be in a palace again," Constantia announced as she removed her shoes and set them on the cushion beside her in the luxurious carriage. She winced and rubbed her feet, even though she had been riding in the cab all day. "I hope the palace at Hadrianopolis has a decent bath."

"Quit your griping," Licinius muttered, and his fat wife fell silent as the carriage rolled along.

The weather today was cloudy and blustery. Though the caravan had pushed hard all day, by sunset they were still short of the city, so the final few miles to Hadrianopolis would have to be completed tomorrow. Licinius waited as long

296

as he could, then told the carriage driver to stop at the nearest suitable place to camp. Soon the troops were preparing to bivouac one last time. Meanwhile, the peasant inhabitants of a roadside cottage were temporarily evicted so the emperor and his wife could have a roof over their heads for the night.

Constantia pointed to the cottage's fireplace. "Put them over there," she instructed the slaves who had arrived to set up the royal beds. "My husband and I don't like to sleep cold."

While the slaves did their work, Licinius ate a meal of pork chunks in gravy over bread, served hot from the cook tent nearby. Though the food was tasty and the wine was a good vintage, still he found himself irritable. When Constantia bowed her head and crossed herself as she was about to tuck into her own dish, Licinius rebuked her sharply.

"I always thank the Divinity before I eat," she protested.

"By all means, thank the Highest Divinity for your food. But he's not the one you're thinking of."

"My understanding of the Supreme Being is different from yours, my love. We have determined that already."

"Our Roman Jupiter is highest and best," Licinius insisted with a scowl, "not that Jewish latecomer. I hate how everyone is so obsessed with him these days! Why not go back to the old gods?"

"Those spirits are called gods, but they're actually demons."

The provocative statement pushed Licinius from irritation to rage. He snatched up his empty dish and threw it against the wall, where it shattered and left a gravy splatter on the plaster. Constantia's eyes were wide, not just with surprise but with fear.

"I thought I told you never to mention the Christian God to me!" Licinius thundered.

"I have not spoken his name," Constantia said meekly. "That was our agreement."

"Your God abandoned me at Cibalae! He fought for your brother instead."

"My lord, if you recall, you renounced the Christian God. Why would he fight on your side?"

"I didn't expect him to," Licinius grumbled, "but I didn't like him aiding Constantine either. Those Alemanni were a divine help brought to him by Christ. He is against me for sure."

"Probably," Constantia agreed, then cast down her eyes and took another bite of her gravy-soaked bread.

A slave approached the emperor. "Your bed is ready whenever you are, O great Augustus," he announced with a bow.

"Good. Now go find Zeno. I wish to speak with him."

The slave left the cottage, and a short while later, Zeno entered. He was a scribe who worked in the imperial chancery—an obsequious fellow, but one who knew how to get the job done. He worked for the Curator of Correspondence, making sure all letters that went out under the emperor's seal had been copied and filed away for future consultation.

Licinius jerked his thumb toward Constantia as he addressed the clerk. "You remember our wedding in Mediolanum?"

"I do. A glorious and splendid affair," Zeno replied with an oily smile.

"So you remember the letter that went out then? From Constantine and me? To the provincial governors?"

"Of course. I copied it myself and filed it among the most important records. It proclaimed tolerance for all beliefs and called for the restoration of Christian properties."

"I favored the Christians back then," Licinius said, "but no longer. Three years have gone by. Now I despise them."

"You despise what is despicable, as a wise man should."

"I like how you think, Zeno!" Licinius rubbed his chin for a moment. "I know we're traveling and things are all jumbled right now, but could you fetch me that letter?"

"Certainly, my lord. I will have it for you in a moment." The scribe departed, then returned surprisingly fast. He was one of those energetic men who always did their work quicker than expected.

"Read it out loud," Licinius said, and Zeno immediately obliged.

When I, Constantine Augustus, as well as I, Licinius Augustus, met on a happy occasion at Mediolanum, we took the opportunity to consider everything that related to the public's best interest and security. We thought that, among the many things we perceived would be profitable for the majority of the people, the first order of business was to secure proper reverence for the Divinity. Thus we granted to Christians and everyone else the freedom to follow the religion each one preferred, so that whatever Divinity is seated in heaven might be favorable and well-disposed toward us and to all who have been placed under our rule.[1]

After the preamble, the document went on with more of the same. As Zeno kept reading, Licinius's ears perked up whenever the Christians were mentioned. He was hoping the Christians had received only vague support. But unfortunately, the wording of the imperial directive was crafted to grant specific rights and privileges to the Christians. The catholic church was now a legal entity, so to clamp down on the Christian masses would invite popular disdain. Licinius would be viewed as a "persecutor" like his discredited colleagues. Over the past three years, the citizenry had become accustomed to the presence of Christians in their midst. A massive persecution like the one Emperor Diocletian had unleashed was now out of the question.

Zeno finished reading the parchment and rolled it up. Before Licinius could speak, Constantia said, "It certainly does favor the believers in Christ."

"So I noticed."

"They are safe as long as they break no existing laws," Zeno remarked. "Of course, criminals can still be prosecuted, even if they are Christians."

Clever man, Licinius thought. He asked the scribe to explain what he meant.

"Just what I said," Zeno went on. "The catholic faithful are safe, generally speaking. But if any particular Christian breaks a law, no one would expect this directive to shield him from Roman justice."

"What kind of laws do you mean?"

"Laws that already exist, Your Majesty, even if no one knows about them. For example, did you know that an ancient statute requires all officers in the imperial chancery to pay homage to the guardian spirit of the emperor? If a Christian refused to do it, that would be illegal on its face."

"Has the law been enforced lately?"

"Not in anyone's recent memory!" Constantia exclaimed, but Licinius only scowled at her.

---

1. This is the famous "Edict of Milan" that ended Christian persecution. The words are my own translation of Lactantius's Latin text, and it appears in my book *Early Christian Martyr Stories: An Evangelical Introduction with New Translations* (Grand Rapids: Baker Academic, 2014), 163–66.

"All laws should be enforced at all times, whether it has been customary or not," Zeno said simply.

"Of course they should!" Licinius agreed. He drummed his fingers on the table, thinking for a moment. "Are there any forgotten laws against secret meetings?"

Now it was Zeno's turn to reflect. "I seem to recall a few old ordinances against clubs and associations. Those are the seedbeds of insurrection. Emperors have always banned them."

"What do those laws say?"

"Typically, the leaders are forbidden from traveling between cities, so their rebellious ideas cannot spread. Sometimes they aren't even allowed to communicate by letter outside of their own city."

"That is exceedingly wise," Licinius remarked.

"It transgresses the freedoms of a Roman citizen!" Constantia countered.

Licinius whirled on his wife. "Stuff a rag in that faucet of yours and stop the drip!" he snarled. "This is a conversation for men!"

Chastened, Constantia lowered her eyes and dipped her chin like a good wife should do.

"What else do the laws say about secret societies?" the emperor asked his scribe after he had collected his composure again.

"There is an ordinance I once saw that says private associations cannot meet under a roof. They have to gather in open air outside the city walls, in plain sight of all. Then everyone can know who belongs to the club."

"The wisdom of our forefathers astounds me once again," Licinius said with a satisfied chuckle. "Return now to your supervisor. Go find those laws. Have the Curator of Correspondence bring me the relevant texts right away."

"Tonight, Your Majesty?"

"Yes, tonight. I want to see those scripts. And bring more lamps. This roadside hovel is dismal now that the sun has set."

Zeno nodded but didn't waste time with more words. Instead, he returned in less than an hour with the Curator of Correspondence, a man who bore the stupid Jewish name of Iosef. The longtime imperial servant was a tall, thin man with a distinguished bearing. He greeted Constantia warmly before respectfully giving his attention to the emperor.

"Hand me the documents," Licinius said gruffly. He took the parchments and shuffled through them by the light of the extra lamps until he found the one he wanted. After scanning it briefly, he held it up to Iosef. "Have you ever seen this statute?"

"Long ago, Your Highness. It concerns the duties of officers in the imperial chancery. To keep accurate records. Never take a bribe. Things of that sort."

"And to worship correctly."

"Yes, it says . . . it includes some outdated provisions along those lines."

"Outdated according to whom?" Licinius rose from the bench where he had been sitting and crossed to the shrine for the household gods. Its figurine depicted the guardian spirit of the cottage's owner, a divine power that lived in the hearth and watched over the father of the family. Licinius removed the little idol and set it on the table. "This isn't just for the householder," he announced. "It represents my spirit too, as the paternal augustus of these lands."

Iosef eyed the blank-faced idol. "So it is believed by many people."

"You do not believe it?"

"I believe every man has a spirit, the part of him that communes with heaven," the curator said diplomatically.

Constantia now came to her husband's side, tugging on his arm. "Iosef has always proven faithful to you, my love. Come now, it has been a long day. Let us leave these legal inquiries for tomorrow. Your servants love and obey you. That is all you need to know."

"It's not all I need to know!" Licinius shook his arm free of Constantia's grasp. "I must also know who is on my side. I cannot allow competing allegiances in my court. If someone follows gods that oppose me, he must be cast from my presence."

Iosef dropped to his knee. "Great Licinius, for twenty-three years I have kept your letters in order. It has been my greatest honor. My allegiance is yours alone."

"Then prove it! Prostrate yourself before the idol. Lie down and swear an oath by my guardian spirit."

"I swear to serve you well!" exclaimed Iosef, though he remained on his knee and did not otherwise move.

"You will not venerate the idol?"

301

"With all humility, Your Majesty, no, I cannot."

"Why not?"

Iosef remained silent.

"Say it!" Licinius roared. "Say it aloud!"

Though the turmoil on Iosef's face was clear, he finally gathered his courage and spoke. "Because I am a Christian," he declared.

"Just as I suspected."

Licinius walked behind the kneeling curator and put his boot against the man's back. With hard pressure from his foot, he forced Iosef to lie prone on the floor.

"Do you smell the dung in your nostrils?" the emperor asked.

"I . . . I do."

"Get used to it. You will smell it often as a slave for the rest of your life in the imperial stables."

"Oh, God, help me," came the pitiful whimper from the demoted officer.

Licinius turned away from the shaking man on the floor and returned to the papers Iosef had brought. Relieved at having decided what to do about the problem of the Christians, the emperor found his optimism had returned. He felt much more positive about the future. After gathering up the statutes that restricted secret associations, he handed them to his scribe.

"Congratulations, Zeno," he said with the broad smile of a generous lord. "Your position as the new Curator of Correspondence begins right now. And your first order of business is to send letters strictly enforcing these laws across my realm."

Sophronia patted Flavia's hand on the cushioned seat beside her. There was no real reason for the action, other than to communicate the depth of her affection. Flavia smiled sweetly in return. Mother and daughter sat close together in the imperial coach that would be reaching Thessalonica within an hour or two.

The journey from Sirmium had been arduous because the travelers had been pressing for speed. Though Sophronia had wondered whether she could endure the rigors, Flavia had been adamant in insisting on long journeys each day. She kept saying she wasn't about to stay in some remote part of the empire while Rex was unjustly shipped out to sea. If she could do anything—anything at all—to prevent his consignment to a navy ship again, Flavia was determined to do it. They departed for Thessalonica as soon as possible after Rex was sent away under armed guard.

Stephen and Cassi came with them from Sirmium, but Bishop Ossius decided his place was to remain at Constantine's side. The emperor was preparing for another confrontation with Licinius, probably somewhere in Thracia. While battle plans were being made, Ossius thought if he stayed nearby, he could still convince Constantine to come around and support the pope's petition. It would just take time and some delicate diplomacy. "I'll tell him positive things about Rex," he had said. "The good outweighs the bad." Staying in Sirmium was the obvious thing for Ossius to do.

But I sure miss him, Sophronia thought. Over the past few months, the stately bishop had provided a wise and steadying presence in her life. Sophronia had come to rely on him more than she realized.

The carriage reached Thessalonica's gate a little over an hour later. The four companions disembarked at the imperial stables. After Stephen loaded their baggage onto a handcart, they all proceeded to the church of Bishop Basil, called the House of Demetrios. A letter had been sent ahead by a swift courier, so the bishop knew they were coming. His gracious hospitality was a refreshment the weary travelers looked forward to.

"Welcome, dear friends!" he said when they arrived at the front door. "Welcome again to the house of the Lord. Please, come in and take your ease."

Though the atrium was warmed by charcoal braziers on this crisp November day, Sophronia thought the warmth of Basil's love was an even greater comfort after the long trip.

A hot bath and a cold drink further rejuvenated the travelers' spirits. That evening, the three women reclined on a couch across a well-laid table from Stephen and the bishop. Basil had no qualms about dining with women. In the catholic church, females often held places of honor. Christian women were accorded a dignity that wasn't common in secular circles. In the right context, they were certainly free to fellowship at the table with men.

Though Basil had insisted on eating a good meal before any weighty matters were discussed, when the dishes were finally cleared, he turned to

303

the subject that pressed on everyone's mind. "I have seen your friend Rex several times," he announced. "He fares well enough in the prison, though he does not have much more time before they put him out to sea."

"The navy ships are in dry dock," Stephen observed. "How would they do that?"

Basil grimaced. "Unfortunately, Rex is not destined to be given a navy post. I'm sorry to say, he has been enslaved. He is condemned to row coastal watercraft and perform menial duties."

The grape that Flavia had been holding fell from her hand and bounced on the floor. She rose from her reclining position on the couch and sat on its edge, gripping the folds of her tunic in her fists. Outrage was etched upon her face. "But he is a mighty warrior!" she exclaimed. "He wasn't supposed to be reduced to slavery. That is a complete waste of his fighting skills!"

"Be that as it may, the decision has been made. No one cares about what he can do in battle."

"I care, and I will do something about it," Flavia vowed.

Sophronia could sense her daughter's frustration and anxiety. "Surely we must have some options," she said, reaching over and patting Flavia on the hip. "Be strong, my love, and let us see what unfolds." Glancing toward the bishop, she asked, "Can we offer a bribe?"

"It is possible. My cousin is highly placed in the judicial apparatus. He does not believe in the Lord, yet he is willing to set our people free with the right payoffs."

"Why would he do that?" Stephen asked.

"It's more common than you might think. Until recently, Licinius was well-disposed toward the church, so his representatives looked the other way when Christian favors were needed. We have often helped our brethren in this way. For example, though it cost us a small fortune, we have freed about forty Greek believers from the mines."

"Praise God!" Stephen exclaimed. "The mines are a long, slow death from overwork and starvation."

Basil nodded. "The servant who brought our food earlier was one of those whom we rescued. He is still gaunt, but he grows stronger by the day." At these words, everyone paused to consider the vast difference between the man's current situation and his terrible fate before. Such ransoms were common in the church. It was one of the many ways that Christian tithes were put to good use.

Sophronia turned the conversation back to the subject that she knew was close to Flavia's heart. "How soon could we arrange a bribe for Rex?"

"I will go see my cousin tomorrow," said the bishop.

Though the promise was a comfort to Sophronia, seeing the relief on her daughter's face was even better. The prospect of freeing Rex with a well-placed bribe caused Flavia's entire demeanor to change from anxiety to peace.

Soon, all will be well, Sophronia thought.

And then the soldiers arrived.

———⁂———

Though the loud banging on the door of the house church was a sign of trouble, Flavia was even more worried about the jangle of armor she heard outside. It meant the men were soldiers on official business.

"Open up!" demanded a raspy voice that bore no goodwill.

Bishop Basil rose from the couch in the dining room. "Friends, let us trust God in this development. I shall go see what the fuss is about. Please remain here and pray. And don't forget to pray for our enemies, as Christ Jesus has instructed us."

After Basil left the room, the others also rose from their couches and huddled together for comfort. Cassi knelt near Flavia and held her hand. "Though we walk through a valley of death," she said, "we fear no evil."

"Because the Lord is our shepherd," Flavia agreed.

From the front atrium of the house, the sound of shouting indicated that Basil had let the soldiers inside. The men were insisting that he go with them, but he was protesting that he had done nothing wrong.

"This is a Christian house! Everyone knows it!" said the gravelly voice that had spoken before.

"Yes, but the church is tolerated now, so that is not a matter for the law," Basil replied.

"Wrong! Licinius don't like the Christians no more! And now he's enforcing the rules against you."

"What rules, sir? I abide by all the laws of Rome."

"There's a bunch of old laws you don't even know about!" screeched the soldier.

"I assure you," Basil replied in a calm and soothing voice, "my ears work quite well, even though I am old. I can hear you just fine. There is no need to shout."

"Quit your stallin' and come with me, priest! Then no one has to shout. You can answer to the centurion for all your secret meetings!"

"Don't forget to collect all his books too," another soldier chimed in.

Books?

Flavia had assumed the soldiers were local thugs who had decided to harass Basil with legal technicalities. However, the mention of books suggested something more sinister was afoot. The confiscation of the Christian scriptures always signaled a widespread persecution. Now a sense of dread took hold of Flavia's mind. A terrible cancer, believed to have been cured, had sprouted a deadly tumor again.

"Go look around," the gravelly voiced leader commanded. "Collect any writings you find. Then we'll be off with him!"

The house church actually did have a good library in an anteroom off the atrium. Flavia could hear the men begin to break into the book cabinets there. Yet it wasn't those volumes she was worried about. They could all be replaced. It was the treasured Thessalonian epistles from Saint Paul's own hand that Flavia feared would be destroyed. In only a few moments, the soldiers would locate them in Basil's private study.

"Where are you going?" Cassi whispered as Flavia began to edge toward the door. "The bishop said stay here!"

"I've got to get those epistles before the soldiers do!" Flavia replied, then was out the door before anyone could stop her.

The study had two entrances—one from the atrium where the men were making a racket and another from the rear garden where the Christians held baptisms. Flavia peeked into the study from the shady colonnade that ran around the garden. No one was in the room, though she could hear the flurry of activity in the adjacent atrium. The ornate wooden box that held the Pauline epistles was inside a cabinet behind the bishop's desk. Once the men barged in, the box couldn't be missed, even by the most half-hearted searcher. Flavia decided to move now while she still had a chance of saving the letters.

In three quick steps, she reached the cabinet. Swinging open its door, she removed the beautiful box. It held nothing but a few fragile leaves of cheap papyrus, yet they were priceless. The Thessalonian letters were the earliest ones Paul had written, predating the four gospels or any other biblical writings by several years. Therefore, the box in Flavia's hand contained the very first pages of the New Testament that God had ever given to mankind.

A sharp interruption startled Flavia. "I'll take that, little honey," said the raspy voice of the soldier in charge.

Flavia whirled to face him. "You have no right to take my hairpins," she said firmly.

"Hairpins! Why would I want that?"

"You wouldn't, but that's what's in this box. They're pretty, and I like to keep them together. I'm getting ready for a banquet tonight, so I need to have them—my hairpins."

"We'll see about that," the soldier said gruffly. He was an unshaven fellow with dried mucus caking his nostrils. "Hand it over."

"I don't have to give you my hairpins," Flavia said, then turned her back on the crude man.

But he was having none of it. Crossing the room swiftly, he grabbed Flavia's shoulder and spun her around. Though she resisted him for a moment, he was too strong, and he soon wrested the box from her grip.

"You have no right to do that!" Flavia cried, trying to snatch back the box.

It seemed this man couldn't speak in any tone but a shout. "My rights come from the augustus himself! Licinius ordered us to clamp down on the bishops. Sorry, Christian girl, but your God don't appeal to him no more. He's out to get you!"

The harsh assertion made Flavia take a step back. *Is it truly a time of persecution again?*

Before that terrible thought could settle in Flavia's heart, Bishop Basil entered the study. "Your men have collected all my books," he said with bitterness in his voice. "Now, please, give the girl back her hairpins and let us be gone. I have decided to speak with your centurion."

"Hurry up, Ares," complained one of the other soldiers from the atrium. "We can't eat until we're done here."

Flavia stared at snot-nosed Ares while he debated what to do. Basil thrust out his hand and beckoned for the lockbox. Finally, Ares set it on the desk and headed for the door—then spun around and grabbed it again.

"Let's just have a look at those hairpins," he said in his gravelly rasp.

The tip of his sword easily pried off the hasp, for the lock was designed to thwart curious eyes, not determined robbers. As soon as Ares raised the lid, a victory cry escaped his lips.

"Hairpins, eh? What do you take me for? You can't fool me that easily!"

"I must have mistaken the box," Flavia said. "But those scraps of papyrus are meaningless."

Basil now intervened more forcefully. "You were ordered to collect books, not old correspondence of mine. Set down those letters and let us be gone, or I shall file a report against you for pilfering household goods."

"You can file whatever report you want! The days of Christian favor from the government are over. Licinius has changed the game."

"That box is valuable," said Flavia. "I shall pay you ten silver pieces for it. Set it down."

Ares chuckled. "Deal," he spat. "You can buy your little box from me. But not what's inside."

And then he did what Flavia feared most. Extracting the pages from their container, he marched over to the charcoal brazier that stood in the corner to warm the atrium.

"No!" Flavia cried. "Don't do it!" But it was too late. Sneering like a fiend, the soldier dropped the original epistles of Saint Paul into the fire.

Basil darted to the brazier and pulled the pages from the coals. The bottom edges were lined with flame, but the words had not yet been destroyed. He began to blow out the fire.

"Drop them!" Ares commanded.

But Basil did not.

What happened next was a blur. There was the sound of a sword being drawn . . . a flash of steel . . . a spatter of red. An angry shout rang out, followed by a cry of pain. Then Bishop Basil was on the floor, clutching the stump of his bloody forearm.

Shocked, Flavia stood rooted in place, trying to comprehend what had just occurred.

Ares gathered the leaves of papyrus and dropped them back into the fire, along with something else—something he retrieved from the floor with the tip of his sword.

"Run away!" Basil urged through gritted teeth as he writhed on the floor. "Hurry!"

It had become clear that Flavia could do nothing more against the wicked power of the soldiers. Before they decided to arrest her too, she turned and made for the door. Ugly smoke billowed from the brazier—the letters of Paul going up in flames. Yet there was something even worse. The last thing Flavia perceived as she fled the room was the noxious stench of burning human flesh.

———

Rex lay on his pallet, dozing in a patch of sunlight that provided the most warmth he could find in the cold cell. His thin blanket and cheap straw mattress weren't sufficient for the November nights. But in a Roman jail, who cared about the needs of the prisoners?

He rolled over, trying to get comfortable, but it was impossible with his wrists chained to a low ring in the wall. The short length of the chain that ran to his handcuffs gave him little room to maneuver his arms. A single padlock bound the manacles together, but it was made of strong iron and could not be pulled open. Rex had strained against it until his wrists were chafed and bloody. Since it had done him no good, he had resigned himself to tossing and turning as he tried to make the best of his cramped position.

The word around the prison was that he'd be shipped out soon. Although the year's sailing season was over now, an old trireme needed to be moved down the Greek coast for overwintering at a repair station. A crew of slaves was being assembled to row it on the next calm, clear day—too few rowers for the number of oars, creating much more work for them all. Soon, Rex would be rolling a shaft again. It was hard to fathom that he was headed back to that life.

No! I won't!

Everything in Rex rebelled at becoming an oarsman again. And unlike before, he couldn't even pretend to be a respectable navy rower anymore. Slavery was his lot now. Rex decided that he hadn't survived mutiny, pirating, poison, and battlefield combat in his quest to be with Flavia only to be

309

dragged away by incompetent soldiers and never see her again. Angered by his fate, he renewed his resolve to escape. There had to be a way. Nothing else mattered. He wanted to be with Flavia above all else. Somehow he had to make that happen. *But how?*

His training as a special-forces operative had taught him to assess a situation rationally and eliminate unworkable options until only the plausible solutions remained. If none of them seemed likely to succeed, he would choose the least problematic choice and run with it. Anything was better than the oar.

At what points were his enemy's defenses the weakest? During any transition from place to place, he would be heavily guarded. Likewise, Rex knew from experience that shipboard life presented few chances for escape. But now? No one was watching him. The oafs around the jail were depending on bricks and chains to do the job of keeping Rex in one place. That meant breaking out of the cell would be the best option. First, he had to get out of his chains. Then he would find a way to escape the prison.

Rex was sitting against the stone wall, examining the padlock that bound his manacles, when the cell door opened and a servant girl entered with his evening meal. She was a pretty lass who had been trying to flirt with him the past few times she had come by. Rex noticed she had started putting up her hair in fashionable braids when she visited. This time, he decided to play along with her seductive banter.

"It's a good thing you're chained up," she teased as she stood just out of reach, "or I might be scared of a man like you. I've heard the barbarians are pretty fierce."

"You might be surprised. I can be tender when I want to be. Tender and slow."

"R-really?" the girl stammered, a little surprised at finally getting the response she'd been seeking. "I . . . I wouldn't have guessed that."

"You needn't be afraid of me. Look here." Rex dipped his chin toward his handcuffs in his lap. "I'm helpless. Completely at your mercy."

"So you are," said the girl, her tone becoming sly. After setting down the bowl and jug of water, she bent over at the waist and put her face close to Rex's. He could feel her breath on his cheek. "I like my barbarians helpless," she whispered.

"You're in charge. Just don't be too rough with me."

Rex's words caused the servant girl to let out a husky groan. She leaned closer and began to nibble his ear. Since Rex was unable to do much with his hands because of the chains, he kissed the back of her neck and breathed in her hair while she made passionate little sighs. She seemed to be lost in rapture when, suddenly, the nearby slam of a door made her jump back.

"I, uh, better go," she said, easing away reluctantly. She tucked a loose tendril of hair behind her ear. "But I'll come again."

"Mm-hmm," Rex replied with a wink.

Once the girl left the cell, Rex rolled his tongue in his mouth until his teeth held the hairpin he had managed to extract from her braids. It was a little sliver of bronze with a pointed tip—perfect for lock picking by anyone trained in the art.

Biting hard on the pin, Rex managed to guide it into the padlock. He understood the mechanism and knew what he wanted to do. It would have been much easier, of course, if he could have done it with one of his hands instead of his mouth. But the padlock kept his wrists too close together for his fingers to do the work. He hunched lower, extending his neck, straining to trip the bolt and spring the lock open. Finally, he felt the hairpin engage, so he began to put pressure on it. A bead of sweat trickled down his nose.

Almost . . . got it . . .

The lock lurched in his grasp and the hairpin fell from his mouth, catching in the folds of his tunic. Though he could pick it up with his fingers, neither hand could insert it into the padlock. Rex put the pin back in his teeth and began once more to jiggle the lock. His shoulders ached from the strain of bending low. At last, he popped open the mechanism and shook loose the handcuffs. He stood up, rubbing his chafed wrists. It felt good to have the shackles off.

There was no time to waste. The jailer, Lucius, and other prison staff were busy outside the door, so Rex wanted to escape before anyone bothered to look into the cell. He crept to the wall beneath the high window. One of its bars was missing, and no one had bothered to replace it. A man could fit through the gap, if only he could climb the wall. Unfortunately, the smooth travertine surface was slick with evening condensation. No one would be ascending that wall without a rope.

Lacking one, Rex used the next best thing. He tore his blanket into strips and braided the lengths into a single strand. Yet once he had used it all, he realized the piece wasn't long enough to stretch from the window to a place he could grasp.

Desperate to get out before he was discovered, Rex stripped to his loincloth and tore his cheap tunic into lengths of cloth as well. By weaving these pieces into a second rope and splicing it into the first, he found he now had a line that was long enough to reach the window. Though it meant he would be running around the streets of Thessalonica in nothing but a loincloth, the embarrassment of that was a small price to pay to escape the jail.

A wooden bucket sat next to his pallet, brimming with his own waste because no one ever came to empty it. Rex poured the filth onto the floor, then broke off one of the bucket's slats. It had a knothole in its center that he was able to knock out with a hard tap from the hairpin. After threading his makeshift rope through the hole, he tied it so it wouldn't come loose from the slat. The piece of wood was long enough to span the bars in the window, as long as it was turned crosswise between them.

After spinning the slat on its rope like a sling, Rex loosed it toward the window, but it hit the bars and clattered to the floor. He winced, thinking someone might have heard. Fortunately, no one came.

The next time he threw it, he was ready to catch the slat before it hit the ground. Six times it bounced off the bars. But on the seventh try, it clanged through the window to the outside. Carefully, Rex drew in the rope until the slat had snagged the bars. It was pressed flat against two of them, so it couldn't be pulled down.

Now Rex shimmied up the rope like he had done so many times in military school. His trainer, Aratus, had been a great believer in the strength and agility that rope climbing provided to his young cadets. Since Rex had to haul himself hand over hand, reaching the window wasn't easy, but he used his feet on the rope as well. A chipped block in the wall gave him enough of a toehold to get the last bit of leverage he needed. By pushing off from the little indentation, he was able to grab the windowsill and pull himself up.

The exertion of wriggling through the gap in the bars was exhausting, and the rough stonework scraped the bare skin of his stomach. After twisting and turning his sweaty body for a long time, Rex managed to drape himself over the windowsill. Now his head and torso were out in the cool evening air while his legs still dangled in the cell. He breathed hard, readying himself for the final stage of his plan.

Since the prison backed up to a deserted alley and the evening shadows were deep, Rex knew he couldn't be seen. However, the distance to the ground was too far to drop onto the pavement, especially headfirst. Yet Rex could tell that if he slid down his hank of rope, he could easily reach the street. All he had to do was switch his slat to the inside of the cell, setting it lengthwise against the bars on the other side. Then the rope would dangle down the jail's outside wall. It would be a simple matter to descend and escape.

Rex had just grasped the filthy piece of wood and was about to turn it around when he heard a feminine giggle behind him. He froze. *Perhaps the girl will let me go?*

But glancing over his shoulder, Rex felt a sudden chill of despair. An archer stood beside the girl with an arrow nocked on his string. Three other beefy men were also there with clubs.

For an instant, Rex considered a sudden dive, but he realized he'd probably break an arm. Then the guards would rush around to the alley before he could get away. It would be pointless. And with the injury, any future escape would be out of the question.

Now the girl started giggling uncontrollably. Clad only in his loincloth, Rex began to feel the indignity of the situation. He was nearly naked and helpless as a baby, with his rear end waving at his enemies.

"That's a nice target," the archer sneered. "Get down now, slave, or I'll put this shaft where you don't want it to go." When Rex hesitated, the skillful man sent an arrow whistling past his shoulder into the dusky sky. "The next one's going in deep!" the archer warned, drawing throaty guffaws from the other three guards.

There was nothing else to do. Disgruntled and humiliated, Rex wriggled back down the rope and dropped to the floor. As soon as his feet touched the flagstones, a weighted net was thrown over him with the proficiency of a gladiator. Entangled in the web, Rex was unable to resist when the guards wrestled him to the ground. They wrenched his arms behind his back and shackled his wrists from behind, then affixed him to the wall again. Now he had to lie on his stomach in an even more restrictive and uncomfortable position than before. And to make matters worse, his clothing and blanket were gone.

"Let him spend the night like that," the archer said. "He oughta be glad we didn't do anything worse for trying to escape!"

Satisfied that their prisoner was helpless once more, the four men left the cell. Only the servant girl remained. Before she exited, she came over to Rex and knelt beside him. Suddenly she spanked him hard with the palm of her hand. "That really is a nice-lookin' target you got there, oarsman," she said with a bawdy laugh. Then, rising to her feet, she closed the door on her way out and left Rex alone with his burning frustration and shame.

"Utter failure."

Those were the words Bishop Melitius of Wolf City had longed to hear. The sound of them was a pleasure in his ears, a bounteous gift from above. God had heard his prayers to destroy the plans of the bishop of Rome. Clearly, Melitius's rigorous fasts had not gone unnoticed by the heavenly eye. God had weighed his works of righteousness and credited them with the rewards they were due.

"It was an utter failure," the Aegyptian Asp repeated to his master. He had just arrived in Wolf City with the good news. "Our mission is complete. The emperor rejected the pope's petition outright. Then he cursed Ossius in front of a crowd of military officers and barbarians."

"Why? What drew his wrath against Ossius?"

"Constantine holds grudges. He recalled that Ossius's traveling companion, a former soldier, had once shown cowardice in war."

"What happened to that man? Was he executed?"

"No, the speculator named Rex has been sent to Thessalonica to serve as a slave rower."

"Excellent! What about Ossius?"

"He no longer has anyone to help him. He is shamed in imperial circles. The rich nuns have abandoned him."

"Those same nuns? The ones who were sent to the brothels in Corinthus?"

"Yes. Clever little things! Somehow they escaped. But now they have left the bishop's side. Their mission was an utter failure, as I have said."

"And Ossius is returning to Rome? Or perhaps back to Hispania?"

"It remains to be seen. But Emperor Constantine is clearly displeased with him. He will not grant Sylvester's petition to build the churches, nor fund the great copy of the scriptures."

"You are sure of this?"

"I am certain of it, my lord."

Melitius stared at the secretive monk with the snake tattoo on his forehead. He had a lean build, yet there was no lack of strength in him. In a previous life, the Aegyptian Asp had been a speculator in the Roman army. He was capable of doing many useful things. Even so, the man was not all-powerful. "You say Constantine will not support the petition," Melitius pressed. "But sometimes the things we believe are not what actually occurs. What if something unexpected happens? What if things turn around?"

"They will not. I planned for all eventualities, my lord, then executed the plan as I conceived it from start to finish. The work of our enemy has come to naught."

"For now, at least. But what about the future? I would have preferred that Rex was killed, or that the nuns had remained in the brothels of Corinthus. I would have preferred that Ossius had already snuck back to Hispania like a rat to its burrow. Yet these things did not happen, despite the execution of your well-laid plans."

The Aegyptian Asp stiffened, yet his face remained placid. "Some eventualities are outside my control," he said evenly. "As a man of God, surely you know this."

The statement offended Melitius. *Who is this monk to lecture me about theology?* However, instead of rebuking his servant, he decided to let the subject go. He had only meant to keep the man on his toes, not alienate him completely. The Aegyptian Asp was too good at getting things done—secretly and without raising suspicions—to lose him over a needless insult.

"Do not take offense. I am pleased with your work," Melitius announced. "No one is perfect, yet you have planned well. Bishop Ossius's wicked schemes have been ruined, without shedding a churchman's blood. Well done."

Upon hearing this compliment, the Aegyptian Asp displayed no obvious pleasure. He was an expert at masking his emotions.

"Tell me about Emperor Licinius," Melitius went on. "We have been hearing some disturbing things. Perhaps he is no longer an ally of any church, whether ours or another?"

The Asp nodded. "That is correct. No longer can Licinius be expected to favor one episcopal see over another. He is a sworn enemy of all Christians now, even to the point of restarting some persecutions. This will continue until his war with Constantine is resolved."

"Hmm. It seems we could use a new imperial patron—one who will favor us here in Aegyptus."

"I have foreseen this," said the Asp, "and I have an excellent suggestion."

Melitius could not contain his smile. *What a useful man!* "Tell me," he urged.

"The commander of Licinius's army is a man on the rise. Some say he is going to be elevated into the Imperial College. And he has Alexandrian connections."

"Who is it?" Melitius asked, sitting forward in his seat.

"General Valerius Valens."

"Ah, I remember him! He was a prisoner of war. The Aegyptian church ransomed him when he was captured in a local uprising. He never forgot that act of kindness."

"Valerius Valens would be very favorable to the bishop of Alexandria," the Asp agreed. "Not the current bishop, of course, but you who sit before me—if you should rise to that place of prominence."

"I will," Melitius vowed.

A servant entered the shabby church at Wolf City and approached the two conspirators with a purposeful stride. He bowed before Melitius. "The ferry boat has arrived, Your Excellency," he said with proper Christian respect for the clergy. "It leaves again in one hour, bound for the Nilus delta."

Melitius dismissed the servant, then glanced at his guest seated across from him. "You must be on that riverboat."

"Tell me my mission, my lord. Shall I go to Hadrianopolis and secure the patronage of Valens?"

"No. Such matters require a command of ecclesiastical politics that you do not possess. I have a better use for your covert skills."

"Command me, Bishop Melitius. Our society is at your service."

Instead of answering, the bishop clapped his hands loudly. A handsome man in his thirties entered the hall from an adjacent room and strode toward the seated pair. The crosses embroidered on his tunic indicated he was a priest. His hair was dark, though peppered with a little gray at the temples. Bowing at the waist, he said, "You summoned me, Holy Father?"

"Indeed, I did." Melitius swept his hand toward the new arrival while looking at the Asp. "This is Father Felix, a priest of the Aventine Hill," he told his seated guest. "He is destined to be the next bishop of Rome!"

For the first time, Melitius thought he detected some kind of emotion on the Aegyptian Asp's face. Perhaps it was surprise, or maybe envy. It was hard to tell. But the man seemed intrigued.

"I am pleased to meet you," Felix said smoothly. "God's peace be upon you, my brother."

The Asp nodded in return, dipping his head slowly and offering the faintest of smiles. It was his only reply to Felix.

"You must return to Rome with me," Felix said to the Asp. "The boat will follow the Nilus to Alexandria. From there, we can catch a ship upon the sea."

Melitius allowed a devious smirk to come to his face. "Yes! I want the two of you to work together. Sow discord in the Roman church. Continue to work against Sylvester's plans."

"There are factions that stand opposed to him," Felix added. "These we must help to grow stronger, until Sylvester is overthrown. Then I can assume his place, as Melitius has commanded me."

At last, the Aegyptian Asp spoke his thoughts. "Since when does the bishop of Rome bow to the desires of Alexandria? If each of you gained the positions you desire, would you not be fierce adversaries?"

Melitius waved his hand dismissively. "In the past, yes, the bishops were rivals. But Felix and I are forging an alliance in which he will be loyal to me. If we unite instead of competing with each other, we can both wield great power. Political power will be ours for the taking! But first, we must obliterate the bishops who stand in our way."

Outside, a dockmaster blew a shrill note on his whistle. "The boat is leaving soon," Felix observed.

Melitius stood up, and the Aegyptian Asp followed. "Your mission is to go to Rome," the bishop told him. "Ensure that Sylvester's plans are truly destroyed. Then replace him with Felix. With God's help, it will happen."

"And what if the Divine Power is not willing?"

Melitius's hand shot out, seizing the cunning monk by his brown robe. He pulled the man close and stared him in the face. The snake tattoo stared back, its eyes beady and bright. "If God is not willing," Melitius said, "then you must do it by the help of another power."

"There are many powers in the world," said the Asp blandly.

"Call upon whichever one is willing," Melitius replied. "Now go and catch that boat."

The oar shaft seemed like a firebrand to Rex. He feared to touch it. Yet touch it he must, or receive the lash upon his back.

On navy ships, the officers did not beat the crew to make them row. The oarsmen were free soldiers who chose the naval life. But the overseers of a slave ship had no such reason to hold back. The whip was a slave rower's ever-present companion.

And so Rex put his hands to the pinewood shaft and bent to his labor. *Forward strokes*, he told himself, and the ship began to move.

Somewhere out there, somewhere in the wide world, was Flavia. But she was behind him now. Rex's future lay at sea. The weather-beaten trireme was headed down to Piraeus for repairs. The trip would be slow as the vessel hugged the coast and dodged November storms. And always, with every turn of the oar, he would be moving farther away from the woman he loved.

"Hail, the ship!" called a voice from alongside.

"Cease rowing!" the overseer commanded. The slaves complied, and the ship's pace immediately slackened to a slow drift.

Someone with command authority boarded the ship, though Rex couldn't hear what was being said up on deck. After several voices conferred for a while, a middle-aged man came below. His uniform identified him as the chief harbormaster from the port authority of Thessalonica.

"Brandulf Rex, raise your hand!" he barked.

Dutifully, Rex did so. The overseer promptly came to him and unlocked the shackles that bound his ankles. Grabbing Rex by his tunic, he hustled him to the harbormaster.

"It's your lucky day, German," the overseer said as he shoved Rex up the steps that led topside.

Rex was ordered into a little skiff that bobbed alongside the trireme. He sat in the prow with the harbormaster while two soldiers took the oars. Both of them had daggers on their belts. Though they did not treat Rex like a criminal, their stern demeanor indicated they didn't want any funny business from him either.

The skiff returned to the port while the trireme sailed on. Rex was taken to the main pier where the port authority office was located. Nearby, he could see the jail where he had been kept for many days. *Am I being returned to the cell? Why?*

The harbormaster, however, did not have incarceration in mind. When Rex entered the office, he found a well-dressed lady standing at the harbormaster's side. Along with them was a prim, birdlike fellow whose box of seals, stamps, and signets identified him as a public notary. Clearly, this threesome was waiting for Rex's arrival. Yet they ignored him when he walked in.

"You look lovely today, my darling," the harbormaster said to the lady. "I'm so glad you could visit me here."

"Let's do the documents," she answered brusquely. "You know I don't enjoy being out here with the commoners."

"This is where I work. I like it here."

"That doesn't mean I have to like it. Hurry up, Cato! Let's get this over with so I can be off."

"Yes, my dear," said Cato. "As you please." Apparently, this man was the master of the harbor but not of his own home.

Rex decided to get clarity about what was going on. "Why am I here?" he demanded.

The notary laid a wax tablet on a table. "If all the parties will sign this, we can finish the transaction." He held out a stylus.

After Cato and his wife had both affixed their names, the notary glanced at Rex with an appraising eye. "Can you write, barbarian, or do you just want to make an X?"

"Of course I can write," Rex said. "In three languages, letters or runes. But what am I signing?"

"Your emancipation."

Emancipation! I am no longer a slave! The news was stunning to Rex. He clasped his forehead and took a step back as he tried to take it in.

"Do you want to sign or not?" the notary asked, impatiently offering the stylus.

Rex grabbed it and scratched his name on the legal document in Latin characters. Then the notary pressed a signet into the wax, and the transaction was complete.

"You are free to go," said Cato.

"But what of Constantine's order? He condemned me to the oar."

Cato sniffed at this. "We do not care what he has decreed! This is the territory of the true augustus, the great Licinius. The commands of that impostor Constantine hold no force here."

"But I was a slave! Who paid the cost of my emancipation? The catholic church?" Rex suspected it was the work of Bishop Basil, but he wanted to know for sure. If so, he intended to thank the bishop profusely. *These Christians never cease to amaze me!*

Yet Cato surprised Rex once again. "The catholic church? Definitely not! The Augustus Licinius no longer has any use for that religion. The bishops are back in disfavor in this part of the empire. We do not conduct business with them, nor grant them any favors. Yours was a purely commercial transaction. You have been redeemed at a fair price of exchange. You are a free man, sir."

"Someone must have paid the price," Rex insisted, bewildered by the sudden turn of events.

The harbormaster's wife finally intervened. "If you must know, it was my doing. The empire has more than enough galley slaves these days, but I have been without a domestic servant for far too long. Good ones are hard to find. Cato finally arranged a solution for me."

"So now your constant complaints can cease, Marcia, my darling," said the henpecked husband.

Rex shrugged and shook his head. "I still don't understand."

"You were designated to serve Cato," the notary explained, gesturing toward the harbormaster. "As a public official, he is entitled to a fixed number of slaves for personal or professional use. To get one for his wife, he had to let one of his rowers go. An even exchange, you see? The girl insisted she wouldn't sign herself into slavery unless you were freed."

Rex felt his heart sink. "What girl?"

"A lovely young thing," said Lady Marcia. "Why that beautiful girl offered herself in exchange for a dock rat like you, I can't fathom. But she did, and I'm glad for it. Rowers are easy to come by. But classy handmaidens are worth a small fortune to ladies like me. They're all the rage among my friends. Everybody wants a pretty one at their side. Now I have the prettiest."

"I'm so glad, my darling," Cato cooed. "You deserve the best."

It took Rex a moment to gather the courage to pose the question whose answer he dreaded to hear. "What . . . what was the girl's name?"

"Fulvia," said the aristocratic lady.

Rex let out a massive sigh. Though the name was similar, it wasn't the same. Apparently, the unknown girl who had become his substitute was someone else.

"Wait! That's not right." The notary pointed to his wax tablet. "Her name is *Flavia*. It says so right here."

"Junia Flavia?" Rex asked, hoping against hope it wasn't her.

"That's her name," the notary declared.

"I guess my memory is failing me," said Lady Marcia. "But who needs to know the name of a slave, anyway?"

"All they need to know is the back of your hand, my buttercup," Cato said with a smile.

Marcia cackled at this. "And that, my husband, is something I certainly haven't forgotten!"

"She's a cruel old biddy," the notary whispered in Rex's ear while the married couple enjoyed their joke. "Be glad she didn't want you as her slave."

"I wish she did," Rex replied.

11

DECEMBER 316

General Valerius Valens dismounted from his warhorse and handed the reins to a groom. The stallion was his favorite, so Valens rode him often to keep their relationship strong. In war, that bond could make the difference between life or death.

And war, by God, was coming soon.

The circuit Valens had just made around the city of Hadrianopolis confirmed what he already knew: the defenses were plenty strong in case Constantine tried to lay a siege. Valens doubted that would happen; a pitched battle like Cibalae was more likely. However, he always liked to be prepared.

After making his way back inside the walls, Valens arrived at the praetorium on the forum that served as the city's military headquarters. Emperor Hadrian himself, for whom the city was named, constructed it almost two hundred years ago. The building was just as solid today as when it was first built.

"Have the reports of the muster come in?" he asked his clerk when he entered the headquarters. "It's first priority for me."

The clerk, a junior officer with a capable, efficient way about him, handed Valens a wax tablet. "Byzantium emptied its garrison and sent almost everyone here. The numbers are there for you to look at, but it's about ten thousand. The messengers from Thessalonica have returned too, and they say Macedonia is providing three legions. And the recruiting of the Goths is going well. We should have a large contingent of mercenaries. I think we're going to have what we need to take Constantine down this time."

"Excellent," General Valens said as he scanned the tablet. "I want to crush him under my foot. And so does the augustus."

"Speaking of that," said the clerk, "Licinius sent a legate for you today. He is summoning you to the palace."

"I will go immediately after my bath. Have my valet polish all my metal. The occasion might be momentous, and I want to look the part."

When all was ready, and he was clean and fully dressed, the general crossed the forum to the palace of Hadrianopolis. It wasn't as grand as many others he had seen, yet it was a decent imperial residence for such a remote province. Valens was admitted by the doorman and ushered to the emperor's private garden. Two benches were there, and a buxom serving girl in a gauzy outfit was setting out wine and olives.

Valens waited for Licinius to arrive before he took a seat. He wasn't anxious, for as an accomplished general with a track record of victories, he knew he had earned the emperor's trust. Yet Valens did have a bit of a jittery feeling in his gut. He had heard rumors about his elevation into the Imperial College. *Don't get your hopes up*, he reminded himself. *You're a former slave, not a noble. It's a long shot.*

Licinius greeted Valens warmly, and the two men sipped their wine. It was an excellent white, bright and crisp on the palate, for Thracia was well regarded as a vine-growing region.

After some initial pleasantries, Licinius took control of the conversation. His question was direct. "Valens, are you a Christian?"

The general savored his wine as he thought about the best answer. Licinius's recent turn against the Christians was well-known. Valens certainly didn't want to seem like a religious zealot of that sect. Yet it wouldn't work to lie to the augustus. Emperors always had ways of finding out the truth.

"It is not clear to me what that word means," he said at last. "Much has been said about Jesus of Nazareth since he walked the earth three centuries ago. His legacy is disputed, and people claim different things about him. Yet they all call themselves Christians."

"Do you call yourself one?"

"I have in the past. But many who go by that name tell me I am not of their number. They say I am a heretic. Others find me acceptable. Who can define Christianity with authority?"

"Are you favorable to the catholic church?"

"When I was captured in war at Alexandria many years ago, I had been attending the church, so the bishop ransomed me. Probably I would be dead if not for that generous deed. I'm sure you can understand, Your Highness, that I feel a certain sense of gratitude."

Licinius did not acknowledge the remark and continued his interrogation with the same crispness as before. "Do you worship with the catholics?"

"No, for they would not have me. I am a follower of Basilides of Alexandria, whom some call a Gnostic. His form of Christianity teaches salvation through illumination of the soul, not the crudeness of a crucifixion. In all my doings, Your Majesty, I have tried to follow the enlightened path of the Christ, who is a manifestation of the Firstborn Mind. He came to earth not in a real body but in the appearance of flesh, to teach mankind the way to ascend to Abraxas, the Great Ruler and Father of All."

The explanation seemed to satisfy Licinius. "Very well," he said. "Your views are aberrant enough not to matter to me. But I want no catholics reigning with me in the Imperial College." A smile crept to his face as he said these words.

The Imperial College! So it's true!

His hands were shaking, so Valens set down his goblet. "Did you say . . . I mean, am I to suppose that you intend . . . ?"

"Yes, Valens. I am elevating you to the rank of augustus. The decree shall go out within a fortnight. Congratulations! You, my friend, are now an emperor of Rome."

"I am humbled," Valens said with his head bowed. "Once, I was but a slave."

"And now you shall reign alongside me. Look at how you have risen in the world! Of course, there will be those who do not like my decision."

Valens couldn't help but offer a wry grin and a nod of his head. "Yes, Constantine is going to be furious indeed. I just wish I could be there when he gets the news. I think his head might explode."

"That would save us a great deal of trouble," Licinius replied with a laugh. "Yet it would also rob us of the chance for glory in war."

Valens knew how inflammatory this action was going to be. As things stood right now, Constantine and Licinius had each acknowledged the other as an augustus. Although they were at odds with each other, their rank was not in dispute. However, the naming of Valens as a second augustus would signal that Licinius no longer viewed Constantine as an emperor. That demotion was precisely the sort of insult Constantine hated. If a second battle had been in question, it wasn't anymore. Constantine would come marching at the head of a mighty column to defend his imperial prerogatives.

"I gladly accept the honor of this position," Valens declared, lifting his goblet in an energetic toast. "Long live the Augustus Licinius, aided in all things by the ever-loyal Augustus Valens!"

"To your health," Licinius replied, raising his own glass as well. "Loyalty is one of my most valued traits in a man. I shall expect it from you always and shall give it fully in return."

If you do, Valens thought, *you will be the first emperor ever to achieve that virtue.* But of course he did not say that out loud. Instead, he simply cried, "Hear! Hear! To the augusti of Rome!" then drained his cup with the gusto of a man whose future was incredibly bright.

It had come to this: drawing water from the neighborhood fountain, then hauling it several blocks in a heavy jug was something Flavia looked forward to. At least it got her out of Cato and Marcia's accursed mansion. That place was a broken mess, a house where no one would want to live.

But it's a small price to pay to free Rex, Flavia reminded herself. *He had it much harder as an oarsman for three years. And his stint as a slave would have been even worse. Just be glad he's free!*

The fountain stood in a quaint Thessalonian plaza with shady pine trees overhead. It was still early, just before dawn, so few people were about. The amphora she had brought would take a while to fill under the fountain's slow trickle and even longer to haul back to the house. But Flavia didn't mind. Anything to be out from under Lady Marcia's watchful eye.

Bending to the fountain, Flavia put her lips to the faucet and took a long drink from the cold stream. The aqueduct brought this water down from the pure, clean heights of Mons Cissus, far to the southeast of Thessalonica. It tasted good, and she was going back for a second drink when she heard someone speak to her.

"Need help with that jug?" asked a man.

"I'm fine," Flavia replied without turning around. She didn't want to make eye contact with the stranger in case his intentions were unsavory. The plaza was deserted right now, and there were enough bushes nearby to conceal a crime. Better not to engage with the fellow.

Flavia's senses were on full alert now, for the situation unnerved her. She gauged the distance to a nearby shop whose door was already open. Someone was probably awake inside. Perhaps the shopkeeper would provide a deterrent.

Flavia straightened and started to move away, keeping her eyes on the distant door. "If you want to help me," she said, "watch my jug until I come back. I will return shortly."

"Don't leave, my beloved," the man said in a tender voice. And in that instant, everything changed.

"Rex!" Flavia cried, whirling toward the sound of the voice she now recognized. He smiled back with unbridled joy. Spreading his powerful arms, he called for her, and she came like an arrow from a bow. Flavia let herself be scooped into his warm embrace. Now she felt safe . . . protected . . . secure. Finally, she was in the one place she would rather be than anywhere else in the world.

"I've missed you so much," Rex whispered, clasping her tight against his chest with an intensity that matched the urgency in his voice. It wasn't a sexual embrace, but something even deeper: the binding of two hearts, the kind of soul-union that sexuality is meant to express.

"Me too!" Flavia exclaimed. "Oh, Rex, how glad I am to see you!"

He separated from her, grasping her shoulders and staring into her eyes. His expression was incredulous. "Why did you do it?"

"What?"

"Sell yourself into slavery!"

"Isn't it obvious? To free you from a terrible fate."

"But I'd rather endure the oar forever than endure your enslavement."

"And I'd rather endure slavery than the torment of a broken heart."

Rex could only gaze back in awe. At last, he said, "You are an incredible woman, Flavia."

"If I am, it is because I was helped to be one by an incredible man."

His face became resolute. "I shall free you."

Smiling sweetly, she said, "I know. I never doubted it. You always make good things happen."

"You can't just run away, though. We have to figure out how to cancel the legal status of your slavery or you'll be a fugitive forever. The empire is obsessive about runaways. You wouldn't be able to lead a normal life."

"How do we do it, then?"

"I could offer to buy you for an unbeatable price."

"No, the mistress wants me as her servant more than money. She wouldn't agree."

"Maybe Bishop Basil could use his connections to invalidate the transaction?"

"Oh, Rex, I wish! But he was cruelly attacked, and his hand was severed. It is infected. Death might take him. We cannot rely on him right now."

"Well, I'm going to think of something."

"I know," Flavia said again. She removed the amphora from beneath the fountain's trickle now that it was full. "I have to bring this back soon, or I'll get in trouble."

"I'll carry it for you." Rex hoisted the jug to his shoulder with an ease that Flavia found unexpectedly attractive. At times, she was stunned by just how powerful he really was.

The pair proceeded through the quiet streets of Thessalonica to the mansion. It took up an entire city block, an impressively large residence with a view of the waterfront. However, despite the house's beauty, it was not a true home but a place of relentless misery. The mistress was a tyrant, and the master was a pushover. That combination made for chaos.

At the door, Flavia fought the urge to run away with Rex. She wanted nothing more than to go wherever he went, to do whatever he did. It wouldn't matter what it was; she just wanted to be with him. Yet the consequences would be, as he had said, permanent. She would forever be a runaway slave. And the law had a way of catching up with fugitives eventually.

Rex set the water jug on the ground. "I'm sorry I can't do more for you right now."

"Do not apologize. Almighty God cares for me."

"Yes, but I want to care for you too."

"You'll think of something. Soon we'll be free of this place." Flavia sighed deeply. "I really have to go now. But, oh! I don't want to!" She paused, uncertain about her next words. "Before I go, would you . . ."

"Yes," he said, and took her in his arms. Sweetly, yet fiercely too, he kissed her on the lips. They lingered for a moment in a tender embrace but finally had to separate. Flavia shuddered at the intensity of her desire for Rex.

"How did you know my request?" she asked after she had caught her breath again.

"You asked with your eyes long before you spoke."

She smiled shyly at this, feeling a little exposed. "Perhaps I did," she admitted. Then, heavyhearted, she picked up the amphora and went inside the house.

The plants in the rear garden were always watered from the public fountain, for Cato was too cheap to use the water that he paid to have piped into the home for such a menial purpose. Flavia had just finished the job when Lady Marcia appeared in the peristyle that surrounded the courtyard. "Where have you been?" she demanded.

"Doing my duties, Mistress."

"Do your 'duties' include gallivanting around the streets with muscular Germans?"

Oh, not this! Lord, help me . . .

Lady Marcia stalked over to Flavia. She was a rotund woman with wide hips and pudgy hands. Her face bore a look of irritation.

"M'lady, I shall—"

Flavia was in midsentence when Marcia slapped her across the face. The hard blow made a gruesome sound, and it felt like the stings of a hundred scorpions. A dizzy fog descended upon Flavia's mind. She gasped a little to catch her breath.

"What do you have to say for yourself, you tramp?" Marcia screeched. Her hand was raised again, ready to deal out another blow.

Various responses occurred to Flavia at once: fight back . . . lie . . . justify herself . . . remain silent . . . beg for mercy. Or did she even dare to complain that such harsh treatment was illogical and unwarranted?

Flavia chose none of these. Instead, the words of Peter's first epistle came to her mind: "Servants, be subject to your masters with all fear, not only the good and gentle, but also the crooked." The scriptural injunction gave Flavia the fortitude she needed. "You are my rightful mistress," she said, "so you deserve my honor and respect. I am sorry if I displeased you."

The humble reply made Lady Marcia do a double take. Clearly, it wasn't the response she was expecting. Her hand dropped back to her side. "Well, don't let it happen again," she said with a little sniff.

"I will help in the kitchen now."

Though Lady Marcia nodded at this, her mind was obviously elsewhere. Only after Flavia had turned to go did the mistress stop her. "Wait!" she barked.

"Yes, m'lady?"

"You have been working hard these past few days. You may return to your quarters and take the rest of the day off."

"Thank you, Lady Marcia," said Flavia with a bow.

And what is that about? she wondered in her heart.

Bishop Basil was clearly suffering. The doctors had prescribed extract of poppy for his pain. Even so, the sweat on his brow and his tight grimace showed that the terrible amputation was tormenting him. To his credit, he was bearing it manfully. Rex felt great respect for that.

Sophronia used a cold compress to mop his brow. "Stay strong," she whispered to him. "The Lord is with you."

After meeting Flavia at the fountain, Rex had come to the Thessalonian house church to learn what resources the Christians might have for emancipating her. He had assumed—correctly—that Sophronia would be pursuing a solution. Though Rex hadn't wanted to bother Basil today, the bishop insisted that Rex come to his bedside. "Bribes won't work now," he whispered through clenched teeth, "but prayer always does." The holy words that he uttered on Flavia's behalf, even in the midst of his own agony, made a deep impression on Rex. He thanked the bishop for the prayers and left him in Sophronia's gentle care.

Unfortunately, though the Christians' prayers were abundant, the earthly options were few. Manumission was a common outcome for faithful slaves, but it typically happened at the end of their lives, after many years of dutiful service. A more immediate solution was needed. Sophronia was working on finding a household servant who could do Flavia's work more efficiently. Of course, it would have to be someone equally beautiful. That, plus an exotic gift of some kind, might incline Lady Marcia to make an exchange in her household staff. The plan was in the works right now. No other option had yet presented itself.

Frustrated, Rex left the church and made his way to the room he had rented at a waterfront flophouse. For one of the few times in his life, he didn't know what to do next. His first order of business was to emancipate Flavia, but what was his role in that? And once it was accomplished—what was next?

The arrival of a ship from the city of Aenus on the Thracian coastline changed things. The innkeeper who owned the flophouse informed Rex that a big barbarian with a droopy mustache had been asking around for him.

"He thought you were still a rower," the innkeeper said. "The guy was glad to hear you were freed."

"What was his name?"

"I forget. Gunther-something."

"Gundomar?"

"That was it."

Rex smiled at the thought that his father's favorite chieftain had found him in Thessalonica. "Send him my way," he said.

Gundomar met Rex in a sailor's tavern with the boisterous exuberance so common among the Germani. After giving Rex a big, booming hug with much backslapping, the two men sat down over rye beer, newly imported from Thracia.

The visitor's news was urgent. "Battle looms, Bruder," Gundomar announced. "Your father calls you to come and fight at his side one last time."

Rex immediately felt torn. He explained the problem of Flavia's voluntary enslavement in exchange for him. "I must free her," he concluded.

"Do you have a way? Or is it out of your hands?"

"I'm still looking for a solution," Rex admitted.

"A son should not abandon his father in his final battle. Emperor Licinius has assembled a fearsome new army. Things might not go like they did at Cibalae. Your father could fall on the field. Any of us could fall. This is war. The Alemanni will be hard-pressed. Your brothers will be dying for their lord."

Words like these were sufficient to prompt just about any warrior into action. Such a call to battle stirred the blood of every true soldier, and this one all the more because it came straight from Rex's father. The fact that King Chrocus wanted his son at his side while Flavia was suffering as a slave in a miserable house put Rex in a terrible bind.

"Go visit her and see what she says," Gundomar finally advised. "She's got a stout heart. I think she will release you to fight. However, war is not the only proper use for a man's strength. A good man protects his woman too. The gods must guide you in this."

The advice was wise, so Rex made the short walk to Cato's mansion. For a while he stood outside because he wasn't sure how to contact Flavia. He was considering ways to sneak in when a slave boy ran up and tugged on his tunic. The boy held a half-eaten raisin cake in one hand and a broken piece of pottery in the other.

"A maid gave me a treat if I brought this to you," he said, handing over the potsherd.

Rex examined the two words scratched into the ostracon: *rear balcony*. He immediately dropped the note and went around back.

Flavia awaited him at a balcony that overhung a narrow alley. It was too high to reach, but at least it allowed them to converse. "I was watering the flowers in the window, and I looked up and there you were!" Flavia said. "When I saw you standing out there, I sent the boy to fetch you. This is the only way I can talk right now."

"I'm glad we can talk face-to-face," Rex agreed. "There are some things I need to tell you, and it's better to talk in person."

"Like what? Tell me quickly, before I get called away."

"For one, I wanted you to know we are still working on your situation."

"Are you *sure* I can't just run away with you?"

"Ah, I wish it too! But just keep reminding yourself, it would only be a short-term solution. Your mother is working on a better way. The plan is to convince the lady to release you in exchange for a true ornatrix who can do her makeup properly, plus a bolt of fine silk from India."

"I'm not too good with face paints or braids," Flavia admitted. "Not even on myself."

Rex smiled up at her. "You don't need that stuff."

"Yes, I do! To look pretty!"

"You look pretty already. Less of those things is more of you. That can only be good."

"Ah, Rex, you're sweet to me."

He winced at this. "You might not think so after what I say next."

"What? Is something the matter?" A worried expression now crossed Flavia's face.

"My father summons me to battle in Thracia. A final confrontation with Licinius is drawing near. The Alemanni are going to be a big part of it."

"Then you must go! Your place is with King Chrocus."

"But how could I leave you in this house of misery?"

Flavia shrugged and waved her hand dismissively. "I'm surviving. It's hard but not impossible. Besides, there's nothing you can do to free me. It sounds like Mother has everything in hand."

"She does."

"And the outcome of the battle is important. Licinius will spread the persecution if he beats Constantine this time." When Rex acknowledged the truth of this, Flavia said, "Please believe me! I want you to go fight in this battle. Not just for your father but for the protection of the church. Evil must be challenged by good men like you. And that is who I see you to be."

A wave of strong emotion filled Rex with admiration and awe. *Gundomar was right—Flavia does have a stout heart!* Here she was, a noble daughter of an ancient family enduring the life of a slave. Long ago, she had done the same thing to spy on the imperial palace. This time, she was doing it out of love! And yet, instead of complaining about her fate or begging Rex to free her, she was urging him to charge into battle like a warrior should. In truth, that is what Flavia always did: she enlarged him, made him greater, more of a man. Rex's appreciation for what Flavia brought to his life led him to a sudden realization. The unexpected insight hit him hard with its certainty and clarity.

She is going to be my wife. Somehow, despite our different religions, I am going to marry this woman.

But first, he told himself firmly, *I must survive a war.*

With two hands, Flavia reached to the back of her neck underneath her silky brown hair. "I retrieved this from your room after they arrested you at Sirmium," she said. Bending over the balcony's railing, she dangled something toward Rex.

"The Christian amulet!"

"Yes, given to you by Constantine. May the power of the cross protect you, and may you find favor once again with the augustus."

Instead of letting the gilded pendant drop from Flavia's hand, Rex pushed a wagon closer to the balcony, then climbed atop its load of hay. Now he could reach high enough so that if Flavia bent low, the exchange could be made.

As he received the amulet, his fingers grasped hers. For a brief moment, the two of them savored the touch—then slowly let it slip away.

Flavia's expression was urgent as she gazed down at Rex. "Come back to me, my love."

"I intend to," he replied, then leapt down from the mound of hay and began to go. But something made him turn back. "I will always love you, Flavia," he added. She nodded in return. It seemed important to say. He wanted her to know it. No doubts.

Yet a shadow now darkened his thoughts. Something else had started to creep into his mind, replacing the exuberance he had felt before. As Rex walked away from the mansion, he couldn't shake the disturbing feeling that these were the last words he would ever utter to Flavia in this mortal life. Turning, he looked back at the balcony one last time.

But sadly, she was already gone.

—⁂—

Although merchant ships rarely plied the seas in winter, a few brave captains were always willing to take the risk if they came across a cargo that would make a big profit. Rex departed Thessalonica on a two-masted trading vessel whose captain couldn't resist taking some Macedonian iron, copper, and hemp to Byzantium in the off-season. The ship would stop at

Aenus, which was where Rex needed to get off. Gundomar was elated to be returning to his king with Rex in tow. The two men reached Aenus in four days and said farewell to the captain at the dock.

Another four days by riverboat took the travelers up the Hebrus River to the vicinity of Hadrianopolis. Constantine had not yet arrived but was somewhere out on the Mardian Plain. Licinius, however, was safely locked inside the city with his troops, though he would probably march out to meet his enemy any day now. Maybe the blustery winds would let up and give the troops a break. Or maybe they wouldn't. The battle would be fought regardless. It was December, a hard time for traveling, much less fighting. Yet this wasn't the age of the Republic, when citizen farmers came out each spring for war and returned home in the fall. The Roman army was now a four-season war machine, and today's professional soldiers had to be ready to fight in a blizzard if necessary.

I hope that won't be necessary, Rex thought as he trudged along the frozen Military Highway toward his father's encampment.

The Alemannic mercenaries had set up their tents near the legions that Constantine had sent ahead to wait for his arrival. The Mardian Plain was a broad expanse with plenty of room for a field camp. Gundomar said that about 3,500 stout Germanic warriors were already here and ready to fight. Morale was high, for after Constantine realized how badly he had offended the Alemanni at the victory banquet, he smoothed things over with the spoils of war. The men had obtained much loot after the Battle of Cibalae, and the capture of Licinius's treasury would supply even more rewards in the form of coins. Horses and arms had been captured as well, so the men felt well equipped for the fight.

As Rex approached the king's tent, he felt a sense of belonging that made him proud. It was a good thing to be a warrior, to fight with brave Germani under their wise and noble king. Come what may, there was glory to be had in war, whether one lived to see another day or died on the field of combat. That was not a very Christian sentiment, but Rex believed it nonetheless.

A smile spread across King Chrocus's face as he emerged from the tent. "My son has returned!" he boomed. His sandy hair, streaked with gray, was tied back in a ponytail. Blood-Maker, his trusted sword, was strapped to his belt. "Welcome, Brandulf!" he cried with genuine affection in his voice.

"You summoned me, Father," Rex said with a bow.

"I did! And like a good son, you came. Perhaps this will be the last time we ever fight alongside each other, like a father and son should do." A conspiratorial gleam came to the king's eye. "Of course, it'll have to be our little secret. Constantine is on his way here from Philippopolis. After what he said at the banquet, I think you'd better keep a helmet on your head when you're anywhere near him!"

"As you wish. I just hope I can finally rid myself of his displeasure."

"Victory has a way of doing that, my son."

Not so far, Rex thought, but he left the observation unstated.

The next day, Rex was equipped with everything he would need for battle: a sword, spear, shield, horse, and armor. On the third day, Constantine showed up, followed by the Licinians soon afterward on the other side of the plain. A tense standoff ensued. Everyone was agitated and irritable. Then, after a week of waiting, on a cold, clear morning, the Battle of Mardia finally commenced.

The two armies had drawn up on opposite edges of a wide depression, so the terrain gave no advantage to either side. They would have to meet in the middle and fight it out like wild animals. It was going to be a mucky pit full of blood and mayhem. Every man who entered it had a good chance of never coming back out.

All day long, the soldiers battled in wave after wave: clashing, withdrawing, and clashing again somewhere else in the depression. Unlike at Cibalae, the forces here were numerically matched. Each army comprised around twenty thousand men. Soon it became hard to fight because so many corpses lay strewn on the field. By midday, about a quarter of the combatants had released their souls into the sky above the Mardian Plain. And there was no sign of a letup.

Late in the afternoon, a lull in the fighting allowed both sides to regroup. Though King Chrocus and Gundomar had the look of battle fatigue about them, their eyes were bright and their spirits were still strong. Dents in their armor and red spatter on their faces showed that the combat had been fierce. Rex knew his own war-torn appearance was exactly like theirs. The comrades munched on hardtack and drank water from a gourd while another legion strapped on their helmets and took their turn in the deadly pit.

After three more forays on horseback, slashing and thrusting as they went, the Alemanni were finally beginning to feel the exhausting effects of the day's fighting. Since it was December, the sun was sinking quickly. Despite the heavy losses on both sides, the battle had been inconclusive. Rex was thinking it might drag on for several days—until a messenger arrived from the commander.

"General Arcadius calls for one thousand Alemanni riders to circle around the enemy and hit their rear," he announced.

"But we'll be under a barrage of arrows the whole time!" Gundomar exclaimed. "Undefended by return fire! Hundreds of us will fall before we engage!"

"Nonetheless, the general commands it before the sun touches the horizon," the messenger said, then rode away without further argument.

"The Alemanni fear no man," King Chrocus declared. "Gather our riders. I shall lead the charge."

And I will be at your side, to share whatever fate comes our way, Rex vowed silently. *Holy Jesus, keep me safe,* he added as his mind drifted to Flavia's imploring eyes.

It was near dusk when Chrocus put heels to his horse's flanks and began to lead the thousand Germanic warriors around the edge of the depression. The substantial distance would require some time to cross before reaching Licinius's rear guard. Since this was an open area of the battlefield and there was no cover from behind, the enemy archers could rush close and loose their missiles without fear of counterattack. It wasn't long before they began to do exactly that.

"Shields up!" Chrocus cried, and then men lifted their arms to the sky, protecting their steeds as much as themselves. To be unhorsed in a battle like this was to be a dead man.

A deadly whistling now mingled with the war cries of the Alemanni. Horses fell to the right and left of Rex as arrows bypassed the shields and struck the unfortunate creatures. Yet the brave soldiers pressed on. Following their king's example, they rose to a gallop.

Licinius's foot soldiers, finally noticing the horde rushing toward them, turned to make a defense. They were the rear guard, so they had no backup. Yet to their credit, they did not yield to their attackers but stayed in formation as the horsemen crashed into their ranks.

Rex now found himself in a dark and furious melee. He slashed with his sword at whatever ferocious, mail-clad figure appeared on either side of his horse. Shouts and groans rang out, along with the clang of metal on metal. It was real war here, cruel and grim. Death was in the air like an insidious fog.

A spearman rose up on Rex's left. The force of his thrust against Rex's shield put him off-balance in the saddle. At the same moment, a lucky stroke from a spearman on the right knocked Rex from his mount's back. Though his good armor absorbed the spear's blow without a puncture, he hit the ground hard and lay prone in the muddy, churned-up earth. Stunned, he grasped for control of his mind, knowing intuitively that he must stand up now or be slaughtered.

Lurching to his feet, Rex found himself in open space. His head cleared enough to realize he held no weapon in his hand. All around him, other combatants were engaged in deadly struggles, but no one faced him—and then a furious war cry sounded from behind. Rex whirled to meet the assailant.

"Die!" screamed a battle-crazed soldier with his javelin raised above his head. Shieldless, Rex bent his knees and prepared to dodge the throw, even though the man could hardly miss at such close range. The javelin would surely impale him.

But then something flashed past: a whirling, spinning thing. The soldier screamed and fell down. His javelin skittered from his hand. Confused, Rex stared at his adversary, who a moment before was about to kill him. Now he was on the ground with a sword protruding from his chest. The look of its hilt was familiar.

Blood-Maker!

Rex ran to the soldier and yanked the weapon from the lifeless corpse. He stared at the crimson blade, panting, astonished to still be alive.

"I'll take that," said a voice behind him.

Turning, Rex saw his father astride his horse like a god. He held out an open palm. In his other, he grasped the reins of a second war pony. Tendrils of hair that had escaped his helmet blew about in the breeze. A broad smile was on Chrocus's face. "Pitch that sword to me, Brandulf, then mount up so we can chase this rabble into the night."

"Gladly," Rex replied. He tossed the sword, butt end first, to his father. Chrocus adeptly caught it by the hilt, then tugged the extra pony's reins,

337

urging it forward. Rex swung onto the animal's back and drew a new sword from the saddle sheath.

"Thank you," he said softly, touching his weapon to the one in his father's hand. A metallic clink sounded as the blades made contact. "You saved my life."

"You saved my life back at Vemania. Now we're even."

"We'll never be even," Rex said, then set out behind his father in pursuit of Licinius's fleeing troops.

Now that the rear guard had been decimated by the Alemannic charge, the enemy's nerve had broken and a rout was on. Even so, remarkably few of the enemy soldiers were captured or killed. Their retreat into the nearby forest was swift, and the limited winter daylight left little time to run down any stragglers. Though the bulk of Constantine's army joined the pursuit, the victors quickly lost contact with the scattered Licinians as they hurried eastward on the Military Highway toward Hadrianopolis.

General Arcadius finally called off the pointless pursuit, opting instead for a few hours of sleep and a quick advance at first light. "They will try to escape to Byzantium," he declared. "It is impregnable. We must catch them before they reach the safety of its walls."

The Constantinian army, weary yet brave, found the strength to rise from sleep the next morning before the sun had yet appeared on the horizon. For several hours, they made excellent progress toward Byzantium. Yet around midmorning, the scouts returned with disturbing news: the Licinians had not rushed toward that city after all but had exited the highway on a side road toward Beroe. Since the Constantinians had moved so quickly, they had overshot the enemy. The Licinians were now behind them, severing their communications with the baggage train. And to make things worse, an envoy from Licinius had arrived, a prideful count by the name of Mestrianus. He announced that his troops had captured the royal entourage, and they were holding Lady Helena as a bargaining chip!

Now the Constantinian army came to a halt as the commanders conferred. Negotiations were going to be necessary in so complex a situation. Yet King Chrocus didn't intend to hold still. "Perhaps we have found an opportunity for the act of valor you need," he suggested to Rex.

"I will never refuse such a chance," Rex answered. "What did you have in mind?"

"To rescue the captured queen. Hit them hard and grab her, if the opportunity should arise. You, me, and Gundomar. Let's go see what we can find."

"Now that's my kind of adventure! Lead the way, Father."

After locating three scout ponies that hadn't been used in yesterday's fighting, the warriors set out. Nobody was on the road, for both armies were regrouping and waiting to see how things would play out. Staying close to the trees that lined the empty highway, the three riders backtracked until they found the side road that turned north toward Beroe. It, too, was deserted. When a squadron on patrol finally appeared ahead under a Licinian flag, the stealthy riders melted into the forest. But instead of waiting for the enemy to pass and returning to the road, they began to pick their way through the underbrush. Their mounts, bred in the scrubby lowlands of Libya, were well-suited to such terrain.

A distant smudge of gray indicated the presence of many campfires. Soon the smell of woodsmoke was discernable too. When the trio finally topped out on a rise and could see the Licinian camp spread before them, the colorful wagon of the captive queen was hard to miss. Helena had not been bound or restricted in any way. She sat on a stool next to a firepit, attended by one of her maids. Evidently, Licinius wanted to parlay for peace, not incite Constantine to further battle by mistreating his beloved mother.

"All those men are exhausted," Gundomar said, flicking his hand dismissively toward the troops lounging in the grass. "Look at them lying around."

"And they've turned their horses out to pasture," Chrocus added. "Who knows where all their tack is?"

"Pursuit is impossible," Rex observed. "So what do you think? A quick snatch and grab?"

Chrocus nodded. "Fast in, fast out, and be gone before they know what hit them. It's the only way."

Gundomar pointed to a gully that passed near the camp, then meandered toward a thick stand of trees. "Let's get into that ditch as soon as we have the lady. We'll be out of bowshot down there. Rex, you take the queen onto your mount. It's the strongest of the three. We'll cover you."

"Surprise is our best defense," the king reminded the other two. "We go in at full speed. Ready?"

"Never readier," Rex replied, and the three riders burst from the thicket.

They reached the edge of the encampment in the span of a few heartbeats. Some angry shouts rang out, but few of the soldiers had their wits about them, for they were dozing and expected no attack. Before anyone could get organized, the rescuers had reached Helena.

"We've come for you, m'lady!" Rex shouted as he galloped up to her.

A few Licinian footmen grabbed spears and began thrusting them at Chrocus and Gundomar. But their horsemanship was too skilled and they easily fended off the attack, leaving Rex free to maneuver.

"Who are you?" Helena cried, confused and afraid.

"Loyalists of the true augustus! Hail, Constantine!"

At these words, Helena relented. Rex bent low from his horse's back and scooped her into the saddle before him. The clash of arms rang out as a few more Licinians joined the attack on his friends, but Rex ignored the melee and urged his mount forward. Bravely, the stallion surged ahead, impervious to its double burden. Its broad chest and churning forelegs cast aside several attackers, then Rex saw only open space in front of him.

"To the gully!" Chrocus cried. "Hurry!"

"Don't let them get away!" shouted an enemy commander. "Kill them if you must!"

Rex had one arm around the queen's waist and a shield draped upon the other. Arrows began to fall from the sky and impale the earth on either side of the galloping horse.

"God save us!" Helena cried.

Angling his arm forward, Rex covered the queen's head with the shield. The gully lay just ahead, a grassy ditch with a stream running along its bottom. Guiding his horse with his knees, Rex headed for the slope that led down into the gully. Only a little farther on, its walls grew steeper and trees loomed over them. Arrows would be useless there.

"Faster! Faster!" he cried to his steed.

Something smashed into the back of his head with incredible force. Although the impact was like a club, there was a piercing sensation as well.

The knife-like stab of pain was the last thing Rex felt before a deep darkness descended on him and he left the conscious world behind.

———◁⦵⦵▷———

It was a raid by a gang of Macedonian bandits that started the slave uprising in Thessalonica. Over the past few decades, the Roman army had gradually grown weaker. Law and order were barely hanging by a thread in some places. Everyone knew it, including the gangs that usually kept to the remote Macedonian hinterlands. But today they had set their eyes on the loot to be gotten in the big city. And in that chaos, the slaves of Thessalonica saw their chance for something other than bondage.

Flavia was bringing a pot of mulled wine to Lady Marcia when a commotion in the distance first signaled danger. After setting the tray on a table at her mistress's side, she went to the window and peered out. "It sounds like a battle," she said. "But it's far away."

"Tell the doorman to lock the doors and close the shutters. Then report back to me."

Flavia obeyed, but by the time she returned to Marcia, two serious concerns had developed. First, thick smoke was rising in the distance, meaning some parts of the city were on fire. Second, a few of the household slaves had banded together and were talking about running away. Flavia informed her mistress about these developments.

"Are they out for revenge?" Marcia asked.

"I believe they would just run from the house. But if a mob got inside and stirred them up, you never know what could happen. Things could turn violent pretty quickly."

"I shouldn't have been so mean to them," Marcia muttered.

Instead of answering, Flavia went to the woodpile by the kitchen oven and returned with a hatchet. "Some of your servants are packing their things," she reported. "Others are talking about breaking into the lockbox. I'm afraid a full rebellion is at hand."

By noon, the looting bandits had reached the waterfront area where Cato's mansion was located. Unfortunately, he was out to sea right now, so he could be of no help. Angry shouts filled the streets as some loyal slaves tried to defend their masters' homes against invasion. But it was no use.

Eventually, the marauders managed to break into the nearby houses. Too many insiders were cooperating with the bandits instead of resisting them.

In the end, it didn't take a broken front door for the looters to enter Cato's home. The slaves who had decided to run away simply let them in. Vile thugs rushed inside and began overturning statues and vases. The lockbox was smashed and its contents greedily snatched, not just by the invaders but also by the rebels from within. Marcia was too scared to protest. She cowered in one of the few bedrooms that had a solid door instead of a curtain. Flavia stood guard over her mistress with the hatchet.

At one point, a greasy bandit came to the door and forced it open. "Be gone!" Flavia warned him, brandishing her weapon.

"Why should I?" he snarled.

"Because soldiers are on the way! Here! Take this and be off!" Flavia picked up a silver goblet from a side table and pitched it to the man. He caught it, smiled at its obvious value, then winked at Flavia.

"Wise girl," he said, then hurried away.

The riot in the streets continued for a long time while Flavia and Marcia waited anxiously in their refuge. At last, the mansion grew eerily quiet. Venturing out of the bedroom, Flavia found all the slaves had left the house. Apparently, a life of banditry in the countryside appealed to them more than Marcia's domineering ways. Flavia returned to her mistress and broke the news.

"What will I do now?" she wailed.

"I am sorry, m'lady."

Marcia grunted, then looked more closely at Flavia. "So you won't leave too?"

"No, m'lady."

"You could hit me with that hatchet and be gone. No one would ever know who did it."

"God would know."

"But would he care? Perhaps it would be his vengeance on me. I've been hard on you."

"It is not my place to wreak God's vengeance on his behalf. The scriptures of the catholic faith are clear. Servants are to honor their masters, whether or not they are abusive."

"That is a remarkable faith you practice! There is nothing else like it." Marcia stared out the window at the smoky horizon. Finally, she said, "I didn't use to be so harsh, you know. When I was younger, I was kind to small animals and the like. My words were sweeter. I used to sing lullabies to my baby daughter."

"You had a daughter?"

"Long ago. But I have changed since then."

"You are indeed a hard mistress now," Flavia admitted.

"I know," said Marcia glumly. "What happened to me?"

"A life lived apart from God, perhaps?"

"Yes. Perhaps."

"There is no reason you couldn't change back."

Marcia smiled wryly at this. "How? By becoming a Christian?"

"Why not? Go talk to Bishop Basil. Explore it a bit. You might find it appealing."

"Many people have, so it must offer them something worthwhile. And yes—all things considered, I would prefer not to be a tyrant."

"To do that, one must first be freed from Satan's tyranny over the soul. Christianity offers the only way."

"That bandit was right," Marcia said with a little laugh. "You are indeed a wise girl. Now follow me."

The two women proceeded to the master's study, stepping over shards of pottery and broken pieces of marble statues. Expensive textiles that once adorned the walls and doorways now lay scattered on the floor. Marcia led Flavia to a cabinet behind Cato's desk. It had been ransacked of its valuables, but the documents inside had been left behind as relatively worthless. Marcia sorted through a stack of wax tablets until she found the one she wanted.

"What is it, m'lady?"

"I will show you. But first, hand me a stylus."

Flavia complied, then the lady scrawled something across the tablet's face before handing it over. Upon seeing it, Flavia sucked in her breath. It was the contract of her enslavement, now overwritten by large letters that read: EMANCIPATED BY LUCIA MARCIA, WIFE OF CATO. The day of the month and the year of Licinius's reign followed.

"You have freed me!" Flavia exclaimed.

"Yes. I shall file this with the court as soon as things have calmed down."

"It is gracious beyond words, m'lady. I thank you with all my heart."

Marcia chuckled. "Well, your face paints always made me look like a circus mime. I think I'll do better with a new ornatrix. But how am I going to replace all the rest of the household servants? That's my real problem now."

"If I may suggest something, Mistress—"

"Don't call me that anymore, Flavia. You are no longer a slave."

"Ah, yes, of course. Thank you, Lady Marcia!" Flavia took a deep breath and continued. "I was going to suggest that you talk to Bishop Basil about replacing the servants. He ministers to many Christians who live in constant poverty, struggling every day, never knowing where their next meal is coming from. If you could run an honorable house, they would be delighted to serve you in exchange for a roof over their heads and regular food. Treat them well, and they will serve you more faithfully than those you had before, who ran away at the first chance."

"This is all new for me," Marcia admitted. "But I shall give your Christian ways a try."

"God will bless you. Of this, I am certain."

"Where will you go now?"

"To my mother, immediately. From there, I do not know. I have a man fighting a battle near Hadrianopolis."

"Is he a good man?"

"Never have I encountered better. My heart is bound to his, though I do not know our future."

"Then you must go to him! Here—take this." Reaching to the back of her neck, Lady Marcia unclasped the chain she wore. It was made of solid gold, and a large ruby adorned the pendant. She offered it to Flavia with a broad smile.

"No!" Flavia breathed. "I cannot take such a gift from you!"

"Oh, my dear Flavia, this is not a gift."

"It's not? Then what is it?"

"It is a sign of my contrition. An act of penance, if you will. A giving up of what I once served."

"And what do you now serve?"

"That remains to be seen," said Lady Marcia. "But the person I shall ask about it is Basil." She pressed the jeweled necklace into Flavia's hand. "Be off with you, young lady, and go see your mother. No doubt she will be delighted to have her daughter back."

"You have no idea," Flavia said as she turned toward the door.

"Oh, I think I do," said Marcia.

———

JANUARY 317

Delirious, Rex reached for the cup that he thought was at his bedside. His hand did not find it, so he released himself once more to the darkness.

Sometime later, he opened his eyes—as much as he was able, for they were sticky with mucus. There was no cup, and no one was in the room, so he closed them again. His face felt hot and his body felt cold. He wiped sweat from his forehead, then shivered and pulled the blanket up to his neck. The fever had ahold of him now.

The doctors had all marveled at Rex's survival, claiming the tough iron helmet had saved his life. An arrow pierced it, yet its momentum was slowed enough by the metal crest, double thick at that spot, so as not to split Rex's head in two. Instead, the point merely buried itself in the back of his skull. Though it had been easy to pull out with pliers, the wound had bled profusely, and infection soon set in. Rex had been abed now for two weeks—a fact he knew only from the doctors' whispered musings, for he was delirious most of that time.

"Water," he croaked. "Th . . . thirsty."

A girl came in, one of the doctors' assistants in the home that had been turned into a makeshift hospital after the Battle of Mardia. Because of the high casualties, local medicine men had been brought in to tend the wounded. The girl tipped the cup to Rex's lips, and he managed to swallow a trickle before a coughing fit overtook him. When it passed, he settled back onto his pillow.

"The doctor is coming with more poultice," she said. "Let me roll you over."

Once Rex was on his side, the doctor applied a mixture of goat dung and the blood of a chicken slaughtered precisely at midnight. He smeared

345

on the goop with a little paddle, working it deep into the wound. "It will make a mess on your pillow," he said, "but I don't believe in bandages. It is better to let the healing spirits have access to the wound if they wish."

Whatever you say, Rex thought, then fell asleep again.

The next day, or maybe the one after, a visitor arrived. It wasn't one of the nurses, but another woman. Her voice was melodious and sweet.

"Rex," she said quietly, stroking his hand. "Oh, Rex, come back to me."

His mind seemed to clear a little at these words. The voice sounded so familiar. Opening his eyes to a squint, he tried to make out the shape of the person at his bedside. She was backlit by the window, so he could only see a shadowy outline. Her face was delicate, and her hair tumbled in wavy tendrils down to her shoulders. Obviously, she was young and slender. That was all he could discern.

"Jesus Christ, I call upon you," the woman said. And then Rex's heart surged, for he knew it was Flavia.

She has come to me!

Seizing her fingers, Rex squeezed them as hard as he could. He tried to form words in a mouth that felt as parched as a desert. "Mm . . . missed . . . you," he managed to say.

"My beloved, I missed you too!"

"S . . . s . . . stay."

"I will! Rex, I won't leave your side. Stephen is coming soon. We are going to heal you the right way, with prayer and simple doctoring, not this superstitious nonsense!"

Rex could not reply to that, so he only lay on his pillow and stroked Flavia's hand with his finger. Eventually, he dozed off again.

When he awoke, Stephen had arrived. "You look terrible, soldier," he joked.

A tiny smile came to Rex's lips, and he tried to mumble, "Shut up." Stephen's chuckle indicated that he understood. Gently, he rolled Rex onto his side so he could look at the wound on the back of his head.

"What is this stuff?" he asked the nurse.

"Magic ointment."

"*Pfft!* It's just filth! I want you to bring me linen cloths and a bowl of water right away. I want boiled water, not what comes straight from the pipe. And a flagon of wine. And honey. You must bring honey."

The nurse disappeared but soon returned with the requested items. Rex lay still while Stephen swabbed away the goat dung poultice with hot water, then applied his own remedies. "The wine is going to sting," he warned. Though it did, Rex did not flinch.

"Why wine?" Flavia asked.

"The scriptures speak of it, when the Good Samaritan healed the wounded man on the side of the road. Christians do not believe in magic spells for healing. We believe in cleanliness, just as God is clean and pure. Washed bandages, pure water, wine, and honey—these things are well regarded in the holy books. We follow God's way of healing."

"I have not heard of honey used in that way."

"One of the proverbs says it brings sweetness to the soul and health to the bones. Many Christian doctors use it. They say it draws out the poison of infections."

"There is one more healing method used by Christians," said Flavia. "It comes from the brother of the Lord. He directed the presbyters to pray over the sick man. Though we don't have a council of presbyters here, Stephen, you are one. So I ask you to anoint Rex with oil upon his head. The *Epistle of James* says that the prayer of faith will save he who ails, and the Lord will raise him up."

"Yes, in truth, we must do it," Stephen agreed. Tugging Rex's shoulder, he rolled his patient onto his back again. Rex gladly complied, settling into the soft mattress. He felt sleepy, as if even the effort of rolling over had sapped his strength.

A lamp was in the corner, so Stephen went to it and dipped his finger. Placing the oil on Rex's forehead, he offered a heartfelt prayer for divine intervention. Flavia held Rex's hand the whole time, stroking it and whispering, "Hear, O Lord," at each request Stephen made.

On the third day of the new regimen, everything changed dramatically. Rex woke up that morning—really woke up, not just emerged from a stupor—with a new sense of alertness and well-being. Flavia was dozing on a pallet beside the bed.

"Hey," he whispered down to her. "How about some porridge? I'm starving."

She sat up with a start. "Rex, you're awake!"

"Awake and hungry. Maybe you could put some berries in it?"

"Anything you want! I'll fetch it right away."

Flavia returned with a bowl and a spoon. Rex had worked himself into an upright position, and he took the bowl onto his lap. He was tired of having people dribble broth into his mouth. He wanted to feed himself like a grown man.

After wolfing down the porridge, he drank a cup of thin beer, then let out a satisfied burp. "I think I'm on the mend," he declared.

"I'm so relieved," Flavia said with a little shake of her head.

On the fourth day, Rex managed to walk around the room. On the fifth, he strolled in the house's garden. And on the sixth day, a visitor came to see him.

It was Stephen who first alerted him to the guest's arrival. "Rex, wake up," he said. "There is someone here to see you!"

"Who?"

"He said not to tell. But be quick! Wash your face and comb your hair. He is on his way."

After Rex did his best to make himself presentable, he resumed his place in bed and awaited the visitor's arrival. Stephen and Flavia also sat by the bed.

A short while later, a tall figure appeared in the doorway. He was alone, and he did not step forward. "Brandulf Rex," the man said—and his voice was unforgettable.

Constantine!

"Your Highness, I salute you!" Rex said with his head bowed. Stephen and Flavia also clasped their hands in front of their chests and dipped their chins.

"They tell me you were wounded at Mardia. Took an arrow point to the head, eh?"

"Nothing a good Roman helmet and a hard skull can't deal with."

"I also hear it was you who rescued my mother. Helena tells me you covered her with your shield while you left yourself exposed."

"The noble lady had to be protected, Your Majesty."

"And then Chrocus and Gundomar got you out. Brave men, you Alemanni."

"Especially when we fight for a cause we believe in."

Constantine entered the room now, his stature big and imposing. He was dressed in the clothes of a nobleman, yet without any fussy adornments to signal a lavish lifestyle. "Here you are again, far from the sea," he observed wryly. "It seems I have a hard time keeping you aboard my ships."

"I am more useful to you in other ways, I think."

"Yes. That appears to be true. You distinguished yourself at Mardia, as well as at Cibalae."

An immediate reply came to Rex's lips, though it was one he hesitated to utter. Perhaps it was foolish to say it aloud, or perhaps it was unbelievably bold. He wasn't sure. In any case, it was true, so Rex decided to go for it.

"And at Verona," he declared.

The room grew still as a stunned silence descended on everyone. Not a single noise could be heard—until Constantine eased his spatha from its scabbard. The scrape of metal on metal was the only sound in the awful hush. With careful steps, maddeningly slow, he approached the bed. Rex heard Flavia utter a little whimper.

The emperor laid his blade flat against Rex's cheek. "When you were a boy, I smacked you with this for your impudence."

Keeping his eyes low, lest he seem defiant, Rex answered, "Yes, you did. And when I became a man, I fought your enemies with a blade just like it."

"You claim to serve me faithfully, Brandulf Rex?"

"I do. I always have."

The steel was cold against Rex's cheek. "Why did you abandon me in battle at Verona?"

"To pursue that turd Pompeianus, Your Majesty."

A chuckle escaped Constantine's lips. "I cannot blame you for hating him. He really was a turd." He paused, his face becoming stern again. "However, there are other considerations. I have made my decision."

With this, Constantine raised his sword toward the ceiling. Flavia shuddered, and Rex felt his heartbeat quicken.

Suddenly the emperor shoved his sword back into its sheath. "Brandulf Rex, I forgive you of the crime of treason. Warriors with your boldness are few. I shall need you in the future. For what, I do not know, but I sense it in my bones."

Flavia could no longer contain herself. "Oh, Your Highness, thank you!" she gushed.

Constantine turned to her. "You have found a brave man here. Be worthy of him."

"I will, I promise!"

"She is more than worthy already," Rex said.

Constantine went to the door, then turned around one last time. "We leave for Serdica in two weeks," he announced. "You are all welcome to come with me at my expense. And tell Bishop Ossius I will require his presence as well."

MARCH 317

The city of Serdica lay westward on the Military Highway in the direction of Rome. Flavia could feel its energy simmering beneath the surface like a volcano whose eruption is imminent. As one of Constantine's favorite cites—"my Rome," he often called it—it was a city on the rise, a place whose time had come.

Yet while Serdica was in contact with western lands, it also wasn't far from the territories where Licinius still had control. Though his holdings were now greatly reduced, Licinius's army hadn't been wiped out, so he had managed to retain a certain degree of power despite losing two battles. And of course, his wife was Constantine's sister. For all these reasons, Constantine's advisers thought it best to reach an uneasy peace with Licinius—though not one in which he would be left with equal standing to the Augustus of the West.

Constantine's imperial entourage had arrived at Serdica about a month ago. Since then, the negotiations had been unfolding at the snail's pace that always marked diplomacy when the stakes were high. Flavia's room in a remote part of the government complex was a comfortable, attractive space that she shared with Sophronia and Cassi. The walls were adorned with frescoes depicting bucolic, scenes, and a large window overlooked a private garden. The weeks of rest had done the women a lot of good—not to mention Rex, who had been able to fully recover from his head wound. Flavia was glad for the peaceful respite after so many months of struggle and travail.

But now the days of rest were over. Things were coming to a head, and the wheel of life was turning again. A big event was planned for tonight: the signing of the treaty that would make peace between the two augusti. It would surely be momentous, though no one knew exactly what the new arrangement would look like.

An ornatrix was working on Flavia's makeup when Sophronia arrived in an upscale gown. "Mother, you look splendid," Flavia mumbled around the brush that dabbed at her lips.

"No talking, please," said the ornatrix, "unless you want your lips to extend to your ears."

Probably not my best look, Flavia thought, although she didn't voice the sentiment aloud out of respect for the girl trying to fix her face.

It was the first day of the month, the Kalends of March, and Constantine had summoned everyone to the signing of the treaty between the two brothers-in-law. However, since Licinius himself wouldn't be in attendance, Count Mestrianus, who had brokered the deal, would sign on behalf of the Augustus of the East. The former adversaries would now agree to occupy, in fraternal peace and harmony, the two top spots in the Imperial College, though with a vast difference in the amount of the empire that each man controlled. This much everyone knew about today's event. As for the all-important question of who the caesars would be, that was the hotly debated outcome everyone was dying to learn.

An imperial page arrived to inform the women that the gathering would commence in one hour. They would meet Bishop Ossius and Rex beforehand, then be escorted to the rotunda where the event would be held. The requested presence of Bishop Ossius seemed to be a very good sign. Coupled with Constantine's forgiveness of Rex, Flavia felt renewed hope that the petition from Pope Sylvester might finally be met with good favor. *Lord, may your will be done!*

Rex and the bishop both looked dashing when the women met them outside their room. As usual, Ossius's wavy silver hair managed to achieve the kind of careless nonchalance that women found irresistible. His ecclesiastical robes were elegant and sober at the same time. The staff in his hand, which was curled at the top like a shepherd's crook, clearly signaled his pastoral vocation.

As for Rex, he looked fantastic as well. His white tunic was beautifully trimmed with red-and-gold embroidery. Beneath the tunic, his trousers were pale blue, and his boots were polished to a rich walnut brown. The cloak draped around his shoulders was made of a crimson fabric that perfectly brought together all the elements of the outfit. With his broad chest and narrow waist, he cut a very handsome figure—the epitome of Roman fashion. Yet his blue eyes and long blond hair, tied at the back of his neck, as well as his full beard, reminded everyone of his wild, barbarian side. Flavia felt honored to be presented into Roman society on the arm of such a virile and dignified man.

"My dear Lady Junia," he said, affecting a kind of playful formality at such an august event, "may I tell you how lovely you look tonight? That gown falls upon you in a most appealing way."

"You like it? I wasn't sure about it."

"It suits your figure perfectly, though I must admit, it took me a while to notice it."

Flavia didn't like hearing that. *I had hoped to take his breath away at first sight . . .*

But Rex only smiled mischievously at Flavia's crestfallen expression. Touching her under the chin with one finger, he raised her face and looked deep into her eyes. "Why would I look first at your dress when I could gaze at your face instead?"

Flavia melted at the sweetness of his words. "Oh, you!" she managed to say. It wasn't the kind of witty banter she knew she was capable of. But on this night, her strong feelings for Rex had tied her tongue into knots. Flavia decided not to fight it and just clung to her escort's arm, letting him take her for a ride.

The proceedings began with an imperial trumpet fanfare. The rotunda at the palace of Serdica was perfect for this event because the treaty could be laid on a table at the center of the room for all the guests to see. Its provisions would be read aloud from start to finish, including its stipulations about the caesars. Then it would be signed by Constantine and Mestrianus, Licinius's proxy, with a fancy pen made of solid gold.

A herald read out the words of the treaty, which began by announcing the joyful cessation of hostilities, then listed the respective domains to be controlled by the two augusti. The only provinces left to Licinius were Thracia, Asia, and the East—maybe a sixth of the empire's whole territory. Constantine would control the rest.

When the treaty finally got to the part about the caesars, the room fell silent as every ear perked up. The herald declared that the first caesar was to be Crispus, son of Constantine by Minervina, which made Helena visibly happy and Fausta visibly annoyed. Yet when Fausta's infant son, Constantine Secundus, was named the second caesar, her mood improved.

An uneasy tension now fell on the room, for the omission of Licinius's heir was obvious, creating an inherently unstable arrangement in the Imperial College. However, a collective sigh of relief was breathed when the herald announced the addition of a third caesar: the child of Licinius and Constantia, whom everyone called Junior. Now all the caesars were either a son or a nephew of the two augusti. It was a dynastic system unlike what Diocletian had originally envisioned, yet it seemed to offer the best chance for lasting peace. As for that "vile slave" Valerius Valens, both of the augusti agreed that the general would need to be executed. The sentence would be carried out tomorrow. Only then could the empire finally be at rest.

After both parties had signed the treaty, a cheer went up and a festive mood broke out in the rotunda. The spectators became jovial as prizes were given out in the names of Licinius and Constantine. Donatives—special distributions of valuable coins—were proclaimed for the troops who had fought so valiantly. In a show of good faith, both armies were compensated for their valor, though Constantine's men were more lavishly rewarded.

At one point, King Chrocus and the Alemanni were singled out for special honor. Constantine summoned the king from his seat to stand before the assembly. "Here before you is a truly fearsome warrior!" the emperor exclaimed. "Long ago, he fought valiantly with me in Britannia. Now he has fought well again, and for this I reward his troops with five gold solidi apiece!"

Flavia leaned over to Rex and whispered in his ear. "Five solidi per man! Those Alemanni are going home with more gold than they ever imagined they'd get."

"What he isn't saying is that it's all coming out of Licinius's treasury. That poor fellow is broke. He won't be threatening Constantine anytime soon. It's going to take a lot of land-grabbing and unfair taxation to build up his finances again."

"He's the kind of greedy ruler who will do it. The East had better watch out in the years ahead."

Rex could only nod his assent.

Chrocus was in the midst of thanking Constantine for his largesse when Rex's name was mentioned. A cheer went up, and suddenly everyone was clamoring for him to come forward. This was no time to hesitate. "Go!" Flavia urged. And with that, he rose and went to stand next to his father.

The king threw his arm around Rex's shoulders. Standing side by side, the two men looked strikingly alike. Rex was slightly taller, yet he was very much the image of his father. Both of them, young and old, displayed a robust manliness and gallant charm.

"Long live King Chrocus!" shouted one of the Alemannic warriors.

"Ever-loyal confederates of Rome!" yelled someone else.

"Prince Rex for the succession!" came a third cry. "Next in line!"

At those words, Flavia's heart sank. In the five years that she had known Rex, he had never spoken about his royal lineage. Only with the recent trip to Germania had the truth come out. Why had he hidden it? And if he could keep such a secret from her, could he also be hiding his desire to rule over his people? To be the respected king of a Germanic tribe was a destiny that many men would covet. It was a high honor . . . an eminent distinction . . . a glorious future.

Did Rex want it? And if so, would it require a Germanic queen?

To Flavia's great relief, Rex smiled, held up both palms, and waved off the accolades. "My friends!" he cried. "Listen to me!" When the crowd had settled a bit, Rex reached to his neckline and pulled out the Christian amulet. "This necklace was given to me when I began my first espionage mission as an imperial speculator. My sole desire is to continue to serve the man who gave it to me"—Rex swept his hand toward the throne—"the glorious Augustus of the West, Emperor Constantine!" More raucous cheers broke out, and everyone seemed to drop the subject of "Prince Rex."

Only when he had returned to his seat did Flavia release her tension with a big sigh. She truly hadn't been sure how Rex would respond to the royal acclamations. She reached over and squeezed his hand gratefully.

"I'm with you," he said with reassuring simplicity.

"Thank you, Rex. I needed to hear that. I'm so glad you got such a sweet affirmation."

"Yes, it's a memory I'll never forget. This might be the last time I see my father for a long time, or maybe forever. I'm glad it could be like this."

"And I'm glad I could share it with you."

With all the formal business taken care of, the emperor was now in an expansive mood. He was smiling, laughing, and even cracking jokes with the boisterous crowd. Turning toward Bishop Ossius, he said, "Most Reverend Father, I believe you recently came to me with a request."

Gripping Rex's arm, Flavia pointed and said, "Look! Here we go!" They both fastened their eyes on Constantine.

Ossius straightened his back in a regal sort of way. "I certainly did, Your Majesty."

"Can you remind me what it was? I might be in a position to rethink it."

"O great Augustus, I shall remind you. The bishop of Rome, Pope Sylvester, has sent you a petition. He seeks permission for two things. One, for your permission to build churches outside the city over the graves of the apostles and martyrs, along with a basilica inside the walls for daily worship. And two, he desires to create a glorious copy of the sacred books. We must determine the canon of our faith in a meeting of esteemed men, then publish a beautiful version of this bible for use in the bishop's new church. Of course, Sylvester also seeks the funds for this endeavor from the imperial fisc, which heretofore has been wasted on the houses of demons."

Constantine stared at the ceiling and stroked his chin thoughtfully. "The senators in Rome are a bunch of crusty old traditionalists. They make a lot of money holding various priesthoods. It's prestigious and time-honored. Some of them even believe in those gods with true devotion! I have a feeling they aren't going to like a bunch of catholic temples cropping up all over town."

"Churches," Ossius corrected.

"Churches, temples, houses of the Lord, whatever you call them. My point is, the politics of the matter have to be carefully weighed."

"I understand, Your Majesty."

"You are prepared to be resisted?"

"We are."

"It won't just be the senators. The churches of other cities won't like it either. They will be jealous."

"We know. Even some factions within the Roman church will oppose it. But we believe it will glorify God and exalt his name, so we are committed to it despite the struggles we will face."

Constantine considered the subject a moment longer, then finally shrugged. Turning, he waved toward a servant. The man ducked out of the rotunda and quickly returned with a lockbox. Based on the effort he was expending to lug it into the room, it seemed to be heavy.

After the servant set the box on the central table, Constantine opened it. A gasp went up as the crowd saw it was filled not with the usual money of silver but with golden coins.

"This should start you on the way," the emperor said to Ossius. "And to finish the job, I will give you letters of credit that can be drawn upon the Roman treasury. I will also have a rescript written up that guarantees you certain essential privileges. Pope Sylvester can have his buildings and his book. The petition is granted."

Ossius responded with more decorum than Flavia imagined she could have mustered in such a moment. "Thank you, O blessed Augustus, for your gracious gift," he said with classy formality. His nod was dignified and restrained. Flavia, however, wanted to jump out of her seat and cheer.

A few more items of business were conducted, then the meeting came to an end and everyone dispersed. But later that night, Rex came to Flavia's room and asked her to go for a walk along a colonnade lit by a line of torches. The place was quiet and empty at this hour, so the two were able to talk privately. After walking hand in hand for a bit, they found a bench and sat down.

"Well, I guess we did it," Rex said after a few moments of contemplative silence.

"Yes! By the strength of the Lord, we finished the mission."

"What a crazy journey we've been on since I found you in that brothel at Corinthus."

"Oh, Rex, I know! We did so many things. Let's see . . ." Flavia began to tick off her memories on her fingers. "Together we toppled an idol of Aphrodite. Addressed the Areopagus. Burned down an island. Rescued the bishop from slavers. Commanded a pirate ship. Overthrew a Germanic tyrant. Restored the rightful king. Roused an army to war. Escaped from prison and slavery. And best of all, we got to see God answer our prayers. Tonight he turned the emperor's heart toward the purpose for which we set out!"

"For which you set out, anyway."

"No, our mission is united, my love. You just joined it late."

Rex fell silent again. At last, he said, "And where will that mission take us next?"

"Back to Rome, of course."

"And then where?"

Flavia thought for a while. Finally, she said with a playful tone, "To Hierusalem."

Rex pulled back from her, examining her face with a quizzical smile. "Hierusalem? That's not what I thought you'd say! Why there?"

"Well, for one, I have always wanted to go there."

"How come?"

"It's the land of scripture, of course."

"And why else?"

A serious mood now descended on Flavia. She took hold of Rex's hand, intertwining her fingers in his. "Because," she said slowly, "all Christians eventually end up in that heavenly city. The New Hierusalem is our final destination. And . . . Rex?"

He glanced at her, meeting her eyes. "Yes?"

"I want you to be there with me."

For a moment longer, he held the gaze, then broke it off. A wry smile came to his lips, followed by a little chuckle. Finally, he shrugged and said, "Who can predict the future?"

"No one. Only God knows what lies ahead."

Rex got to his feet. Looking down at Flavia with a charming grin, he held out his hand. She beamed back. Accepting his hand, she let him pull her up. He drew her close, encircling her waist in a loving embrace.

"Want to go to Rome with me, pretty girl?" he whispered in her ear.

"I do," she replied.

And all the way to Hierusalem.

ACT 3

REVELATION

12

Like many spring days in Rome, today was cool and rainy, though not with-out some passing spells of sun. Pope Sylvester peered out of a window in the former reception hall of the Lateran Palace, now the gathering space of the neighborhood Christians. The field outside was muddy—a rain-soaked bog that used to be the cavalry camp of Constantine's rival, Maxentius. Stakes and ropes marked out a rectangular area for a future church, the same shape that Sylvester had once traced in the dirt with a javelin. Rocks had been piled where the altar would someday stand, if God should be so kind. *Do it for your holy name*, Sylvester prayed, then turned away from the window.

The reception hall's interior had been rearranged today for an important meeting. In the open space where the congregation normally stood, benches had been brought in and placed in a semicircle before a wooden sign, newly painted and now covered by a curtain. Once everyone arrived, the billboard would be revealed—and Lord willing, the assembled clerics and wealthy craftsmen would embrace the vision Sylvester would cast before them.

Primus, a faithful slave whose face was blemished by a wine-colored birthmark, approached the bishop. "Your Eminence, some of the guests have arrived early. Shall I offer them calda?"

"Yes, but mix very little wine into it. Mostly water and spices. I want everyone to be warmed on a day like this, but I want them alert too. Bring the urn into the room and serve it judiciously while we speak. Keep it nice and hot."

"As you wish," Primus said with a bow, then withdrew.

When all the attendees had arrived, Sylvester welcomed them into the hall with genuine affection. In addition to the priests of various Roman congregations, there were working men of different social ranks. Common carpenters and stonemasons sat alongside wealthy business owners and even a few noblemen. The clergy were mixed among the laity. Only Felix, the priest of Saint Sabina on the Aventine, was absent. He was under discipline for his public confrontation of the bishop last year.

"I have gathered you today for an important purpose," Sylvester declared after he had welcomed his guests. "Perhaps you are wondering what is behind this curtain you see before you."

"A painting!" blurted out an overeager bricklayer of the common class.

Sylvester smiled. "It was more of a rhetorical question, my friend. But yes, this is a painting. Can you guess what it is?"

The bricklayer now seemed chastened. "A decoration for a church, Your Eminence?"

"No, although it does relate to churches."

"Go ahead and show us," said the gruff owner of a construction business who sat on the front row. Though he was not a nobleman, he had a lot of imperial building contracts, so his wealth was substantial. "We're curious. Let's get on with it."

Rather than irritate his guests, Sylvester drew aside the curtain. At first, no one could understand the markings on the sign. "Who knows what this is?" asked the pope.

"A map!" someone finally exclaimed.

"Yes, a drawing of the walls of Rome, with its gates and roads. It is the best that our surveyors can produce." The bishop picked up a thin willow wand and pointed to a triangle. "Look here. Do you see the Pyramid of Cestius? Then what road is this?"

"The Ostian Way," observed one of the senior priests, who was also a monk.

"Yes. And a mile and a half outside the walls, we have the tomb of Saint Paul. It is right there. Now follow the line of the Aurelian Walls to the east. What is this?" Sylvester tapped a spot with his wand.

Few in the room could understand maps in relation to the actual landscape, so there was a long silence. Finally, the same monk said, "The Appian Gate."

"Exactly. As you all know, that road is the site of the Apostolic Monument and the Catacombs, where the relics of Peter and Paul now reside. Sebastian the martyr is there too. And farther to the east? What is this, right here?"

"Where we are now," said the sharp-minded monk. "The Lateran Palace."

"That's right. And if you keep going around, you come to the other roads. The Labicana Way and the shrine of the martyrs Marcellinus and another Peter. The Tiburtinian Way, where Lawrence is buried, who was roasted over a grill-fire for his faith. The Nomentana Way and the cemetery of sweet Agnes, treated so cruelly by the men of Rome. Each of these is an important pilgrimage destination. Have some of you been there?" After discerning the nods of many heads, Sylvester traced his wand all the way around the walls of Rome. He stopped northwest of the city, across the Tiberis River. "What lies here?" he asked his audience.

"That is the Vatican Hill," said the wise old monk.

"And what is there of Christian significance?"

Now the hall fell silent, for no one knew the answer, not even the monk. Sylvester waited, letting the tension build. Finally, he pointed to an oblong structure painted onto the map at the Vatican Hill. "Whose circus is this?"

Still, there was silence.

"Good!" Sylvester exclaimed. "It seems the great evildoer has been forgotten, and all he constructed has been lost to memory. But this was once the site of deadly entertainments. It is the Circus of Nero, where Christians were crucified and set on fire or attacked by fierce dogs. Now the circus is in ruins, and the wicked emperor is the one burning in the flames of hell."

"God's vengeance is just!" cried the energetic bricklayer.

"God's vengeance is his own," said Sylvester, "and except for the cross of our Savior, it would rest upon us as well." He spread his arms like a professor addressing his class. "Tell me, any of you who knows the history of his faith: Who was crucified by Nero in that circus?"

"Peter!" came the reply of many voices, for he was the foremost of the apostles and the most cherished saint of Rome. That was one story everyone knew, even if the actual location had been forgotten.

Sylvester smiled warmly. "Yes! He was Jesus's right-hand man. According to the gospel of Saint Matthew, our Lord gave Peter the keys to the kingdom of heaven. The worldwide church is built upon the foundation of the apostles. Peter is the rock of that foundation, we are its living stones, and Christ Jesus himself is the Chief Cornerstone."

"And Peter was the first bishop of Rome," added the old monk.

Sylvester nodded. "According to our earliest traditions."

The gruff owner of the construction business finally spoke up. "If your purpose today was to lecture on theology, Master Bishop, why did you bring us craftsmen here? It seems a gathering of your clergy would have been enough."

The pope arched his eyebrows at the speaker. "No, my friend! Theology is for everyone, not just those in holy orders. But that point aside, your concern is valid. I do have a practical reason for summoning you here today."

"Be on with it, then," said the businessman. "There are hundreds of projects that need my attention. I cannot spare much time."

"So I shall." Sylvester inhaled deeply, then took the plunge. "As I have told you before, I desire to embark on a great building plan around Rome. Though many will oppose it, those of you gathered here today are in favor. Now let me give you some details about the plan. My proposal is before you on the map. I intend to erect a civic church for the episcopal congregation of Rome right here, where we are, at the Lateran Palace. That muddy field outside, Maxentius's old cavalry barracks, shall become the Church of the Savior. Next, at our important burial places along the suburban roads, I propose to erect covered halls over the graves of our apostles and martyrs. Going around the city in a circle, that would include the apostle Paul, the Catacombs of Sebastian, Marcellinus and Peter, Lawrence, Agnes, and the greatest of all, Simon Peter, the preeminent apostle of Christ and first bishop of Rome."

"Master Bishop, that would cost a fortune!" exclaimed the businessman. "There aren't enough Christians in the whole empire to fund a job like that."

"Of course not. It is my hope that Emperor Constantine will pay for it. I have sent a mission to ask this of him, led by Ossius of Corduba. Though the emperor is far away in the east right now, we have all heard how he was victorious over Licinius. My prayer is that his triumph in war will have made him generous toward the God who granted him the victory."

The businessman still looked skeptical. "When does the mission return?"

Sylvester could only shrug. "When the alpine passes thaw or the winter storms cease upon the seas, I expect they will return. With good news, I hope."

"It is certainly a bold undertaking," the businessman mused.

"Indeed. Yet does it not glorify God?"

An anonymous critic shouted a quick comeback. "God or the bishop?"

"Aha! The question is a legitimate one," Sylvester admitted. "Is this plan simply a way to advance our church against others in the empire? Is it just the whim of my own personal vanity? I have reflected much on this and have made it a matter of earnest prayer. The Lord has given me, I believe, a vocation to do this thing. Yes, it's true—this action will solidify our place as the most eminent of Christian cities. But is that wrong in itself? Did not the two most glorious apostles die in this place? And consider our greatest rival of the east, Alexandria. That city is rife with Gnosticism. Melitius is trying to undermine our brother Alexander. Is it not wise, then, to build a strong base of support here in Rome, where our faith is orthodox and our legacy apostolic?"

"The Alexandrians claim to be apostolic too," someone else protested.

"But they aren't. Those legends about John Mark founding the Alexandrian church are just that—legends. We have no good evidence that Mark ministered there. The church fathers of Aegyptus make no mention of him until much later. The roots of Alexandrian Christianity are Gnostic. Even Clement and Origen skirted close to that false doctrine."

"Heretics, all of them!" the businessman exclaimed. "They deny the risen Christ and speculate about a bunch of nonsense. And the Aegyptians overcharge for granite and marble like no people I've ever seen. Even the Christians there do it. A plague upon Alexandria! They're the worst!"

"Let us not curse our brethren," the pope warned.

"I suppose not," the businessman muttered. "But I will at least curse the growth of heresy."

"Which is why Rome must be made strong," Sylvester said with a pointed stare at the rich tycoon in the front row.

"It is the emperor's responsibility," he replied.

"I would suggest it is everyone's responsibility here in Rome. To the degree that each one is able, each one should respond."

After folding his arms across his chest and doing some mental figuring, the business owner finally asked, "Is there a lesser project than all these huge churches? Something small to get the initiative started?"

Sylvester suppressed the smile that might have made him look greedy. *This is your doing, Lord*, he reminded himself. *It is the beginning of something great. I praise you!*

"Rome desperately needs a baptistery," Sylvester said aloud. "The house next door is unoccupied. It has some fine baths that are never used. We could tear down that old building and reuse the plumbing in a beautiful new structure for baptisms. It would stand alongside the Church of the Savior for centuries to come."

The businessman rose from his seat. "Alright! I pledge a hundred thousand denarii." He pointed to the bricklayer who had been so earnest in the earlier discussions. "And you, sir, shall lead the team that builds it. I know your skill with masonry. May God use your abilities and reward your faith."

"And may God reward your generosity!" Sylvester replied with genuine gratitude for the man's great gift. When other rich donors also rose from their seats and made pledges, Sylvester knew his prayers had been answered. He turned toward the door and clapped his hands. "Come, let us be glad! Primus, bring more calda at once, and double the mixture of wine. This is a time for celebration!"

"As always, your wish is my command," said the birthmarked slave with a pious dip of his chin. Then, grinning broadly while he worked, he began to distribute hot wine to the jubilant Christians of Rome.

———⟨𝒆/𝒆/𝒆⟩———

At last, Flavia was in Italy again. It felt good to be home, even though the surrounding region of Venetia—a wide, flat plain—didn't look much like the Italy she was used to. Nevertheless, Flavia took comfort in knowing that this easternmost Italian region truly was a part of her homeland, no matter what the local geography had to say about it.

The trip west from Serdica had progressed slowly, for the travelers were accompanying the Second Italian Legion on its return from the two battles. Rex insisted that was a good thing, for he was escorting the lockbox with its huge treasure. Bandits probably would have tried an attack were it not guarded by a substantial force. The presence of Rex's old legion made the travelers more secure as they went along, even if it meant taking longer to reach Rome.

Two wagons had been appointed to carry the six emissaries: Rex and Flavia, Sophronia and Ossius, and Stephen and Cassi. Sometimes they traveled in their natural pairs, while other times they intermingled. At one point, Rex mentioned that he'd had some interesting theological discussions with Stephen and the bishop as the three of them rode along. But when Flavia later asked Ossius about it, he was less enthusiastic.

"Rex is far from the Lord," the bishop said. "Though he doesn't despise Jesus, and he's even willing to worship him, he sets him alongside other gods. The old ways die hard."

Flavia grunted and shook her head. "Sometimes he seems so close to believing! Why won't he just bow the knee to Christ?" The topic bothered Flavia greatly, though she tried to hide from Ossius how much it really did.

"It is partly pride—he wants no master in heaven. And like I said, he was formed by his upbringing to believe in many gods, not one. Yet beyond this, there is something deeper."

"Do you know what it is?"

"Shame," Ossius said emphatically. "He has thrust a blade into an enemy's flesh and watched the light in his eyes fade away. Rex has killed many men, Flavia—and not always in the context of battle, which is perhaps easier to justify. On some deep level, Rex feels that the peaceful Christian God couldn't forgive him, whereas his own gods celebrate warfare and combat."

"But the gospel teaches grace! It is free and abundant from a loving God, no matter what a person has done."

"For Rex, those are abstract truths. They apply to 'good' people like you and Stephen, not men with lots of blood on their hands."

"I shall continue to pray," Flavia said sadly.

"It is all you can do. And it is what matters most. May God do a mighty work in your friend."

The next afternoon, the legion reached the Venetian capital of Aquileia. It was a splendid city near the head of the Adriatic Sea, with a thriving river port and an important status as the gateway to Italy from the east. A noteworthy Christian church was also there. Since a rest stop had been proclaimed for the marching troops, Ossius decided that the six travelers would take hospitality with the eminent Bishop Theodore while they remained in town.

The church of Aquileia had recently made an innovation that few other churches had ever tried. Instead of meeting in a private home, or in a house refurbished into a Christian meeting space, the pioneering Bishop Theodore had constructed a brand-new building that was not domestic in its architecture. Ossius was interested to see it, for he thought it might serve as a model for the new halls that Sylvester wanted to build around Rome.

Theodore was waiting at the church when his guests arrived. Flavia had seen him once before, three years prior at the Council of Arelate. But she had never personally met him. He was a short, bald, chubby fellow with obvious zest and energy. "Blessings to you in the name of the Lord!" he exclaimed as the travelers exited the wagons. "The brethren of Aquileia welcome you!" He spoke in mellifluous Latin, a sound that was like music to Flavia's ears.

After greetings were exchanged and introductions made, Theodore asked Ossius to sit on a stool and remove his sandals. He then proceeded to wash his guest's feet in a bowl of water. The other five travelers received cloths moistened with fragrant rose water for their faces and necks. Once everyone was refreshed, Theodore led the party inside the church.

The building consisted of two spacious halls that sat side by side, connected by a third chamber to form an overall U-shape. "One hall is for the liturgy of word and sacrament, while the other is for baptismal catechesis," Theodore explained. "Come along, now! You must see the mosaics. Their artist was a true genius. They're exquisite!"

Upon entering the hall for the instruction of catechumens, Flavia could immediately see that the mosaic floor was indeed a masterpiece. It was divided into four bays, each with distinctive themes. Human portraits mingled with scenes from nature and abstract designs. One bay depicted Jesus as the Good Shepherd. Another depicted a winged Victory surrounded by children and birds.

But by far the most amazing bay was the fourth, which told the biblical story of Jonah against the backdrop of intricate fishing scenes. Flavia traced the story in three parts with her eyes. First came Jonah being thrown overboard, his body half swallowed by the sea monster. Second, Jonah could be seen bursting from the mouth of the deadly monster. And third, Jonah was at rest under the shady vines of a pleasant garden. *Death . . . resurrection . . . paradise. The Christian's hope, prefigured in an Old Testament story.* "I will give them the sign of Jonah," Jesus had said. And here it was, in pictorial representation.

Ossius craned his neck to examine the dedicatory inscription on a medallion set in the midst of the Jonah saga. He began to read: "'O blessed Theodore, with the help of Almighty God, and the flock entrusted to you from heaven, you have happily made, and have gloriously dedicated, all these things.'" He turned to his new friend. "Truly you are an energetic pastor!"

The chubby bishop could only smile and shrug. "I serve a great God. Should I sit around, passive and complacent, or should I press on toward the upward call of Christ Jesus?"

"Press on!" Stephen said with an enthusiastic pump of his fist.

"And speaking of pressing on, let's go see the second hall. It is this way." Theodore motioned for his guests to follow him.

Like the catechetical hall, the hall for Eucharistic celebration was also adorned with a glorious mosaic floor. In addition to geometric shapes, many real-world scenes of frolicking animals and pleasant greenery met the visitor's eye. There were partridges, rabbits, goats, hens, donkeys, deer, dogs, and even lobsters. The Aquileian bishop paused beside a tortoise and a cock facing off against each other. "Do you know what this means?" he asked his guests.

"Morning defeats the night," Rex said. "The turtle is a night creature, and the rooster crows at dawn. It is an age-old battle."

"Yes," Theodore agreed, "and in scriptural understanding, the turtle is also an unclean animal, unfit for sacrifice. He hides in his own little tomb, but the light of dawn defeats him. See that victory cup? The sun will triumph over darkness."

Flavia subtly opened her palm toward heaven as she listened to the conversation. *Lord, defeat the night and bring Rex out of darkness!*

Stephen pointed to an inscription next to a picture of a ram. "'Cyriacus, may you live,'" he read aloud. "Who was Cyriacus?"

At this question, Theodore's face fell and a look of deep sadness came over him. "My wife was barren for many years. But eventually, we conceived, and she bore a son. We named him Cyriacus, which means 'belonging to the Lord.' And now he does! Our boy died before he reached his second month. Though we buried him in the earth, we know he will rise again in the final resurrection when the Savior blows his trumpet. See that ram? It reminds me of Abraham, who sacrificed a ram so that his own son might live. So, too, the Lord Jesus is the sacrifice that the Father has provided for us, so that death will not win the victory over my son."

Flavia placed her palm on the bishop's shoulder. "I am sorry for your loss, brother. Even a loss in the Lord is painful to those left behind."

"Thank you," said Theodore, then everyone quietly moved on.

When the tour of the church was finished, the six travelers retired to Theodore's house, which was only a few steps farther along the street. On the way there, Ossius again marveled at the innovation of not using domestic architecture for a church. Though there was a "Hall of the Church" in Rome's Trans Tiberim neighborhood, a building that had never been a private home, it was nothing but a converted warehouse. Houses and rented banquet halls were commonly used for Christian worship. In no way could such buildings compare to the incredible beauty Theodore had commissioned in the church of Aquileia. This was truly a sanctuary for the worship of God, imagined as such from its very inception.

"I will remember this," Ossius declared.

The evening meal was shared by the bishop, his wife, Thecla, and the six guests. A great variety of seafood was on the menu, which Flavia found delightful since she had been far from the coast for so long. She reclined on a couch next to Sophronia and Cassi, stealing glances as often as she could at Rex, who was positioned across from her. He looked especially handsome by the light of the olive oil lamps.

The subject of Cyriacus came up again, and everyone expressed gentle condolences once more. Yet this turned the conversation in a surprising direction. Bishop Theodore was married, like many priests of the catholic church. Yet Bishop Ossius believed in celibacy for the clergy. He had even led an important council in Hispania whose decrees demanded this principle. The council also insisted that priests must not cohabit with women in so-called spiritual marriage, supposedly acting like siblings to one another. No couple, said Ossius, could withstand the temptations of such intimacy and remain celibate in the privacy of a shared home.

The ensuing discussion was lively, though Flavia could tell that Rex was a little uncomfortable. Theodore and Thecla made their case for clerical marriage by emphasizing the goodness of holy matrimony and the example of Saint Peter. They also pointed out that the first letter to Timothy spoke of bishops being the "husband of one wife."

However, both Ossius and Sophronia were firm in their conviction that *First Corinthians* taught that married people are "divided" and cannot focus solely on God. Saint Paul's words were meant for good, Ossius reminded his friends around the dinner table. He quoted the Pauline text from memory. "'I say this for your benefit, not that I might place a snare upon you, but to promote what is appropriate, that you might be devoted to the Lord without distraction.'" Ministers of the gospel were called to adopt a celibate life, lest they be divided and distracted.

"It is very difficult to live such a life," Theodore observed.

Ossius nodded his agreement. "Indeed, it is. But if God asks martyrdom of some, should we not expect him to demand this lesser sacrifice as well?"

Theodore glanced at his beloved wife, who was reclining beside him at the table, then looked back to Ossius. "Is it truly a 'lesser' sacrifice, my brother? The pain of martyrdom is momentary. The pain of denying true love goes on and on."

"Such pain is . . . yes, it is a very tormenting pain," Ossius admitted.

"It might hurt even worse than death," Sophronia remarked, fiddling with a ring on her finger as she spoke. "Yet God—" She paused, collecting herself before continuing. "God often calls us to the hardest path of discipleship."

"But what if a man and woman find themselves in love?" Thecla asked.

"Marriage is a blessing from God," Ossius insisted. "Those lovers should get married, just as the apostle said. His words were, 'It is better to marry than to burn.' I am only talking here about clergy."

"So then, what if a priest falls in love?"

For a long time, the room was silent. Ossius stared at his empty plate, and Sophronia also had no ready answer. Eventually, Ossius said, "I suppose there could be a kind of spiritual marriage between them. It would be a holy friendship, a union of souls in chaste love. But at no time could it include cohabitation, as some priests and monks try to do. The temptation of that is too strong. It is the height of foolishness—like a man scooping coals into his lap. Would he not surely be burned?"

"He would, my brother. On that we can heartily agree." Theodore smiled broadly. "And now that we have enjoyed some gracious discourse seasoned with salt, as the apostle says, should we not also enjoy the taste of something sweet? My cook is an excellent baker, and sweet cakes are his specialty. He makes them with creamy cheese and thick grape sauce. You have never tasted anything like it! They are ready now, and still warm."

The servants immediately brought in the cakes, and Flavia found them just as good as Theodore had claimed. A little more light conversation finished off the evening, then everyone adjourned.

It was a cool night, late in the month of March. Since the dining room had been rather stuffy with its lamps and charcoal braziers, Flavia found herself wanting some fresh air. She caught Rex's attention as he passed nearby. "Escort me for a walk?"

He smiled and extended his elbow. "There's not a man in the empire who could say no to that."

"And there's not a man in the empire I'd ask except you," Flavia replied as she clasped Rex's arm and tipped her head against his shoulder. His satisfied chuckle sounded sweet to her ears. Gladly, she let him lead her into the night.

The pair made their way back toward the church. They stopped outside its dark façade. Gazing at it, Flavia let out a deep sigh. "It was so beautiful in there, wasn't it? The mosaics were stunning."

"Truly beautiful. No question about it." Rex glanced over at Flavia with a mischievous grin. "Would you like to see it by moonlight?"

"Oh, Rex, of course! But I'm sure it's locked now."

He scoffed. "Yes, but with a latch any street urchin could pick! That thing is pitiful. I hope this church doesn't keep its sacred vessels out in the open, or they won't last very long. Come on, I'll take you inside."

The door to the Eucharistic hall sprang open after Rex jiggled the lock with a rusty nail that he had pried out of an old board. He entered first, then beckoned Flavia to follow when all seemed clear.

Stepping inside, she sucked in her breath at the sight before her eyes. The church lay quiet and still, its marble-lined interior bathed in a milky glow. Distinct moonbeams shone through the high windows, each of them made starker by the velvety darkness on either side. The mosaic floor shimmered with a luster so vibrant it could have been the pavement of Zion's own streets. This was a sacred place, a holy place, a juncture between two worlds. Although Flavia's feet were planted on earth, her soul was instantly lifted to the heights of heaven.

Rex was a few steps away. She reached for him and brought him near. "I want you next to me in this place," she whispered. After she said it, the request struck her as more profound than she first realized.

"I'm glad you could see this," Rex said, slipping his arm around her shoulders.

"I'm in awe. The Christian faith is so beautiful."

"It is. Though not without its hard parts. The conversation at dinner showed that."

Flavia glanced at Rex. "What did you think of what Ossius said?"

"About celibate marriage? It sounds a lot less fun than actual marriage," Rex replied with a little laugh.

"I think so too, actually."

The honest statement drew a sudden, wide-eyed look of surprise from Rex. He gawked at Flavia with his mouth agape. Blushing, she turned away, relieved that he couldn't see her face clearly in the dim light.

Rex stared at the ceiling for a time, his mood growing more pensive. He seemed to have something important to say. At last, he spoke. "All that talk about marriage got me thinking," he admitted.

"R-really?"

"Yes. Some things became clear to me."

Though Flavia wanted to cry out for him to go on and tell her what they were, she managed to remain quiet and give Rex time to process his thoughts.

A few more moments of silence passed. Then, after taking a deep breath, Rex said, "I really do think you would make a great wife." Since Flavia found herself unsure how to respond to that, she just waited, though her heart was beating fast. After another long pause, Rex continued. "I'm just not sure I'd make a good husband," he concluded.

The words immediately presented Flavia with a dilemma. *Should I contradict him? Tell him how much I admire him? Call him to faith in Christ?*

Offer to wait as long as it takes? Express my undying love? She was about to provide a counterargument to Rex's assertion when a voice spoke to her—and everything seemed to turn on its end.

Let it go, Daughter, said the voice that came from . . . where? From everywhere: the moonbeams, the mosaics, the breeze through the doorway, even the recesses of Flavia's own heart. *Let it go, Daughter,* the voice repeated. Then there was only silence again.

Rex glanced at Flavia, but when she didn't respond, he gave a little shake of his head, as if to clear his mind. "Well, anyway, enough about those heavy topics for one night, eh? We should probably head back. I think we should return separately, lest anyone think poorly of you, coming in from the dark with me."

"Alright," was all Flavia could manage to say.

"The street is safe. This is a quiet neighborhood. But I'll watch you from my window just in case."

"Thank you. It will give me some time to pray in this lovely place."

"I'm sure you'd like that. Well, then . . . good night, I guess."

"Good night, Rex."

Though he smiled at her, the action seemed forced, lacking in real emotion. Turning, he exited the church and left Flavia alone in the cavernous hall.

For a long time, she stood utterly still. Tears would have come, but Flavia's body sensed that now was not the time for that. All she could do was stand in place and contemplate the lonely future to which God was calling her. The church's mosaic floor, which before had been so lovely, now seemed full of monsters and demons. Even the glorious moonlight had dimmed to a pallid gloom. The sanctuary of God seemed like a prison, a place to escape at all costs. At last, too troubled to remain immobile any longer, Flavia tore her eyes from the church and fled into the cold night air.

———

Minucius Felix had always known he would become a priest. He just never guessed it would be such an easy pathway to power. Lately, however, that truth had become readily apparent. And he intended for it to continue.

Named after a famous theologian of earlier times, Felix had sensed from the beginning of his studies that he had a bright ecclesiastical future. He had come up through the ranks of the church, starting at age ten when he became an acolyte to assist at the altar. Blessed with a sharp mind, Felix had been educated in not only the Latin classics but also Greek. Secular writers such as Plato, Aristotle, Cicero, and Tacitus had been interspersed with church fathers like Justin Martyr, Irenaeus, Tertullian, and Origen. Yet the best of them all had been Valentinus the Gnostic. His writings weren't allowed by the church authorities in Rome—certainly not the narrow-minded Sylvester, who considered it raw heresy. Even so, Felix had drunk deeply of Valentinian Gnosticism over the years. He found it much more palatable than the "orthodox" teachings of the mainstream catholic church.

"Hand me my wrap," said the girl lying beside Felix. The two had spent the night in the bedroom that used to belong to the aristocratic daughter of the house when it was a private residence. That daughter's name was Flavia, which happened to be the same name as the spiritual wife Felix had taken into his home. Such women were known as "beloveds," or those "brought under" the protection of a generous benefactor, such as a priest or monk who had decided not to marry. It was an arrangement that provided many benefits. Sometimes it even provided the most pleasant of benefits when the girl was cooperative, which wasn't always the case. Fortunately for Felix, the nubile, young Flavia in his bed—unlike the one who used to live here—had a reputation for libertinism rather than piety.

Felix gave the pretty girl her shawl so she would be covered enough to leave the room. After she exited, he rose from the bed and went to a bowl on a stand, where he splashed water on his face and combed through his hair in front of a bronze mirror. He was a handsome man, and he knew it. Surely that was part of the reason he had risen so quickly through the ranks of the church. Everyone liked attractive people.

Having become a priest while still in his twenties, Felix's ascendance had been unusually speedy. Now he presided over a prominent and wealthy congregation that used to meet in the house of Senator Neratius Junius Flavianus atop the Aventine Hill. Today, however, the building was a full-time church instead of a private home. Yet it was named not for the senator, who was a divorcé and a defiler of children, but for his modest wife, Sabina

Sophronia. She had stabbed herself to death in this very house rather than be taken to Maxentius's bed to be ravished by the lusty emperor. It was a famous story among the Roman Christians. Ever since that martyrdom, the church here had borne her name: Saint Sabina on the Aventine Hill. The previous pope, Miltiades, had even placed a large plaque above the door with her name on it.

Flavia Lucilla poked her head back inside the bedroom. "Your snake-man has arrived," she announced. "And the stained slave is with him."

"Good! Usher them in."

"I'm not doing that!" cried the girl. "I can't look at them. The tattoo is scary, and that blotchy stain repulses me."

"Tell the doorman to do it, then," Felix said with a wave of his hand. "Send them to the back garden where we can talk in private. And have him bring raisin cakes. I'm hungry."

The rear garden of the church was centered on a deep cistern that collected rainwater. A few of the household servants from the days when the church was a private residence said that two Germanic speculators had once fought a great duel here, but Felix didn't believe those stories. It didn't seem likely that such an odd event would happen in a rich senator's mansion. However, a noble suicide did occur, so perhaps the other rumors were true as well.

A moment after Felix arrived in the garden, the Aegyptian Asp and the slave Primus were led in as well. The men seated themselves in wicker chairs around a low table with a tray of cakes on it. Primus eyed the cakes warily, so Felix said, "Go ahead, have some." With that permission, Primus snatched up two pastries and began to stuff his face.

The Aegyptian Asp, however, didn't seem to notice the food. "Our enemy has advanced his plans," he announced. "We must move quickly, or the building program will be a foregone conclusion."

"Are you sure?"

"Absolutely. This slave heard every word of Sylvester's conniving."

"Tell us what you heard," Felix instructed.

"Bishop had a big sign," Primus mumbled around a mouthful of food. "Showed all the walls and roads."

"What about them?"

The slave swallowed his last bite, then reached for a third cake. "He has plans for churches over the martyrs' graves. Plus a big one, right at the Lateran Palace."

"Inside the walls?" Felix rubbed his smooth chin, which was the latest fashion among Christians in the know. "The senators will be furious."

"It's not on the Forum," the Asp pointed out. "It's barely inside the walls, on the fringe of the city."

"Even so, it would be a prominent Christian edifice. Such a building would detract from their ancient temples." He paused, thinking a little more. "Which martyrs will get churches?"

"The usual ones that get mentioned. Sebastian, Marcellinus and Peter, Agnes, Lawrence. And also the apostles—Paul and Peter."

Felix sat up straight at this. "The apostle Peter, you say? At the Catacombs?"

Primus shook his head. "Nero's old circus. The Vatican."

At this announcement, the Aegyptian Asp and Felix exchanged glances. "That is very unfortunate," said the tattooed assassin.

Felix felt the same concern. "The *Gospel of Matthew* invests Peter with the power of the keys," he said with a sense of foreboding. "If the Roman bishop takes up the mantle of Peter, he will have power that far eclipses Alexandria. And a pilgrimage church over the grave of Peter would make it certain. People would come from all over the world to visit it. The Roman pope would become the spiritual father of everyone."

"We must stop it," the Asp agreed.

For a moment, there was only tense silence. Then, slowly, a devious smile spread across Primus's disfigured face. "It is worse than you think," he declared.

"How so?" asked Felix.

Primus's expression turned coy. "A simple slave like me overhears many things not publicly known." He licked his fingers after finishing the third raisin cake. "Of course, we are often punished when we tell our secrets, so it is not worth the risk to speak."

"*Pfft!* Sylvester punishes no one," said the Asp with a dismissive wave of his hand.

"Even so, my secrets stay with me unless I have a reason to tell."

One flick of the Asp's wrist was all it took for a sharp razor to appear in his hand. The look in his eyes was stern as he brandished the blade. "Perhaps some free surgery on that birthmark would convince you?"

Primus immediately shrank back, but before he could jump out of his chair, Felix intervened. "Now, now! There is no need for a confrontation," he soothed. "We have many kinds of incentives for Primus, who is our fellow servant in the Lord."

Looking over his shoulder, Felix shouted for Flavia Lucilla. She soon appeared in the garden, dressed now in an expensive silk robe.

"You called for me, my brother?" she asked in a sweet voice.

"Yes, dear sister. Might you bring me my purse?"

"Of course! I shall return with it in a moment."

When she came back with the purse, Felix reached into it and withdrew a silver coin. "Some charity for you, Primus," he said as he laid the coin on the table.

"Times are hard, Father Felix."

"Indeed, they are," replied the priest, adding a second coin. The Aegyptian Asp snorted and looked away.

After scooping up the coins, Primus reached into his tunic and tucked the money into a hidden pouch around his waist. Looking up again, he gave the two waiting men a broad smile. "It seems you do not like the idea of a basilica being built over Peter's grave."

"We do not," Felix agreed. "For the reasons we have already said."

"Well, you might be interested to know that no one knows exactly where that grave is."

"What do you mean, slave?" the Aegyptian Asp asked suspiciously.

Now Primus's expression turned smug, for he possessed information his superiors did not have. "Only two other people know what I am about to say," he boasted. "I listened secretly while Sylvester told it to Quintus. The grave of Peter has been lost—not just forgotten by the masses, but lost by the bishop and his clergy. It is somewhere near the ruined circus on the Vatican Hill, but there are probably five thousand burials in that cemetery. No one can visit Peter's grave anymore. It would be like trying to find a walnut in a wheat field."

"So where will they build the basilica?" asked Felix. "They won't just take a guess and put it up anywhere. It would have no value as a pilgrimage site if it's not directly over the actual grave."

"Oh, Sylvester intends to find it! There are some old records in the archives. He knows as well as anyone that a funerary church without a grave is useless."

The Aegyptian Asp turned to stare at Felix. "We must find it first, my friend, and obliterate it, along with all the records."

"Can you do that?"

"There is nothing I cannot do when the Divine Spirit helps me. And I am certain she will assist me in this holy endeavor."

Felix wrinkled his nose at the strange sound of the feminine pronoun. "You consider the Holy Spirit female?"

"Many of my sect believe this. She whispers often in my ear. Accept it, if you will."

"I will think upon it," Felix said with a slow nod. He shook his head a little, then went on with his main point. "Primus is right. Sylvester won't build a church unless he's certain the altar rests above the apostle's true grave. But there's more to this than just getting those records or destroying the grave so no one can find it."

"What else?"

"We had a spy at Serdica, and his report was grim. Constantine gave our enemies his full support. We're going to need to steal the rescript that authorizes the construction along with the treasure chest of gold." Felix leaned close to the Asp in a conspiratorial way. "Take away Sylvester's holiest site, his permission to build, and his funds—then we've defeated the catholic church! Its membership will shrink, and the Gnostic church will rise to take its place."

"I will do all these things," said the Asp. "No new churches can be allowed to go up in Rome. Especially not the Peter church! It would be a mighty base of power."

At these words, Primus spoke up again. "A slave like me might know one more thing of interest to you gentlemen," he suggested with a greedy look in his eye.

"What more could you know?" the Asp scoffed.

"Perhaps something of great significance. Or maybe it is nothing."

Felix reached into his purse and laid another silver coin on the table. Though it was valuable, when Primus saw it, he frowned. "More is needed," he said. "I promise you, it's worth it."

The Asp flicked his wrist and brought out his razor again. Instead of threatening Primus with it, he only began to trim his fingernails—yet the sight of the blade was fearsome nonetheless. Felix sighed and laid a second coin on the table. "Spit it out," he snapped, finally feeling irritated with Primus's moneygrubbing.

After he had collected the reward, Primus straightened his shoulders and announced with a haughty air, "His Eminence, the bishop of Rome, does not intend to find only the grave of Saint Peter."

"What else, then?"

"He intends to find the bones."

The Asp's head swung around, his eyes narrow and mean. "What are you talking about? Everyone knows the bones are at the Catacombs on the Appian Way. They are in the Apostolic Monument. People have banquets there for that reason."

"Everyone *thinks* that," said Primus. "But the pope knows otherwise. The sacred relics of Saint Peter were moved there during the persecution of Valerian. But they did not remain. After the persecution passed, somebody moved them back to their original resting place. That was almost sixty years ago. Today, nobody knows exactly where it was. The bones themselves are lost, along with the grave."

"Then what is out on the Appian Way?" Felix demanded. "I have banqueted there myself."

Primus shrugged. "No one really knows what is encased in the Apostolic Monument. The Christian masses assume the relics are there. Pope Sylvester knows they aren't. That is why he wants to find Peter's grave on the Vatican. In so doing, he will recover the mortal remains of the Lord's greatest apostle. And then, directly over the original grave and its bones, he will erect a colossal basilica."

"The bones and the grave together!" Felix exclaimed. "It would be the greatest church in the Christian world."

"Forever surpassing Alexandria," the Asp agreed with bitterness in his voice.

"I told you it was worth an extra coin."

The Aegyptian Asp produced a fifth argenteus from somewhere inside the folds of his brown robe. "Yes, it was," he said as he handed it to Primus. "Continue to keep your ears open, slave. You are a valuable asset inside our enemy's lair."

—◦◦◦—

Stephen didn't know which he liked more: being the first of the traveling party to arrive back in Rome or getting to do so with Cassi.

The couple had been sent ahead while Bishop Ossius was delayed at a country inn near the Milvian Bridge, a few miles north of the city. Unfortunately, he had come down with an illness that required bed rest for several days. While Sophronia and Flavia were taking care of him, it had been decided that Pope Sylvester needed an update about the mission. For planning purposes, he should be informed that the emissaries would arrive soon with a report. Stephen felt honored that Rex—who was staying back with the bishop to guard the treasure chest—had trusted him enough to charge him with the task. The hardest part, Stephen thought, would be not giving away the secret of the mission's success. The honor of bringing that good news to the pope belonged to Bishop Ossius alone. Stephen was only supposed to speak of an "important" announcement coming in a matter of days.

Feeling optimistic and excited, he stared out the window of the rolling wagon. Another one of the benefits of being given this assignment was spending quality time with the lovely Cassiopeia. The two had become close friends during their travels over the past few months. Fortunately, in these days of married clergy and spiritual marriages, no one would question a priest and a nun traveling together during daylight hours.

While Stephen did not consider Cassi a romantic partner, neither was he oblivious to her good looks. In fact, he had to admit, though she was truly a friend, he also felt attracted to her as a woman. Her long-lashed eyes, curly hair, and smooth, dark skin had an exotic appeal. She was a beautiful young lady, slender and charming. Stephen often had to snap his mind back to reality, reminding himself that Cassi was a nun from a Sicilian convent, sworn to a vow of chastity.

For how long, though? Forever? He didn't know what Cassi intended to do with her life. Generally speaking, many nuns left their convents for marriage. Celibacy was expected to be maintained while they were devoted sisters, not necessarily for their entire lifetime. The vow of a nun wasn't always permanent. Stephen sometimes found himself hoping that Cassi's wouldn't be.

"I see the walls," Cassi said in Latin, having reverted to that language now that Rome was near. Her Greek was better, and she also spoke her native Aethiopian tongue, though that was of no use here. Yet Cassi's command of Latin had improved over the past year. She was close to fluent now.

Stephen followed Cassi's gaze out the wagon's window. "You're right! And look, there's the gate. We will enter through that one."

"I know, Stephen. It is the Flaminian Gate." Cassi smiled primly as she spoke, and Stephen reminded himself not to underestimate the sharp intellect behind his friend's shy and retiring demeanor.

When the wagon reached the gate, the coachman dismounted and arranged for a nice litter with curtains to take the pair all the way to the Lateran Palace at imperial expense. Stephen and Cassi were carried down Broadway to the Capitoline Hill, through the Forum to the brand-new Arch of Constantine, around the Flavian Amphitheater, and out to the southern wall of Rome. The palace of Pope Sylvester, given to the catholic church by Constantine, lay just inside the walls.

Cassi pointed to some ropes and stakes that formed a rectangle over the ruins of Maxentius's horse camp. "Look!" she said with a delighted expression. "Sylvester has made a plan already. The bishop's church."

"It is going to be so hard not to tell him about our success!"

"Do not," Cassi warned. "It is for Ossius to do." Stephen nodded at this, then the two of them clambered out of the litter and approached the palace.

They were welcomed warmly once they identified themselves. Cassi had been part of the original embassy sent by Pope Sylvester last May, almost a year ago now. Though Stephen was unknown to the palace staff, he was a priest from Gaul, so he was accorded all due respect. A message was sent to the bishop, and word quickly returned: Sylvester wanted to see them immediately. He was combing through old records in the library when the visitors were ushered into his presence.

"You have news of the mission?" Sylvester asked after he had greeted his guests.

"I can only say that our news is important," Stephen replied. "Everyone will be here in about a week, with a full report."

"Where is Ossius now?"

"The Milvian Bridge, recuperating at a country inn. He has taken ill."

"The nuns are there to care for him? Flavia and—" Sylvester arrested his words, taking a closer look at Stephen.

"I know the identity of the other," Stephen said to reassure the bishop. "Lady Sabina Sophronia, whom all in Rome believe to be dead from noble suicide. The secret is safe with me. I know she wishes to retain her anonymity."

"Very good. See that you do not tell."

"I will not, Holy Father." Stephen's eye caught sight of an ancient papyrus on the desk behind which Sylvester stood. "Is that the original *Letter to the Romans*?"

The bishop gingerly picked it up. "Alas, it is not, but it is a copy from fifty years later. All the originals of the New Testament epistles have been lost."

"We have seen some, Your Eminence," Cassi said.

Though Stephen was surprised that his demure friend had spoken up, Sylvester seemed more intrigued by the assertion itself. "Really? Where?" he asked.

"In Thessalonica. Bishop Basil showed us both of Paul's letters. Then some bad men burnt them."

"Yet you saw the originals?"

"Yes, sir."

"Ah, how exciting! What a delight to know that they existed into our day, even if they are now lost. Of course, those epistles are not in question as being scriptural." Sylvester turned to a cabinet and removed a slim codex. "Stephen, I take it that you are literate, since you recognized the *Romans* manuscript?"

"I am. My studies for the priesthood took me to the great school at Alexandria. I can read both Latin and Greek."

"Ah, the Alexandrian school! Impressive indeed. I am curious about what you may have learned in Aegyptus. Behold this volume, which I only recently discovered."

"What is it?"

Sylvester opened it. The text was Greek, and it looked to be quite old. "It is an anonymous dissertation on the church's rule of faith. It comes from the time of Pope Soter, around a century and a half ago. One of its most interesting portions is its discussion of which books belong in the New Testament and which are heretical. Whoever this writer was, he spoke wisely when he said, 'It is not fitting that gall should be mixed with honey.' The catholic church must be very discerning about its holy books."

"Certainly the Thessalonian epistles belong to the canon," said Stephen. "In fact, all the genuine letters of Paul should be included."

"Indeed, those are not in dispute. Neither are the four gospels, nor the *Acts* compiled by Saint Luke. The churches have always accepted them. But there are other books about which theologians disagree. Look here." The bishop pointed to a passage of his codex, where the New Testament books had been listed. "What is erroneous in this canon, in your opinion?"

Stephen quickly scanned the text. "It adds two books strange to me: *The Apocalypse of Peter* and *The Wisdom of Solomon*. I was not taught at Alexandria to accept them among the church's scriptures."

"We in Rome do not consider those valid either. What about any omissions? Is anything overlooked?"

After examining the text again, Stephen said, "I have always heard that James, the Lord's brother, had a legitimate epistle. And the *Epistle to the Hebrews* should be included. And also two by Peter, though his second one has only recently been discovered. None of those are mentioned here."

Sylvester nodded sagely at this. "You are absolutely correct. Clearly, whoever wrote this dissertation did not know about those epistles, or he would have mentioned them. A hundred and fifty years ago, the church of Rome had not yet received all the sacred writings."

"Perhaps not in Rome. Yet *The Epistle of James* has always been well regarded in the east, along with the *First Epistle of Peter*. Admittedly, the second is more debated. The scholar Origen of Alexandria mentions all three, with varying opinions of each. As for *Hebrews*, it remains controversial in the church to this day."

"Here in Rome, we do not consider it to have been written by Saint Paul," said the pope.

"I cannot deny, it bears significant inconsistencies with his style. It is a subject for further consideration by the theologians of the church."

"You speak wisely, Father Stephen! I can see you are erudite. You shall be welcome at my convocation of scholars—if such is to be allowed."

An awkward silence now descended on the threesome. Stephen could see that Pope Sylvester wanted him to hint at whether Constantine intended to sponsor the meeting about the holy scriptures, then pay for a beautiful bible to be used at the bishop's church. Though Stephen knew the permission had been granted, it was not for him to relay the exciting news. He struggled to hold his tongue, even as Sylvester refused to relent. The pope kept waiting for Stephen to speak.

Cassi finally broke the tension. "Holy Father, the Lord is the writer of the scriptures. He has sent the Spirit to lead us into all truth. He, not Constantine, will guide our thoughts on the canon."

A big smile broke out upon Sylvester's face. He turned to Cassi and approached her, then took her hand in his, patting it lightly. "Well said, Sister Cassiopeia! You have shown more wisdom today than all the men of this house put together." After kissing her gently on the forehead, he released her hand and turned back to Stephen. "I will arrange rooms for—"

A loud crash interrupted the pope's words. Everyone turned toward the sound, which had come from the library's window that gave a view into the garden. Stephen saw a man standing there, his face marred by a purplish birthmark across his right cheek. He wore the garb of a palace servant.

"I am very sorry, Your Eminence!" the servant said. He held up the handle of a broken pitcher. "I was bringing you drinks, and the jug toppled from the tray!"

"Drinks from the garden, not the kitchen, Primus?"

"I was . . . I was decorating the tray with some flowers."

"How thoughtful! A nice touch. Well, you can clean up the mess in a moment. But first, please do bring some drinks to my guests. Then you may lead them to—" Sylvester paused, turning to Stephen. "Are you two married?" he inquired under his breath.

"No, Your Holiness. Just friends of a spiritual nature."

"Ah, I see." Sylvester returned his attention to Primus. "Lead my friends

385

to two bedrooms in the guest wing. Not adjoining, please. They shall have hospitality here until the rest of their party arrive."

"As you wish," Primus said before scurrying off.

"I hope your party shall have good news," Sylvester remarked to the two visitors.

Stephen could not suppress the grin that came to his face. "Good things are in store for the Roman church," was all he would say.

"So be it," Sylvester replied, then began to return his books to the shelves.

<hr/>

"The emperor was right over there, near the end of the span," Rex said, gesturing to the Milvian Bridge in the distance. He could see its cream-colored arches bathed in pale moonlight. "Maxentius was at the other end, hurling insults at Constantine. And I was riding toward them at a full gallop, with arrows landing all around."

Rex gazed across the table at Flavia, who was leaning on one elbow while she ate. Their two couches sat under a sheltered pergola beside the Tiberis River. A single lampstand lit the intimate space, its light flickering on the gentle contours of Flavia's face. "So what did you do?" she asked breathlessly.

"Took off my armor, if you can believe it, while never slowing down."

Flavia's mouth fell open as Rex's story about the famous battle kept getting more dramatic. "You took off your armor with all those arrows flying? Why would you do that?"

"I had to stop Constantine from going out onto the bridge. There was a trap in it, to make it collapse. This was the only way."

"To gallop faster?"

"No, to jump into the river."

Flavia blinked and shook her head. "You jumped from the back of a galloping horse into the Tiberis?"

"I sure did. Right over there, where that clump of bushes is. I decided to spring the trap from under the bridge before the emperor could ride out. So I got my feet up onto the saddle and leapt sideways while the horse went down from a javelin. I hit the water at full speed."

"Did it hurt?"

"Not as bad as getting kicked by the horse when it fell off the bridge. I

NaNNaNNaN

was really woozy after that. The rider wore chainmail and it snagged my tunic, so he pulled me down. We got tangled pretty bad. My feet sank into the mud like glue. I grabbed my sword and cut myself free of the guy. But by then I had been under a really long time. It was completely black down there, and my lungs hurt so bad. I remember just wanting to open my mouth and end it all. My body started to shut down. My mind went dark."

"Oh, Rex! You could have died at the bottom of a river!"

"Almost did, for sure. And I would have never been found."

"That is so scary! How did you get up?"

As Flavia gaped at Rex in amazement, he was struck by how beautiful she looked tonight, with her elegant makeup and her hair done up in braids. "I saw something above me in a halo of light," he said. "It beckoned to me."

"Ah! It must have been an angel."

Rex looked across the table and met Flavia's eyes. "No, it was *your* face that I saw. Your eyes . . . your hair . . . your lips. You said to me, 'I need you, my love. Fight for me.' So I did. I kicked my feet and didn't stop until I reached air."

A silence descended on the little nook behind the country inn where Rex and Flavia were sharing a meal. It was a cozy spot, a private place, well suited for affectionate conversation. Yet now, instead of talking, the two just stared at each other, neither knowing what to say.

Flavia broke the silence first. "You . . . you saw *me*?"

"I did."

"What did I look like?"

"Actually, like an angel. Turns out you were right about that."

Flavia smiled shyly at his remark, so to lighten the mood, Rex reached for the decanter on the table between them. "This wine is good. Would you like some more?"

"Perhaps not. I've had too much already."

"Can there be such a thing?" Rex asked with a grin. When Flavia nodded her agreement, he refilled her cup and handed it to her. She took a sip, acknowledged its excellence with an arch of her eyebrows, and drank some more.

It was a pleasant night, and the dinner of wild boar and roasted chestnuts had been divine. Poor Bishop Ossius was inside the inn, restricted to a diet of

387

plain bread and thin soup while he recuperated. Sophronia had been caring for him since sunup, attentive and compassionate as always. Though they had both retired now after a demanding day, neither Rex nor Flavia had been ready for sleep, so they found the pergola behind the inn and ordered a meal from the kitchen. Because the inn catered to powerful guests who were arriving in the capital, the staff had been happy to serve the visitors who were here on imperial business.

Setting down her cup, Flavia said, "I'm glad you survived that battle, Rex. And all the ones after it. You are an incredible warrior."

"I do what I'm made to do, I guess."

"And you do it well." She traced her finger around the rim of her goblet, contemplating her words. Finally, she blurted out, "I just have to say this. You look so handsome tonight!"

He chuckled, both surprised and delighted by the compliment. "Thank you. I'm glad you think so."

"I really do. You should wear your hair like that more often—swept back tight like that."

He reached to the crown of his head, where his long blond hair had been pulled into a knot. "I prefer it free, actually." With a tug of the leather thong around the knot, he sent his locks tumbling to his shoulders with a vigorous shake of his head.

"That's . . . uh . . . good too," Flavia admitted.

He stood up and walked around the table between them, towering over Flavia as she reclined on her couch. She lay still, gazing up at him, and for a moment Rex wasn't sure if she planned to rise. Finally, he extended his hand. "Let's go look at the moon," he said. "We should be able to see it well from the middle of the bridge."

Taking his hand and not letting go, Flavia walked beside Rex along the riverbank until they reached the marble span. "Is this where Constantine was standing when you galloped up?"

"Approximately. But the bridge that day was a temporary one because this one had been cut. Let's hope the masons have repaired it well since then."

Flavia clutched Rex's arm. "I hope so! I don't want to go for a night swim!"

"Not in that white gown," he replied with a wink, then led her onto the bridge.

Rex was correct about the view of the moon. It had risen above the horizon, its swollen orb casting amber light upon the waters of the Tiberis. Where the moonbeams shone, pale yellow rose petals seemed to flutter on the river's surface. Flavia placed both hands on the bridge's railing, gripping it as she looked over. A little shiver went through her. "Oh, Rex, if you had died down there . . ."

"Then what?"

Flavia thought for a moment. "Then we wouldn't have gotten the permission from Constantine to build the churches. Nor the great treasure from him, nor the letters of credit, nor the right to convene a council about the scriptures. There would be no new church at the Lateran. No new copy of the holy book. You have done so much, Rex. Or I should say, the Lord has done it through you."

"I think God did it as much through you as through me."

"But your actions were bolder than mine," she countered. "Braver. More courageous."

"I can't accept that, Flavia." Rex reached to his neck and began to unfasten his cloak as he talked. "Remember when you stepped up to speak before all the councilors of the Areopagus on Mars Hill? Or when you sold yourself into slavery? Or when you faced all kinds of horrors but didn't break? How can you say I was braver than you, just because my actions came on the field of war?"

"I guess you might be right. I just don't normally think of myself as courageous."

"You are courageous, my beloved. You have it within you."

Flavia shivered again, for the night had grown cool. Now Rex stepped behind Flavia and spread his cloak around her shoulders. She sighed as its warmth—and the embrace of his arms—enveloped her. "I like who you are," he said in her ear with tender affection.

"I like who you make me," she whispered over her shoulder.

"I don't make you into anyone, Flavia. I just make space for the real you to emerge."

"Ah, Rex, you're sweet to me! You're the key that unlocks who I really am."

Rex smiled at this, then made a motion with his hand, as if inserting a key and turning it. "Click," he said with a little laugh.

"I'm open," Flavia replied with a playful giggle of her own. She leaned back into Rex's chest, turning her head and looking up at him with an arched neck. He gazed down at her, cradling her in his arms. The two of them exchanged warm smiles, then the gentle laughter of shared closeness.

"Shall we head back?" he said at last.

"I guess so. It's probably time."

Flavia took Rex's arm as they walked along the uneven riverbank. It was a short stroll back to the inn, which was located in a forested and rural setting. The place had grown quiet, for it was the second watch of the night now and everyone had gone to bed.

When the party of travelers had arrived at the inn a few days earlier, they had obtained three adjoining bedrooms: one for the women, one for the sick Ossius, and one for Rex. Each room had a solid oaken door with a lock on it. Rex had chosen the middle room with the sturdiest lock of the three, for he was guarding the treasure chest. It was chained to his bed for extra protection. He paused outside his bedroom, examining the lock.

"Everything looks good," he said after inspecting the keyhole for scratches. He spoke in hushed tones because a deep silence had come over the inn.

Flavia also spoke in the quietest of whispers. "Did you fear theft?"

"No, but it's still nice to see that all is safe."

"I can't believe how much money the emperor gave us! And letters of credit too. Sylvester is going to be so happy."

"The mission was a great success," Rex agreed.

"We work well together, don't we?"

"Yeah, we do. We're a natural fit. Like you said: a lock and a key."

Stepping closer, Flavia murmured, "I love striving alongside you toward a common goal. It's what I've always wanted in life."

The implications of Flavia's words had an immediate effect on Rex, snapping his mind from the present to the future. Two competing emotions now flooded him; and since he had felt them both before, he knew them well enough to recognize each.

On the one hand, he felt a deep longing for this utterly desirable—in fact, nearly irresistible—woman. Yet in that very recognition, Rex's sense of moral inadequacy became all the more apparent. The closer he drew to Flavia's goodness, her purity, her Christian virtue, the clearer he could discern his own unworthy past, his violence and bloodshed, his crude pagan ways. The clash of these feelings created a storm inside him. Now, on this intense evening, at the culmination of an epic journey, the unstoppable impetus of Rex's desire crashed headfirst into the immovable wall of his disgrace. More than ever before, the terrible smashup made him want to run far away.

"I like working with you too," he said stiffly. "Our dinner was a great way to celebrate the end of our mission." A yawn came to Rex, and he stretched his arms. "Well, it's been a long day. We should get to bed, I guess. I hope you sleep well."

"No!" Flavia hissed. "Please, Rex, don't leave me. Not like this."

"I'm not leaving. Just letting you sleep for now."

"I mean in the future. I can't keep having you come close, then pull back like that. I want a different sort of life with you."

"That life won't work," he grumbled.

"Oh! Don't say that."

"Why not?" He put his hand on the doorknob. "It's true."

"It doesn't have to be." Flavia stepped close, then reached up and intertwined her fingers in Rex's long hair. Straining, she brought her lips close to his ear. "I can't live without you, my love."

"Stop!" he exclaimed, more loudly than he intended. "We have no future!"

"Yes, we do! Surely we must!"

The look of desperation on Flavia's face churned Rex's emotions even more. He felt a strong urge to comfort her, and at the same time an urge to flee. He stepped back. Yet even as he pulled away, trying to avoid a coming disaster, the cumulative effect of their romantic tension began to take hold of him. *Maybe we should just go ahead and . . .*

No, countered a voice in his head. *Flavia is too good for that. You can't!*

But one glance at Flavia's wide, fearful eyes weakened his resolve. She wanted him now. Maybe even needed him. *Can you really say no to her heart's greatest desire? Can you leave her weeping and alone on a night like this? Don't do that to her . . .*

Tentatively, Flavia grabbed the fabric of his tunic. She began to pull him, then stopped and lowered her eyes. But after a moment of indecision, she met his gaze again and began drawing him toward her room. With her free hand, she unlocked the door, then opened it a little. The darkness beckoned.

"Your mother is—" Rex began.

"Asleep on a pallet at the foot of the bishop's bed," Flavia finished.

And with that, Rex succumbed to the demands of his desire as well as the ferocity of Flavia's fear. He embraced her, feeling her body against his own. Though he dared not kiss her, he could still utter the words he so urgently felt.

"I want you now," he whispered, overcome with longing.

"I want you forever," she replied, and drew him in.

———✿✿✿———

The Aegyptian Asp did not concern himself with the things he knew were happening in Flavia's room. He had learned long ago to dispense with such behavior. It was something that lesser beings were absorbed with. Enlightened souls did not need it.

Nevertheless, the Asp was glad for one thing: the activities next door would give him plenty of time to pick the lock to the man's room. That was a good thing, for the lock was well constructed.

After fiddling with it for some time, and even breaking one of his more delicate tools, the stealthy assassin finally tripped the mechanism and pushed the door ajar. He entered Rex's room and closed the door behind him. The place was dark and empty.

By the light of the moon from the window, he spotted the heavy chest. It was fastened to the bed with a chain that would take far too long to cut. Fortunately, the Asp's pick set contained tools for opening smaller locks like the one on the chest. He would have its latch open more quickly than the one on the door.

Lifting the lid a few moments later, he was astonished by what he found inside. He had known, of course, that there would be coins. He just hadn't expected them all to be made of gold. They were stored in sacks, seven in all, and there wasn't a bit of silver among them. He stuffed the seven bags into his knapsack, knowing they would be heavy, yet feeling delighted instead of encumbered because the sum was so substantial. There was enough money here to hire a construction firm for a year. The Asp smiled as he realized that the funds would never be used for their intended purpose.

Rising to listen at the wall of the adjoining room, he discerned that all sounds had finally stopped. Yet that didn't necessarily mean trouble. His years of robbery had told him that couples rarely parted quickly. Even so, it would be wise to get moving.

Affixed into the lid of the chest was a tubular scroll case that Latin speakers called a *capsa*. After extricating it and opening its cap, the Asp discovered one item he had expected and another that excited him even more than the gold.

The expected item was the rescript from Constantine that detailed the rights and privileges of the Roman bishop to erect churches at imperial expense and convene a meeting to discuss the books of scripture. But the unexpected thing—truly a marvel!—was the unlimited line of credit that could be drawn from the treasury at the Temple of Saturn. The income from various properties in newly conquered lands would fund these loans, repaying them over time, all at no cost to the catholic church.

Sylvester could have built so many churches with this—but no more! O great Mother Spirit, I thank thee for snatching these ill-gotten funds from him!

Immediately after this prayer, the Asp had a clever idea, no doubt an enlightenment from she who had been thanked. *The letters of credit are extended to the catholic church. I wonder if, with Felix's help as a priest, we could trick the bankers . . .*

The Asp's scheme to commit bank fraud was interrupted by the sound of creaking hinges from the room next door. Instantly, his sleeve-razor was in his hand. The Germanic warrior was probably on his way back to his room. If he entered now, he wouldn't be expecting an attack. The Asp knew he could injure the man quickly enough to cripple him. Then he could escape, even while carrying the heavy knapsack. However, fleeing through the window was an option too.

The Asp had to make a tactical decision, and he did not hesitate. Instead of trying to leap from the high window with the heavy pack, he decided he would slice the man's eyes when he came through the doorway. The cut would be deep, blinding his opponent in a cascade of blood. Escape would be easy after that.

Taking a position next to the door, the Asp waited in deep shadows for Brandulf Rex to enter. After his juvenile cavorting with Junia Flavia, he would have other things on his mind. He would not be in a defensive posture. Surprise would be complete.

In the hallway outside the room, the Asp heard the couple whispering back and forth. But soon they would separate and the man would come to his own bed. The Asp tightened his grip on his blade, rehearsing how he would make a swift slash that would disable his enemy as soon as he entered.

Now the talking outside ceased. For a moment, there was nothing but silence. Then, after the creak of hinges, the latch next door clicked into place again. *Here he comes. Be quick. Like a serpent!* However, nothing happened. No footfalls sounded in the hallway. No hand touched the doorknob. The man did not come.

Carefully, the Asp put his ear again to the wall of the adjoining room. A smile crept across his face as he listened. The man would not be reentering his room anytime soon. With a snicker, he sheathed his razor in his sleeve.

Now he picked up the knapsack and heaved it onto his shoulders, then slung the capsa around his body by its leather strap. Opening the door, he peeked into the hallway. All was quiet, so he stepped out. From there, it was only a short distance to the stairwell. Descending, he left by the inn's back entrance. No one disturbed him as he left.

As soon as the Aegyptian Asp slipped into the moonlit forest, a feeling of exultation washed over him. His mission was complete, for he had obtained the gold and the documents. God's will had prevailed. He gloated as he considered the fleshly weakness of his adversaries. *What fools they are!*

And then, once again, the Holy Spirit spoke to him. This time her voice was from the sacred text called the *Song of Songs*. "'I adjure you, daughters of Hierusalem,'" she murmured upon the breeze, "'do not awaken love until the time is right.'" *Aha! Junia Flavia has surely done this. It will be her doom. A curse now lay upon the daughter of Hierusalem.*

The Asp shivered at the mystical revelation from the Goddess. She was the Beautiful and the True. He used the words of the *Song* to form his reply.

"'Make haste, my beloved,'" he whispered to the moon.

13

MARCH 317

It was dawn. Flavia lay under the rumpled covers of her bed, wishing she weren't awake; for there was no guilt in sleep. But while she was awake, the guilt gnawed at her soul.

The lovemaking with Rex had been like nothing Flavia had ever experienced. Its intensity had overwhelmed her. Unlike the horrible liaisons with Aoric, which could only be endured until they were over, this had been a mutual experience. While Rex was in her arms, all seemed right in the world. But now, in the clear light of dawn, things did not appear so beautiful. Flavia was filled with a shame much deeper than after she had been with Aoric. Because this time, she had been a willing participant.

Willing? Flavia sighed and shook her head. *I was hardly just "willing." I invited it to happen!*

She knew why she had been so bold with Rex—reaching for him, bringing him close, drawing him in. It was partly because of love. Their hearts were joined by an inexplicable unity, an understanding of one another so natural and innate that it demanded tangible expression.

But it was more than that. It was fear too. Those two things weren't separate. Flavia fiddled with the bedcovers as she contemplated how love and fear were intertwined in her heart. *I love Rex so much, I can't imagine living without him!* A future in which he played no part was unimaginably bleak. So when he pulled away . . . rejected their life together . . .

The deepest of fears set in.

"I know it's idolatry," Flavia whispered to the window. Tears brimmed in her eyes, obscuring the lovely springtime view of leaves and vines outside. A morning bird chirped, its cheery song incongruous with the sorrow in Flavia's heart. Her prayer was simple: "Forgive me, Lord, for I have sinned."

But despite the plea for mercy, which Flavia knew she would receive from Jesus Christ, the burden upon her soul did not lift. Sin could be forgiven, yet that didn't mean its pain would be whisked away. The feel of it was a deep, dull ache that would not relent. She had taken foolish risks, drunk too much wine, worshiped the security that a man could provide, and finally, succumbed to her fleshly longings. Last night's passion was a guilty pleasure, not sanctioned by God except within the bonds of holy matrimony. Flavia knew this—knew it deep within her soul—and it spoiled what should have been lovely and bright. Morning regret gave Flavia a bloated, yucky feeling after a night of sensual indulgence. Though she wouldn't have said it at the time, when everything seemed new and exciting, she now wished she hadn't made love with Rex—not as anything other than his lawfully wedded wife.

A deep-throated cry from next door snapped Flavia's attention away from her remorseful reflections. Something was terribly wrong, for Rex rarely cried out in pain. Yet this wasn't the sound of a physical attack. It was something emotional. *Maybe guilt is overwhelming him too?*

Flavia quickly dressed in her tunic and sandals, ignoring her tousled hair. She opened the door and peeked out. No one was in the hallway. But in his room, Rex was still grunting. He even seemed to be moving furniture around.

Before Flavia could decide what to do, Rex burst into the hallway. Since it was early and everyone was asleep, he wasn't yelling. But his face was contorted into a mask of frustration and rage.

"Rex! What is it?" Flavia whispered urgently.

"It's gone!"

"What's gone?"

"The money! And the documents! They're not in the chest!"

An icy fear seized Flavia's heart. "Oh, no! Show me!"

She followed Rex into his room and hurried to the sturdy chest, its lid ajar. Inside was nothing but the wooden bottom. Rex insisted he hadn't opened the lockbox since the night he had chained it to his bed. The reality of what this meant settled onto Flavia's shoulders like a millstone.

"Someone stole it," she said forlornly.

"Yes. I checked it this morning and found the box unlocked. There are tiny scratches on the latch, and on my door. Someone very skillful broke in and took everything."

"Who did it? It sounds planned! A robber wouldn't have taken the documents."

"You're right. And he would have rummaged through my other things. This wasn't a robbery. It was an operation. The thief was someone with insider knowledge who knew we were here." A determined look came to Rex's face. "I'm going to get that money back, no matter what it takes."

"Do we need to ask for help?"

"Right now, we should limit who knows."

"I won't tell anyone, then."

"Good. Let's keep it to ourselves until we've solved the crime. I'll fill the chest with sand and guard it like it's still precious. We won't show it to Sylvester until the very last moment—hopefully with the gold back in it."

"But how will we find the gold? It could be anywhere!"

"The trick here is to discern motive. Anyone would have a motive to steal so much money, but taking those documents along means two things. One, the thief is someone who doesn't want churches built in Rome or the scriptures to be copied. Taking our authorization from Constantine puts an end to that. For anyone else, that piece of parchment is worthless."

"The thief must be an enemy of the catholic church."

"Exactly. And two, stealing the letters of credit means he thinks he has a chance to commit fraud. Those letters are worth even more than the gold, but only if he can trick someone at the Temple of Saturn into releasing the funds."

"He might just throw them away. Maybe he only wanted the permission document from Constantine."

"That's possible. But that amount of credit is tempting. It's worth keeping an eye on the treasury to see who shows up."

"I don't think the bankers would give so much money to some lowlife criminal. The letters are made out to the catholic church. It would have to be someone from the clergy."

Rex glanced at Flavia. "Now you're thinking like a speculator," he told her with an appreciative nod. "Our enemy is someone from within the church who opposes Sylvester's building program. They knew we were here, so it must be someone highly placed in the church hierarchy, someone who had heard the news that we were on our way."

"But also someone with expertise at breaking and entering."

"High up in the church, yet a skilled burglar." Rex pursed his lips and shook his head. "I have to admit, it's a strange combination."

"Maybe the enemy hired an expert thief? There are men who will steal things for pay."

"Not likely. With that amount of gold, a hired hand would just take the money and run. This has to be a person who believes in the cause, someone with a higher purpose than just getting rich." For a few moments, Rex paced around the bedroom, considering all the options. Finally, he turned back to Flavia. "You know church politics in Rome better than I do. Is there a faction that opposes Pope Sylvester?"

"Yes, there are still some Gnostics around. They disagree with Sylvester's doctrines about Christ's incarnate body. They say it didn't really happen, it was just an illusion. Their goal is to purge themselves from everything physical. To them, what matters are secret ideas from the world above. So they say we shouldn't erect halls for churches because that is something physical and earthly."

"Who leads that faction?"

The query made Flavia sigh. "I hate to say it, but my old pastor is one of the foremost. His name is Felix. He was in charge of the church that used to meet in my house on the Aventine."

"It doesn't seem like your church would be led by a heretic."

"Felix didn't start out that way. He changed over time. He's handsome and likable, and he seems orthodox until you get to know him."

"Where is he now?"

"When my father abandoned us to marry a little girl, he put our house up for sale. The bishop at that time bought it and made it into a full-time church. Do you remember Pope Miltiades?"

"I do. He was a righteous man."

"He truly was! Miltiades cared about all the flocks of Christians under his care. When my father ran off with his bride, the bishop didn't want our congregation to dissolve. So without my father knowing it, Miltiades bought our house. And with my own money, I paid for a marble plaque to go over the door. The church is now called Saint Sabina in honor of my mother. And Felix is still its pastor because he's tricky. No one has been able to prove his Gnostic leanings."

"Alright. This is enough information to begin with." Rex's voice brimmed with firm resolve. "We can start with Felix and learn what we can about the faction that opposes the new buildings. And if they try for the funds at the Temple of Saturn, we can catch them there. We have two places we need to watch: the temple and your old house. I'd like to leave here immediately and get some reconnaissance in place."

"So early? The sun is barely up."

"I know. But this is pressing on me." Rex looked down at his feet, wagging his head with a look of consternation. "No sooner do I get forgiven by Constantine, than I turn around and fail Ossius and Sylvester by allowing the treasure to be stolen. I'm ashamed of myself."

"No! It's not your fault."

"Then whose is it?" Rex's tone was bitter. "While I was next door with you, I let a thief steal everything you've worked for. I didn't just let those churchmen down. I let *you* down."

And I let God down, Flavia thought, though she couldn't bear to utter the words aloud. Instead, she said, "We should ask the Lord to help us." It was an attempt to reach again for the God whom she had rejected last night.

But Rex shook his head. "I don't want to do that. I don't dare draw his eye upon me."

"God isn't like that, Rex. He's merciful."

"Maybe he is, and maybe he isn't. You go ahead and say your words. I'll listen, but I don't want to stand too close." Rex left the bedroom and went out to the hall but didn't shut the door.

Though Flavia knew Rex was misunderstanding God's ways, she acquiesced to his wishes. Lifting her hands to the red sky out the window, she asked the Lord to help them find the stolen funds and documents. Strangely, while Flavia's words were heartfelt, she could feel an incoherence to them

399

as well. Sin had a way of doing that. It always disrupted relationships, whether human or divine.

When the prayer was finished, Rex reentered the room. "It's convenient for you Christians to be able to pray anywhere," he observed. "In my religion, we have to go to temples and make sacrifices to get the gods' attention."

"Christianity has temples too. But that's not what our buildings are." Flavia put her hand over her heart. "Our bodies are the temple of the Lord."

"Does your book say that?"

"Yes. It says, 'Do you not know that your body is the temple of the Holy Spirit who is within you, whom you have from God?'"

As soon as Flavia uttered those words, the preceding sentence rushed into her mind. Paul's admonition to sinners reawakened the sorrow in her soul. "Flee from sexual immorality!" the apostle had written. "Every sin a man commits is outside the body. But the one who fornicates sins against his own body."

Flavia glanced at Rex, wondering if he could read her guilty expression. But his mind was already on other things. He turned to leave the room, his purposefulness about his mission having taken over.

"I'll go wake up the coachman," he said. "We'll head straight into Rome and find that priest Felix. He might have our money and papers. I intend to get them back from whoever has them. Maybe before too long, we can go back to how things were before."

"Maybe we can," Flavia replied with forced optimism.

Or maybe things have changed forever, said a quiet voice in her heart.

When Rex entered Rome's northern gate on the Flaminian Way, a surge of memories came back to him. He recalled coming here for the first time with his friend Geta and his centurion, Aratus, more than five years ago, when they were beginning a secret spying mission in the capital. He also remembered coming back from Verona, victorious in war yet ashamed of having abandoned his oath-sworn lord. And he even remembered riding through this gate as part of a triumphal parade after Constantine defeated Maxentius at the Milvian Bridge. Maxentius's head, which Rex had severed from his body, was mounted on a spear at the front of the column. On that day, Rex had honorably carried the flag of his former unit, the Second Italian Legion.

It seems so distant, Rex thought as the imperial carriage rolled through the gate. *Like memories from another life.* Yet here he was again. Life had a way of coming full circle.

After transferring from the coach to a litter that their travel certificate allowed them to use, Rex and Flavia were carried through Rome's streets to the Aventine Hill. They alighted a few steps from the former mansion of Senator Neratius Junius Flavianus. Rex pointed to a spindly umbrella pine behind the house. "See that broken branch?" When Flavia spotted it, he said, "I once fell from there onto your roof, and only barely kept myself from hitting the pavement below."

"You're so brave," Flavia said with genuine admiration.

"And foolish," Rex added with a smile. He knew how close he had come to death that day.

The pair stood in a deeply shaded alley between two apartment buildings. The front door of the mansion was visible from here, lined on either side with the street-front shops that most Roman houses rented to the locals for extra income. A doorkeeper stood outside the entrance to the home, though it wasn't Flavia's faithful servant, Onesimus. This was a stockier man whom neither of them recognized.

"I've got to find an excuse to get in that house," Rex said. "There might be some papers lying around the study. Maybe I could even find the gold. Did your father have a vault?"

"No, there's no vault that I know of. His money was kept at the banks, and smaller amounts in lockboxes. Our servants were all Christians, so we trusted them not to break in."

"I just need to look around for a while. I don't think anyone would recognize me with my beard and long hair. It's been too long since I was here, and I was a soldier then. Maybe I could pose as a kitchen delivery man. Just bringing some groceries for the cooks. No one would think twice."

Flavia's eyes lit up, and she gave Rex a mischievous grin. "I think there's a better way to get you inside. They'd let you right through the front door! You could snoop around as much as you want."

"How?"

"You tell me, speculator," Flavia replied coyly. She was clearly delighted with her good idea.

"A repairman? I was thinking of that too. I could break some roof tiles by night, then come back the next day with the tools to fix them."

"Not a grocer, nor a repairman. Something even easier!"

"What?"

"Rex, think about it. What's the best way to get into a mansion like that?"

"I've already given you my best ideas."

Flavia's smile was wide now. "Think harder," she teased. "Remember, it's not a regular house anymore . . ."

"Aha! A religious scribe? Delivering some holy books?"

"No, just go to the church service!"

Now a big grin broke out on Rex's face too. "You trickster!" he exclaimed. "You're trying to convert me!" Yet he had to admit, the plan was excellent. No fake identities were needed, and the house's residents would be expecting visitors—in fact, welcoming them into their midst. "That is actually a great idea. Much better than what I had in mind. Let's do it. When do they meet?"

"Every Sun Day. But Pascha is coming soon. That's when we should go."

"Pascha?"

"The day of the Lord's resurrection is called Pascha. It comes around each spring—the holiest day in the Christian year. It culminates a week of fasting and spiritual preparation. There will be a huge crowd of people who aren't normally around."

"Which would help us blend in."

"Yes. With your beard and a veil over my face, I think we can pass unnoticed. Felix knows me because I was the master's daughter, but he will be too busy to pay attention. And the people who attend the church now are Felix's followers. We're strangers to them."

Rex agreed that the plan was the best option. In the meantime, constant surveillance of the house was essential. Over the next few days, he hired some local idlers to watch the mansion from an inconspicuous distance. The men reported that they often observed Felix coming and going with various ecclesial associates. Rex himself kept an eye on the Temple of Saturn, but he never saw Felix show up there, nor anyone from the catholic church. Apparently, the enemy was laying low for now. Rex found it frustrating, yet he hoped that entering the Aventine mansion would provide immediate results.

When the Paschal day arrived, Rex accompanied Flavia to the church that used to be her home. A deacon welcomed the pair at the door without any recognition in his eyes. Inside, they discovered that some of the former walls had been demolished to create a gathering hall, though it wasn't decorated in any way. The only freestanding objects in the room were a marble altar and a plain lampstand whose clay lamps burned brightly. Light also entered the space through the translucent crystal panes that filled the high windows.

"There are four parts to the service of the Eucharist," Flavia whispered to Rex through her veil. "Entrance, word, sacrament, and dismissal. But we can't stay for the sacrament, since we are unbaptized. The doorkeepers will make us step into a side room. Sometimes they let you listen to the liturgy, but you can never see the sacrifice of the bread and wine until you have been washed in the laver of life."

"Very mysterious," Rex observed.

After separating from Flavia and going to stand with the men, Rex watched the clergy enter the hall. They seemed a little bored and distracted as they made their way to the front of the church. Finally, Felix arrived, walking slowly as if to lend the occasion a solemn air. He took a seat on a throne that had been carved into a semicircular nook at the far end of the hall. The other clergy sat on either side of him.

The second part of the service consisted of readings from the sacred scriptures. Rex found the words beautiful—some from the *Book of Isaiah* about a suffering servant and others from the *Gospel of Luke*, describing the arrest, trials, crucifixion, and resurrection of Jesus. One gospel reading stood out to Rex: an account of the postresurrection Christ talking with his disciples as they walked along a road. Though they could not understand what had just happened to their Lord, he explained to them what it meant and how it had been predicted by the Jewish prophets. "Was it not necessary for the Christ to suffer these things and enter into his glory?" Jesus asked.

Unfortunately, Felix's sermon had nothing to do with these texts. When it was time for him to speak, he received another gospel into his lap, the Gnostic one called *Gospel of Thomas*, from which he proceeded to explain the inner enlightenment that the Heavenly Fullness can bring. Felix concluded with a request from Saint Peter in that gospel: "'Make Mary leave us, for females are not worthy of life.'" But Jesus responded to Peter with the promise, "'Behold, I am going to draw her to make her male, so that she too might become a living spirit, resembling you males. For every female who makes herself male will enter the kingdom of heaven.'" Felix's inference from this text was simple: the true message of Pascha was that all duality must be absorbed into oneness with the Heavenly Fullness. Rex thought this message was nothing like the disciples' response to the empty tomb in the *Gospel of Luke*.

After the portion of the service devoted to the word was over, the door-keepers came to remove people from the congregation, just like Flavia had predicted. The unbaptized were not allowed to partake in—or even see—the Holy Eucharist. Dutifully, the visitors and catechumens exited the hall. Some of them left the church now, but others were allowed to wait in the room that had once been the master's study. Fortunately, the doorkeepers did not stand guard over the worshipers, but left them alone in silent contemplation.

"Now is the time to snoop around," Rex whispered to Flavia. Her face was hidden by her veil, yet he saw her nod in return.

The two of them slipped from the study and went to the rear garden, where the bedrooms were located. Several had been turned into storerooms for charitable goods, while others now served to lodge the monks and deacons who lived here. Most of the rooms were marked off with curtains, and where there were doors, none had locks. Only the mansion's outer doors were bolted against intruders.

"This is my old bedroom," Flavia said, sweeping aside a curtain to peek in. "Now it definitely looks like a man lives here. Look at that rumpled bed."

Rex had been investigating the other rooms but returned and joined Flavia in her bedroom. He went to a cabinet against the wall, the only container that could have held the gold. As he had discovered everywhere else, the implements inside were simple and inexpensive.

Rex had just exited the bedroom and let its curtain drop when a deacon came around the corner. "Can I help you?" he asked in a tone that was both polite and firm.

"The lady seeks a private place for the chamber pot," Rex said smoothly. "It is extremely urgent, or we would use the public facilities."

"You may use this room," the deacon said, gesturing to a small closet with a heavy drape. Flavia went inside while the two men waited at the doorway. After an extended time, she exited again, and the deacon escorted the pair back to the waiting room in awkward silence.

"Thanks a lot, Rex," Flavia whispered through her veil after the deacon left them. Her tone was playfully angry. "That was so embarrassing. Why is it always me?"

"You need to go a lot! It seemed like the most natural explanation."

"It's true," Flavia agreed.

Despite the interruption, Rex's mind was still on the mission. He kept peeking out the doorway of the waiting room. "Are you sure there's no vault in the house?" he finally asked.

"There's no vault, but being here reminded me about the storeroom. It's in the cellar. When I was a girl, it was always locked. However, I hid a key behind a stone because . . ."

Rex glanced at Flavia when she arrested her words. "Because what?"

"Ah, I hate to admit it!"

"You can tell me. What was it?"

"I used to sneak inside and take sips of wine!"

Rex could only chuckle at Flavia's reluctant admission. "What a terrible Christian girl you were," he teased. "Come on, let's go see if your naughty key is still there."

When no one was watching and the way looked clear, the pair once again left the waiting room and hurried to the kitchen. Although the stairs down to the cellar were open, the storeroom in the cellar was secured behind a heavy oaken door.

"Every other room in this house is left completely accessible," Rex said, "which tells me there's something secret in there."

Flavia was inspecting the stones in the cellar wall. "This is it! The one with the streak of quartz." She dug her fingernail behind it and pried it loose. Spinning to face Rex, she swept aside her veil so he could see her bright-eyed look of triumph. A key was in her upraised hand. "Got it!"

"Well, look at that," Rex said with a laugh. "I might even let you have some wine as a reward."

The storeroom door creaked open on its unoiled pivot. Inside, Rex found a dark and musty space much larger than he was expecting. A wine vat was in the middle of the room, about half full. Beyond it was an old winepress that hadn't been used in years. Shelves lined the walls, mostly bare. Empty crates lay scattered around the room as well.

Something on the floor behind the winepress caught Rex's eye. He went around the contraption to discover a pallet with a blanket and a few personal belongings. He was about to inspect the boxes nearby when a deep, resonant voice assaulted him from behind.

"What are you doing here?" the voice demanded in a threatening tone.

Flavia gasped at the same time that Rex whirled to face the speaker. He was a tall, lean fellow in a brown robe. Yet the most distinctive thing about him was not his build but the serpentine tattoo on his brow. A green snake slithered up the man's left jawline and bared its fangs from his forehead. It was an eerie sight, even in the storeroom's gloom.

"Please, sir! Don't report us to the bishop!" Flavia exclaimed. "My friend is a Christian, but he struggles with wine. He can't stop drinking! It has a hold on him, and he does bad things. He's trying to overcome it!"

"Many pleasures of the flesh ensnare the weak," said the olive-skinned man with the tattoo.

Rex came to Flavia's side, staring at the new arrival, whose eyes were cold and beady, his expression unreadable. Yet Rex sensed power in this man—power both human and otherworldly.

"I am glad you interrupted my drinking," Rex said, adopting Flavia's ruse. "I shall leave without having imbibed any of that wicked poison."

"There is no wine over by that pallet," observed the snake-man.

"No, but I was seeking a cup to dip into the vat."

"And did you find what you seek?"

"I found no cup. But I discovered something greater—an insight"

"And what was it?" asked the menacing stranger with an arch of his eyebrow.

"That danger often lies hidden in the harmless things we seek."

The man folded his hands into the sleeves of his brown robe. "The scriptures say, 'Seek and ye shall find.' Be careful, O seeker, or you just might find the danger of which you speak."

"We will be careful," Flavia said in a shaky voice.

"And we will be prepared for whatever we find," Rex added.

The snake-man did not reply. Instead, he approached Rex slowly, inspecting him up and down. Flavia put her hand on Rex's arm, which he understood as a request not to get in a fight. Rex remained still while the tattooed man looked him over. He even went behind Rex, then finally came back to face him.

"Leave," he said simply.

Flavia tugged Rex's sleeve, and the pair headed for the storeroom exit. At the door, Rex noticed that the man had removed Flavia's hidden key from the latch. Apparently, he missed nothing.

The pair had crossed the cellar and begun to ascend to the main floor when the snake-man hailed them one last time. "A word of warning," he called from the storeroom doorway.

Rex looked over his shoulder. "Yes?"

"You have met your match, Brandulf Rex," the man said, then slipped behind the storeroom door and shut it fast.

Rex and Flavia came up from the cellar to the kitchen. Instead of going back to the church's waiting room, they exited through a delivery door to the street outside. The spring sunshine seemed bright in contrast to the cellar's gloom.

"He knew me," Rex said when they had found a quiet place to collect their wits and figure out what just happened.

"He knew both of us."

"How do you know?"

"Because I've seen him before. In Germania."

"What?" Rex was astounded at this announcement. "Why didn't you tell me?"

Flavia shrugged. "He wasn't threatening, so I never thought of it again. It was when we were staying in Brigantium. I found him snooping in your bedroom, but he claimed to be the bread delivery man. He even left you a loaf. Then he went away, and I forgot about him. But that snake tattoo is hard to forget when you see it again."

"Posing as a delivery man is an old speculator's trick," Rex said. "The guy did have the look of an operative. Light on his feet. Trim and agile. We can often recognize each other."

"Is he working against us?"

"Probably. My clothes were poisoned around that time. They were stored in my bedroom. Now, a few months later, my treasure chest was broken into. It seems like too much of a coincidence that my room was infiltrated twice, then bad things happened and this man was nearby both times. And he knew my name. It all adds up."

"He's also living here with Felix. He didn't expect us to be snooping around his bedroll. Those two are working together, obviously."

"I bet our gold is somewhere in your house!" Rex cried with indignation.

He started to move back toward the mansion, but Flavia caught his tunic. "No, don't go! You won't find it now. It would be too well hidden. You'll only reveal yourself to them, and maybe get arrested."

Knowing Flavia was right, Rex acquiesced. For the moment, he was stymied. Yet he was much closer to recovering the gold and documents than when they were first stolen. "You give good advice for a female," Rex said with a mischievous expression. "Maybe Jesus will make you male so you can go to heaven."

"Ugh! I hate how Felix brought that devious book into the Paschal homily. You know it's false, right? The catholic church doesn't accept that fake writing."

"I did know that, actually."

"What did you think of the rest of the service?"

"I thought the liturgy was beautiful. And I will admit, I found Jesus more attractive than I ever have before."

Flavia remained quiet. Rex couldn't tell if she was praying for him or just didn't know how to respond.

"Shall we go?" he finally asked.

"Where to?"

"The Temple of Saturn, to keep watch."

"We're visiting a heretical church and a heathen temple on Pascha," Flavia said with a little shake of her head. "It just doesn't seem right."

"Nothing is right these days, Flavia. It's all a mess."

She paused for a moment, then glanced up and met Rex's eyes. "Not everything," she said. "He is risen."

"He is risen indeed," Rex replied. And for the first time, the words did not feel strange upon his lips.

April 317

The Aegyptian Asp mounted the steps of the Temple of Saturn with Felix beside him. He paused on the porch and gazed up at the temple's high pediment, supported by impressive Ionic columns. Ever since ancient Republican times when the spoils of war flowed into Rome, Saturn's temple on the Forum had served as a bank for the Senate and other rich men. Then, with the rise of single emperors under Caesar Augustus, the temple began to house the imperial treasury in the capital city.

But today, the Imperial College had multiplied the number of emperors and spread them across the realm, along with their respective mints and treasuries. Other banks in Rome now catered to wealthy locals. The imperial financial system was vast and incredibly complex. Even so, the Temple of Saturn still retained some of its ancient prerogatives. In time-honored fashion, it made loans and disbursed funds from its convenient location across from the Senate House. And God willing, it would do so again today, if the Aegyptian Asp's plan worked like he hoped.

"Is the bank in there with the idol?" Felix asked, peering through the main temple door. The reluctance in the priest's voice was obvious. No Christian, not even a Gnostic, wanted to get near idols.

"The treasury is around the side and underneath. I just wanted to see the view from the porch. Let us go down now. And remember your role."

The two men descended the stairs and went to a side door that led to a room in the temple's massive platform. It was really just an opening in the giant tufa blocks that supported the temple above. *Nobody will be breaking into this place by force*, the Asp thought as he ran his hand along the impenetrable stone wall. *However, breaking in by trickery is another matter!*

A bored-looking man behind a counter greeted the visitors. "Hail," he said gruffly.

The Aegyptian Asp strode to the counter with a confident, though not intimidating, demeanor. He looked the banker in the eyes as he spoke. "We have come to collect a loan granted to us by the Augustus of the West, His Imperial Majesty, Flavius Valerius Constantine."

"He is far away," said the banker, "and I have heard nothing of this."

"Of course not. How could you? The papers have only just arrived."

"And who are you? Senators don't wear brown hemp-cloth, nor have tattoos on their faces."

"Did I claim to be a senator?"

"Who else gets big loans from Constantine?"

"The catholic church. Surely you know of his conversion to Christianity and his generous patronage of that sect?"

"Everyone knows about his conversion. But if you want any money, you're going to have to produce the right documents."

"We have them right here." The Asp brought around the tubular capsa that was slung on his back. He unbuckled its end cap and withdrew a rolled parchment. The seal on it was still unbroken. "These loans are to be disbursed in payouts of one million denarii. That is the amount we seek today. Later, we shall come back for more."

"We shall see," said the banker. He picked up a water-filled magnifying globe and inspected the seal for longer than seemed necessary. At last, he shrugged and glanced up. "It looks legitimate."

"Of course it is. Now open it."

The banker broke the seal and unrolled the scroll. His eyes scanned the page as he read the Latin words. Setting it down, he said with grudging admiration, "Fifty million denarii, to be paid in increments of a million. The emperor must really like the Christians."

"It is his chosen religion. We are two of its top representatives."

Glancing over the Asp's shoulder, the surly banker asked, "Who's this fellow?"

"You do not recognize the eminent bishop, Ossius of Corduba? Do you not see his elegant robe, emblazoned with crosses? He is one of the most important men in the empire, for he has Constantine's ear at all times. The loans may only be paid out to him or the pope."

"I have heard the name, but I thought he would be an older man."

Felix now stepped forward and assumed a place next to the Aegyptian Asp at the counter. "I am older than I look, yet not so old as to forget obstinate bureaucrats who thwart the emperor's wishes. That is just the sort of thing I often mention to my friend Constantine. It frustrates him greatly! Fortunately, he usually corrects the problem by decreeing a harsh punishment."

"Hey, now! I'm not being obstinate! Just doing my job."

"Then let's get on with your job," Felix said, "lest you start to seem obstinate in my recollections."

"One thing at a time!" the banker exclaimed, a little nervous now. "Before I can give you any money, I need two witnesses to vouch that the payee is who he claims to be. Both witnesses must sign an affidavit. And one must be a known senator of this city."

"I shall serve as one of the witnesses," said the Asp. "I am Eutychius of Alexandria, abba of the monastic commune of Saint Anthony and prelate of the suffragan diocese of Thebes."

From the bewildered look on the banker's face, the Asp knew he didn't understand all the fake ecclesiastical jargon. But the words were lofty enough to sound convincingly Christian.

"The affidavit is here," said the banker, sliding the document across the counter along with a reed pen and inkpot. "Bishop Ossius must sign first. Then you may sign as well. But a senator known to me must countersign it, or the transaction is not valid."

Felix bowed his head in a solemn fashion. "The Christian senator who intended to come with us today has taken ill. We had hoped that you might know a cooperative senator to help us complete the loan."

At this, the banker's face grew sly. "Excuse me for a moment while I go get the funds. And . . . would you gentlemen like some wine?"

"Wine would be appreciated," said the Asp.

The banker disappeared into the rear vault for a long time. Eventually, he came out carrying a crate with rope handles. Heaving it onto the counter, he opened it and took out ten sacks bulging with coins. The sacks were the same size as the seven that the Asp had pilfered from the treasure chest of his enemies, each of which held a hundred thousand denarii in gold solidi. *One million here, plus seven hundred thousand before . . . an incredible sum!* A fortune like this would go far in helping Melitius take over the Aegyptian church—and it would destroy Rome's architectural aspirations at the same time. *Praise God!*

Now the banker returned his attention to his affidavit. He wrote down the numeral X for the number of sacks being disbursed today. The signatures of "Bishop Ossius" and "Abba Eutychius" were affixed next. Yet the third blank still required a senator's name. Dipping his reed into the pot, the banker put its tip to the page—then removed it and set down his instrument. "I am thirsty," he declared.

"By all means, take a drink," said the Asp.

A jug and three glasses were brought from under the counter. The banker, who now seemed even more nervous than before, poured wine for himself and his customers. After taking a long draught, he set his cup aside and resumed his writing. He scrawled a messy name on the page, then glanced up from beneath his prickly eyebrows. "You are taking nine sacks away today, yes?"

"Nine!" exclaimed Felix. "Ten are sitting here!"

With a swift movement, the banker snatched one sack and set it under the counter. "No, kind sir. As you can see, there are only nine. Count them."

"You're taking too much!" Felix complained.

"I'm taking much risk," the banker replied.

"Extortion!"

"Compensation," came the quick response.

The two men glared at each other, but the Aegyptian Asp soothed them both. "All is well, friends," he said. "Both sides are satisfied. We are willing to let some of it go. Let us finish the transaction."

Smiling, the banker picked up his cup and sipped from it again. Then, after dipping his finger, he dribbled a crimson droplet onto the senator's indistinct name. "Oh! What a mistake," he said with mock alarm. "Perhaps I can fix it." He smeared the wine around, mixing it with the fresh ink, until the name was completely illegible. After making a little *tsk*, he said, "How unfortunate! I have accidentally obscured the signature that attests to this disbursement of ten moneybags from the vault."

The Aegyptian Asp gave the dishonest banker a friendly grin. He replaced the nine sacks in the crate and closed the lid. Lifting it by the handles, he tested its weight for a moment, then set it back on the counter. "Strange how this box of ten bags feels a bit lighter than it should."

"That is indeed strange," the banker agreed with a straight face.

Felix leaned close to the Asp as the two men prepared to leave. "This is a large amount, even with the deduction," the priest whispered to his companion. "Will we be safe in the streets?"

The banker overheard the remark. Waving his hand around, he dismissed the concern. "Do not worry about that, my friend. The Urban Cohorts have a station outside. They will escort you to your destination. You may leave now with your loan."

"Then let us be going," said the Asp as he hoisted the box from the counter.

"Stay right where you are," said a stern voice from behind the men.

——◦◦◦——

Rex's bold words to the two swindlers had the ring of authority that came from his deep voice and imposing stature. Nevertheless, Flavia knew he would have preferred to have a good spatha on his hip to back up his commands. As a civilian, he couldn't carry a sword in the streets of Rome. Rex was going to have to win this battle with his words—and maybe his fists, if it came to that.

The tattooed man set down the box, then turned and stood side by side with Felix at the counter. A look of recognition came to the priest's face as he spied Flavia. Several years back, he had been her pastor, when the Aventine congregation met in her private home.

"You've grown up, Lady Junia," he said with little emotion in his voice.

"And you are much the same, Felix." Flavia didn't think the priest deserved the honorable title of "father" when he was in the midst of committing fraud.

Rex took a step forward, though he didn't make any sudden moves. Even so, Felix positioned himself between Rex and the man in the brown robe, as if to defend him. "It is a sin to harm a priest of God," Felix declared.

"You might be surprised by how quickly I can sin."

"God would curse your heathen soul, German!"

"Maybe he already has," Rex shot back. He interlocked his fingers and cracked his knuckles as he took another step forward. "So what have I got to lose?"

The man with the snake tattoo finally spoke up. "Bishop Ossius, let us be going now. I'd like you to carry the load. Pick it up, please, and we shall be off."

"Don't touch that box," Rex warned.

A haughty smile came to the snake-man's face. "We have all the right paperwork, sir. This loan legally belongs to us. If you interfere, you shall be arrested."

413

Flavia knew the assertion wasn't true. She and Rex had been watching the Aventine house church for many days, even paying some pickpockets to follow the devious priest on his errands. When he and the brown-robed monk set out this morning with a capsa of documents, Rex had known immediately that something was up. He had followed the sneaky pair to the Temple of Saturn, then eavesdropped outside the bank until the fraud was complete before confronting them.

Rex's reply to the snake-man was a bold challenge. "If you have the letters, let's see them. Bring them forth! I suspect we will find they are made out to Bishop Ossius of Corduba."

"I am he," said Felix.

"You lie. And it will soon be known." Rex glanced to the frightened banker cowering behind his counter. "Hey, you! Yes, you there! Stand up."

The man finally rose to his full height, which wasn't much. "I'm just a c-clerk," he stammered.

"Did you make a disbursement to this priest under the name I just mentioned?"

"Yes, but he had all the proper witnesses! How was I supposed to know what this Ossius looks like?"

"He's a lot more distinguished than that faker," Flavia accused, jabbing her finger at Felix.

Rex crossed his arms over his chest. "I think it's time we call the Urban Cohorts in here to sort this matter out."

"No!" the banker cried. "They're idiots and ruffians!"

"Maybe so, but they can read those letters of credit and authenticate the witnesses."

Rex had just started for the door when the banker did something that changed the dynamic in his favor. Grabbing a handbell, he began to ring it furiously. "Thieves!" he shouted, though it was actually he who was the thief. "Help me! Come quick! Thieves!"

"Oh, great," Rex muttered, and the chase began.

Still wearing the leather capsa over his shoulder, the snake-man made a dash for the door before the policemen could arrive. Though Rex reached for him, the fugitive was surprisingly agile and eluded the grab. "Stay here and explain!" Rex shouted to Flavia as he followed his quarry out the door.

Four husky policemen from the Urban Cohorts burst into the bank while the bell was still clanging in the clerk's hand. "The girl is with them! She's a thief!" cried the lying banker.

"No, it's a scam! They're the thieves!" Flavia shouted in reply.

"Silence, everyone!" barked the police captain.

Though the handbell stopped ringing, the hubbub in the little room did not immediately abate. Both the banker and Felix started accusing Flavia of trying to defraud respectable citizens. They portrayed Rex as a "hired thug" to carry out her bidding. Strangely, the policemen seemed inclined to believe the banker, despite his unwillingness to show them his ledger book. He kept insisting it was too messy for them to read, so they should focus instead on the lady committing fraud.

"You're coming with us, little miss," the police captain said. "Step outside."

"But these men—"

"Shut your mouth and step outside," another policeman snapped.

Right then, Flavia realized she wouldn't get a fair hearing from the Urban Cohorts no matter what she might say. Stepping into the bright sunshine, she glanced around while the men were guffawing at some crude joke that one of them made. A nearby oxcart provided what she needed. It was situated next to a wall, with a gap behind it that only she could fit through. Before the men could stop her, she darted to the narrow space and slipped past the cart.

Although one of the policemen yelled for his comrades to go after her, the captain countered with a command of his own. "Stay put! The money is still here. Our job is to make sure it goes safely with the priest. We aren't paid to be prosecutors. Just let her go."

Flavia hurried away from the Temple of Saturn, glad to be free of the wretched place. A commotion up ahead made her raise her eyes. Across the Forum, the brown-robed fugitive was nearing the House of the Vestal Virgins. But Rex was close behind!

As quickly as she could, Flavia made her way to the house of pagan priestesses. She felt tired and weak under the hot sun, because ever since her transgression with Rex, she had been fasting in penance. Yet she pressed on. Winding through the crowds that paid her no mind, she finally reached the beautiful building.

The sound of shouting from inside indicated that the two men had invaded the precincts where only women were supposed to go. Flavia tried the main door but found it bolted. However, she knew a secret way in. Years ago, she had taken refuge here when evil soldiers were trying to kill her. A kindly maid in the house, moved by pity, had shown Flavia a hidden door. Unfortunately, the soldiers captured her nonetheless and slapped her in chains. It was just after this when Rex—a total stranger at the time—stepped from the crowd to promise rescue. And he had been rescuing her ever since.

The secret entrance was around back, in a narrow alley at the foot of the Palatine Hill. She went there now and found the little door to be even more obscured by woody shrubs than before. Trying its handle, she felt it give and slipped inside.

The House of the Vestals was centered on an oblong courtyard with three reflective pools. Marble statues of famous Supreme Vestals adorned the space, and rooms for the virgin priestesses and their servants lined the two-story colonnade that surrounded the courtyard. But the noise wasn't coming from the center of the house. The disturbance had moved to the rear annex, which enclosed the ancient temple of the goddess Vesta. It had been standing there since the beginning of Rome itself. The city's second king had built the rotunda more than a thousand years ago. It served as the ceremonial hearth of the citizenry, just as in every good Roman home it was the job of the virgin daughter to keep the hearth fire going.

Hurrying there, Flavia found the annex full of frightened servants, as well as two of the six noble priestesses. Yet they were young ones, still children who lacked authority. Like the servants, they were paralyzed into inaction. All the women just stood there gawking at the Temple of Vesta, whose round shape imitated the huts of Rome's original settlers. Its ornate wooden doors were wide open.

"Call the Urban Cohorts!" a cherubic little priestess exclaimed.

"No! Never let a man enter!" replied someone else.

"In times of extreme need, we can!" a third voice insisted.

"Call for the Supreme Vestal," said the little girl. "She will know what to do!"

Instead of hesitating to debate the ancient rules, Flavia pushed her way through the crowd and approached the temple. A portico supported by

Corinthian columns ran around its exterior. High above, a column of smoke rose from the hole in its roof.

Shouts and threats from inside could be heard when Flavia reached the porch. Glancing in, she saw Rex on the near side of a huge brazier made of bronze, while the snake-man was trapped on the far side. Each time Rex's enemy would circle toward the door, Rex would move to intercept him. The man would retreat the other way, only to be blocked again. The two adversaries were in a perfect stalemate. Flavia resolved to help Rex change the odds in their favor.

"You go left, and I'll go right," she called to Rex.

He glanced over his shoulder, surprised to see her. "No, stay back! He has a deadly razor. He'll cut you!"

Flavia saw that Rex was right. The man had a wicked-looking blade in his fist. He held the leather capsa in the other.

"The Urban Cohorts are coming!" Flavia warned the evil monk. "You won't get away with your theft!"

"I already have. Your gold is mine."

"We'll get it back!"

"Not likely, little one."

Rex drew Flavia's attention to a handcart stacked with firewood. "Push that cart next to the brazier and block him on that side," Rex instructed. "Then scatter some logs on the floor. But stay back from his blade if he gets close."

Flavia did as Rex requested, obstructing the right side of the brazier with the cart and logs. In the small, round temple, it wouldn't be easy to dart past the barricade. Now Rex began to move left. As the snake-man backed away, he looked angry and desperate. Rex was likely to catch him as he stumbled around the cart on the log-strewn floor.

"You're mine now," Rex warned.

Outside, sharp male commands and female shrieks indicated that the Urban Cohorts had finally been admitted into the house. In a moment, they would be at the temple.

"Give me those papers!" Rex cried, making his move.

Three things happened in such quick succession, they seemed to Flavia like one event. First, the policemen arrived in the doorway and began to follow Rex around the brazier's left side. Then the snake-man darted right but was slowed by the obstruction. Rex was about to grab him when the third thing happened—a terrible and shocking surprise.

Turning toward the bronze basin, the man hurled the capsa into the lively flame. It came to rest in a bed of white-hot coals. The leather case immediately began to curl and burn.

"Get it out!" Flavia cried.

Aghast, Rex stopped his pursuit and turned toward the fire tools. A long iron poker leaned against the wall. He ran to get it, but as he picked it up in two hands, the snake-man lunged and slashed Rex across the back of his thigh.

"Argh!" Rex cried, dropping the poker with a loud clang. Bright red blood spattered the floor.

"God curse you," the assailant snarled as Rex staggered away. Then, with an evil grin on his serpentine face, he turned and fled from the Temple of Vesta.

———◦/◦/◦———

It was almost a week before Rex could finally stand on both legs. Even then, it was difficult, for the wound had bled a lot, leaving him weak and nauseated. The surgeons had closed the gash with silk thread, fifty stitches in all. Fortunately, Rex had sensed his enemy's lunge at the last moment, so he had flinched just before the razor swept past his leg.

"It's a good thing you moved," the surgeon had told him, "or you would have been hamstrung and crippled for life."

The catholic church had been generous to provide for Rex's medical care. Even so, he was anxious to be out and about again. It wasn't like him to lie abed for days on end. Yet he couldn't help but feel that the boring recuperation at the Lateran Palace was preferable to the event scheduled for today: a formal audience with Pope Sylvester. Although Rex had stalled as long as he could, the church leaders had finally learned of the theft at the inn. Now it was time to give an official report of the mission, even though the basic facts were already known. Rex was dreading it, and he imagined Flavia was too. They had nothing to report but failure.

A litter arrived, the simple kind used indoors. It was really nothing more than a chair on poles carried by two slaves. With difficulty, Rex got himself into the chair and was lifted from the floor. He could walk only a few steps before needing to sit down. Riding in a litter was a necessary annoyance for now.

As he was borne along, he examined the lavish architecture of the Lateran Palace. It felt strange to be staying here as a guest of the bishop of Rome. Rex had been here once before, not as a guest but with the intent to kill the master of the house. Centuries ago, the Laterani family owned this place. It then passed to Constantine's wife, Fausta. But when her brother Maxentius ruled Rome, he took it from the sister he despised and gave it instead to the cavalry commander he trusted: Ruricius Pompeianus. That man was Flavia's mortal enemy, so Rex had briefly considered assassinating him. Though the plan failed, Rex later killed him in war.

How things have changed since then! When Constantine took over the city, he awarded the palace to the catholic church and razed the cavalry fort to the ground. Ever since then, Pope Sylvester had been hoping for permission to build a glorious church on the empty lot. And just when it was about to happen, Rex had let the necessary documents go up through the smoke hole at the Temple of Vesta.

Ach! It's all my fault, Rex thought glumly as the litter arrived at his destination. He stepped down and leaned on his crutch. Resigned to his fate, he prepared to enter the palace's audience hall that served as the temporary—or now maybe permanent—Lateran Church.

"Rex, wait for me," said a voice he immediately recognized. Turning stiffly, he saw Flavia coming toward him. Her downcast face showed that she felt just as dejected as he did.

"Come stand by me," Rex said. "We've done this whole mission together. We might as well finish it that way."

Flavia sighed heavily. "Oh, Rex! Do you really think it's finished?"

"What else? We can't go back to Constantine. He's far across the empire. And even if he would issue new letters, the bishop wouldn't send us to get them. We had our chance. Our mission failed."

"So be it. God's will be done." Flavia punctuated her statement by making the sign of the cross over herself. Rex thought she looked gaunt from her penitential fasting.

"Let's get this over with," he said, beckoning Flavia toward the door with a nod. Side by side, they entered the room.

The church hall had been set up with seats for everyone, which wasn't the normal case during Sun Day worship when the congregation stood. Sylvester wasn't sitting on his formal cathedra today but had drawn up a chair among his circle of guests. In addition to the pope, Bishop Ossius was there, finally recovered from his illness. It had turned out to be much more serious than anyone had anticipated, so he had spent several weeks recuperating at the inn. Sophronia, who had nursed him so faithfully during those dark days, was seated beside him. Stephen and Cassi were there too, for each had played a role in the mission. The archdeacon Quintus also had a place—and Rex noticed that for some strange reason, his seat alone had thick cushions upon it. Two empty chairs awaited the final guests. Rex hobbled over and sat down with Flavia at his side.

"I welcome you to this gathering with all due solemnity," Sylvester said, speaking with the stiff decorum of a council host, or perhaps with the sternness of a displeased master. It was hard to read the bishop's somber tone. Rex hoped it was due to the gravity of the occasion.

After the opening formalities were finished, Ossius was asked to give a full report of all that had transpired since he departed Sicilia with the three nuns. Rex had to admit, the telling of the tale was astounding: the capture by pirates, the rescue of the women from enslavement, the oration at Mars Hill, the escape of Ossius from a burning ship, the adventurous life at sea, the assistance from Bishop Basil of Thessalonica, the journey to Germania, the toppling of Aoric, two mighty battles, and the final defeat of Licinius. After all this, Constantine's grant of the rescript and gold, followed by the safe journey back to Italy, formed what should have been a grand conclusion.

"But then, Your Holiness, things took a different turn," Ossius said blandly. "I will let another member of our party continue the report." He swept his hand toward Rex with a disapproving glare.

Though Rex felt ashamed, he also realized that he had endured too much on behalf of his comrades for him to grovel in this moment. The final failure of the mission didn't mean that many brave and sacrificial deeds hadn't been done along the way. Even so, the sting of guilt was acute. Rex didn't like to fail at anything. He certainly didn't like having to admit it in front of people he respected. But worst of all was the realization that his own failure had brought shame upon Flavia. He wasn't sure how much the people in the room knew about the night at the inn, but they probably had their suspicions. There was no good explanation for why Rex wasn't in the room when the treasure chest was pilfered. He resolved not to let that subject come up here.

"Your Holiness, there are powerful forces working against your plan in Rome," Rex explained. "Enemies within your church have recruited skilled allies, men who are adept at theft and poisons and secret plots. One enemy in particular stands out—a man with a serpent tattoo on his cheek and forehead."

"We have learned he is called the Aegyptian Asp," said Sylvester. "A fitting name for a venomous man."

"I have heard that name!" Flavia exclaimed. "Long ago, when I attended a council of bishops in Arelate. I followed Melitius of Wolf City into a shop, and he wrote a letter to this wicked person."

Sylvester frowned at this but did not reply.

"It was the Aegyptian Asp who slashed me and gave me this limp," Rex said. "Probably it is he who stole the gold and documents from my room. And he appears to have poisoned my clothes in Germania with essence of bitter almond, which nearly killed me."

Sylvester's face was grave as he nodded. "He is as crafty as the Serpent he serves."

"That man used our letters of credit to make a withdrawal from the treasury at Saturn's temple," Rex went on. "Father Felix, the priest of Saint Sabina upon the Aventine, posed as Bishop Ossius and countersigned the documents. Then they bribed the man at the counter and forged a third name. We believe they made off with one million denarii in gold coins, minus whatever they paid the clerk."

"The Lord take vengeance on him!" Ossius cried, clearly outraged by the devious trickery. Though he didn't dare curse his enemies, he was certainly willing to invoke divine justice.

The pope did not rebuke the Spanish bishop. He only regarded him with a brief stare before turning back to Rex. "And the imperial rescript? The permissions from Constantine that he granted at Serdica?"

"Burned to ash," Rex replied, looking the bishop in the eye, though not with disrespect. "The man you called the Aegyptian Asp hurled them into the fire when I cornered him in the Temple of Vesta. He then injured me with a razor before he escaped."

Ossius could contain himself no longer. "Why did he have the papers in the first place, Brandulf Rex? You were supposed to be our guard!"

These hard words caused Flavia to burst into the conversation. Her eyes were fiery as she said to Ossius, "Esteemed bishop, he *was* our guard! A courageous one, again and again! Think of how many times Rex defended us at the risk of his own life. But this time . . ."

Though Flavia's words trailed off, her mother jumped in to finish the thought. "This time, our enemy got the best of us. He is a skilled man too. He caught us unaware. It happens to even the greatest warriors."

"But he stole the documents from your room, Rex! Do you slumber like a log? I thought you speculators were light sleepers, always ready for nighttime attacks!"

Rex stared at the floor as he weighed his reply to Ossius. He was about to speak when Sophronia intervened again. Turning to the handsome Spaniard, she rested a hand on his sleeve. "Do you remember, my friend, when you were sick at the inn?"

"Of course."

"Do you remember what you asked me to fetch from Rex's room?"

Rex and Flavia exchanged nervous glances. They had no idea where this conversation was going.

"I do remember," Ossius admitted.

"Are you willing to say it?"

Embarrassed, the bishop muttered, "A second chamber pot."

The implications were obvious to everyone: Rex had no chamber pot in his room that night. If he had needed it, he would have had to go out. Although Sophronia's insinuation was not a lie, neither was it the reason that the Asp was able to carry out his theft. Sophronia had only mentioned a circumstance that could be understood in various ways. An awkward silence descended on the group, for no one wanted to press the matter.

"I am very sorry I let the gold and papers be taken from me," Rex said at last. He glanced to the faces of everyone around him. "I humbly ask your forgiveness."

Sylvester smiled gently. "It is granted, young Rex. We shall speak no more of this. The story is now fully told. And praise be to God, his grace has prevailed."

With those words, the bishop motioned to Quintus. The archdeacon rose from his chair and went to the door of the grand hall. Opening it, he held it aside as a plump yet stately matron swept into the room. She wore a diadem on her brow and was clad in a sumptuous gown of blue and gold.

Queen Mother Helena!

Everyone jumped to their feet. Pope Sylvester alone seemed unsurprised. Rex leaned on his crutch and bowed as low as he could while the royal lady approached. All the others bowed as well.

"Greetings to each of you in the name of the Lord," Helena said. "You may straighten up and take your seats. I shall sit among you, as a fellow Christian should. We are all brothers and sisters here."

After making herself comfortable in Quintus's cushioned chair, the queen explained the reason for her visit. "I arrived in Rome only two days ago, unannounced to Pope Sylvester. He has informed me of all that has recently transpired. Now I share with you what I have already told him. Among many other matters of business, I have been sent to inform the Roman Senate of a new position my son has created. A chosen man shall have supreme financial authority in the realm, aided by a large team of clerks. His name is Marcus Sextus. He is to be called the Count of Sacred Benefactions."

"We shall humbly abide by the count's wishes," Sylvester said, "and we are grateful for his generosity to the catholic church."

"Indeed, the count is generous—but a stern master too." Helena's eyes narrowed with disapproval. "His new office will pursue that fraudulent priest of yours with the full authority of the law and recover the embezzled funds as soon as possible."

The pope closed his eyes and dipped his chin in a gesture of humble respect. "We will cooperate to the utmost, Your Highness."

"See that you do. And in the meantime, I want you to continue with your existing plans. I have come to inform you that while the rescripts from my son may have been stolen and burned, the will of Emperor Constantine still prevails. He approved of your buildings and your book. His will must go forward, and I am in Rome to make sure it does. You may proceed with the construction, receiving full funding from the count's new office."

Though it looked as though Ossius would nearly burst from his chair at this announcement, he managed to stay seated by gripping the armrests. "God be praised!" he exclaimed. But then he paused for a moment, his jubilation seemingly curtailed. "Will the Senate and the treasury accept your word?"

Now it was Sylvester's turn to make a surprising revelation. "They had better, for this is no private citizen who sits before you today. Not anymore! The great Constantine has declared his mother to be a Most Noble Woman of the realm, holding all the rights and privileges that such a designation gives her. It is one step below the rank of Augusta! Our Lady Helena is now one of the supreme rulers of the empire. Her every command has the force of law."

"God be praised!" Ossius exclaimed again. This time, his chair could not hold him, so he leapt from his seat and crossed to a signboard that stood behind the gathered friends. On it was drawn a map of Rome. "We shall build the Lateran Church of the Savior right here," he said, pointing to a mark just inside the Aurelian Walls where everyone now sat. "Then we shall surround the city with martyr churches—here, here, here, and here!" Ossius's finger stopped at various points outside the walls, from the Tomb of Paul on the road to Ostia to the Apostolic Monument on the Appian Way.

Everyone smiled at the bishop's enthusiasm. Helena's grin was the widest of all. She clapped her hands in agreement. But Pope Sylvester then beckoned the friends to come near. "There is one more thing you must know," he said mysteriously. "Your mission is not quite finished."

Intrigued, Rex leaned in, though he wasn't the only one whose curiosity had been piqued. Everyone wanted to hear what Sylvester was about to reveal.

"The relics of Saint Peter rest inside the Apostolic Monument," the pope declared. "Does everyone believe this?"

"Yes, of course," Sophronia said. "I once celebrated a love feast there, paid for by Flavia at her behest. It is a lovely garden, and the meal takes place in the presence of the holy bones."

"It isn't true. The bones aren't there."

At this revelation, a stunned silence descended upon the group. For a long moment, no one said a word. The pope did nothing to break the tension. He simply waited.

"If the bones aren't there . . . then where are they?" Ossius finally asked as he returned to his seat.

"Right now, no one knows where the relics reside, for the grave in which they rest has been lost to memory. Or, at least, no one at the top of the catholic hierarchy remembers it. There may be some old-timers who know. Or there may be records in the archives. We must learn the truth. I am entrusting all of you with the mission of finding out."

"You still trust us?" Rex asked, astonished that the pope would want anything from him any longer.

"Of course, young Rex," Sylvester replied. "Did I not say that God's grace has prevailed? With true grace comes true restoration."

Humbled, Rex fell silent. Thankfulness and amazement flooded his soul at this unexpected turn of events.

"Of all the churches outside the walls, the one devoted to Saint Peter shall be the foremost," Sylvester went on. "It shall stand above the grave of the apostle, out on the Vatican Hill. The whole world will come and visit this great marvel! But of course, it must be located in the proper place."

"That is essential," Ossius agreed. "What is a pilgrimage church without real relics and a tomb? Only a circus show for the people. Never should such a thing be built! It is the bones of the saints that localize their memory. And it is the exact place of their burial that serves as an especially appropriate destination for prayer."

Now Sylvester rose to his feet. With stately dignity, he addressed the group, though he spoke especially to the queen. "Our brother Ossius is correct. Once we have located the grave and relics of Saint Peter, foremost of the apostles, we will build our basilica there. Then the church of Rome will rise to great prominence. Its orthodox doctrines will go forth, and its holy scriptures will be embraced by all believers. The Gnostics and other pretenders will be diminished. We will strike bonds of unity with like-minded churches across the empire, the ones that also stand for truth. Heresy will be defeated, and the risen Christ will be exalted in every place. Truly, it is a noble and sacred task that lies before us."

A strong emotion welled up in Rex—a feeling of gratitude that impelled him to speak. "I have failed you once," he said solemnly, "but I will not fail you again. I will accomplish this task and regain my honor."

"And I will be at your side," Flavia declared.

"Me too," said Stephen.

Even timid Cassi chimed in. "I will help too, if I can, for the glory of Jesus."

Ossius and Sophronia gave approving glances to the four comrades. "Our role shall be to support you in prayer," Sophronia said, "an invisible role, yet one that is most vital of all."

Satisfied by the decision, the queen commanded that it should be so. "I am confident in this endeavor!" she added. "Well do I remember that day when Licinius captured me, then brave Rex came galloping to my rescue. My son remains grateful for that bold deed. You are all fine and faithful Christian people. I know you will accomplish this task."

"Yes, they will," said Sylvester, "by the grace of God." The pope lifted his hands toward heaven in a prayerful way. "Soon, Saint Peter's Basilica will house the greatest relics in all the Roman Empire."

Helena, however, had another idea. "They shall be the greatest for a time," she countered, "until an even greater relic might be found." The unexpected statement made all eyes turn toward the queen.

"Like what, my lady?" Flavia asked.

A gentle smile came to the queen's lips, and the gleam of pious aspirations was in her eyes. "The True Cross," she replied, "but that is a matter for another day."

<hr />

MAY 317

Flavia's admiration for Cassi's humble Christian spirit had always been high. The girls had been drawn to each other since the first day they met in the Sicilian convent. Now, having spent almost a year on a journey with her Aethiopian friend, Flavia adored Cassi even more.

Although Cassi was not Flavia's servant, she took joy in serving Flavia in a Christlike manner. She often performed the household duties that needed doing without ever being asked. Today the young African nun had just returned from the laundry room, having washed the women's tunics, and hung them to dry in the sun. Their undergarments were clean too, along with the linen rags that the women used each month.

"I thought you might be needing these," Cassi said as she set down the basket of menstrual rags.

"I would have thought so too, by now." Flavia smiled and shrugged. "But I'm not complaining."

Cassi gave Flavia a strange look. "How late?"

"Quite late. More than a week, actually."

Flavia was seated on her bed in a guest room at the Lateran Palace. Cassi came over and sat beside her. Both of them were lost in thought for a time. Finally, Cassi said, "Your emotions lately have been more turbulent than normal."

To this, Flavia could only sigh. "I am sorry, my friend. Life has been hard."

For a while longer, the two girls remained silent. Then Cassi suddenly poked Flavia's breast.

"Ouch!" she squealed. "That hurt!"

Cassi stared wide-eyed at Flavia, and with dawning horror, Flavia discerned her friend's suspicions.

"No, Cassi . . . I don't think . . ."

"Perhaps not. Perhaps it is nothing. But is it possible?"

Flavia hung her head, and she could feel her cheeks burning. She scrunched her face, trying to hold back tears of shame. After a long time, she nodded. "It is possible," she admitted.

"It has been too long since Germania for it to be . . ."

Again, Flavia nodded.

"Then could it be Rex?"

A third nod.

Cassi sighed deeply at this. "If it is true, it usually makes men run away."

"I know," Flavia whispered. "That is my greatest fear."

14

MAY 317

It took three long weeks for Rex to finish recuperating at the Lateran Palace. Although he did not, of course, share a room with Flavia, he did find it strange to be living in the same house with her like an older brother. "Maybe it's a spiritual marriage," he had quipped, but she didn't laugh at the remark, and the joke fell flat.

Yawning and stretching, he swung his feet to the floor. Early morning sunlight poured through the shutters, so he opened them and looked outside. It was late May now. The weather was warm and sunny, and all the flowerpots overflowed with color. Spring had come in full to the Eternal City.

He turned back to the room and removed his tunic and Germanic trousers from a peg, then put them on without any trouble. The doctor who removed Rex's stitches last night had pronounced him completely healed. Yet he would always have a scar across the back of his leg to remind him of his encounter with the Aegyptian Asp.

Who is that man? he wondered. Although Rex didn't know much about his enemy, he felt confident they would run into each other again.

A busy day lay ahead, but Rex was ready to be out of the house and on a mission again. It was Flavia who had proposed the idea for the day's sleuthing. "If we're going to find out about Saint Peter," she had said, "we need to learn everything about him in the church's traditions. No one has a better library of the church fathers than Alexamenos."

Rex agreed, so a message was sent to their old friend to let him know that a visit was imminent.

The morning sun was still low in the sky when Rex, Flavia, Stephen, and Cassi reached Alexamenos's home, known as Gelotiana House. The Greek schoolteacher's job was to instruct the page boys who served the imperial palace on the Palatine Hill. Though no emperor was in Rome anymore, the palace still had a huge bureaucracy. Its important dignitaries required the page boys' constant service.

"Welcome, dear friends!" Alexamenos cried when he saw Flavia and Rex. He was a slender man with dark curly hair that was beginning to show a little gray. After he was introduced to Cassi and Stephen, everyone adjourned to the house's notable library.

The sacred scriptures of the canon were examined first. Most churches these days agreed that the list included the four gospels, the *Acts of the Apostles*, and the letters of Paul. But other works were debated—among them, the second letter attributed to Peter. It was part of a large body of Petrine writings that many Christians enjoyed, though some texts were thought to be forgeries. Those were called *apocrypha* in Greek, meaning "hidden," for they did not receive public reading in church.

"Look here, this is important," said Alexamenos in his teacherly way. He had two codices open before him as he made a comparison. "*Second Peter* makes a reference that can be correlated with the *Gospel of John*. Peter writes that 'the putting off of my tabernacle'—he means his body—'is coming soon, just as our Lord Jesus Christ has made clear to me.' But when did Jesus ever speak of Peter's death? Does anyone recall?"

Stephen, a highly educated priest, knew the answer. "In *John*, the Savior predicted Peter's denial before the cock crowed. Jesus said to him, 'Where I am going, you cannot follow now, but you will follow later.' And the time did come when Peter followed the Lord on the road to crucifixion."

"That's right," said Alexamenos.

But Rex was skeptical. "Did Jesus mention crucifixion? I didn't hear him say anything about that. He said Peter would 'follow' him. Maybe it just means death. How do you know Peter was crucified?"

Alexamenos flipped a few pages to the end of John's gospel. "Lady Junia, will you read this passage aloud, please?"

Receiving the book, Flavia read from it, translating the Greek into Latin for easier understanding among her friends. In the selected text, Jesus said to Peter: "Truly, truly, I say to you, when you were young, you tied your clothes around you, and you walked where you desired. But when you are old, you will stretch out your hands, and another will gird you and bring you where you do not want to go." After this, the apostle John added the remark, "Now he said this to indicate by what kind of death Peter was going to glorify God."

Rex motioned to Flavia. "What was the Greek verb that you translated as 'stretch out'?"

"*Ekteneis.*"

"Interesting," Rex mused. "That's the same word soldiers use when they crucify someone. They 'stretch out' his hands on a cross."

Alexamenos nodded emphatically. "You see? This certainly seems to be a reference to martyrdom by crucifixion."

Although Rex could see the connection, he retained his skepticism. Too much was on the line to be making decisions based on hunches and conjectures. "I don't know, my friend," he cautioned. "At best, it is only an allusion."

"True. But do you know Tacitus?"

"Of course I know Tacitus," Rex replied. "Do you think I'm some kind of primitive barbarian?" He winked playfully at Alexamenos, although with someone else, he might have taken offense at the presumption that he was uneducated.

Now the curly haired schoolteacher withdrew a secular codex from his cupboard, the *Annals* of the historian Tacitus. He flipped the pages until he found what he wanted. "This is an account of Nero's terrible persecution of the Christians, just after the great fire of Rome. Since I do know that you are no illiterate barbarian, Brandulf Rex, please read this passage to your friends."

The text was in Latin. In a clear voice, and without stumbling over any words, Rex read it out loud: "'And mockery was added to their deaths; so that, while covered in wild animals' furs, they were shredded to death by dogs; or they were fastened on crosses, and when daylight faded, they were burned alive as lamps to illumine the night. Nero had offered his gardens for the spectacle, and he gave a show in his circus, mingling with the crowd in the outfit of a charioteer and riding around in his chariot. And so, despite the guilt which had earned the Christians this most exemplary punishment, a feeling of pity arose, out of the sense that they were being sacrificed not for the best interest of the state, but due to the fierce cruelty of one man.'"

Stephen couldn't contain his outrage. "May God judge that wicked emperor forever!" he cried. "Nero died in shame, for his deeds were so evil!" Everyone nodded quietly as they reflected on this first Christian persecution and the courage of those earliest martyrs.

"Do you see how this fits with what the Lord predicted about Peter?" Alexamenos asked after the silent moment had passed. "Not only did Jesus speak of 'stretching out' the hands. He also said that others would 'gird' Peter in clothes and lead him forth. Are you familiar with the 'terrible tunic' that is sometimes used in the cruel spectacles of the circus?"

From Flavia's involuntary shudder, Rex could see she knew of it. But since Cassi did not, he explained. "It's a tunic soaked in flammable pitch and oils. Those substances burn long and hot. For the entertainment of the audience, criminals are nailed to posts and set aflame. They writhe in agony, and people laugh at their extreme torment."

"That seems to be what happened to Peter, just as Jesus predicted," Alexamenos said sadly.

"How do you know Peter was in Rome during Nero's persecution?" Rex asked. "Tacitus didn't mention him by name in his account."

"All the church fathers agreed on this, right from the beginning. It is stated by Clement of Rome, Dionysius of Corinth, Irenaeus of Lugdunum, and Tertullian of Carthago."

"But those are not your original scriptures."

"Rex, you are a difficult skeptic to convince!" Alexamenos exclaimed with a shake of his head. "Yet I am grateful for your skepticism, for we must be certain about these things. To prove Peter's presence in Rome from the scriptures, I offer this: the apostolic letter of *First Peter* sends a greeting from the church at 'Babylon.' And in our *Revelation of John*, Babylon stands for Rome. So this letter was written from Rome, though Peter used a code word to convey it. There is no evidence that he ever went to the actual Babylon.

The traditions about Peter are unanimous. He came to the capital city in the reign of Claudius and was killed by crucifixion and burning during Nero's persecution at the circus and gardens on the Vatican Hill."

"Can we go there?" Rex asked.

"The whole area is ruined now. The circus hasn't been used for centuries. There is a vast necropolis out there, but it's all overgrown. It's like a maze. The Christians buried Peter in it somewhere, but the exact spot is forgotten now."

Rex frowned and let out a little grunt. Though the evidence did seem to show that Peter was killed and buried at the Vatican Hill, only the general location was known. Rex wasn't sure how he was going to carry out Sylvester's mission without some way of discerning which specific grave was the apostle's.

More out of frustration than actual inquiry, he asked, "Why didn't your people mark his name on the grave?"

Once again, the scholarly Alexamenos had an answer. "It wasn't considered wise to write the apostle's name on a tombstone. However, let me show you one more book. It is by a Roman priest who lived about a hundred years ago. His name was Gaius, and he makes a very interesting boast to a heretic whom he was refuting. Gaius wanted to prove the orthodoxy of Rome's church by referring to its apostolic founders. Listen to what he says."

After locating the book, Alexamenos read an excerpt from it: "'I can show you the trophies of the apostles. For if you decide to go to the Vatican or to the Ostian Way, you will find the trophies of those who founded this church.'"

"I know the trophy of Paul very well," Flavia said. "My family has a vault in the same burial ground on the Ostian Way. Our vault is only a few steps from the marker of Paul's grave."

"And Gaius declared there was another like it at the Vatican necropolis. So this priest knew, in his day, that there was some kind of structure to mark the graves of Peter and Paul—the two founders of the Roman church."

"But you no longer know where the Vatican trophy is?" Rex asked.

"No," Alexamenos admitted.

At this point, Cassi spoke up. "I do not know what you mean by 'trophy.' It is not a word I have heard."

"Soldiers build trophies after a great victory," Rex explained. "They hang the enemy's armor and shields on tree branches or on spears stuck in the ground. Eventually, some of these trophies became fancier, made of bronze or marble at the site of the battle. So a trophy is like a giant victory monument."

"The martyrs are victors," Flavia added. "Their tombs are places not of defeat but of triumph. The tombs are sometimes adorned, as was the case with Peter and Paul. Evidently, this priest Gaius had seen those monuments. I can still picture how Paul's looks. It has little marble columns and a kind of canopy over the grave."

"What about Peter's?" Cassi asked.

"That is the lost one. Its appearance has been forgotten." Alexamenos spread his hands to his guests. "My friends, to research this mystery further, you must go to the archives at the Hall of the Church in Trans Tiberim. A charter of the trophy's construction should be on file there. At the time of its erection, the bishops of Rome were keeping records of such things. The Hall of the Church is our oldest episcopal seat, so that is where the archives are kept. But please! First come to my table and have some refreshments while I arrange for transport. After you have eaten, you can go visit the monk Damasus. He knows the history of our catholic faith better than anyone."

The meal was a pleasant one, expertly served by the page boys in training. Between the courses, Rex thought back to the days, which seemed so long ago now, when Flavia lived here and he would sometimes visit. He was just a lowly soldier then, and she was posing as a kitchen maid to spy on the imperial palace. In all that time, neither of them had ever been served a meal in the formal dining room at Gelotiana House.

Life is strange, Rex mused. *It has a way of coming full circle.*

The sun was at its midday zenith when two litters, each borne by four stout slaves, arrived at the domus. The men carried their passengers to the Hall of the Church on the far side of the Tiberis River. Rex had seen this church before yet was surprised again by how plain it was. Except for a little colonnade that ran down one side and a couple windows along its length, it looked just like a warehouse—which is what it originally was.

But Flavia nonetheless insisted the building was special. It wasn't a house, nor had it ever been one. This building was one of the first in Rome to serve as a full-time worship hall. Its interior dimensions allowed a large congregation to gather there. Christians had continuously occupied the Trans Tiberim neighborhood since the original days of the apostles.

The monks associated with the congregation lived in a house adjacent to the church. Since Stephen was in clerical orders—though it had been many years since he had led a congregation—he hailed the doorman of the house and asked to see Damasus. Christian hospitality required that fellow clergy be admitted right away and be greeted with honor. It wasn't long before Damasus came out to meet the arrivals.

Rex found him to be an interesting little fellow. He was probably close to seventy years old, short and humpbacked, though still quite spry. His legs were bowed and his fingers gnarly. The top of his head was bald and freckled. Yet a bright light of intelligence shone in his pale blue eyes.

After Stephen had explained the party's quest, which had Pope Sylvester's full backing, the elderly monk walked everyone across the street to a room at the rear of the church. The air inside was musty when he opened the door. Rex inhaled the familiar smell of leather and ink: the age-old aroma of learning.

Damasus searched through a stack of barrel-shaped capsas. They were the large, wooden kind designed to store documents, not transport them. He found one with writing on its top: *Bishop Anicetus.*

"This is the one," said the monk as he set it on a table.

"When was his ministry?" Stephen asked.

"About a hundred and fifty years ago. It was during his time that the trophies of Peter and Paul were erected. The charters should be in here." However, after rifling through the capsa and pulling out some documents, a frown came to the monk's face. "The financial contract for the Vatican construction is intact, but the sketches and plans are missing."

Rex grunted. "How will we recognize it without a drawing?"

Damasus fixed his blue eyes on Rex and gazed at him for a long time. Finally, he said, "Not all drawings are made with ink, you know."

To this, Rex gave no response. It was the kind of cryptic statement that religious men often made. Rex waited to hear whether the monk would explain further.

And he did. Tapping his forehead, Damasus said, "I have another drawing in here."

Everyone was taken aback, and Flavia's mouth fell open. "You've *seen* it?" she gasped.

"Aye. Long ago, when I was but a lad."

"And could you still recognize it?"

Damasus tapped his forehead again. "My ink hasn't faded yet, young lady, despite my age."

"Sir, you must accompany us to the Vatican Hill immediately," Rex said.

"I think old Saint Pete would enjoy a visit," Damasus agreed.

Though it had taken every bit of clandestine skill that the Aegyptian Asp possessed, in the end, he had evaded the dogged pursuit of Helena's financial police. The fraud at the imperial treasury had agitated them like a bear stirring up a beehive. For civilian men, they were quite good at persisting through the Asp's expert countermeasures. He suspected that some former speculators must have been recruited into Constantine's new Office of Sacred Benefactions, for these investigators seemed well versed in the tradecraft of spies. It was all the Asp could do to stay one step ahead of them.

Surprisingly, Father Felix had proven himself more than capable of learning the devious arts of evasion and escape. At first, the Asp had been worried that his companion would be a hindrance. But he kept up well, even when the pursuit drew near. The pair had flitted about the Italian countryside, always on the move as they dodged the tenacious police.

They'd had a close call at Tibur when agents raided their inn at dawn. And down at Three Taverns, there had even been a fight. Capture would have led to torture, and the Asp suspected the handsome priest wouldn't have held out long on the rack. He would have confessed to the theft of 1.6 million denarii—though at least he didn't know the treasure was hidden at the Aventine church beneath the wine vat, which had a false bottom. Some secrets should be possessed only by the strong. But in the end, it hadn't mattered. The Asp's razor had left Helena's two agents gagging on the blood of their slashed throats. Escape had been easy after that.

The relentless game of cat and mouse finally ended at Portus when a few coins bought a forged manifest that indicated the fugitives had taken passage on an Alexandrian grain ship. The huge vessel had been forced to overwinter in the Italian port, and now it was heading home with the arrival of spring. After it cast off, the financial police embarked for Aegyptus on the next available departure. Father Felix and the Asp watched the ship sail away from a dockside tavern, snickering and toasting its receding stern with good wine.

"They're going to have a hard time picking up our trail in Aegyptus!" Felix crowed, then poured himself another cup.

Freed at last from pursuit, the two men made their way to the abandoned necropolis on the Vatican Hill. It lay across the Tiberis River from the city, surrounded by a rural area of swampy lowlands, scrubby forest, and old ruins. Before their hasty departure from Rome, Felix had used his ecclesiastical connections to gain access to the historical archives of the catholic faith. After rummaging through the documents at the Hall of the Church, he had stolen the charter for the construction of Peter's victory monument. The two men held it before them as they gazed at the tangled Vatican field from the brow of the low hill. A sketch showed them what the little edifice should look like: two columns, a horizontal slab for a canopy, and a gravestone set into a niche in a wall.

"The necropolis is obscured by many later buildings," Felix observed. "Maybe the trophy over the grave was destroyed?"

"I doubt the catholics would have let that happen. They'd buy the surrounding property before they'd let a builder have it. Peter is too important. I think the tomb is still out there somewhere."

"Look how overgrown it is! How are we going to find it in that big mess?"

The Aegyptian Asp glared at the priest. "Father Felix, where is your faith? Are we not empowered by the Holy Spirit? Will she not shine her light upon our every step?"

"Perhaps she might," the priest agreed with a shrug. He had recently come around to the idea of considering the Holy Spirit as female.

Since it was not long past dawn, the day was still cool. The Aegyptian Asp and Felix decided it would be best to get an early start and take a rest break during the heat of the day. They agreed to split up and rendezvous back in Nero's ruined circus at noon. An obelisk, the age-old symbol of the sun god Ra, would be their meeting point. Emperor Caligula had imported the stone spike from Aegyptus. It sat on the spine of the circus and was visible from a long way around as a prominent landmark.

"While you walk about, be looking for a wall like this," said the Asp, gesturing to the sketches from the stolen charter. "It is covered in red plaster. So keep your eye out for that color."

"I will, God help me," Felix replied.

The morning's search proved fruitless, however. The tangled shrubs and vines made it hard to proceed through the maze of tombs that once had open alleys between them. When the Asp met Felix at the obelisk, neither could report having seen anything that looked like the trophy of Peter. In fact, neither man had even encountered a red wall like the one depicted in the sketches.

After a meal and nap in the shade, the comrades decided to search together during the late afternoon hours before dusk. This time, however, they resolved to pray to the Mother-Father before searching—and the prayers worked. No sooner had the Aegyptian Asp finished the incantation than he looked up and saw a hawk circling in the empty sky. Suddenly it folded its wings and dove into an area of the necropolis that had not yet been examined. *A divine sign!*

Proceeding there with haste, the two men followed a narrow lane and discovered a tiny courtyard enclosed on three sides. A flowering bush almost completely obscured the entrance, so they moved some branches and peeked in. On the tiled pavement, a yellow-eyed hawk stood with a bloody rabbit in its talons. And behind that noble predator was a red wall.

"It's just like the sketch!" Felix exclaimed.

The trophy of Peter consisted of two slender columns supporting a horizontal slab that abutted the red wall and formed a canopy. It covered a plain, flat gravestone in the ground. The pair of columns and the canopy clearly marked this spot as important. The gravestone was specially highlighted by this structure, though without any identifying words or images.

The Aegyptian Asp pushed aside some flowery branches and took a step into the courtyard. With a screech, the hawk snatched its prey and flew away, leaving a bloodstain upon the white tiles. The Asp knelt by the apostolic gravestone and ran his hand along its smooth surface. Unfortunately, it was cemented tight into the pavement. Great effort would be needed to pry it out.

"What is this strange thing?" Felix asked.

Raising his eyes, the Asp saw the priest investigating a thick, stubby wall that protruded from the red wall. It was clearly a later construction, for it ruined the proportions of the grave marker. One of the two marble columns had been bumped over to accommodate the blocky addition. Its surface was smooth and plastered, giving it a pale-blue color. It was an odd and ungainly edifice, one that marred the right side of the trophy's original symmetry.

"It covers a fissure in the rear wall. Look there." The Asp pointed to how the red wall had shifted over the years, necessitating the construction of the perpendicular blue wall to camouflage the crack. "It is an ugly solution. It looks as if someone pushed a wardrobe against the wall."

"I think it also hides the gravestone from the sight of anyone passing by the courtyard," said Felix. "That tells me this is a secret place."

The Asp stood up from his kneeling stance. "Sylvester's dream is about to come to an end. By sunset tomorrow, nothing will remain here, neither the trophy nor the relics. You arranged for the fossors, yes?"

"They are encamped along the road, near the pyramid. They await our command."

"Then let us go fetch them and see what can be done today, before the daylight fades on us completely."

The pair left the necropolis and made their way back toward Rome on the ancient Cornelian Way. Before reaching the city gate, they arrived at a slender pyramid that served as the tomb of some forgotten senator who had the audacity to bury himself like the pharaohs. The fossors were assembled there, eight of them in all. They were the beefy gravediggers who burrowed through Rome's soft rock and created the underground cemeteries of the Christian church. After Felix conferred with them, they packed up their tools and food, ready to move to the newly discovered grave.

The leader of the fossors was a burly fellow with his hand on a pony's halter. He led the creature to a wheeled cart upon which was mounted a small crane. From its long boom, a great iron hook dangled. A block-and-tackle system of pulleys would allow the fossors to lift the heavy stone from Peter's grave after it was pried up with iron bars. Then whatever was in the earth below would be discovered.

The Aegyptian Asp beckoned Felix to stand beside him. "You know the *Gospel of Matthew*?"

"Of course. It is one of the four gospels that the catholics read. They ignore the Gnostic accounts of the Savior's teachings."

"If you know *Matthew*, you know this saying of Jesus: 'You are Peter, and on this rock I will build my church.' How does it finish?"

"'And the gates of Hades will not prevail against it.'"

A sly grin came to the Aegyptian Asp's face. Reaching up, he grasped the iron hook attached to the crane's boom. "The gates of Hades might not prevail against the rock of Peter, but I have a feeling this crane is going to do just fine."

The wagon ride along the Cornelian Way was bumpy, making Flavia fret a little about the baby growing in her womb. She had heard of women losing their infants after being jostled too hard on the road. "Please keep me safe," she whispered to the Lord, "and give me your strength." *The strength to tell Rex*, she added to her prayer, though only in her mind.

Damasus the monk had used church funds to rent a carriage at the city gate that led onto the Aelian Bridge over the Tiberis. A massive mausoleum—a huge, round monument that housed the ashes of Emperor Hadrian—lay across the river. There the road took a sharp left turn and headed toward the abandoned Vatican area. Stephen sat on the wagon's bench, driving the pair of mules with Damasus as his guide, while Rex, Flavia, and Cassi rode inside the cab. They passed a pyramidal tomb where some men were camped out. Other than that, they saw no one on their ride out to the ancient necropolis.

"Rex, where should we park the carriage?" Stephen called down from above. "Damasus says we are as close to the area of Peter's grave as we can get."

After glancing out the window, Rex pointed to a thicket with a grassy meadow behind it. "That should do well. Let's unhitch the mules and stake them out in the grass as quickly as possible. We're all anxious to start looking around."

When the animals were cared for and the wagon hidden in the bushes, the five searchers hiked over to the necropolis and began to pick their way through the maze. Though the elderly Damasus was unsteady on his feet, the others managed to clear a way for him. Every so often, he would stare around to get his bearings. "Not far now," he would say, and they would all resume walking.

It was late afternoon when the old monk spotted the red wall that identified the grave of Saint Peter. The place really was a hidden little nook. The tiled courtyard was almost completely enclosed so that it couldn't be seen by a casual passerby. Only someone who knew what to look for could find it. The seekers entered the courtyard with a sense of holy awe.

Flavia ran her hand along one of the smooth columns of the trophy. "It's a lot like what they built at Paul's grave."

"That's a good sign. It means we've found the right place," Rex said.

"This is certainly the place," Damasus insisted.

Cassi examined a strange blue wall that protruded into the courtyard, perpendicular to the red wall. It was a thick structure, almost like a tall box. "What is this for?" she asked.

Damasus walked around beside it and gestured to the pavement at the foot of the red wall. "See here? The earth has settled, so the wall shifted and cracked. This was put up as a buttress, I believe."

Stephen took a step back and curled his lip. "It's ugly. It messes up the look of the trophy."

"Sometimes you have to adapt as best you can," Damasus said.

Now Rex knelt beside the gravestone of Peter, directly below the travertine canopy. He tried to insert his fingers beneath it, but the surrounding mortar was tight. Even the knife from his belt was unable to loosen any chips. "This is a job for hammers and chisels. And then pry bars. We can come back tomorrow and do the job. But I doubt we can get that heavy slab out of the ground without some more men."

Damasus agreed. "I could recruit some monastic brothers tomorrow. Monks love any chance to get out of the house. They would be happy to come out."

"Be sure they have masonry tools," Rex added, receiving a nod from Damasus.

"In the meantime," Flavia said, "let's cover the opening to this courtyard with some branches." She went to an oleander bush near the entrance, draped with delicate pink flowers. As she rearranged the foliage to obscure the courtyard even further, something darted past her feet. "A bunny!"

The rabbit hopped to the far side of the courtyard but found itself enclosed by the walls. It froze in place, twitching its little nose. Suddenly a hawk dove from the sky and pounced on the unsuspecting prey.

Flavia started to shoo the bird away, but Rex stopped her. "The hawk is God's creature too," he said with a serious face. "It must kill to survive. Don't judge a creature for doing what belongs to its nature."

"Alright," Flavia said, sensing a deeper meaning behind Rex's words.

The five explorers turned their attention away from the bird and back to the trophy of Peter. Christians often marked their prayers to the saints on the walls of places like this. Yet here, nothing of the sort was to be found. When Stephen remarked that he would have expected some graffiti, Damasus reminded him that the catholic church had forgotten this place over the past sixty years. The veneration of Peter and Paul, with plenty of prayers and graffiti, had been transferred to the Apostolic Monument on the Appian Way. Since then, no one had been coming here.

Rex hushed everyone with a sharp command and an upraised fist. "Shh! I hear voices!"

Flavia heard them too. It sounded like a conversation between two men, not a large group. But they were coming this way.

"Let's hide over there," Rex said.

Leaving the hawk alone with the rabbit in the courtyard, the group slipped into a nearby tomb whose closing stone had fallen ajar over time. Fortunately, the tomb was the dovecote type. The niches in the walls held urns for cremated remains, which meant that no exposed bones lay about. Murals depicting mythological scenes were painted on the walls. Everyone huddled in the dark while Rex peered past the outer stone. Flavia crept over and knelt beside him so she could watch too.

The two men arrived a few moments later. At first, Flavia was surprised to see it was Father Felix and the mysterious Aegyptian Asp. Yet as she considered it further, it made sense. These men were hostile to Sylvester's plans. If he wanted something, by definition, they wanted the opposite. They had spies in the Lateran Palace, so they probably knew what the bishop was trying to accomplish. Their evil plans had brought them to this courtyard for the same reason she had come: to find the bones of Saint Peter. However, they had much different intentions for the holy relics.

"It's just like the sketch!" Felix exclaimed as he peeked into the courtyard.

The hawk flew away with its prey when the Aegyptian Asp and Felix stepped into the hidden space. After inspecting the trophy for a while and conversing among themselves about it, the two men finally left. Rex snuck out of the tomb and made sure they were truly gone, then signaled for everyone to emerge.

"We're in a race against those men," Stephen said. "We need to return to the city and get reinforcements. Should we head back to the carriage now?"

Rex shook his head. "I'm not willing to leave this place unguarded overnight. There's no telling what they might do before we can return. Stephen, I need you to go for me. At first light tomorrow, bring men here with digging tools and pry bars. Pick ten good men who can fight if necessary. It might come to that."

Stephen clasped Rex's hand in both of his. "I won't fail you."

"What about the rest of us?" Cassi asked.

"You can all go back to Rome with Stephen. I will spend the night here and watch over the trophy."

Flavia shook her head. "I'm not leaving, Rex. Not now. We've come so far together. It has all come down to this. I'm here to stay."

"And I'm too tired to travel any farther tonight," Damasus added. "A monk can wrap himself in his cloak and fall asleep anywhere. It won't be a problem."

"I will go with Stephen, to aid him as needed," Cassi said.

Stephen rummaged in his knapsack and brought out some rye loaves and a hunk of cheese, along with a fire striker, which he gladly left with his friends. After Stephen and Cassi departed, the remaining three settled in to wait. They collected sticks and piled them beside the tomb, which would be their shelter for the night. Their meal would be cheese toast and rainwater. Flavia thought that sounded just fine.

The red light of dusk was in the western sky when the sound of voices came to Flavia's ears again. This time, it was a much larger group. Rex hustled his friends back into the tomb to hide from whomever was arriving.

Felix was at the head of the party, while the Aegyptian Asp brought up the rear. Between them were eight gravediggers and a pony pulling a cart. Tools and torches were loaded on the vehicle, as well as a crane with a high boom.

"Clever," Rex whispered. "That crane will lift out the stone easily."

The new arrivals entered the courtyard with the red wall. Immediately, the fossors began to chisel away at the mortar around Peter's gravestone. The continuous *clink! clink! clink!* of iron on stone filled the air.

"Hurry up," Felix urged. "We only have an hour more of light."

When the mortar was cleared, the two biggest fossors inserted rods into the new crack. Using them as levers, they began to pull down on them with great exertion. At first, nothing happened—until suddenly there was a loud pop.

"You got it," said the Aegyptian Asp. "Saint Peter, breathe new air."

Though the gravestone was now ajar, it still ended up being difficult to remove. There was much shouting and confusion as the eight men, each with his own ideas, tried to get ropes and slings around the stone, then attach them to the block-and-tackle of the crane. Darkness had nearly descended when the workers finally lifted away the slab. Venus, a bright pinprick in the evening sky, gazed down on the proceedings with her approving stare.

"Want us to start digging?" asked the foreman of the gravediggers.

The Aegyptian Asp shook his snaky head. "Too much chance of missing something in the dark," he said. "Even one bone left behind would be enough for the catholics to build their basilica here. Let us withdraw to a wooded place to camp for the night. There is a brook nearby where your men can refill their gourds. We will return at dawn."

"Good," said the foreman. "I want some hot soup."

The party of ten left the spot without bothering to gather up their digging tools and torches. When all was quiet again, Rex and Flavia crept from their macabre hiding place. Damasus followed close behind.

The marble slab that had covered Peter's grave now rested to one side. Bare dirt was visible where it had once lain. Rex scratched the soil with his fingers.

"Are you thinking what I'm thinking?" Flavia asked.

He nodded. "It's now or never. We find the bones tonight, or our enemies get them in the morning."

"Yes. I'll go get the fire striker and get us some light."

"And I'll start digging."

By the flickering glow of a single torch, Rex began to dig into the hard-packed earth. The going was slow, but eventually he managed to excavate a knee-deep hole.

"Nothing yet?" Flavia asked, probably for the tenth time.

"I'll widen it. Pass me that hand spade."

The night wore on, but still they made no discovery. Though Damasus dozed in a corner of the courtyard, Flavia felt it was important to keep this vigil with Rex. She refused to fall asleep on him like the disciples did in Jesus's moment of need. Together, they would face this task until it was seen through to the end.

Sometime late in the night, thunder began to rumble in the distance. Rex finally clambered from the hole, which was chest deep now. His face was streaked with sweat and dirt. "I went deeper than any grave would need to be. My shovel was hitting bedrock by the end. There was nothing but soil. The bones of Peter aren't here."

"Where could they be? This is the trophy, right?"

Damasus wasn't asleep at the moment. "Yes, this is the place, my friends. I came here as a youth with the bishop. I was just an acolyte at the time. The bones were returned here from the Apostolic Monument after the persecution of Valerian had passed."

Another thunderclap reverberated across the sky, which was now covered with dark clouds. A few big drops spattered the pavement tiles. Sunrise was still an hour away. It would be a gloomy morning.

"Did you see the relics put into the ground?" Rex asked.

"I did not. A hole was dug here. That I saw with my own eyes. But when the time came for reinterment, all the gravediggers and attendants were dismissed, for this was a secret event. No one remained for the holy ceremony except the bishop and a few chosen priests."

"Clearly, the bones weren't actually buried at that time. Either that, or someone has dug them up since then."

"I have no explanation," Damasus replied.

Rain began to fall now, so the monk pulled up his hood. Flavia did the same with her cloak, but Rex did not, for his head was already soaked with sweat. The drops were steady, yet it wasn't a drenching rain.

Exhausted, Rex propped his shovel against the strange blue wall that abutted the red one. He leaned against it with his head tipped back and his eyes closed. Flavia's heart went out to him. She knew he was feeling the burden of defeat. His vow to deliver the relics weighed heavily on him, for their discovery was to be his redemption for his earlier failure. But now he had failed again.

As she approached Rex to provide comfort, she noticed something unusual on the blue wall behind him. Rainwater was dribbling down the face of the block-shaped addition, yet upon reaching a certain point, the flow was disrupted by a horizontal crease in the plaster. It was the faintest of lines, a mark that, except for the rain, wouldn't have been noticeable.

"What's that?" she asked, pointing.

Rex turned. "What?"

"That line. Look—there's four, actually. They make a rectangle. See?"

Now Rex stooped and began inspecting the rectangular shape in the plaster. He scratched at it a bit, then pried out a small chunk of masonry. After inserting his finger, he cried, "A hole!"

Flavia felt the excitement of discovery. Though it was raining steadily now and lightning flashed occasionally, she hardly noticed her surroundings. "Open it!" she exclaimed.

Rex pulled away a big piece of brick, revealing a hidden rectangular compartment. Damasus came over too. Both men peered into the gap but could see nothing.

Flavia brought a flickering oil lamp, shielding it with her hand from the rain. "Let me have a look," she said, holding the flame next to the hole. The men stepped aside, so she bent over and peeked in. "It's lined with marble, just like a burial niche in a cemetery."

Rex craned his neck over Flavia's shoulder. "Can you see the bottom?"

"No, it's too deep. But I can see the red wall, where it's cracked." Flavia gasped and turned to Rex with her eyes wide. "There's graffiti on the wall! I see letters! Someone scratched some words in Greek!"

"What does it say?" Rex asked, unable to hide the excitement in his voice.

Flavia squinted at the letters. "P . . . e . . ."

And with that, Flavia drew back and stood up. For a moment, she couldn't speak, but could only stare at Rex in astonishment. He stared back, his eyebrows arched and his mouth agape as he awaited her stunning news. "What is it? Tell me!" he begged.

"It says, 'Peter is within!'"

The three explorers stood like statues in the driving rain. The discovery was overwhelming, even though it was exactly what they had been searching for.

"Reach into the cavity, Rex," the monk said at last. "Dig down and see what you find."

Rex immediately obliged. He widened the hole a bit more, then thrust his arm inside. After groping around a bit, his face lit up. He pulled out a sack made of expensive purple cloth, interwoven with golden threads. Bulky objects were contained within it.

"It's the bones," he said with breathless awe. "Someone moved them up here from the ground."

A menacing voice shattered the holy moment. "Nice work! Now give that bag to me."

The three friends whirled to face the speaker. The Aegyptian Asp stood there, drenched with rain. Felix was beside him, along with a crowd of mean-faced fossors with pickaxes in their hands. They blocked the exit from the courtyard.

"You can't have it," Rex snarled.

"Yes, I can," said the Asp. He started forward, his blade gleaming in his hand.

And then the world exploded.

—————

Everything was spinning. Stars flashed before Rex's eyes. His vision was cloudy. Strangely, there was no sound, only a deafening roar inside his head. It felt like moss was stuffed in his ears.

He lay on hard pavement. It was . . . wet? Was the air sizzling and crackling? Rex's mind struggled to comprehend what was happening around him.

In his nostrils was the pungent aroma of charred wood. And also, a kind of clean smell. Sweet and tingly, like a rainstorm that had just passed. *But isn't it still raining on my face?*

Sound began to return. Human voices, moaning and muttering. And a ringing in his ears—piercing, like a whistle.

Rex pushed himself to a seated position. His body felt achy and sore. He squinted and shook his head to clear the mental fog. Around him, people were lying upon the ground. One of them was . . .

Flavia!

Rex crawled over and knelt beside her, then helped her sit up. Tendrils of wet hair hung in her face.

"I'm . . . I'm alright," she said in a shaky voice. "What about . . . the bones?"

Awareness came flooding back to Rex. The explosion that had stunned everyone was lightning. He turned and looked at the iron hook that dangled from the crane in the courtyard. Steam rose from its sizzling surface, and dark singe marks streaked the wooden boom.

Where are the bones? Rex glanced around for the sack. He started to rise. And that was when something smashed him in the back of the head.

Flavia shrieked as Rex went tumbling across the courtyard. Yet now his battle instincts kicked in. He rolled over and caught the boot of the Aegyptian Asp as it came flying at him, attempting to stamp on his face. Instead of letting the attack crush his nose, Rex used his enemy's momentum against him. He ducked his head and pulled the boot hard, extending the Asp's leg. In the same motion, he rolled toward the man's other foot. Knocked off balance, the Asp crashed into a heap on the wet pavement.

The two adversaries scrambled up at the same time. They eyed each other warily, primed for battle. Although the Asp had his razor out, Rex had whipped his own knife from his belt. Unfortunately, a pry bar leaned on the wall near the Asp. He grabbed it, and its length gave him an unbeatable advantage. The heavy iron rod was a weapon that no knife could match. Recognizing this, Rex used the only strategy available to him: flight. He would draw his enemy into a chase by taking the one thing he desperately wanted. Snatching the purple sack from the ground, Rex dashed from the courtyard.

Running at full speed despite the driving rain, he dodged among the tombs with the Aegyptian Asp close behind. A dreary daybreak had arrived, so the sky was light enough now that Rex could see the way ahead. Branches clawed at him as he passed, but he ignored them and pressed on. He chose a random path through the necropolis, trying to break free of the maze.

But as he rounded a corner, he came up short as he faced a dead end. Without pausing to think, he whirled and made a stab at his enemy. The

Asp, caught by surprise when he turned the corner, barely eluded the thrust. While the Asp was off-balance, Rex darted from the dead end. Yet the Asp recovered quickly and brought his iron rod around with two hands. A hard strike from it would surely break a bone. This was a weapon Rex feared; so instead of continuing to confront a losing proposition, he took off running in a different direction.

At last, a gap appeared between the tombs. Rex could see a tall structure comprised of high arches. Leaving the necropolis, he found himself at Nero's ruined circus. Though the Asp was close behind, Rex believed his superior speed would make the difference on an open field. His enemy wore encumbering garments and was lugging a heavy rod. An all-out sprint should be enough for Rex to get away. After darting through the crumbled arches that supported the circus's seats, he ran onto the grassy racetrack where forgotten heroes once drove their chariots.

The circus was oblong in shape. Rex headed across its narrow width, his arms pumping as he ran. His knife was in one hand, and the purple sack of relics was in the other. The grass was tall and slick—more of a hindrance to the Asp than to Rex. Glancing over his shoulder, he realized he had indeed increased his distance from his pursuer.

Now he approached the midpoint of the track. He was about to vault over the low wall of the center spine when something clobbered him in the back of the legs and took him to the ground. Pain blazed in his calves. He gasped as he hit the turf. The purple sack flew from his grip.

Before he could recover the relics, the Asp was upon him. Although the pry bar, hurled from behind like a javelin, had struck Rex and made him fall, at least the dangerous weapon was lost in the grass now. Yet the razor still presented its deadly threat.

Rex rose from the soggy racetrack just in time to leap away from the Asp's thrust. The two adversaries circled each other in the driving rain, feinting and jabbing, each seeking some way to gain an advantage. But since both men held a blade, neither could advance for a strike without suffering severe damage in return. All they could do was continue their deadly spiral beneath the obelisk of an Aegyptian god.

Lightning flashed on the Asp's face, illuminating his fearsome tattoo. The serpent's eyes seemed to blaze like twin embers of hate. A deep disgust rose up in Rex, for he sensed the evil that indwelled his opponent. Such a fiend must not be allowed to prevail.

Though it was a terrible risk, Rex decided to hurl his knife at his enemy. The attack was so unexpected that the Asp was forced to make an extreme move to evade it. His dodge was successful and the blade missed. But while the Asp's attention was on evasive maneuvers, Rex closed the distance and immobilized the razor with a two-handed hold on the Asp's wrist. A wrenching twist forced the weapon to fall from his grasp.

Now the two enemies clinched, body to body and eye to eye. Each man tried to throw the other to the ground. The Asp snarled in Rex's face, gnashing his teeth like a wild animal. And while he was making that terrible noise, Rex headbutted him as hard as he could.

The blow stunned them both, and they staggered backward. Yet Rex did not fall to the ground like the Asp, who had taken the worst of the impact. Before Rex could finish him off, the fierce combatant rose to his knees. Water and blood dribbled down his face. With a guttural cry, he dove across the grass, snatched up the purple bag, and made a break for the risers on the far side of the circus.

Rex followed him, but the Asp now seemed to run with supernatural speed. He leapt up the risers like a mountain goat, taking the steps three at a time. Reaching the rim of the circus, he began to run along its length above the top tier of seats. Yet Rex did not give up. He, too, reached the rim and began to pursue his enemy down the long, narrow catwalk.

The drop-off outside the circus was a long one, and no guardrail protected against a fall. Though the stones were slick, nothing seemed to hinder the Aegyptian Asp. Rex decided he would run with just as much abandon as his enemy did—for the true God was on his side.

Up ahead, Rex could see that the rising slope of the Vatican Hill, into which the circus was built, would gradually decrease the height of the rim above the ground. In fact, the drop-off would be eliminated as the catwalk drew even with the surrounding terrain. A man stood at that far spot, waving frantically. He had two horses on the grass, only a short jump down from the circus's rim.

"Over here!" cried the man with the horses. The voice was that of Felix. "Bring the bones to me!"

Desperate to stop the escape, Rex picked up his speed, striving to find his last bit of strength. Yet he could tell he wasn't going to make it. The fleet-footed runner had too much of a lead. And that was when Rex spotted movement on the circus risers ahead.

Flavia!

She charged up the steps on an intercept course, striving to gain the rim before the Aegyptian Asp could reach the spot where Felix waited with the horses. In her hand was a torch, its sizzling pitch impervious to the rain. A trail of black smoke rose behind Flavia like the war banner of a mighty champion.

The Asp halted when Flavia reached the narrow catwalk ahead of him. Her torch dripped with sulfurous tar, the gooey stuff that could so easily set garments ablaze in a deadly wreath of flame. She waved the torch back and forth, preventing the man from advancing.

Rex closed on his enemy from behind. "You're mine now!" he cried as he drew near. Bunching his fist, he leapt into the air. The Asp spun just as Rex descended. His fist crushed the man's nose, showering him in blood and sending him staggering along the catwalk. He stumbled toward Flavia. As he neared, she swatted him with her torch. The Asp's brown robe burst into flames.

Yet the man's endurance was superhuman. Even as the blaze engulfed him, he did not release his hold on the sacred relics. Rex rushed at him, but the Asp would not give in. Like a pair of stags with their antlers locked, the two opponents pushed against each other in a desperate struggle for supremacy. The tar on the man's robe, alive with dancing flames, set Rex's tunic afire as well. Hot pain seared Rex's shoulder as he tried to drive his adversary over the rim and hurl him onto the hard seats of the risers below.

"Give . . . that . . . to me!" Rex cried, lunging for the bag.

"Never!"

"Then die!" Rex yelled as he grabbed a wad of burning tar from his shoulder. Thrusting out his fiery palm, he smeared the burning sludge on his enemy's serpentine face.

A colossal howl burst from the hellish depths of the man's dark soul. The ragged sky responded with a thunderclap of its own. Seizing his advantage, Rex sent the Asp hurtling toward the jagged stones of the circus risers. Yet as he wrenched the bag from his enemy's grip, the sudden release of tension sent Rex flying backward as well. Careening across the narrow catwalk, he crashed into Flavia and knocked her toward the external edge of the circus. For a long moment, they tottered above the drop-off.

She screamed.

And then, together, they plunged over the rim as wicked Nero took his final revenge.

———◦◊◦———

It was the stomach pain that woke Flavia from her stupor. She was flat on her back in the soggy grass when something seemed to stab her in the gut. Terrified that the snake-man had knifed her, she cried out and squirmed away. But no one was there. The pain receded, and Flavia was left with a dull ache. Fortunately, it was the generalized ache of a sore body, not the sharp agony of a broken bone.

Time passed, though Flavia didn't know how long. The next thing she perceived was Rex at her side, helping her sit up. He was wearing his gray woolen trousers but was bare chested. The skin of one shoulder was red and inflamed, and his tunic was wrapped around his right hand. He was soaking wet, for the rain had not let up. Water ran down his cheeks and into his beard.

"Are you hurt?" he asked, his eyes wide with concern.

"I . . . I'm achy. Wh-what about you?"

"Surface burns. Painful, but I can endure."

Flavia glanced at her surroundings. There was a grassy slope, and above her, the outer wall of the circus. But no people. "Where is that evil man?"

"His body was broken upon the risers. On this side, the ground was softer."

"And the relics?"

"I have them. I will return them to the pope. Can you stand? We need to get out of here."

Flavia nodded. She was about to clamber to her feet when another sharp pang pierced her belly—much harder this time. She cried out, clutching her lower abdomen.

"Flavia! What is it? Where does it hurt?"

"Ahhh! My stomach!" she groaned.

"You're bleeding!"

Rex was right. Glancing down, Flavia saw blood on the grass. A terrible fear came over her as she recognized the blood as dark and clotted, not bright red like a fresh wound. That could only mean one thing. She grabbed Rex's arm, seeking solace from him. Yet comfort was all he could provide, for he couldn't prevent what was happening.

"No, Lord!" she cried. "Please! Not that!"

"Are you cut somewhere?" Rex lifted the hem of Flavia's dress to inspect her bloody legs.

But Flavia knew this was no gash from a sharp stone . . . no broken bone protruding from the skin . . . no knife wound she hadn't noticed. It was something much worse than all these. In the way that women always knew their bodies, Flavia clearly understood: *I'm losing my baby.*

And I haven't even told Rex! Oh, Jesus! How can I do it now?

"Carry me, Rex" was all she could say. "Take me out of the rain."

He complied, scooping her effortlessly from the ground. The arches of the circus created a long colonnade along its length. Rex gently laid her beneath a barrel vault that provided shelter from the elements. Though the stone paving was hard, at least it wasn't wet. Kneeling beside her, Rex sought details about her symptoms. Most military men knew how to staunch the flow of blood from a wound. But this was a different kind of wound than what soldiers encountered on the battlefield. "It's inside of me," she told him.

Before Flavia could explain further, another agonizing pain wracked her entire body. This time, she could feel her womb convulse.

Rex unwrapped the tunic from around his hand—the only cloth he had available. "You're losing a lot of blood. Should I . . . ?"

Flavia shook her head. "Just hold my hand," she gasped. The pain was strong now. Another contraction had its fierce grip on her.

She lay back and drew up her knees. Her tunic was hiked up. Rex had a look of terror on his face. There was a series of intense and agonizing convulsions. Flavia threw back her head and cried out. Tears mingled with the rainwater on her cheeks.

"I'm here with you," Rex whispered helplessly. His fingers interlocked with hers.

And then it happened: Flavia felt her baby go. Though the fetus was tiny, nonetheless, she knew exactly when it passed. Life was a fragile thing, delicate and uncertain. Yet it never slipped away without leaving agony in its wake.

Rex sighed deeply. "Ah! You were pregnant with our baby." His eyes were tender and compassionate. "I didn't know."

Quiet sobs kept Flavia from responding right away. She covered her face with her hands, and her shoulders shook as she cried. At last, she said, "I wanted to tell you. I was afraid."

Surprisingly, Rex said nothing. Instead, he rose to his feet. "I hear a wagon," he said. "I will come back for you."

After spreading his tunic over her—it was wet but better than nothing—he left the arches of the circus and went out into the gray mist. The rain had let up a little. Flavia lay still for what seemed like a very long time. She had dozed off, or maybe fallen into a daze of exhaustion, by the time Rex returned. A gentle hand upon her shoulder roused her.

"Stephen has come, like he promised."

"I can walk," Flavia said, though she did not move.

"I will carry you," Rex answered.

He lifted her and took her to the coach. Stephen was on the bench, driving the mules. The monk Damasus was beside him. From the window of the cab, Cassi's sweet and welcoming face smiled at Flavia. A mattress had been fashioned inside the cab from seat cushions wrapped in a spare cloak. Another cloak served as a top blanket. Flavia gratefully accepted the ministry of her friends, allowing herself to be laid in the makeshift bed.

"Ready?" Stephen asked from his bench.

"Not yet," Flavia whispered. She clutched Rex's sleeve beside her.

"What is it?"

"We must . . . we must give Christian burial to our baby."

At first, Rex started to protest, but one glance at Flavia's face apparently changed his mind. He looked behind him until he spied an earthenware jar among the provisions. After opening the little crock and dumping out the contents, he stepped outside. But before he could leave, Flavia stopped him again.

"Rex," she pleaded, "I need you to look at something for me." When she was met with a kind and willing expression, she continued. "Please look and see . . ." Now her words broke off as tears flooded her eyes. It took her a while to collect herself. At last, she said, "See if it was a girl or boy. I need to know."

Rex nodded. This time, he wasn't gone long. He returned with the crock clutched to his bare chest, its clasp tightly fastened. He climbed into the cab and sat down beside Flavia.

"I believe it's a boy," he said quietly, then knocked on the cab's wall to signal Stephen to leave. After a jangle of the reins, the mules leaned into their harness and the coach lurched ahead.

The threesome rode in a sad and pensive silence. Sensing the somber mood and interpreting it correctly, Cassi said, "I shall ride outside with Stephen and Damasus."

Now Rex and Flavia were alone in the wagon as it rolled along the Triumphal Way toward Rome. Flavia watched Rex from the corner of her eye as she lay in her bed. He stared out the window with a dejected expression. Though he was normally confident and capable, she could tell that the weight of great sorrow was upon him. His eyes were heavy-lidded, and his face drooped in a way Flavia had never seen before.

"Rex . . ." she whispered. He did not respond, nor even seem to hear her. "Look at me," she insisted.

Finally, he turned, though he remained silent.

"I love you," Flavia said.

"You don't blame me for . . . the loss?" He eyed the earthenware crock as he spoke.

"No. It was not your fault."

"But I knocked you from the height! The baby is dead because of me. And it was my sin against the Christian God that got you pregnant in the first place."

"That sin was committed by both of us. As for my fall—nothing happens that isn't part of God's will." Now she pulled Rex's injured hand to her lips and kissed it. "I do not blame you, my beloved," she repeated.

"But I am full of sin, Flavia! I have so much blood on my hands. And now it includes the blood of my own son."

"It is a great loss," Flavia agreed. "What could be greater?"

"Nothing! I am so dirty. Stained with bloodguilt since my youth. And now my foolish actions have led to your greatest pain."

"Then surely, Rex, you need God's forgiveness."

"God could never forgive me."

"Of course he could. God has a washing that can make you clean. These three testify together: the Spirit, the water, and the blood. Believe it, Rex! God loves you—yes, even you."

"Ahhh!" he cried. "Such love cannot exist!"

"With God, it can. It is the love of the cross, which you wear around your neck. God gave us his only Son so that your sins might be forgiven. Such love is given by no other god. Accept his free gift, my beloved."

For a long time, Rex said nothing, only gazing out the window at the gloomy sky. At last, he turned back to Flavia. His voice was strong when he spoke. "I bow my knee to the Lord Jesus," he said simply. "I will be baptized a catholic Christian."

"And I will join you in the fountain of life," Flavia replied, "for the Mighty One has done great things for me."

15

Pope Sylvester himself conducted the funeral at Saint Sabina upon the Aventine. It was a concession of love and respect, for he did not perform many funerals. Yet for Flavia, a bereaved mother, he had agreed to do it. "It is the least I can do for you, dear one," the bishop had said to her. "I know how much you have sacrificed." As a pastor, Sylvester understood that the loss of her baby was a far greater sacrifice than the fortune she had spent on a year's worth of travel.

While Sylvester recited the funeral liturgy, Flavia glanced around the worship hall she knew so well yet didn't know at all. The mansion felt empty and quiet, for with Felix gone, everyone had abandoned the place. Back when it was her mother's house instead of a church named for her, the congregation had met in a room that Flavia's no-good father begrudgingly allowed to be enlarged for the congregation. It was a more beautiful space now, enhanced with crystal-paned windows through which morning light streamed. Yet today, those cheery rays felt out of place to Flavia. This was a day not for beauty but for mourning.

No, it is a day for beauty too, she reminded herself. *The hope of the gospel adorns even the specter of death.*

A wooden box, stuffed with straw, held the little crock into which Rex had put their baby's mortal remains. The boy's name, they had decided, was Nikasius. It was a word that meant victory. The name had seemed right to both parents, for the baby was born in the context of a victorious defeat of evil. Also, through Jesus Christ, little Nikasius would gain victory over the forces that had snuffed out his much-too-short life.

"Our great God and Savior, we commit this child to you," intoned Sylvester with his hand upon the box. "We are but dust, and to dust we shall return."

"Amen," said Rex and Flavia in unison. They made the sign of the cross on their foreheads.

After the funeral—attended by no other mourners, since the circumstances were private—Flavia and Rex descended from the Aventine Hill and made their way by foot out to the Vatican necropolis. Somehow it seemed fitting that Nikasius would be buried in the same place where he had been born. In fact, the baby would await the final trumpet of Christ alongside the relics of Saint Peter himself.

It was a hot day as the pair trudged along the Cornelian Way beneath the June sun. Rex paused and mopped his face, leaning on the shovel he had brought along. "Do you want some water?" he asked, passing Flavia a gourd.

She accepted it gratefully. After taking a long drink, she stared at the container. "It's such a primordial substance, isn't it? We are conceived in water. Birthed in it. We need it to live every day. And we are baptized in water for eternal life."

"It is used at marriages too. Brides are washed in water."

Flavia smiled shyly at this reminder yet said nothing more. She handed the bottle back to Rex, and they resumed their walking.

The open-air courtyard where Peter's body had originally been buried looked much different than when Flavia had seen it last. Gone were the tools and the crane. The pavement had been swept clean and the shrubbery cleared from the entrance. A gate of stout wooden poles with an iron lock had been erected over the opening to regulate access to the grave. Pope Sylvester had posted a permanent guard station nearby, and the man sitting by the gate had instructions to let the visitors in.

After the gate was opened, Rex led Flavia inside. The pale blue wall, which turned out to be a secret receptacle for the relics of Peter, had been replastered and sealed. The relics were back inside the cavity now, hidden in their second resting place until anyone should ever find them again.

Everything in the courtyard was as it had started, except the gravestone of Peter's original burial had not yet been put back into place.

Kneeling, Flavia scratched the bare earth and picked up a handful of it. Rex had dug a hole here, fruitlessly searching for the holy bones, but now the dirt was filled back in. The soil was rich and dark as it slipped through Flavia's fingers.

"'To dust we shall return,'" she said quietly, repeating the bishop's words from the *Book of Genesis*. She stood up and looked at Rex. "The scripture says, 'It is appointed unto men once to die, and after this comes the judgment.'"

Rex stood quietly for a moment, leaning on his shovel, then finally let out a heavy sigh. "Then praise God for his mercy," he said, and began to dig.

The hole didn't need to be wide or deep. Rex excavated it quickly and set the shovel aside. He had just removed the wooden box from his backpack and was about to unlatch it when footsteps and voices signaled the approach of visitors to the courtyard. Rex picked up the shovel again, but there was no need for alarm. The visitors were Sophronia and Bishop Ossius.

"Greetings, Mother," Flavia said, bowing a little awkwardly, "and to you, Bishop. I did not expect to see you here."

"But we are glad you came," Rex added.

"We just learned of your sad news," Sophronia said quietly, "and we wanted to be with you in your grief."

Although Flavia felt shame at these words, she also felt relief. It was good to have her mother nearby in a time like this. She nodded gratefully, then motioned for Rex to continue.

Rex unlatched the box and removed the earthenware jar. It had not been opened since he first collected their son's tiny body. Now the jar's rim was sealed with wax. He placed it carefully in the hole, while Flavia stood above him, peering over his shoulder. Though sorrow was not absent from her heart, her eyes were dry, for Christian hope filled her too. Rex's presence was a tangible comfort. And she was glad her mother stood next to her, along with the respectable bishop.

When Rex picked up the shovel to fill the grave, Flavia stopped him. "Let me do it," she said. He passed her the wooden handle, and she scooped the dirt into the hole. Just like that, the jar was gone, swallowed up by the earth.

When the hole was full, Flavia smoothed the soil that once lay beneath the gravestone of Peter. It was hallowed ground, sanctified by the former presence of a man who had walked with the Lord himself.

Ossius approached the blue wall that now held the sacred relics in its hidden repository. He caressed the smooth surface. "Blessed Peter," he whispered, "take this boy Nikasius by the hand. Lead him straight to Jesus, your Savior and Friend."

Flavia came and stood beside Ossius. Removing her hairpin—the lioness one that Rex had given her—she scratched a message into the plaster: *Nikasius may you live in ☧.* Stepping back, she examined the inscription.

"I hope many other believers add their prayers to this graffiti wall," she said.

"I am sure they will," Ossius replied.

The two of them turned away from the wall and returned to Rex and Sophronia at the grave. "It is strange to think that all this is going to be filled with rubble," Sophronia said, gesturing to the courtyard around her. "Every tomb and alley will be packed with landfill. It will make a solid platform for a huge new church."

"And the altar will be directly above the grave," Ossius added, lifting his eyes from the trophy to the sky above it. He pointed to the empty air. "Right there."

Like her mother, Flavia could only marvel at the audacious plan that would soon become a reality. It consoled her to think that her baby would await the last trumpet within the confines of such a magnificent structure. "It will be a destination for pilgrims from all over the world," she said, awed by the thought. "They will receive the Eucharist here, and find forgiveness from Christ for all their sins."

"It is not the sins of the world you should worry about, but your own," said Ossius.

And with that severe admonition, the nightmare began.

Rex immediately came to Flavia's side, slipping his arm around her shoulders. "Both of us understand our sins, Reverend Bishop," he said mildly. "You may be sure of that."

"The sins of the flesh violate the temple of God. Such transgressions are especially grievous."

"We know that, sir."

Strangely, Sophronia seemed to side with Ossius in this unexpected indictment. "How could you have done such a thing?" she cried, her stern gaze accusing her daughter. "I almost died trying to preserve my chastity. I was willing to kill myself rather than be defiled! Could you not do the same?"

"I tried, Mother. But temptation took me!"

"It is a very serious matter," Sophronia continued. "A great moral evil. God's prohibition of it is clear."

Flavia's face fell. She stared at her feet. "I know. I feel ashamed."

"Yet there is grace in Christianity," Rex said.

Ossius took command of the situation with authority. Though he tried to strike a more pastoral tone, his displeasure was clear and his conclusions were firm. "My friends, Rex is right. The Lord offers grace to the repentant sinner. But sin does have its consequences, and I am afraid it is going to affect you both. The two of you must be enrolled in the order of penitents. A child's life was lost in the course of this travesty. And your bodies were used impurely. These things must be dealt with through a penitential process that cannot be rushed."

"What does the 'order of penitents' involve?" Rex asked. His arm was still around Flavia's shoulders, protecting her. Yet he also was respectful to the bishop, which she appreciated as well.

"It is a helpful and godly process of humbling oneself, repenting of sin, and performing actions that demonstrate your true sorrow."

"What kind of actions?"

"Almsgiving is always good. Fasting regularly. Praying without ceasing. And deeds of humble service, like scrubbing dishes or garden labor." Ossius's face grew sober. "And of course, abstinence from sexual union."

"But . . ." Flavia said, then let her words trail away.

"What is it?" her mother asked.

"Rex and I were hoping to be . . ."

"What?"

"Well . . . to be wed."

At this, both Sophronia and Ossius drew back with horrified expressions.

"Of course you cannot be wed!" the bishop exclaimed. "Not while you are in penance!"

460

"How long does that last?" Rex asked. Though his inquiry was polite, there was restrained frustration in his voice as well.

"Three years at least. That is the normal duration for fornication. Only with a time of such length can you truly contemplate the gravity of your sins before God."

Now it was Flavia's turn to be horrified. "Three years?" She glanced at Rex, who was aghast too.

"Why so long?" he demanded.

"The sin was great. The restoration must be equal to it."

"But we're in love!" Flavia cried.

"Which is why," Sophronia said gently, "the bishop and I think spiritual marriage is right for you. It doesn't have to be forever. But it does have to be for now."

Though Rex's jaw was clenched, he still managed to keep his tone measured. "What are we supposed to do during our penance? Just fast and pray all the time?"

The older couple glanced at each other, then Ossius motioned for Sophronia to explain. She turned toward Flavia. "We have a beautiful plan. You and Cassi can return to Sicilia with me, and we can once again resume our lives in the convent at Tauromenium."

"But that place was an agony to me! I longed for Rex every day!"

"We understand, dear child," Ossius soothed. "We have made an accommodation for that. Rex can serve the esteemed Bishop Chrestus of Syracusae. He is in need of a helper, a man who can do physical tasks and provide protection."

"Why should a bishop need protection?"

"The island of Sicilia is divided into huge imperial farms. A criminal underworld functions there—a mob that runs gangs and engages in illegal activities. The countryside is unsafe, but the bishop's duties often take him there. He needs a bodyguard."

"Would I ever see Rex?" Flavia asked woefully.

"He could visit you in public places, so long as you had formed a spiritual marriage. Never could you be alone in private. Yet you could still see each other from time to time. Under the circumstances, this is the only way for you to be together."

And just like that, the matter was decided. The bishop's terms were clear, and Sophronia stood in firm agreement. She would accept nothing else. Flavia realized that to reject the plan would be to become a true orphan, bereft of her mother as well as her father. No other option existed. And yet, as bad as it was, the plan wasn't the worst that could be imagined. It wasn't permanent. It held out the hope that Rex could someday be her husband. And while she waited, he would still be in her life.

"I suppose I can live with this," Flavia whispered.

Rex, however, was silent for a long time. Finally, he said, "The Christian way is hard—as hard as I can possibly endure. But I have agreed to follow a new Master. So I must accept his hard calling or my faith is meaningless."

"That is the spirit of Christ," Ossius agreed.

With agreement having been reached, the foursome departed the necropolis. The walk back to the Aelian Gate of Rome was long and somber. No one felt like talking. At the gate, two litters were waiting for the travelers. But when Rex started to climb into Flavia's, the bishop stopped him. "Rex, you should come with me. I have arranged for Lady Sabina and Lady Junia to stay alone at the house church on the Aventine. It is empty now."

Flavia felt bewildered by the announcement. The hits just kept coming. "I can't stay at the Lateran Palace anymore? There is plenty of room for us there!"

Sophronia gave a little shake of her head. "It just doesn't seem appropriate, given that there has already been one nighttime transgression. It could happen again."

Although Flavia was certain it would not happen again, she did not protest. She settled onto the cushions inside the litter with her mother. The curtains were drawn for shade, but she peeked past them. Rex was also looking out of his conveyance. She met his eyes. His face was sad, for he clearly also understood that their paths were about to diverge—perhaps for a very long time.

Reaching past his curtain, Rex held out his fist toward her. A leather string was wrapped around his hand. Opening his fingers, he let something drop from his hand, dangling from the string.

The cross amulet given to him by Constantine.

"Jesus is Lord," Rex said. And with that strong affirmation, he let the curtain fall back into place so that he disappeared from view. The finality of it took Flavia's breath away. It was all she could do to hold back tears. She let her own curtain close as well.

The porters carried Flavia and Sophronia across the Field of Mars toward her old home on the Aventine. On some other Roman street, Flavia knew her beloved Rex was riding along to a different destination. *When will I see him next? When will we leave for Sicilia? How often will I see him there? Will I ever be his wife?* She had no immediate answers to these questions.

Late that night Flavia was awakened by a panicky desperation roiling inside of her. A dewy sweat was upon her forehead. Swinging her feet to the floor of her old bedroom, she stood up and went to the door. After grabbing a wrap, she slipped out. She knew where she had to go. The beautiful worship hall of Saint Sabina was the sanctuary in which she needed to pray.

She pushed open the rear doors of the hall and closed them behind her. At the far end stood the marble altar, illumined by a pale shaft of light. Slowly, mindlessly, Flavia began to walk barefoot across the floor. The irregular patterns of its stones seemed to warp and shift as she passed. And yet, straight down the middle of the church, a bridal path gleamed in the moon's soft glow. Flavia walked this path, one foot in front of the other, all the way to the altar.

She stood before the solid block of marble. Staring up into the rafters, she cried with upraised hands, "What do you want from me?" Before the echoes had even died away, the awful answer returned.

Let it go, Daughter.

The surface of the altar beckoned. The gospel book lay open upon it. Without thinking, Flavia laid her left arm on its pages. Somewhere, she had heard that a nerve from the ring finger on the left hand ran straight to the heart. Marriage rings were worn there for this reason.

But Flavia's fist was clenched. "My God!" she pleaded. "I don't want to let it go!" This time, there was no mysterious reply to her outburst, only a dreadful hush in the church.

Outside, a cloud lifted from the face of the moon. The light that caressed the sacred book intensified, making its words clearer. It was the first page of the *Gospel of Luke*. Flavia dreaded to look more closely. She feared what she would find. Even so, she made the choice to examine the words of God.

"Noooo . . ." she groaned as her eyes fell upon the text beneath her wrist.

I will not read it aloud, she vowed.

But it was a vow she could not keep. An intense pressure inside her—the accumulated habit of a deeply Christian heart—forced her to give voice to the words that leapt from the page like living things.

The words were in Latin. Mary's song. The handmaiden of the Lord.

Now Flavia could no longer contain her tears. They burst forth as from a wellspring, streaming from her eyes, running down her cheeks, sprinkling the holy altar like a bloodless offering—her bodily oblation, her living sacrifice, her spiritual service of worship.

And so, at last, she summoned her voice. Loudly, boldly, and with great fervor, Flavia declared the words on the page to the heavens. She embraced each one, making it her own, weeping as her bridal fist lay upon the altar. "'Behold . . . I . . . am . . . the . . . handmaiden . . . of . . . the . . . Lord,'" she read, then shuddered so violently she could not continue. Her boldness collapsed. Flavia felt that to finish the reading would be to cast herself into a future she could not bear.

Yet soon enough, new courage welled up inside her, or perhaps came flooding into her, for the Holy Spirit was filling her now. Flavia's voice grew strong once more, and her emotions seemed to stabilize. Now she dropped to her knees, bowing before the altar, yet with her arm still laid upon it. Slowly, she unclenched her fist and laid bare her open palm.

"Let it be done to me according to your word," she prayed, "whatever that may be."

———✦———

July 317

Rex stood upon the massive defensive wall of Rome near the Lateran Palace, gazing across the Italian countryside. Dawn was coming, but it wasn't here yet, so the stars were still spangled across the dark sky. He stared at them without really seeing them. As he held Flavia's hand in his own, he was surprised to find that his heart was beating fast. Though he didn't normally feel nervous around her, he did now. Today would be a momentous day. Rex was about to become a catholic Christian. And he would also be taking a spiritual wife.

Under the new limitations of their penitential discipline, Rex never let pass an opportunity to be with Flavia. It had been a hard adjustment over the past few weeks. Fortunately, the couple was allowed to be together on the walls right now. Since night watchmen were stationed nearby, sin was impossible in such circumstances.

Even so, as Flavia stood silently beside him, she yawned in a way that Rex found surprisingly enticing. A wave of tender affection surged through him. *I would gladly wake up to that sleepy yawn every day for the rest of my life,* he thought. But he couldn't tell her that, of course. It would be inappropriate, for it would lead to temptation.

"Feeling tired?" he asked.

"Mm-hmm. Very much. I hate to admit it, but I fell asleep during my prayers in the deepest part of the night."

"I did too!" Rex replied with a laugh. "Night vigils were no part of my previous religion."

A wry smile curled up Flavia's lips, then she shrugged at their little failure. "We're probably not the first catechumens to do it."

"Nor the last."

Over the past forty days, Rex had learned well what the Christian catechumenate demanded. It was an intense time of spiritual preparation and focused instruction. The teacher, called a catechist, taught the catechumens the stories of the scriptures, the moral requirements of God, and all the orthodox doctrines of the catholic faith. Fasting and praying were required, including an overnight vigil in the church before the ritual of baptism happened at dawn. The appointed time would arrive in less than an hour. But Rex and Flavia had taken a quiet moment to slip away before the rite began.

"You know what's out there?" Rex asked, sweeping his hand to the south.

"The Ostian Way. The road to the port."

"Yes. And the long peninsula of Italy. But what is beyond that?"

Rex felt Flavia squeeze his hand. "Our new home, for as long as God requires it of us. The island of Sicilia."

"Life has a way of coming full circle," Rex observed, and the two fell silent.

In the east, the black sky had begun to fade to a deep ocean blue. A faint streak of light lined the horizon. Flavia glanced over her shoulder at the shadowy bulk of the new building that stood next to the Lateran Palace. It adjoined the empty field that would soon see the rise of Sylvester's city church.

"We should go to the baptistery now," Flavia said, tugging Rex's hand. "Dawn is almost here."

"One more thing," Rex replied, then held up a shiny object. "This is for you."

"A ring! It's beautiful!"

The delicate ring was made of silver, and its gemstone was brilliant blue. A Christian cross was incised upon its face. "Let me put it on you," Rex said. With Flavia's left hand cupped in his, he slipped the ring onto her finger.

"Oh, Rex, it's lovely," she cooed. "Why blue?"

"Because even if I cannot be your husband now, I consider us married already in heaven. The gem will remind you of our marriage above, until we can be married below."

To these sweet words, Flavia could only utter a long, satisfied sigh.

"You're right, it's time to go," Rex said at last. "Dawn is coming. We can't be late. Let us go and be baptized and wash away our sins, calling upon his Name."

"Aha! I see someone has been reading *Acts* in his catechesis," Flavia replied saucily as they descended from the walls of Rome.

The brand-new Lateran Baptistery had been built next to the palace and the empty field that once was a cavalry fort. A smaller house with a private bath complex used to stand here. But that building had been razed. In only four months, a new building of marble-faced brick had been erected over the bath's main pool, reusing the plumbing that was already in place. The Lateran Baptistery was shaped like an octagon.

"Why eight sides?" Rex had asked his catechist, a tall, red-haired Celt named Vincentius. He had become the priest of Saint Sabina now that Felix had disappeared.

"Because seven is the number of completion," Vincentius had replied, "and eight is the first step into a new era. The scripture says, 'If anyone is in Christ, he is a new creation. The old has passed away; behold, the new has come!'"

Stepping inside the baptistery for the first time, Rex found it to be beautifully decorated. Eight porphyry columns stood in the corners, two of which were linked by a tight cable for hanging a curtain. Flickering lampstands illuminated the dim interior, aided by the light of dawn, which was just now breaking. The water in the central pool was absolutely still, its surface as smooth as a mirror. A single column stood in the water. On top of it was a golden censer sending up the aromatic smoke of balsam incense. A lamb made of solid gold and seven silver stags adorned the font's rim. They were connected to the plumbing so that they could spout water into the pool. A statue of John the Baptist stood next to one of Jesus, with the inscription "Behold the Lamb of God, he who takes away the sins of the world!"

After being led with a few other men to a private changing area behind a screen, Rex disrobed until he was naked, then approached the baptismal font. Pope Sylvester stood across it, wearing a long robe made of pure white wool. Steps led down into the water, and another set rose up the other side. The women were not yet present in the baptistery, of course, because the men were nude. But the symbolism of nakedness was important. For both genders, it signified that the catechumens were leaving behind all vestiges of their old lives.

A deacon came forward with the oil of exorcism. Rex had been taught exactly what to say at this point: "I renounce thee, Satan, and all thy followers and thy demons." When these words were uttered, the deacon anointed Rex's forehead and pronounced him free of evil spirits. He was invited to enter the water.

Descending, Rex found the water cool yet refreshing. It was waist deep when he reached the floor of the font. The deacon waded in after him, barefoot and clad in his plain tunic. Now it was time for the bishop to hand over the creed.

"Do you believe in God the Father Almighty?" Sylvester asked.

Rex replied, "I believe in God the Father Almighty." After this there were some affirmations about Jesus Christ—his virgin birth from Mary, crucifixion under Pontius Pilate, death, burial, resurrection, ascension, and return for judgment—as well as some statements about the Holy Spirit, the holy church, the remission of sins, and the resurrection of the flesh.

"Upon your confession of these truths," Sylvester said when the creed was finished, "I welcome you into the Christian faith. You shall henceforth be known as Brandulf Vitus Rex, for you are not a killer but a life-giver to many. And the Life that is the Light of men has come to you—even to you, a sinner."

"Amen," said Rex, and the deacon in the font took hold of him.

The bishop of Rome lifted both of his hands. "Brandulf Vitus Rex! I now baptize you in the name of the Father"—the deacon plunged Rex beneath the water—"and the Son"—another plunge—"and the Holy Spirit!" After the third plunge, Rex was led across the pool like the Israelites leaving Aegyptus through the sea. He climbed the steps and was met by Pope Sylvester with a confirmatory kiss.

"Take a drink," said the bishop, handing Rex a cup filled with a thick, sweet syrup. It was milk and honey, for the Promised Land had just been reached.

Now another deacon gave Rex a white linen robe, then touched his forehead with the oil of thanksgiving. Rex was led to a waiting area while a few other men were immersed as well. They were the first people ever to receive the rite of Christian washing in the Lateran Baptistery.

Once all the men had been baptized, a thick curtain was drawn between two of the marble columns. The bishop stood next to it so that his voice could be heard on the other side of the curtain. "Deaconess Zoe!" he called. "Bring forth the precious lambs!" Though Rex could not see, he knew the women were being led to the font by the deaconesses. They also were baptized in the nude, shielded from male eyes, though not the eyes of the God who had formed them in their mothers' wombs. Using the same liturgy as the men, Pope Sylvester baptized them as well. Each woman was given a new garment, for she, too, was being clothed anew in Jesus Christ.

The baptistery's high windows were now rimmed with the orange light of a distant sunrise. Joyfully, the women came around the curtain to greet their new Christian brothers. Rex's eyes immediately went to Flavia—so holy and pure in her gleaming white robe. Her delicate feet were bare, and strands of wet hair dangled onto her shoulders. *Candida*, meaning "white," was her baptismal name. She waved demurely at him but did not approach.

However, when Pope Sylvester saw Flavia offer the tentative greeting, he hurried over and confronted her. His back was to Rex, and his position blocked Flavia from view. Yet Rex could tell the conversation was intense.

Don't intervene, he told himself. *If it is a rebuke, Flavia can handle it. But she might be in distress . . .*

No, stay put! Newly baptized Christians do not interrupt the pope!

But I do, Rex decided. *I will always go to Flavia's need, no matter what.* And with that, he started to approach the bishop from behind.

At the same moment, though, Sylvester turned. A troubled expression was on his face. His gaze was fixed upon Rex.

"You two must come with me," he declared.

═══◊◊◊═══

Tenuously, Flavia followed Pope Sylvester and Rex out of the Lateran Baptistery. The palace was nearby, but the bishop did not take them there. Instead, he brought them to the empty field where construction of the church had just begun.

"Do you see the outline made by the foundations?" he asked with a wave of his hand.

Flavia could see what he meant. Concrete had been laid to support the walls of the basilica. The lines formed a large rectangle, with a semicircular apse at the far end.

"We see it," Rex said. He sounded abrupt, like he was in a suspicious mood.

The bishop's tone, however, was neutral. "The church that will rise here is one of several that will make Rome prominent. Saint Peter's is another. And Saint Paul's, when we start that one. And all the martyrs. Rome is about to become the foremost diocese of the catholic church."

Both Rex and Flavia already knew these things. Rex's face was guarded. He seemed to be evaluating where the bishop was going with these assertions. "Praise God," was all he said.

"Although it will be quite unbecoming," Sylvester went on, "other churches are going to be jealous of our rise. The worst of them will be Alexandria, in Aegyptus. I don't mean Bishop Alexander, of course! He is a humble and righteous man, a true brother in the Lord. But Melitius of Wolf City is seeking to supplant him. We have also heard that a popular priest leads a faction that seeks to undermine Alexander. Many Aegyptian believers follow that man, even though his doctrines about Christ are false."

"What is his name?"

"Arius," said the pope. "A man on the way up—but up to no good."

Flavia folded her hands and assumed a humble posture. "If I may ask, Your Eminence, what does this have to do with us?"

"You are headed to Sicilia, I hear?"

"Yes, that is our plan."

"Well, I have a different plan for the two of you. I am sending you instead to Aegyptus, to spy out the situation there and report back to me. You have proven yourselves skillful in such matters. And I want you to support Bishop Alexander in all he does."

Aegyptus? With Rex at my side?

The strange announcement excited Flavia, though it confused her too. Fortunately, it also caused Rex's former skepticism to evaporate. "Holy Father," he said with a much more respectful tone, "you know we will not disobey your direct commands. And yet . . ."

"What, my son?"

"We are . . . that is . . . well, Flavia and I are penitents. We are to be joined in spiritual marriage for quite a long time. Wouldn't it be improper for us to travel together to Aegyptus and take up residence there?"

"I intend to send Stephen and Cassiopeia with you."

"Even so, I believe . . ." Rex's words trailed off, but the bishop urged him to go on. "The temptation would be too much to bear," he finished.

"Yes, of course it would. The apostle Paul has instructed us about this. 'It is good for the unmarried to remain apart. But if they cannot exercise self-control, they should marry. It is better to marry than to burn.'"

At these words, Rex and Flavia exchanged glances. "Bishop Ossius says—" Flavia started to say, but Sylvester cut her off with a dismissive wave of his hand.

"That strict man says many things, my child. Yet that does not make them right. He cannot contradict the scripture I just quoted."

"But my mother—"

"Must obey her own bishop," Sylvester insisted. "Marriage is no sin, but a good gift of God."

Flavia's heart was racing now, and her knees felt weak. As the full import of Sylvester's words hit her, she staggered a bit. Rex stepped close to hold her up. It felt good to let him support her—very good indeed.

470

Sylvester smiled warmly at the couple. "Dear ones, please recognize this. The catholic church always oscillates between strictness and leniency, between holiness and grace. Some say the Bride of Christ must be without spot or wrinkle of any kind. Others say the church is a hospital full of sickly sinners trying to get well by the medicine of the Lord."

"And what do you say?" Rex asked.

Sylvester straightened his shoulders and stood fully erect. The awesome dignity of a Roman bishop settled upon him as he spoke. "I declare to you," he said in his rich and resonant voice, "that the one, holy, catholic and apostolic church is no man-made institution. Nay, it is the mystical body of our Lord Jesus Christ! Therefore, its command to you is this: 'Be holy, just as he is holy.' But when you are not, 'God is faithful and just to forgive your sins and to cleanse you from all unrighteousness.'"

"We sinned grievously," Flavia said with her head bowed.

"Yes, you did. And because of it, you must follow a pathway of penance for your own spiritual benefit. For the time being, you and your husband must seek a deeper journey into Christ."

Flavia struggled to reply, but her intended words could barely form in her mouth. "My . . . my . . . *husband?*"

Sylvester nodded. "That is what I said. Penance can occur in the marital context too. Ossius is wrong about that."

Rex took Flavia's hand in his, gripping it tightly. "Holy Father, are you saying we could be married? Right here on earth? Physically, and not just spiritually?"

"Yes, my friends. That is what I am saying. And I am also saying you should do it right now, in the short time we have before we go inside, so that you can partake of your first Eucharist as husband and wife."

Married here and now? Mighty God! How can it be? The sudden turn of events hardly seemed possible to Flavia, yet she knew it was real life and not a dream. This was truly happening, right before her eyes. Rex, her beloved soul mate, was becoming her own. *Thank you, Father! Thank you for giving me my heart's greatest desire!*

"We shall do it at the future altar," Sylvester announced. "Follow me. I will keep the ritual simple and succinct."

The threesome walked across the packed earth inside the rectangular foundations of the future basilica. Bits of discarded military refuse lay strewn upon the ground, left over from the days when the place had been the cavalry fort of Maxentius. Since Rex and Flavia were still barefoot, they picked their way carefully through the debris.

"I once rode the Cantabrian Circle to join the cavalry right about here," Rex observed as he crossed a bare patch of dirt. "I never could have guessed that someday I'd be married here!"

A jumble of stones was piled where the altar of the Lateran Church of the Savior would eventually stand. Sylvester stopped there and faced the couple. "Join hands," he instructed. After Rex and Flavia obeyed, Sylvester bowed his head, closed his eyes for a moment, then began to speak.

And so it was that by the light of the rising sun, the bishop of Rome took Brandulf Vitus Rex and Junia Flavia Candida through the marriage liturgy of the Christian church. Rex had already given Flavia a ring, so only the exchange of vows remained to be performed. Flavia knelt before the makeshift altar, voicing her promises earnestly, while Rex knelt across from her and uttered his with equal fervor. Finally, they stood up, overcome with great joy. But as the ceremony ended, one thing was left undone.

"We have no marriage crowns," said the bishop, "but do not worry. God does not require them."

Rex disagreed. "My bride must have a crown," he insisted, "for her deeds are glorious in God's sight. She is worthy of honor."

A few paces away, a laurel bush was growing in the stony soil, watered by a nearby fountain. Not long ago, its boughs would have provided wreaths for soldiers who had performed well in drills, or even in war. But now, as Rex broke off some branches and wove them into a crown, Flavia realized that these leaves would honor triumphs of a different kind—victories over rebellious souls that had bowed before the Risen Lord.

Rex returned to where she and Sylvester were standing. His steps were slow, but Flavia did not mind. She remained quiet and let Rex come to her at his own pace.

"You have waited a long time for me to get to this point," he said when he had drawn near. His handsome face was gentle and his countenance was full of light.

"And you have been worth the wait," she replied.

"Please bow your head, my beloved."

Flavia willingly complied.

"You may crown the bride," said the bishop.

"The handmaiden of the Lord has become a queen," Rex declared, then placed the wreath on Flavia's waiting brow.

※※※

As always, the Forum of Trajan bustled with activity. Unlike Rome's older forum, which was more of a political center, the forum built by Emperor Trajan, with its attached market, served a commercial purpose. Rex marveled at the amazing architecture of the giant complex, bedecked with columns, statues, and gold ornaments everywhere. A towering marble spire, carved and painted in brilliant hues, depicted the exploits of the great emperor in a spiral around its entire height. Yet all these decorations couldn't match the beauty of the object Rex was about to pick up at a bookseller's shop: a brand-new copy of the Christian scriptures, the very words of God himself.

"This whole place is a temple to human vanity and greed," remarked Vincentius as he surveyed his surroundings. He stared up at Trajan's Column. "That thing is a new Tower of Babel, erected in the new Babylon."

Rex had discovered during his baptismal catechesis that Vincentius's moral scruples were often strict like that. The tall, lanky Celt from distant Hibernia had little stomach for the pride of man or the arrogance of empire. And yet, while severe in his attitude toward the world, he was nonetheless a warmhearted and generous fellow—and an excellent theologian. No wonder Pope Sylvester had elevated him from the status of a catechist and made him the new priest of Saint Sabina on the Aventine. Rex could tell the young man was going to have a long and illustrious ecclesiastical career.

"The bookseller is over here," Vincentius said, leading Rex to one of the hundreds of shops and stalls in the Market of Trajan. The pair jostled through the crowds and finally arrived at their destination.

The shop owner, a freedman named Nereus, was no Christian but instead was a devoted follower of the ancient gods. Yet he was reputed to be one of the best publishers in Rome, perhaps in all the empire. His scribes were known for their remarkable accuracy. They never made copying mistakes, which had been Pope Sylvester's primary criterion when he commissioned the job. In addition to the accuracy of the words, the bookbinders were excellent craftsmen, fashioning works of art that didn't only convey information but did so with elegance and style. This publisher was worthy to create the church's new book.

"Welcome, Father Vincentius," Nereus gushed when the two visitors entered his shop. "I see you have brought a strong guard with you. Excellent! You will want to protect this book once you see its cost on my final bill."

"Your exquisite work is worth any price, my friend," Vincentius said.

The compliment appeared to please Nereus. Without delay, he brought out the codex and laid it on a table. It was bound between two coverboards wrapped in rich leather. Gold and silver tracery was all over them, both front and back. The pages inside, made of the finest calfskin called vellum, were written in an elegant script using the highest quality ink. The original Greek text was on the left page and a Latin translation was on the right. Truly, this was a precious artifact that would serve the Roman church well.

"It is very big," Rex observed. "I have never seen a book so large."

Vincentius nodded. "Our western scriptures tend to be a little longer than those of the churches of the east. The wording in our manuscripts is a bit more detailed and colorful than what our eastern brethren have copied down over the centuries."

"Let me show you the scriptorium before you go," Nereus said. He beckoned for his two customers to follow him.

The scriptorium was a large room with south-facing windows that gave good light. The desks for the scribes were littered with scraps of parchment, inkpots, and reed pens. A few of the most diligent copyists were laboring at their tables, but most were off at the baths or napping, for it was the height of summer and the afternoons were too hot for work.

Nereus gestured to a long table strewn with manuscripts of every size and shape, some of them very old. "These are the earliest biblical texts that your bishop possesses. My calligraphists copied them meticulously. Your whole Christian faith lies right here on this table."

"Which writings did you put in the bible?" Rex asked.

"Just what your bishop ordered. We included everything from your Greek Old Testament, the *Version of the Seventy*. Then we put in your New Testament books, twenty-seven in number—the very same ones that were selected in your recent meeting. In addition, we copied some of the Jewish books from between the two testaments, in case you should wish to consult them. And lastly, there are several Christian treatises of much value, which your bishop said to include for good measure, even though they are not divinely inspired. You have a whole Christian library between those two coverboards!"

Rex searched among the papyrus texts spread on the table until he found a copy of the *First Epistle to the Thessalonians*. He moved aside a tattered manuscript with his pinky so he could see the page he wanted. Though his reading knowledge of Greek was meager, he could make out the letters well enough. His roving eyes finally found the word *epioi*, or gentle. It occurred in Paul's phrase, "We were gentle among you." Rex called Nereus's attention to it. "This should say *nepioi*," he said.

"With an *n*? 'We were infants among you'? That makes less sense than 'gentle.'"

"Which is why it's more likely to be the original. Scribes tend to correct things like that, and over time, they gradually change the wording. But Saint Paul himself wrote *nepioi*. I am sure of it."

"Oh, you Christians!" Nereus exclaimed to Vincentius. "Even your bodyguards are textual scholars!"

Rex and Vincentius both laughed. "I'm no scholar," Rex admitted, "but I have been to Thessalonica. Bishop Basil showed me the original letter from Paul's hand. I saw with my own eyes that it said *nepioi*. 'Infants among you' is the correct reading."

"Then let us make sure the error does not creep into the western scriptures," said the bookseller.

After retrieving the codex from the front room, he opened it to the beginning of *First Thessalonians*. Nereus scraped the vellum clean at the proper place, then inked a pen and set it to the page. Carefully, he inserted a letter *n* before *epioi*. Since the previous word also ended in *n*, there should have been two *n*'s together, which was probably why some copyist along the way had made the accidental omission. It was easy for a tired eye to skip over a second letter like that. Such errors would then be perpetuated down through the centuries. But fortunately, the mistake had been caught. The text now read *nepioi*, like Paul intended.

The three men returned to the front of the shop. While Vincentius settled the bill with Nereus, Rex wrapped the book in soft cloths and bound it with string. Then he put it in an old flour sack. Admittedly, no one was likely to try to rob him in the middle of the day. Yet a book like this was expensive. Neither Rex nor Vincentius wanted to offer temptation to an opportunistic thief.

With the transaction done, the pair proceeded from the Market of Trajan to the Roman Forum. As they passed the New Basilica, Rex asked Vincentius to stop, for he had powerful memories associated with this place. He wanted to see the colossal statue of Constantine inside.

"Go ahead, we have the time," said the Celtic priest. His bushy red hair flopped as he nodded.

Inside the grand hall, with its high, coffered ceiling, the air was pleasantly cool. Rex walked slowly toward the statue, which sat enthroned in an apse at the far end. Constantine's carved head—instead of the originally intended head of Maxentius—now sat atop the statue's body. His placid face smiled upon the cavernous hall, and his eyes were lifted upward in a heavenly gaze.

But perhaps the most striking thing about the statue was the item the emperor held in his hand. It was a wooden pole with a transverse bar. A plain banner hung from the crossbeam, making it possibly a military flag or a Christian cross. The symbolism was open to interpretation. Rex decided it was probably intended as a cross, though displayed in a way that wouldn't offend the old pagan aristocracy. Nevertheless, one thing was clear to Rex as he left the hall and returned to Rome's main square: Christianity was coming to the empire in a bigger way than ever before.

Resuming their walk, the two men passed the Flavian Amphitheater, where Rex had rescued Flavia from lions almost six years ago. Next to it stood the brand-new Arch of Constantine. It was an impressive triple arch, a monument to Constantine's victories in war. The emperor was surely establishing his sovereign presence in the city. An inscription at the top of the arch claimed that he had won his battles "through the inspiration of the Divinity." The monotheistic wording was yet another sign of Christianity's triumph over paganism in the Eternal City.

At last, Rex and Vincentius arrived at their destination: the huge estate known as the Sessorian Palace, home to Queen Mother Helena and thus

476

the new center of imperial power in Rome. With no emperors in the city, the Sessorian Palace, not the Palatine Hill, had become the focal point of Constantine's bureaucracy. Helena, the Most Noble Woman of the Empire, along with the new financial officers whom she controlled, were running the civic government out of this stately palace on the southeastern edge of town. Since Emperor Constantine had paid for the official copy of the scriptures, the presentation of the book to Pope Sylvester would take place under Helena's watchful eye.

Rex and Vincentius handed over their expensive delivery to Archdeacon Quintus, who thanked them warmly for their assistance to the bishop. After another hour of preparations, the presentation ceremony was ready to begin. Rex was granted a seat next to Flavia, his new bride of less than a week.

A short while later, Stephen and Cassi entered and took their seats next to their friends. They had been surprised and delighted to hear about the recent wedding. In fact, even Ossius and Sophronia had begrudgingly given their blessing to the marriage once they heard it had already taken place. "Very well, so be it," Bishop Ossius had said stiffly when he found out, for no Christian was willing to call the pope's decisions unwise. As for Sophronia, she seemed relieved that everything had turned out this way. Rex had even seen her wink at Flavia, though the dashing Spaniard hadn't noticed it.

But now, Ossius was seated at the front of the hall on a marble chair. Sophronia, unfortunately, wasn't able to attend the ceremony lest she be recognized by anyone who used to know her. However, she had made sure to ask Flavia to give her a full description of the momentous proceedings.

A trumpet fanfare announced the arrival of Queen Helena. Though the reception hall wasn't the biggest one in the Sessorian, it was still a large space within the sprawling estate. It was divided into three sections along its length. Imperial bureaucrats and top church officials were seated in the first section closest to the royal throne. Rex and Flavia were in the middle, while the rear section was designated as standing room for local believers who wanted to attend the proceedings. The area was packed with curious Christians, all of them craning their necks to see the queen or the pope.

"Welcome, fellow believers in the Lord!" cried the herald who conveyed Helena's words to the audience. "It is truly a momentous day, one for which we have long been waiting. Your glorious emperor has paid for a great book of the scriptures to be used by His Holiness, Bishop Sylvester, in his new church. As you know, that building is to be constructed a short walk from here, along with many others to be built over the graves of the apostles and martyrs. And all of this comes from the largesse of your generous patron, the God-loving augustus, my son, the Emperor Constantine!"

A cheer went up in the hall, the loudest section being the third that was thronged by the common folk. After a short but raucous celebration, the herald quieted the crowd and continued. He introduced Pope Sylvester, who offered his own words of greeting. Then there was a hymn, followed by a skillful oration by a rhetorician of the imperial court. The flowery speech, known as a panegyric, extolled the Christian virtues of the emperor and his mother. Once the man had finished his extravagant words, the time came for the presentation of the sacred book.

It was Bishop Ossius's job to make the handover, for he had been the leader of the papal mission. On either side of Helena's grand throne, lesser chairs had been set up, each one facing the other. Ossius sat on the left side of the hall and Sylvester on the right. At Helena's command, the men rose from their seats and began to walk toward each other. Ossius carried the beautiful book flat upon his palms, held out in front of him as he paced toward Sylvester.

"Halt!" Helena cried, rising from her throne in the center. Both bishops stopped and looked at her. Silence reigned in the hall as everyone waited for the queen to speak.

The queen lifted a glass bottle and removed its crystal stopper. Slowly, she began to pour dirt upon the floor in front of her throne, where the two men were about to meet. At first, there were gasps in the hall, but Helena's words silenced them.

"This is earth from the sacred city of Hierusalem," she proclaimed, "so that the scriptures may be passed to the Roman bishop while he stands upon the Holy Land itself!"

"Hurrah!" cried one of the commoners at the back of the hall, and immediately the cheer caught on. "Hurrah! Hurrah!"

"Proceed now with the presentation," Helena commanded, so the two bishops continued their walk. They met face-to-face in front of the imperial throne, with their feet upon the scattered soil of Israel.

"A beautiful gift from Emperor Constantine," Ossius said as he handed over the book.

Sylvester received the scriptures into his bosom. "Thanks be to God," he replied, though his words were nearly drowned out by the cheering in the hall.

Flavia leaned over so she could speak in Rex's ear while the crowd went wild. "Buildings and a book for the catholic church. Our mission was long and hard, but we did it."

"It was the Lord who did it," Rex said.

"Holy is his name," Flavia replied.

———✺✺✺———

The harbor at Portus had not yet awakened from its nighttime slumber when Flavia rose from her bunk in the hold of the Roman warship *Dominant*. She had found that the predawn hour was the best time to find a little solitude along the busy waterfront. The sailors, soldiers, and rowers who manned the trireme were off at whatever barracks or brothels had provided them shelter for the night. Only two groups slept aboard the ship while it was moored alongside the pier: the crew of officers and the passengers who had paid the fare for the voyage south. In these peaceful times, most navy captains made a little money on the side by dividing one of the ship's storerooms into tiny cabins for high-paying customers. Bishop Ossius had bought three cabins for the six travelers who were making their way out of Rome.

Yet it was quiet worship, not the upcoming trip, that had gotten Flavia out of bed so early. "Thank you, Lord, for all you have done for me," she whispered to the morning sky. Although the stars had faded now, one was still left: the bright Morning Star. The pagans called it Venus, and the prophet Isaiah called it Lucifer, but the *Book of Revelation* identified this star with the true Light of the world. Though Flavia did not superstitiously pray to the stars, Jesus's own words gave her reason to believe that this heavenly body, which ushered in the dawn each morning, was a reminder of himself. She uttered another scripture that came to her mind, letting the sacred words apply to herself: "'Awake, O sleeper, and rise from the dead, and Christ will shine on you.'"

"I sure feel like I was dead," said a groggy voice behind her. Flavia smiled at the unexpected interruption and turned to greet her husband.

"Good morning, handsome," she said playfully.

"Give me another hour to wake up, then greet me again," Rex replied, rubbing his eyes. His long hair was tousled, his feet were bare, and his tunic was on backward. Yet Flavia didn't mind. Rex truly was handsome, even when rumpled from sleep.

He shuffled over to her and slipped his arms around her waist from behind. She leaned backward into his warm embrace. For a long while, they remained like that, enjoying the early morning stillness together.

"We made it, sweet girl," Rex said at last.

"Oh, Rex, we did! Many times, I thought we'd never see this day. I thought God had other plans for us."

"Me too. But that's something I've learned about God. You can never guess what he's up to. You just have to wait and see."

Now Flavia separated from Rex and turned around. Raising her hand, she stroked his bearded cheek. "I don't mind waiting to see what lies ahead, as long as I can wait with you. I was prepared to do it alone. But I'm so grateful that God let us be together."

"I will always walk beside you," Rex said. "Hand in hand. Let's go forward and discover God's plans for us."

A little cough behind the married couple signaled the arrival of someone else. They turned to see Stephen, who had just come up from the hold. He was bunking in the same cabin as Bishop Ossius, while Cassi had volunteered to go with Sophronia so the newlyweds could have their privacy. Gradually, the others came up too, as each of them awoke. By the time the eastern sky was fully bright, all six of the friends stood at the rail. They watched the crewmen arrive and trudge up the gangplank from the dock—ready, though not eager, to prepare for the day's departure.

No wind stirred the harbor, so the sail remained furled during the preparations. Eventually, tugboats with eight-man crews moved the great trireme out of its mooring. The inner enclosure of Portus, built two hundred years ago by the ever-busy Emperor Trajan, was shaped like a hexagon. Since the passageway out of the port was narrow and the lagoon was clogged with vessels of all types, warships like the *Dominant* couldn't extend their oars.

All the rowers sat below deck, awaiting the captain's signal. Only after they reached the lighthouse and hit the open sea would they put the blades into the water and begin to pull the pinewood shafts.

The captain's name was Abantus, a swarthy, middle-aged seafarer whose military career was on the rise. Emperor Licinius, though now at peace with Constantine due to the treaty at Serdica, was building a stronger navy in Byzantium. Many warships were being summoned to that city. Flavia often wondered why it was necessary. "Because of the pirates," was the answer usually given. But there couldn't be so many pirates. It seemed more like preparation for a future war.

Captain Abantus intended to make a stop in Sicilia, where Sophronia would depart and resume her cloistered life in the convent. The *Dominant* would then set sail for Alexandria, meeting a fleet there before continuing to Byzantium. However, while Bishop Ossius would go all the way to Constantine's court, Flavia and Rex would not be part of any travel beyond Alexandria. They, along with Stephen and Cassi, would disembark in Aegyptus and make a new life there, just as Pope Sylvester had commanded. The catholic bishop of Alexandria needed good Christians in his congregation to fight for what was right.

The swarthy captain approached his fare-paying passengers while the ship was being towed from the harbor of Portus. "You're a strong lad," he said to Rex, looking him up and down. "Ever pull an oar?"

"Aye. Did a stint in the navy for a time."

Abantus's face lit up. "I knew it! Those broad shoulders have the look of a rower's build. How would you like to make some money?"

"It never hurts," Rex replied.

"We're undermanned until we reach the navy base at Neapolis," said Abantus. "I could use you on an oar each day until sunset. I'd pay you well."

Now Rex glanced over to Flavia, seeking her input with his eyes. Though she had wanted to spend her days at sea with him, in truth, she didn't mind letting him row. He would be given breaks throughout the day when the wind was fair, and there wasn't much else to do anyway. Rex never liked to sit around doing nothing. He needed to be moving toward a goal. Flavia knew it would help his mental state to be accomplishing a physical task, while earning income as well.

"Sure," she said agreeably. "You should do it. As long as you're finished by sunset."

"Oh, I will be," Rex said with a sly smile. "I have a new reason to come back each night." His frank statement made Flavia blush, yet she couldn't disagree.

After squeezing Flavia's hand affectionately, Rex followed Captain Abantus to find his place at the oar. Flavia watched him go—not a criminal, nor a slave, but a free Christian man providing for his wife. It was a beautiful thing.

When he had disappeared below deck, Flavia made her way to the front of the ship. The prow was outfitted with a bronze ram that cut through the water like a great finger pointing into the future. She stood at the front rail and gazed across the whitecaps at the western horizon. As the *Dominant* neared the outer lighthouse and left the shelter of the harbor, a stiff breeze picked up. Its coolness felt good as it stirred Flavia's hair and ruffled the folds of her dress. The morning sun gleamed on the water ahead. Droplets spritzed her cheeks with the ocean's familiar kiss.

"Tugboats away!" the first mate cried as the towlines were released.

"Clearing the lighthouse now," another crewman called to the captain.

"Steerboards, hard left!" shouted Abantus. "Prepare to turn south for Neapolis! Oarsmen ready?"

"Ready, sir!" came the cry from the beat-keeper below deck.

"Then, forward strokes!"

At once, the beat-keeper's mallet began to beat out a steady rhythm. The ship's great oars, three banks per side, rotated in unison as if guided by a single hand. As soon as the blades caught the choppy surf and swept back against it, the *Dominant* lurched forward like a chariot bursting from the gate, its horses eager to run.

Flavia gripped the ship's rail and lifted her face to the sky. Exuberance filled her as the warship rounded the lighthouse and slipped smoothly into the open sea. A bright future lay ahead. Rex was propelling her along. The catholic church was sending her out. And high above, Jesus Christ sat upon his heavenly throne. "My soul magnifies the Lord," cried the handmaiden of God, "for the Mighty One has done great things!"

Epilogue

I had never seen a priest of God be so rude to his bishop. Unfortunately, such bad behavior was, I had discovered, all too common in the Alexandrian church. There was a lot of fighting among the Aegyptian Christians. For a naturally respectful woman like me, it had come as quite a surprise. Even Rex had commented on it—and he is much more comfortable with conflict than I am.

My husband had invited me to join him at a gathering of churchmen whom he had gotten to know at the Catechetical School. While we had been living in Alexandria over the past year, he had started taking theology classes. He was even considering becoming a subdeacon, an entry-level position in the church. Rex had found a new love for theology, and that made my heart glad.

On this pleasant autumn day, the esteemed bishop of the city, Alexander, had gathered a convocation of his civic priests, as well as some country bishops from around the Nilus delta. Many theology students were in attendance too, along with some nuns who had shown up unexpectedly. It was the bishop's intent to give some lectures on a very important subject: the eternality of the Son of God. He was in the middle of doing that when the rude priest Arius interrupted him.

"Blasphemy against Almighty God!" Arius shouted.

The audience hall at the Serapeum immediately fell quiet. Even the chattering students were dumbstruck. The silence was awkward and tense.

But Arius filled the empty space with more righteous anger. He was a man of about sixty, with a trim physique and his gray hair tied in a ponytail. No question, he was eloquent and charismatic. Everyone said he was an expert in logic. His parish church in the suburban Boukolia neighborhood was booming.

"You follow the errors of Sabellius!" he accused.

I leaned over to Rex and whispered, "Who is Sabellius?"

"Libyan theologian," Rex replied. "He said the Father and Son are the same being."

I shook my head at such an insane accusation. *Alexander doesn't believe that! The scriptures are clear. Jesus isn't the Father—he was sent by him!*

No sooner had I thought this than the bishop proved me right. "I am not committing that foolish theological error, Father Arius," he said sternly. "My belief is that Father and Son are both eternal, and have always existed. Did you not hear my affirmations just now? Listen to them again: God always, the Son always. As the Father, so the Son. The Christian church teaches that the Son is everlasting, forever coexistent with the Father."

"If they're both eternal, then they are the same being!" Arius shot back. "You must reject the heresy of Sabellius, which you clearly believe."

"What I believe is the clear teaching of scripture, not the doctrine of any man! The Father and Son are distinct. Yet both have always existed. Recall that the apostle John instructs us, 'In the beginning was the Word, and the Word was with God, and the Word was God.' Think also of the sayings in *Hebrews*: 'Thy throne, O God, is forever and ever,' and 'Jesus Christ is the same yesterday and today and forever.' Clearly, our scriptures teach that the Son is eternal and distinct from his heavenly Father. Yet they are one God."

"It is logically impossible for them to be one God," Arius replied. "If the Son is eternal, as you claim, yet he is distinct from the Father, then you have two eternal Gods. But this is blasphemy! In your attempt to reject the teaching of Sabellius, you swing the other way. Now you are teaching two Gods, against the clear words of divine revelation. In either of these views, you are condemned as a heretic."

Alexander was about to reply when one of the deacons stood up and joined the conversation. Though I did not know him, I immediately liked his demeanor. He was a short fellow whose dark color told me he was native to Aegyptus. His eyes were bright and lively, and he gestured as he spoke. He looked to be a few years younger than me, perhaps not even twenty years old. But despite his small frame and obvious youth, I could feel the force of his personality across the lecture hall.

"So you claim to use logic today, Father Arius?" he challenged. "Then let us see where your logic leads! You agree that the Son of God exists right now, do you not?"

"Of course," Arius replied with a wave of his hand.

"And he is our Lord Jesus Christ?"

"Yes. That is a belief of all Christians."

"But if Bishop Alexander is wrong when he says the Son is eternal, it must mean that he has not always existed."

"That is correct. The Son has a beginning. Before that, there was a time when he was not."

"So where did the Lord Jesus come from?"

"God made him."

At this bold assertion, a ripple of discomfort ran through the room. The doctrine sounded unnatural, not only to the churchmen's ears but to mine too. I have been a Christian all my life. Never have I been taught that our Lord Jesus Christ was one of the creatures made by the Father.

Now the dark-skinned deacon pressed home his point. "What you are saying, Arius, is that God made the Son. But the maker is always greater than what is made. A creator is superior to his creatures. So then, God must be greater than the Son."

"He surely is," Arius agreed.

"So the Son is not fully God?"

"Not fully. A lesser kind of divinity," said Arius.

"And the Son is Jesus Christ?"

"Of course. As I told you before."

The young deacon now turned to the crowd in the room, spreading wide his hands. "Who here is the true blasphemer? The bishop, who teaches that Jesus Christ is fully equal to God? Or this man here, this arrogant priest, who teaches that God made Jesus? Is our blessed Savior a lesser being, a creature just like us? Surely not! Who is the true blasphemer?"

"Arius the Blasphemer!" someone shouted, and others quickly joined him.

Although I agreed with those shouts, a certain man did something then of which I did not approve. He was one of the stretcher-carriers employed by the church to bring sick people to the hospital for care. Reaching into a pouch at his waist, he drew out a stone and hurled it at Arius. The rock struck him on the temple, leaving a trickle of blood down his cheek. Some of the other stretcher-carriers drew stones from their pouches to follow the first man's lead.

"Stop this, immediately!" Alexander barked. Then he spoke to Rex, addressing him by his baptismal name. "Vitus! Escort Father Arius out of this room to a safe place. There shall be no violence among Christian brothers!"

Rex hurried over to Arius and put an arm around his shoulder. The poor man looked woozy as Rex led him from the hall. Once he was gone, the mood settled a bit. It looked like most of the troublemakers had slipped out in the confusion.

"This is not how we should debate theology," the bishop sharply rebuked. "The Holy Spirit is not among us right now. I hereby adjourn today's meeting until a future time."

With those words, everyone dispersed. Since I didn't see my husband outside, I decided to walk home by myself. I was passing a small public garden when I saw, under an olive tree, the youthful deacon who had refuted Arius's argument with logic of his own. His eyes were downcast and his expression was gloomy. I could tell he felt bad about the unexpected turn of events, so I decided to encourage him.

"Those rock throwers were out of line," I said, "but your confrontation was needed."

Glancing up, the youth seemed grateful for my words. "False ideas must be refuted with truth," he agreed.

"Yet never with violence. I know you did not intend it."

"I did not. But violence comes quickly for some."

"Logic is the better way. A careful argument from scripture, reasoning from the text, to discover divine truth by the light of the intellect."

The young man smiled at my words. "Aha! A wise and godly woman. What is your name?"

"I am Junia Flavia, a Christian wife. We recently arrived here from Rome."

"Welcome to our great city, sister! I have lived in Aegyptus all my life. I trust you will come to love it as much as I do."

"I hope to," I replied. "And who are you?"

"I am a deacon of Alexandria and a loyal servant of the bishop."

"And your name, sir?"

The deacon came over and took my hand. "I am Athanasius," he said to me with warmth in his eyes, "and I hope we shall become good friends."

Bryan Litfin is the author of the Chiveis Trilogy, as well as several works of nonfiction, including *Early Christian Martyr Stories*, *After Acts*, and *Getting to Know the Church Fathers*. A former professor of theology at the Moody Bible Institute, Litfin earned his PhD in religious studies from the University of Virginia and his ThM in historical theology from Dallas Theological Seminary. He is currently a writer and editor at Moody Publishers. He and his wife have two adult children and live in Wheaton, Illinois. Learn more at www.bryanlitfin.com.

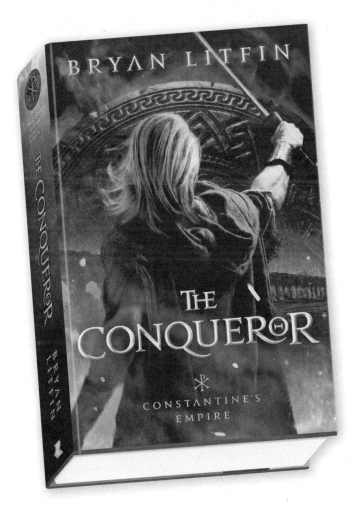

MEET BRYAN

Follow along at

BRYANLITFIN.COM

to stay up to date on exclusive news,
upcoming releases, and more!

  Bryan.Litfin

LET'S TALK ABOUT BOOKS

- Share or mention the book on your social media platforms. Use the hashtag **#EveryKneeShallBow**.

- Write a book review on your blog or on a retailer site.

- Pick up a copy for friends, family, or anyone who you think would enjoy and be challenged by its message!

- Share this message on Twitter, Facebook, or Instagram: **I loved #EveryKneeShallBow by @BryanLitfin //** **@RevellBooks**

- Recommend this book for your church, workplace, book club, or small group.

- Follow Revell on social media and tell us what you like.

RevellBooks

RevellBooks

RevellBooks

pinterest.com/RevellBooks